Roger Sayer

GW00858370

THE
SECOND
AQUA
CHRONICLES

PublishNation
www.publishnation.co.uk

PROLOGUE

Dawn broke early in midsummer and the band of men who roused themselves as the sky lightened grumbled good naturedly at the old man who led them in their task.

One man rubbed the sleep from his eyes and rolled up his blanket.

'We don't want to do this twice Brother Scribe,' he said. 'Are you really sure this is the right hill?'

'Ask your brother.' The oldster told him. 'He helped me dig the hole and line it properly. I can't ever remember seeing you with a spade in your hand.'

'Neither can I,' somebody said.

'Hey,' he called. 'Has anyone ever seen Bjarn do any work?'

A chorus of denial greeted his words. Bjarn looked sheepish at the unjust accusation. They made a hasty breakfast and turned to their task.

'Come on lads. Bjarn and Olaf, you go at the back with the poles, and everyone else to haul on the ropes. Not you Brother Scribe, or you Grandpa Erik. Your years have earned you a rest.'

'Bah! Never in my life have I shirked hard work youngster, and I'm not starting now. I can still pull my weight.'

'And I,' growled Erik the Elder to his young namesake.

'Have it your way. I'm glad you thought to have runners under the box, it does make the pulling a little easier.'

'Aye, and when the time comes it will make it easier to raise it out of the pit and down to the bottom of the hill.'

Brother Scribe was dwarfed by his companions, most of whom were as fair-haired as their ancestors had been.

The box that they laboured to heave up the craggy hill was stoutly built and the wood was bound with iron. At last, at the end of a long day, it was lowered into the chamber that had been prepared for it and the pit was carefully roofed over.

Brother Scribe and old Erik made a thorough inspection of the work.

1

'Old friend, we've done all we can,' Erik said eventually.

'Aye, that we have,' Brother Scribe agreed. He raised his voice for all to hear. 'Thank you all. It was hard work, but a promise made is a promise kept. I think we may be satisfied with what we have accomplished on this day.'

'It was a heavy box,' one man replied.

'It had to be. It will be in the ground a long time,' Erik spoke for Brother Scribe.

'How long?'

'More than a thousand years will pass. It will see the light of a changed world when Clive Boarslayer uncovers it.'

'Do you really believe that?'

'I believe it and I know it,' Brother Scribe declared firmly.

***

Dusk at the end of a long day. White smoke from somebody's fire coiled lazily into the air until it stopped rising and spread out in a flat grey haze. A flock of black birds flew high above the two men who strolled beside the shore of the Lake. Rooks, on their way home to roost.

The tallest of the pair gestured towards the smoke.

'It took me a long time to discover why smoke lingers in the air like that sometimes,' he remarked.

He was past the years of his prime and walked with a staff.

'You could have asked,' his small companion replied in a voice that was strangely high pitched.

A long cloak of rich dark blue hung from his shoulders.

'It's never been my style. I always had to think things out for myself, and then think of ways to prove whether I was right or wrong. Heh! It got me into trouble more than once!'

'I know. You launched me out onto the Lake without a paddle once. To see what would happen, you said.'

Atta nodded.

'I remember I did and I soon found out what would happen. How could I ever forget? One of the fishermen found you and towed you back behind his canoe. Vocca's grandfather, he was the man. Then he laid into me with his paddle and I suppose I deserved it. To this

2

day I still don't know if he found you by chance or whether you managed to influence him in some way but, heh! I still remember the sting of that paddle!'

'Do you want the answer?'

'No. It ceased to be important a very long time ago. There were always three of you in those days. It wasn't until Tarn began his bloody business that I ever saw any of the knowing ones alone the way you are now.'

The plop of a rising fish caused both men to stop and regard the surface of the Lake and the spreading circle of ripples.

'You know,' Atta said thoughtfully, 'the Lake has always been good to us since we all came here. I have lived here all my life and so have Vocca and a good many others but there are more people now, ever since the time when Tarn came to make slaves of everybody. The newcomers brought a lot of new ideas with them when they came and we learned a lot from each other. Each of us benefited by it.'

They began their slow walk again.

'It was just a place then, back when I was a boy, but it's a good deal more than that today. The new people brought... well we can talk about it later when we've had something to eat. My house is only a few paces away, let's go inside.'

Dusk had given way to darkness by the time the meal was over.

Atta set a pair of earthenware drinking vessels on a sturdy table and filled them from a stoppered earthenware jug.

'I think you'll like this, Wint,' he said as he offered one of the vessels, 'it's a blended drink.'

He sipped appreciatively at his own goblet.

'It's something new,' he continued. 'I don't know any of the songs for brewing, but I do know that one of the ingredients was left to freeze during the winter and the ice that formed on the surface was discarded. I believe that was done three or four times, and what was left was blended with the juice of several fruits. That's the sum total of my knowledge of brewing and wine making, but I do know a good product when I taste it.'

Wint agreed.

'I don't know who the brewer was,' he informed Atta, 'but I'll wager at least one was named Alfrid.'

3

'Two of them are!' Atta cackled. 'And that brings me back to what we were talking about while we walked by the Lake. New people and new ideas.'

Atta's comfortable chair that was woven from the willow that grew by the Lake was positioned near a shelf on the wall. He reached for his pipe rack and tobacco, and selected a long stemmed pipe, which he stuffed with tobacco while he talked.

'I my lifetime I have seen more changes than any of my forebears ever saw. I've met and talked with more people than they ever knew.'

He took a glowing stick from his fire and puffed his pipe into life.

'I learned this from Beowulf. Oh, I forgot to thank you for your gift of tobacco.'

'It is a small payment for your hospitality,' Wint told him as he tested his drink. 'Mmm, this is very good.'

'My thanks all the same. I do like a pipe in the evening, and I find a stroll along the shore eases my aching knees if I don't go too far. My age is catching up with me.'

'New people and new ideas,' Wint prompted him.

'Metal. I never had much use for metal and I still prefer to peel an apple with a good stone blade. I carved my pipes with stone tools too, but more and more people are using metal these days and I'm forced to admit it has its uses.'

Atta was known to be conservative in his views about metal, believing it to be no more than a passing fad.

Stone had served him well through all the years of his long life and he saw no need to change his opinion now. All the same, he was a scientist and he wondered...

'People have even begun to make metal on the Lake,' he informed Wint, adding, 'and before you ask, there is an Alfrid involved there too.'

'It's a common name.'

'It is now. All the Alfrids came from across the water, some on Shipmaster Cadric's vessels and some on foot like Alfrid the shoemaker. Beowulf told me once that the first thing Alfrid the shoemaker said to him was that Alfrid is a common name. For a common person, that's what he said.'

'There's nothing common about Alfrid the shoemaker.'

'That there isn't,' Atta agreed readily. 'I've never had better shoes in my life than the ones he made for me. And there was nothing common about the way he fought the Battle of the Lake either. He learned fast from the Vikings, and what Beowulf and Freya didn't know about war wasn't worth knowing. Between the three of them they kept hope alive at a time when we had little hope for. Nobody wanted war but we knew it was coming and the Vikings bought time enough for us to learn how to fight.'

Atta stopped talking and pushed a burning log further into his fire.

'We did things that no civilised person should ever be asked to do,' he continued sombrely. Staring into the flames he added, 'It was the price we had to pay for our freedom, and what would have happened if Tarn had won is something nobody cares to think about. We paid the price in full, but it left its mark on us. We don't want to remember those days, but we don't want to forget them either. It's important that our children and our children's children never forget the price of freedom.'

Wint finished his drink and refused Atta's offer of a refill.

'Speaking of children,' he said with a chuckle, 'I believe small Alfrid isn't short of ideas either.'

'Small Alfrid! Bah! The boy's a pest. Always up to some mischief or other. I've never seen behaviour like it. Never in all my days!'

'I have,' Wint smiled broadly. 'Small Alfrid reminds me of the boy who set me adrift on the Lake, on a raft without paddle.'

Atta ceased his ranting.

'Was I really that bad?' He asked.

'You caused more trouble on your own than the rest of your generation put together,' Wint told him. 'Hardly a day passed when I didn't hear somebody yelling Atta at the top of his voice, and see you running from the scene of your latest misdemeanour!'

A look of pure delight lit up Atta's face.

'Then perhaps there is hope for the little menace after all. Heh! Did I ever tell you about the time...'

***

The sound of a horn came from somewhere in the mist that had formed on the Lake during the night. Breakfast was hastily swallowed and they made their way to the jetty, arriving in time to see a raft appear out of the swirling greyness. Cheerful greetings were called as the raft bumped the jetty and one of the two men at the poles leaped ashore and expertly looped his mooring rope around a stout wooden bollard.

'I'd like you to give some thought to the matter we spoke of last night,' Wint said in his high-pitched voice.

Atta nodded.

'My curiosity is overcoming my misgivings,' he replied seriously. 'I'm not convinced it's a good idea, but, well, dammit, I can't see anyone passing up the opportunity. I'll put it to the Council of Seniors for their approval and I think, at all events I hope, that I can persuade them. It won't be easy, what you're proposing is... Have you anyone in mind?'

'I'll accept the recommendation of the Council,' Wint replied.

'Very well. I'll see to it that your proposal is added to the agenda. I could call a special meeting but the next scheduled session is only two days away.'

Wint was helped aboard the raft and Atta gestured to the man on the jetty.

'Hop aboard son, I'll unhitch the mooring rope myself.'

The departing raft was quickly enveloped by the swirling mist.

Know the Lake. Learn its ways and it will serve you well. Atta recalled the words of the knowing one who had spoken them at a time when the future of civilisation had hung in the balance.

We're learning, he thought. In those days there was no one who would have dared to set out to cross the Lake on a raft until the mist had lifted. Now the Lake had been charted, distances and directions had been carefully calculated, a project that Atta had been heavily involved with, and the currents were known. Every crossing of the Lake added to the store of data, which was put into new Songs of Knowledge that were constantly updated.

This is a good time to be alive, he told himself.

Chapter 1

Clive Bowden panted for breath as he scaled the rocky hill with a spade in his hand and a coil of rope over his shoulder. There was nothing to be gained by hurrying, he knew that but his impatience had got the better of him. Below and proceeding at a more leisurely pace his father Lawrence Bowden followed him, and behind Lawrence, Henry Rudd and Henry Whiting, the navigator and pilot respectively of a World War Two Mosquito bomber plodded in his footsteps. Age had slowed their footsteps but not their determination. Lawrence Bowden carried cameras to record their mission.

Lower down the slope Brian Gleaves and Jack Smythe brought up the rear, each man carrying more equipment.

Henry Rudd had parked his Range Rover in a lay-by at the foot of the steep hill and Brian Gleaves had drawn up his pick-up vehicle close behind it. The road was narrow but they had encountered no other traffic.

Clive reached a level patch of ground and threw down his equipment with a sigh of relief as he sat down on a large grey boulder. He began to regret his haste as a light but persistent breeze made him feel cold and clammy.

When everybody had arrived at Clive's resting place the equipment they had laboriously toted up the hill was dumped without ceremony on the ground and each man found a place to sit and rest for a while.

Brian Gleaves was the first to speak, making a wide sweeping gesture, 'Blimey,' he panted, 'that's what I call scenery. A proper landscape and no mistake, that's what it is. I ain't never been in these parts before.'

'You wouldn't want to see it in the winter Brian. Not from up here,' Henry Rudd commented.

'Prob'ly couldn't even get here,' Brian replied readily, 'I reckon as how my pick-up would have been snowbound miles back.'

All nodded agreement.

'Whatever Beowulf buried here, it's going to be a bit of a struggle getting it down to the road,' Jack said, calculating the distance and the steepness of the slope by eye.

'We're going to have to be careful how we go,' Lawrence Bowden suggested. 'We don't want it to get away from us and go tumbling down the hill on its own.'

Brian Gleaves agreed.

''S'right, we don't. And we don't want anyone getting in front of it neither, just in case. Well, we'd best get started I reckon, because we might be up here a good few hours. Sort of depends on how we make out. Me an' Jack'll start with putting the hoist together and rigging the block and tackle. Can't do a lot else until some digging gets done an' we know what we're dealing with.'

'And the one who carried the spade can be the one to start digging,' Jack Smythe said with a meaningful look at Clive Bowden.

Leaping to his feet Clive turned to step up onto the rock that had been his seat.

Jumping down he took a few paces and said 'Here, just here where I'm standing. At a depth of one sword, that was what Beowulf said. This is the place!'

He set to work with enthusiasm.

The hole was about four feet square and there was a sizeable heap of earth and small stones beside it when Lawrence Bowden, whose turn it was to dig, measured the depth against the spade handle.

'That's about the depth of one sword,' he estimated, 'it can't be far now.'

Clive hoped so. The blisters he had raised on both hands were painful and he wished he had listened to Henry Whiting when he had advised him to take it more slowly.

Lawrence suddenly held up his hand for silence.

'Listen!' He exclaimed. 'We're there! Can you hear how it sounds hollow when I put the spade in?'

'That's it!'

'We're in!'

'I was starting to think we'd never find it!'

The last few inches of soil were removed very carefully. Merlin's instructions to Beowulf had been to construct a roofed chamber and to have the box supported above the level of the floor. It was soon obvious that more soil would have to be removed.

Jack Smythe took over the task of digging.

8

'Try a few inches that way Jack,' Lawrence told him. 'I think I have found one edge of a stone slab that covers the roof, so if you can find the opposite edge we should soon know how big the chamber is.'

'There's some writing on the slab,' Jack Smythe soon reported. 'I reckon we can brush it clean when we get it up for a look at it. Don't suppose we can read it though, not unless anyone knows Viking. Or maybe it's Latin.'

Lawrence Bowden took a few pictures before the excavation was resumed. He wondered what the Vikings had left for their many greats grandchildren to recover. How many greats should that be? Nobody knew, but Lawrence and Anne Bowden, Clive's father and mother, were researching their family tree, helped by other members of the bell curve community.

Lawrence was suspected by many of hoping to find more evidence of cattle stealing in his ancestry.

Beowulf and Freya had looked on cattle rustling as a sport with a bit of give and take on both sides and they had admitted between peals of laughter that their departure from Denmark in a Viking longship had been precipitated by a cattle raid that went wrong. They had stolen an entire herd from a Viking chieftain and were hotly pursued by a Viking army when chance took a hand and they jumped aboard a Viking raider as their only means of escape. Freya had come by her double headed axe when one of their pursuers threw it at them. There had been another claimant but Freya, who stood nearly two metres tall in her bare feet, landed a punch that made him change his mind with alacrity.

Lawrence was brought back to the present by a cry of excitement from Brian Gleaves.

'It's Latin!'

Brian Gleaves had changed places with Jack Smythe. His dirt stained forefinger traced the words chiselled into the stone slab.

'It says, "Freya put me here," that's what it says. Or it could mean Freya had me put here. It's a bit like saying Christopher Wren built Westminster Abbey. Not on his own he didn't, an' I reckon he never touched a stone with his own hands. He was in charge all right but dozens of builders did the actual building.'

Lawrence exchanged knowing looks with his son Clive and Jack Smythe at Brian's knowledge of Julia's native tongue. Julia Calpurnia

Florentina Pantera, the Lady of the Lake and the last citizen of the Roman Empire. There had been a good deal of speculation about Brian and Julia and it was starting to look as if there might be some truth in the rumours. He wondered how far Julia would permit the rumours to spread. She was known to be aware of the gossip. Did Brian know too? Hard to say.

'I didn't know Freya knew Latin,' Brian concluded doubtfully.

'She didn't,' Clive confirmed as he knelt to examine the words more closely.

'She might've learned it when she went home,' Jack suggested, 'but somehow I don't think so.'

'Nor me,' Clive added. 'And why isn't Beowulf mentioned?'

No one had an answer for him.

The work was soon done and the Viking's legacy to their descendants was uncovered.

'It's a lot bigger than I expected,' Clive commented as he examined the find.

'Our ancestors thought big,' his father reminded him.

Brian Gleaves felt his way along each side of the box.

'There's a set of lugs,' he reported. 'I sort of thought there might be. Pass the rope Jack, and I'll get us hooked up.'

'Brian, how long are we looking at?' Henry Rudd asked. 'I want to let the folks back home know when to expect us.'

'Ain't sure mate. About an hour maybe to get the box out of the ground, and then another hour to get it down to the road, most likely a bit longer, an' then we've got to swing it onto the pick-up and get it lashed down under the tarpaulin what I brought along special. It'll be tea time by the time we get back to your farm.'

'Any margin of error?'

'Not much.'

Henry Rudd made a call on his mobile phone.

'Do we want any sandwiches brought out to us?' He called.

Lawrence Bowden thought not.

'We ought to have planned this better, but I'm for working through without a break.'

There were words of agreement from everyone.

Henry Rudd spoke into his phone again.

'Expect six very hungry men about tea time,' he said, 'and brew up a gallon of tea, and another gallon of coffee.'

'Message to everyone,' Henry announced when his phone call was ended. 'Merlin will be waiting in your yard when you and Jack arrive back home Brian, along with Janet and Julia, Frank Holley, Anne Bowden, and mostly everyone you can think of, including the vicar. He's with Merlin right now. Special message for you, Brian; Julia says Button has been fed and watered.'

Button was Brian Gleaves' Alsatian dog. Brian looked startled and pleased, and Henry Rudd swiftly turned away with a knowing look.

***

'I reckon the Vikings prob'ly meant the box to be easy to open,' Brian Gleaves said. 'It's a fine piece of workmanship and the wood was prepared special. It should polish up and make a nice piece of furniture.'

He removed his cap and scratched his head.

Jack Smythe agreed.

Addressing the small group of onlookers who were assembled in Brian's workshop he said, 'The smith who did this was an artisan and it wasn't just the smith, there was a woodworker who knew what he was about. I'd like to know how they did it.'

'Me too,' Brian agreed.

Following some discussion and further examination of the box the Vikings left for them to find, Merlin and Clive's father Lawrence Bowden agreed with Brian Gleaves and Jack Smythe.

'It won't be a quick job,' Jack warned everyone. 'Best thing is to leave us to get on with it and we'll give you a call when we're ready and then when everyone's here we'll have a shot at lifting the lid.'

With care and patience the lid was finally lifted from the box that was Beowulf's legacy to the future. Lawrence Bowden tilted his camera to get a picture of the contents.

'Another box,' he reported, 'but this one has handles and I think the lid is hinged. And the metalwork isn't iron, it's brass. That is, I think it's brass. Jack, what do you think?'

Jack Smythe leaned forward to examine it.

'Brass,' he reported, 'and Lawrence is right, the lid is hinged. The metalwork is in good condition and I can't see any corrosion. Self lubricating,' he concluded.

'Huh? I'm not with you.'

Brian Gleaves proceeded to give Lawrence Bowden a quick lesson in metallurgy.

'Brass is a mixture of copper and zinc, it's what we call a yellow metal. It's softer than iron, which I expect everyone knows, and the thing about it is that when you cut it or drill it you don't need to lubricate it with oil like you do with ferrous metals. Ferrous metals are the ones that have iron in their makeup.'

'Which is why Beowulf used brass,' Jack Smythe interjected. 'I think the inner box will open with a good stiff pull on the handles.'

'You're Beowulf's nearest relative Lawrence,' Merlin prompted. 'It's your privilege.'

The engineers were proved right. Though stiff after more than a millennium under the earth the hinges creaked in protest but they did allow the lid to be raised. Lawrence's hands shook as he retrieved the first item and placed with care on Brian's cloth covered workbench.

'It's a book, and quite a hefty one at that. I don't think I'd better open it, I don't want to do any damage.'

Merlin approved.

'I can work on it in the cave. I believe I can soften the leather covers and avoid cracking the spine, but I won't open it Lawrence, that's your right. Your's and Clive's.'

Lawrence Bowden thanked Merlin sincerely. He returned to the task of examining the contents of Beowulf's time capsule.

'This is fabric, some sort of tapestry perhaps. I think it best to leave it to you Merlin. I could make a real mess of it if I tried to unfold it. Hello, what's this?'

Lawrence straightened up with a curious artifact in his hand.

'Even I know this is not Viking,' he said hoarsely, 'but where did it come from?'

Merlin examined Lawrence's find.

'It's a stone knife and it's well made, exceptionally well made,' he said. 'Late Stone Age I believe. What was Beowulf doing with it? It must be important or he wouldn't have sent it to us. There's a story behind this knife and I'd give a lot to know what that story is.'

Chapter 2

Lawrence Bowden donned a pair of cotton gloves that Merlin had provided before he touched the book. He held his breath and opened the cover and revealed a richly illuminated title page.

'It's beautiful,' he breathed, 'but I can't read a word of it.'

He turned the page.

Merlin stepped forward and examined the work.

'Hmm. Saxon. Not what I expected, I thought it would be written in Latin. Saxon writing is very rare. Very, very rare, but with the help of Master Gerni and Julia I'm sure we can translate it. It'll take some time, say three months to get the gist of it, and a lot longer to produce a full and accurate translation.'

'I'm sure the wait will be worth it,' Lawrence declared.

'I think so too,' Merlin concurred.

'I've got another surprise in store for you,' he continued. 'You remember that fabric you thought was a tapestry? Well, it's a flag. I've taken a liberty with it and hung it in the dragon cave along with the banners of old Wessex. Shall we...'

Merlin led the way to the cave that was hidden behind the wall of his cellar, and Lawrence was soon standing in front of the flag.

'The wavy blue lines represent the Lake, I knew that, but Beowulf only knew about it from what he heard when he was here. And what are we supposed to make of a hedgehog with horns?'

Merlin pulled a face.

'We might never know that but... well, maybe. Maybe we will know. There might be something in the book that will explain the mystery. It wasn't penned by Beowulf unless he learned to read and write after he left Bath and returned to his own time, and the same can be said of Freya. Freya could turn out a fair drawing though; we both have some of her pictures and so have Clive and Copper and half a dozen others. I'm mentioning this because she sent some more of her art work.'

'What!' Lawrence exclaimed.

'There was a leather folder in the time capsule that turns out to be her portfolio. It's upstairs in my study.'

Merlin smiled enigmatically as he added, 'There's something rather odd about them.'

'Am I supposed to ask what that something is? All right, I'm asking.'

Merlin led the way from the cave, talking over his shoulder.

'I want to see if your reaction matches mine, and I also want you to see it before anyone else sees it, especially Clive, because as an historian he might read more into them than Freya intended. Um, what I really mean is that Clive might be able to put a date on some of the things Freya drew. I think perhaps I've said enough.'

Lawrence still wore his cotton gloves and he handled the drawings very carefully. Merlin had placed tissue paper between each one.

'These are drawings of Beowulf's farm I imagine,' Lawrence commented, 'and these are their cows. They must be priceless but I'm not surprised at her choice of subject. They thought the world of their cows.'

Merlin agreed.

'Hullo, what's this?' Lawrence said as he removed the tissue paper and revealed another picture. 'It's a head and shoulders portrait but is he Viking? They weren't all big and fair haired but this chap, well his hair might be fair but he just doesn't look like any Viking I've ever imagined,' he continued. 'Of course I'm probably wrong, but maybe he was just a non-Viking neighbour. Pointed nose, close set eyes, and hair that looks as if it belongs on a scrubbing brush. I just can't see him as Viking.'

Once again Merlin agreed with Lawrence.

'I think the next series of pictures will confirm that, and they are also the reason why I wanted you to see them before Clive does. I'll say no more than that until you have examined them and drawn your own conclusions.'

Lawrence removed the tissue paper from the next drawing that Freya had made. Merlin watched his expression change. Lawrence removed another tissue paper and jumped as if he had been struck.

'They... these aren't Viking,' he gasped. 'They're, well, they're older than Viking. Merlin, I know enough to know that this kind of building is Celtic, the Celts built round houses, which I don't believe the Vikings ever did. Viking buildings were straight sided long houses, so how did Freya know about Celtic round houses? She had never seen one but I know she drew these pictures, I recognise her style. What... what... where...?'

Lawrence sputtered into silence.

'Your reaction matches mine, I rather thought it would. Lawrence, I can't add much to the story of your Viking ancestors yet, but I can say this: Beowulf and Freya didn't only visit us in the future, their future that is to say, they went back to the past as well. Quite a long way back. Wint was at the heart of it, that much I do know, and I'm fairly certain that Beowulf orchestrated a battle of some sort. The battle was won, but at a cost. Beowulf was killed, laying down his own life for something more important; civilisation itself was at stake. Freya returned alone to the Viking age and the book she left for us contains a narrative of their adventures in the past. I hope and expect that further translation will clear up a lot of old mysteries.'

'Oh. The Legends of the Lake,' Lawrence managed to blurt out.

Merlin nodded.

***

The vicar waited until he was sure he had everyone's attention before he began his narrative. Some people were taking notes. The midweek weather had been unusually hot and the vicar's arms and face showed the redness of sunburn. Much of the afternoon had been spent tending his garden and he made no secret of the fact that he was proud of his efforts. From seven o'clock in the evening his guests had begun arriving and his large living room was crammed with as many people who could pack themselves into every square inch of space.

The vicar's talks were always well received, especially on the occasions when he had managed to unearth something new around which to construct his improbable theories. There were times when he had to admit that they verged on the limit of the gor-blimey as he sometimes put it, and these were the ones that his audience looked forward to most of all. This evening had promised that he was going to deliver something so outlandish that he had wondered whether or not to confide his thoughts at all. A long and serious talk with Edwin Mallory had finally persuaded him that he should.

The room fell silent as he started to speak.

'I said I wanted to share my thoughts about Wint,' the vicar began, 'and I'll be interested to hear what you have to say about my latest theory, which may or may not be so crackpot as to be verging on insanity. Before I do I have a piece of news that Janet Smythe told me over the phone a week ago. It appears that she has managed to convince Suzanne Fluteplayer that the knowledge of Viking music and their language, which I remind you she speaks all too fluently sometimes, is too valuable to be lost and she should take a tutor on board to help her with getting it all written down and put into some sort of order.'

His last comment drew a ripple of amusement. Suzanne was the daughter of Jack and Janet Smythe and her language could be colourful at times. Fortunately for her Suzanne was the only person who really understood what she said.

The vicar continued.

'Merlin agrees with Janet and he has managed to ferret out a suitable person, who will be brought into the fold so to speak. I don't know who she is but Merlin told me she lives somewhere near the Royal Crescent in Bath so travel is not an issue because Suzanne can easily make the trip, and her qualifications are impeccable. One can only hope that the lady is broad-minded as well. We all know what sort of songs Beowulf and Freya sang!'

'They weren't prudes, that's for sure,' somebody commented.

'They certainly weren't, and now I shall turn to the business in hand, which is Wint and his ilk. Little People appear in folklore on a world-wide scale,' he informed his audience, 'and I'm sure you'll be interested to know that the tales, stories, fables, legends, call them what you will, are deep rooted. Very deep rooted. I've done a little reading and I have discovered that many tales go right back to the Stone Age. Hah, I thought that would make you sit up!'

He waited for chatter to die away and continued, 'It surprised me too, but perhaps it ought not to have done. What I'm going to say will probably surprise you still more, and I don't doubt that it will provide material for thought and discussion for a very long time.

'Consider elves for a minute. Children's story books are full of them, and usually those stories are told to younger children as fairy tales. Everybody knows elves are small, it's knowledge that we grew up with.'

The vicar paused for a brief moment, then he said, 'Except that in folklore elves may be only inches tall or they can be man sized. Another thing about elves in folklore is their ability to travel in an instant from one place to another. Putting two and two together and making five, I can now state that my latest crackpot theory is that our friend Wint is an elf!'

'Elf!'

Doctor Andrew Simpson was the first to find his voice.

The vicar looked pleased by the reaction to what he had called his crackpot theory. His special talent and self-appointed task in the matters concerning the Bell Curve Society was the collection of myths, legends, and folklore, and knitting them together to construct a theory that he then put forward to be tested.

'I've been working with Merlin and Clive Bowden on this,' the vicar continued. 'To begin with I found myself in a difficult position, and to a certain extent I'm still uncomfortable with the notion of elves as, well, as human beings. You see, when Christianity reached these isles some two thousand years ago, belief in elves and spirits et cetera was discouraged. It still is. Then the discovery of some complete skeletons of fully grown but small human beings threw me a lifeline.

'These skeletons were found not too long ago, on an island in the Indonesian Peninsular, and were dubbed Homo Floriensis, you may remember reading about them in the papers at the time.'

The vicar frowned as he added, 'Some people who ought to know better called them Hobbits. I attribute that to an unconscious rejection of what is apparently the case, namely that these small people were a branch of the human race, in much the same way as Homo Neanderthalis, or Neanderthal Man as he is more commonly called. The importance of this is that the Neanderthals were our nearest relatives until they disappeared from the scene about thirty thousand years ago, or so it seems but more recent discoveries indicate that the Neanderthals weren't the only surviving branch of the human race apart from ourselves, and not only that, it now transpires that many of us have about four percent of Neanderthal genes in our genetic makeup. Mr and Mrs Bradley, I'm afraid you miss out because your ancestors didn't leave Africa soon enough.'

'We can live with that Vicar,' Mrs Bradley laughed.

'Without going into details I'll just say there was a branch of humanity which we call Denisovians, and yet another branch called the Red Cave Men. The skeletons of Floriensis are a mere twelve or thirteen thousand years old, and not only that, the other inhabitants of the island claim that they are still around. Naturally this is disputed, and some scientists claim the skeletons are normal people who had a pathological condition that would account for their lack of stature. However, there seems to be mounting evidence that this is not the case. I believe the bones in the wrist are subtly different from our own, but don't quote me on that, I might be wrong. Other evidence seems to show their teeth to be somehow different from ours. What does seem certain is that these, um, Little People were very intelligent despite having small brains in a small skull. Small, but proportional to their skeletons that is. Their brains were structurally different from ours, as was shown by the casts that were made of the inside of their skulls, and perhaps it was that difference that accounts for their intelligence.

'So, with a gigantic leap of imagination I began to wonder about other Little People. Ireland has its Leprechauns, and Scotland has the Wee Folk. All over the world there are legends of small people. Cornwall for instance has the knockers, named so by the old Cornish miners because they believed that they knocked on the rock walls of the mines as a warning that a cave-in or some other disaster was coming and it would be wise to get out of the way. In their various languages miners all over Europe had their own equivalent. Had, and for all I know they still have. I'd offer to provide a complete list of the names of these little people but there so many of them that I doubt whether such a list has ever been compiled.

'I confess to being rather relieved that I no longer have to believe in sprites, pixies, and so on. The possibility that other kinds of humans still exist is something I can not only live with, but I find it exciting both spiritually and intellectually.'

'Blimey!'

'And so say all of us.'

'Vicar,' Doctor Kate Fawcett pleaded, 'you're not going to sing God Moves in a Mysterious Way are you? Please don't.'

The room rocked with laughter. The hymn was the vicar's favourite but his singing voice and ability to hold a tune was bad by anyone's standards.

The room fell silent as he started to speak again.

'I'll begin by saying that the ideas that I'm about to present are, um, well, scary. Which is to say that they frighten me and they may very well frighten you too. The implications of my notions could cause trouble in a big way. They could be twisted to prove or disprove a theory, or they could be biased to support an argument, and that holds true whether or not I have stumbled across something that would be better left alone.'

The vicar paused for a moment and regarded the ceiling thoughtfully while he mentally reviewed what he was about to disclose.

'I'm passing a picture around. This little chap is called Wilberforce, according to the lady in the library who found this picture for me. Wilberforce is, as you can see, a chimp, or to give him the respect he deserves, a chimpanzee. He's not just any chimpanzee either. Wilberforce is a bonobo chimpanzee. I'm no scientist but I can tell you from the information I gained from reading one or two books and some articles I found published on the internet that we humans are very closely related to the chimpanzees. Does anyone know what percentage of DNA we have in common?'

Doctor Andrew Simpson glanced towards Doctor Mallory, who probably knew the answer from his talks with the vicar and said, 'I'll open the batting. It's a high figure; upwards of ninety percent I believe.'

'Any advance on ninety percent?' the vicar invited the assembly.

'Don't look at me,' Copper Beach said, 'but I expect my know-all father knows.'

'I dare say he does but Merlin isn't here. Have a guess.'

'Ninety two percent. No, ninety-three.'

'Getting warmer. Anyone else?'

Jack Smythe stirred. Seeing than nobody was going to speak he decided to stick his neck out.

'Somebody's got to say it. Ninety-nine percent.'

The vicar looked pleased with the answer.

'I can't put an exact figure on it,' he informed his eager audience. 'The actual figure seems to be closer to ninety-eight point seven percent, which is an astonishingly high figure, I think you'll all agree, and I found some suggestions that it is even higher. Ladies and gentlemen I repeat that I am no scientist so I cannot dispute those figures but it appears that about one fraction of one percent of our DNA is shared with Wilberforce and his kind. The small amount that we don't share makes a huge difference but if you'll excuse me for putting it in a way that I can understand, we are more than just a collection of genes.'

'Vicar,' Copper interrupted, 'if that's true for us isn't it just as true for the chimpanzees?'

The vicar nodded agreement.

'Copper, you've beaten me to the punch,' he told her, 'and I'm going to stray into the territory that rightly belongs to the anthropologists. I suppose nobody just happens to know an anthropologist?' He asked hopefully. 'No? Well I'll muddle along as best I can. I'm groping for words. I know what I want to say but I don't know how to say it, so if I'm not getting my thoughts across to you I'll try to do better. Remember I'm not a scientist.'

'I'm an engineer so if you can get through to me you can get through to anyone,' Jack Smythe commented.

The vicar looked relieved.

'Thank you for that Jack,' he said. 'Here we go then. Culture and intelligence. Culture shapes our daily lives, and Wilberforce is part of a culture too. Chimpanzees are social creatures, just as we are. Wilberforce's kind are clever, but only as clever as a small child, but young children have a culture too, and despite the best efforts of the politically correct brigade every child in a group of toddlers knows the ground rules and the pecking order and tries to change both from time to time.'

'To continue then,' the vicar said, 'I have stated that Wilberforce is intelligent, if only in a limited fashion. He's a tool user, chimpanzees are known to use stones to bash open hard nuts and there are other examples that I won't bore you with but which are easy to look up and which show a remarkably high level of reasoning.

'Now, this is where it gets interesting. Six million years ago or thereabouts the tree of evolution forked and humans and chimpanzees went their separate ways. Just as an aside let me add that it's pointless to say which of us left the mainstream of evolution. The ultimate arbiter is Mother Nature and she hasn't cast her vote yet even though humans, or Homo Sapiens to give us our scientific name, outnumber chimpanzees by millions to one. Perhaps in another six million years she will have made up her mind. It's an interesting thought and one that might not sit comfortably with a lot of people.'

The vicar sipped some water and continued.

'At a later date there was more branching and one result of this was Neanderthal Man who was human beyond all doubt; the fact has never been disputed. Now then, I'm going to repeat myself because I think this is important. Recent discoveries in Indonesia have revealed another branching. Homo Floresiensis, sometimes unkindly called the Hobbit, walked onto the stage as it were. Homo Floresiensis were small people, about three feet tall, they made and used stone tools, and there are native Indonesians who maintain that they are not extinct. Imagine that! I ought to have mentioned that their brains were, or are, smaller than the brains of a chimpanzee.

'And here is where once again I mention even more recent discoveries. There were other humans, who have been named Denisovians because their remains were found in Siberia, in the Denisova cave, which is in the Altai Mountains. Not much has been discovered, just a finger and a tooth, but that was enough for the scientific people to determine that the Denisovians are genetically distinct from us Homo Sapiens and the Neanderthals, and that we all share a common ancestor although it seems that Denisovians are more closely linked to Neanderthals than they are to us. They got around a bit; apparently they are related to the Australasians, who show around five percent of Denisovian DNA.

'So we can say that Homo Sapiens, Denisovians, Neanderthals, and Homo Florienensis all co-existed until only a few tens of years ago. Four distinct species of humans and maybe even more! And did I mention that apart from recent migrants from Africa, which is to say post-Neanderthal migrants, our particular branch of humanity shares four percent of our DNA with the Neanderthals? Did I mention that?'

'You did Vicar when you told Mr and Mrs Bradley they miss out on Neanderthal genes,' Copper said wryly.

'Does that mean I am more of a pure modern human than you are Vicar?' Mrs Bradley enquired.

'Forgive me, I can't answer that question. I doubt that there is an answer,' the vicar replied seriously.

He sipped more water.

'If Homo Florienensis is still around there are still two branches of the human race in existence,' he continued, 'and I rather hope that to be the case. I've almost reached the end of my sermon, but before I stop spouting I'll mention the thing that I said scares me a little and fascinates me even more. I promised you something sensational and the easily qualifies. It's outrageous, preposterous, and borders on lunacy. I have been wondering if perhaps… excuse me while I get my thoughts together. You might have wondered why I have talked about chimpanzee intelligence. Well, I had the thought that perhaps there was more branching of the tree of evolution and…'

'Wint!' Clive Bowden exclaimed.

'Sorry,' he apologised, 'it just came out.'

The implications sunk in and there was a stir of interest. The vicar was obviously pleased. 'Yes indeed,' he said.

He continued, 'My proposition is that we and Wint are humans of different species. Perhaps our DNA differs from Wint's by the same amount as it differs from Wilberforce's DNA. One fraction of one percent, and that small, almost insignificant difference accounts for Wint's obvious intelligence which, while it may or may not be superior to our own, is different by an order of magnitude.'

It seemed that everyone was talking at once. The vicar was called to participate in several separate discussions and notes were jotted on whatever paper was available.

'Where are they?' Clive wondered out loud.

William of Salisbury had an answer.

'Where's the best place to hide?' He asked and answered his own question. 'In plain sight, living in the same street as you or I. They're probably a little on the short side but I wouldn't take that as gospel.'

'Oh, the Little People,' Copper interjected, adding, 'they're everywhere. I mean Leprechauns in Ireland, Tylwth Teg in Wales, and so on. They're all over the world. They're the real elves and fairies and you-know-what's.'

'I'll be…'

Clive beckoned Edwin Mallory and ushered him into the conversation and gave a brief outline about what had been said and posed a question.

'How could you tell them apart from us, um, ordinary humans?'

Characteristically, Doctor Edwin Mallory gazed at the ceiling while he considered his reply.

'Hmm. Interesting question. I don't know. It's possible that the Little People aren't even aware that they are different, it probably depends on the degree of separation. If the divergence hasn't gone far, and it would take hundreds of thousands of years to do so, then I woudn't be at all surprised if it isn't possible to tell without taking their DNA apart and even then you'd have to know what you are looking for. It's a fascinating window into the wonders of evolution. Wonderful stuff! Perhaps you and I are representatives of two different species and neither of us know it!'

He stopped and paused for breath.

'It's too early to call us and Wint different species, but give or take a million years, well, you never know.'

'What about their intelligence?' Clive wondered.

'Is it so significant? However you define intelligence it is only a measure of potential, and how many people do you know who do reach their full potential? How many people know how intelligent they are if it comes to that? My personal view is that if there is a divergence, which is by no means certain, it is very subtle and incomplete. Not yet, and maybe never. Perhaps there is only one branch of humanity after all but something in me wants there to be two. Or even more. Nature hedging its bets so to speak; it has an intellectual appeal.'

'Not everybody might see it that way,' Clive objected.

'Sad but true,' Mallory agreed.

He added, 'George Green had a leap of intuition that he told me about over a pint of best beer a few days ago. Listen to this if you will. George put forward the notion that the Beach Buggy virus might have been deliberately genetically engineered. It would be staggeringly difficult but now I've heard what the vicar had to say I'm starting to wonder if the Wee Folk all share a common blood group and the Buggy was designed by them and for them specifically. Whenever our branch of humanity catches it, it's always been by accident.'

'Not any more it isn't,' Clive corrected him, 'not now you and Patti Driscoll have cracked the problem.'

Hearing her name mentioned Nurse Patti Driscoll shot a glance at Clive.

'There is a hole in my argument,' Mallory admitted. 'I wouldn't expect you to know this but having a number of different blood groups might have some advantages for the human race. Some say that some groups have a greater immunity from certain diseases than others. If that is so I would imagine the net result to be better survival chances for humanity as a whole. It's a marvel of evolution really, a small and largely insignificant difference that might have kept humanity going when things got tough.'

'Has anyone checked the relationship between disease and blood group?' Copper enquired.

'I'd be surprised if they haven't,' Mallory replied, 'but there is an example of a definite relationship between disease and, um, the state of an individual's blood. I expect that everyone has heard of sickle cell anaemia. It's an unpleasant condition where the red blood cells are sickle shaped instead of the round shape that is normal, and it results in a big reduction in the amount of oxygen the blood can carry. It isn't found in Europeans but in Africa it's not uncommon and on the face of it there is no evolutionary advantage to having it, but it is known that those who do suffer it are less susceptible to malaria than those who do not. Evolution is fighting back and hasn't got it quite right yet but given time, well, who knows. Until then I can only suggest that nature regards it as a step towards the survival of mankind as a whole.'

'I'm gobsmacked.'

'You know what Copper? So am I.' Mallory pulled a face and replied. He continued, 'My point is though, that nature has produced more than one species of human in order to keep humanity itself in existence. Darwin's theory of natural selection is what I'm getting at.'

'Now I'm gobsmacked again!'

Patti Driscoll had a question.

'Doctor,' she asked, 'it sounds like fighting fire with fire but you were the one who told me the medical profession did the same thing once by having malaria bearing mosquitos bite patients with syphilis, so it seems to me it's a case of art imitating nature. Am I right?'

'I can't remember saying that but that is correct Nurse. Nature fights malaria with sickle cell anaemia and medicine fought syphilis with malaria. It was crude but it was better than nothing I suppose. I don't know what the rate of success was but I doubt it was much. I could be wrong. I daresay our friends at the Institute of Tropical

Medicine could tell us but speaking off the cuff I'd guess the unfortunate patient wound up with two diseases instead of just one.'

'I was the one who told you Nurse,' Matron interjected, 'and I might have added that it raises difficult questions in the matter of ethics. I for one would not like to defend the rights and wrongs of it. Or to advocate them.'

'Now I'm doubly gobsmacked,' Doctor Mallory declared.

Chapter 3

The vicar closed and locked the doors before striding up the aisle and turning to face his expectant audience.

'I think the presence of so many vehicles is bound to draw attention to our church so I have let it be known that we are gathered together for a private service of remembrance. It is a fitting distortion of our exact purpose for we are indeed gathered to remember Beowulf and Freya, the Viking forebears of Lawrence Bowden, Clive Bowden, and Lawrence Bowden junior, the young son of Clive Bowden and Copper Beach. I ask you to join in a silent prayer while we remember them, each in our own way. I had the unique privilege of uniting them in marriage in this very place, and it is this service I shall remember. Now let us pray together in silence.'

The vicar and the packed assembly bent their heads in silent prayer as they recalled their own experiences with the Vikings.

For a few brief minutes there was quiet until the vicar said amen and commented that the true business of the assembly which was eagerly awaited by so many people could begin.

Opening the proceedings he declared, 'We are in for a long session, which is unavoidable because there is much to be said. Our presentation will be skimpy at best, and in many respects downright inadequate. We hope to be able to rectify this in the very near future and present a written paper. Let us begin and start with Mr Brian Gleaves who engineered the recovery of Beowulf's box, the Viking's legacy to the future. Brian, the floor is yours.'

The popular engineer left the pew he occupied.

'I 'spect you know I was Beowulf's best man when he got hitched to Freya. Most of you were here anyway,' he began.

'Well, I went up the hill with Clive to have a look about and test the ground. It's a pretty steep climb I can tell you, and we weren't even at the top. Jeepers Creepers, you can see half of Yorkshire from up there! We had a pretty good idea how deep the box was because Beowulf said it would be at the depth of one sword. Well, a bit of probing by whacking in an iron rod soon showed the truth of that.

'Then I got to thinking about what we would need to lug up the hill to get it out. Spades o'course, shearlegs, block and tackle, some lengths of rope, that sort of thing. We had a good look at the lay of the land and figured out how to get the box down on the road in one piece without it running away out of control. That was the first trip, to find out what we had to do. The second trip was when we got down to doing it.

'This time we had Lawrence Bowden along with the camera to keep a record of the digging work. I could say excavation but it weren't that grand! What we found first was the stone slab that covered the box. I'm by way of knowing a bit of Latin so I worked out as how it said Freya put it there. That could've meant the slab or the box but I reckon as how it meant the box. I had a word with Julia and she thinks like I do. Jack and me took it out of the hole and it's in Merlin's cave right now.

'Then we hoisted the box out and it weren't difficult because the smith what made the iron straps fitted lugs to ease the hoisting. And the lowering when it was stowed in the pit o'course. There were wooden runners what showed signs of wear so I reckon that's how it was hauled up the hill but it weren't an easy job to get it down, even with the runners, and it took all of us pushing and tugging and holding on for dear life when it nearly got away from us. Odin's Ghost! The skid marks where we dug out heels in was twelve feet long if they was an inch!'

Brian took a long pause for breath before he continued his narrative.

'That was the end of getting it out of the ground, but there was one funny thing. When we got the box back under control we heard people laughing as plain as day. Lawrence got it all with the video camera and you can see us jump like we'd been shot. It were Viking laughter, honest it were. Beowulf and Freya was looking over our shoulders, I swear they were.'

There was a buzz of excited chatter. Brian waited for it to die away.

'We took the box to my workshop but we didn't touch it until everyone else had taken a look. It was photographed and measured and weighed and William of Salisbury even took its fingerprints! That ain't quite true but he had a go at it. Mostly he found out that me and Jack and Clive had all handled it but we could have told him that!

'The box was made from fine lengths of oak timber and bound with iron, and it's a real good piece of craftsmanship. I can tell you the weight and dimensions but that ain't important just now. It's longer than I thought and it turned out there was a good reason for that because it had to be big enough to put a sword in. There were a real Viking sword for Lawrence, what was put in box inside a box. This one was metal sealed up airtight with a big letter sort of scratched into the top, a big letter F it were, and anyone what's seen Freya's writing would know her fist anywhere. Freya put it there an' no mistake.

'Then we knew it weren't Beowulf's box at all. It was Freya's!'

Once again Brian waited for the babble of excited voices to die away.

'Well,' he said, 'that about ends my bit of talking and it ain't a patch on what happened next,' he told his spellbound listeners.

'It was pretty dramatic and no mistake but it ain't my job to talk about it, 'cept to say one more thing, and it's this. Beowulf and Freya weren't done with travelling in time. They went somewhere else! Or somewhen else, I ain't sure how to put it.'

There was an eruption of voices.

Clive Bowden took over where Brian Gleaves had left off.

'I want to take you back to a time in prehistory, and the Legends of the Lake,' he began.

'Working independently, Merlin, Julia, and Gerni have nearly completed their task of putting the Legends down in writing and by comparing each account against the other two we feel that at least some of the gaps in our knowledge will be filled.

'Very little is known about the Legends but they do tell of events in the past and events that were yet to come when the Legends began to emerge, and some which have not come about but may yet do so. One Legend says the Lake will be drained. Well, as we all know, it has been drained and today there is good farming land where once there was water, and of course there are towns and cities too, but the Legends also say the Lake will fill again. They don't say when, but some large areas have already been returned to wetlands as part of the land management scheme. Also, the summer of twenty twelve and the following winter brought vast flooding over many square miles of the Somerset Levels. Perhaps this is what the Legends are talking about. We don't know and we have no way of telling. Which begs one very important question. How in the world did the ancients know? Travel through time is the obvious answer. Obvious that is to anyone who knows Wint, and if time travel really is the answer it lifts the Legends from fable to fact. Admittedly the facts have almost certainly been distorted over time but the difference between fact and fable is a difference of major importance. I don't think anyone would argue with that.

'The legends are old. Exactly how old is another unknown. The First Legend says that three things are true. Firstly,' Clive ticked off the points on his fingers as he made them, 'the people who first settled on the Lake came from somewhere else. Secondly, there was a battle. Thirdly, the red dragons and the blue dragons went their separate ways.'

Clive drew a deep breath.

'Thanks to Freya we now know what that was all about. Ladies and Gentlemen, Freya was present at the foundation and settlement of the Lake!'

As Clive had anticipated this item of news caused an uproar that took a long time to die away. Clive used the time to review his own thoughts.

Taking a deep breath he continued, 'Those strangers, some of them at least, who settled on the Lake came from Wales, or I should say they came from the land that was to become Wales. The red and blue dragons are a subject that I shall return to later, and the battle that became known as the Battle of the Lake was fought by Beowulf, my Viking ancestor!

'I won't go into more details until Merlin and Julia have completed their translation of an account of the battle that Freya dictated to a certain Brother Scribe, but I can say that the battle altered history and it was fought against someone or something that was unspeakably evil. Beowulf won the Battle of the Lake but his opponent, who was named Tarn, fled the battlefield. Beowulf followed him to Wales and it was there that he met his enemy face to face. Beowulf was armed with his sword and shield but his opponent had something far more potent, the power of the stones.

'There can be no doubt that Beowulf fought himself and his enemy to a standstill but there was only one way to settle the matter once and for all. Badly injured, Beowulf managed to impale Tarn on his sword and lift him clear of the ground, denying him the power of the stones. Without hesitation Beowulf walked into certain death in a stone circle, giving Tarn to the stones, which was the only way of killing him, and saying only to Freya that he would be waiting for her in the Hall of Warriors when her own time came.

'Freya returned to the Viking age and lived to become an old lady before, in the words of Brother Scribe, she went to her rest according to Viking law and custom, but before she left the Lake she made a curious promise that if ever the Lake Dwellers needed Viking aid again they would come if the Lake Dwellers played their pipes and drums.'

Interlude

'Find the Lake! It's your only chance, you must find the Lake. It won't be easy and you're only a boy but you can do it. You mustn't let yourself be captured, so only ask for directions if you are sure you won't end up in Tarn's hands.'

The boy nodded obediently. The howling wind tore at his hair and waves crashing on the beach flung up a salty spray into his face. The wizened old crone who had found him gestured towards the wreck of a boat that had been driven onto the rocks, and at the cairn of stones that the pair had built to cover two bodies.

'What were their names?' She demanded, bending to shout in his ear.

'She was Reve and his name was Gelf but those weren't their real names. They were stone turners,' he shouted back, 'and my name is…'

A bony hand clamped over his mouth.

'No names boy, what we don't know we can't tell.'

It was strange, the words seemed to come from inside his head.

'They weren't your parents, that much is obvious.'

The hand was withdrawn.

'They were just people I know. I haven't got any parents, I think I'm an orphan. I was just found, that's all I know. We were trying to sail to the Lake but the sea is so big and our boat was broken. When it started sinking they put the way to the Lake in my head the way some of them can, so I would know where to walk.

'They were always kind to me. They made me a toy,' he pulled a carved wooden animal from inside his cloak. 'It's a cat but it's got black stripes all over and they said there are lots of cats like that where they come from, and they're big, not like our wildcats. As long as two people,' he concluded doubtfully.

'It's a tiger,' the old woman identified it. 'It's many a long year since I saw one of those. I was a girl then boy, not the old woman I am now. Your friends were long-lifers.'

'I know. Did you go to their homeplace?' the boy asked.

'I did, and many were the wonders I saw, but it will be a long time before anyone goes there again. Not in our lifetimes boy, not in our lifetimes.'

Beginning to walk up the beach she said roughly but kindly, 'Well boy, you'd best be on your way. Get as far from this place as you can before nightfall. You have a pair of good stone knives and you can make fire. Be careful not to make smoke. Your journey will be long, you'll be older before you reach the Lake, but reach it you will. Do you understand?'

Chapter 4

Merlin spotted Edwin Mallory and Kate Fawcett walking in the hospital grounds as he approached the building. He changed direction and hailed them.

'I was on my way to find you,' he said as he got nearer.

'I didn't expect to catch you both but I'm glad I have,' he continued when he caught up with them.

'You look like a man with something on his mind,' Kate Fawcett observed.

'I am. More than one thing actually. I've been talking to Marcel and Françoise Land. I thought I'd run their ideas past you.'

Professor Marcel Land and Doctor Françoise Land were the French psychologists who had helped Copper come to terms with her condition before Merlin revealed himself to her.

Merlin continued.

'Marcel thinks it would be a good idea if we brought some more people in to our society. Specifically he suggests some younger people who have no connections with us via their families. His reasons are that sooner or later we will become known to everyone and Marcel believes that teenagers will be more, well I was going to say accustomed to us but what I mean is that they will be ambassadors for us. If they already know and can be seen to have taken it in their strides it will make it easier for the general public when they find out. Teenagers are more likely to be flexible in their thinking and acceptance of the situation, he thinks. I must say I tend to agree but I want your opinions.'

'He could be right,' Edwin Mallory said.

'Agreed,' Kate Fawcett echoed.

'I'll set the wheels in motion. Françoise recommends a mixed group of four to six people. That seems about right to me. I mean to have a word with Clive Bowden and George Green because as schoolteachers they are the most likely people to know who should be recruited. It does mean they will be sailing close to the wind so to speak.'

'It certainly does!' Kate Fawcett exclaimed. 'And I hate to think about the repercussions if anything goes wrong.'

Edwin Mallory concurred.

'It requires careful thought. I'll approach them anyway and spell out the risks although I'm sure I won't need to,' Merlin said.

'Keep us informed Merlin. I think Marcel is right and I'm all for it in principle but it's a dodgy business all round. I would like to add a suggestion, and that is that not only are the teenagers in question carefully selected, so should their parents be,' Edwin Mallory said very seriously.

'Noted and taken on board.'

'You said there was more than one thing on you mind,' Kate Fawcett reminded Merlin.

Merlin nodded.

'This one came to me from pre-history. I had a surprise visit from Wint and I've been mulling it over for a while before I spring it on anyone. He dropped a bombshell and I'm at a loss to know how to handle it. In a nutshell he proposed an exchange visit between four people from the time about five years after after the Vikings fought the Battle of the Lake and two people from out time. The numbers are disproportionate but Wint pointed out that there are far fewer people on the Lake than there are in the city of Bath. What do you think?'

'I'd go without thinking twice,' Mallory said, 'but it needs careful selection. That's my way of saying I'm all for it.'

'Me too,' Kate Fawcett echoed.

'I'll take that on board. There's another thing.'

'I'm half expecting what you are about to say,' Mallory said.

'This one is nearer to home. Julia has spotted something that I have only noticed myself these last few minutes. You've broken Clive Bowden's rules about who should have the bugs in their bloodstreams, haven't you? How did you do it?'

'Umm, I was hoping nobody would ask that question for a while,' Edwin Mallory said.

'Blame Julia for putting me on to you.'

'Merlin, it was my fault,' Kate Fawcett intervened, 'I raised the question of medical ethics because it was an untried medical procedure, or maybe I ought to say experiment. The authorities come down heavily on that sort of thing and rightly so. I offered myself as a guinea pig and I think I was careful about breaking any of Clive's rules about who gets it and who doesn't, apart from being less than seventy years old, but I couldn't do anything about that. I told Edwin to make it a secret trial because failure was possible and we, I, didn't want to disappoint anyone if Edwin had got it wrong and he couldn't… well, you know. So I'm the one to blame.'

'Side effects? How do you feel?' Merlin asked directly.

'My joints ache and I've lost a tooth that was more filling than tooth anyway. I can't feel a new one growing through yet but it's still early days.'

'Who else knows?'

'Matron possibly. I'd think very carefully before I tried to keep anything from her. I'd like to tell Nurse Driscoll because it was her insight that made it all possible.'

'I'll tell her myself. I haven't seen Patti for far too long. As for you Edwin, I don't think Clive's rules will be too badly broken if you prepare a dose for yourself and match your age to Kate's more closely, not forgetting to do the same for Janet Smythe. You still haven't told me how you managed it.'

'Actually I had intended to call Janet and Jack as soon as I was sure and I ought to have called them days ago. As to how I did it, I made some tests and confirmed a theory. The strain of buggies in the Roman Baths is the one that survives the trip. The strain that I found in the luminous patches on the trilobites is equally tough but it doesn't make the trip. The idea of a second strain came directly from Clive Bowden. I managed to find it and culture it and I would have tried it on myself first my blood group can take the same strain as you and Copper have in your blood so it wouldn't have proved anything. Kate can't take your strain but she can take the one I found. It was that easy.'

'I think you're underselling yourself but I must say I'm delighted with what you have discovered and what you have done with it. Do you think anyone would call us stark staring mad if we joined hands and danced round in a circle?'

'Who cares?'

***

'I knew all along that my rules about the beach buggies would never stand up,' Clive said to George Green as they walked along a deserted corridor at the start of the school day. 'I didn't know it would happen like this though.'

'It raises interesting possibilities,' George replied.

'So does Marcel Land's idea of getting a few teenagers on board. Kate Fawcett is dead right about it being dodgy, but the idea itself is sound and speaking for myself, I'm all for it. Actually, I have been thinking about getting another staff member recruited, purely for selfish reasons but if we do go ahead and pick out a mixed bag of pupils we ought to have a female staff member too. It might possibly give us some added protection if it blows up in our faces,' Clive said.

'Which it could. I want to give it some thought before I go along with it. Presumably you have a staff member in mind already?'

'Miss Collins. Angela Collins, she teaches English. I've been working on the Shakespeare play that was written about Merlin and it's hard going, quite apart from the fact that his penmanship was, I suppose I should say is, his penmanship is almost unreadable. I'm hoping that together we could unscramble it but I need somebody with a better knowledge of Shakespeare than I have to ferret out the proper meaning of some of the things he wrote, and she'll have to give an opinion on some new words I've run across.'

George nodded his agreement.

'As I remember he invented dozens of new words and got them into the English language,' he replied.

'And his use of insult and invective is impressive too. You could certainly say he had a way with words.'

'I remember that as well. You're starting to think like the Roman military, killing two birds with one stone. You get someone who understands Shakespeare and you get female staff member as well.'

'I can't take any credit,' Clive replied after a short silence while another staff member passed, 'I just wanted a translator, but I have to admit it is rather convenient.'

'What teenagers have you got in mind? I'm assuming you've considered one or two candidates?'

'I'm assuming you have too,' Clive answered him.

George agreed that he had.

'It's still early days. What say we each put a list together and compare names? Let's see what we've got. I do recollect an article I read in one of the teacher's journals that can be summarised in a sentence, namely that when a group of bright pupils get together they spark off each other, apparently it's self perpetuating. Unfortunately the converse is true. If I remember right the groups have to form of their own accord, you can't put the pupils into an ad hoc group and expect a result. They'll split up as soon as their task is done.'

'Putting a list together seems as good a way as any. Somewhere between four and six of our pupils. I can name one or two I wouldn't have at any price until they grow up a bit but at this stage I'm not prepared to rule anyone in or out.'

'Suits me. Ho hum, back to work.'

They parted company and went off to their respective classrooms.

***

It was the end of the week. Brian Gleaves stood next to his pick-up vehicle and gazed around his yard. There had been extra work during the middle of the week when an emergency job had to be done for a local farmer but somehow they had managed. More than one of his customers was feeling the pinch and made no secret of the fact but there was still plenty of work for his engineering business. Regular maintenance work on machinery on half a dozen farms meant Brian had to stick to a tight schedule and it was a referral from a regular client that had brought in the extra work. Wolftamer Agricultural Engineering had a reputation for quality work and good service.

He had operated as a one man band until a bewildering series of events had seen the old workshop go up in flames one night, leaving nothing but ash and twisted metal. It was replaced by a new building thanks to the help given to him by Police Superintendent Francis Holley, more commonly known as Frank, an old acquaintance and friend who, to their mutual surprise, had taken on a new career with Brian when he retired from the police force. Superintendent Holley's account of the event, in which he was involved, ensured prompt action on the part of Brian's insurers and the new building that went up was bigger and better than the one it replaced. It was also designed to be easily extended, which was something Brian was contemplating.

37

Frank Holley handled the tasks of administration and was also prepared to take on anything else that came his way and he was presently driving a newly acquired Land Rover into the yard, towing a small trailer that bore a tracked digger that he had been using at a nearby farm where new drainage was being laid. The vehicle and the digger had been bought as a job lot in an auction, used but in good condition, and it came with a full set of attachments to perform a number of jobs.

Brian had a lot on his mind. There was more work around than he could easily handle and he had begun to wonder if expansion would be a good idea. On balance it seemed that it would. He had taken advice from several sources. He considered his suppliers and his customers. If he expanded he would be dealing with more suppliers, people he had never dealt with and products of unknown potential. Take his new digger. Well, new depends how you look at it. It came cheap but it didn't take much brainwork to figure out that it was up for sale because it wasn't making money for its owner. Brian felt it was a good purchase but he wasn't going in for wishful thinking.

Agricultural engineering had changed a lot since the early days. Machinery had got bigger for a start. Tractors that used to be the same size as cars had become huge and had electronic equipment that controlled and monitored performance and reported any problems automatically. Once a plough never had more than four shares, and they were considered big. Now the big new machines could turn over eight furrows at once. Computer diagnostics had become an everyday part of the business and he often went out to the farms with his equipment. It wasn't like the old days when the machinery was brought to his yard as often as not. You couldn't get a combine harvester into the yard any more, they were that big. They had satellite navigation equipment that kept them positioned to within a gnat's hair and the drivers could go hands off for much of the time. The computers did it better. He had a library of manufacturer's manuals and maintenance instructions and more brochures arrived with every post it seemed to Brian. Farming was changing and no mistake, and so was agricultural engineering. Like it or lump it, you had to move with the times.

Frank Holley interrupted Brian's reverie.

'That's another job finished Brian,' he said, 'and there'll be more jobs like that coming our way. When the Somerset levels flooded people started to pay more attention to their ditches. We're going to be digging more trenches for drainage to be laid and I've had enquiries for ditch clearing from the farm where I've just been. I told him we had the attachments for both jobs. We're going to be asked to do more drainage work from now on, of that you can be sure.'

'I've had a couple of phone calls myself mate,' Brian admitted.

He realised he was holding his dog's water bowl and dragged his thoughts back to what he was doing. He had inherited his alsatian dog on the night his business burned down and the first thing he did was change her name from Sheba to Button when Superintendent Holley as he was then told him that any amount of large bitches were called Sheba which he claimed said more about their owners than it said about the dogs and it wasn't meant as a compliment.

The bowl was quickly cleaned and filled. Button was nowhere to be seen but Brian knew she was not far away, the dog never strayed from the yard. Her kennel stood next to the new building and she was probably sleeping.

Brian and Frank were talking about the amount of work that had been accomplished that week when a red van drove into the yard and the driver got out with a package of mail bound with a red elastic band.

'Quite a bundle you've got there Brian,' the driver said cheerfully and added, 'hello Button,' when the dog came out of her kennel.

She stroked the alsatian's head and picked up the ball which was dropped at her feet. She threw it Button raced off to fetch it

'More stuff from the tractor people,' she commented as she indicated the package she had delivered.

'Most likely,' Brian agreed, 'and I'm waiting for a new servicing manual from the combine harvester rep who comes round. It's ring bound so I can slip new pages in and take the old ones out. I was sort of hoping it would be on this delivery.'

'There's always tomorrow,' the woman replied. 'Well I've got three kids and a husband and to pander to and I've stretched my legs for long enough, it's time to get back on the job.'

Weighing the package in his hand Brian watched with a thoughtful look as the van left the yard and only then did he remember that Frank Holley had collected an envelope full of the red elastic bands that the

Post Office used to keep bundles of letters that were to be delivered to one address. He had meant to hand them over when the post was delivered. Waste not, want not. Well, tomorrow would be soon enough and besides, Frank hadn't remembered either. He picked up the ball that was dropped at his feet.

'Just one more time,' he said as he threw it. 'I've got work to do.'

The door was open as the two men walked inside. Brian knew Button would not come in. She was a dog that hated to be indoors, ever since she was a puppy. Brian found Jack Smythe placing the tools he had used on his last job onto a silhouette board so that each tool could be accounted for.

'I'll have the paperwork on your desk in a couple of minutes Boss,' Jack told him, 'and we could do with a new packet of fine toothed hacksaw blades, we're down to just two or three.'

'OK mate, I'll put it on the list. Anything else what's a bit short?'

'No, I don't reckon, not in my department anyway. Frank said something earlier about tea bags and a jar of coffee but that's his thing, not mine, and he's probably told you already.'

'I was getting round to it,' Frank said, 'and I left a note on your desk before I went out.'

'Blimey mate, we're getting organised. That don't happen often!'

Jack's boyish grin belied his age. Apparently in his mid-twenties he was actually in his fifties. It was believed that he had got the beach buggy virus when he was baptised in a font after a small dragon had been hastily removed and thrust into the vicar's pocket as his family approached for the ceremony.

'Organised,' he said. 'I don't reckon I could stand the boredom!'

Frank Holley had been told about Jack's condition shortly after he had been taken on as an engineer, and after Merlin had given a convincing demonstration of the reality of the situation they had metaphorically shrugged their shoulders and got on with the job.

'Tell you what mate, you organise the kettle and I'll get the mugs.'

There were things to discuss and he started the ball rolling.

'I got a letter here what's just come an' I reckon it's from the surveyors. Hang on while I just open it up... yep, thought as much. There's a surveyor coming in next week to do a bit of work. I've said he can park in the yard, there ain't a lot of other places. So anyway, he's going to measure us up. All the ground around the place and a fair way back, and it adds up to quite a bit of ground.'

'Is someone after it?' Frank Holley was quick to ask. 'I haven't heard of any developers sniffing around but that's no surprise. Keep quiet and there's no competition and that means prices stay low. Most probably they'll hang on to it for a while and then sell building lots. It could be bad news Brian,' he warned.

'Well mate, that ain't likely to happen, I know for sure.'

'Who owns it anyway?' Jack Smythe asked. 'It's no use as farmland, not even for grazing a few sheep. Most likely the council just wants to be rid of a few plots that aren't making any money.'

Brian picked up his mug and moved it to one side without tasting his coffee and then dropped his bombshell.

'Fact is,' he said, 'the bloke what owns it is me.'

'You! You own it?'

''S'right mate, me. I own it, me and nobody else and what you said about it not being any use for farming and grazing is the same as what I was told. It's what they call a craggy outcrop and scrubland but what with building machinery, bulldozers and such you could clear enough ground for a new building, which you couldn't have done once.'

'I'll say one thing Brian, you're full of surprises,' Frank Holley said as he put his own mug of coffee on the table with an unsteady hand.

'Sort of surprised me too,' Brian informed him.

'I better begin at the beginning,' he said, 'and it's this way. It ain't any secret about how I stood a few years ago before the old barn burnt down but it goes back further than that to when me and my sister Marge inherited a bit of money. It weren't a lot but it came in handy and I managed to buy my place here. I don't kid myself that I would've got it if anyone else had wanted it but I had ideas back in them days and I thought I could make a go of it. Anyway, there was the land that went with it and its mostly rocky scrubland what nobody had a use for. I never asked for it and I never had any use for it either so I just forgot about it and that was that.

'Like as not it was a good thing I did because if my wife had known she would have most likely wanted a share of it when she took off. She can't now because the births and marriages and deaths people was on the case when I asked about her and she was on the bright life in

London with drink and drugs for a little while until the day she took too much. She never cared about me and I stopped caring about her a long time ago so nobody has to say sorry.

'I was on my uppers and no mistake but I had my work and I kept myself going and I never had to spend much, it weren't like I had a social life and so I put away most of my money into an account. My sister Marge does that for me, regular every month. I sort of did it for years and it's still there and what with me having regular work and the interest on the account I suddenly found I ain't badly off. I still can't hardly believe it.

'And that's pretty well up to date, more or less, and I'm sort of thinking. I've talked about expanding from time to time and the work is there. That's the reason I changed the name of the business to Wolftamer Agricultural Engineering. Fact is, it never had a proper name before; it was just Brian's place. Anyway, I could have another building or I could make the one I've got bigger. I might knock the house down, it don't hold any special memories for me and the site could be used for something else. Thing is, it depends on how much land I own because it's marked on the papers but I ain't even seen all of it on account of not having any use for it. So I just don't know how much I own or anything. And there it is.'

'Wow!' Jack exclaimed.

'Brian, haven't you any idea how much land there is? You might be sitting on a couple of acres or hectares or whatever measurement they use,' Frank Holley enquired.

'It's a bit more than that mate. More like a square mile.'

'Jeepers Creepers!'

'Bilmey!'

Brian Gleaves looked sheepish.

'It don't change anything and it ain't money in the bank. I just thought about taking on a bit more work in a bigger building but I ain't put in for planning permission and it weren't until I thought about making the business bigger that I remembered I had a bit of spare land. There's some people at the Land Registry what told me it's all been one piece for as far back as the records go so there's no doubt it's mine. There's never been any building there but they said it maybe that somewhen in the last couple of hundred years there might've been a bit of quarrying or something so I got to thinking I could find out and so that's why the surveyor bloke is coming to have a look and do a bit of measuring and do a satellite fix or something and just plain see what's there.'

'If it hasn't ever been used it might be what they call an SSI. Site of Scientific Interest, I saw a programme about it once. That would stop the property speculators bunging up a housing estate but it might stop you putting up a new building as well,' Jack Smythe said.

Brian made a note in the small notebook he kept on his desk.

'I'll have to find out but I don't reckon as how I'd have any trouble knocking down my house like I said and getting a new place put up there. I suppose it won't hurt to drop a line to the chronicler either and get it in the records of the Bell Curve stuff.'

'What did Julia say?' Frank Holley enquired. 'Not that it's any of my business, I'm just being nosy.'

Brian coloured slightly and the experienced ex-policeman spotted it instantly.

'You haven't told her have you?' He said not unkindly.

'I don't know how to. I know I should but I just don't know what to say,' Brian replied unsteadily.

'Brian, Julia is the Lady of the Lake. A little thing like that won't even make her blink.'

Chapter 5

George Green glanced out of the window as he and Clive Bowden walked the school corridor towards the staff room. It was Thursday afternoon and the forecast light rain had arrived. The forecaster was Merlin. It was a weak weather front coming from the west and after it's passing the rest of the week the rest of the week would be warm and dry, Merlin had said. Copper's father was never wrong when he predicted the weather though his methods remained a mystery.

As they approached the English classroom they slowed their pace. Clive glanced at his wristwatch.

'She's running late,' he said.

'She won't be long. If we stop here and look as if we're having a conversation nobody will take much notice.'

Inside the classroom Miss Angela Collins pulled down the rolling whiteboard to reveal a pair of sentences she had written previously. She read it out loud.

'You would think a business like ours would have a branch in every street. So we do.'

After a brief pause she asked, 'Can anyone tell me what is wrong with that?'

A boy raised his hand.

'Yes?'

'The verb has been changed Miss. The second sentence should use the same verb as the first. It should be "So we have."'

'Correct. Christine, you look as if you want to say something.'

'We do use two verbs in the same sentence sometimes. I could say "Have you got a spare pen." We do it all the time,' Christine Appleton said.

'We do. It would be more correct to say "Have you a spare pen?" It has been said that the English language is in a mess at times as a result of new words being introduced, and the legacy of some old ones. Speech forms alter over time too, so what was once considered correct is now thought of as wrong.'

'It isn't always logical though.'

'Logical. There speaks Spockette.'

Miss Collins made no attempt to hide her smile as she issued a gentle rebuke. It was hard to read Christine Appleton's expression.

'I see. Miss, that was an advertisement wasn't it? I'm sure I've heard it before.'

Miss Collins smiled again and not for the first time she wondered whether Christine Appleton remembered everything she read or heard.

'Well remembered. It is an example of a poor sentence constructed by copywriters who ought to know better. It's getting late, so class dismissed.'

The classroom door opened and loosed a class of pupils, all in a rush to go home.

Seconds after the last pupil emerged Miss Angela Collins appeared. Her teacher colleagues matched her pace although she was unaware that their encounter was planned.

'Did you bring your umbrella?' Clive enquired.

'No,' Angela Collins replied ruefully, 'I wasn't expecting rain.'

'It won't last, I have it on the best authority and by a remarkable coincidence an umbrella awaits you in the staff room, and not only that there is somebody waiting in the car park to have a few words with you.'

'What are you talking about?'

'Wait and see,' Clive replied as he opened the door for her. Nobody else was present. Clive produced a folding umbrella from his locker.

'It won't rain any more after this evening, the rest of the week will be fine and dry and so will the weekend but on Monday you'll need your coat,' he told her.

'Have the two of you gone raving mad?' Miss Collins demanded, 'And why are you grinning like Cheshire cats?'

'Patience. Contain yourself and all will be revealed,' George replied, obviously pleased about something.

Without a word Angela Collins followed George and Clive out of the building.

'Well,' she said, 'am I to be told what this is all about?' She asked as she unfurled the umbrella she had been given.

Clive indicated an approaching woman whom until now Angela had not noticed.

'Meet my wife, Copper Beach,' he said as he made the introductions. 'Copper uses her own name,' he added unnecessarily, 'and she'll put you in the picture.'

'Have these reprobates been playing games? They have a guilty look about them.'

Without waiting for a reply Copper added, 'Angela, I'm to invite you to a barbecue on Saturday. My father is rather good at that sort of thing and Mrs Bradley makes the most delicious dips and sauces. I must tell you that we all want you to come and we have an ulterior motive. I don't think you will be disappointed but, well, this is difficult but I must play all mysterious and not say any more than that.'

'Please,' Clive entreated, 'we need you.'

'Need me? Me in particular? Does it have to be me?'

'Actually, it does,' Clive told her.

'Very well, I'll play along. I'm not sure why but I will.'

Copper looked pleased.

'Mr and Mrs Green will pick you up because they know the way and it would be silly to use two cars when one will do. And of course you can bring someone with you.'

For the first time Angela smiled.

'I'll come alone,' she declared, 'I'm footloose and fancy free until the next one comes along. I've just been dumped. And I'm intrigued.'

The weather on Friday was what Clive had said it would be and Angela Collins returned the umbrella she had borrowed. Neither Clive nor George answered her questions and she was unsure whether she was annoyed or not. Something was going on, she was sure of that, but what? Tomorrow would tell and until then she would have to learn to be patient. It was a hard lesson to learn but Saturday came at last. Copper Beach greeted them as Angela arrived with George and Hilary Green.

'Do come in,' she urged, 'my father is waiting to see you Angela and there are one or two other people who will explain what this is all about. We'll do that indoors and by then my father will have the barbecue going, he's in the garden now. First let me introduce Julia, Alison, and the vicar, who has a name but it never appears in print. You'll soon know why.'

More than ever, Angela Collins was starting to wonder what was lying in store for her. Opening her mouth to protest she was interrupted by the vicar.

'In at the deep end I think,' he said, 'ready, steady, and...'

The jostling crown in London's Globe Theatre fell silent when the actors appeared.

'Tush! Never tell me Iago; I take it much unkindly that thou, Iago, who hast my purse as if its strings were thine, should know of this.'

Angela Collins mind raced. William Shakespeare's Othello, Act 1, Scene 1, Roderigo addressing Iago she thought as she recognised the play. Her surroundings changed before she was able to answer her own question.

Standing and facing her, a woman gave her a gap toothed smile.

'Experience,' she said, 'though noon autoritee, were in this world is right ynogh for me to speak of wo that is right in marriage. For lordynges, sith I twelve year was of age, thanked be to God that is eterne on lyve, housbonds an chirch door I have had five -'

Abruptly and before she had finished what she was saying, the woman was gone.

'That was the language of Geoffrey Chaucer,' Angela muttered, and then realised she was the centre of attention.

'I ... Chaucer,' she raised a hand to her temple. 'I think I had better sit down,' she gasped.

Solicitous hands caught her as she staggered towards a chair and lost her balance.

'Angela, that was my fault,' Julia apologised.

Angela shook her head as the words seemed to come from a long distance.

'I was in the Globe Theatre,' she forced the words out, 'and then somebody talked to me and it was, I mean she was reciting the prologue of the Wife of Bath's Tale in Chaucer's Canterbury Tales. I knew who she was because I know the words and I've heard recordings of the language that was spoken in his day.'

Lifting her head she addressed Alison.

'She looked just like you.'

'Angela, she is me,' Alison told her. 'I'm much older than Copper and I had an affair with Geoffrey Chaucer that was quite scandalous at the time. He spiced up the Wife of Bath's Tale because he knew what his readers wanted but even so I was no better than I should have been.'

Alison laughed. It was plain that her memories were happy ones.

'This is not the time,' she added, 'but one day I'll tell you all about the Miller's Tale which was true in every word but even Geoffrey dared not name the person he wrote about.'

She laughed again.

'By the way Angela, my name is Alison. I'm six hundred years old, more or less and Copper is a hundred or so but a girl's age is her own affair don't you think?'

'That's enough ladies,' the vicar interjected. 'Angela, you might have noticed that Julia and Alison are wearing scarves now, which they put on while you were, um, otherwise engaged. From now on you qualify for a scarf yourself, and here it is. The ladies wear scarves and the men wear ties with the same motif. No doubt you recognise the dragons, which are blue because the Wessex dragon is blue as opposed to the Welsh dragon which is red. The red beastie is a trilobite. They are well known from fossil finds but you might not have heard of them.'

'I haven't,' Angela Collins said unsteadily as she accepted her scarf with a faint but noticeable reluctance, 'and I'm not convinced. I know something happened to me but not what you said. I think I'd better leave.'

She stood up, leaving the scarf on the chair.

'As you wish,' Julia said, 'but Copper will be disappointed. Come with me,' she added, 'and say your goodbye. She's not far away.'

Angela Collins followed Julia reluctantly, not really wanting to but somehow unable to resist.

They found Copper outside and looking slightly uphill towards the barbecue that her father was attending.

'Angela wants to leave,' Julia informed her, 'but,' she turned to face Angela, 'we might still be able to persuade you to stay. Copper has a little pet which is guaranteed to persuade you to at least give you a chance to change your mind. He's very timid so try not to startle him.'

Plainly displeased, Angela compressed her lips.

Raising her forearm Copper looked towards one of the apple trees in the garden and said 'Peep' and waited.

'Peep,' she said again and with a flash of blue wings a creature launched itself from the tree and swooped down to land on Copper's bare arm.

'Peep,' it piped.

'That's, that's a dragon,' Angela Collins stammered.

'He's called Peep because that's the noise he makes,' Copper informed her. 'I think he'll let you stroke him,' she added.

Hesitantly Angela stretched her hand out and then quickly withdrew it.

'Go ahead,' Copper encouraged her.

Nervously Angela reached her hand out again and very cautiously managed to stroke the small creature.

'Peep,' it said.

'Now you know why your scarf has the blue dragon of Wessex on it,' Julia informed her and continued, 'and if you are still with us I'll show you why it has a red trilobite as well. This way.'

Julia led everyone to the barbecue area and handed paper plates to everyone.

Merlin introduced himself.

'I'm Copper's father,' he said, 'call me Merlin and pass your plate. Try this, I think you'll enjoy it.'

Merlin used a pair of tongs to put something on Angela's plate and then spooned a little sauce over it.

'Orange sauce,' he informed her, 'but I have tangy lemon or ginger too.'

'What is it?'

'Trilobite. Try it.'

Cautiously Angela nibbled a small bite.

'It's delicious. I don't know what it tastes like but I do like it.'

Merlin looked pleased.

Suddenly Angela gasped, 'I've just touched a dragon! It's just hit home!'

'And now you've eaten a trilobite,' Copper told her, 'and they are extinct. They were sea creatures and there were lots of different kinds, the same as there are lots of different sorts of fishes. Then they died out millions of years ago.'

Angela looked at her, open mouthed.

'Except they didn't, not quite. These are fresh water trilobites but they haven't been discovered. Uh, I'm not doing this very well am I?' Copper continued.

Merlin intervened.

'Perhaps I can explain. Copper, look after the barbecue for a while and Angela and I will find some seats. Just a second,' he said as he ladled a drink into a plastic beaker and handed it to Angela.

'Copper's own recipe for punch, more or less. Let's seat ourselves over there.'

Merlin indicated a rustic seat and led the way.

'I made all the garden furniture myself,' he said, 'but that's beside the point. What you want are answers to your questions. Hmm, where to begin?'

'Alison told me Copper is a hundred years old, which quite obviously she is not, and you are supposed to be her father. I don't know why I was fed such a nonsensical story. And then she called a dragon and it flew out of a tree and, and my head's in a whirl.'

'You left out the part about watching one of William Shakespeare's plays and then hearing Alison speaking some lines from Geoffrey Chaucer's Canterbury Tales,' Merlin said.

'Mr Merlin, what is going on?' Angela Collins demanded.

Merlin chuckled, then apologised.

'Sorry. I'll explain. Just a sketchy outline but you will leave here with an information pack which will go some way to filling in the gaps. To begin with my daughter is as old as she claims to be. Plainly then, I am older. Not only that, Julia and Alison are exactly what they say they are.'

'Julia hasn't said anything yet,' Angela Collins protested.

'Has she not? Then it falls to me to tell you that Julia, whose full name sounds rather grand, she is Julia Calpurnia Florentina Pantera and she came to our shores during that period of history when Britain was ruled by the Romans. Julia is the last citizen of the Roman Empire. Your next question is why some people live so long.'

'Is it? I suppose it is. Why am I taking this so calmly?'

'Because some part of you accepts the truth and another part is trying to reconcile that with what you know. Professor Land will put it better when you meet him. Or Doctor Land; they are French, man and wife, and in all probability they are going to be furious that they aren't here tonight because of previous engagements. They have been told about you and you can be sure that one or both will meet you before long. But your first question concerns the length of some people's lives.

'Angela, a few years ago Copper was found to be carrying a sort of virus. She isn't the first, I carry it too, as do Julia and Alison. If I may second guess your next question neither Clive Bowden nor George Green are carriers. It isn't something you can catch but very recently one of its secrets has been cracked and now we know how it can be put into anyone and from then on they are immune to anything and everything. It has been done very recently and if I may say so, rather clandestinely. Speaking for myself, I couldn't catch a cold if I wanted too, and the Black Death back in the Middle Ages never touched me. The virus also has an effect on the aging process as you will find out. There are rules about who will and who will not be offered it and I know that George and Hilary Green won't mind me telling you they turned it down flat.

'Now as to me, I did say call me Merlin but you called me Mr Merlin. Well that isn't wrong but whereas everybody has one or more given names and a family name, that doesn't apply to me. I am simply Merlin.'

'Oh,' Angela Collins said faintly. 'That Merlin? Merlin the Magician?'

'The same, but I'm not a magician, far from it. I do know a trick or two though and so does Julia. Our knowledge came from different directions. I learned from, well, schools is as good a description as any, schools that were set up by the ones we call the Old People after a major upheaval that we will discuss at a later date.

'Julia's case is very different. She came to Britain with her parents when she was a very young girl and at some point when she was still young she got the virus into her system. Rome fell and in the early years of then fifth century the last Roman Legions left Britain to its own devices. Julia went to live in what we now know as Somerset, which at that time was extensively flooded. Her arrival turned out to be expected by the native Britons who lived around the edges of a vast lake. How they knew she was coming is a mystery that has only recently been cleared up, thanks to some Vikings named Beowulf and

Freya. They were Clive Bowden's ancestors as it happens but that too is another story.

'Anyway, Julia became well known to legend and literature as the fabled Lady of the Lake.'

'Oh. I don't know what to say. Uh, is Mr Bowden, you know..?' Merlin smiled.

'No, but one day perhaps. You see it was Clive himself who ruled on that. In essence nobody younger than seventy years old will have it, neither will anyone who demands it. Especially those. My daughter was very old by the usual standards when, as somebody said, lightning struck the same place twice, and it is sheer coincidence that she got it. All through her life I have stood on the sidelines, unable to be a father to her until, well until lightning struck again. She will tell you all about it, and more details will be in the information pack we will give you. Starter pack would be a better way of putting it.

'There is one other thing; you can walk away whenever you wish. We hope you won't. Did Clive mention that we had a special reason for asking you to join us?'

'He said he had an ulterior motive.'

'Mmm. He could have phrased it better but it is true. He will be here in five minutes or so, bringing my grandson Larry for me to spoil, and when he does I think he will make you an offer you can't refuse.'

While they waited and made small talk a man whom Angela had not met previously whisked her plate away and replaced it with another.

'Last piece,' he told her, 'and this time it comes with a lemon dip. My favourite as it happens. Enjoy.'

Angela had just enough time to notice that he wore an unusual hat before he was gone and she lost sight of him. She had a question for Merlin.

'Why did Mrs Bowden, Mrs Beach, uh, I suppose she'll tell me which, but why did she say these trilobite things are extinct? Trilobites, is that right? They're not and I'm eating the evidence but I don't quite understand what this is all about. Any of it.'

'My daughter kept her own name when she and Clive were married but you might have noticed how we tend to use given names rather than family names. In my own case I only have one name but to the world at large I'm called Marlin. More than one of us is in the same boat as it were; William of Salisbury for instance, who is a Police Constable and he's standing over there. Obviously he cannot insist on William being his only appellation so he uses a fictitious family name for the sake of convenience. He is a policeman.'

'You just said that.'

'Oops, so I did. Well, as to the trilobites, they really did become extinct millions of years ago after a run of three hundred million years or so. They were all salt water species save for the ones you have had on your plate, which found an ecological niche and carried on as if nothing had happened. To the best of my knowledge no freshwater trilobites have ever been discovered in the fossil record so the many books that have been written trilobites have no reference to them. More recently, in the light of deep water exploration it has been speculated that maybe, just maybe, one or more colonies might still be around.'

'Oh. Like coelocanths?'

Merlin looked pleased.

'I knew George and Clive had picked the right person,' he said.

'Quick on the uptake and doesn't mess around, that was how they described you. Coelocanths are a very good anology. Angela, you're going to fit in very well. And here comes my grandson so I must leave you now and George and Clive will take over. Oh, one more thing; do remember to collect your scarf from where you left it and wear it around the city. You will be surprised at the number of people who will come up and talk to you, and sometimes you'll be surprised at who they are.'

The garden seat was not big enough for five people. Angela Collins stood up as Clive Bowden approached, accompanied by Copper Beach and George and Hilary Green.

'It seems that I'm in then, but in what exactly I'm none too sure.'

Copper Beach placed a large polythene bag on the seat that had just been vacated.

'We call ourselves the Bell Curve Society. Members are all the people who know about us, which includes you as of this evening. Everyone gets a scarf or a tie and, wait for it, a hat to be worn or not, depending on how you feel,' Clive told Angela.

Copper had brought two of her three cornered hats in the bag.

'There are more indoors. These are a sample of styles and colours and trim and so on. And I forgot to show you this.'

She produced a mangled fifty pence piece.

'Peep did this,' she explained. 'The dragons are so strong you wouldn't believe it, which is one reason why nobody ever sees one. Well, not often,' she amended.

'Don't worry, they're not dangerous,' Hilary Green said, 'they run away from trouble, which is just as well.'

'Oh.'

'Hats,' Copper said. 'These are all your size. I made sure to have some ready in my father's house and I had your measurements as soon as I saw you. Take your time about deciding which is the one for you.'

'I've just seen a man wearing one. He gave me the last piece of those trilobite things and then disappeared.'

'He's rather good at that,' Clive declared, 'but George and I want to raise another subject.'

'The ulterior motive you spoke of I presume?'

'Correct,' Clive confirmed her supposition, adding, 'we want your help with one of Shakespeare's plays. One that is not, uh, not well known.'

'I might be interested. Go on.'

'Here it is then. William Shakespeare penned a play about Merlin. It hasn't been played, not in public at any rate, but the script was left with Merlin. I'm trying to get it down on paper but his handwriting is littered with crossings out, re-written lines, repetitions, and so forth. In short, it would be returned unmarked if it was handed in by any pupil in the school and I imagine that you would have harsh words with the culprit.

'Well, it's a bit late for that but we are asking for your help. You're a lot closer to Shakespeare than we are. Will you do it?'

'Will I? Of course I will. An original manuscript in Shakespeare's own hand, it's a dream come true! How soon can I see it?'

'Before we leave the barbecue. Is that soon enough?'

'It's my birthday!'

'There's more. Alison has offered to have any amount of sessions with you in Chaucer's English. How does that sound?'

'Two birthdays on the same day!'

'We hoped you would see it that way,' George Green said and added soberly, 'there is another matter we would like you to be in on but it's a sensitive issue and it could lead to serious trouble. Really serious trouble.'

'I'm still listening.'

'OK. Angela, when Clive and I caught you in the corridor on Thursday it was not by accident, it was because we want to bring some younger people into our group. I'll explain why later but in brief it is because we think the extended lives of some people is something the youngsters will take in their stride much more easily than adults. We want it to be seen as commonplace. Obviously the place to recruit them is from inside the school because these are the people we know and because we will be on hand at all times if things get out of hand so to speak. Having a lady teacher on board will balance things out a bit and any girls who are recruited will perhaps be more inclined to come to you instead of us.'

'Serious trouble is an understatement if ever there was.'

'You don't have to play along.'

'I have a feeling that I'm already in too deep to back out now. What do you want me to do?'

'Help us to choose a group of bright pupils, a mixed group up to six in number,' George Green told her.

'George and I have made lists of our own already. Do you think you can make one too, so we can compare notes and agree who we should take?'

Angela nodded thoughtfully.

'I'll have a list ready for Monday morning,' she replied.

***

As good as her word, on Monday morning Angela Collins produced a list which she handed to George Green in the staff room without comment. George scanned the names rapidly and made a brief nod. It was lunch time before he caught up with Clive Bowden. The afternoon passed and Angela Collins was lingering in the corridor when George and Clive caught up with her.

Making sure nobody was within earshot Angela said, 'How does my list compare with yours?'

'We'll tell you in the car park. Say, ten minutes?'
It did not take that long.
'Christine Appleton, James Wilson, Yolanda Walker, and Derek Thorpe. Those are my immediate choices, all from the same year,' George read the list of names.
'All four of those are on the lists of candidates that we made separately,' Clive told Angela. He handed over a typed list of names.

1. Derek Thorpe, aka Deke
Tall, good at athletics, especially track events
Shows leadership potential
Career interest; Botany

2. Yolanda Walker, aka Yo
Average height
Dark hair
Swims well and has a life saving certificate
Career interest; Astronomy

3. James Wilson
Average height
Very outgoing
Career interest; Engineering

4. Christine Appleton
Tall
Fair hair, pert ponytail
Swims well and has a life saving certificate
Very intelligent
Career interest; ???

'Each one is an outstanding pupil,' Clive continued. 'They get together at the weekend for a homework session in one of the burger bars on Saturday mornings and help each other with their homework if any of them are in difficulty, which rarely happens. It's a sort of homework club that they organized for themselves and it's certainly paid off. It's an ongoing thing and when some pupils move on there are usually others who to take their places. Miranda Bradley was one club member and she went on to study electrical engineering at university. There was a boy called John Lambe who used to be more than friendly with a girl named Lyon if the rumours were true. I don't think they were but it made for good classroom gossip. Today's bunch revise for any exams that are due and then they either go their separate ways or carry out some other plan. The girls have life-saving certificates and they go off to the sports centre quite often. There is one other candidate but George isn't so sure about her.'

'How so? And who?'

Jasmin Tyler. I'd take her in like a shot but she's two years behind the other four and we are not so sure about mixing year groups. It might not work.'

'I agree that age can be a big issue with some teenagers. Second years don't mix with fourth years, and fifth year students are far too grand to mix with third years. It was the same when I was at school. I know Jasmin Tyler and she's a good student,' Angela replied.

'How would you describe her?'

'Diligent. Clever, but not pushy. She socialises well but she has, not an air of remoteness, but some sort of self-sufficiency, as if she can go it alone if necessary. Can and will; she shows determination. All in all, I would say she's not as developed as the others but she certainly has the potential.'

'My own assessment is that she's not a joiner. I'd be a bit concerned if some of her contemporaries acted the way she does but Jasmin Tyler is as stable as they come. It's just that she has a place of her own and I'm not sure where it is or what it is. That fits in with what you said about self-sufficiency. I'm eighty percent for her and twenty percent wait and see,' George stated his own position.

'Fair enough, but I don't think we ought to wait too long.'

'Agreed, we'll keep an eye on her and keep our fingers crossed.'

'There's another thing,' Clive said. 'Our stumbling block is the way they are to be approached. According to Marcel and Françoise Land the best thing we can do is to approach their parents first and be mindful of siblings, and we can't invite the parents into the school, that goes without saying.'

Angela Collins agreed.

'That would be asking for trouble, but so will any contact anywhere, but all is not lost. I happen to know Yolanda's parents fairly well so perhaps I could ask them to get the other parents together somewhere where they could be told. If we can get them on our side we will arrange another meeting with both parents and students. What do you think?'

'It's as good as any plan. In fact it's our only plan,' George told her.

'Go through your info-pack thoroughly before you make your move,' Clive advised although he felt it was unnecessary, 'and base your approach on that. In fact,' he continued, 'showing your material before you make the invitation will give you a chance to gauge their reactions and clear the way.'

'I will, and I know it's been said before but we must hang together or you may be sure we'll hang separately,' Angela said seriously.

Angela Collin's Diary

Here begins my diary. I have been asked (told?) to put all my thoughts, deeds, interpretation even, of my induction into what is known as the Bell Curve Society and everything that follows into writing. This, as I know from my info-pack, will be transcribed by Robert Robertson and put onto a disc or memory stick for subsequent collation and circulation and quite possibly publication. My fifteen minutes of fame!

I believe I was targeted long before I was approached. That, as Christine Appleton would say, is logical. She is a mental powerhouse and knows it but never flaunts it. She has no need to and I think she knows that too. Last week one of the pupils called her Spockette. Very apt, she adores logic.

(Afterthought, two days later; which is not to say she suppresses her emotions, nor is she afraid to express her doubts.)

(Yet another afterthought. I'm still getting to grips with this. In one memorable day I talked to a citizen of ancient Rome who was and still is the Lady of the Lake, and the woman who was, I mean is, the Wife of Bath who featured in Chaucer's Canterbury Tales after she had an affair with him, and there was Merlin who isn't a magician after all but he invented much of what has been written and rewritten about him. I'm all agog to find out what Shakespeare wrote about him! I stroked a dragon and they don't even exist and then I ate a trilobite that went extinct millions of years ago. Is it any wonder I'm all mixed up?)

And I got a new hat and a scarf.

Chapter 6

'This is very unusual Mr Bowden and I'm telling you right now that I'm within an inch of contacting the education authority but for some reason I've decided to speak to you before I do,' Derek Thorpe's father said bluntly.

Clive was not surprised and he was prepared for this scepticism.

The room was crowded. Angela Collins had somehow persuaded the parents of all the older students they proposed to admit into their circle that they should attend a meeting. The subject of Jasmin Tyler had been put on hold for the time being.

'As you say Mr Thorpe, the situation is unusual,' Clive agreed, 'and ordinarily I wouldn't have asked for your involvement you in this, any of you. However, this is anything but ordinary. I believe each of you has seen the information that was given to Miss Collins?'

'Seeing is not believing,' was the curt reply.

Clive was ready for him.

'Peep,' he said, 'come out from wherever you are.'

Something cautiously poked its head round an open door.

'Peep,' it squeaked.

Copper held her forearm level.

'Come here Peep,' she commanded.

Slowly the little dragon took a few paces towards her and then launched itself with a flutter of blue-green wings and flew to its mistress.

'Peep,' it squeaked again.

'Convincing, isn't he?' Clive said cheerfully, adding, 'Would anybody like to hold him?'

'We read about them but are they… is it safe?' Mrs Thorpe asked nervously as Copper lowered her pet into the woman's cupped hands.

'Quite safe. Our son plays with him all the time. They're very timid and Peep is the only dragon that comes into contact with humans. He's a little short of his sixtieth birthday, which is barely half grown. In fact I don't believe that even Merlin knows for sure how long they live,' Copper told her.

'Your son? I… I…'

Copper laughed.

'Women who are in the region of a hundred years old don't often have infant children, do they?'

'I suppose this would be as good a time as any to apologise and admit I believe your story now,' Mr Thorpe said gruffly.

'Can they really chew metal?' Another parent asked.

That was Mrs Wilson.

'Sure. You could whack a dragon with a sledgehammer and it wouldn't hurt it in the slightest but your hammer would be a scatter of iron filings in less than a minute.'

'Wow! It really is all true then?'

'Every word, except for some things that have yet to appear in print and a few others that have been, um…'

'Obfuscated?' Another parent suggested.

Clive chuckled.

'That's a good way of putting it.'

'How does this affect us?'

Mrs Wilson again.

'We want to draw more youngsters into what we call the Bell Curve Society, and it was thought that we should find a small group of pupils from our school because we know them and they know us. We selected them on the grounds of their maturity, common sense, intelligence, and so on. In other words we picked the most outstanding group we could, with the added proviso that they should also be a, well, a set of friends. I think we got lucky. I'll explain our motives more fully but before I do I want to emphasise that we do offer something in return.

'For some time there has been a feeling among us that sooner or later word is going to get around that not everyone is what they seem. Copper for instance.'

'And you and Mr Green?'

Clive shook his head.

'Not us. In my case I intend to abide by a set of rules that I put together some years ago, one of which is that nobody will jump the queue and get an increased life expectancy before they have reached the age of seventy years. As far as Mr Green is concerned I am at liberty to tell you that if the offer is ever made to him he will turn it down flat.'

Angela Collins spoke for the first time.

'Clive, excuse my interruption but may I say to everybody that the trade-off for me is the opportunity to assist in the transcription of a play by William Shakespeare that was never published or acted and along with that I'm learning to speak the English that Geoffrey Chaucer spoke. My teacher grew up speaking the English language of that era. You really couldn't put a price on that.'

'What will we have to do?'

'Initially, be our back-up crew. It's going to be vital. We're asking a lot of you and your children. They will need your full support and both you and they will need ours.'

'Your first reward will be scarves for the women, like the scarf I am wearing, and matching ties for the men. Clive, take your tie out of your pocket and put it on,' Copper said.

Clive Bowden was soon wearing his tie and Copper was distributing scarves and ties to the parents.

'My father is nearly here,' she announced suddenly.

'How do you know that?' Mr Wilson asked, 'Can you read minds or something?'

'No,' Copper smiled, 'but I do know what time he said he would arrive and I can see the clock on the mantelpiece.'

'Can he show us a trilobite? I'd love to see what they look like.'

For the first time one of Yolanda Walker's parents spoke.

'I'll ask him,' Copper promised as the doorbell announced Merlin's arrival.

Lawrence Bowden junior skidded to a halt at the sight of a room full of strangers and whooped, 'Peep! Peep!'

Soon he was holding the dragon as he would have held a soft toy, while inspecting the company and making for Copper's outstretched arms.

'Just call me Merlin,' Copper's father said as introductions were made. 'I've spent most of my life without a title except for the times when it saves having to answer awkward questions that I would sooner avoid. Copper, the look on your face says you are going to ask me something.'

'Can Mrs Walker see a trilobite? I said I would ask you.'

'Hmm, yes. Hmm, I've an idea. If you can all find room for an aquarium I can catch a few and you can take them home. I think the students might like the idea of having pets that are as unusual as my daughter's dragon. Three trilobites to a tank of about this size.'

Merlin held his arms out.

'Alternatively, we can set a date after you have had time to think about it and I'll show you and them the dragon cave and they can have a shot at catching their own trilobites. How does that sound?'

Chapter 7

Copper Beach welcomed the group who had arrived in response to an invitation to a barbecue in Merlin's extensive garden.

'Some of you are no doubt thinking that this is an elaborate hoax and wondering why it is being perpetrated but by now you have all been told about my father Merlin and the Lady of the Lake. All of what you were told is true.' Copper addressed them.

'I'm Copper Beach,' she continued,' and as you know I'm married to Clive Bowden. Among ourselves we are normally on first name terms but that might be difficult for some of you, especially the students, so feel free to use whatever form of address suits you best. That completes the formalities, and now for the hats. I'm wearing one of my own creations which I adapted from the old fashioned tricorn hat that went out of fashion a long time ago. Yes?'

A student raised his hand.

'I've seen Miranda Bradley in a hat like yours. I don't know her but she was at our school once and I've seen her around town.'

Copper smiled.

'Miranda got her hat when she was about your age and when I know what colours you choose you will all get one, there are men's and women's designs.'

'Was she still at school when she got one?'

'Ask her yourself, she's at the far end of the garden helping with the barbecue along with some other people you will recognise, and some you won't, but all of them will answer whatever questions you ask, and don't be afraid to ask them their ages. Don't forget to talk to my husband either, and your English teacher Miss Collins. Clive and Miss Collins are transcribing a play by Shakespeare that never saw the light of day. Shakespeare's handwriting is hard to read and his spelling was out of this world. He used to cross out whole chunks of text sometimes and then change his mind so nobody can be sure what was to be included. That's the introductions, and now my father is going to put on a display which will go some way to telling you what all this is about, so if you look towards the barbecue you will see what I mean. And don't forget to ask her to put a trilobite on your plates. You try out different dips and see which ones you like best,' Copper said with a smile tugging her lips.

'My father said something about trilobites,' Deke Thorpe told her. 'He said we could put some into aquariums. I knew they were extinct but, well, you know…'

He stopped talking as his mother turned up.

'I'm just off to eat a trilobite Mum, and I remember Dad saying about putting some in an aquarium. I could have it in my bedroom.'

'And when has your bedroom been fit to be seen?' His mother replied with a look that said butter wouldn't melt in her mouth. 'You'll bring your friends round to see them and what will they think?'

'Mum I'm a teenager and having an untidy bedroom isn't only expected, it's demanded.'

'We'll see about that.'

'Mum I promise…'

'Don't make promises you know you won't keep,' Mrs Thorpe told him and then softened her tone and added, 'you can have an aquarium but a tidy room is a quid pro quo.'

'Thanks Mum. Imagine that! Trilobites!'

'Steady on youngster,' Merlin had arrived without being noticed. 'Let's not run before you can walk. What do trilobites eat?'

He passed his grandson Lawrence to Copper when she held her arms out.

'I … I don't know,' Deke Thorpe said unsteadily.

'Then I'll tell you. Is everybody listening?'

All the students said they were.

'To begin at the beginning then, millions of years ago trilobites numbered thousands of species and they occupied every ecological niche where they could gain a foothold. They were creatures of the oceans. Some were free swimmers, others were bottom feeders, and some were predators and quite likely cannibals. The biggest trilobites were about the same length as my arm but most were a lot smaller and some were only the size of my fingernail. The remarkable thing about them was their curious compound eyes, which were unique to trilobites. They were made up of calcite prisms.' Merlin said.

'Calcite? $CaCO_3$… That's rigid. Our eyes have lenses that are flexible. That's how we focus.'

Merlin recognised Christine Appleton and her instant recollection of the chemical formula for calcite came as no surprise, given what he had heard about her.

'As it happens Christine the eyes of the trilobites have been called the best eyes that any species ever possessed. Nature and evolution had about three billion years to get it right,' he told her. He added, 'Seawater isn't always crystal clear and the trilobites lived in water that was often murky but their eyes were splendidly developed for their environment. Their vision was remarkably good. The water in my cave is fresh but caves are not noted for the quality of light so the eyes of the trilobites there are fit for purpose as they say.'

'Sir, what about aberration and focus and depth of field?' Yolanda Walker asked.

Merlin took her meaning instantly.

'They got round that too, it's amazing what time will do. For instance, I believe you are the one who is interested in astronomy?'

'Yes sir,' Yolanda replied.

'Then you'll be aware that the lenses in your telescope, and for that matter you camera too, are made up from a series of lenses, some concave and some convex, all fitted together very precisely to prevent spherical and chromatic aberration. Trilobite eyes are made the same way and the trilobites have a splendid depth of field. As predators they were unsurpassed. The trilobites in my cave are free swimmers and bottom feeders but they also eat fresh water shrimps, and there are plenty of those in the cave.'

'Are the shrimps unique to your cave sir?' Deke Thorpe enquired seriously.

Merlin considered this.

'Quite possibly, even likely,' he replied. 'Shrimps are ubiquitous little critters, they get everywhere, including the deepest part of the oceans and around the bases of hot smokers on the sea bed, and they live in fresh water streams and caves where they feed on detritus that is washed in, and they scavenge the dead bodies of anything they can find.'

'They seem too valuable to feed to the trilobites. Could I keep some in a separate tank?'

'Derek you mustn't. Don't you think Mr ... I mean Merlin has done enough already?'

The use of his proper name made Deke aware that he had overstepped the mark.

'I suppose. I mean yes. Sorry sir.'

Merlin smiled.

'No need to apologise. I was a bit like you myself once; impatient, always wanting to see everything and find out all I could about it. One of our Bell Curve Society members has a saying; "Learn to discover. Discover to learn." It goes round and round because each of those things leads to the other. Short and to the point.'

'I see. Do one in order to do the other. They're interdependent which means doing one without the other isn't possible, or at least is inefficient,' Mrs Thorpe said. 'I couldn't have put it better.'

'The question was what to feed the trilobites and shrimps,' Copper reminded everyone. 'My fishes get dried flakes and dried daphnia, or sometimes live ones. They're water fleas. I think I would feed them all with that and see what suits them best. I've seen fresh water shrimps and they're fast movers and they'll eat anything. I know of one keeper who put shrimps in with his goldfish as live food. It turned out the other way round. The shrimps are aquatic hooligans and they ate most of the food and grew quite large very quickly and then they ate the fishes.'

'Wow!'

'He told me he wanted to see how big they would grow but he never expected to see his fishes eaten,' Copper told them. 'He discovered and learned and no mistake. I did a lot of reading when I was given my little aquarium. I discovered to learn and so will you. Learning is going to come first and one thing you need to know is what water suits your shrimps and trilobites best. The answer is alkaline water with a high level of dissolved calcium so they can grow their exoskeletons which they all shed from time to time.

'Plainly then, the best water is the water they are in now, which will have to be maintained of course. Mr Green will advise you what to do and you can buy testing kits from any aquarist. You'll need thermometers too, or maybe not because the water in the cave is cold. Then I'll speak nicely to my father and talk him into taking you to the cave where they all live and you can practice your tests there. If we're lucky you'll see some trilobites too but probably not any shrimps because they don't swim through very often. What about it father?'

'As soon as you're ready. Copper has omitted to tell you that you can reckon on one inch of fish to one gallon of water, excluding the tail, and the same formula will probably do for the trilobites. I'm old fashioned and I still use feet and inches instead of metres, and gallons instead of litres, but I know you can all convert to metric measurements if you prefer. There's some real scientific work to be done. Are you up for it?'

'Up for it! Try and stop me!'

'Then it's settled,' Merlin declared. 'I'll go ahead and arrange a session with George Green and you can come and see for yourselves where the shrimps and trilobites live and you can make a few tests to find out more about the state of the water. I'm going to call him now. Now if my daughter will give me back my grandson she will give ties to the men and a scarf for the ladies. Later on you will get your hats, after you have decided on such things as style and colour. You were measured for them the moment Copper set eyes on you.'

'Umm. I read about that.'

'One of Copper's many talents is her gift for knowing anyone's measurements at a glance. For the most part the men don't wear their hats except for gardening and barbecues and nobody wears a tie as much as they used to but the ladies and, I hope, the girls, will wear their hats and scarves more often.'

After a moment's thought Merlin added, 'My daughter has a tendency to adjust my tie whenever I wear it.'

Chapter 8

It was an astonished group that found itself in a cave with a solid wall behind them.

'Something I learned to do when I was a boy,' Merlin told them.

Sloping uphill, the cave was easily wide enough for three people to walk abreast with Copper leading the way. There was an abrupt turn to the right.

'This is the way the cave was discovered,' Merlin explained. 'Two brothers were mining for lead during the days of the Roman Empire and they accidently made their discovery when they broke through a wall. Eventually they explored for quite a long way but they never saw the full extent of the cave. They widened the entrance where they had broken through and being of an entrepreneurial turn of mind they went into the tourist business and made a good living by charging an entrance fee. They did find the metal they were looking for and extracted a small but profitable amount but mining ceased to be their main source of income.

'This is where we split into two groups. George is going to supervise the youngsters at the pool so off you go, and I'm going to be a tour guide to this part of the cave.'

Merlin waited until he was alone with the parents group before he started his narrative.

'Those two Roman mining engineers carved a flight of steps down to the floor but they were too steep so I re-worked them to make them less steep and I built the balustrade as well. That was about a hundred and fifty years ago. I did a bit of work here and there where I found it necessary. From up here where we are standing you can see what we call the dragon cave with the pool on the far side. The trilobites often swim through from a larger pool that connects with the cave via a submerged passage. I have swum through to the other side many times, it isn't far. That large pool is in a cave of course and the cave itself fairly large and the trilobites appear like sparks because of the luminous patches they carry. If one happens to swim through to this side today George will try to net it. The large pool and its surrounds is the main home of the dragons.

'As you see there is more than one passage into the further reaches of the cave. It was many years before I made it to the furthest extent and even today I have not passed through some of the submerged passages although I do know where they lead to.'

'Isn't there a chance that somebody might come in through the back door, so to speak?' Christine Appleton's father wondered.

Merlin shook his head.

'No. There is a constant flow of water from the cave but not through any passage wide enough to be negotiated. The dragons come and go as they please but nothing except dragons can manage it.'

'Is there a chance of seeing dragons today?'

Merlin smiled.

'Not likely,' he said. 'They will see us if they haven't already but they avoid contact with humans. My daughter's little pet Peep is an exception but even he won't show himself if it can be avoided. Which reminds me,' he continued, 'I've turned off you phones in case anybody happens to call you and startle the dragons that might hear your alert tone. One of my little tricks.'

'I wouldn't have thought a signal would get through to the cave. If I had thought of it at all, but I didn't. I'm guilty, I'm carrying a phone in my bag,' Mrs Walker told him.

She was not the only one. Several phones were produced.

'I can let signals through or block them but as a rule I simply turn off all phones. Forgive me for not mentioning it earlier, it was an oversight. I can turn them on again if you like, with the ring tone suppressed. The vibrating alert will have to do.'

Merlin's offer was appreciated but there were no takers so he picked up the thread of his talk from where he left off.

'The banners that hang in the cave used to be flown over the castles and villages of the Kingdom of Wessex over a thousand years ago and I confess I still miss them sometimes. They made a fine sight but they were more than that, they were a statement. Every single person could fly a blue dragon banner; it was their right and a reminder of the responsibilities that they gladly accepted.

'Over there,' Merlin continued and indicated with his pointing finger, 'you will have noticed three figures carved into a niche in the wall. That carving is fairly recent and how they were carved is a mystery but they are figures of Wint who is a scientist from a period of pre-history. I said is, not was. Wint describes time as a sphere inside which he can travel at will, though perhaps not to everywhen, so it would be wrong to use the past tense when we speak of him. I'm afraid English grammar doesn't deal with time travel very well,' he concluded wryly.

'We read about Wint in the material we were given,' Mr Appleton commented. After a second or two of thought he added, 'But now it's a lot more believable.'

Merlin allowed his guests a few minutes to study their surroundings before he resumed his narrative.

'From up here we have a good view of the floor of the cave. The mosaic you see was laid by Ulpius, a Roman craftsman, and Sabina who was a freedwoman. Sabina was responsible for the border; the pattern and the colours are her trademark. Sabina assisted Ulpius with his measurements and drawings and the mosaic floor they laid here is perhaps the finest work they ever produced. I can tell you it cost a pretty penny, they were very much in demand and they could name their own price for their work. Their drawings and all the contract documents together with bills and samples are part of my collection of artifacts that one day perhaps I shall loan to the British Museum. We shall see.

'Actually I have a very large collection that goes all the way back to the time when the Stone Age was giving way to the Bronze and Iron Ages. Some pieces are, hmm, surprising, shall we say'

'Surprising? Are we permitted to ask what is surprising about them?' Mr Wilson enquired.

'Some Stone Age technology was much further advanced than anything you would expect. I'll show you some things at a later date and you can actually handle some tools and examine their work for yourselves. They knew a thing or two that is hard to match even today,' Merlin replied and then added, 'the offer is open to everyone of course. I think it would be useful to have Brian Gleaves or Jack Smythe come into the cave and give you a talk about pre-historic engineering. Your boy James would be especially interested; I'm informed he is a born engineer.'

Mr Wilson looked surprised and Merlin changed the subject.

'I was going to say more about the mosaic floor,' he said. 'The people you see there are wearing Roman clothes, both civilian and military. My daughter has designed a collection of ladies evening and day wear based on what you see below and one of her first customers was Hilary Green, George Green's wife. Clive Bowden is more interested in the military uniforms worn by the men.'

A shout of excitement and a sudden commotion by the pool put an end to what Merlin was about to say. Looking pleased he said, 'I rather think the youngsters have caught a trilobite. Shall we go down and see?'

There was no need to ask twice; the parents were as excited as their offspring.

'There you are,' George said with a huge grin covering his face, 'not quite as exotic as everyone thinks. It won't do it any harm to be out of the water for a minute or two. Notice the shell, how it isn't all one piece like a tortoise shell but made up of a set of plates which are shed from time to time as the trilobite grows.'

'I've been meaning to ask you about that Mr Green. How big will it grow to?'

'On average about fifteen centimetres or six inches if you prefer. Millions of years ago the oceans were full of them and some were smaller than your little finger nail,' George said, repeating something that Merlin had said once before. 'Sixty centimetres would have been big; that's about as long as my arm. What I want you to notice is the way it's built. Most people seem to believe that the three lobes which is how they got their name are the equivalent of three parts of an insects body.'

'Head, thorax, abdomen,' Christine Appleton recited.

'Exactly. When I turn this one over we can see that the lobes are longitudinal and not lateral, which is not to say that trilobites couldn't curl up like woodlice because many of them could.'

'I wonder if there are places in the sea where there still are trilobites,' Christine said thoughtfully.

'I'd like to think so,' George Green replied, 'and so does the vicar, he's a closet marine biologist who keeps himself up to date with marine exploration, especially in the tropical deeps around the Indonesia region where seismic activity generated devastating tsunamis in recent years and resulted in intense scientific interest in the region. That interest is second to seismic monitoring and so it ought to be but it would be foolish to ignore the benefits of exploration on those grounds. To return to your question, every now and again somebody claims to have found them but it always turns out to be something else. Run a computer search and see what you come up with.'

'Convergent evolution?'

'I'll admit the possibility Deke.'

'I've read something about the discovery of new species in the seas around Indonesia,' Yolanda Walker said.

'Me too,' James Wilson declared, 'and Antarctica as well, and I know some unwelcome species migration is happening there. I don't know what but I'll look it up.'

'Some sort of crab,' Deke Thorpe told him, 'and maybe jellyfish and that's all I know. Which doesn't add up to much,' he added wryly.

'It's a start. We all need to crank up our computers. James and me to research the warm seas, Deke and Yo do Antarctica,' Christine Appleton said.

George Green found himself very impressed with their knowledge and enthusiasm.

'I'll pop this specimen back into the water and if Merlin will dim the lights you'll see how these small patches on its shell are bio-luminescent.'

The lights dimmed and the trilobite slipped away when George released it. The glowing patches on its shell were plainly visible. George shook the water from his fingers.

It was some time before the party retuned from the cave and found that Clive and Copper had prepared a mountain of sandwiches and soft drinks and transported them to Merlin's garden.

'I've heard mention of trilobite eyes,' Deke Thorpe's father said to George Green, 'but I never expected to see one.'

'They lasted for three hundred million years or thereabouts until the mass extinction at the end of the Permian period and they were all salt water species except that there is evidence beginning to emerge that some, probably very few, adapted to fresh water. It probably is no surprise that some found their way to Merlin's cave. Look at it this way; does it make any sense that fish should only live in salty water? Of course it doesn't. There are thousands of fish species so it's inevitable that fish would migrate to rivers and streams. There were thousands of trilobite species too. No fewer than seventeen thousand have been discovered and who is to say how many are lying in the fossil record waiting for their turn?

'Trilobites diversified, just as fish have diversified. Sea bed dwellers were predators, scavengers, filter feeders, somewhat analogous to plaice, halibut, turbot, and the other flatfish. Swimmers ate plankton and most likely anything they could catch. I touched on the size of the trilobites when Deke asked me but most were only as long as my little finger so a diet of plankton makes sense and that puts them on a par with crabs. Crabs are found everywhere and by and large crabs and trilobites are similarly sized. One other thing before I get booed off the stage. When we were below ground I mentioned the vicar and called him a closet marine biologist. Well, while I was rambling on Merlin called him and you'll find him standing behind you. Hello Vicar.'

'Hello everyone,' the vicar said loudly enough for everyone to hear. 'For those who don't know me just call me Vicar. I'm afraid George Greens description of me is quite true and if ever a living trilobite species is discovered at the bottom of one of the earth's oceans I'm going to make a real pest of myself until I can go and see them. I'm not sure what I'll do but God moves in mysterious ways and, well, let's wait and see.'

Very soon he was the focus of attention which, George Green observed, prevented him from singing his favourite hymn. The vicar's singing voice matched Merlin and Copper's in loudness and not one of them could carry a tune.

Chapter 9

Cool air, crystal clear, had blown the clothes dry and Mrs Rudd unpegged the last few items and glanced up at the sky. The forecast was for a warmer afternoon and evening as the trailing edge of a cold front drifted away to the east and warmer air took its place. With the experienced eye of a Yorkshire farmer's wife she confirmed the weatherman's predictions.

She carried the heavy clothes basket indoors and acknowledged that both she and her husband Henry were fast approaching the time when their days on the farm must come to an end. They had already left it too long and they knew it. She wondered what their future would be. Not what they had expected, that was certain. Together with Henry Whiting and his wife they had been offered the opportunity to have the strange pseudovirus injected into their bloodstreams, the organism that would vastly increase their lifespans. All four had immediately insisted that Walter and Anneleise Pfaffinger were to be included in the offer or there would be no takers.

'Funny you should say that,' Doctor Edwin Mallory had replied when they delivered their ultimatum, 'that's what Walter and Anneleise said about you when Julia made them the same offer. It had to be Julia who told them of course, I can't speak German and Anneleise can't speak English but Julia was on the train like a shot. Anneleise met her in Cologne when she arrived. So there you have it. I'll take your answer as an affirmative, all six of you together with Robert and Victoria Robertson and as soon as your preparations are made for your retirement to sunny Spain or whatever story you choose to put about I'll have you all in at once.'

The ringing telephone pulled her thoughts back to the present as she laid the laundry basket on the table in the kitchen. The interruption was not unwelcome but she hoped the call would be short because she wanted to finish what she was doing. The caller turned out to be Henry Whiting, and he sounded excited.

'I've turned up something interesting,' he told her, 'it goes back to our wartime days and I'd all but forgotten I had it.'

Briefly, he told her what he had found.

'I'll tell Henry the moment he comes in,' Mrs Rudd said, 'I know he'll be pleased.'

Deep in thought, she returned to her task.

***

Henry Rudd reached into his inside pocket and produced a small white cloth bag.

To his former pilot he said, 'Does this bring back memories? I've had it since our days in the RAF but it's been a few years since I thought about it and then I turned it up when we were getting all our belongings ready for when we move out of the farm, but suddenly I've been wondering how things turned out for them.'

Henry Whiting took the bag into his large hands.

'I wonder,' he breathed, and more soberly he added, 'there's a good chance they're not around any more, it's been a long time. It's a small miracle that we've beaten the odds, us and the Robertsons and Walter and Anneleise Pfaffinger. They might not have been so lucky.'

'Mmm. All the same I'd like to know. We were close knit back then and...'

Henry Rudd ended his sentence with an expressive shrug of his shoulders.

The vicar looked from one to the other and asked, 'Are you going to let me in on this?'

'Ooops! Sorry Vicar, we were getting carried away with old memories. This little bag carries a few coins. It still does.'

Henry Rudd shook the bag and the vicar heard the clink of loose change.

'It all came from an idea that...'

... Leading Aircraftman Harrison, Lofty to all who knew him, indicated to the crew of an approaching Mosquito bomber the spot where he wanted them to park their aircraft in its dispersal area. It rolled to a stop and Lofty's hand signal told the pilot that he wanted the bomb doors open, and as soon as that was done he drew his hand across his throat to indicate that the two Rolls Royce Merlin engines could be shut down while he hurried to collect a pair of wooden wheel chocks from the grass at the edge of the tarmac and place them in position, one in front and one behind the wheels of the main undercarriage to prevent the aircraft moving when the brakes were released.

'Chocks in, brakes off!' He called as one of the crew opened the entry hatch in the floor of the cockpit.

The pilot released the brakes with a hiss of escaping air. The Leading Aircraftman was known to want the brakes released as soon as possible because the brakes heated from repeated operation when an aircraft was taxied and the inflation bag that applied the brake pressure could become stuck to the hot metal of the brake drum if the brakes were left on for too long. That would mean work that could have been avoided. A replacement would have to be fitted and Lofty would be the man who had to do it.

He grasped the canvas map bag that the navigator handed down to him while at the same time he steadied the crew ladder as Flying Officer Rudd climbed down.

'No snags Lofty,' he told the airman.

'We'll have a walk round and see anyway, you might have damage you don't know about.'

The two men walked around the aircraft, leaving the pilot to catch up with them after he completed his shut down checks. They could hear the metallic tinkling noise of cooling exhausts as they walked around the port wing and made for the tail of the aircraft. Lofty Harrison walked with a pronounced limp, favouring his left leg.

Stopping to gaze at the tail wheel he said, 'That's odd,' almost to himself.

'I can't see anything,' the navigator replied. 'What's odd?'

'The tyre inflation valve, it's in the same position as it was when I saw you off. Look sir, it's exactly as close to the ground as it gets. I bet he can't do that again.'

'I bet I can.'

The big pilot, Sergeant Whiting, had approached unheard.

'OK then Sarge, how much?'

'Sixpence.'

'Sixpence it is. I'll tell you what, I'll scrounge a tin of paint and we'll all go in for a tanner, Lizzie Engines included. Winner is the one whose bit of the tyre touches the ground. Four quarters, one each. I'll mark them off. Pilot, top left, navigator opposite at bottom right, me, top right, and Lizzie at bottom left. How's that?'

'Suits me. Where is Lizzie, she's usually here to meet us?'

'Engine change in number two hangar. She got called away to lend a hand.'

The three young men sat on the tarmac and regarded the tail wheel carefully and turned their heads when the noise of a bicycle bell drew their attention.

'Something the matter lads?'

It was Flight Sergeant Johnson, the man who was in charge of the aircraft servicing crews.

'Nothing wrong Chief,' Henry Rudd replied, 'but we want to paint the tail wheel if it's all right with you, and mark it into quarters.'

He explained the reason for his request.

The veteran NCO chuckled.

'Can't do any harm. OK Lofty, take my bike and see what you can scrounge from the tyre bay, get the white paint they use when they paint the creep marks on the tyres, and don't forget a paintbrush. Finish your inspection before you go.'

Whistling a dance tune he pedaled away to complete his rounds of all the returned aircraft. 'It's going to be over soon,' Henry Whiting declared. 'They can't last more than a few weeks now.'

'Can't come soon enough for me.'

'Me too. You were at Dunkirk weren't you Lofty?'

'Yeah, turned up driving a bren gun carrier that someone had left behind,' Lofty said. 'I piled my lads aboard and jump started it and away we went. It took me a while to get the hang of it but it had a fair turn of speed. We should have been picked up when the aircraft were sent back to Blighty but it never happened, we were left to fend for ourselves. I was the senior man so I decided to head for Dunkirk because I'd heard that the navy was evacuating everyone from there. I thought it was a port. We were shot at on the way by a couple of fighters and a bloody tank and then we were dive bombed. The beach at Dunkirk was orderly chaos and we were still being bombed and RAF uniforms weren't popular. Everyone wanted to know where the RAF was and to be honest I was asking the same thing. An army corporal told me to take off my jacket so as not to draw attention to myself and I told him I was a Leading Aircraftman in the Royal Air Force and I'd thump his head in. He was only trying to do me a favour but I didn't know that. I owe him a pint if we ever meet up again. I was damn lucky to get a place on a boat.

'I'm going to be kicked out as soon as it's over, or maybe even before. I've still only got fifty percent hearing in my left ear on account of the bombing at Dunkirk and there's my leg as well.'

Henry Rudd took up the tale.

'Lofty Harrison never did get around to his painting on account of Squadron Leader Kirk bringing home a flak damaged aircraft that needed immediate attention and TLC so Chiefy Johnson did the job himself as soon as he got a spare minute and from then on the first thing we did after a raid was look at the tail wheel. The chief was like that, there was nothing he wouldn't do for his men and women, and he was the final adjudicator if there was any doubt and we had a right old time with plumb lines and protractors and combination sets.

'Lizzie Engines was a corporal in the Women's Auxiliary Air Force, I forgot to mention that. According to Chiefy Johnson, if there was anything she didn't know about our engines there was a good chance Rolls Royce didn't know it either. She was called Lizzie Engines because there was another Lizzie who was an armourer called Lizzie Bombs. Their first names were Elizabeth but you know how these things work. Of course,' Henry Rudd chuckled, 'it would have been too easy to use their surnames. Most of the girls were recruited as cooks and clerks or drivers but some were more technically minded.

'Looking back on it I suppose we were all a bit shell shocked after years of war and our little game was a way of winding down. We'd been bombed, shot at, torpedoed and sunk, and Lofty, well he'll tell you his story himself I hope, but he'd been through sheer hell at Dunkirk and then he'd had his leg smashed and as if that wasn't enough he lost every member of his family in the blitz. We needed our own little cocoon and that was it.'

'That and the Wheatsheaf.' Henry Whiting was the speaker.

'The Wheatsheaf,' he continued. 'Home from home; a place to wind down and where the usual rules were frequently disregarded. Grievances could be aired and arguments settled, sometimes at the top of the voice and it didn't matter who you were. As often as not the argument or row ended with two people heading for the bar, the best of friends. What went on in the Wheatsheaf was a matter for the Wheatsheaf only and the rules came back into force when anyone stepped back outside. It worked, and that's what mattered. The place was a typical country pub, run by a bloke called Jim and his misses; umm... Gladys. Jim and Gladys Moreley. They had a son named Graham, we saw him now and again when he was home on leave from the army. He was a Sergeant Major and I was damned glad he was on our side, believe me.'

Henry Rudd picked up the narrative.

'The Station Padre used to sit at a table in the corner sometimes, with a glass of beer left untouched. Anyone who wanted to could sit down with him and talk about anything. Lofty did. In the ordinary way he would've had to be dragged in chains to a church but the padre's corner table was a different matter and I know he wouldn't mind me telling you he was in tears when his family were bombed out and killed in the blitz, every last one of them. The padres must have had the worst job of the war sometimes, and sometimes the best.'

… Flying Officer Rudd came in first, closely followed by Sergeant Whiting.

'Two pints of your finest please landlord. My driver will pay,' Henry Rudd said grandly.

The landlord chuckled.

'Wheel of fortune, eh? Three in a row?'

'Four. Serves him right.'

Henry Whiting laid a ten shilling note on the bar and picked up his pint.

'Ah, that's the stuff to give the troops,' he said and added, 'put one in for Lofty and Lizzie, Jim, and one for you and Gladys.'

There was not much change for his money. He checked to make sure that a sixpenny piece was included so that he had one to put into the linen bag that held the cash, ready for the next flight.

'It's a bit quiet tonight Jim' he observed.

'It is that.'

The bar-top was wiped with vigour.

'It's going to be over soon, they can't go on much longer, and people are starting to wonder what they are going to do. Our Graham for one. He's still got his job on the buses if he wants it but he's a Sergeant Major now and he's seen a bit of the world and been in the thick of the fighting everywhere he's been. He was in the Normandy landings on D-Day and now he's in Holland or Germany, I don't know which. Me and Gladys, we told him he'd do well to come into the pub with us when he was home last time. We were here before it started and we'll still be here for a few years yet but we won't be here forever.'

'I'm going to have a herd of cows. It's what I've always wanted,' Henry Rudd said.

The conversation was brought to an end with the breathless arrival of Lofty Harrison and Lizzie...

'I wouldn't go back there now,' Henry Whiting said when the narrative was over, 'it's probably called the Slug and Parking Meter or some nonsense and full of the wrong people. People who don't know....'

Chapter 10

As he approached his destination the vicar paused for a moment and unfolded a sheet of paper in order to remind himself of the address he was calling on. He reckoned it must be no more than a five minute walk from where he stood. The pause was unnecessary, he thought wryly, because he had learned the information by heart. He resumed his walk and for the umpteenth time he rehearsed what he was going to say.

The gate was open and he heard the sound of a lawnmower as he walked the length of the short drive and encountered the gardener who was trimming a well maintained lawn. The man noticed him and flicked a switch to cut off the engine of his mower.

'Can I help you?' He asked.

The vicar detected the trace of a limp as he approached.

'I think you must be Mr Harrison,' the vicar replied with a note of hesitation in his voice.

'That's me.'

'I'm, um, well I'm usually called Vicar since that is my calling.'

He told the gardener his proper name.

'And I'm usually called Lofty.'

'I've brought you something you might recognize,' the vicar said as he produced the small linen bag with its content of coins that jingled when he shook it.

'I'll be sideswiped!' Lofty Harrison gasped. 'The wheel of fortune! That takes me back a bit.'

A woman who carried a pair of secateurs in one hand and a basket of dead-headed roses in the other came from the side of the house.

'Look Lizzie, look at this!' Lofty called out, holding the bag for her to see.

'Oh!' She exclaimed as Lofty had done. 'The wheel of fortune! Where did you get it and how did you know about us? You must know something.'

'I do,' the vicar told her after the introductions were made.

'Our aircrew had the bag with them on their last flight during the war. Such a long time ago. They were killed you know, and it seemed so unfair. The war was nearly over and they wouldn't have had to fly many more times. So unfair,' Elizabeth Harrison repeated quietly.

'As it happens they weren't killed,' the vicar was able to tell her. 'They were shot down, they think it must have been a shell that failed to explode but it went through a fuel tank and they made a crash landing because there was no chance of making it back to England with half their fuel gone. They headed for anywhere they could behind the Allied lines and crash landed while they still had enough fuel to pick an open space. It took them a few weeks to get back home and by the time they did it was all over.'

There was a moment of silence.

'And now,' the vicar continued, 'I'd better show you my proof. This is called a tablet.'

Producing something from a pocket on his luggage, he held the device so that Mr and Mrs Harrison could see the screen. Henry Rudd and Henry Whiting looked out at them.

'Hello Lofty, hello Lizzie,' Henry Whiting greeted them. 'Right now you're probably thinking we look a bit older than our years but there is a good reason for that. We thought a reunion would be a good idea but there are certain complications. Over to you Vicar it's your show now.'

Lofty Harrison whistled softly.

'That's a nifty gadget and no mistake. I've never seen anything like it and your luggage is a bit unusual too,' he said as he pointed to the dark green case the vicar wheeled behind him.

'The case doesn't belong to me. I borrowed it from a chap who flies out to Turkey fairly frequently. He stuck the yellow patches of tape on to make it easy to find when it comes out of the carousel. He's pretty experienced at that sort of thing and he travels fast and light. I've brought a few bits and pieces to show you and they're all in there along with my toiletries and a change of underwear. I need to find an hotel for the night but enough of that later. I'd like if I may to plug a DVD player into the mains.'

'A what?'

'A DVD player. It...'

'We'll go indoors,' Elizabeth Harrison decided, leading the way.

The vicar was not long in setting up his equipment.

'I'm going to show you something remarkable,' he said, 'and however far-fetched it might appear, and believe me it will, I can assure you that every word is true. It will take about forty-five minutes.'

Nobody spoke while the DVD played through, when Elizabeth Harrison said in an unsteady tone, 'So you're a man from the future?'

The vicar nodded and replied, 'Yes. I'm not telling you which now I come from, that would be frowned upon to say the very least. At the same time I, we that is, we know that all you need do is pick up a newspaper or listen to the news in my time and you'll know the date exactly. The fact is, and any question you ask will be answered truthfully and in full, but…'

'You could meet yourself while you are here,' Lofty commented.

'In theory I could but in practice I couldn't because I would already know it but I don't. We don't fully understand how it works and I for one am not going to try experimenting.'

'I suppose I couldn't check to see which horse will win the Grand National for the next five years,' Lofty said with a smile. 'I imagine that would be frowned on too.'

The vicar returned the smile.

'I don't think it would work,' he said.

'It would be asking for trouble, it seems to me,' Elizabeth declared.

The vicar agreed.

'Now I've shown you the DVD I can give you a couple of presents from the future. First, for Lofty a tie like the one I am wearing myself. Elizabeth, the ladies all get a silk scarf. The motif is blue dragons and red trilobites on a grey background. Dragons aren't supposed to exist but they do, and trilobites are supposed to be extinct but they're not.'

He distributed the gifts and added, 'I've something else, a present from Copper Beach.'

He passed a carefully wrapped item to Elizabeth Harrison for her to open it.

'I wouldn't let your neighbours see it,' the vicar beamed.

'I should think not. Look Lofty, look at this.'

She showed her husband what she was holding.

'Good grief! A royal wedding souvenir plate and it hasn't happened yet! I'll be d… darned.'

Lofty hastily amended what he had been about to say.

Elizabeth stood up.

'I'm going to put the kettle on,' she declared.

'You'll stay the night Vicar,' she said half an hour later, 'and never mind hotels, and if I've got this right it won't make any difference if you go back to Merlin's stone tomorrow or even sometime next week. Or any other time.'

'That's correct,' the vicar confirmed.

'Good. Then it's settled.'

'And I've got something to say,' Lofty Harrison said, 'and it's about what you haven't said. We're no longer alive in the now that you come from, are we? Otherwise you wouldn't have come to this now. Don't look so surprised, I reckon we both figured it out when we watched your film.'

'It was obvious from the start,' Elizabeth confirmed.

'Um, I was wondering how to break it to you,' the vicar replied sheepishly.

Elizabeth smiled but said nothing.

Remembering something that Henry Rudd had mentioned the vicar said, 'I think Wint might approve of your nickname. He is a prehistoric scientist and Wint is a small part of a name that he claims we couldn't pronounce but it incorporates his name, his title, and his function, whatever that is. Speaking of wartime events, I'm curious about the wheel of fortune. Henry Rudd and Henry Whiting laughed when I asked them and they said it was your idea so you ought to be the one to tell me about it. I'm guessing it was something to do with a roulette wheel.'

'Far from it,' Lofty chuckled. 'It was when…'

Elizabeth Harrison interrupted him.'

'Hold your horses. I'm going to alter your plans a little Vicar so we can get to know each other better. We'd like to know how the others got on and then in a couple of days we can get one of the boys to drive you to your stone so we will know where it is when it's our turn to go.'

Lofty had a thought.

'Would it matter to anyone if we all go back to your now at the same time? I'm thinking that when we come back we can just jump back into the car we came in and come straight home. That way there would only be one journey and we would only have been gone for a few seconds if I've got it worked out right.'

'Why in the world didn't anyone think of that!' The vicar exclaimed. 'It makes perfect sense!'

'I'll ring our Kenneth and tell him to take some time off work,' Elizabeth declared, 'he can do the driving.'

'His boss might have something to say about that,' the vicar objected.

'I am his boss. Well, not exactly because we've signed part of the business over to him,' Elizabeth explained and added, 'we have three sons and a daughter. We only meant to have three children but number three and number four are twins. All our affairs have been settled a long time ago. We're comfortably off Vicar and there's no point in denying it but what matters is family, not money.'

'I couldn't agree more. I must say you've all done well for yourselves,' the vicar concurred.

'Mr Rudd got his farm then? He had a sheaf of aerial pictures and a way of plotting his course home that took him over the place for another look.'

'He got his farm and his cows and kept a few turkeys and hens. The Vikings thought turkeys are the stupidest birds on earth, they never had them in the Viking Age. And then there were the tailnoses.'

'The what?'

'Tailnoses. Elephants to you and me. One of the last things Beowulf said about them was that he still wasn't sure if their heads were at the wrong end. When we go to my now there'll more for you to see. More DVDs, our info-tech man has prepared a sort of jump in at the deep end presentation to get you up to speed fast. Oh, and you will each be given a phone like mine, with a set of numbers pre-programmed into them. You can talk to whoever you like and you can send text messages, I'll tell you all about that later. It's a pity you can't bring them back, or maybe you can but you'll have to wait until the right communications satellites are put into orbit before you can use them and I don't know when that was. Or when it will be, if you want to put it that way.'

Later, after dinner, the vicar learned more.

'I'd known for years that I was going to be kicked out of the RAF as soon as the war was over, because of my left leg. I was knocked down by a car in the blackout in London and I got run over. My shin bone was shattered and bits of it poked through my skin. It hurt like hell but that was the least of my problems. The blackout was the cause of more accidents and deaths on the roads in London that was caused by the bombing up until then. There was no street lighting and all vehicles had to be fitted with shades over the headlights. The driver got a fine of fifteen pounds and he probably thought he was hard done by.

'While I was in hospital I was told that I was being given a discharge. That got me bloody annoyed, not to mince my words Vicar. Maybe I couldn't march and go on parades but I could still do my job and I wasn't taking it lying down. I told the medical board to take a jump and I refused to go and if they wanted to court martial me that was up to them. There was a hoo-hah but I stood up to them and they decided I could stay but only as long as the war lasted and I could forget about promotion for ever. I was going to be a Leading Aircraftman and that was that. Looking back on it I was damn lucky not to have been court martialed but the RAF needed all the mechanics they could get so they kept me on.'

'You were the most bloody minded airman I ever met,' Elizabeth Harrison remembered fondly.

'I probably was but I'd been abandoned in France and been shot at and bombed and I wanted to get a bit of my own back. That bloody mindedness was all we had and it was what got us through the war when things were especially bad. But I'll tell you one thing Vicar; and that is that Winston Churchill was wrong when he told the nation to brace itself for their finest hour. It's become a legend about the Battle of Britain in it's own way and you can call me disloyal if you like but to my dying day I'll say our real finest hour came when Dunkirk was evacuated. The lads over in France are in trouble, they said, and we need your help to bring them back. And they did. Weekend sailors put out to sea in their little river boats and away they went; scores of them. It was meant to be a strictly naval affair but there weren't enough sailors to go round so the boat owners more or less took the law into their own hands. They didn't have to come and get us but they came anyway. I wish I knew who brought me back but I never found out. I do remember seeing the Medway Queen going back for more and she was a paddle steamer pleasure boat. I think she made nine trips altogether. Dunkirk brought it home to everyone that we were in the war good and proper, more than any speechifying could ever have done and we dug our heels in and rallied round.

'Anyway, I stayed put in the Royal Air Force and then after years of walking with a bit of a limp I had my leg broken and re-set and a couple of metal plates were put in and now it's a bit hard to tell. That was after my discharge. Well, I did get booted out, just a few weeks before it was all over. This time I didn't argue, we all knew it couldn't be long. I was peeved more than a bit to be leaving Lizzie behind but as it turned out it might have been a good thing. Lizzie's parents took me in as a lodger for a spell. Uh, I don't know if anyone told you my family was killed in the bombing not long after I came out of hospital?'

The vicar nodded.

'I never had a home to go back to and there was nobody left in my family, so what we planned to do was for me to go up to the midlands where Lizzie came from and start out from there after we got married. Well as I said, it turned out to be a good thing...'

Mr Alan Harrison, known to the world as Lofty, crossed the road and walked around the corner – and there was Lizzie Engines running to meet him.

'I didn't know you were coming,' Lofty gasped after he had got his breath back.

'I purposely didn't write to mum and dad to let them know. They're awfully mad with me. You know dad; we'll have no hanky-panky in this house my girl.'

Lizzie laughed as she imitated her father.

'I got an early discharge,' she continued,' so now I'm a civilian. I'd forgotten how it feels.'

'Me too,' Lofty agreed.

'Dad moved me into the spare room but we'll need to find new lodgings for you or we'll never hear the end of it. He's got a bit of news for us but he isn't saying what it is.'

They found out later that evening.

'It's like this, lad,' Mr Richardson said, 'A lot of youngsters like you will be coming home from the war in the next few months and they'll all be asking for their old jobs back. I've no quarrel with that; it's the way things ought to be. You're going to be pushed out though, you can count on that, and finding a new job isn't going to be easy. You haven't had much luck so far have you?'

Lofty admitted the truth of what Mr Richardson said.

'Well lad, you can't live forever on odd jobs here and there and I've been keeping an eye open and I might be able to help you out, both of you. How are you fixed for cash?' Mr Richardson asked bluntly.

'Not too bad,' Lofty was able to tell him. 'After my family was bombed out in the blitz I had nowhere to go, no family any more, and nowhere to spend my money. I just shovelled it all into a savings account.'

'Aye, that was a good idea,' Mr Richardson approved. He continued, 'I've been looking around a bit and passed the word here and there. I'm well known in these parts, and I've heard about something that I reckon will suit you both if you play your cards right.'

Lofty leaned forward to hear more.

'There's an ironmonger's place up for sale, not too far away. The people who own it, well, they haven't got anyone coming back from the war, not now, and they're looking to sell up and they got on to me. The price is steep but it's a fair price and you'll pay it. No arguments. I won't have anyone say they was taken advantage of.'

'...and that's how it all began Vicar,' Elizabeth Harrison told him. 'We borrowed from the bank and put all our savings into it and we had our own little shop. We worked hard at it and our business was good. Everybody knew that Harrison's was the place to go for ironmongery and advice too, as often as not. We were lucky, we both had good trades behind us but some of our customers who could shoot out a gnat's eye at a thousand paces didn't know how to knock a nail into a piece of wood.'

'We had a proper storage for paraffin too,' Lofty added, 'and it sold like nobody's business, especially in the winter. I tell you Vicar, the winter of nineteen forty-seven was the worst I'd ever seen. Snow and ice everywhere, and bitterly cold, it seemed to go on forever. Back then there wasn't luxuries like central heating, so paraffin heaters were the order of the day. We supplied paraffin heaters and the paraffin to fill them and the wicks to burn. We sold mountains of candles as well. Sometimes it's hard to remember how things were back then but candle lighting was common, along with paraffin lamps of course.'

'And tin baths,' Elizabeth reminded him.

'I should say so,' Lofty Harrison agreed. 'The sight of a tin bath hanging on an outside wall was an everyday thing. In it's own way it was a sort of status symbol. I don't know if you've ever seen them Vicar but they came in two sizes, one was long and flat bottomed and the other was smaller and oval shaped and the bottom was corrugated. Just the job for bathing the kids in front of the fire and for doing the family laundry before washing machines came on the market. We couldn't get enough tin baths to meet the demand, it was like... well it was as if people were trying to wash away the war so they could get on with the peace,'

'Well put, I think,' the vicar responded, 'ritual cleansing in one form or another is common to nearly all races and religions.'

Lofty and Elizabeth agreed with him.

'We started our delivery service with the bath tubs,' Lofty took up his narrative. 'I got hold of a clapped out Royal Enfield motorbike and sidecar that had seen one careful owner and a dozen not so careful. We stripped it down and made it serviceable and the sidecar chassis was just the thing for me to make a wooden platform on it and I regularly loaded it with baths, paraffin, and anything else the customers wanted delivered. That old bike was a kick starter like they all were back then but it was on the right hand side which was a good thing because my left leg wouldn't have been up to it. And to cut a long story short that is where it all began,' Lofty concluded. 'From humble beginnings to meeting the demand for garden tools and seeds when people started to pick up from where they left off. Lawnmowers, mostly the ones that had twelve or fourteen inch width cutters and you had to push them yourself. You got a good cut though.'

'Merlin still uses one of those,' the vicar told him.

'They were well built, and no mistake. We didn't know whether to expand or keep our business small but there were more and more demands and so we opened our garden centre and there are two more hardware shops with Harrison written above the door. It was damned hard work but we found plenty of time to enjoy ourselves as well. We were lucky, we could always see where we were going,' Lofty said.

'We loved our little shop,' Elizabeth declared, 'but things do move on. And on top of that we managed to raise a family but I've told you that already,' she added with justifiable pride.

There was a short period of silence until Elizabeth spoke again.

'Vicar, we don't mind knowing that we will have died before the time you come from. We've got our song you see and for us it's a way of life. It's an old song that we heard way back when we were still in uniform so you might have heard it. It's called 'I'll Walk Beside You' and the words have stayed with us and they will, right up to the end.'

'I don't think I know it,' the vicar confessed.

Lofty Harrison said, 'Over here Vicar. Lizzie embroidered the words years ago and this was hung on our wall on our first wedding anniversary and it's been on the wall ever since, wherever we have lived.'

The vicar stood up and approached the framed embroidery and read out loud.

'I'll walk beside you through the world today
While dreams and songs and flowers bless your way
I'll look into your eyes and hold your hand
I'll walk beside you through the golden land

I'll walk beside you through the world tonight
Beneath the starry skies ablaze with light
Within your soul love's tender words I'll hide
I'll walk beside you through the eventide

I'll walk beside you through the passing years
Through days of cloud and sunshine, joy and tears
And when the great call comes, the sunset gleams
I'll walk beside you to the land of dreams

I'll walk beside you through the world today
While dreams and songs and flowers bless your way
I'll look into your eyes and hold your hand
I'll walk beside you to the golden land.'

'It's beautiful,' he breathed.

'You must hear it before we go to your time in the future and the record label will tell us who wrote it, because for the life of me I can't remember.'

'I can. It was Alan Murray and Edward Lockton. It was very popular during the war years and I suppose half a dozen people have recorded it.'

***

Kenneth Harrrison (call me Ken, everybody else does), regarded the vicar thoughtfully.

'I'm impressed,' he admitted. 'I wouldn't have believed a word of it but your phone and tablet gadget and you what do you call it, DVD player, make a convincing argument. I want the answer to just one question and it's this; is there any intention to compel my parents to have this virus thing planted in them?'

The vicar was ready for the question.

'There is not,' he declared firmly. 'I won't deny the offer will be made,' he added honestly.

'I believe you. I don't know why but I do believe you.'

'They are well aware that they are no longer alive in the now that I come from so it follows that the offer will be turned down.'

'It doesn't. They could take it and be spirited away somehow. To me it seems certain that you have the resources to arrange that.'

'Not me personally but perhaps Merlin... I honestly don't know whether he has or he hasn't but it would be unethical to say the least. I don't believe the question will arise.'

'Mmm. Once again I believe you. Shall we go and find my parents? I'd like to take you on a tour of the garden centre.'

Kenneth Harrison, the oldest of the Harrison's four children, picked up the DVD player and the vicar's phone.

'I'll take my phone but not the DVD player because they'll bring home a shed load of DVDs from all over the place. Better keep it under lock and key because the technology behind it is in advance of anything that is available in this here and now,' the vicar told him.

'We've had an idea Vicar,' Lofty said when the four people met in an area taken up by pot plants. 'If you stay another night Kenneth can drive us to your stone and wait for a minute or two until we come back, which might be weeks for us. That cuts the car trip to just one and there'll be no chance of anyone getting lost. Will it make a difference

92

if we all arrive at your now all together? Perhaps we aren't expected for a few days; I still haven't got used to your way of doing things.'

'Why didn't I think of that? You will be earlier than expected but that where you will stay and who you will stay with has been settled so it won't matter. Actually I think Alison is giving you the keys to the flat she keeps in Bath because it goes without saying that you won't have your own transport. Anyway, your early arrival will give me the chance to show you round my village and see the sights, and there'll be a horde of people wanting to see you. I wish I'd thought of it myself.'

As an afterthought he added, 'The village pub is a popular hang-out too, and the locals are a friendly bunch.'

Luggage was packed in the evening in preparation for an early start and when Kenneth Harrison arrived everything was ready. The vicar was to take the front passenger seat and give directions in the final stages of the journey. Kenneth Harrison stopped at a filling station and as well as petrol he purchased a selection of daily papers.

'You can read them as we go or keep them and take them forward in time. Some of your people might find them interesting.'

'The younger ones will, I'm sure,' the vicar replied, 'and Clive Bowden might be able to use them when he teaches modern history and I'll be interested myself to see what jogs my memory.'

'Stop and have an early lunch somewhere or keep going?' Kenneth said after said after they had passed the halfway point of the journey.

'I say keep going,' Elizabeth Harrison replied. 'Does that suit everybody?'

It did.

'I'm looking forward to meeting our wartime friends again,' Lofty declared.

'That goes both ways,' the vicar replied.

The drive was a trip down memory lane. The vicar commented that roads and road transport had changed dramatically, more than he had realised.

'You don't notice it when you live through it because the changes take place gradually but looking back as I am now I'm beginning to see any amount of differences. 'I've seen, oh, half a dozen makes of car that either merged with other manufacturers or went out of business or both.'

Kenneth Harrison tapped his steering wheel.

'What about this one?' He joked.

'Gone. The last Rover rolled off the production line some years ago. I can't recall when exactly,' the vicar replied.

'Rover!' Lofty Harrison exclaimed. 'I never would have thought it but if you say it I believe you,' he continued. 'I was expecting changes, we both are, but not that. Rovers turn out good models and that's why we bought this one. It's like having the carpet pulled from under your feet.'

'Well there are other makes and models. Cars are still cars and lorries are still lorries except that both cars and lorries are a lot bigger now. I mean in the future. Roads have improved to a certain extent. Urban roads are what they always were but long distance travel by road makes more use of motorways and dual carriages. Some of the biggest changes are in the field of communications. All the predictions that were made have been outstripped by a very wide margin. I carry a phone everywhere I go and so does everybody else, including children from about twelve years onwards. The even make children's models for the younger ones.

'There is a group of pupils who are itching to meet you; all of them are in their mid-teens and each one carries a phone, and in addition to that they all have laptop computers that are far more powerful than anything in you're here and now. They pack more computing power into a portable personal computer than, hmm, I'm not sure but I believe some of the larger organisations here have computers that take up as much space as a tennis court. I've seen pictures of rooms crammed with huge metal cabinets but all that is pocket sized now. I mean in my now.'

'What puzzles me most is how that prehistoric man can open a door into the past and future,' Elizabeth Harrison said from her seat behind the vicar, who swivelled round as far as his seat belt would allow when he delivered his reply.

'We don't know what he does and how he does it but there is nothing in the laws of physics to say it can't be done, or so I'm told, but according to those who know more about science than I do there's no way we can generate enough energy to make it possible. It's a complete mystery but I've done a lot of reading and discovered that the myths and legends of folklore do say that the standing stones have a certain power, including some form of weather control apparently, and they can age people as well. I ought to say they could do that once but whatever happened thousands of years ago put an end to it and the stones were deactivated, either by design or accident. Some stones are still active though but Wint the prehistoric scientist is the only person who knows how to operate them properly. Merlin can use the stones, or some of them at any rate, as a sort of remote camera and communications system. We're doing our best to unravel the mystery but we are treading very carefully.'

'I'm looking forward to meeting Merlin,' Lofty Harrison remarked.

'So am I,' Elizabeth said.

The vicar answered what questions he could as their journey continued and occasionally he commented on the things they passed and eventually Kenneth Harrison stopped the car at the place that was as near as possible to the place from where the vicar had stepped back into the past. He remarked that he wished that the car he drove had a little less room for luggage as he carried a large suitcase.

'It will be heavier on the way back,' his mother prophesied.

The vicar halted and put down the green case he had borrowed.

'This is the place. There's nothing to see but Merlin will erect a new standing stone just here some years from now and this is where I came through. When Wint opens the gate we step through while Kenneth stops here for a second or two until you come back in a few weeks time. Seconds here, weeks there. It does sound weird doesn't it?' He said.

There it was. The vicar approached confidently and gestured.

'After you.'

He said a brief goodbye to Kenneth Harrison and stepped through the open gate that looked like a hole in the air.

'I sort of neglected to mention the reception committee,' he said but his words were lost in the noise of explosive greetings as old wartime friends were reunited.

***

Morning. Lofty Harrison studied the printed page that he and Elizabeth had been given. It was a list of suggestions about what the Harrisons might like to do and see during their stay in Bath. A set of stapled papers rested on the breakfast table beside his empty plate. They carried a list of contact numbers with short notes about the people who wanted to meet the Harrison's and talk to them. It was a long list.

'They made sure we're well stocked,' Elizabeth said, 'but I still can't get over the fact that the owner of this flat is over six hundred years old or even more. She keeps this place for, well for this sort of thing I suppose. It's hard to believe.'

'Right now I'd believe the moon is made of green cheese,' Lofty Harrison replied.

'She'll be here in about half an hour. I'll wash the breakfast things and you can do the drying. The tea towels are over there,' Elizabeth pointed, 'and we're supposed to talk over the things on that paper you are looking at to see if it suits us. I can't see any problems except that I don't know what to wear for the big get-together tomorrow night in the village hall where the vicar's church is. There's bound to be new fashions and I know what the vicar said about our clothes being just like anybody else's clothes but what does a man know about fashion?'

'What indeed,' Lofty said wryly.

'And what about tonight? There's a reunion dinner at the restaurant that belongs to a Roman woman named Julia. Goodness knows how old she must be.'

Alison was not long in arriving and she towed a suitcase on wheels that the Harrisons recognised.

'Everyone wants to meet you,' she said briefly.

'We were just talking about it. Tonight and the Roman lady.'

'Julia, or to give her name in full she is Julia Calpurnia Florentina Pantera. It's a bit of a mouthful isn't it?' Alison replied cheerfully. 'She owns the restaurant but the name over the door isn't hers. The nominal owner is two hundred years old and doesn't know how to boil water but the chef is out of this world. I'm babbling on a bit aren't I?' She finished breathlessly.

'Elizabeth has been complaining that she hasn't a thing to wear' Lofty told her, 'but I've heard that before.'

Alison smiled.

She indicated the suitcase that she had brought.

'I've borrowed this from the vicar who borrowed it from somebody else. You probably recognise it. Help me unpack and you'll find a pile of dress designs that you can talk over with Copper. She's got your measurements and what she doesn't know about dress materials and fashion isn't worth knowing. Trust me.'

'My measurements? I don't think so,' Elizabeth Harrison objected.

'Copper kept a low profile yesterday when you arrived and she had your height, weight, and everything else down pat. I've heard Clive Bowden say her eyes are calibrated. Clive is Copper's husband. Copper works in feet and inches because she is about a hundred years old and we didn't use the metric system in those days. She can work in metric if she must but she doesn't like it. And I'm still babbling aren't I?'

The suitcase was eagerly unpacked.

'A scarf for Elizabeth and a tie for Lofty. Everyone will be wearing them this evening. Tourist guides and brochures to help you find your way around the city; we thought you might like to walk around and discover Bath for yourselves and do a bit of souvenir hunting.'

Alison produced two books.

'This is a book that was written to tell the world about us in a fictional sort of way. One for each of you. Some things in the book are obviously made up and some are not and some things are just plain wrong but for the most part you can rely on it. The chronicler did his best to make it easy to read and I think he did a fair job although I wouldn't tell him so because his ego is big enough already,' Alison finished with a light laugh.

'Will we meet him?'

'Probably not,' Alison thought. 'Perhaps you will meet him but not know it. There is a schoolteacher called Angela Collins who accepted a trilobite on a plate from him at one of Merlin's barbecues but her head was in a whirl because she had only just found out about us and what was going on. She saw him walk away and I have no idea if she knows yet that he is the chronicler and you can be sure she wouldn't recognise him again. He comes and goes a lot and he really does try to avoid publicity, but you never know. Perhaps he will turn up. I really don't know but this suitcase belongs to him so he might turn up to claim it back.'

Lofty Harrison made a decision.

'First things first. Yesterday was along day for us and we don't intend to do a lot today, especially with tonight's session in front of us and the meeting in the village hall tomorrow. After that we do want to see the city and do a bit of rubbernecking and we want to go to the Roman Baths and see for ourselves where all this started. We might not dip our fingers in the water though,' he declared.

Alison smiled.

'The chances of anything happening are nearly zero,' she said.

'It's the nearly that's stopping us,' Elizabeth told her, 'and I understand that you never had a choice, it just happened and it must have been an unnerving experience, but we don't want to catch the virus thing either by accident or intent. Good luck to everyone who has it or wants it but that's not us.'

'Fair enough,' Alison replied. 'You can rest assured that it won't be forced on you, which I understand was a concern of yours. Nobody who demands it will get it either and that's a rule which is unlikely to be broken, and the surprising thing is that nobody that I know of has ever said they want it, not now or at sometime in the future. Another rule is that everybody has to live out seventy years first but that rule has certainly been broken.

'And now I'm going to cease my rambling and leave you to your own devices for the day. Merlin says it will be a fine day so you won't need to wrap up if you do go out later so it's goodbye for now and no doubt we shall meet again before you return home. Adieu for now.'

***

'Trilobites, brought in fresh from Merlin's cave this morning,' Henry Whiting replied to Elizabeth Harrison's question. 'It's a pity they went extinct because they make a perfect starter to a good dinner.'

'You really should sample the different dips. I prefer orange but lemon and lime come a close second and third,' Mrs Rudd said.

'I can't get over it. I mean, first being told they are extinct and then seeing them on the plate in front of me,' Elizabeth said as she tried a cautious bite.

'Mmm, it's like nothing I've ever tasted,' Elizabeth said. She added, 'But it is delicious.'

'According to Merlin they can be frozen and he will catch a couple of dozen for you to take back with you when you return home. Actually I suspect that you will be given a tour of his cave and given a chance to catch your own and if he turns the lights off the little patches of light that they have will dart around in the pool and put on a display. It's not something that many people have seen,' Henry Rudd told her.

'I'm still wondering what else is in store for us,' Lofty Harrison said.

'Walter Pfaffinger for one thing. He's just itching to meet you. He and Robert Robertson are the best of friends who go back to our wartime days when they did the best they could to kill each other because Robert was a guardsman and Walter commanded a panzer tank for the opposition. They fought each other in the desert in North Africa and Italy. Walter never got to Dunkirk to shoot at you because his army was halted for a few days and you had time to be evacuated from the beaches. That turned out to be a big mistake because we might have lost the war there and then.'

'I've heard that said over and over and with the advantage of hindsight it's plain to see that they ought to have pressed on. I'm damn glad they didn't though.'

'Aren't we all.'

'There are some pupils on our contact list. What will they want to talk to us about I wonder?' Elizabeth Harrison asked.

'Anything and everything,' Henry Whiting chuckled. 'Those youngsters are all beyond clever. Each one has more than enough qualifications already to get into university but George Green told us they are staying on at school for another year to study for more subjects. They won't attend school every day and their study will be self-guided to a certain extent. George said they have special dispensation or something, whatever that means.'

'Clive Bowden told us that,' Mrs Whiting corrected her husband. 'There is another girl who is two years behind them at school but the year groups don't mix but she's another clever one but she isn't in the group on account of her age. I can't see a problem with fitting her in but I'm not a schoolteacher.'

'Jasmin Tyler. She isn't on your list of contact numbers as far as I know. I wish they would make up their minds about her,' Mrs Rudd said, echoing Mrs Whiting's opinions.

Chapter 11

The grass in Merlin's garden had been newly mown by Copper, who pushed the hand mower up and down with enthusiasm.

'Call me old fashioned but for me it's one of the sounds of summer,' she declared. 'You can keep your electric mowers, this is the way grass should be mown.'

A large area was left to grow wild. Merlin was a beekeeper and he liked to see wild flowers growing among the trees in his orchard.

'My daughter is laying down the law again,' Merlin said to Clive as they arranged the barbecue in preparation for the coming evening.

'She told me she is making her own brand of punch. Lord only knows what she puts into it but it seems to work. She just puts in this and that and adds fruit and gives it a stir. It's never the same twice,' Clive replied.

'Variety is the spice of life, as they say.'

Clive agreed and changed the subject.

'The homework group are as keen to meet Lofty and Elizabeth Harrison as the Harrisons are to meet them. Also, Lofty and Elizabeth are looking forward to meeting up with Walter Pfaffinger and Anneliese. Her English is getting better by the way.'

'Has any told you what Lofty's proper name is? Apparently Elizabeth never calls him anything except Lofty,' Clive asked.

'Alan Reginald Harrison or Reginald Alan Harrison, according to my sources. They can't both be right and they might both be wrong for all I know. Whichever it is it seems that Lofty is Lofty and that's all there is to it,' Merlin replied. 'Hand me that spatula will you?'

Clive located the spatula among the pile of paper plates where he had misplaced it. He was certain that somewhere in the garden a small dragon was watching them. Peep had attached himself to Copper and become a household pet but like all the dragons he steered well away from strangers. Considering what they could do this was a good thing but he did hope Peep could be persuaded to show himself to the Harrisons.

'It's going to be quite a gathering,' he commented. 'Old friends, old enemies, pupils, teachers, a citizen of the Roman Empire who … has Julia talked Brian into coming?'

'Julia can be very persuasive.'

'Enough said. It's a good thing your garden is big, it's going to be quite a crowd. Are you putting trilobites on the menu?'

'Not tonight,' Merlin replied. 'I had intended to but Mrs Bradley has something new in the way of beefburgers but for the time being the recipe is a closely guarded secret. She put twenty or so in my fridge this morning and when she turns up at six or thereabouts she will bring twenty more. Probably more than twenty if I know her. Have I mentioned that Miranda Bradley will be her assistant chef?'

Clive looked surprised.

'I thought she was doing something at a power station somewhere. Her degree in electrical engineering is paying off but I haven't seen her in ages. Hardly at all since she left school in fact.'

'Miranda intends to get your current pupils to go round with jugs of Copper's punch and keep everyone's plastic beaker topped up,' Merlin replied, 'and teenagers and beefburgers go hand in hand so Mrs Bradley wants to hear their opinions of her new recipe.'

'Roman Army thinking. Killing two birds with one stone.'

'Precisely.'

Lawrence Bowden junior tottered up to his father and grandfather with his arms outstretched. Clive picked him up and commented that he was getting heavier by the day.

'That will do for the time being,' Merlin decided and dusted charcoal from his hands. 'I don't know if anyone has told you but Brian Gleaves and Julia are arranging a barbecue at Brian's place. Brian's yard will be a car park and the barbecue will stray all over the place. Brian and Frank Holley have started clearing the undergrowth for as many people who care to turn up, and that probable means as many as a hundred.'

'Summers are made for barbecues.'

Copper had approached unseen.

Merlin and Clive agreed.

Merlin had forecast a hint of a cooling breeze and when his guests began to arrive the temperature had dropped a few degrees and it was pleasantly warm without being oppressive.

Mrs Bradley was ready with her beefburgers and jugs of punch were placed in everyone's hands. George Green was quick to spot Lofty and Elizabeth when they arrived in Alison's car and he beckoned the student group over and made introductions.

'These are some of our pupils. Derek Thorpe, who will only answer to Deke; call him Derek at your peril. James Wilson, Yolanda Walker, also known as Yo, and Christine Appleton. They will keep you topped up with Copper's own brew of punch, which is never the same twice because Copper adds various ingredients whenever the level of punch in the bowl is getting low. It always has ginger beer in it but Copper just pours in whatever comes to hand and adds fruit and so far no one has died from it.

'Alison has made sure to arrive early so you can meet Merlin and get a chance to catch your breath.'

'Sir, you forgot to mention Peep,' Yolanda said.

'So I did. Well, if you happen to spot a small dragon, which isn't likely, your eyes are not deceiving you. They stay out of sight with good reason but more of that later. No doubt you will be approached by Merlin's dog. His name is Blackie, which is the name the local children gave him but he is normally known as Hungry Dog because he will scrounge for food from anyone. And everyone probably,' he added.

'We were told about dragons Mr Green,' Elizabeth replied.

'Please call me George. We don't go in for formality.'

Guests arrived in groups. A ferrying system was usual on these occasions to save on parking space. It made perfect sense.

'I'm Angela Collins,' a young woman introduced herself. 'I came alone because my latest boyfriend dumped me. I teach English to the students who are practicing their social skills by acting as waiters.'

'They seem a bright bunch.'

'Believe me they are. All four of them are top scorers in every subject in the school curriculum. There is a girl named Jasmin Tyler who we want to bring in, partly for continuity as old pupils leave and new ones join, and partly because we think she would fit in well with the others. Her class is two years behind the other students and year groups don't tend to mix much so she might refuse to join and that would be a pity,' Angela Collins replied.

She accepted a plate that was being offered. Lofty and Elizabeth did the same.

'I've been telling Mr and Mrs Harrison all about you,' she said.

'Yes Miss. Did you mention how polite and attentive we are?'

'Be off with you James or I'll tell them the real truth.'

As the youth went on more errands Angela said, 'I expect you have already met them but if not, that was James Wilson. He's irrepressible. The girl is Yo Walker.'

'Polite but cheeky,' Lofty commented.

Angela shook her head in denial.

'No. Among our little society everyone is on a level footing and we treat each other as equals. It's a different matter when we are in school. It's a delicate situation to put it mildly but they are sensible about it and so are their parents.'

Robert Robertson hurried towards them and put an end to the conversation.

'Angela be a good girl and find yourself an unattached male. I've seen one or two looking your way. Lofty and Elizabeth, come and meet the enemy.'

Robert made the introductions.

'Lofty and Elizabeth Harrison, Walter and Aneliese Pfaffinger. Walter and I exchanged shellfire in North Africa and in Italy we came close enough to shake hands. There might have been other times but dates are a little hazy.'

Anneliese's English was halting but adequate.

'The vicar said you are a physiotherapist who used to drive a tank and he did say your story is an epic,' Lofty said.

'He said the same thing about you. I believe you were at Dunkirk? We all thought we had won the war but how wrong we were. How wrong I was,' Walter finished quietly.

'Tell us your story Walter,' Elizabeth prompted.

Robert quickly found them a table where they could talk and departed to attend to other matters'

Walter began to tell his tale.

'When war broke out I was too young to join the army. I was like every schoolboy and my only ambition was to be a train driver. The war put an end to that and as soon as I could I went into the army. In my youthful foolishness I thought it would soon be over and I would return home covered in glory and then I would drive a train. It didn't turn out that way.'

Walter paused and called to Deke Thorpe.

'Deke will you tell Mrs Bradley that her beefburgers are the finest I have ever tasted and please may I have another one?'

He looked to Lofty and Elizabeth.

'Four more, whatever my wife says about her waistline.'

After a short pause Walter continued, 'I went into the army and I learned how to march up and down and sing patriotic songs and fire a rifle and keep my kit clean. Especially that! Kit inspections were brutal. At the end of our training we clustered round the notice board to find out where we were to be sent. One of my friends shouted. Walter, we're in tanks! That meant more training and I was sure the war would be over before I had a chance to face the enemy. All the papers said it would be. I still can't believe how anxious I was to get to the battlefields, but that's youth all over the world. I have no other explanation. So I became a tank driver and I felt pleased with myself because tank soldiers were thought to be elite and our uniforms stood out in a crowd. Perhaps some of the glory would rub off on me!

'Then I went off to North Africa to fight in the Western Desert. The inside of a tank is no place to be in the desert heat but... ah thank you Christine and James.'

Walter interrupted his narrative as their beefburgers were delivered.

'Your beakers are empty,' Christine noted. 'I'll fetch more punch. Copper has topped it up with more ginger beer and I think pineapple juice and I saw her drop slices of lemon into the bowl. I'll make sure you get some.'

She sped away.

'So there I was in the desert and we fought up and down, advancing and retreating and all the time I had more training and I qualified to be a tank commander. I never got to do much commanding, and never in battle. I was still a driver but I did command when we were moving from place to place. Our gunners and loaders often came out of the turret to sit outside in whatever fresh air there was. They changed places with the radio operator to give him a chance too and it meant that each crew member could do at least two jobs.'

'That's five people. Gunner, loader, commander, radio operator, driver. I never knew that,' Lofty said.

'Five men in a small space. We came to know each other pretty well,' Walter chuckled, 'and we talked about our families and how long it would be before we saw them again. If we had thoughts that we might never see them again we kept them to ourselves. You only thought about that at night when you couldn't sleep. And we trained and kept our tanks in order and practiced loading again and again so we could fire as fast as possible. The loaders could make or break a tank battle and we knew it. And so we fought on.'

Christine Appleton reappeared with Deke Thorpe.

'More punch. I said to Copper it needs a spring onion to stir it up and add more tang and the next thing she did was take them straight out of the garden and I'm to give them to you,' she said.

'Stir, then bite off a piece of spring onion and chew it and wash it down with punch,' Deke advised. 'That's what works for me,' he added.

Anneliese Pfaffinger was the first to try it.

'It is nice I think. Danke, thank you.'

Walter continued his narrative.

'The English Eighth Army kicked us out of Africa and by that time I was no longer the starry eyed youth who had been so keen to fight the enemy. I was evacuated and I wanted to go home and see my parents. I had a brother who was in the army like me and another brother in the navy but I had no idea where they were. I just prayed they were still alive. I didn't get sent home though; I was sent to Italy. I had leave owing to me and I was given a few days off but I had nothing to do. I wrote a letter home but I couldn't tell my parents where I was but I could give them my address as a field post office and hope that any reply would reach me.

'I liked Italy, especially after the deserts of North Africa and I felt safe for a while. I was put in with a new tank crew and for a while life was routine. Nineteen forty-two ended and nineteen forty-three began and privately I wondered if the war might soon be over. The towards the end of summer the allies invaded Italy. Everyone had been saying they would invade southern France because it didn't make sense to have to fight all the way through Italy.

'Optimism and barrack room talk had got it wrong again. My tank unit was at the front of the counter attack and we came under fire from the American Fifth Army and the Royal Navy and I had never been so frightened. I drove my tank like a madman and nearly stripped every gear and toothed wheel and it's a wonder I didn't shed a track. We were on the run and we knew it.'

Walter stirred his punch and bit off a piece of spring onion before cautiously sipping his punch'

'Mmm. Refreshing. From then on we retreated. There were minor battles but nothing like the large scale battles that I had previously known. I got promoted to corporal and was made a tank commander. That made me proud but all I really wanted was to drive a train in Germany. The countryside is so beautiful. I wrote to tell my parents of my promotion and I secretly wanted to receive a letter addressed to Corporal Pfaffinger. It took a long time to arrive. And then I was sent back to Germany, straight to a training school without being allowed to visit my home.

'I trained new recruits, youngsters mostly who still believed in the war and talked of new wonder weapons that would give us victory. It would have been cruel to tell them the truth. I trained them to their limits, not because I thought we would win the war because it was obvious that we had already lost. No, I trained them to give them a fighting chance of surviving.

'And then I was fighting for my life on the soil of my homeland. I had a brand new panzer tank and a crew that was as good as I could make them. Allied aircraft were everywhere and their black and white invasion markings said here we are and there's nothing you can do about it. They were right. An American unit was in front of us but I wasn't sure where and together with another tank we crept towards them in the early dawn and hoped to get into a position to take them by surprise, but we were the ones who were surprised and it wasn't a pleasant one. Daylight was breaking as we crept forward and...'

The tank commander spotted a hollow.

'Over there!' He barked. 'To your left. It will hide the hull and give us a low profile!'

The tank began to spin on it's tracks.

Bang! The tank halted.

'What the hell?'

'Out! Everybody out!'

Their companion tank was a burning wreck.

'Are you all right corporal?'

'Just about. That was a rocket firing aircraft that scored a near miss because of our sudden turn. Let's see what we can do.'

The damage was inspected.

'Repairable but it will take time. Look out, he's back!'

The aircraft roared overhead. The commander knew what to look for.

'His rocket rails are empty but he still has his machine guns and there must have been two of aircraft. One for us and one for...'

There was no need to complete the sentence.

'Gunner, you keep a look out. The tank will give us cover if he returns. If you spot anything with rockets on the rails yell out and scatter. Loader and radio get the tool locker open. Look sharp!'

An hour of frantic work was starting to show results when the lookout screamed, 'Herr Corporal! Americans!'

Machine gun bullets bounced off the turret.

'Don't fire back! Whatever you do don't fire back!'

Taken completely by surprise they were surrounded. That would never have happened in the old days, Corporal Pfaffinger thought. They were spoken to in German.

'Face the tank and get your hands up. Up!'

The corporal knew that many United States personnel were the descendants of German and Italian families that had emigrated so it came as no surprise to hear German spoken.

'Let me see. Emil, Herman, Willi, Fritz, and Heinz. Just to be sure...'

A grenade was thrown up to a soldier who had climbed onto the tank. It was dropped in.

'Who is in charge. You, Willi? Are you in charge?'

'Walter. My name is Walter. Corporal Walter Pfaffinger. I am in charge.'

'I don't care if your name is Adolf Hitler. Turn around all of you.'

Two soldiers patted them down. Corporal Pfaffinger noticed an officer for the first time. A lieutenant.

The officer remained silent but the corporal suspected that he spoke German.

'My… my picture,' the loader said in a trembling voice.

'What?'

'Herr soldier, he has a photograph in the turret. Will you allow him to retrieve it? Please?'

The lieutenant did speak German.

'Fetch it. Any tricks and you're dead. Let's see what your girlfriend looks like.'

The loader had tears in his eyes when he emerged with a torn photograph. He handed it over.

'Mein hund,' he snivelled.

'I'll be… Lieutenant, it's a picture of his dog.'

'Give it back,' Corporal Pfaffinger said. 'He has little else now.'

He was taking a chance but…

'Give it to him.'

The lieutenant mellowed slightly.

'Do any of you speak American?'

Corporal Pfaffinger came to attention.

'Herr Lieutenant I was in north Africa and Italy. I have learned from the Americans and the English.'

'Stand easy. You're out of the war now. Behave yourselves and you might see it out.'

He jerked a thumb over his shoulder.

'There's a village over there. Two of my guys are going to take you there. You'll be walking and they will be in one of the jeeps. One false move and I don't need to tell you what will happen…'

'… and so I became a prisoner of war. We were well treated but there were so many prisoners and nowhere to put us so we were herded into a field and we slept in the open. When it rained we got wet. Every day a water carrier came and my cup was a tin that had held field rations and I shared it with my men. Men! They were boys and I was a veteran soldier who had yet to see his twenty-fifth year. I remember another soldier who walked up and down asking if anyone had seen a Hans Schmidt. His brother perhaps or a comrade in arms. I never knew.

'Then I was moved and I had a roof over my head at last. I was documented as we all were. I need only have told them my name and rank and number but what was the point of hiding anything? I told them I came from Cologne and their officer said that would help with my return home. I think we both thought that would be soon. The allied armies were advancing everywhere and I was told the authorities in Hamburg threw the city open to avoid more senseless killing. And so the war ended.

'I was still confined. All the roads were choked with military traffic and the railways were a mess of bombed bridges and tracks and so we were low on the list of priorities for transport. It was understandable but frustrating and I made up my mind to go it alone. Some infantrymen were put onto a lorry one day and I saw my chance and scrambled on and kept my head down. I discovered we were being taken to a discharge centre and I thought perhaps I might bluff my way through the procedure.

'It didn't work. I found myself in Hamburg which was a port. It had been bombed nearly flat. My tank uniform made me stand out and I knew I was in trouble because I was technically an escaping prisoner and I could expect harsh treatment.'

Walter managed a smile.

'Harsh treatment was what I got. The allies had taken over a hospital and I was packed off there to do menial work. The head nurse was called Schneider and she seemed to have a special hatred of Herr Corporal Pfaffinger. All the dirty jobs came my way. I cleaned bed pans. I scrubbed floors. I scrubbed walls. I washed dishes. I mopped and I swept. I was in and out of the wards to clean windows and do all the tasks I was given to keep the place spotlessly clean. I talked to the patients when I could and sometimes I ran small errands for them. We got to know each other and many times they tipped me off when Schneider was coming and I made myself scarce.

'One day I stopped to watch a physiotherapist treat a bedridden patient who was trying to squeeze a rubber ball. It was painful for him I could see that, and he dropped the ball and it rolled to where I stood so I picked it up and put it back in his hand and I closed my hand over his and put my other hand on his shoulder while I squeezed his injured hand gently to encourage him and he tried again. I went back to my mop and bucket but from then on I made sure I was there when the physiotherapist was in the ward and gradually he allowed me to do small things while all the time I kept watch for Schneider. And so I helped men walk up and down the wards and lift themselves up and squeeze rubber balls and so on. One day I was caught by Schneider and I thought I was in trouble but she said nothing.

'I wrote some letters home but I wasn't allowed to leave Hamburg and I was getting impatient. I shared a room and a washbasin with other workmen, mostly labourers clearing rubble, and it was like being back in barracks. Then one day I was summoned to see the commanding officer. I didn't know what to expect. He...

... said 'Come in Pfaffiger. Sit down.'

He picked up a file.

'These are your discharge papers. You're free to go. Here is a ticket to Cologne. Do you know what you are going to do now?'

'I shall try to become a train driver sir.'

'Well Pfaffinger you can if you like but I want you back here. I've written you a return ticket and a ten day pass. Your conduct here has been good and I have been kept informed about your interest in physiotherapy. Read this.'

Incredulously Walter Pfaffinger read a recommendation that was written by head nurse Schneider.

'I want you back here. You will assist the physiotherapist form a few months and then if all goes well you will transfer to a hospital in or near Cologne and start to gain formal qualifications. Schneider has contacted the right people and she will push it through. Between you and me Pfaffinger I'm a colonel and she scares the hell out of me. What's it to be? Train driver or physiotherapist? It's a choice between one or the other. Germany is getting back to normal and the railways are the lifeblood of the nation but physiotherapists are needed too. The choice is yours but I think you can do more good here. Look, I'll give you time. If you come back when your ten days are up I'll be glad to see you. If not, then I wish you the best of luck.'

Walter left the colonel's office with a dazed expression and a travel warrant. He collected his few belongings and walked out of the building a free man. No longer a soldier, no longer a prisoner of war, no longer... no longer what?

'My family was one of the lucky ones,' Walter continued. 'I was the last to return home and my brothers were already there. I met some old acquaintances and learned that there were far too many people I would never see again. I talked to my parents and I decided to return to Hamburg until I could come back to Cologne. And that is what I did. I was four months in Hamburg and then I was given a position nearer home. I worked and I studied and I passed all my tasks and examinations and at last I received my diploma. I was Walter Pfaffinger the physiotherapist!

'But the railways always called to me and in my spare time I used to go to the Cologne railway station and be a train spotter. And then one day a very pretty girl with a suitcase stepped off a train and I rushed up the platform and told her I was a porter and I would carry her luggage for her. And so it was that the first thing I ever said to Anneliese was a lie and I've never been allowed to forget it!

Walter's laughter was infectious.

'I came to Bath to treat Copper Beach and make sure her old joints were in working order. Doctor Mallory had heard about me by means I have never discovered and I was dragged out of retirement to come to Bath on and off and now here we are getting younger by the day and I'm going back to work as soon as I can. Once again Doctor Mallory will pull strings and he has a lot of people on his team. I shall be a physiotherapist again and do voluntary work on an English steam railway. Or perhaps Welsh or Scottish, we shall see, and one day I will achieve my boyhood ambition and drive a steam engine. And that is the story of Walter Pfaffinger.'

Chapter 12

As she had done several times already Angela Collins reached for the folded paper that she had put on the empty passenger seat of the car and slipped it into her pocket with a smile of inward amusement. One glance at the watch told her that she had arrived early at the school where she taught English. This was no accident; Angela wanted to catch Clive Bowden and, if possible, George Green before they went inside the school building. They could speak freely if they talked in the car park and neither arriving pupils nor other staff members would take any notice of them.

Her patience was rewarded when Clive backed his car into a slot two places away from hers. George Green sat next to him.

Angela approached from the passenger side so George spotted her first and as he got out of the car he called a greeting. Within seconds he was joined by Clive Bowden, and Angela produced the folded paper from her pocket.

'I wanted you to see this first and tell me what you make of it. It's a description by Shakespeare of one of the characters in the play I'm working on,' she explained.

The play was something that William Shakespeare had penned about Merlin, Copper Beach's father and Clive's father in law. It had never been produced in public and Angela Collins had taken on the task of using Shakespeare's original hand written manuscript and put it into a type written form. The work was complicated by the author's almost illegible handwriting and his constant crossings out and alterations. Words and phrases that Shakespeare had invented had become part of the English language and were often used in everyday speech by people who were unaware that they quoted him. Angela had already encountered two unfamiliar words which she was almost sure were never used in any other of his plays although it would be some time before she could be absolutely certain of it.

George Green was nearest so Angela handed him to paper to pass to Clive for him to open and read it.

'He is faced as is Janus faced and tongue'd as is Janus tongue'd,' Clive read.

'What might that mean?'

'Umm, Janus was a god who was worshiped by the Romans. He faced both ways, backwards and forwards and he looked backwards to the past year and forwards to the next and the month of January is named after him. He was also the god of doorways and he looked out and in and from that we get the word janitor. Some Roman coins have been found that show him as having two faces on one head, one face looking backwards and one face looking forwards. How's that for an answer?' Clive said.

'It's only half an answer. Why did Shakespeare compare one of his characters to him?'

Clive shook his head.

'My thought is that he, well he saying that his character had two faces. It was Shakespeare's way of calling him two faced. It wasn't meant as a compliment,' George Green guessed.

'Right so far. Is there more?'

Clive studied the paper again.

'I'm feeling like a third form pupil,' he confessed, 'but look, this man had two faces and two tongues. He was a two faced liar,' he concluded triumphantly.

'Go to the top of the class.'

'Who was he talking about? Do you know?' George Green enquired.

Angela looked serious.

'I do. It was Merlin.'

'Merlin? Shakespeare called Merlin a two faced liar,' Clive gasped. 'I had the impression they got on well together. I know Shakespeare could hand out insult and innuendo by the dozen but this isn't making sense.'

'Actually it is. Who else do you know who is a two faced liar?' Angela countered.

'Well I wouldn't like to say but...'

'Then I'll tell you. You are.

Did Clive Bowden's face show a trace of Viking fury? It was gone in an instant and George Green was never sure. Angela Collins missed it.

She continued, 'You are a two faced liar and so am I and so are you George in the sense of what Shakespeare said about Merlin. He has one private face and one public face and he tells one story in private and a different story in public and that is exactly what we members of the Bell Curve Society do day in and day out. It is not just us; everyone does it to some extent. It's a part of everyday life.'

Clive relaxed and admitted it was true, adding, 'He would have got that past me.'

'I don't think he would. Don't forget I've read the whole thing in context and that passage is intended to be humorous,' Angela said and told him, 'I have a sneaking feeling that it was Merlin who put him up to it.' She finished with a wide smile.

'Knowing what I do know I tend to agree,' George Green backed her up.

Angela had more to say.

'Shakespeare also described Merlin as casting more shadows than a lawyer and he wasn't being complimentary to lawyers. It was a nice turn of phrase and I suspect that when he wrote that piece he had run foul of the legal profession again. I can also say with a fair degree of certainty that this play was comical and Shakespeare intended to involve the audience. It is a pantomime and he was inviting a certain amount of cat-calling and lampooning and when I have finally sorted it out I shall be looking for a cast of players so be warned.'

'Ohh no you won't.'

'Ohh yes I will.'

Some arriving pupils might have wondered what the loud laughter was all about.

Clive folded the paper into quarters.

'Do you mind if I keep this? I'd like to show it to Copper and Merlin. Merlin first I think.'

'Of course, but don't tell me what they say about it because I don't want my work to be coloured by their opinions,' Angela replied.

'Mmm. Makes sense. OK, we have a deal.'

Clive checked the time.

'We'd better shift ourselves or we'll be late for school and that would never do.'

They moved off.

The school day had begun.

***

'I didn't put him up to it. Miss Collins was wrong about that,' Merlin said.

Sunday lunch was over and the washing up was done. The family relaxed at home. Lawrence Bowden junior played with his coloured wooden blocks and kept himself amused.

'Shakespeare's play was a comedy and I was being lampooned. She was certainly right about that. It was uproariously funny and the audience loved it. Most of them were victims of his humour too.'

'Father you told me it had never been performed,' Copper objected.

'Never performed in public, I said,' Merlin corrected her, 'but there were half a dozen or so private performances in front of, shall we say selected audiences. Some people attended more than one performance because they knew Shakespeare could be depended on to make alterations here and there. He frequently poked fun at them and they loved it.'

'I can hardly wait for Angela to finish working on it but it seems to me there might be more than one version. There must be,' Copper declared.

Merlin agreed.

'It was never the same twice and that was the beauty of it. Shakespeare didn't invent audience participation, not by a long way, but he knew how to get his audience involved. Miss Collins has grasped the sense of the thing exactly. It was pantomime at its best and whenever a pantomime goes on tour there is reference to some local event or person as often as not. It's always been a way of getting the audience to identify with the cast and the play. I remember the play was acted twice with the introduction of a town crier to change scenes and spread the news about the peccadillos of some of the audience. It always went down well.'

'Did they have town criers in those days?'

'Town criers go back for centuries in one form or another. Shakespeare was quite familiar with them. He was manipulating his audience. You only have to watch television to see how an audience can easily be manipulated for instance when a comedian walks onto the stage and points a finger at someone in the audience. It could be just anybody and the performer is working the audience. They come prepared for it but I'm sure that most of them don't know how puppet-like they are. It's always been that way,' Merlin said.

'Manipulation. Politics. Propaganda destroys objectivity,' Clive mused.

'That is its purpose. When it is done subtly and cleverly the greater mass of the population doesn't even recognise that it is propaganda and their thinking is being directed. Added to which there is a natural desire to conform. Professor Land could go into detail about that I have no doubt. I'm beginning to sound like a lecturer,' Merlin said.

'Is it really fair to say propaganda destroys objectivity?' Copper asked.

'Let's say that conformity is an ally of propaganda,' Merlin replied.

Young Larry Bowden tired of his bricks and tottered towards his grandfather with his arms outstretched.

Peep the dragon snored softly in his basket.

It was a perfect afternoon.

***

Clive turned off his bedside light and sank back into his pillow.

'Shakespeare had a lot to teach us. I always though the person in charge of what I think is me,' he said.

Copper rolled towards him.

'I'm going to have a big influence on your thoughts for as long as I can stay awake,' she whispered.

Chapter 13

'My trilobites have settled down in their tank,' Deke Thorpe reported to the group members. 'They go for fish flakes and dried daphnia but I haven't tried them on live food yet. I don't want to over feed them so I'm taking it easy.'

'Where do they feed?' Yolanda enquired. 'As far as I can tell they aren't surface feeders.'

'True. I think. They know it's there but they won't touch it until it starts to sink and then they go like crazy. It takes an age for the dried flakes to sink. I'm wondering if their eyes have anything to do with it; maybe they can't even see it on the surface. It could be they pick up the ripples when it hits the water.'

'They haven't got lateral lines,' Christine Appleton objected.

'I know but I'm checking out their behaviour, not their anatomy.'

'Point taken,' Christine admitted. 'Perhaps their shells are sensitive to the noise of something dropping into the water but I can't see the point of that unless there is something in the cave that doesn't swim through and we don't know about. It might be a creepy crawly or detritus dropping in with a splash.'

James Wilson agreed.

'Ask me about my dad's shrimps,' he said.

'No.'

'I'll tell you anyway. He scrounged some shrimps from Merlin and put them in a tank in the shed and covered half the bottom of the tank with marbles and a plastic washing up scouring pad. It's a tip he got from the internet. Ask me why?'

'No.'

James grinned.

'Well get this. Two of the shrimps are females that were carrying eggs and when they laid them they dropped to the bottom of the tank where they can't be eaten because the marbles and the scouring pad keep the adults away. They'll come out when they are big enough to be safe but my old man is going to put a plastic fence across the tank to keep the adults separated.'

'How many layers of marbles?' Yolanda demanded.

'Two,' James replied. 'That should be enough. The water won't stagnate because the shrimps will keep the water aerated. Their legs go non-stop. The marbles are info from the internet according to my dad.'

'It does point the way to experimentation,' Christine said. 'With marbles, without marbles. With light, without light, that's because the cave is dark except for the light patches on the trilobites. Is your dad keeping records?'

'You bet. And photos.'

'I wonder how big they will be when they are grown?' Deke said. He added, 'I bet Mr Green knew we'd get a project going but I bet he never expected our parents to get in on the act.'

'Don't underestimate Mr Green,' Christine said.

**

'So this is where you gang up on Saturday mornings,' Mrs Harrison commented as she looked around. 'Mr Green said we would find you here. We're having a wander around to see what your time is like. There seems to be a lot of changes. Your pocket telephones are like something from a science fiction film and as for your computers and tablets and talk of uploading and downloading it's like listening to a different language.'

'Haven't you got phones yet?'

'Not your kind of phone. Mine is ten times bigger than any of yours and I have to pull the aerial out when I use it. I never dreamed that one day they would be cameras as well as phones,' Elizabeth Harrison told them.

An untouched cup of coffee sat in front of her until Lofty Harrison pointed out that it was getting cold and she took a few sips.

'We usually get together in here on Saturdays and get our homework finished and have a bit of a chat, you know, catch up on the gossip and that sort of thing. We just talk about anything that comes up and then just drift off when it starts to get crowded. People mostly do their shopping and get it over before they come in so it gives us plenty of time, and the staff know us and they don't mind when we join a couple of tables together or yank up a couple of chairs,' Deke Thorpe informed the Harrisons. He added, 'Yo brings her astronomy pictures in sometimes, and shows them off on her lap top computer. We've all got those, and tablets. Nearly everyone has.'

'Our now is too early for us to have them,' Mrs Harrison said, 'but I've just told you that.'

'I haven't got any pictures today but I've been getting ready all week for a look at the Pleiades tonight. It's a perfect viewing night, the forecast said it's going to be nice and clear and there's no moon so I might get some really good pictures. The Pleiades is a star forming region and there are lots of bright new stars and you can really bring the colours out. If I get anything good, which I think I will, I'll make some prints,' Yolanda informed everyone, 'and I'll post them to your computers anyway.'

She stopped her speech to bite from her half-eaten muffin.

'Don't look now but Jasmin Tyler has just walked in. She's at the counter,' Christine Appleton said suddenly. 'She's on her own, I'll wave her over,' she added.

'I know that name,' Lofty Harrison said. 'Isn't she the one everybody is wondering about bringing her into the bell-curve set up?'

'Society,' James Wilson corrected him.

Lofty laughed.

'If you say so. Let's hear what she has to say.'

Jasmin Tyler approached uncertainly. She knew who the teenagers were but they were two years ahead of her in school and they didn't mix.

'Is it all right?' She asked anxiously.

'Sure. James, budge up a bit. We don't often see you in here. By the way, this is Mr and Mrs Harrison who are visiting Bath for a few weeks. They know some friends of ours and were showing them around,' Christine added.

'I don't come in here much,' Jasmin admitted, talking while she pushed a straw into a carton of orange juice, 'but I've just picked up my magazine and I told my dad this is where I'd be.'

She indicated the plastic bag that held the publication.

'They've printed a letter I wrote to them. I can't wait to show my dad,' she said with pride.

'Can we see it too?'

Jasmin looked pleased at Mrs Harrison's request and slipped the magazine out of the bag. Mrs Harrison looked surprised. It was a gardening magazine, which was not what she had expected.

'The letters page is near the back,' Jasmin told her, 'and this edition is all about garden pests.'

'Yuk! Bugs and slugs!' Yolanda shuddered. 'I hate creepy crawlies.'

'Insects are pollinators,' Jasmin protested, 'and if we didn't have insects we wouldn't have gardens. Or anything else much,' she added, 'and birds eat insects and their larvae because they're all part of nature.'

Yolanda wasn't quite finished.

'What about slugs?' She asked with an air of revulsion.

'My hedgehog will eat them,' Jasmin Tyler said positively.

To the Harrisons she said, 'I haven't got a hedgehog yet but I've been trying for ages and I've made some special hedgehog places for them to live in my garden. I know one will come.'

'Aren't you supposed to put out a saucer of milk and some tinned meat for them?' James enquired.

'No. hedgehogs drink water like every other wild animal and if you put tinned meat out you'll get rats before you get hedgehogs. Or foxes. Whichever gets there first.'

'I never knew that.'

Lofty looked interested.

'Will you go to university to study horticulture?' He asked her.

'No sir. I'm thinking about a diploma course in garden design, you can see advertisements for that in the very last pages of my magazine. It's going to be very important because of climate change and gardens are going to have to change too. Different grasses perhaps, and different flowers and vegetables. Stuff that isn't grown now very much but will be because some things will have to go or be grown differently. Things like potatoes because the wet years ruin the crop so there might have to be new varieties. But proper garden design is not just growing things, it's about making the garden fit the space around it and what sort of buildings there are and what sort of a garden somebody wants, like if there are children who want a swing or something and is there room for trees. You have to get everything to fit together so it looks nice and it has vegetables and flowers and, well, everything,' Jasmin finished breathlessly.

'You do know your stuff,' Lofty Harrison complimented her and Jasmin looked pleased.

'I like doing gardening and I'm going to try and get work experience in a garden centre but I still need to do a garden design course and get my diploma,' she replied.

'That's interesting,' Lofty said, leaning forward and adding, 'I'm a bit of a gardener myself.'

The Harrisons exchanged surreptitious glances, Christine Appleton noticed. She interpreted the exchange correctly.

'I wonder if I should send a text,' she said.

'I think you should,' Mrs Harrison told her.

Jasmin looked perplexed.

'We've a surprise for you,' Mrs Harrison told her, 'just wait and see.'

'More like a big surprise,' Deke said, 'it knocked me sideways when I found out. You're going to love it.'

Jasmin Tyler opened her mouth to say something but before she could utter a word a voice said, 'Found you!'

'Dad! That was quick!' Jasmin exclaimed. She added, 'I'd better go.'

'Not so fast young lady,' Lofty said.

'I'm Lofty Harrison, Mr Tyler. Please sit with us for a few minutes. We've just told your daughter she's in for a big surprise, and so are you. A pleasant surprise, I think you'll find.'

'Deke said it knocked him sideways when he found out Dad, but I'm still waiting for someone to tell me what it is.'

'That's me. I'm Deke, Mr Tyler.'

'You've got my full attention. Spill the beans.'

'I think we're supposed to wait for someone to come first Mr Tyler,' Yolanda told him.

'I'm Yolanda but everyone calls me Yo, and this is Christine Appleton and James Wilson, we all go to the same school as Jasmin. I don't know who's coming but, well, Christine has just sent a text and by now phones will be ringing all over Bath. I can't explain. I'm allowed to, we all are, but none of us knows quite what to do next.'

'That's true, Mr Tyler. Bear with us a minute,' Lofty said.

'Patience isn't one of my virtues but…have I got time to get myself a cup of coffee?'

'I don't even know that. Probably. Allow me to do the honours just in case someone turns up a little sooner that I expect.'

Without waiting for a reply Lofty made for the counter. When he returned George Green had just arrived.

'Oh! Mr Green's come in and he's coming this way. He's my science teacher Dad.'

George managed to find a chair.

'Morning all,' he said briskly, 'I've been tipped off and I'll put you all in the picture as much as I can. Christine, you'll probably get a few phone calls soon. I'm George Green, you must be Mr Tyler, Jasmin's father.'

'Yes,' was the brief reply.

'Good. Well, we've got something going. Let's call it a sort of club for the sake of convenience. You'll notice that Mr Harrison and I are wearing the club tie and Mrs Harrison wears a matching scarf. The boys don't go in for ties much but the girls… how about it?'

Christine and Yolanda each produced scarves.

'By the end of the day you will have a similar tie and scarf,' George continued. 'You don't have to join the club if you decide not to but you'll be in the know. You'll still have the, um, regalia, and whether or not you choose to wear it is up to you. Jasmin, who is your English teacher?'

'Miss Collins sir.'

'Look out for her scarf on Monday when you get to school. She won't say anything but she will be aware that you know what it means.'

'We don't know,' Mr Tyler said bluntly. 'Are you going to get to the point?'

'Text, Mr Green,' Christine Appleton interrupted.

'Ah, perfect timing.'

George read the message on Christine's phone.

'Well, things really are moving!'

Yolanda's phone rang while George was speaking.

'It's for you sir,' she said, and added, 'it's Julia.'

'Mr Tyler excuse me for a minute but needs must.'

George listened to Julia for a moment.

'Hang on, I'll ask him. Mr Tyler, can you be free tonight at about seven o'clock?'

'If I must.'

'Good. Julia the answer is yes. I'll make the arrangements with them, such as I can.'

Retuning the phone to Yolanda, George let out a 'Whoosh!'

He put his thoughts together and said, 'You're being carried along on the tide I'm afraid, and so am I. Mr Tyler, here's the plan. Challenge it if you like but it goes like this; I'm going to pick you up a seven o'clock and drive you to Julia's place. You've just heard Yolanda mention Julia. When we arrive there will be quite a few other people waiting to see you, including these few.'

He indicated the group of pupils.

'No can,' Yolanda wailed, 'I've set up an astronomy night and it's not just me. I can't get out of it.'

'Um. Can't be helped but you'll be kept informed. Mr Tyler, we have a policy of complete openness. No secrets. Some of the people you will have met already. Between us we're going to…'

'Knock us sideways, Deke said,' Jasmin interrupted him, adding, 'sorry sir.'

'No need to apologise. I can't say more at the moment and in any event the place is starting to get crowded and I for one have just had a whole lot of work dumped in my lap. Well, there it is. Can I let everybody know you will come?'

'Yes. Not without misgivings but we will be ready at seven o'clock.'

'Good. One other thing; wear a shirt that goes with a tie like mine. Now I really have to leave in a hurry so if you will excuse me…'

'Wow! Julia! Blimey!' James Wilson gasped.

'She's high powered,' Deke Thorpe added. 'More high powered than you'd believe but I'd better shut up.'

George Green was out of the door before he had finished speaking.

'One small point,' Christine said with the logic that was typical of her. 'Mr Green probably doesn't know where you live. I can text your address to him just in case.'

Mr Tyler nodded dumbly.

Christine did so, and after a hectic day George green and his passengers arrived at Julia's large house to find the door opened by Julia herself.

'Do come in. we're a bit crowded tonight but I've saved some seats for you. Others are sitting on the floor, which is not uncommon at these get-togethers because they're always well attended. Three of your fellow students are on the floor over there Jasmin, and I'm sure you recognise your history teacher.'

Julia smiled as she spoke.

'I'm Clive Bowden Mr Tyler. We haven't met before but I don't doubt that from now on we'll be seeing more of each other.'

'Mr Bowden will start things off. Over to you Clive,' Julia said.

'Here we go then. As you know, I'm a teacher. I'm married and I have an infant son who is spending the night with his grandfather who spoils him but that's what grandfathers do. My other half, some say my better half, is here though and there she is.'

Copper raised her hand.

'She's a thoroughly modern girl and she kept her own name when we got married. It's a rather unusual name, she's Copper Beach. Actually the name Copper came about because of her sun-tanned appearance and the colour of her hair.'

Clive paused for a brief moment and then continued, 'The story I'm going to tell has it's origins about five thousand years ago. The exact date is uncertain but before we go back to that period of history I must talk about more recent events. A few years ago in the city of Bath a rather peculiar organism was found in a blood sample that was taken from a local resident. It's a dual identity organism for want of a better way of putting it, and one part of its persona is a bacteria and the other and far smaller part is a virus. We call the thing a pseudo-virus and I believe it is unique but there are two strains of it, which turns out to be important. It doesn't happen anywhere else and some people believe it was genetically engineered. The strange thing is that although it can be cultured it was impossible to introduce it into samples of anyone else's blood. It just died. Then Doctor Edwin Mallory, who is sitting crossed legged on a cushion over there, had a breakthrough.'

Edwin Mallory raised his hand to identify himself.

'I share the credit with Nurse Driscoll who unfortunately isn't able to be present this evening. Patti Driscoll got me pointed in the right direction,' he told Mr Tyler and his daughter.

'So now the pseudo-virus could be put into somebody else's bloodstream, but as it turned out there was only one blood group that was able to take it. We only knew that from donated samples of blood, it was never injected into anybody,' Clive said.

'Why would it be?' Mr Tyler interrupted, 'I wouldn't let anyone deliberately infect me. Sheer stupidity.'

Displeasure was apparent in his tone of voice.

'Who would?' Clive replied calmly.

'However,' he continued, 'the organism had an unusual effect on the, um, carrier. There is documentary evidence by the way. The effect I'm talking about is that the, ah, carrier, the carrier's biological clock was reset so somebody who is about one hundred years old looks decades younger.'

Clive grinned boyishly and said, 'I'm told that if I reveal the lady's exact age I shall never hear the end of it but the lady in question is here in this room.'

Mr Tyler and Jasmin stared hard at the assembly of people.

Clive said, 'She's Copper Beach.'

'Your... your wife!'

'My wife, and now I have to tell you that Copper is not the only one who carries the virus. Pseudo-virus I ought to say. It turned out that others had been infected long before Copper. Julia, it's your turn.'

Julia stood up.

'I'd like you to look closely at this portrait,' she said, 'it was painted about two hundred years ago. The artist was Gainsborough. The sitter looks a bit like me doesn't she? That's because she is me.'

The room seemed to shimmer.

'And this is how I looked in that dress.'

Julia walked a few paces and gave a twirl to show off her outfit.

'Stylish, don't you think?' Julia smiled as she spoke.

'If all this is as true as it seems to be I'm knocked sideways and back again,' Mr Tyler said hoarsely.

'You can't say you weren't warned,' Julia laughed lightly.

'I go back further than this though, to the time of the Roman occupation of Britain, which lasted about four hundred years. I lived in Bath, which we called Aquae Sulis, and this is the way I dressed then.'

Once again the room shimmered.

'Here I am in a rather formal outfit, not my day clothes. Fashions change over the years and I had a number of different styles over a long period. I believe I got the virus in my blood when I was a little girl not long after my parents came to Britain from Rome. I used to play with other children and make mud pies near an outlet from the Roman Baths in the city. Eventually Rome fell and I am the last Citizen of the Roman Empire. My name in full is quite a long one for the women of my era. I am Julia Calpurnia Florentina Pantera.'

'I don't know what to say. Is everyone else seeing what I'm seeing?'

'Yes, but I can limit it to just you and Jasmin if I choose to or if you want me to.'

'No. It's fine just as it is. I think. I don't know.'

'It is rather a lot to take in,' Julia sympathised, 'and there's more to come. This is probably as good a time as any to tell you that we're expecting a mystery guest later but for the time being I will continue to say my piece.

'The Roman Empire in the west collapsed, although the Eastern Empire continued to flourish for many years. I left Aquae Sulis and went to live not far from here on what are now the Somerset Levels but at that time were flooded. I was expected by the Lake People which was something of a mystery to me but tradition held it that they had been told thousands of years earlier to expect someone from a race as yet unborn. In other words, Roman. Today we know who told them but more of that later.

'I lived on the Lake in a fairly small village that was so important it gave its name to the whole district. It was called Avalon.'

'That's a legend!' Jasmin gasped, adding, 'Sorry Miss.'

Julia smiled at her.

'Jasmin, please call me Julia,' she said, 'everybody else does.'

'I'll try M… Julia.'

'Good. I didn't wear Roman clothes while I lived on the Lake of course and as usual fashion changed over time but in those days change was gradual. Typically I dressed like this.'

Once again the room shimmered.

'Or on more formal occasions like this,'

Now Julia wore a long flowing garment.

'My stay on the Lake lasted some three hundred years,' Julia continued,' and over a period I learned to do the things I am doing now. The knowledge came from what we call the Old People who stretch way back into pre-history. We now know the original settlers on the Lake, some of them anyway, called them the knowing ones. These knowing ones were somehow different from everyone else. To begin with they were small with high pitched voices and they always went in threes. It was rare to see one alone and most people never did so.

'So it came about that I became quite powerful. Let's not beat about the bush, I was very powerful. I was, and I still am, the Lady of the Lake.'

'Oh. I mean…oh!'

'I'll give you time to catch your breath Mr Tyler and I'll show myself as I was when you came in, which is the way I normally appear.'

Julia did as she said.

After a brief halt she asked, 'Are you ready to go on now?'

'Uh, I think so. And if you are to be called Julia may I not be called Mr Tyler? I notice that first names seems to be the rule.'

'Of course. You can adopt an alias if you like, for the purpose of reporting. There's a book you see, that was written about us. It's a chronicle but padded out to make it readable. The chronicler is writing for the present and the future. Who knows what the world will be like centuries from now? What shall we call you?'

'Not Wat Tyler for sure, I've been trying to rid myself of that nick-name all my life. It made sure I never forgot the date of the Peasant's Revolt because the original Wat Tyler was the leader. I'll just be any old Tom, Dick, or Harry.'

'Tom Tyler. Alliterative but it doesn't suit you, and neither does Dick Tyler. Harry Tyler sounds more like you.'

'Then I'm Harry Tyler.'

'Excellent. Everybody say hello to Harry Tyler.'

'Hello Harry,' they chorused.

'It's settled. I mentioned the book-cum-chronicle. You'll get a copy before you go home. One each so you won't be able to argue who is to read it first. There are some discs as well. Our computer wizard has transcribed a mass of video tapes and put them into an up to date and more compact form. George,' Julia continued, 'this would be a good time to give Harry and Jasmin a tie and scarf respectively. The motif is a dragon and a trilobite for reasons that shall become clear.'

'It's lovely,' Jasmin said as she accepted her scarf. 'Is it all right if I put it on now?'

'Go ahead, you're one of us now, and I did advise your father to wear a shirt that would go with the tie,' George said.

The girl was soon adjusting her father's tie.

Clive took over.

'This is where we go back five thousand years or thereabouts and introduce a new character. He's called Wint, which is apparently a contraction of his name, his title, and his function. Shall I carry on Julia, or do you want to?' Clive finished with a question.

'You Clive, and I'll step in when it's necessary. Which it will be,' Julia added to Harry and Jasmin Tyler.

Clive nodded assent.

'Right then. Way back in pre-history the knowing ones lived side by side with the people who lived on the Lake. Small people with high pitched voices, both the men and the women. The vicar has a theory that they were a separate branch of humanity in much the same way as the Neanderthals were. He suggests that they were a lot more intelligent than we are. He isn't present tonight but it won't be long before you meet him,' Clive began.

There was a short pause before he continued.

'One thing the knowing ones could do defies belief. They had the secret of time travel.'

'What!'

'I can show you the proof. Rather dramatic proof as it happens. Wint can also move other people in time, as well as himself. He did that to me and Matron who I'm afraid is another absentee. We were thrown back in time and landed pretty well at the feet of the Lady of the Lake, who was tending a badly injured man but lacked the skill to do anything much. Matron had the skill but she was very relieved when a very competent surgeon arrived. In the meantime I was rushing off along a causeway to stop a wild boar returning to finish the job it had started on the injured man. I hadn't a clue what I was going to do and while I was trying to work something out a boy came rushing up behind me and he handed me a sword that he said belonged to Lady Calbia.'

It was Julia's turn to speak.

She explained, 'The People of the Lake had a taboo about speaking the first name of anyone they considered important and their pronunciation of Calpurnia came out as Calbia. I learned to live with it. Back to you Clive.'

'That boy was a nuisance, not to put too fine a point on it. He claimed that everyone called him Pest, and they weren't wrong. I wanted to be rid of him but he wanted to stay and see me kill the wild boar, and all I wanted was to be somewhere else, I can tell you. Then I discovered I had a small pot of a culture of the pseudo-virus in my pocket. I was meant to pass it on but I hadn't had time and I'd forgotten about it until I put my hand in my pocket for a handkerchief to wrap around the hilt of the sword.'

Clive stopped and licked his lips.

'I told the boy to take it to Matron because it was a special medicine that would help to heal the injured man, whom he called Master Gerni. When he arrived Matron was assisting the surgeon who, by the way, was about fourteen years old and went by the name of Rufus. Matron told the boy to rub the culture on Master Gerni's hands. Anything to keep him quiet. Umm… it might have been Rufus who told him. Right now it doesn't matter who it was.

'Around this time the boar attacked me. The size of the brute was unbelievable. And then out of the blue a pair of Vikings turned up. I couldn't believe my eyes. They weren't there in person, they were more of a hologram. They didn't think much of my ability with a sword and one of them, a woman, favoured a double headed axe. Their names were Beowulf and Freya.'

'How do you know that?' Harry Tyler demanded.

'I'm coming to that. I was on the ground having my leg chewed by the boar when I remembered something I'd been told about the standard sword of the Roman Army. It was a stabbing weapon. So I stabbed. I got lucky and the sword slipped between the boar's ribs and into its heart. The blasted thing fell on top of me but that was the least of my worries. Things got a little hazy then. Master Gerni woke up with his hands covered in the virus culture that the pest of a boy had

130

rubbed on them and he grasped Matron's wrist and without going into detail the virus got into his blood. He's sitting over there… well he was. Gerni where are you?'

'Over here. I found a more comfortable piece of floor to sit on.'

Gerni raised his hand to identify himself to the Tylers.

'It was at this time the sword was given a name,' Julia interjected. 'It's called Excalibur.'

'I'm steamrollered,' Harry Tyler gasped. 'Have you got anything else to hit me with?'

Clive's grin was infectious.

'We have. And how!'

'We're ready.'

'No we're not Dad,' Jasmin Tyler objected.

'You're right. We're not ready but go ahead anyway, let's see how much more we can take.'

'I'll stick to the essentials and keep it as brief as I can,' Clive Bowden promised.

He continued, 'I mentioned the Vikings, Beowulf and Freya. Well, they hadn't done with time travel and they went back to the founding of the Lake and they fought a battle to save civilisation from a dark age that probably would have continued until today and into the future. As it turns out they were my ancestors, which accounts for my fair hair and blue eyes. That was after they had come to Bath when Copper and I married and since they had never had a wedding of their own, which is a story in itself, the vicar performed a double wedding. I'm getting slightly ahead of myself so let's get back to the pest of a boy who brought Excalibur to me.'

Once again Clive grinned.

'He took me to task for sending him away when I saw him for the second time. Master Gerni and Merlin had turned him into a king. You'll have heard of Merlin of course, everybody has, and the boy became King Arthur. Actually he never referred to himself as a king but he never had to. Everything about him gave the game away.

'As I said, we met again, and this time the Vikings were there in person. Arthur used Excalibur to tap me on one shoulder and he borrowed Beowulf's sword, which was called Ravager by the way, to tap me on the other and so he made me Clive of the Lake, a title of which I am immensely proud. Not Sir Clive, just Clive of the Lake.

Arthur joked that he was supposed to tell me to rise but as I was in a wheelchair from the mauling the boar gave me he suggested we simply shook hands on the deal and that's what we did. He told me I ought to have a flag of my own and described it as having wavy bars to represent the waters of the Lake, and a black boar pierced by a sword with a gold hilt. Uh, I forgot to mention that Excalibur has a gold hilt.

'Arthur said it was always what he wanted, that every man, woman, and child could have a flag of their own so they could have anything on it to tell the world who they are and what their accomplishments are. Beowulf was given a flag with a hedgehog on it when he fought the Battle of the Lake and because his Viking helmet had horns so did the hedgehog.'

Tentatively, Jasmin Tyler raised her hand for attention.

'Mt Bowden sir, does that mean I can have my own flag too?'

'Jasmin, that's exactly what it means,' Clive told her.

'I don't know what to put on it though,' the girl said excitedly, 'but I'm sure I will think of something. And I just want a small flag so I can have it on a small flagpole in my back garden. Will that be all right?' She asked anxiously.

'Of course.'

Deke Thorpe signalled for attention.

'I think the size of the flag that you see on cars now and again would be about right,' he suggested, 'I've seen Mr Green's car with a Welsh flag sometimes and Union flags are common, as well as Saint George's flag. I expect Saint Andrew's flag is common in Scotland but I've never been to Scotland so I don't know,' he concluded.

'I'll have to decide what my flag will be like first,' Jasmin Tyler said half to herself, 'and I don't know how to use a sewing machine either. Just think, a flag of my own!'

'But I do know how to use a sewing machine,' Copper interjected, 'and I know a thing or two about dyeing cloth. I can help you with the design and I think I can make a flag.'

'Something botanical for me when I design mine and most likely a telescope for Yo but I'm jumping the gun so I'll shut up,' Deke said. He continued, 'If this catches on I reckon people all over the place will start making flags for themselves. Everyone can have a personal flag'

Harry Tyler stirred and studied the assembly thoughtfully.

'It looks as if King Arthur will have his wish then. Everyone and anyone can have their own flag. I never would have believed it,' he told them, 'but Julia's demonstration was pretty convincing. So there was a King Arthur after all, and a Lady of the Lake and a sword called Excalibur. I draw the line at Merlin the Magician though. He was a made up character if ever there was.'

'I expect he'll be quite amused when you tell him,' Copper purred. 'He's my father.'

The room rocked with laughter.

Harry Tyler managed a wry smile.

'I walked right into that didn't I? I hope he won't turn me into a frog or something.'

'He's a clever clogs but he's no magician, whatever people say. You're safe.'

Copper smiled.

'That's relief. Is there more to come?'

'More,' Julia took charge again, 'and stand by for a big surprise.'

'A nice surprise?' Jasmin Tyler sounded anxious.

'I think so and I hope you will too.'

Lofty Harrison indicated that he wanted to speak.

'I'm not scheduled to say anything but I'd like to have a shot and in view of my situation, well, can I have a go?'

'Seconded,' Clive said quickly.

With the comment that she wished she had thought of it earlier, Julia assented.

'I've made a plateful of sandwiches in the expectation that this might go on until the early hours. An expectation based on experience I might add. To take a break before you finish because I don't know when our guest will arrive. If that happens we will have a stand-up buffet and listen to what he says. Paper plates I'm afraid, and plastic cups. I would like to finish at eleven o'clock or thereabouts because some of you have further to go than others and some like George are acting as taxi drivers. So we might finish on time or we might not,' she ended with a gesture of helplessness.

'Right, here I go then,' Lofty said after drawing a deep breath.

'In the first place Clive isn't the only time traveller in the room. I am and so is Elizabeth.'

Eilizabeth Harrison smiled at Jasmin Tyler who gaped open mouthed.

'We have come for a re-union with some old friends. Our own place in time is not so far back, but far enough. If you look at those four conspirators scrunched together on the sofa over there,' he indicated, 'I'll make some introductions. The chaps in the middle are Walter Pfaffinger and Robert Robertson who is our computer wizard. The two gentlemen at each end are Henry Whiting and Henry Rudd who crewed a Mosquito bomber during the Second World War.'

'Gentlemen? You never called us that before,' Henry Rudd commented.

'I used the term loosely Henry.'

'And some of the things Elizabeth said about the way I treated my engines were decidedly impolite and unladylike,' Henry Whiting laughed.

'The word is mistreated and those were my engines if you don't mind, and I always said it under the Wheatsheaf rules,' Elizabeth told him with mock severity.

'If you could see the look on your face,' she added to Harry Tyler.

'I'll tell it how it was,' Lofty Harrison continued, 'and try and get it into some sort of order. The thing is we were all in the Royal Air Force during the war. Henry Whiting and Henry Rudd flew the Mosquito and Elizabeth and I looked after it and we all looked after each other. Elizabeth owned the engines and the rest of it was mine from nose to tail and wing-tip to wing-tip. When the war ended Elizabeth and I thought we were the only two left because we were told that the bomber was shot down with no survivors. And that was that. The war was all but over and I was discharged straight away and Elizabeth followed soon afterwards.

'Recently we found out that our information was wrong and a re-union was arranged. Elizabeth and I had to come forward a few years because you see in the here and now we are dead. Apparently we lived to a ripe old age but not for as long as these reprobates. We don't know when we died and we don't want to know. That's how things happen.

'Moving on a bit, I have already identified the, uh, gentlemen in the middle of the sofa. Walter was a tank commander during the same conflict, he was in charge of a German Panzer. Robert was a Guardsman at that time and it seems certain that their paths crossed at least twice and they did their best to blow each other to pieces. Fortunately neither succeeded.

'All four have been infected with the virus, if infected is the right word to use, and they are going to look a lot younger very soon. At this very moment all their wives are having a hen party and discussing what they will wear when they are thirty years old again. Shoes, handbags, hair-do's, it's going to cost them a small fortune.'

'Don't underestimate them Lofty, it's going to cost us a very large fortune,' Robert Robertson retorted.

'And at this point,' Julia interceded, 'I'm calling a halt on the proceedings while we take a break. I need a volunteer to help me load the table with the buffet I prepared and I have a feeling that our mystery guest will arrive very shortly. He will have a few words to say and then it will be a case of mix and mingle for a while before we press on with something else we have arranged.'

'I'll help with the buffet and so will James,' Christine Appleton declared.

Soon the room was filled with groups of people and the babble of conversation.

'I used to drive a stagecoach between Bath and London in the days before railways and motor cars,' a smiling stranger told Jasmin as he poured orange squash into a plastic cup for her.

Lost for words and clutching her cup tightly the girl could only nod.

Groups formed and broke up and reformed. Conversations arose and a mixture of gossip and serious discussion circulated round the room.

Harry Tyler had his cup filled by the same man who had served his daughter.

'It's a lot to take in, isn't it?' He said sympathetically. 'The worst is over though. I think.'

'You think?'

Harry Tyler sounded suspicious.

'The mystery guest. I have a sneaking feeling that we're all in for a surprise, all of us, not just you.'

'Do you know who it is?'

'I can only guess, and my guess is that it's someone I've never met before but – cripes! Look!'

'It's Wint!' Somebody gasped hoarsely.

He wasn't there. Then he was. He was in his three-state although nobody could be sure if he was in the same place three times or whether he was three look-alike people. He was small and appeared to be incredibly aged and when he spoke his voice was high-pitched. The three figures threw back the hoods of their long blue cloaks. Standing side by side, the hems of the cloaks touched.

Julia greeted him warmly and welcomed him into her home for the second time that day.

'As if you hadn't guessed,' she told the assembly, 'this is Wint.'

Quick thinking Christine showed her presence of mind. Far taller than Wint, she approached him with a jug in her hand.

'Perhaps you would like some squash sir,' she said, and added, 'Julia has filled these jugs with orange squash, lemon squash, and I think this one is summer fruits.'

'One of each,' Wint smiled, 'it is one of the perks of appearing in threes.'

'Hmm, pleasant and unusual,' one of the figures voiced his opinion after sampling his drink.

'I think you must be Christine,' he continued.

Christine's face was a picture of astonishment.

'I'm to tell you that Yo managed to make some pictures of the stars. She allowed me to peer into her looking device and I found it as good as anything I have ever seen. We have our own devices as I believe you know. She has another device that she used to show me some pictures of the moon and so I was able to tell Yo of a place on the moon that will be of interest to her one day.'

James Wilson looked at his wristwatch.

'It's too early,' he objected.

'I don't always do things in the same order as you James,' Wint replied to a ripple of laughter and applause.

'I have come here with a purpose,' Wint continued. 'I don't know if all of you are aware of something I suggested to Merlin at a previous meeting I had with him. I have spoken with Atta, who heads the Council of Seniors that most of you have heard about. Those who have not will catch up soon. The Council has approved a suggestion I made, which is to arrange an exchange visit. The People of the Lake are as interested in you as you are in them. They have said that if you are agreeable they would like Alfrid and his family to come to your now, and they think two people from your time might spend a little time on the Lake. Two for four appears uneven but their society is small compared with your own so I am inclined to agree with their views.

'Alfrid has a wife named Eathl and a son who is simply called small Alfrid, and a daughter whose name I unfortunately do not know. The people who will come from this now to visit the Lake are a matter of choice for you, they will accept your decision. Shall I tell them that this, what do you call it, is cultural exchange the right way to say it? Shall I say you will accept?'

'That's wonderful!' Copper exclaimed.

Hilary Green had taken little part in the proceedings so far but she nodded enthusiastically.

'I don't usually speak for everybody but just this once I will,' Copper said. 'We accept! We need time to get ready so perhaps you will talk to my father about the arrangement. Will that do?'

'It's easy to see that you are Merlin's daughter, even if I didn't already know it,' Wint chuckled.

'I will speak to him about it.'

As suddenly as he arrived, Wint was gone. All that was left was what Freya the Viking had described as a hole in the air, which quickly faded.

'Who should go?' Clive wondered.

'Not me. Much as I would like to go I'm already a part of pre-history,' Julia said. 'I don't think you ought to go either because you have already been to Avalon once when Gerni was attacked by a wild boar.'

'So was I but I take your point. Who then?'

'We're already time travellers so that rules us out I suppose,' Elizabeth Harrison said with a sideways glance at her husband.

'Marcel Land? He'd jump at the chance to study their psychology.'

'I'd jump at the chance to see their clothing and fashions,' Copper declared, 'but if Clive can't go then neither can I so I'll have to be patient and wait to see what they are wearing when they come here.'

'I'm too new to this to even think of it,' Harry Tyler said. 'I've had enough of surprises to last me for a while.'

Julia spoke again.

'There is a candidate who would fit the bill perfectly. Somebody who is no historian so he has no preconceived ideas, but he is

137

interested in everything he sees and gets on well with everybody and he would make an ideal observer and more than that, a participant. I believe he would, embed himself is the expression I think. He would embed himself and integrate into the life and times of the early days on the Lake. In short he is what I would call a man for all seasons. I'm looking at you George.'

'Huh? Huh? I mean, what?'

'We will go,' Hilary Green said in a voice that brooked no argument, 'and I dare anyone to try and talk us out of it.'

Harry Tyler chuckled.

'And I thought I was due for a surprise. Wow, this has been a night to remember and no mistake.'

'How can people who live in different times talk to each other? It isn't logical,' Christine Appleton asked.

'That's a question that has been asked many times. You've read about Beowulf and Freya who came from the Viking Age and spoke to us in English. How did they know the language? We don't know but it's probably a trick of Wint's. That explains nothing of course. We simply don't know.'

Julia addressed her guests.

'There is more to come. This is the point where I had originally planned to bring out the sandwiches and let everyone meet Mr Tyler and Jasmin and welcome them into the Bell Curve Society, but things have got a little out of control. The best laid plans of mice and men, as it were. I'll try and get us back on the rails now.

'This afternoon Christine came out with something that stopped me in my tracks and I think you ought to hear it. If Mr Green has recovered from his shock enough to help me with the flip chart board I asked him to bring, we can let Christine tell you what she told me, and I promise you won't be disappointed.'

'You refused to tell me what you wanted this for and it will be a while before I get my feet back on the ground,' George said as he set up the easel. 'I brought a handful of felt tip pens that you didn't ask for,' he added.

'I knew I wouldn't have to,' Julia replied, smiling as she said it.

'And the video cameras?'

'All set up while her back was turned,' George replied after making sure the girl could not hear him, adding, 'I'm not too happy about that but I'll bow to your judgement for the time being. This must be pretty important.'

'I think it is. There, we're ready' she said more loudly for everyone to hear.

'Christine, off you go.'

Christine Appleton drew a deep breath.

Sounding slightly nervous she began, 'I'm still trying to sort this out in my own mind so this might not come out in the right order. To begin with, I was thinking about time travel and how Wint manages to do it. Well, time is really just another dimension, so I drew a cube like this.'

She sketched swiftly on the flip chart.

'These are the three dimensions, length, breadth, and height. They all start from this corner, here at the bottom left. Actually they could start from any corner of course. When the big bang set things off the dimensions got bigger and bigger but not fundamentally different. The big bang is where, I mean when, time started as well and so the space-time continuum got going. So I can draw an arrow of time which you can imagine is at right angles to the other dimensions. Actually I can't begin to imagine how that would look but my arrow is the best I can do. The thing about time though, is it doesn't behave itself. If I put a black hole into my little universe its intense gravity bends light and time as well. Some theories say time can even run backwards. And why shouldn't it? You can move in both directions along the other dimensions; up and down for instance. In fact it's not possible to do anything else. You can't have a universe where you can only travel up but not down, it doesn't make sense.

'All of us have read in the Chronicle that Wint says time is a sphere. It makes sense to me in a funny sort of way.'

She flipped the sketch and started a new blank sheet.

'The big bang started a universe that expanded in all directions so my drawing of a universe in a cube can't be right,' she explained.

'I thought it was but then I realised that I couldn't fit the time dimension in because time spreads all over to fill the space but, well, I tried to think of it as like a ball of string that started in the same place as the other dimensions and so to go from one time to another you had to travel along the string, which seemed right, or jump from one place to another, I mean from one time to another, by hopping across.'

Christine paused for a moment while she arranged her thoughts in her mind.

'That didn't seem quite right and then I saw where I was going wrong. In saw that time must behave like a wave spreading in every direction from the, the, um, middle of the big bang. That seems to be a better way of looking at it. Then I thought of something else. I was looking at Zeno's paradox. He was a Greek philosopher and there was actually more than one paradox but the one I'm talking about is about the arrow that Zeno said could never reach its target because however far it flew there was always more distance for it to travel. The arrow can get half way and then fly half the remaining distance and do the same again, fly half way, and so on.'

On the sketch chart she drew a reasonably straight line and made a mark half way along its length. Then she halved the remainder. It was easy to see what she was getting at. 'However many times you divide the distance by two, or in other words halve the distance, there is always a remainder so you could divide until the end of, uh, time,' she smiled faintly, 'but you would never come to an end. It's logical and I do like logic, but it's wrong. That's what makes it a paradox. I realised a long time ago that if it did hold true the arrow would never be able to start, let alone finish. I wondered if Zeno realised that but it turned out he did. What he probably didn't know was that he could never have fired an arrow in the first place, and that's because that action needs movement, you can work it right back to the firing of synapses in the brain, but that requires movement, and once again if you halve the distance for nerve impulses to travel and halve it again you can see that motion is impossible. Zeno could never have shot his arrow.

'For centuries the paradox remained an unsolved problem, right up until calculus was invented. Invented? Well, until it came along. I'm not sure how to say it.'

Christine pulled a face.

'Anyway, when you measure a distance, any distance,' she resumed, 'what you are measuring is the sum of a number of particles. A very large number, but finite, you will get there in the end. But particles are weird. I'm talking about sub-atomic particles; they can behave as particles or waves. I think they have to because they would never have the energy to be particles all the time. It's called dualism. Thank you for my science Mr Green,' she acknowledged, 'so the universe which is made up of matter, has a split personality. It's schizophrenic. That's really weird. I don't think I'm saying this very well,' she apologised.

'You're doing fine, you can polish it up later,' George Green encouraged her.

Julia was right, he thought, this was something that really merited recording. Food for thought and many hours of discussion. He looked forward to it with keen anticipation.

'Yes sir. Thank you. Where was I? Oh yes. Well, at the start of the big bang it wasn't space that was expanding, it was time! My private definition of time is that time is when things happen. You can see that if time doesn't exist nothing happens and that means space could never have happened because it took time for space to expand and become, well, to become space. Time and space, you can't have one without the other. I can draw the universe with all the dimensions radiating out from the centre where the big bang started. I can draw them as lines all coming from the middle and going out to the very edge. There, height, width, depth, all these radius lines are going out in all directions away from the middle.'

Christine sketched them in.

'What I can't draw is a radius line in the fourth dimension, which is time. I can't do that because time is a single dimension which is everywhere. Where there is space there is time, you can't have one without the other. I think I've already said that, but anyway it seems to me that time is an ever expanding wave and the wave front is the edge of the universe. Time and the universe expand together.'

She paused while she turned over to a fresh sheet of paper and took up her narrative once more, making another swift sketch while she talked.

'This is our galaxy, it's a view from the side and it's shaped like a discus. It's huge. It measures one hundred light years from one side to the other and the speed of light is one hundred and eighty six thousand miles per second. Just to give you an idea of its size light takes eight minutes to reach the earth from the sun which is ninety-three million miles away so imagine how far light travels in a year! Out at the edge it measures ten thousand light years thick but at the centre it is more than that. Some estimates are more than ten thousand light years. The average thickness is thirty thousand light years. I phoned Yo this afternoon and she gave me the dimensions so this is not just my own work,' she acknowledged.

'I suppose I could work out the volume of the galaxy but there doesn't seem to be any point. Also, there isn't enough mass to hold the galaxy together. Well there is, but nobody can find it, which is why it's called dark matter.'

George Green noticed that Christine was beginning to look uneasy, but she pressed on.

'The thing is that if time is just a wave the universe would surely just settle down once it had passed, just like ripples on a pond, and that doesn't seem right. So,' she drew a deep breath, 'I think there must be time particles. They must be so small as to be undetectable but however small they are they must have mass, and that must be immeasurably small too but they are everywhere and our galaxy has a volume of, well perhaps I should have worked it out but there must be thousands and thousands of cubic light years. Millions more like. And there's the missing mass that holds the galaxy together. It's time particles!'

Christine bit her lip.

'There's more,' she said hesitantly, 'but I'm, well, it's silly.'

Julia encouraged her.

'It is unusual,' she said, 'but what you told me this afternoon made me stop and think, and you did say the universe is weird. Christine, it's too late to back out now. In for a penny, in for a pound.'

The girl shuffled her feet awkwardly. George Green thought he had never seen her off balance like this before and he wondered what was coming. There was a long silence. Eventually, and in a voice that shook, Christine Appleton resumed her narrative.

'It seems to me,' she began hesitantly, 'that there is something missing from the big bang theory.'

George nearly jumped out of his chair and only kept quiet with an effort.

'When it started there had to be all the dimensions, including time, all in one place and ready to go. But it wouldn't work. The other three dimensions need time to expand in a giant explosion, but until they have expanded time has nowhere to go. It doesn't make sense.

'So I think that perhaps there was another particle or wave or something. I'm not sure what, but I have read that the universe needs about eleven or twelve dimensions to work properly. Um, eleven. Or perhaps more. The dimensions seem to be all folded up, like screwing up a piece of paper. So perhaps something from a fifth dimension gave it a push and set off the big bang. Then the stuff of the universe formed into matter, atoms and molecules formed after the universe cooled down enough, but anti-matter formed as well. What happened when matter and anti-matter collided was mutual annihilation, but there was more matter than anti-matter and so what was left over became our universe.'

Once again the girl paused.

'I wondered if the anti-matter sort of leaked through from another universe that was made of anti-matter. Perhaps we got some of theirs and they got some of ours, which would make us part of a back-to-back universe. It seems logical but at the same time it seems silly. I don't know,' she said in a small voice, 'but I have heard of multiple universes, multiverses was the word they used.'

'You said something about symmetry as well didn't you?' Julia prompted her.

Christine nodded.

'Oh yes, I remember. Well there was another theory of the universe that said it exists in a steady state. It had to give way to the big bang theory but it had what they, the scientists, called symmetry. Both theories say the universe has spatial symmetry; in other words it looks the same wherever you view it from. I don't quite understand that. Anyway, the big bang universe hasn't got temporal symmetry, which is all about time. The steady state universe has it because the theory says it was always there and it always will be. The big bang universe has a beginning and quite possibly there is no end, it just keeps expanding forever so temporal symmetry is missing. It's a bit like have left but no right, or up with no down. It doesn't work so I was wondering if that can be explained by having a back-to-back universe like I said just now. It does preserve symmetry. I just don't know,' she concluded doubtfully.

Chapter 14

The car that drew up at the vicarage gate carried two occupants, both women. Two cardboard boxes rested on the rear seat and when the vicar, who had spotted them from where he was working in his garden, arrived the driver was removing one box and passing it to her companion.

'Hello Vicar,' Alison greeted him, showing the gap between her front teeth when she smiled.

'Vicar, this is Pauline,' she continued, and added, 'she's wondering how she managed to get talked into this.'

'Pleased to meet you,' the vicar said, 'but excuse me if I don't offer to shake hands. I'm putting a new weathervane on my shed and I'm covered in grime. Just call me Vicar, everyone else does.'

Two more women appeared.

'Julia and Janet,' the vicar introduced them. 'They're supposed to be helping me but I'm the one whose hands are dirty.'

'We're supervising,' Janet said airily. 'Let me give you a hand with these.'

Rather bemused, Pauline found herself indoors where the vicar's wife soon had everyone seated. The vicar disappeared to wash his hands at the kitchen sink.

Alison directed the conversation which, unknown to Pauline, was carefully rehearsed.

'I'll begin by telling Pauline exactly what this is all about. I'm afraid one or two things were left were unsaid when I press-ganged you into this.'

'You told her it was about music, and that was the sum total of everything you said,' Janet interrupted.

'Gulp. Mea culpa,' Alison replied.

'Getting down to business,' she continued, 'I, that is, um, we, we have some music, quite a lot of music that we want you to listen to and give us your opinion as to it's… well, I don't quite know how to put it.'

'Its origins, authenticity, nature, the manner of its arrangement, and so on. In short, we want you to pull out every scrap of information you can,' Julia said crisply.

Alison spoke again.

'The recording starts with about two minutes of play by two instruments, I can tell you that much. The rest is up to you.'

The vicar's wife switched on a very sophisticated machine and inserted a compact disc.

'Ready?' She enquired.

Pauline licked her lips.

'I feel like a new student who is being examined,' she answered, 'which I suspect is not far from the truth. Very well, I'm ready.'

Her face gave nothing away while she listened to the short recording but nobody failed to notice that she tapped her knee as she picked up the melody. She hummed a few bars.

'Folk music,' she said eventually, 'and played on improvised home-made instruments. Some kind of flute. The tune is simple and probably repetitive but I haven't heard enough to be sure. Let's say I'm seventy percent certain. The tune belongs to a close-knit ethnic group. Not African or Native American. I place it tentatively at Northern European from the eastern side of the North Sea coast. At a pinch though, it could be Faroese or Icelandic. Correct me if I'm wrong.'

Julia complimented her.

'Alison said you were good,' she told her, 'and I believe you are semi-retired?'

Pauline agreed.

'I like to think I'm reasonably good at what I do. And yes, I am in semi-retirement. These days I do private teaching. It takes two or three of my afternoons each week.'

She pulled a wry smile.

'Why do I think my answer is important?'

Returning the smile Julia said, 'Because it is important. Very important.'

Consulting a page of notes Janet said, 'Let's hear a little more. This time there is a third player. Oh, I nearly forgot, I'm supposed to tell you that the tunes are very old. There is a counter on the on the machine so I can go back to any part of the recording if you want to hear it again.'

Pauline listened with intense concentration. When the recording was over was able to say, 'The third instrument is a recorder.'

With the hint of a frown she added, 'The tune was not written for that instrument but it could be arranged to fit. The third player is not of the same ethnic group as the first two players,' she concluded.

'She certainly isn't,' the vicar said jovially.

Pauline looked startled. She had failed to notice his arrival from the kitchen during the playing of the last piece of music.

'Do you know where these tunes came from?' The vicar asked her.

'No, except that they came from Northern Europe. Where exactly is anybody's guess.'

'Not a guess, as it happens,' the vicar admitted, 'we do know where they came from and when they were written. To within a few years anyway, and we know brought them to these shores. Not to mention the manner of their arrival.'

The vicar seemed amused.

'Then I fail to see why you need me,' Pauline retorted with some asperity. She was plainly not pleased.

'I'm coming to that. We do need you, but there are things I must tell you first. Number one, we investigated your academic background very thoroughly. Number two, and this is of utmost importance, what you are about to see and hear is not to leave this room if you decide you want no further part in it.'

Holding up his hand to forestall any comments and questions Pauline might have the vicar continued, 'I'm going to show you a recording that was made not far from here. Two singers are singing to a tune they first recorded on their instruments, the ones you have correctly identified as flutes of a kind. Nobody else knew the tune and could play it so it had to be done that way, which I admit was rather clumsy.'

'Not as clumsy as your explanation Vicar,' Alison said as she readied the machine.

'Ready when you are,' she told Pauline.

While Pauline watched the screen everybody else watched Pauline, waiting for her to react.

As soon as it was done she said, 'A re-enactment group. They're good, whoever they are but I fail to see how that concerns me. I don't know the words, I don't even know the language.'

'That's a relief,' Janet commented, 'because the words would, well, they're rude, and now I've come to the tricky bit. The girl who played the recorder is my daughter Suzanne Fluteplayer, which is a Viking name. The thing is, the language is Old Danish and the couple who sang it were Vikings. Real Vikings I mean. Julia…'

Reality slipped away. The sound of Viking music filled the air and the clang of a blacksmith's hammer in a smithy by the shore of the dark North Sea was heard above the babble of voices as a square rigged ship that carried a red and white sail ran up the shingle beach. Acrid smoke from the smith's fire stung the nostrils and made eyes water.

Pauline wore a stunned look.

'What was that?' She gasped weakly.

'That was a picture from the Viking age, something fairly typical that Freya left me. The singers on the recording are Beowulf and Freya, who are no longer with us, although you might doubt that when you set eyes on Lawrence Bowden who is their direct descendant. Lawrence and Beowulf can pass for brothers. I ought to have put that in the past tense, they could have passed. Sometimes it was hard to tell them apart. This is when I must tell you that Alison and I are much older than we look. Hold on to your sanity, the vicar has something to show you.'

'This is a little pet that belongs to a friend of ours. He's timid and easily frightened but he's stronger than you would believe. His name is Peep.'

The vicar reached into a basket that Pauline had assumed contained firewood and carefully picked up the creature that had been curled up out of sight.

'It's, a, it's a dud, dud, dragon!'

'I'll pop him back in his basket.'

With typical English understatement Pauline said, 'I think I would like a cup of tea.'

Swiftly and succinctly Julia explained the reality of the situation to Pauline.

Her strong brown tea was almost finished when Julia said, 'What we would like you to do is take Suzanne under your wing. Her knowledge is far too valuable to be lost and Suzanne is no musician in the usual sense of the word. She speaks excellent Old Danish and she has written the down tunes and the words the best she knows how to. She needs something from you that she could never get from a conventional musical education but,' Julia smiled wryly, 'any attempt to contaminate her knowledge will be met with, well let's say you'll have a golden opportunity to learn some Old Danish yourself.

'Contaminate isn't the word I would have used myself but Suzanne guards her knowledge passionately and fiercely. Incredible though it might seem she learned the Viking language in a matter of weeks and we have played some carefully selected conversations to an acknowledged expert who is more than impressed and wants to know where she was educated. Needless to say, he was fobbed off with a cock and bull story.'

The vicar passed a book to Pauline and explained, 'So far we have told you very little about what is taking place. There are a number of discs you should watch, discs and tapes and memory sticks, we're still in the process of getting our computer records arranged properly, and there is an information pack that will be here shortly. This book is presented as fiction, it was always intended that it should be, but it does contain certain facts and I'll tell you now that sorting fact from fiction is not always easy, but what it will do is ease you gently into something that will turn your life upside down.'

Pauline accepted the proffered volume, studied the front cover briefly and turned to the rear cover.

'I don't recognise the writer,' she commented.

She put her cup down.

'That's typical of him,' Julia said. 'He claims he likes to keep a low profile and for the most part he does but that didn't stop him sneaking his name into the text in a manner that can only be described as childish. To be fair it might not have been entirely his doing and it could have been done without his knowledge. One of our group can't resist bad jokes and this is typical of his idea of humour. In any event he isn't here at the moment, I happen to know he's on holiday in Alanya in Turkey on the Mediterranean coast.

'According to him a day in Alanya is wasted if it doesn't start with an hour or two of snorkel diving before breakfast and by this time he'll be at a beach bar talking to whoever happens to be there while he has something to eat.'

'He'll have his phone in his pocket but he'd rather throw it in the sea than answer it,' Janet added.

'I might be able to force his hand and make him say more about himself,' Julia mused.

'How? He's the author, he can say what he likes.'

Julia disagreed.

'Actually he can't. He has a certain amount of leeway but he's a chronicler first and an author second. He doesn't like to be called an author. He's constrained to write about events and the part played by the people involved and he may or may not comment on them, but only within limits. At the same time he does choose not to tell all he knows, and he is aware that he doesn't know everything. By his own admission he isn't altogether comfortable with the way things are and there have been instances when circumstance has pushed him in a direction he wouldn't have taken through choice. He aims to include a certain amount of detail into his work because other chroniclers, especially those who penned the Anglo-Saxon Chronicle, were often content to record the passing of a whole year with just a single word. He has incorporated an extract from the Chronicle into the book you are holding so you will see what I mean when you read it. The writers never included what they regarded as commonplace but might have been invaluable to future generations.

'For instance, in your book it is recorded that a police constable crossed the road in front of the railway station and then he walked through the bus station. Since then the bus station has been relocated across the road to the front of the railway station and the old site is full of shops. The chronicler was furious when they did that. He doesn't like the new buildings but perhaps in two thousand years somebody will use the information to put a precise date on them. I mean when they were built because I can't see them lasting for two thousand years. It's a small contribution but it might be important one day. You see Pauline, he's writing for today's readers in a style which is easy to read in order to reach as many people as possible, but he is also writing for readers from today until as many as two thousand years from now.

It doesn't make his task any easier. He tries to be factual so you won't find what they call gratuitous violence and other such nonsense. You know what I mean.'

'No blood and guts.'

'Precisely. Now and again he records what he thinks he hears and gets it wrong, and sometimes he says the same thing twice, that's when his information comes from two or more sources and he isn't sure which version is correct and which is false. It describes matters from more than one point of view so it does have it's uses. Future historians might not agree but it will compel them to examine and sift the evidence thoroughly, which can only be a good thing.

'Copper said she made a mistake when she told the chronicler that the railway porters shouted Bath Spa Station when the train arrived with George Shore as the fireman. Apparently it was plain Bath Station in those days. I might also add that Copper was every bit as annoyed as the chronicler about the moving of the old bus station but not for the same reasons. She has a sense of ownership of the railway station and its surroundings and her toes have been stepped on and she doesn't like it, and when Copper says she doesn't like something it pays to tread carefully.

'I have heard the chronicler complain that putting things in the order in which they happened is impossible. His sources are all over the place and only a few of them keep him regularly up to date so his chronicle is often out of sequence. To put it in his own words the result is a patchwork quilt of a chronicle which contains inaccuracies and mistakes. Some mistakes are his own and some are not and there is no way of knowing where and what they are. It does make it hard for him to produce an acceptable piece of work.

'Having said all that you will find things in the book that are plainly works of fiction, but it's easy to separate the wheat from the chaff. Most of the time anyway, because there are some things that are unbelievable on the face of it but are actually true. The reason the chronicler included them is to add a little insight into our affairs and it has to be said he plays games from time to time.

'I think he might be ready to put a little more of himself into his accounts of our affairs. I seem to have strayed a long way from the subject. How am I doing so far?'

'You haven't asked me whether I'll take the job. Umm, the task.'

'Will you?'

'Like a shot.'

'I hoped you would say that. Your name will appear in the book and be exposed to public gaze but you can choose an alias, as many do. Janet does and so do I, and now you are one of us I'll tell you why. I'll leave it up to you but you will be identified unless you choose not to be.'

***

'How did it go?' Copper asked Janet eagerly.

'Considering what we did to her it was a one hundred percent success,' Janet informed her.

'We showed her the boxes of recordings but there was no time to play them of course so she saw just the ones we decided to tempt her with, not to put too fine a point on it. She agreed to see Suzanne and teach her,' she hesitated, 'to teach her all about music I suppose. I don't know enough to be able to ask the right questions.'

Copper's hair caught the light as she nodded her head in agreement.

'Janet told me it worked out quite well,' Copper said later in a reply to a question from Clive.

'I was never too sure that Suzanne Fluteplayer would agree to it or whether she would fly off the handle, but she genuinely wants to lean more. Her new tutor has chosen an alias so for the records she'll be written into the chronicles under the name of Pauline Grant.'

Clive Bowden looked up from his task of turning the pages of a picture book for their son Larry.

'She's taken on a big job,' he commented briefly.

'She's up to it. She drinks Sergeant Major's tea.'

'Is that a qualification?'

'If you're an Englishwoman it is. It's tea so strong that only an Englishwoman or a Sergeant Major can drink it. There's nothing pussy footed about her.'

Clive grinned.

'I'm sure you're right.'

'Trust me.'

Larry called for attention and Clive turned the pages of the book again.

'This is a cow. It goes…'

'Moo!'

Another page turned.

'What's this?'

'Duck.'

'How does it go?'

'Quack. Quack quack quack!'

'And this is a sheep.'

'Baa.'

The final page had been pasted into the book by Clive.

'Dragon!'

'How does it go?'

Larry clapped his hands together.

'Peep! Like that. Peep peep peep!'

Copper declared that it was time to think about dinner and made to leave her husband and son to their own devices.

'You two men can lay the table,' she told Clive as she stood up.

Chapter 15

'I'm still trying to make sense of this time travel business,' Harry Tyler admitted.

'I haven't given it much thought until now, but why should I?' He continued.

Christine Appleton was the one who replied.

'It's new to us too Mr Tyler but we've got a head start on you and Jasmin,' Christine pulled a face and said, 'I've got a sort of mental picture but it doesn't explain anything, not really.'

She found a pen in one of her pockets and drew a paper napkin towards her.

'For instance,' she said as she sketched, 'time is just another dimension, like length, width, and height, except that you can only go one way. I mean, you can't jump from being thirteen years old to being sixteen, you have to go with the flow and there's no going back. Except there is. There's nothing in physics that says it can't be done and when I tried to look it up it said that time doesn't always run at the same speed and there was a load of stuff about black holes. So my not very good drawing of an arrow is wrong.'

'I'm listening but I can't honestly say I understand,' Harry Tyler admitted.

'Well, it's like this – oh hang on, Jasmin's just arrived so I'll wait a sec so she can get a look in.'

Chairs were shuffled as space was made for Jasmin Tyler to sit next to her father.

'Have you got your hedgehog yet?' Yolanda Walker asked her.

Jasmin shook her head.

'Not yet,' she said ruefully, 'but I'm sure I will. There aren't so many as there used to be, they're an endangered species.'

Yolanda looked startled.

'Are they? I never knew!' She exclaimed.

'Their habitats are being destroyed and they get run over and squashed on the roads and if nothing is done there won't be any left and that will be sad. I like hedgehogs and really want one in my garden. I know one will come but I've tried for so long.'

'I'll keep my fingers crossed for you.'

Jasmin looked grateful.

'We're talking about time travel,' Harry Tyler informed his daughter in an attempt to get back on track.

Christine Appleton explained what she had done so far.

'That prehistoric man said time is a sphere,' Jasmin Tyler commented.

'I know,' Christine agreed, 'you've been reading the book.'

'I've read it all the way through,' Jasmin confirmed enthusiastically, 'and it was, well, I thought it was going to be heavy going but it wasn't, it was easy to read.'

'The Chronicler meant it to be,' James Wilson interjected.

'Just as well or I wouldn't have got far,' Harry Tyler observed with an expressive shrug of his shoulders.

He continued, 'Do you know how he, the prehistoric man that is, um, how he does it? Has he got a time machine or something? I seem to remember that something on the internet says the reason we haven't been visited by time travellers from the future is because we haven't built a time machine yet but that doesn't seem to fit in with what's going on here.'

'I've heard the same, we all have,' Christine agreed, 'but what does a time machine look like? I mean, if you saw a time machine would you know what it was?'

'Good point. Something you get into and start the motor and… and you're right, I haven't a clue what a time machine would look like.'

'Mine would be red,' James Wilson joked.

'James, if you had a time machine it would be in bits and pieces because you would take it apart to find out how it works,' Deke Thorpe told him.

James grinned.

'Most likely,' he agreed cheerfully.

'And it would have whizzy things that go whiz and there would be flickering lights and it would nearly shake itself to pieces. Good Hollywood stuff but poor science. I don't think it would be anything like you would expect,' Christine continued, 'because I think it's a field generator.'

'That's still a time machine isn't it?' Jasmin Tyler asked.

Christine agreed.

'Yes, but, well, sort of. Jasmin, I think it's a force amplifier. No, that's not right either. I'm not making much sense am I?'

Christine pulled a face. 'I'm still putting this together so I'm not saying it properly yet,' she said, unconsciously implying that she was certain she would be able to do so at some time in the future.

'I might be wrong but I think I'm starting to catch up with you,' Harry Tyler continued to Christine, 'what this is leading up to is that your time is in contact with itself in a sort of side by side way and not just, uh linearly. So to travel in time you jump sideways to another place in the string, the time line I suppose, and that takes you to where you want to be.'

'When, not where,' Christine corrected him, 'but that's pretty much how I think it works. Bearing in mind I'm not a scientist,' she added.

Yes and no, Harry Tyler thought.

'You've got an idea, that's plain enough, but you don't know how to put it into words,' he encouraged her.

'I'll try. The thing about time is that it isn't constant. It is for us but if you move fast enough it slows down, which is what happens to the astronauts and cosmonauts.'

'That's true,' Yolanda Walker confirmed, 'people returning from the International Space Station are a little younger than they would have been if they had stayed on Earth. It's just a tiny amount, it's only a small fraction of a second even if they stay in space for a year but one day it might be a very big amount if long distance space travel becomes a reality. Which it will.'

'Very true, which is why I think the time machine isn't a machine at all.'

Christine paused.

'I think the standing stones, some of them anyway, are time machines.'

'Is that why the Old People stopped what they were doing with the standing stones do you think? I read about that in the book. I mean the chronicle.'

'I'm not sure Mr Tyler,' Christine replied seriously, 'but I don't think so because there is no mention of the reason for stopping. It seems to me they had a meltdown of some sort.'

'I read it the same way,' James Wilson interjected. He explained, 'I wouldn't be surprised if they controlled their stones with some sort of feedback mechanism and the system oscillated out of control.'

'It got away from them, is that what you mean?'

James nodded.

'The same thing happened to that footbridge over the Thames in London. The Millennium Bridge. When people walked across it swayed so they all leaned the other way to get it back on an even keel but they went too far and it swayed the other way so they leaned back and so it went on swaying one way and then the other. It's called positive feedback and it just made the swaying worse. Two days after it was opened they had to close it and a lot of money was spent to make it stable. It was two years before it was opened again. I spotted what was wrong as soon as I saw it happening because I'm sort of into engineering,' he explained.

As an explanation it left something to be desired but his listeners let it pass, if indeed they realised it. James was sure that some at least did.

Jasmin Tyler broke her silence.

'I don't know about those things,' she admitted, 'but I expect I'll learn one day.'

Clive Bowden's arrival went unnoticed until he spoke. He came accompanied by his son Lawrence in his pushchair.

'I can't stay, I thought I would find you here and I've just popped in to give you this.'

He handed a large package to Jasmin Tyler.

'Copper said for me to tell you she hopes you like it. It might not be quite what you expected; it has a message, or perhaps I ought to say it makes a statement. See what you think.'

With a look that said she half expected it to blow up in her face the astonished girl took the package and unwrapped it very carefully.

'It's a flag. It must be my flag but I don't understand... I mean, I can see it's a green hand on a playing card but I thought playing cards have hearts and clubs and things on a white background but this is light blue and I don't know how to play cards,' Jasmin stammered.

'I think I get it,' Harry Tyler said. 'What card is it?'

'It's a spade. The ace.'

'And?'

'I don't know. It's just a spade.'

'And who do you know who uses a spade?'

'Well me for a start. I do. I use them in my garden. Oh!'

'Mrs Beach has put a green hand on the spade but I don't get that. There's a county badge somewhere with a red hand but I don't know where it is.' James Wilson told her.

'I think I know. I do know!' Christine Appleton exclaimed. 'The red hand is the badge of Ulster in Ireland and the fingers are held together. Jasmin's hand has the fingers spread. And that's it. It's green fingers! Green fingers because you're a gardener. And I wouldn't mind betting Merlin put Mrs Beach up to it,' she added.

She glanced at Clive Bowden for confirmation.

'My lips are sealed but you could be right. Copper thought the light blue background looked better than white. She kept the flag unclutterd so if you ever do something that you want to tell the world about there is plenty of space to include it. And now if Yolanda and Christine have quite finished spoiling my son I must be on my way.'

'You haven't said whether you like it or not,' Harry Tyler prompted his daughter.

'I love it! My own flag! I'm going to make a little flag pole in my back garden as soon as get home.'

'Leave that to me. You're all off to the covered market.'

'Are we? Why?'

'I was telling Mr Tyler before you came in,' Christine told her. 'Deke had the idea that the nail in the market might be a standing stone put up in plain sight for anyone in the know to recognise so he's brought a compass along and we're going to see if the needle swings when we stand close to it.'

'I've seen it a million times but there's a notice that says it was a place for trading and that's why we say cash on the nail. It would look nice with a jardiniere filled with plants standing on it.'

'There speaks Jasmin Greenfingers. That's your Viking name now. Come on Jas, let's go!'

***

George Green tilted his chair backwards and regarded his computer screen thoughtfully while he waited for the call he expected. The wait was longer than he had anticipated but a glance at the foot of the screen told him that he had logged on earlier than he needed to. Finally, his wait was over.

'Peter Birkett, it's been a while since I last saw you. I've kept an eye on your doings for some time and I've read your publications. All the ones I've come across anyway. I'm glad to see that at least some of my pupils turned out well.'

'Hello Mr Green. I don't get back to Bath very often. Work gets in the way, you know how it is. I got your letter and a copy of the recording you sent me. It's interesting and I've shown it to a few people who are here with me now.'

Introductions were soon made.

'What did you make of it?'

'It's interesting and original. There appears to have been some editing.'

George agreed. He had no intention of revealing Christine Appleton's allusion to time travel, at least not yet.

'What was deleted isn't important. It didn't add anything.'

Two lies. The recording that George Green had sent to his erstwhile pupil had been edited but the original was untouched. That was the first lie. The second was the denial that anything important was involved. George regretted his actions but considered they were justified under the circumstances. Apologies were due but they must wait.

'I was wondering what conclusions you have drawn, if any,' George continued.

'Some and some, is the best answer. Opinion is divided. For my part I like the concept of time particles, not because they may or may not exist but because it opens up the possibility of looking at time and space from a different perspective. We've given the particles names, by the way. The first one mentioned by Christine Appleton is the Appleton Special Particle One, or ASP 1, the time particle, and the other is ASP 2, the particle that started it all off. Actually I buy in to ASP 2 more than I buy into ASP 1 but my opinion isn't shared,' Peter Birkett replied.

'I go for ASP 1, the time particle,' one of his colleagues put in.

'Can you explain why?' George asked.

'I'll have a stab at it.' The speaker was a curly haired man in his mid-forties. 'In the first place we can't actually measure time at all, we only measure the fact that the hands on our watch dials move a certain distance during the course of events. Time could run fast or slow at different times for all we know, and it follows that events could take more time or less time from start to finish and we would never know it. Having said that, I think maybe we can start to consider the true nature of time. So far we have never reduced it or expanded it. Time just is. But if I can use an engineering analogy, a lot of our equipment and component parts are made for us by our own engineers, you can't buy our kind of stuff off the shelf. Let's suppose you want to drill a series of holes in a block of metal. The engineers say to the machine, let's start here, this is our datum point. Drill a hole here and then move ten centimetres to the left and drill a second hole. When you have done that, move a distance of twenty centimetres from the datum point and drill a third hole. After that, move a distance of thirty centimetres from the datum point and drill a fourth hole. That's what we call absolute measurement.

'But there is another way of programming your machine. As before, we establish a datum point. Then we tell the machine to drill a hole there. Then we say move ten centimetres to the left and drill a second hole, just as before. But for our third hole we say move a distance of ten centimetres from our second hole and drill there. You see the difference? Our second hole becomes our datum point. The holes are drilled just as before but the distances are measured incrementally. Now, here's where the science kicks in; if we can get a grasp of time as an incremental dimension it might open up a whole new way of looking at the cosmos. It could even be possible that we live in a flickering universe that switches on and off. For my part I like it. I might call it my Granular Theory of Time.'

George was uncertain whether the last statement was meant to be taken was seriously.

'Christine Appleton might be on to something then?'

George made a question of the statement.

'I think it possible.'

There came a chuckle.

'I just don't know where to begin though. Not yet, anyway.'

Peter Birkett, George Green's one-time pupil, took over.

'It has interesting possibilities but it's only one point of view. Our resident graduate student,' he nodded towards a slightly built girl, 'has a different opinion.'

Thus invited the girl began.

'I don't see time that way at all, but I'm learning the hard way not to dismiss an idea just because I don't think it's right. I think ASP 2 is worth investigating, if only because it preserves the symmetry of the universe. I even think, or at least speculate that when one universe is formed it must have a twin as postulated by Christine Appleton. I'm insanely jealous. Nobody has had a particle named after then since Professor Higgs claimed there must be another particle lurking out there somewhere, the Higgs boson. It took forty years to find and Professor Higgs was awarded a Nobel Prize when it was.'

'It doesn't go down well with everybody,' Peter Birkett told George with more than a hint of laughter. 'Doctor Sheldon Cooper for instance.'

George's mouth dropped open.

'This isn't right, she's just a schoolgirl. She can't discover new sub-atomic particles. Even I haven't discovered one.'

'Sheldon, she hasn't discovered anything, it's a hypothesis.'

'And she's postulated an entire universe right next door to us. You haven't done that either.'

'How did she do that? How could she? She has no right.'

'Are you saying that anybody could do what she did? Even if they aren't Doctors?'

'Of course not Penny. Science isn't for everyone. It demands superior intellect. Such as mine'

'Sheldon, they could.'

'But Christine Appleton might win a Nobel Prize. She might even win it before I win mine. Oh, that's unthinkable.'

'Sheldon, nobody is guaranteed to win a Nobel Prize.'

'I am.'

'Wait, let me get this right. Howard, suppose there is someone who is a waitress in a cheesecake factory and isn't a Doctor, could she win a Nobel Prize?'

'Yes.'

'No. It's wrong. Whoever heard of a Penny Particle?'

'Sheldon, why don't you invent an undiscovered sub-atomic particle detector and get it aboard the International Space Station to make its search.'

'Well maybe I will Wolowitz, maybe I will.'

'And I'll be the astronaut who goes into space and installs it.'

'I'm going to my room.'

George joined in the laughter as the scene descended into chaos.

When Peter Birkett managed to restore some sort of order he claimed, somewhat tongue in cheek, that the only reason his team watched The Big Bang Theory was to keep an eye on the opposition. Suddenly he became serious.

'Wait! Wait a second! I read something a couple of years ago, I've just remembered. There's a region in space somewhere that some scientists claim shows evidence of a collision between our universe and another. It's called the Universe Cold Spot, heaven knows why. Apparently there are too few galaxies there, which I wouldn't accept as proof of anything but I only read the first few paragraphs because it hasn't anything to do with what we do here. Perhaps, and I'm thinking on my feet here, but perhaps there is a reason for the lack of galaxies and that reason is that the matter in that region was annihilated by anti-matter when the big bang resulted in our universe and the mirror image universe as proposed by Christine Appleton. There was some leakage of matter and anti-matter between the universes. Comments, anybody?'

'Bimey! Is blimey a comment?'

'No. Or possibly yes. It'll do for the time being. The Appleton Interface Region makes a good acronym. AIR. I'm wondering if the connection is not severed. It need only be, oh, no more than a few square centimetres across but I'd guess it's more like millions of square light years. That's pretty big, as we scientists say. I'm imagining something hourglass shaped and the narrow part of the hourglass is where our universe and the mirror image universe come together but don't ask me what the implications of that are. The cold spot of the universe might be worth a second look. It's huge, really huge, and it has been speculated that its existence is a result of contact with another universe. Food for thought wouldn't you say?'

'I'm not up to speed on that but I'll see what I can find on the computer, and I'm starting to think that article might have more to do with your work than you thought,' George commented, his mind reeling.

'Hmm. Me too. You know, Christine Appleton is brilliant, and no mistake. I won't be disappointed if she finds her way here one day.'

George considered his reply carefully.

'Neither would I be, but she's unusual in that she has yet to say what she wants to do. Most of her contemporaries have done so but not her. I can't steer her...'

'Like you didn't steer me,' Peter Birkett interrupted.

'You were already headed that way. I simply might have casually mentioned something within your hearing,' George said meaningfully.

'To Christine Appleton her speculations were a thought experiment that took her into places that were unexpected, she simply followed her logic, but her conclusions were the reason for her shaky delivery. She couldn't let go of them because they were well founded but in her own words they were outrageous,' he continued.

'Some thought experiment.'

'I encourage my pupils to be bold.'

'I remember that too.'

'I have one or two other people who might well be amenable to suggestion,' George continued. 'One is a budding astronomer and the other is an engineer and has been since he was about ten years old and was caught using a slide rule during an examination. His claim that it wasn't a calculator fell on deaf ears but in made one hell of an impression. I gave detentions to the pair of them once.'

'How so?'

George chuckled at the memory.

'I was wrapping up a lesson on lenses and prisms. I'd been speaking about the way the prism splits light into the colours of the spectrum, the same lesson I delivered to you about thirty years ago, if you remember.'

'I do remember. Violet, indigo, blue, green, yellow, orange, red. You followed it up with that mnemonic, Richard Of York Gave Battle In Vain, but you said it first in the order that I just did and it went in and stayed in.'

'I'm glad to hear it. Returning to the matter of their detentions, I touched on the subject of chromatic aberration, and the reason that camera lenses are made up of a number of separate lenses so that the image is reproduced without unwanted colours and shades. The rainbow effect as some people call it. Yolanda Walker, better known as Yo, turned to the boy who sat next to her and said "So anything that is coloured and abnormal is a chromatic aberration. James, that's you, you're a chromatic aberration." They had hysterics and literally had to prop each other up. I had no choice, I had to dish out the punishment but I confess to having trouble keeping a straight face. It didn't end there. James has a business card template on his computer and the next day he handed me his card with his phone number and email address. The card read James Wilson, followed by the words Chromatic Aberration beneath his name. I still have it. Normally they both say black instead of coloured but the opportunity was too good to pass up.'

'Sounds like my kind of guy.'

'James Wilson is everyone's kind of guy. The girl I mentioned, Yolanda Walker, she's the up and coming astronomer. They're part of the group that includes Christine Appleton and a couple of others, a bit like that bunch you used to hang out with. Do you ever hear from them? I meant to ask you earlier.'

'Phone calls once or twice a year plus the occasional text message. I'll remember you to them.'

'I'd be glad if you would. There is just one more thing. I'd like to hear your opinions about tachyons. Anybody?'

'I'll take that one.'

It was the curly haired man speaking.

'Tachyons, tachyonic particles if you like, are particles that travel faster than light. They can't slow to sub-light speed. They come with two other particles; one is the luxon which travels at light speed, neither faster nor slower, and the other particles are called bradyons and they always move at sub-light speed. What is interesting is that luxons and bradyons do exist but tachyons may or may not. If they do exist they have yet to be found and it's not for want of looking. It goes without saying that you couldn't see them coming so the way to search for them is to find and identify evidence of their passage. I think you are less interested in the answer to your question than you are in exploring what, if anything, they might have to Christine Appleton's ideas. Am I correct?'

'You have me there,' George replied with a chuckle.

163

'Ask me again in a year or two and I might have an answer. I admire her logic, we all do, and you can tell her we will look into it. Not immediately of course but, well you never know.'

'Speaking of logic,' George informed him, 'she has been called Spockette and not without reason. Actually, she doesn't know she was filmed, we, uh, didn't want to put her off saying her piece. I'll have to show it to her and her parents and the rest of the gang.'

'Then I'll send you the recording of my end of this session,' Peter Birkett promised. 'I think she ought to know that some, ahem, very clever physicists admire her way of thinking, whether or not she decides to join us.'

George turned off his computer when the connection was broken and regarded the ceiling thoughtfully while he considered what to do next. Report back to Julia and Merlin of course. Then tell everybody what he had done and who he had spoken to, and their reaction. How would Christine Appleton take it when he told her what he had done, and the comments of some pretty powerful particle physicists? He was in for an interesting few weeks.

***

'The needle always points north when I walk around it. Magnetic north I mean,' Christine Appleton said as she examined the compass she held in her left hand.

'Put it on the nail and see if anything happens,' Deke Thorpe suggested.

'Still north. I'm going to stand it on its edge and move it around a bit and if there is a magnetic field it should show up.'

'Nothing,' she reported eventually.

'That could mean the nail isn't a standing stone or it might mean it is a standing stone but nobody is using it,' Deke said.

'Variables. Temperature. Humidity. Lunar phases.'

Yolanda Walker could be sparing with words sometimes.

'I still think it should have a jardinière standing on it,' Jasmin Tyler declared.

Chapter 16

Copper pulled up in the place reserved for Clive on the school car park. It was Friday, the end of the school week and she had come to pick Clive up after school. The afternoon was warm and she decided to unstrap Lawrence junior from his car seat and let him walk around while she kept him close by and watched out for the vehicles of departing teachers. A glance at her watch confirmed what she knew already, that her husband was running late. Some pupils passed by, all in a hurry it seemed. Well, hadn't she been the same when she was their age? She smiled inwardly. If they only knew how long ago that was!

Clive appeared. She noted that he carried a few exercise books, probably intending to mark some work at some time during the weekend, and she strolled to meet him while holding tightly to their son's small hand.

'You're late,' she accused him.

'Sorry. I had to go back for these,' he indicated the exercise books, and continued, 'I want to get them out of the way before Monday. It shouldn't take long.'

'Did you manage to speak to the gang?'

'All five of them. I don't know which of their parents will put in an appearance. Harry Tyler almost certainly will but as for the others,' Clive shrugged his shoulders, 'we'll wait and see.'

'What about the other arrangements?'

'No problems, I said we will meet in front of the Royal Crescent where we can find a suitable place to sit ourselves on the grass. Merlin has already said the weather will turn out warm and dry. James Wilson and Christine Appleton regularly pass through the park anyway and the others won't mind going out of their way. I've primed the other participants. It should be interesting to watch what happens,' Clive ended with a chuckle.

'You can say that again!'

They climbed into the car and drove off.

Merlin was right as he always was when he forecast the weather. When Clive and Copper arrived they found James and Christine already present in a spot they had chosen, about half way up the slope from the path that ran through the park. They seemed interested in two people who sat on the other side of the path.

'They were having a blazing row when we got here,' James told them.

His father had been in conversation with Mr Appleton as they trailed behind their children and they both agreed.

'They had musical instruments with them and my guess is that they might be buskers because you often hear buskers in the city and some of them are very good. They seem to have simmered down now but they were going at it hammer and tongs,' Mr Appleton observed. 'By the way, I can see Mr Green in the distance,' he added.

It was no more than a short wait until everyone who was coming had arrived. Clive's prediction that Harry Tyler would be present was proved to be correct and each pupil was accompanied by a single parent.

George Green opened the proceedings by saying he could only stop for a few minutes.

'I've got a beehive that needs my urgent attention. It won't take long but I don't want to lose a hive of bees so I'm afraid I can't stay. And I have more preparations to make for my impending visit to the past. I've come to ask how you are making out with your trilobites. Any problems?'

'They eat anything, I've discovered that,' Deke Thorpe told him.

'I show mine a coloured card when I'm going to feed them. If it's red they get fed at one end of the tank and if it's white I put their food in at the other end. They seem to be catching on,' Christine Appleton informed him.

'Jasmin, you haven't got any trilobites yet but I want to ask you a question. Do you know what triops are?'

Jasmin Tyler looked towards her father before she answered.

'No sir.'

She shook her head.

'Triops. Doesn't that mean three eyes?' Deke asked in disbelief.

'They have three eyes. The third eye is not as prominent as the other two and it seems to be a prehistoric hangover that tells the triops which way is up. You can buy triops eggs in some of the larger toy shops and they'll make a good science project if you're interested.

They don't live long, about ninety days as a rule, but by all accounts they live life in the fast lane. I don't know anyone locally who has ever kept any but I can pass on the telephone number of a couple of people who live in Norfolk if you like.'

'I think we can find a space for them,' Jasmin's father said. 'They sound interesting.'

'Good. As it happens they have sometimes been mis-identified as trilobites. Now tell me, do you know what isopods are?'

'Yes Sir, they're woodlice. And scorpions too I think. I've got a place for woodlice in my garden where they can break down an old log and recycle it back into soil. They live under the bark.'

George agreed.

'Woodlice are isopods, but there is another creature called a giant isopod that lives in the sea, which is where the isopods all started out. I believe they have been mistaken for trilobites too.'

Christine Appleton made a mental note to look them up.

George got to his feet.

'And on that note I must make my departure,' he declared.

Mentally he reviewed the shopping list that he carried in his pocket. Disposable lighters for a start; he thought they came in multi-packs. Refill pads for note taking. He and Hilary would each keep diaries. Too many refill pads would be better by far than too few and what they didn't use could be left behind. Ball point pens. Once again too many would be better than too few. Coloured felt tip pens by the dozen, and two reams of plain paper for sketches. Hmm... make that four or five. Clear plastic pockets to keep them in. All of these would not take up much room. Batteries for the pocket cameras he was taking. Small items, no problem. More memory cards? Wouldn't do any harm.

As George left the park Clive swiftly got down to other business.

'We can't afford to make mistakes,' he began. 'Alfrid and Eathl and their children will be totally out of their depth when they arrive but they are keen to see all that they can so I want to cover a few points. Firstly, the matter of traffic. Small Alfrid wants to strike out on his own of course and he wants to mix with people of his own age. You are older by a few years than he is, even Jasmin, but I'd like you to take him under your wings so to speak. Talk to him about your lives and ask him about his. It's a golden opportunity so make the most of it. Show him the sights but never let him out of your sight, and make sure he can see at least one of you at all times. In the pedestrian precinct he should be free to roam around a bit but remember he has no idea about things we take for granted, like crossing the road.

'Your Saturday meeting place in the burger bar is ideal for your first meeting with him so what I propose to do is wait until you are ensconced and then I will come in with Copper and Alfrid and Eathl and all our children. I'll make the introductions and then hand small Alfrid over to you while the rest of us find a place for ourselves not too far away but far enough. Don't stuff him with burgers and chips but do show him what's on offer and make suggestions as to what you think he might like to try but remember he will have eaten his breakfast before we bring him in.'

'Sir, why can't he have his breakfast in the burger bar? We do sometimes. Usually we have a drink and a muffin but they do a proper breakfast or brunch.'

'Good point Deke, I hadn't thought about that. He won't be able to read the menu but he can look at the pictures and you can tell him what's what. Money is no object, this comes out of the Bell Curve Society contingency funds. Now, where was I? Oh yes, secondly, listen carefully to everything he says because the more we find out the better we will be able to make his stay enjoyable.

'Thirdly,' Clive ticked off another point on his fingers in the manner of his Viking ancestor Freya, 'don't take it for granted that he will be interested in the same things that interest you. On the other side of the coin, I think he will be interested in anything and everything so if you want to talk football or astronomy go ahead. He might be interested in the sports centre; I understand he can run like the wind. He can swim as well because apparently all the children on the Lake are taught at an early age.'

'That makes good sense,' Mr Thorpe commented.

'He might have to be restrained from stripping and jumping straight in,' Copper said wryly. 'The custom back home is skinny dipping.'

'Is there anything in particular that you want to ask him, or will you play it by ear?'

'Play it by ear sir,' Yolanda Walker said straight away.

'We don't want to work to a script,' Deke Thorpe added.

'I begin to suspect you have already talked it over,' Clive told them.

Harry Tyler confirmed his suspicion.

'They have, and I heard it from Jasmin at second hand. Did everybody else?'

All the parents confirmed that they had.

'And are all agreed on our plan of action?'

All were. Clive felt pleased at the total involvement of everyone concerned.

'One question from me,' Copper said, 'and it has nothing to do with the forthcoming arrival of our guests from the past. Have any of you decided what your flags should look like yet?'

'Not yet Mrs Beach,' James replied, 'but I'm sort of thinking about a simple hydraulic diagram. It's just a jack and a pump and a control valve and a hydraulic reservoir plus connecting pipelines. There's a standard way to show hydraulic components so it will be easy to do but I'm still deciding.'

'Me too,' Deke Thorpe said in response to Copper's enquiring look.

'Sir, when Alfrid and Eathl come to our time can I talk to them? I want to ask them about their refrigeration,' James said.

Clive frowned slightly.

'Leaving aside the inconvenient fact that they never had refrigerators five thousand years ago, what do you expect them to say?'

James Wilson's grin was irrepressible.

'Well sir, I think they did and you more or less said so when we covered that period.'

'I can't remember saying that. Explain,' Clive demanded.

'I got there by a roundabout route sir. It started me off when Jasmin asked us to test her on her English set piece. She's doing a poem by Tennyson called The Lady of Shallot, the same one that I did when I was in that year. When Jas got to the bit about the mirror it triggered off something in my mind.'

'The mirror,' Clive echoed.

'Yes sir. The poem says, um...'

Deke Thorpe prompted him.

'The mirror crack'd from side to side

The curse has come upon me cried

The Lady of Shallot.'

169

'That's it,' James said. 'Well sir, if you tap a mirror or a window with a hammer it cracks because the hammer blow sets up a shockwave that travels through the glass which is too brittle to flex as the wave passes so it breaks,' James said, 'and then I thought that ice behaves like glass. The shock wave propagates too fast for the ice to flex and so it cracks, you can test that by throwing a heavy stone onto a frozen pond. When the ice is water the shock wave shows up as the ripples on the surface. Well sir, that got me thinking because I came across some strange stuff a little while ago when I was researching engineering materials. It's called Pykecrete and…'

'Pykecrete!' Copper exclaimed. 'I know about that!'

'I don't. I've never heard of it,' Clive said to both Copper Beach and James Wilson.

'It's a mixture of water and sawdust,' Copper remembered. 'Eighty-six percent water and fourteen percent sawdust if I remember it properly. When I worked for the Admiralty in Bath during the war there was a Mr Pyke who developed it. He made a lot of it in Canada but I can't remember exactly where. They have cold winters and a logging industry so Mr Pyke had all the sawdust he needed. Am I right so far James?'

The boy nodded.

'Yes Mrs Beach.' He continued, 'Well, I know they made experiments with Pykecrete and some was put into a pond and months and months later it still hadn't melted even when the warm weather came. The thing about it was that it was hard and difficult to crack. It was tough enough to stop a bullet and I know that because somebody shot at it with a pistol and it bounced off and nearly hit somebody.'

'It nearly hit Lord Mountbatten,' Copper interrupted. 'It made a hole in his trouser leg. We weren't supposed to know that but everybody did.' She laughed at the memory.

'I read about that too,' James told her. 'I think it was a General in the army who did it but whoever it was he didn't have a clue about kinetic energy. A direct hit would have dissipated the energy by flattening the bullet but a glancing shot meant it ricocheted around the room. What a nimlet!'

'A what?' Clive demanded.

'Nimlet sir. It's a village you go through on the way to the M4 motorway. We were doing an exercise in local geography and I said it sounds like a person who isn't very bright,' Deke Thorpe told him.

Copper smiled inwardly but her face gave nothing away. She could remember the hearing the word nimlet commonly used for that sort of person ever since she was quite small but Deke had evidently got there under his own steam and his interpretation matched what others had said in the past. She said nothing.

'I see. Carry on James, I'm waiting to hear what I said that has anything to do with this.'

James looked pleased with himself.

'Mr Pyke didn't invent Pykecrete sir, but he developed it. It seemed to me though that in Alfrid's now they might have discovered Pykecrete for themselves. At first I thought they might use wood chips instead of sawdust because they did use axes to fell trees and they knew how to hollow out a log with an adze to make dugout canoes. It wouldn't work though because there would be too much ice between the woodchips unless you make a really big pile but I don't think that was likely,' he explained.

'Hold on a minute James. What is it about sawdust that makes Pykecrete work?' Clive demanded.

'Flexibility for one thing sir. Sawdust can absorb an impact in a way that ice can't and the other thing is the area of interface between the water and the sawdust is immense when you add up all the grains of sawdust. The grains are quite spiky and so they have a sort of grabbing power because of their surface area. It's like if you imagine a fractal in three dimensions. I think the sawdust keeps the ice from melting because ice always melts at its surface but the sawdust sort of conducts heat away from the surface so it stays cold. Sheer volume means that the heat is dissipated harmlessly and so the Pykecrete doesn't melt. I mean it will melt eventually of course but not for a very long time.'

Clive tried to visualise a three dimensional fractal and found that he couldn't, and clutching at mental straws he decided that neither could James. It was a concept of the imagination, used as an aid to get the feel of Pykecrete.

'Alfrid's people haven't got sawdust so it seems to me that making Pykecrete was, I mean is, it's beyond their abilities,' he objected.

James Wilson agreed up to a point.

'I thought so too sir,' he explained, 'but then I had an idea that might work. I think it would. I thought that if dried wood and bark was pounded with a stone hammer you would end up with a substitute for sawdust. Also sir, if you raided wood ants nests you could get masses of chewed up wood and a little more hammering would make it the next best thing to sawdust. Perhaps even better and so the Stone Age and Iron Age people can make Pykecrete after all.'

'Very well James, they can make Pykecrete. Then what do they do with it?'

'They refrigerate meat for a short time, but they freeze it in solid in Pykecrete for long term preservation. They can do it during the winter, which makes good sense if you are short of animal fodder. They can do that and you more or less told us they did.'

Clive looked startled.

'I did? James, I can't imagine that I ever told you that.'

'You did sir. You said it a long time ago but I remember when you told us that meat had been found that had been wrapped very tightly in cloth and placed under water to preserve it. In ponds, that's what you said. Well, they can do the same thing on the Lake and in places like the fens in the east of England, and in peat bogs on the moors. They can do it sir, and I'm sure they did.'

Clive thought back.

'I believe I might have mentioned it as an item of interest once but prehistory isn't a part of the school curriculum to any large extent. You put forward a convincing argument James but where is your evidence? I don't believe any traces of Pykecrete have ever been found.'

'It's never been looked for,' Christine said with her usual incisive logic.

James had an answer ready.

'Those wrapped up joints of meat are evidence sir and I don't know how much has been found but if they did it once they could do it hundreds of times every winter when Pykecrete is easy to make and you need to slaughter your livestock. The sawdust or whatever else they used has long rotted or been washed away or maybe it has been found near preserved meat but nobody figured out what it was so they didn't take any notice. I don't know about that but I bet the Stone Age and Iron Age people knew about fridges and freezers. They just don't look like ours. I want to talk to Alfrid about it.'

'James, as of now so do I.'

As if by way of an afterthought he added, 'Those two people who were having an argument when you arrived,' Clive pointed them out for the benefit of the late comers, 'What do you make of them?'

'They aren't English,' James said, 'because when I walked past with Christine we heard them speaking. Actually the younger one was yelling. It sounded like mother and daughter having a row.'

'It probably wasn't polite but I don't know the language. It wasn't like French or German because that's taught in school so we would have known it,' Christine added.

Copper laughed.

'I didn't hear it but I can positively guarantee that it wasn't polite. It was Old Danish and the younger one who was doing the shouting is Suzanne Fluteplayer. Her music sessions often include arguments with her tutor. Anyway, they want to meet you. Off you go.'

Watching the rapidly departing teenagers Yolanda Walker's mother remarked, 'That was a set up.'

Clive agreed.

'It was, but they often hold outdoor music lessons in the park and they really do want to meet everybody so I thought we might do as the Roman Army used to do and kill two birds with one stone in a manner of speaking. Jeepers Creepers! As if it wasn't enough that Christine has put a new twist on cosmology and come up with a new theory of whatever it is, now James has opened up the possibility of finding something of historical significance. I'm truly staggered.'

'What are they like to teach?' Mr Thorpe enquired out of curiosity.

'Nerve wracking verging on scary. Even more scary when I think about how we are really sticking our necks out. Exhilarating. Enjoyable. It's often hard to believe they're still in their mid-teens. Each of them pushes you to do better. I'm waiting to see what they're going to throw at me next.'

'I've been doing the same for years!'

Mr Thorpe paused briefly and then said, 'Deke has told me that the chronicler got it wrong when he wrote that Alfrid used to put conkers on a string for his son. Apparently there weren't any horse chestnut trees around until fairly recently. A few hundred years, no more.'

'He's right,' Clive confirmed. 'The chronicler picked up on that but he was reporting what he was told so he took it at face value. As it happens it's quite possible that Alfrid could have threaded conkers after all. You see, horse chestnut trees are natives to the Mediterranean countries, specifically Turkey, or so I'm told. The chronicler knew that and he also knew that some coins that were minted thousands of ago in Turkey have been found in England, in the west country. Our conjecture is that whoever brought the coins here also brought conkers. Perhaps a few trees were planted, but not many and eventually they died out until they were re-introduced.

'Anyway, it set the chronicler off on a visit to Turkey and he had two reasons for going, one being the trees and the other being the fact that when the Roman Empire collapsed in the west if continued to flourish in the east. Turkey boasts a wealth of Roman history and by a weird piece of reasoning he wondered if any soldiers or civilians who had been in this country at some time had picked up the pseudovirus and were still around.

'So off he went and by his own admission his only plan was to walk out of the airport and turn left. He has seen an avenue in Istanbul that has horse chestnut trees along the side of the road. It's within sight of the place where all distances in the Roman Empire were measured from. He didn't find anyone who is a lot older than they look but he says he's made enquiries. He claims that it doesn't matter whether or not he is taken seriously as long as he has planted the seed in the minds of the people he has met. Mostly they are medical people and others who come into contact with a lot of people. He's been back more than once and returned with dozens of pictures of mosaics, which he passed on to John Smythe. They're spectacular. John is the one who got hooked on mosaic floors as soon as he saw the examples in the Roman Baths here in the city.'

'Clive, you must tell everyone about the headstone that he found,' Copper reminded him with a laugh.

Clive laughed too.

'It was classic,' he gurgled. 'He found a headstone in a cemetery and the inscription claimed that the grave belonged to a man who was born in the year thirteen ten and died in nineteen fifty, which would have made him over six hundred years old. The chronicler fired off text messages all over the world. I can remember the dates because I had one of those texts myself. Nobody had the heart to tell him that in Turkey they used to use the Julian calendar which was Roman and it was Julia who tipped us off because she's Roman herself. I can't remember when that changed and the Gregorian calendar was adopted but it was something in the region of seventy years ago. In Turkey headstones like that are not unusual. If I could only have seen his face when he found out.'

Copper dissolved into peals of laughter.

Harry Tyler waited to ask a question.

'What you said about being taken seriously. We've been wondering about that, at least I've been wondering. I have to believe the evidence of my own eyes but most people will only learn from the chronicles what's going on here in Bath. How many of them will believe a word of it?'

Copper answered Harry's question.

'That's been asked before and according to Marcel Land the believers will be few and far between. Almost everyone will read through the book and take it as fiction or fantasy, and some of it is. A few will believe it and hope it isn't true. I can't tell you why that is but Marcel can. Some won't believe it but would like it to be true. That leaves a very small minority who will believe it and try to search us out. Possibly fewer than one in a thousand. In other words hardly anyone but as the chronicler said about the people he met in Turkey, it doesn't matter as long as the suggestion has been implanted. Speaking of the professor, has anyone told any of you that he is watching the pupil group from a distance?'

The parents exchanged glances.

'Just as I thought,' Copper said, 'so I'll put you in the picture. Marcel is convinced that having the teenagers involved is a good thing and I agree with him. He doesn't want to have any contact with them himself because of a study that happened when I was a lot younger, somewhen in my mid-twenties. There was a man called um, Clive what was his name?'

Clive Bowden strained his memory. 'Elton Mayo,' he said eventually.

'That's him. He studied a small group of people who worked in America at a factory called Hawthorne Electrical. At least I remembered that. Anyway, they worked in the mica splitting room, which I think must have been a dirty job. Mica was an insulator but I don't think it's used quite so much nowadays. Mr Mayo was a professor and he arranged to change the working conditions of the people in the study group, and when he lowered the intensity of the light he expected production to fall but it didn't. He did other things and his discovery was that the group behaved differently from the way everyone thought they would because they knew they were being studied. The group set their own pace of work and they punished any member who produced too much by punching them on their upper arms. It was called binging and some of the punches were quite hard but nobody complained. Am I right so far Clive?'

'That's how I remember what Marcel said,' Clive Bowden confirmed.

'The group knew they were being studied, I've already said that, and so the tail began to wag the dog, so to speak, and the study was ended. What Marcel wants to avoid is altering the behaviour of our group be letting them know they are observed, because he wants them to act naturally. Am I making sense?'

'Perfectly,' Christine Appleton's father told her, 'and I imagine the study includes us as well.'

He indicated the assembled parents.

'He hasn't said as much but I wouldn't be at all surprised,' Clive replied.

Interlude

Email from Peter Birkett to George Green

Hello Mr Green. Here are some thoughts about the Appleton Interface Region. They won't make a lot of sense and in my defence I quote first the English scientist JBS Haldane; 'The universe is not only queerer than we suppose, but queerer than we *can* suppose,' and an American scientist named Carl Sagan; 'Imagination will often carry us to worlds that never were. But without it we go nowhere.'

That's a staggering thought.

I imagined Christine Appleton's matter and anti-matter universes to have the appearance of two soap bubbles joined together. The interface would be large as any kitchen sink experiment will show. You remember I mentioned the universe cold spot? That's where I though the interface might lurk. That was my Theory 1.

However, whenever the question of where the big bang took place is asked the answer is it happened everywhere. Proof: wherever you stand in the universe everything is receding from your position. Mind boggling, but no more so than the fact that light always travels at a constant speed with relation to the observer no matter where the observer stands. It isn't logical, as I'm sure Spockette would agree but that's the way it is. That being the case it is reasonable and logical to expect that the Appleton Interface is everywhere too. I pictured it as touching our spherical universe way off in the distance where our universe ends. In other words the interface surrounds our universe. That was my Theory 2.

Theory 2 didn't last long because the question of which universe encloses which immediately sprang to mind.

However, if the big bang happened everywhere then logic says the interface is everywhere too. The big bang and the interface are inextricably linked. That was my Theory 3; that our universe and the anti-matter universe occupy the same space.

The universe queerer than we can suppose? You bet!

The next time I manage to get time off and come to Bath I would like to meet you and your student group. We might have some lively discussions and I would like to keep you informed about the work I'm doing.

I have a distinct feeling that Christine Appleton would understand it straight away!

Regards.

Peter Birkett.

Chapter 17

'Deke, it's me, Yo. Where are you?'

'Bus station.'

'When you get home have a look at the picture I've uploaded to your computer. It's a giant isopod, you remember Mr Green told us about them. I got the picture from Christine and she likes it but it's like a creature from a horror film, not even its mother could like it. It's yuk! The description says they haven't evolved for more than a hundred and thirty million years and get this, some restaurants in Taiwan serve them up on a plate. You can eat mine.'

'OK Yo, I'll check it out ASAP when I get in. Call you in an hour or so. Is there anything else? Like, how big?'

'Anywhere between nineteen and thirty seven centimetres, weight one point seven kilos, and they're crustaceans. Somewhere between crabs and shrimps. Loads of legs, and they lay eggs. They're yuk!'

'Sounds like it. Call you in an hour.'

'OK. No wait! There's something else. Do you remember that bit in the Chronicle where it says they're doing geomagnetodynamics? Well Christine says that's all wrong because there really is a science called that already. I don't know what it is but Christine told me she texted Merlin and he said it's true and they wanted to put the Latin word for water into it.'

'Aqua. It's called the Aqua Chronicles.'

'Yes but the geo bit is Greek and the Greek word for water is hydro or something like that and the Latin word is aqua and they never decided to go all Latin or all Greek so they got stuck with it the way it is.'

'How did Christine know? No, don't bother to answer, you know Christine.'

'See it, hear it, remember it, know it.'

***

Interlude

Mrs Walker's Notes

I have to start somewhere and this is what I know so far:
Fresh water shrimps are egg-layers that like nutrient rich alkaline water and require high levels of dissolved calcium to develop their chitinous exoskeletons which they frequently shed.

Suzanne Fluteplayer's Notes

Today I had a music lesson in the park. It is nice there when the sun is out and it's warm and we often have our sessions outside when I have a lesson at the weekend. I have been writing down the words of some Viking songs for Pauline Grant, my music tutor. The words aren't meant to rhyme, they are a story sung to music. Actually I had just about finished when some students from the school where Mr Bowden and Mr Green teach came running down the slope to where we sat.
Their names are
Derek Thorpe
Christine Appleton
James Wilson
Yolanda Walker
Jasmin Tyler
I put that in to get it straight in my mind
Thorpe is a Viking word for a village but I don't know if Derek Thorpe knows that. They wanted to know if I can speak Old Danish, which I can. I speak it quite well because I learned the words by singing some songs first and then writing them down with Beowulf and Freya to help me, so we had to sing and talk a lot. My accent is good too. Well it has to be because I've only heard it from the people who grew up speaking it.

Merlin says I'm the only person in the world who knows Viking music as well as I do but I must know it better than anyone else because of the way I learned it. Also I know how they think, so I know seals and hedgehogs and mice are persons and so are tailnoses (elephants) but cows and dogs and sheep are not persons. I don't think Beowulf and Freya ever saw giraffes but I know they would not be persons.

Merlin says I think like a Viking now. Sometimes, not all the time. Imagine that! Even Clive Bowden can't do that and he very nearly is Viking. His father is called Lawrence and I think he can think like a Viking but he doesn't speak Old Danish like I do.

They (DT, CA, JW, YW, JT) wanted to know if I know the swearwords. I do. I also found out that a stupidhead (which is the English translation of the Old Danish word) is a nimlet.

Nimlet is the name of a village between Bath and the M4 motorway.

I already knew that.

Pauline Grant's Notes

Today's music session in the park consisted of an argument conducted at the tops of our voices and I am pleased to say that I am beginning to hold my own in the language of the Vikings.

If I am to make any headway with Suzanne Fluteplayer I must have a working knowledge as a bare minimum. To call Viking humour robust is not telling the half of it but I have heard worse. Where and how is my own business.

Viking songs fall into distinct categories.

1. Heroic accounts of wars and battles and the men who fought them. Viking women were not above fighting either; it appears from some of the songs that they were downright enthusiastic.

2. The songs of travel, including who made the voyage (travel equals ships to a Viking) and where they went, what the weather was like, how long the voyage took, and who they met along the way.

3. Songs of domestic affairs, including great feasting, partying, and general celebration. The Vikings certainly knew how to enjoy themselves!

4. Songs to be sung when winter was over. These are partly in anticipation of the start of the growing and raiding season and partly a form of thanks that winter was over. Northern winters can go on for a long time of course and there must have been occasions when supplies ran perilously low.

5. Love songs, which are often suggestive, raucous, and bawdy. Quite fun actually.

I had been primed to expect a bunch of five students to descend on us. They arrived at the run and that finished the music session for the day. Did I behave like them when I was a student? I sincerely hope I did!

Chapter 18

'Sir, can you spare a minute?'

Clive Bowden stopped and turned to face his questioner.

'Haven't you got homes to go to?' He asked good humouredly.

It was Friday afternoon and most students had bolted from their classrooms at the earliest opportunity.

Christine Appleton ignored the question.

'Sir, I want some careers advice. It's important.'

Deke Thorpe remained silent.

A moment of swift thought was all Clive needed to assess the situation and he guessed correctly that although there was careers advice to be found elsewhere in the school the matter of the girl's membership of the Bell Curve Society had some bearing on her request. It was a valid point.

'Fifteen minutes and no more,' he said, 'in my classroom.'

The trio made their way back along the corridor. Christine wasted no time.

'Sir, what do you think about career decisions made on the spur of the moment? You know, you find out about something that presses your switch and…well. I know it worked for John Smythe when he saw the mosaics on display at the Roman Baths. He took one look and made up his mind straight away. If it worked for him it could work for me or anybody couldn't it?'

Hmm, that was interesting. There might be more to this than meets the eye. Let's see.

'It worked for me too,' he told the girl truthfully. 'Do you want to hear about it?'

'Oh. Yes please sir.'

Clive chuckled.

'Well I put the blame fair and square on Iris, who is my distant relative.'

The students looked baffled.

'This is how I came to be here,' Clive continued. 'To begin with I expect you remember that my family comes from Sussex?'

'It's in the book sir,' Deke Thorpe said.

'Correct. Now, the place where they live grew up around a Roman cross-roads. They're quite proud of that and rightly so, and in fact there are signs set up on the roads in that show Roman figures, and there are other signs that indicate something of the later history of the place.

'One of the roads runs from Chichester in the south to Tower Bridge in London so we're talking about a road that runs roughly south to north. The other road runs east to west but the place where they cross has shifted over the centuries so there is a joggle of about five hundred metres but you should be able to identify it if you use a map. The section that runs off to the east is very straight for miles once you leave the built up area. There is a church which at one time served as a landmark because it stands on a hill beside the roads. Nowadays it is less visible because there are more buildings than there used to be.'

'Saint Michaels Church sir?' Deke Thorpe enquired. 'I found out from the book that churches dedicated to Saint Michael were often built on hilltop sites.'

'Good guess, but wrong,' Clive grinned, 'this is Saint Mary's Church and it has a direct bearing on how I chose my career. The church has stood for nine hundred years, and by the way it has a tower. That should help you find it because I'm certainly not going to tell you. Consider it part of your homework. As churches go it's not spectacularly big but it has a wealth of history, and this is where my aunt Iris enters the story, and as it happens she walked past the church every day on her way to and from school. It was a walk of not less than two miles each way and she took the footpath that runs through the churchyard. Everybody did, it saved a fair amount of walking and it was a public footpath. The school she attended was closed shortly after she left and a big new school was built.

'In nineteen fifty-five I think it was, the church put on a pageant during the run up to Christmas. Everything came from the parish records and of course the pageant centred around the events of the church. Iris went along one evening with some of her school friends. Actually I believe a slot was reserved for her school on that particular evening but I can't be sure. Apparently the pageant was very good and all the parts were played by local people. The whole thing held fourteen year old Iris spellbound. I was about the same age as you when she told me about it. I have to say I didn't know her well.

184

Anyway, what stuck in my mind was a scene where a woman who had attended the church all her life and occupied the same pew week in and week out suddenly found she was ousted by somebody else. She was one against many but wasn't having any of that so she went to war. It was something of an event and the lady won her case and the right to sit in her pew from then on.

'It was that one incident out of hundreds of years of events that rang a bell with me. Suddenly history became a living thing. I think young Iris felt the same. That woman was a real person who had a problem that might seem small but it wasn't small to her and for the first time I got an appreciation of what went on in the minds of real people, all the millions who never performed great deeds and who wanted more than anything to be left alone to get on with their lives. They weren't generals, they weren't admirals, they had no votes or any say over who ruled them and nobody ever asked their opinion about anything. National and local government was administered but whoever had the most muscle, but the ordinary people weren't quiet and this is something that history is belatedly coming to grips with.

'My parents had to sit through the dates of various kings and battles and who was prime minister at such and such a time and as far as both of them were concerned history was boring. I'm not surprised; you see Christine and Deke, history as taught back then was often all about kings and queens and wars and plagues and very little else. Important of course but those things are only the skeletons of history. They need real people to put the flesh on the bones. People like you and me.

'And that, in a nutshell is how young Iris got me hooked in an instant.'

'Did Iris go into history too sir?' Deke Thorpe asked.

'No. Things back then were not the same as they are today. She left school the following year when she was fifteen years old and was expected to go straight into a job. She worked in the Post Office, that much I do know, but that's the sum of it.'

'All those people, all those lives,' Deke mused.

'Are you going to change direction?' Clive enquired tongue in cheek.

'No sir. It's still botany for me. Botany and the chemistry of plants, that sort of thing. I'm still sorting it out but that's what I'm going to do.'

This was no surprise.

'Christine, what about you? You raised the subject so I assume you've made your career choice at the drop of a hat like John Smythe and I both did.'

'Yes sir. Mr Green put me up to it when he told us about the giant isopods that live in the sea. I've looked up everything I can find about them and I discovered marine biology and remotely operated diving capsules that can go anywhere under the sea. And there are manned submersibles. Some of the marine life is really strange and we don't even know the half of it. I'm, well sir, I'm going to be a marine biologist,' the girl replied seriously.

'Good for you,' Clive approved. 'Have you talked it over with your parents?'

Christine shook her head.

'Not yet,' she confessed, 'but I know they'll go for it.'

Clive agreed.

'Well I think you allotted fifteen minutes are up now,' he said.

'Just a minute sir please. I want to show you something on my laptop. It's a giant isopod.'

In next to no time Christine was able to bring up the picture.

'Jeepers Creepers!'

'That's what Yo said. And yuk! But it's beautiful in its own way, and strange. Why are its eyes that shape and why are its eyes like mirrors? What does it see? I have to know!'

Chapter 19

The walk to the place that Wint had directed them to was too long for small Alfrid's liking. His feet ached, he complained. It seemed that half of all the people who lived in his village had come along to see them off and many of them carried some of the things that the people of the new time/place had shown their interest in.

Alfrid had loaded a cart with clothes, tools, samples of leather, stone implements, cooking utensils, and, as Atta had put it, all the comforts of home. Eathl had made sure that enough clothes had been packed, knowing all the time that the clothes of her time would look out of place in the new time/place. Someone she was about to meet had insisted that every sort of clothing was of great importance and Eathl could not imagine why that should be so but if that was what they wanted that was what they would get.

It was a hot day and everyone had brought some water but there was little left for the walk back. Not enough, they would be very thirsty before they reached home. The middle of the day was long past when, at last, the place was reached. All anyone had to do now was wait. For how long was anyone's guess. Eathl moistened a finger and wiped small Alfrid's face for dirt that only she could see. He was glad to escape this ordeal but Twiss was waiting for him.

'You might meet more girls in the new time,' she said.

Small Alfrid could hardly see how this mattered since he would be back soon and never see them again. It was certain they would never meet again but Twiss was a girl who never gave up easily. What was small Alfrid to say? Twiss was right and so was he and it was said on the Lake that they were made for each other. Inwardly small Alfrid squirmed at this thought because he knew full well that what everyone meant was that small Alfrid and Twiss were trouble makers. There was that time when... well, if he were completely honest it was all his own fault and no one else's. And anyway, hadn't Vocca's paddle on his bare hide been enough punishment? The Council of Seniors hadn't thought so and he had spent every spare moment digging out a new piece of ground for the growers. Twiss had been put on a raft and told not to step ashore before her next birthday. Ouch! But you had to be philosophical, they had it coming and they knew it.

How long were they to wait? Small Alfrid accepted a drink from his father's dwindling supply of water and tried to be patient. There was a small standing stone where everyone was gathered and according to Atta it was somehow connected to the future. More than that, it had been erected in the future. That was strange and many older people claimed that this was not unusual but this stone was further away in time than any others had been in the old days. As if that made a difference. Weren't all the stones in the same time/place, only moving when their power was needed for something? Mostly they didn't work any more anyhow and nobody he knew was going to chance messing about with them.

Snap! What Freya had called a hole in the air appeared. Alfrid's cart was swiftly pulled through. Eathl carried her young daughter through and then all the things that would be wanted were swiftly passed by willing hands to someone unseen in the future. Then it was small Alfrid's turn; he stepped with confidence and anticipation into the future, closely followed by Alfrid, and snap! The way through closed behind them.

'That went off without any problems,' Atta remarked to no one in particular.

'Now all we have to do is wait a moment and they'll all be back.'

Alfrid was a fast thinker. Quickly taking stock of his surroundings he saw that everything that was meant to accompany him and his family had arrived. There seemed to be a lot of stuff but Eathl had deemed it necessary. He found there were four adults, three men and a woman who carried an infant who had been waiting for their guests in this place in the great sphere of time. He licked his dry lips.

'I'm... I'm Alfrid,' he stammered, 'and...' He stopped, not knowing what to say.

Eathl took two paces forward.

'I'm Eathl and this new one is Elfrey. It is not a proper name but one I made up. Half Eathl and half Freya.'

Copper Beach smiled warmly.

'I'm Copper,' she replied, 'and this is little Lawrence who is named after his grandfather. We call him Larry for short.'

The ice was broken and a babble of disjointed conversation broke out.

'Hello, I'm…' 'welcome…' 'I hope we…' 'can run faster than…' 'to see everything…' 'make shoes…' 'know all about…' 'hand cart…'

'Do men everywhere all talk at once?' Eathl said to Copper.

'It seems so. They say the same about us. Look Larry, here's Elfrey come to see you.'

Two children reached out to each other.

In later years small Alfrid, no longer small, used to say he never knew what hit him.

'It was all so confusing,' he told his grandchildren who listened attentively to all his stories about the future. 'We had a bit of an idea, thanks to the Vikings I told you about.'

'Beowulf and Freya.'

'That's right. They had already been there but some of the things they said, like flying for instance, we found a little far fetched.'

'Grandpa, did you ever do any flying? Up in the air with the birds?'

'Higher than that lad, much higher. No I never did. I saw the thing that does it but it was just a small one for only two people. Some of the other flying things were for, oh, half a village all at once.'

'Half a village! But that's… and how did they flap their wings?'

'Whoa girls, one at a time. I'll tell you all about it, and I'll tell you about the fish as well. There were three fish…'

Chapter 20

Doctor Edwin Mallory gazed thoughtfully at the ceiling, a habit when he was in deep thought.

'A football,' he said eventually. 'Every boy ought to have a football.'

'Every boy? I thought we were talking about one boy.'

'We are but by extension we are talking about all the boys on the Lake.'

'A hundred footballs then.'

'Why not?'

'No reason now you mention it. I'll add footballs to the list.'

'Does anyone know what footballs cost?'

'Does anyone care?'

'Not really. I've seen some decent balls for less than a fiver. Depends where you buy them and the time of the year.'

'I suppose.'

'Anything else while we're about it?' Mallory asked.

'Teapot. Stainless steel, unbreakable. And a tea service, not just the teapot but cups and saucers, plates, the whole kit and caboodle.'

'Your department Hilary,' George said decisively. 'Your's and Copper's and Janet's. Find out what patterns she likes first. Freya liked flowers on hers, roses were her favourites but Eathl might go for something else. Or nothing at all.'

'Women don't change that much,' Copper objected. 'She'll be sure to want a tea service. Traditional design if there is such a thing. China sets come in any amount of patterns and shapes.'

'Solar lamps!' Jack Smythe exclaimed. 'For lighting up the path or hanging around the garden or the porch. The youngsters have already got that sorted out. There's about a million different kinds and colours and they are pulling out all the stops on this one. Butterflies and hanging lanterns and whole strings of lights, you name it and it will be in there somewhere. The Lake is set to be ablaze with solar lighting if they have anything to do with it.'

Jack's son John who appeared to be only a few years younger than his father added, 'Wind up torches might go down well.'

'Wish I'd thought of that,' George Green said. 'I'll get Robert to put it onto the computer and send it to everyone for their comments and suggestions. I've got one of my own but I'm not really sure… it's a bit big. About ten feet long and four or five feet wide but it could be bigger.'

'Stop beating about the bush and get on with it,' Hilary Green told him.

'Well then. Pool liners. I was wondering if pool liners would be something they might be acceptable. I could lend them a hand to get it fixed up; dig a hole and lay a roll of pool liner in and if necessary overlap two lengths of roll. The hole would have to be lined with clay before the roll goes in but I don't see that as a problem.' George replied.

'Solar lamps around the pool! George, you and Jack have got it made, it'll go down big I know it will!' Mallory exclaimed.

'I thought perhaps some lilies, the Lake is bound to have lilies. And fish but I don't know what fish would be suitable. Minnows or something like that maybe.'

'Roach, mate,' Brian Gleaves spoke for the first time. 'We used to catch roach when I was a boy, they're silver with red fins and tails, and there were little gudgeons that are brown and I reckon as how they'd be handy for keeping the water clean.'

'I've already solved that part of the problem,' Copper said. 'The two Alfrids spend hours at a time looking at the fishes in my aquarium so I've searched out a book of freshwater fishes, it's one of those books with lots of pictures. I never dreamed of anything like taking a pool liner back to their village. It's inspired!'

'I know about minnows,' Brian Gleaves said. 'They're little silver fish about three inches long. They're shoaling fish so you wouldn't keep them in an aquarium but in a big pond you could put in about twenty or thirty. Alfrid could keep a shoal of little fish or three or four big ones. I reckon a shoal of minnows and a few roach. Roach grow to about seven or eight inches so they should do all right.'

'Settled then.'

'What about carp? I'm asking because I know that in mediaeval times the monasteries kept carp ponds for the days when meat was banned.'

'Sorry Jack,' Merlin said, 'but carp were introduced by the Romans long after Alfrid's time. They were brought in from somewhere in Europe. I can't remember where exactly but Julia might know. Has anyone got a garden design package on their computer I wonder' he continued, 'because at this stage it might be a good idea to try out different designs. Alfrid and Eathl live in a round house, we all know that but what we don't know is how much ground they have that they can use. Quite a lot I believe because the houses aren't huddled together but we need a little more information before we can get much further. A plan of the whole village would be helpful, one that shows houses, doors, pathways, animal pens, boundaries, and so on. It would be useful to have a map like that.'

'I know Jasmin Tyler has a package on her computer but she doesn't use it much because she likes to use bigger sheets of paper. I heard that from Harry. Jasmin might like to have a bash at making a village map and do a bit of town planning and maybe I could swing it for her to do a school project of some kind without disclosing the fact to the authorities that her source of information is going to be Alfrid,' George replied.

An idea occurred to Jack Smythe.

'Garden string!' He said suddenly.

'How come?'

'To anchor pond plants. It's bio-degradable and it won't leave any chemicals in the water. Also I have a gut feeling that Alfrid and Eathl want to get a pergola going, at least I think that's what they were talking about. That means climbing plants. Deke Thorpe is your man, him and Jasmin both, and Lofty and Elizabeth Harrison too.'

'I'll add it to the list,' George said.

'You know,' Copper said thoughtfully, 'they make cane chairs and things from willow. Eathl told me about that. Perhaps they weave hanging baskets too. Merlin, did they do that?'

'I don't know,' her father replied. 'Alfrid and Eathl are a bit before my time but the method is only a step away from weaving eel traps which has been done for thousands of years. If they haven't any hanging baskets now it only needs a nudge in the right direction. It's a kind of home decoration and where one leads the way others are bound to follow.'

'Jeepers Creepers, Stone Age snobbery!' Doctor Mallory exclaimed. 'Who would have thought it?'

'Anyone with half a brain,' Copper told him.

***

'Clive will be down in a minute, he's making Larry presentable,' Copper told Eathl.

'I don't know what you usually eat for breakfast. I don't even know if you eat breakfast, but we usually begin the day with something to eat and drink. I can do cereal, eggs and bacon, tomato, beans, sausages, bread and butter, or…'

Copper saw the look that passed between Alfrid and Eathl and stopped abruptly.

'Have I said something wrong?' She asked anxiously.

'We don't eat eggs out of season,' Eathl said stiffly, 'and we don't offer them to our guests.'

'Oh dear,' Copper sounded distressed.

'I didn't think about that because we eat eggs all year round and we cook with eggs when we make cakes and things. Look,' she said, holding up a brown egg, 'I'll crack it into a glass and you can see for yourselves.'

She did so and placed the glass on the table.

'It does look all right,' Eathl admitted after she had examined it closely, 'but I don't know what laid it. There's a strange mark on the shell and it's too big to be anything I know except for duck's eggs and they aren't brown. Is it a turkey's egg? Beowulf and Freya told us about turkeys. Freya said they're stupid.'

'Too stupid to know how to fly,' Alfrid added.

Copper explained the British Lion stamp on the shell but she felt sure she was not entirely believed. Her eye fell on a picture book that her young son had left lying around.

'Here,' she said, 'this is a picture of a chicken. Chickens laid the eggs I put on the table.'

Eathl examined the picture with care.

'There are more pictures on the other pages,' Copper said, showing Eathl how to turn the pages.

'Suddenly Eathl exclaimed, 'Oh look! Oinky pig! We know that one. And a cow. We own two cows so we know about those too. Look baby,' she said to her infant daughter Elfrey, 'pig, and cow, and sheep. We know all of those. And ducks!'

Whew, Copper thought, crisis over. For the time being anyway. She made a decision.

'I'm going to change everyone's plans,' she said crisply, 'and we're off to the shops. In at the deep end as the saying goes.'

'I think that means jumping into the water instead of wading in,' Alfrid contributed to the exchange.

Copper nodded agreement.

'It does, but it means, well, taking a risk as well. We're going to see all we can in a short time and we're going to buy some things like food and drink so you can see how we do our shopping. Do you know shopping?'

'I think so,' Eathl replied, 'it's a place where things are kept so if you want a new thing like a pot you can look and see the one you want. Is that right?'

'That's the way of it, and there are shops for all sorts of things. Food, drink, books like the one you are holding. Shoes!' She exclaimed. 'We can go to the shoe shops and you can see shoes and boots and, and, everything,' she finished slightly out of breath.

'Will you make your Range Rover take us?' Small Alfrid wanted to know.

'We'll go in our car,' Copper corrected him.

Small Alfrid looked perplexed.

'But Beowulf said it is a Range Rover,' he stammered. 'He told us he knew how to, to, how to do it.'

He searched for the right words.

'Beowulf was right, he was taught to drive. That's the word Alfrid, to drive a Range Rover, but there are other, um, vehicles, and Range Rovers are just one kind. I'll tell you what, we shall find a book with pictures of cars for you to look at and you can see them for yourself.'

Copper hoped her inadequate explanation was sufficient. Hastily she changed the subject.

'We were talking about breakfast,' she reminded her guests from Stone Age Britain.

'I'll put everything on the table and you must tell me what you would like to eat and drink. Then we will… Oh Clive, you're just in time,' she said as Clive Bowden appeared with their small son, 'can you tell Merlin to let everyone know we're going shopping and sightseeing. We're going to look at shoes and clothes and groceries and books, we must find a car magazine for small Alfrid, that's your department.'

'I'm on it. Are you thinking of going straight after breakfast?'

'Yes, I think so.'

'I've got a better idea. I'll give Merlin a call but I'll also rope in a few other people as a safety measure which means leaving later, say after lunch. What I will do though is load everyone in the car and drive around pointing out the landmarks. The railway station, the Abbey, and so on. It means you staying behind to look after Elfrey or I can do two trips. What do you think?'

'I think that makes sense and small Alfrid will get to ride in the car again.'

Small Alfrid seized his opportunity.

'If I go with my dad first and then go with mum I can go two times,' he said quickly.

Clive made an expressive gesture.

'It's decided then. Two trips it is. Give me time to talk to Merlin and we'll be off.'

***

'Remember everybody,' Clive addressed Alfrid and his family, 'if anybody becomes separated make your way here to the front of the Abbey where Mr and Mrs Rudd will be and you will soon spot them if they don't spot you first. Are you all sure you can do that?

'If we have to,' Eathl said confidently. 'It is only our son who is likely to go astray and our sense of direction is good. Better than yours I believe.'

What she said was true and Professor Marcel Land had speculated that living in wide open spaces might have something to do with it.

'Where is the railway station?' Copper asked small Alfrid.

'That way,' the boy pointed, 'and the river is over there and Pulteney Bridge is upstream in that direction and there is a weir downstream of the bridge. Over in the other direction is the Royal Crescent.'

'That puts me in my place,' Copper said ruefully.

'Off we go then,' Clive said to small Alfrid, 'and we'll find you pictures of all the cars we can, plus trains and aircraft and ships. We shall have quite a load before we've finished so we might go back to the car and leave them there and then go back for more. Does that suit you?'

Evidently it did.

Small Alfrid was almost bouncing with excitement.

'So many people,' Eathl whispered to Copper. 'What are they all for?'

Copper found the question hard to answer.

Eathl spent a long time looking at chinaware. Freya the Viking had told her about cups and saucers and teapots. Eathl was spoilt for choice and she was unable to make up her mind. So many colours and shapes! Cutlery too; knives, forks, spoons, all with different uses and different styles. Eathl admitted that she knew the use of almost none of them but she made it plain that she rated fish knives as a waste of the time and the metal it took to make them. Why would anyone make something so useless?

The women gathered all the brochures they could and decision making could come later. Eathl wanted a hairbrush and a mirror of her own. Alfrid wanted to see more shoes and polishes, along with laces and leather dyes. His cutting tools were all of stone and he was content to leave it that way but perhaps he might use just a little metal. Well he would see. And that tool that made holes in the leather for the metal eyelets looked useful. Coloured eyelets too. Black, blue, green, white, and plain metal. Perhaps he would try them out because after all there was no harm in trying. What about ready made heels? Surely there was a market there? Useful for repairs. Thread, mustn't forget thread. Alfrid had two spools already and he knew they were not to be had easily and he was grateful for them. He was glad of a supply of nails too. He wondered how he was going to make new styles of shoes. Nobody was going to want high heels that much was certain, and some shoes were too narrow for his and Eathl's liking.

Alfrid only made leather shoes but he had seen other materials used and his professional interest was aroused. Leather was the material available to him and he had the skills and knowledge to get the best from it. He regarded the shoes he was wearing now, brown sandals with an open toe, fastened with a metal buckle. The sole was not leather but in most other respects they differed little from some of the shoes he made at home. Alfrid considered the buckle to be inferior to the leather ties that he stitched to his shoes. Some people preferred short ties and others liked then long so that they could encircle the ankle before being tied. They were practical, roomy, light, and very comfortable, and if they got wet they were simply hung up to dry. The substances that he made to keep the leather in good condition gave a measure of protection against wetting.

He wriggled his toes; he thought it important to have room for even the broadest feet and his new sandals did not disappoint him. In his opinion sandals were the best daily footwear.

Some tradespeople liked thicker soles and heels. The herders preferred them but Dendric and his hunters wouldn't wear them even if you paid them to. His new stock of nails was going to be very useful until new ones were made on the Lake and he knew that production was set to begin.

He wondered about boots with metal toecaps. Their use was compulsory for workers in some occupations in this new time. Perhaps the raft workers … no, they liked open sandals that allowed water to run out if they got wet, as they often did, and if they went for an involuntary swim their lightweight sandals wouldn't carry them to the bottom as heavy boots might.

Alfrid wriggled his toes again and the action brought back a memory of Freya and her fashion socks. Colourful they certainly were. Socks like Freya's were a fashion symbol all over the Lake for a while and he was sure they would make a come-back as sure as fashions changed.

George's prediction that Eathl would be likely to want a tea service proved correct. Copper had brought clothing off the peg for her visiting guests after she greeted them on their arrival and as usual they were a good fit. The city of Bath was a tourist haven and Alfrid and his family attracted no attention.

'Now we will go our separate ways,' Copper said. 'We girls are going shopping for lingerie and chinaware and you men can find car magazines for small Alfrid to look at. Eathl will need more shoes but that can wait until another day. Has everyone got a phone?'

Everyone had. Clive knew that if Copper called any of the menfolk it would be Alfrid or his son who received the call. Hmm, not if but when, and the caller would be Eathl and not Copper. In at the deep end and the practice would make everyone confident about the use of their phones.

Eathl was amazed to see so much chinaware and Copper picked up a brochure with the comment that Eathl could decide later which she liked best. Eathl agreed that it was something she would have to think about very carefully. Copper made up her mind to collect every brochure she could find. Any brochure, no matter what it was advertising. Already she was thinking that they would be a talking point for years when her guests returned home.

'The sports shop first,' Clive said to Alfrid and his son as they strode off. 'Small Alfrid will need a football because boys everywhere play football. Something to carry it in too, so we'll get you a rucksack, and one for you too Alfrid. Nearly everyone has one and the schoolchildren you'll meet in a few days use theirs to carry their books and other things, and we're going to search out books with pictures of cars. Alfrid, you will be able to see a whole range of sports shoes. Different sports require different shoes. Swimwear too, not to mention snorkels and flippers.'

'I don't know those things,' Alfrid said. 'What do they do? What are they for?'

'I could tell you but you'll understand better when you see them. I can't say for sure but I have a feeling that flippers are not to be used in the swimming pool at the sports centre but snorkels might be. Goggles are permitted, I do know that much. Two of the schoolchildren use the pool fairly often so we can ask them about it.'

'I can swim quite well,' Alfrid said.

'I know,' Clive replied. 'You pulled Beowulf out of the water when he knocked a horse and its rider off a jetty. I'm glad you did, Beowulf was my ancestor. Freya wrote about it when she returned back to the Viking age.'

'I can swim too,' Small Alfrid claimed. 'Everybody can because we have to learn in case we ever fall into the water, and there's a swimming place where everybody goes. We don't call it a swimming pool though.'

'If you go to the sports centre you'll soon see why,' Clive told him, 'and here's where we cross the road so we have to be careful.'

'At the kerb, halt. Look right, look left, look right again. Then, if the road is clear, quick march,' small Alfrid recited.

Copper had taught him the words.

'It sounds a bit military,' she had said, 'but that was the way road safety was taught in the late nineteen-forties after the end of the Second World War. It's never been bettered, if you ask me.'

Clive allowed small Alfrid to lead the way, which he did with confidence.

The sports shop was a bit crowded but Clive soon found what he was seeking.

'Rucksacks first, and you can choose whichever ones you like.'

There was some discussion before the selection was made.

'You can see there are pockets on the sides of the rucksacks,' Clive pointed out. 'Small things go in there, things like water bottles and anything else you can think of.'

The trio moved on and examined a range of footballs.

'Football is an all year round sport except for a few weeks in the summer but kickabout games go on all the time when a few lads get together. We have talked about getting more footballs for you to take home with you. I wouldn't be surprised if football catches on fast.'

Clive gave the best advice he could about the purchase.

'Football teams have eleven players but kickabout games have fewer; it's a matter of who turns up. Over here are football shirts. The teams all wear the same colour so you know which side a player is on. The shirts all have numbers on the back, each player has a different number and his name is above the number. Women play football too so I ought to have said his or her number,' Clive continued.

'We don't know numbers very well,' Alfrid admitted. 'We know how to look at the pictures in the book that George Green made for us so we can look at the pictures and press the buttons on the telephone things we were given because the numbers are next to the pictures. It seems simple enough but we don't know which number is which.'

Clive had a burst of inspiration.

'We can fix that in no time Alfrid. You're going to have a wrist watch and learn to tell the time!'

He indicated the watch he wore on his own wrist.

'Am I?'

You both are, and so will Eathl. I'll show you how. You'll know the first twelve numbers in no time! Come on, we'll pay for you rucksacks and football and the we're off to find watches, just for the two of you for the time being because Eathl might want to choose a watch of her own.'

It crossed his mind that it might be possible for Alfrid and his son to have football shirts printed with their own names of the back. He was sure it could be done but he was not sure where. Hmm, Deke Thorpe would know, he was certain. He would ask him.

Chapter 21

Merlin had predicted a fine day. As usual, he was right, and Brian Gleaves bustled about putting the finishing touches to the preparations he had made. Jack Smythe and Frank Holley assisted.

A workbench had been moved into the yard, along with a makeshift table that held a miscellany of engineering bits and pieces. Jack was adding to the collection when Janet Smythe arrived with their two grown up children. Frank Holley indicated the spot where he wanted her to park, next to the pick-up that belonged to John Smythe that had been left in the yard overnight.

'We're expecting more vehicles,' he remarked to the newcomers. 'I'm not sure how many exactly but Julia will come and Alison will be with her as like as not. Merlin's coming with George and Hilary Green and as far as I know Alfrid and Eathl will come with Clive's parents in a hired people carrier. That's so Elfrey and small Alfrid can ride with them in the same vehicle.'

Suzanne Smythe appeared to be concealing something. Exchanging a conspiratorial look with her mother she went off to see how her own display was taken care of.

'It's ever so exciting,' Janet said to Frank, 'they want to see all they can about metal. I've no idea how much they use at home but Alfrid does own a few metal tools and at the same time he uses a stone knife and a stone hatchet.'

Frank Holley agreed and placed an empty oil drum at the side of the yard, next to a drum that was already in position. They were meant to be a depository for the expected barbecue debris, tins into one drum and paper plates and napkins into the other. His attention was drawn to flashes of light coming from behind a screen. Someone was welding. He looked surprised; he thought Suzanne Fluteplayer had finished the work she had been doing and besides, she stood nearby.

'Who's welding?' He asked.

'Pauline.'

'Huh? Pauline Grant? Your music tutor?'

Suzanne was spared an explanation when Pauline emerged from behind the screen, removing a welding mask and patting her hair into place.

'Welding? I didn't know... I mean... you're a musician.'

The astonished man was lost for words.

Wearing a smile like a Cheshire cat Pauline said, 'You're not the only ones who know people here and there. Wallis the Welder taught me years ago. He lives in Kent and I've told him all about you and Merlin and Copper. It's on Robert's database. I never mentioned it when I was recruited into all this but why shouldn't a musician be a welder as well?'

'Uh. No reason. I'll be ...'

'Very likely, but that's your problem. I've just put the finishing touches to a new weather vane.'

Frank looked at his watch partly, as he admitted later, because he didn't know what else to do.

Preparations for the barbecue continued.

'I've heard. Brian and Jack are pretty keen to get a look at stone tools just as much as Alfrid wants to see metal. From what I can gather they live in a period of transition where stone is still used but metals are beginning to appear. I only know from what Freya left in the Viking time vault. Not being an historian myself I always imagined a situation where they went to bed in the Stone Age one night and woke up in the Iron Age. Bingo! There it was. The Iron Age had begun. I'd have probably known better if I'd given it some thought,' Pauline said to Janet Smythe.

'I was the same,' Janet replied. 'We don't know how long the transition period lasted though. I asked Clive and he told me there's no way of knowing for sure. He did say it might have happened quite quickly in some places but Alfrid and Eathl seem to have lived in a quiet backwater before they came to the Lake, and they didn't use much metal. Mostly it was for buckles and jewellery I think, but not for much else.'

More preparations were being made elsewhere in the yard. Mrs Bradley and her daughter Miranda were arranging tables and seating around the temporary barbecue area while Julia and Copper ran errands for them and Larry helped in his own way, which wasn't helpful at all.

The concreted yard sloped slightly uphill from the road. Concrete gave way to roughly cut grass and it was there that the barbecue was to be held.

Brian Gleaves had the fleeting thought that this might be a good place for a new building to go up if he could get planning permission, and then he remembered that he was the owner of a large piece of land and the location of any new building could wait until he could come to terms with it and make a few decisions. He had never had a use for it and it had been a long time since he even thought about it.

An arm slipped through his.

'They'll be here soon Brian,' Julia said, 'and you are wearing your thinking face.'

'I've got a surveyor bloke coming in for a day or two,' Brian confessed. 'I was going to tell you later but there ain't no time like the present. I've got a bit of land that goes with the property and he's going to say where the boundary is exactly 'cause I'm not sure. It's on the deeds of the property but it's all scrubland with crags and gorse and brambles and there ain't no path anywhere, I don't think. It don't seem to be a lot of use and it never was but I might as well find out because I'm sort of thinking of having a new building and making the business bigger.'

'That should be interesting and having a properly fixed boundary seems like a good idea to me. It will take a few days I suppose but no longer,' Julia replied.

Brian shuffled his feet.

'Might be a bit longer,' he said awkwardly. 'The thing is, it stretches along the each side of the road for about a hundred yards each way and I really don't know how far back it goes. I told Jack and Frank there's about a square mile but it probably ain't that much. Maybe it's more. I just don't know.'

'Then perhaps the surveyor can find us a nice place for a picnic.'

Frank Holley and Jack Smythe were putting the finishing touches to a workbench that was laid out with two sets of tools.

'All set mate?' Brian asked Jack.

'Ready and rarin' to go,' Jack confirmed. 'We're getting to the stage where we start pacing up and down and looking at our watches.'

The wait was short, which was fortunate fore everyone's stretched nerves. Lawrence and Anne Bowden had managed to borrow a people

203

carrier and Alfrid and his family jumped out and stared with wide eyed curiosity at the activity in the yard.

Brian forgot his nerves and stepped forward to greet them.

'I'm Brian and I'm glad to meet you,' he said, 'and this here dog is called Button.'

'Beowulf said you had a tame wolf,' small Alfrid said.

Brian had learned not to dispute the matter.

'This is where I do my work,' he continued, 'and Jack and Frank too.'

Each man raised his hand in greeting.

'What we're going to do,' Brian explained, 'is go inside for a look round and while we're doing that so more people are going to turn up so you can talk to them and sort of get to know what they do and so you can find out all about us in our now and tell us how things are in yours.'

Leading the way into the building Brian stopped at a workbench where an array of equipment had been laid out.

'We do engineering in here and for us that means taking care of the machinery for agriculture,' he explained.

'We know about agriculture because we grow corn and other things but you grow more than we do and you have things to turn the soil and plant your seeds,' Eathl said confidently.

'That works both ways because I know you grow some things that we don't,' Brian replied. He picked up a brochure from a pile on the bench.

'I've got all the pictures I could get hold of from the people who make the machinery so when you go back home you can show everyone how they look. There's plenty of folk who will go through them with you, which I'm told has already been started with Eathl's clothes and hair styles and your magazines with shoes and boots and small Alfrid's book of cars,' he said, and added, 'you'll have quite a pile stacked up and I reckon as how Jack and me can rig up a trolley to wheel them along. What I reckon we'll do is make a couple of four wheeled trolleys. We can do that dead easy, an' on top of that we can search out some more wheels and axles so when you get home you just need some planks to make more trolleys what I reckon'll come in handy for hauling all sorts.'

Alfrid thanked Brian for his thoughtfulness. He added, 'We are not very good at making wheels yet, which was a good thing for us because if the wheel on our cart hadn't broken we would have been caught by Tarn but instead of that the Vikings found us first and then they showed us how to fight back and that was how we won the Battle of the Lake. We are getting better all the time though.'

Brian picked laid the brochure aside and picked up a nut and bolt.

'Now for a bit on engineering,' he began, 'an' to start with maybe the greatest engineering invention ever, the screw thread…'

The tour that Brian and Jack gave, together with their detailed but easy to understand explanation held their visitors attention and drew out some very intelligent questions. It was hard to remember that they came from a time and place where Stone Age methods went hand in hand with newly introduced metals that were not yet fully understood, though as Eathl insisted, 'We will learn about metal as we are still learning the ways of the Lake and what we learn we will learn well.'

As Frank Holley said later, 'Eathl is one proud and determined lady. Together with Alfrid she got us all off to a good start.'

Eventually Brian checked the time and said, 'That's about it for now but any time you want to see some more it'll be all right with us. More people are turning up and we'll have a bite to eat in about half an hour, which is just enough time for Jack to show you a little thing he made when he was learning his business as a youngster.'

Many cameras were produced as Jack Smythe led the way to his workbench.

'Here it is Alfrid, I made this little g-clamp when I was fifteen years old. It's a small version of the g-clamps you saw when we walked around and now I'll make another one like it. All the tools I need are on the bench so here goes. I know my measurements off by heart so first I'll cut two inches off this metal bar, which is a piece of mild steel. See the measurements on the ruler? I mark off two inches with this scriber, like so, and I pop the bar into the vice and use this hacksaw to cut the piece I need.'

The job was soon done.

'Right,' Jack said. 'Now I need to file down the metal to make it smooth so I'll pop it back into the vice and, well look, there's another vice on the other side of the bench so maybe you'd like to measure off a couple of inches and cut a piece yourself?'

Eagerly Alfrid did as he was shown and made his cut while Jack filed his piece of metal.

'Neatly done,' Jack told him. 'Here's the file I've been using. See what you can do with it.'

Alfrid soon had a piece shining piece of metal that matched Jack's.

'You know a thing or two about handling tools Alfrid,' Jack complimented him.

'I was well taught.'

'Knowledge Sustains,' Jack quoted. 'That was the motto of my technical training school where I was taught my trade and it's stood me in good stead all my life and it's doing the same for you. Now for the tricky bit; I'm going to cut away some metal so I mark out what I want to remove and I'll use the same tools as I did before and it should match what I did years ago. I'm using a handbrace to drill the corners and then I'll drill more holes between the two I just drilled. Then I use the saw again and cut down to the first holes I drilled. Now I can easily knock out the metal I don't want and then I just need to file all the edges smooth.'

The work was quickly and expertly done.

'You try that with your piece.'

'Uh. I'm making a g-clamp aren't I?'

'I wondered when you'd catch on,' he told Alfrid with a laugh that had Alfrid and his family joining in.

'The next thing to do is drill into the metal where the screw thread will go and when I've done that I'll round off all the corners with the file the way I did the first time I made one of these. We could file them first and then drill but I like to leave as many straight lines as I can when I'm measuring.'

It was Alfrid's turn to smile.

'I've cut away some pieces of leather sometimes when I'm making shoes and then found out that I've cut away the piece where my, um datum point is the right word I think, and all my measurements have gone with it,' he admitted.

'Anyone who works with leather, wood, metal, cloth, or anything else has probably done that at one time or another,' Jack replied, 'I know I have.'

The two workmen were soon at the point where the internal thread was to be cut.

'Here's a set of taps and dies,' Jack explained, 'and we're using he old BA sizes because that's what I used before, when I made my g-cramp. BA stands for British Association and BA threads aren't used a lot nowadays but engineers don't throw away good tools because you never know what's going to come in handy. The die is the tool we need now and there are two dies to use and they're called taper and plug.'

Jack showed the tools to Alfrid.

'Bigger sizes need three dies, taper, second, and plug. Taper goes first and here's the way of it.'

Quickly and efficiently he had his thread cut and Alfrid swiftly followed suit.

'Well done. Now let's cut two inches off this metal rod. After you.'

Once again Alfrid demonstrated his familiarity with the use of tools and Jack and Brian were impressed with his skill. Jack cut off a piece for himself.

'Nearly there Alfrid,' Jack said, 'just pop it into the vice and clean up the ends with a file so we can cut a thread. Great. Now we just bend about half an inch of the rod to about ninety degrees; the exact measurements aren't important so we can save ourselves a little time here. Next we put the die in position and push down firmly and give it a half turn; you'll feel it catch. Turn it back a bit, and then forward so you cut a little further every time. About an inch of thread will do. Keep going just another fraction and there you have it. Now I'll do the same while you fit your two pieces together.'

Alfrid's face was a picture as he held up his finished little g-clamp for all to see.

'That's a nice bit of work Alfrid, especially for a man who's never worked with metal,' Brian Gleaves broke off a discussion he was holding with Lofty and Elizabeth Harrison with Julia in attendance and complimented him.

'I made that,' Alfrid said as if to remind himself of his work.

'You did make it and it'll last for years,' Jack said. 'Just keep a thin film of oil on it to stop any corrosion. Hang on, I'll give it a squirt from this spray can and there you are, you've got something to show off back home. Take mine too and you'll have a pair.' He checked his watch and added, 'Brian said it would take half an hour and we did it with a minute to spare.'

'My dad's clever,' small Alfrid broke the silence that, for him, had been unusually long. Out of the corner of his eye he saw James Wilson beckon him and he raced away.

'Copper sent me to tell everyone to come and eat,' James told him. 'You go on and I'll fetch the others.'

'Are there chips?' Small Alfrid asked hopefully. 'I think chips might be good for me.'

James shook his head.

'No, but Mrs Bradley has laid on just about everything else. She makes burgers with a secret recipe but I heard her say she'll let your mum know what it is. She said you can make burgers in your time. Is that true?'

Small Alfrid nodded.

'We don't do bread the way they do here but my mum knows how to make the inside. It's chopped up meat and she puts an egg into it when there are some and then some other things but I don't know what they are,' he told James. 'Perhaps my mum will tell Mrs Bradley.'

Before long he was seated with his friends and tucking in happily.

'I never dreamed I would see a Stone Age boy munching on a burger and drinking fizzy drinks from a can,' Clive said. 'Is everyone taking pictures?'

Copper told him they were and pointed to where Elfrey had her arms wrapped round Button's neck.

'A Stone Age girl playing with a wolf is something you don't see every day either,' she said, 'and don't bother telling me Button isn't a wolf. Your Viking ancestors thought she is and that's good enough for Elfrey. It's a good thing we don't use roll film any more; I've taken dozens of snaps. By the way, I can see James talking to Alfrid. I wonder if they're talking about Pykecrete.'

'I wouldn't be surprised. I'd like the answer myself. And all because of a throwaway remark I made in the classroom a long time ago.'

Yolanda Walker produced her phone and took a picture of small Alfrid.

'I took pictures of your dad while he was making that little clamp. We all did.'

'Oh. I forgot. I've got a picture maker camera thing too. And a phone so I can talk to people and that takes pictures too but I don't really know how to do that.'

'A phone.' Yolanda echoed. 'How do you know the numbers?'

'And how do you know the people's names?' Christine Appleton asked curiously.

Small Alfrid rummaged in his rucksack.

'This is my phone thing and Mr Green made me a book with pictures and numbers. This picture is my dad and next to his picture there is a number so I have to press the numbers and then he hears the noise it makes and he answers.'

He showed off his makeshift telephone directory with its pictures and the numbers next to each picture. The list included Merlin, Julia, George Green, Clive Bowden, Copper Beach, and William of Salisbury among others.

Quick thinking Christine Appleton drew a simple sketch on a clean napkin.

'Who's this?' She asked.

Small Alfrid identified it immediately.

'It's you,' he said. 'That's your head and pony tail hair.'

The sketch was nothing more than an oval shape with two curved lines attached. Christine carefully added a string of numbers and told small Alfrid to try and call her. The ring tone that came from her pocket showed that he could.

Christine and Yolanda added small Alfrid's name and number to the stored information in their own phones.

'Deke and Jas are over there,' Christine pointed. 'This is Deke's number. Call him and tell him and Jas to find James and come over here.'

She penned Deke Thorpe's number onto the napkin.

James was quick to draw a picture on the napkin. He drew a circle and coloured it in, leaving two smaller circles for his eyes. It was topped by a spiral of tightly curled hair.

'It's not politically correct but you've drawn something that looks a bit like a golliwog,' Deke commented, 'and if you make your hair a bit more like the cogs on a gear wheel it will look even more like one.'

'Politically correct phooey. My aunt's got a golliwog stashed away. It belonged to my grandmother and my mum didn't get it because she's the youngest but she wanted it. You should hear her go on about it.'

James did what Deke suggested.

Jasmin grew excited.

'I've got the card that James made for me. It's got my flag with my name and phone number on it and it says Jasmin Tyler, Ace of Spades.'

She gave one of her cards to small Alfrid.

'You and James have just drawn your own flags,' she added to Christine Appleton.

James and Christine looked at each other.

'Have we? I suppose we have. Cripes!'

Deke Thorpe put two empty drinks cans together and placed a third can on top of them. Yo put her empty can alongside and looked for another to place on the second tier. George Green noticed what was going on and decided to try an experiment.

'Have you all got something to write on? Good. Suppose you lay a bottom row of ten cans and then you place nine cans on top of them and then go up to the next row. How many cans will you have when you reach the top?' He said.

Pens were produced.

'Ten plus nine plus eight plus seven...' Deke mused.

Christine Appleton wrote something down and leaned back.

'Solved it,' she claimed.

'That didn't take long. Anyone else?' George enquired.

'I know the answer but I don't know about writing it down,' small Alfrid said.

Tell me then,' George suggested.

'Fifty-five,' small Alfrid said confidently.

'Christine, what about you?'

The girl passed her note to George.

'Hmm... Christine has given me a formula.'

'I solved it for any amount of tins along the base. Ten, two, seventy-nine, any number you like.'

George read it out.

'The square of the number of tins on the bottom row, divided by two, then add half the number of tins on the bottom row.'

'How did you figure it out?' George asked curiously.

210

'It was logical to assume there is a universal solution so I...'

'Stop! Christine I can keep up with some of the time but Spockette leaves me standing. I'm glad I didn't make a bet that you couldn't do it. Let me ask you something; have any of you heard of Carl Gauss?'

'I think he had something to do with magnetism,' James replied.

'He had, along with many other things. He was a German mathematician and it used to be said that he was the last man to know everything, by which I mean everything that had been discovered in the eighteenth century, which was his now. He was set that problem once. I can't remember the exact details but he cracked the problem in about the same time as Alfrid and Christine. Were any of you close to solving it?'

'I was thinking the answer might be found in Pascal's triangle,' James replied, 'but I never found it.'

'I've never heard of Pascal's triangle,' Terry Michell said mournfully.

'I'll talk you through it, you and Jasmin. Its full of surprises.'

'Deke? What about you?'

'I thought there might be some way of using a Fibonacci series but I didn't come up with a solution,' Deke Thorpe replied.

'You're trying to make me look stupid,' Terry Mitchell accused him. 'I'm not, even if I don't know these things. I might as well go.'

'Nobody said you are stupid. I can talk you through the Fibonacci series and maybe we can find the solution that Deke couldn't find, always supposing there is one.'

Christine turned to a fresh page in her A4 refill pad

'I'm drawing this freehand but I can show you how Fibonacci numbers work,' She told Jasmin and Terry. She turned the page on it's side.

'First I'll draw a line down the page on the right hand side so the right side is half the area of the left side. Then I divide the right side into two parts so the bottom part is half the size of the top part. Half the area. After that I draw another line in the bottom part and make the left side of it half the area of the right side. Nearly there. One more line divides the top part of the left side of that into two equal parts and that's the drawing nearly done. I'll put numbers into each of the areas I marked out. Starting at the right side of the last division I make it nought, or zero. Next to that is number one. Under those is number two and then I move to the right and make the next part number three, which is the sum of the last two. one plus two equals three. Above that I put the number five, which is the sum of the last two and that leaves one area without a number so I add the last two figures again and it comes to eight. If I had a bigger sheet of paper I could go on forever but I don't need to. Now I'll start in the bottom right corner of the first area and draw a diagonal to the top left corner and from there I'll draw another diagonal to the bottom left corner of area one. Then I'll draw another diagonal to the bottom right corner of area number two and do the same again to the top right corner of area number three. From there I go to the top left of area number five and lastly to the bottom left of area number eight. Nature doesn't like straight lines so I'll make the diagonals into curves and now I've got a spiral like a snail's shell.'

Christine finished talking and passed her sketch to Jasmin and Terry for them to scrutinise it carefully.

Eventually Terry demanded, 'What good is it?'

Deke answered him.

'Good question. That spiral is all over the place if you look out for it. You can see it in the way sunflower seeds are arranged and some flowers show it in their petals. Its nature's way of packaging in the most efficient way.'

'Galaxies have spiral arms,' Yo added.

'Romanesque broccoli. Do you grow it?'

'No, but if I had some seeds I could. I know I could,' Jasmin replied.

'It's a perfect example.'

'That's answered the question for Jasmin but it was Terry's question and the answer is I don't know how it applies to sports coaching but that only means I don't know enough about sports,' Christine declared.

'I might know,' James interjected. He reached for Christine's sketch.

'A4 paper is thirty centimetres by twenty and the first line Christine drew divided it into a twenty by twenty square and a twenty by ten oblong,' he said. 'Hang on a sec.'

James folded the paper along the line he had indicated and turned it over.

'That's the golden ratio and for some reason it's a shape that seems to be…' James reached for the right word. 'Attractive,' he concluded. After a short pause he added, 'I've just had a thought. Flags, I haven't measured a flag but I bet the golden ratio is there too.'

'I'm not sure about this but I think the dimensions of a football pitch match the dimensions of the A4 sheet. Its just a bigger scale. The same for tennis courts. Basketball and netball as well. They might be one and the same, I don't know. It seems likely that arcade games follow the same rule. That doesn't say what use it is to a sports coach but something might come out of it if you get on your computer.'

Terry looked stricken.

'I don't know any of these things,' he mumbled.

George Green decided to intervene.

'Neither did anyone else when they were in your school year,' he assured Terry. 'You and Jasmin are not in any way less able than anybody else and two years from now you will be telling what you know to new members of your group. By the way,' he added, 'Let me know what you find out.'

***

George sought Christine out when she waited at the barbecue.

'Terry and Jasmin were struggling to keep up with you. I think you should go over it again in your next get together in the burger bar,' he said.

'Oh. I didn't mean to do anything wrong.' Christine sounded upset.

'You didn't do anything wrong. Christine, you're smarter than I am and we both know it so let's not have any false modesty, but sometimes you go too fast for most people. I have the advantage of years of teaching experience and observing people and that gives me a slight edge but there will come a day when you overtake me. Try to be a bit more Christine and a little less Spockette sometimes. Now shall we have another of Mrs Bradley's burgers?'

Chapter 22

'Brian told me about you,' his sister said. 'He said it was all right to and he said to just call you Julia but I don't know... you're a Lady aren't you?' She concluded doubtfully.

Julia smiled.

'He told me to just call you Marge,' she said. 'I am the Lady of the Lake but it's not a title in the usual way of thinking. Marge, just how much did Brian tell you?'

'Everything I think. Brian did say he is allowed to tell me everything because Mrs Copper Beach wants to bring it out in the open. She did at first anyway, but that was before she found out about you and her father. Merlin's daughter? Well I never! He wouldn't have made it up, Brian hasn't got a dishonest bone in his body, but I don't know what to make of it, I'm sure. Are you really a Roman? You know, from the time when Julius Caesar was here?'

'Almost from that time. Julius Caesar came to Britain in 55BC, but as an invasion it was not a success, however much he tried to dress it up. The Roman invasion proper came nearly fifty years later, in 4AD when Claudius was Emperor of Rome. My family came some time afterwards when I was a little girl. Bath was an established city by then. We called it Aquae Sulis.'

'Oo-er, it gets me in a flummox to think about it!'

After a short pause she added, 'I think he would have told me anyway, with or without permission, but he wouldn't tell anybody else and you can be sure I haven't breathed as much as a word to anyone.' She giggled. 'I know about that Mr Green and the time when somebody asked him if he would like to tell anyone, and I don't want to be called a raving lunatic any more than he does!'

Julia smiled too.

'That's one of the reasons the book about us was written as fiction.'

Marge nodded her understanding.

'I know the matron at the hospital said anyone would think it's fiction but there could be people all over the world who have visited the Roman Baths and they would know better. Am I allowed to ask if there has been anybody yet?'

'Of course you may,' Julia told her. 'We all agreed there should be no secrets about that, and the answer to your question is no. So far no one has turned up looking younger than they ought to look but we are better prepared now than we were when Jack Smythe came looking for answers. You seem to be well informed,' she added.

'Well Brian gave me a copy of the book some time ago, but it was after the Vikings went home. I'd like to have met them but you can't have everything. Brian was fair knocked sideways by it all!'

Marge crossed the room and returned with the book, which Julia could see was well thumbed.

'I've been to the Roman Baths now so I know what they are like. I expect one of your, well you know, one of your people wrote the book.'

Julia smiled again.

'He prefers to be called a chronicler rather than a writer because his task is to record events. At the same time he has to present his work with observations and interpretations because what we accept as commonplace today might be seen differently in say, a thousand years from now.'

'A thousand years! Oh, my word!'

'He has to think well ahead so as to fill in what he calls the little gaps in history that make it more real to the reader. You can ask him about it when you meet him.'

Marge gasped.

'Me meet him! Oh my, I'm sure, well…'

'He won't bite,' Julia laughed.

'What's he like?'

'He's been called an enigma, but so have I for that matter. He collected all the things we have written about ourselves, we're all supposed to do that, and if I may stray from the subject, so are you now. It isn't compulsory but we all do it and we can talk about it later. Some of what went into the book was a surprise to all of us, things nobody ever got round to mentioning. Copper Beach took him to task for saying that Freya complained that modern shoes made her feet ache. What Freya actually said was feets, she never did get singular and plural sorted out.'

'And she always said sheeps instead of sheep!' Marge exclaimed. 'It's in the book! I don't understand why Mrs Beach always says fishes though. Even I know the plural of fish is fish.'

'I don't know either. Copper told me once she's always said it that way but as for Freya, she never got the hang of singular and plural.' Julia agreed. She added, 'I've just said that haven't I?'

She continued, 'Some things in the book were written out of sequence or altered slightly. Needs must, occasionally. It's a lot to take in all at once,' she said, changing the subject slightly, 'and Brian didn't believe it either until Merlin showed him and Mr Holley, Francis Holley that is, but everyone calls him Frank. You know him, so I'm told.'

'I've known him on and off for years and he was always fair and square when he was a policeman and I expect he still is. Brian told me you were all on a raft and then King Arthur came along. It all sounded a bit far-fetched to me.'

'I imagine it did. Merlin showed them a small slice of what life was like on the Lake. It was a fine place in those days. It's nearly all drained now but the wetlands are being reintroduced in some places. One day the whole Lake will fill again, according to the Legends of the Lake, but I don't pretend to understand the Legends. They speak of the past but they quite often mention the future.

'The Lake was always a strange place and it could be a dangerous place too. The Lake Folk knew the Lake and understood it and they used it well, but to outsiders it could be a hostile place. Outsiders were always made welcome and the wise ones took the help they were offered. As for the foolish ones, well the Lake was no place for fools.'

'I expect I'll get used to it sooner or later but unless I'm very much mistaken you want to talk about Brian. Am I right?'

Julia blushed.

'I thought so.'

Chapter 23

'To bring everyone up to date, here's the way things are going and I must say I'm rather pleased with developments. Bringing the younger people into our society has been an interesting experience on both sides, starting with the fact that not one of them or their parents reacted with anything more than a calm acceptance of the way things are. Except for one thing,' Merlin showed a wide smile, 'which is that my daughter of…'

'Father my age is my own business,' Copper interrupted. 'I know what you were going to say.'

'My daughter of about a hundred years old but whose exact age is a not very closely guarded secret, has brought them up short because she has a young son, Lawrence, or Larry for short. That took them all by surprise,' Merlin amended. 'Will that do?'

'I want more free babysitting,' Copper demanded.

'Granted.'

'And you're not to spoil him any more.'

'Not granted. Grandchildren are there to be spoiled. It's a time honoured tradition.'

'Huh!'

'What I was about to say,' Merlin continued with a huge smile on his face, 'is that while nothing was said it did not pass unnoticed that eyebrows were raised.'

'Hardly surprising,' the vicar's wife commented.

'They'll be talking again,' Copper told them, 'because another time honoured tradition is that young children are always to be admired and talked about and their mothers are to be envied and I'm going to see to it that tradition is maintained to the letter!'

Merlin's orchard rang with laughter.

'Get out of that if you can Merlin,' Clive Bowden said gleefully.

Raising his hands in a gesture of resignation Clive's father in law admitted defeat.

'I've an item of news that might not have reached everyone yet,' George Green interjected, 'and that is that Christine Appleton has decided to become a marine biologist. Hah, Vicar, I thought that would interest you.'

'I always had a hankering to be a marine biologist myself but the church came first. I'll watch her career with interest though.'

'Won't we all. John Smythe heard about it in an indirect way from Suzanne Fluteplayer and he produced a picture of the mosaic that the chronicler took in Alanya in Turkey. Is that right? Alanya?'

'That's right. It's on the Mediterranean coast and somehow the chronicler made his way there when he was looking for anyone who might possibly be a Roman who had served with the Roman Army in Britain. He saw the mosaic in the grounds of a museum,' Merlin confirmed. 'There is an information board that says it was relocated there from somewhere else, I forget where, and apparently it is thought to be the floor from a Roman bathhouse for fishermen. It's a beautiful piece of work.'

'Work of a very high standard,' George Green confirmed. 'What I'm leading up to is that John Smythe told Christine that one day he would lay a replica of that mosaic in her bathroom or he could cover a wall with it if she preferred. I've a feeling that Christine will be pressing her parents to have it laid on their bathroom floor long before she has a bathroom of her own.

'Christine has thought up a few experiments for the study of her trilobites,' George continued. 'She needs to write them up properly and present them but she knows what she's doing and in due course I'm expecting a professionally written paper that will stand scrutiny and peer review.'

George chuckled.

'A few years down the line and her peers will be hard to find, I guarantee. I modestly claim it stems from the good teaching she received,' he continued.

'Modestly? Huh!'

'As I was saying,' George continued unabashed, 'she and John are sharing information about their work. As well as marine biology she intends to study oceanography and a host of other ologies and ographies if I'm not mistaken. She doesn't realise the full extent of her potential yet but one day I'll be able to boast that I taught Christine Appleton.'

'Starting today,' the vicar observed.

'And completely ignoring the fact that one or two other people have taught her,' Clive added.

'Details, details,' George replied grandly.

'Are we going to hear what the others are up to?' The vicar's wife enquired.

'They're all pitching in with their own trilobite experiments but so far nobody has anything to report. Jasmin Tyler has no trilobites but she has started to keep triops. She picked up a few tips from James' father, via James, and she has laid marbles in the bottom of her tank so the triops can't devour their own offspring. Mr Wilson is looking after an aquarium of cave shrimps if you remember.'

'I have had reports from Robert Robertson,' the vicar said. 'He tries to keep me up to date with affairs and he's given me copies of everyone's diaries. Apparently the chronicler is wondering how to record them. In the past he has inserted them as he thought proper but he is wondering if he ought to lump them all together and open a new chronicle just for them. Any suggestions?'

'Hmm… Interesting. There's a lot going for it,' Clive Bowden said.

'They won't necessarily be in sequence but I do think they might paint a broader picture of what takes place. Historians might take me to task for that one day.'

'That's the way history is written; a little piece here and a little piece there and any amount of points of view,' Clive said. 'Speaking for myself I would rather have it that way because it makes more interesting study than a mere list of dates and facts that may or may not be correct. The Anglo-Saxon Chronicles are a good case in point. They list dates and the events that the chronicler of the period considered to be important; they are invaluable but all too often there is too little information or none at all.'

'Perhaps the lack of information says more than the information itself.'

'You have me there,' Clive conceded, 'but I still believe in putting as much as possible into the chronicle but in a way that makes it readable to everyone and not only to historians.'

The vicar nodded.

'I'll take that under advice and pass it on. There is one other point and it poses a question; is our student group too elitist? You selected the brightest and I can see why but the Bell Curve Society is meant to be accessible to everybody. Are you setting yourselves up for a backlash?'

'Have you been talking to Françoise Land?'

'She has mentioned it.'

'I thought as much. The best answer I can give is that the students we picked are undeniably intelligent but at the same time each of them is level headed. I think they are smart enough to see trouble in the offing and counter it before it becomes a problem. The other thing is that we have Julia as our secret weapon and I for one wouldn't ruffle her feathers. But we do need to be more inclusive and that was the whole point of recruiting a set of younger people. The watchword is stay alert.'

Interlude

Lots of happenings.

I took my life in my hands and told Mum and Dad I'd changed my mind about what I want to do when I go to university. I've already been offered places because of my results even before this year's exams. So have Yo and James and Deke. We were all bumped up last year and we all got good marks.

I thought they would hit the roof but they didn't. They never even asked me what good it would do me for my work in the future. Then I found out they had been spying on me. That's not the right word but it will do. They have already talked to Mr Green and Mr Bowden who both said too many people look at university as an end rather than a means to an end; like they are saying they went to university and that's all they need to do. They're nimlets and I came close to being one too. That won't happen again. For me it will be a stepping stone to do more things.

If Miss Collins ever reads this she's going to come down on me like a ton of bricks because I'm rambling all over the place. Sorry Miss, I still haven't got it all sorted out in my mind.

So anyway I've got my subject at last and it's Marine Biology. Mr Green says I'll have to follow it up with Oceanography, which I had already thought of and I think they all talked to Merlin but they won't say. I forgot Ecology. It's strange to think we know more about the moon than we do about the sea bed and what lives in the sea. I've spent hours on my computer and discovered creatures that are really strange and quite beautiful and others that are strange and not beautiful at all but they are all part of the ocean's diversity of creatures and anyway beauty is in the eye of the beholder. I don't really mean I discovered them because somebody else did but I do know that one day I will go down to the sea bed myself. I might even find trilobites but I don't really think I will because their niche seems to me to have been taken over by crabs and arthropods like the giant isopod and lobsters. But the oceans are big so you never know if they might still be down there somewhere. If they are ever discovered I think it might be by accident because it would be silly to go looking for them when there is so much else to do. So that's my future.

The others have known what they want to do for ages. Yo got her first telescope when she was about nine years old and she's going to be an astronomer. James is going in for engineering with computers and robots and production techniques and other things he understands but nobody else does. Deke is up for botany and biology. He is another one who always knew what he wanted to do. He has to do environment/ecology as well and most likely climatology because of global warming and climate change and the effect that will have on geography and what trees and plants grow where. And we're supposed to be enjoying our teenage years! Jeepers Creepers!

I left Jas out. She is not going to university (she says!) because there are no courses for gardening and she wants to be a gardener. She already is. I don't know if she has really thought very far ahead but I'm a fine one to talk.

I left Terry out too. He wants to go in for sports coaching but I don't know much about that.

I know all of us are taking on a lot and I think it's because we think differently ever since we were taken into the Bell Curve Society. I'm not sure how but one day I might get the chance to talk about it to Professor Marcel Land and Doctor Françoise Land. I know about them but I haven't met them yet. They are psychologists. They are French, as you can tell by their names.

I left something out. When I asked Mr Bowden about careers he told me about a girl called Iris and how he got into history and he described how Iris walked to school every day and it was quite a long walk. Mr Bowden set me the problem of finding out where it happened. It took me about five minutes with one of my dad's driving maps. He has a satnav in the car but he says the map gives him an overview and that makes sense to me.

Chapter 24

The ferryman's youthful son led the way up the wide path from the solidly built jetty. Looking back over her shoulder while she regained her breath Hilary Green remarked that the structure was bigger than she would have suspected it to be. The boy had a ready explanation.

'It has to be,' he informed her, 'because the hospital barge is big and sometimes there can be a whole eight of healers waiting to receive a patient, and then there will be bargemen and others ready to carry the litter up the path. Usually the growers do that when they are on the island but if they are not here there are plenty of volunteers. You never know when you might need help yourself so only a fool would refuse to help, and since the time of Eadmon there are few fools on the Lake.'

The turncoat Eadmon had defected to Tarn before the Battle of the Lake and everyone knew what his fate had been. Chained to a stone, he had paid a dreadful price for Tarn's misuse of the power that came from the stones.

Pleasantly situated in a grove of trees the hospital was located here because the ground was high enough to remain above the mists and damp air that could rise from the Lake and low lying ground. Clear visibility was important; day or night a visual signal could be easily seen and a healer cold be summoned. At other times, either in poor visibility or for other reasons a horn was blown. George knew that there were different signals for different things, for instance to announce the arrival of the regular raft traffic or to request a special stop if a passenger had an urgent journey to undertake.

They had expected to be met by Gwenve but instead of the Senior of the Healers a stocky man hailed them, his blue eyes revealing that he had not been one of the refugees who had fled from Alfrid's old homeland.

The young boy exchanged a few sentences with him and hurried away to return to the raft.

'Domric,' the man introduced himself. His name was another clue to his origins.

'I'm one of the growers. Gewnve and the healers are busy at present, she sends her apologies. At least,' he amended, 'I'm sure she would have done if she had thought of it but with Gwenve her work comes first, second, and last.'

Domric gestured expressively.

'That's how healers are. I don't mind, it gives me a chance to show off my work. All the growing on this island is for the infirmary, I've a fine collection of medicinal plants, and some of the food is grown here too.'

George Green declared he was mightily interested. He pointed at the trees that surrounded the infirmary.

'I notice you allow yew trees to grow here. I thought yew trees were chopped down because they are poisonous.'

'It's true they are poisonous to cattle so they are often burnt down where cattle are kept. They are poisonous to humans too if anyone is stupid enough to eat the berries. Actually the red fleshy part can be eaten but I wouldn't want my children to eat even that, in case they accidently swallow the berry. We grow the trees here because they have medicinal uses if they are used properly.'

'That would account for the fact that nobody uses bows and arrows then,' George guessed.

'No yew trees equals no bows.'

Domric smiled.

'No offence but the Vikings said you had some weird ideas about us. Dendric and the hunters don't use the bow much because they hunt in the forest with spears and believe me there is no shortage of yew trees there. They like it that way but they know how to use the bow if they want a change. He'll tell you all about it. Come this way, I want to show off my work.'

Domric's garden was extensive.

'This plant grows yellow flowers that keep flies away. Very useful. I make a small profit on the side through selling it for rubbing on meat and I'm planning to plant more next year.'

He led the way to a straggly bramble.

'This one is an experiment,' he said proudly.

'I think it may be possible to breed a thornless blackberry bush. Several generation of cross breeding have gone into this. I admit it doesn't look much but I think I'm on to something.'

'Awesome,' George Green murmured.

His reaction obviously pleased Domric but the grower was quick to point out that his new strain would not be much use as a hedge to prevent cattle straying. Their animated conversation was cut short by a message from Gwenve that the visitors should present themselves at the infirmary.

Promising to resume at the first opportunity they moved towards the building.

Small of stature, Gwenve wore a robe that reached the ground. Anne Bowden wondered if she was wearing built up shoes underneath it but it was impossible to tell. The assistant healer wore the tunic that was universal among the men. Each healer wore a curiously shaped clasp at the left shoulder. Noting his visitor's interest the man smiled a broad smile.

'The badge of the healers,' he informed them. 'By the way, my name is Nerthi.'

Gwenve was waiting to conduct the first of her daily rounds of the infirmary and she made it plain that the only reason she was prepared to tolerate strangers at her patient's bedsides was because the patients themselves insisted on seeing them. Like all the Lake People she was polite but her chief concern was the well-being of the community and no matter who her visitors were she was averse to the interruption of the routine of the infirmary.

The tour began with a talk by the assistant healer. Gwenve listened intently and George suspected that the assistant was under examination.

'This place was built above the mists,' he explained in his opening remarks.

'I expect you are aware that some dwellings are raised on stilts for the same reason, plus the fact that gnats and mosquitos don't fly very high. Well usually anyway. They can be a nuisance.'

'We thought it was to keep clear of wet ground and flooding,' Hilary told him. 'From what little has survived it was always thought that they were, are, clear of the water most of the time but were constructed so that in poor weather the people who live in them can stay dry. Everyone we have met says our ideas about you are strange but you left no written records and our knowledge is gleaned from what can be inferred from the little that has been preserved.'

'So I have heard,' Nerthi replied. 'Much of the healer's work is done by house calls but some patients are brought here if their convalescence is expected to be long term or if intensive healing processes are required. At present there are two resident patients, one of whom is ready and impatient for discharge. I'll take you to see them and at the same time I will check their progress.'

The first patient was an old man who had broken an arm in a fall. Nerthi stood at the foot of his bed.

'Ready to leave us Brin?' He enquired.

'I'm ready, Healer Nerthi. You did a good job on me.'

'Squeeze my fingers,' the healer instructed. 'Hmm, very good. Open and close. Again. No pain? Excellent.'

'I healed faster when I was younger.'

'We all do. At your age your bones are more brittle than they were when you were young. Have you eaten a good breakfast?'

'I have, and I thanked the girl who prepared it. I ate a slice of meat and a meal-cake, followed by an apple washed down with a hot infusion.'

'Very good. I'll have the barge called to take you home. Take it easy for a few days and I think you'll have no trouble. Remember Brin, you're an old man so don't try to do too much too soon.'

The oldster sighed.

'How can I forget my years,' he said, 'when all the girls can run faster than I can?'

Nerthi laughed and even Gwenve raised a smile.

'There's nothing wrong with you. Our guests are becoming impatient with me, they want to meet you. They are George and Hilary Green.'

Old man Brin was visibly proud to have been invited to talk to them.

The next patient was a lot younger.

'Nedrenn is a hunter and he had an encounter with a bear. Unusual, they normally run away before you get close but this one must have been having a bad day. I had to operate on his hand.'

Nedrenn showed off his scars.

'Hmm, nicely healed, but as you can see, Nedrenn has been left with one finger that won't bend.'

The hunter tried to make a fist. Nerthi felt the hand gently.

'I think you're ready for a course of exercise, starting with gripping a block and holding it for a while before you release. I want you to work with big blocks to begin with and work your way down to smaller ones and see if we can get you back to normal.'

'My finger is still very stiff Healer Nerthi. Will it ever be of any use to me? I'd sooner have it amputated than be left like this.'

'I don't know,' the healer replied honestly.

To the interested onlookers he said, 'Nedrenn is a very busy man and if his finger will not become supple through exercise it will be a serious handicap to him. I'm hoping the exercises will do the trick but if they don't and your finger is still stiff after, let's see, three eights of days, come back and see me again Nedrenn and I'll take it off for you.'

'We use stone for all our work,' Nerthi explained afterwards, and added, 'I've heard of your preoccupation with metal but we have little or no use for it.'

'We are surprised you have any metal at all,' George replied. 'I'm not a proper authority but it seems that metals have been used from a period far earlier than we thought. It goes without saying that the spread of metal technology was faster in some places than in others.'

'There are metals that required the heat that only the stones could produce to make them,' Gwenve added, 'but they are in short supply now. Their lack makes little or no difference.'

'I know that your stone tools are sharp,' Hilary Green said, 'but how do you perform operations? It must be agonising for the patient.'

Gwenve looked pained.

'Of course it isn't. We use a form of hypnotism. Our patients feel nothing and there are no after effects.'

'Wouldn't work on me,' George claimed. 'I'm not susceptible.'

George's attention was drawn to the way Gwenve's fingers strayed to the intricate brooch she wore and she made a gesture that George could not follow.

'Of course not.'

George whirled to face Gwenve who now stood behind him.'

'What? How?'

'She had you cold,' Hilary told him. 'Not susceptible my foot,' she added.

227

'You will have your medical examinations now,' Gwenve directed. 'It will not be a complete examination, merely a quick check-up. Nerthi will examine George Green and I shall examine Hilary Green.'

Hilary's examination was not what she expected.

'How long have you known,' Gwenve demanded.

'I don't know what you mean,' Hilary denied.

'Don't fool with me.'

It was no use trying to hide anything. Gwenve stamped her foot.

'About a week. Seven or eight days. I… I haven't told George, he doesn't know. I don't want to bother him with it.'

'You shouldn't have come,' Gwenve told her bluntly.

Hilary hung her head.

'I know but… I couldn't let George down, Gwenve, you don't understand…'

Gwenve softened her tone.

'I understand perfectly but you place me in a difficult position.'

'I'm sorry,' Hilary apologised miserably, 'but George was so looking forward to coming here. I just couldn't bring myself to do anything that would stop him coming.'

'I would probably have done the same thing myself if I found myself in your position,' Gwenve told her.

'I never though anyone would guess there was anything wrong,' Hilary said.

Gwenve's professional pride was touched.

'It was not a guess,' she said sharply. 'I saw you come up the hill to the infirmary. I know how much you weigh, how fast your heart was beating, the length of your stride, how many breaths you took, and I can judge your temperature accurately.'

Hilary apologised again.

'What will you do?'

'Nothing. It is nobody's business but yours. Have you brought any medication with you?'

Hilary nodded.

'Good. I have something that will help if you need it but I would hesitate to prescribe anything because of my ignorance of your treatment, but I will prescribe if I must, and I think I have shown you something of the power of the healers.'

George questioned Nerthi.

'How did she do it? I genuinely thought I couldn't be hypnotised and yet she, well, as Hilary said, she had me cold.'

Nerthi smiled.

'It is a mixture of the healer's brooches and certain hand movements. It takes a long time to learn. Look at it this way; how many ways of putting your hands together do you think there are? Just touching fingertips, for instance. Look, I can put my first fingers together with my palms flat or pressed together or anything in between. The ways are uncountable.'

'Well it certainly works,' George commented wryly. 'I can't even begin to describe her hand movements, but her fingers seemed to flow in a way I can't describe,' he added 'but suppose you have a blind patient. What then?'

'There are other ways. Even new-borns can be reached.'

He hesitated for a moment.

'We couldn't do anything for the men we captured from Tarn. He had reached them first and any prisoners who were taken died as soon as they were questioned. Some managed to tell us a little but it was an effort and it was no use. They died and there was nothing we could do about it. They weren't all bad people but after Tarn had got at them they never stood a chance and to be honest I believe they preferred to die rather than return to Tarn. We had a pretty good idea of the treatment they would have received at his hands.'

***

Atta and Alfrid stopped at one of the children's play areas and regarded the dozen or so children at play. The game they played was football; the balls that Alfrid had brought back from the future were a hit with everyone.

'Gwenve and Nerthi will have a few questions for them, I have no doubt and I know that Domric the grower on the island will want to show them around. They probably won't be back for a while,' Atta remarked.

'They'll have plenty of questions to ask us,' Alfrid replied.

'I imagine that every person on the Lake has heard about the camera things that George and Hilary have been using,' he continued. He said, 'George has shown me how to use them. They made a host of pictures for me and Eathl to bring home with us and our son was given one to use as well. Eathl has agreed to cross the Lake to the school and show off some pictures and give a talk about the now that we went to. She'll take a camera with her. You can take pictures and the camera keeps them inside and you can see them if you, um, the playback button, you have to push it the right way and then you can see every picture there is inside it. George was concerned that people might think they were captured in some way when they had their pictures taken. I wonder where he got that idea?'

Atta was amused.

'I knew from what Beowulf told us that George's people could be strange at times or even downright weird but that is the weirdest thing I've ever heard.'

'Apparently some people really did think that once. They thought their essence had been stolen from them and locked away,' Alfrid was able to tell him.

He bent down and plucked a blade of grass.

'Of course that nonsense didn't last but there are still societies and individuals that don't like their pictures taken.'

'Very odd.'

Alfrid agreed.

'They have a saying; there's nowt so queer as folk. It probably holds good through all the sphere of time.'

Atta pulled a wry face.

'That's scary,' he said.

The pair sat a while with their thoughts. Alfrid was the first to break the silence.

'They had the forethought to bring a number of camera things. Apparently they thought everyone would want to see pictures of themselves and their families and from what people have said to me as Councillor Alfrid it seems they were right. George says the Games will be a good time for that. Half the population will be there and some of the cameras can make instant pictures that you can take away. George wants to show some people how to make the cameras work because the people of his place want to know what is important to us.'

'That does make sense,' Atta agreed.

'Last night he said he would ask Wint to bring back copies of the pictures that are stored inside the cameras in some way so everyone can see how they look. I don't suppose Wint will appear until it's time for George and Hilary to go home but I for one would be interested,' Alfrid continued.

'Hmm. For what it's worth my idea would be to hand out cameras to enough people to represent the Lake and let them make pictures over, say, an eight of days. They could make pictures of their homes, their work, their entertainment and so on.'

'Not to mention the way we dress. Copper Beach in the other place is very interested in that. I'll talk to them about it but I think it's a good idea.'

'I've seen pictures of the way they dress in the magazines. Is that the right word? Magazines?'

'Yes.'

'Hmm. I've seen one or two being passed around and I must say I never would have thought there are so many ways of dressing and wearing clothes. It seems to be very important to them.'

'It is,' Alfrid agreed. 'They lead very complicated lives.'

'I have a feeling that some of those clothes will be copied before very long. You know how women are.'

'You should see the waiting list for my shoes,' Alfrid complained. 'Atta, when the Games are over I really want to stand down from the Council. I've served for more than long enough. So have some of the other Councillors but we can't go on forever and I need more time to myself and my family.'

'You've more than earned it. As a matter of fact I intend to stand down myself.'

***

By mid-afternoon Atta and George Green had begun their walk back to the village. When Atta suggested a short cut through the forest George was only too happy to agree.

'I'm not as fit as I used to be,' he admitted, 'and to be honest I've been surprised that the people of the Lake are far healthier than I expected. I don't get enough exercise, and in my time I'm not the only one.'

'We do enjoy good health for the most part,' Atta agreed. 'My knees give me gyp in the early morning sometimes but at my age it's to be expected so I don't complain. Not much,' he added with a wry expression.

'Gwenve takes good care of our health and she will always see a patient, day or night, and if she's not available one of the other healers will always turn out. Day and night, storm and shine, the healers will always come to a sick individual. Man, woman, or child, it makes no difference. The healers will come.'

'I never knew medicine was so well organised,' George commented. 'I was told before we came that there is evidence to show that serious operations were performed in this age, even procedures that involved the removal of portions of the skull to treat injury or relieve pressure on the brain.'

'We turn off the main track here,' Atta said, 'and it's a bit of a climb but believe me it cuts our journey by half.'

Returning to the subject of their discussion he continued, 'It's the Law of the Lake. The Law has two arms, one that says do as you would be done by, and one that says be done by as you did. So the healers act according to the way they expect people to behave towards them. It was something we learned from Beowulf and Freya when they were here.'

'Weren't there any laws before the Vikings came?' George asked with surprise.

Atta paused for breath on the steep stretch of trail and chuckled. 'That's the trouble, there were too many laws,' he said. 'It was like this George; the Lake people come from all over the place, and some like Alfrid and Eathl had travelled a very long way. Each group brought their own laws, which caused many an argument between neighbours, as you can imagine.

'The Council of Seniors voted to abandon the old laws, which were good laws for the most part, and adopt the law that came with the Vikings. Do as you would be done by and be done by as you did. It leaves a little room for manoeuvre and you can be sure that there'll always be someone who pushes his luck or hers, but it did away with the complications that came from having too many laws, and it replaced them with just one law that any fool can remember. Not,' he added, 'that we have many fools on the Lake.'

Making unhurried progress they resumed their upward climb. The magnificent panorama that spread out before them made George whistle his admiration. A canoe was visible on the shimmering water, probably Vocca engaged in his trade as a Lake fisherman George guessed, and a large raft was being expertly poled towards the shore. George saw that it was loaded with reeds intended for replacing the thatch on one of the houses. More than one load had been delivered during the past days and the house owners for whom it was intended had collected the loads that were meant for them and deposited the reeds next to their dwellings. Everything appeared well organised. George had accepted an invitation to lend a hand and assist with the thatching to gain experience of the work and the methods used. The thatchers expected the work to be finished in half a day.

Another task was to be involved with the building of a raised footbridge or causeway that would run between two points of higher ground that were islands during the winter. This work was not local; he would spend at least one night away. George had wanted to be fully involved with life on the Lake and he was delighted with the way he was being treated.

'From now on its downhill all the way,' Atta said after they had admired the view for a while.

'We'll arrive at the jetty about the same time as the raft I should think. Home is over there, you can just see it through that belt of trees. Coming over the ridge has saved us a long walk round the headland and the view makes the climb worthwhile, I always think. Can you recognise anything from your own time?'

George shook his head.

'Not so far. I wish I could. I'd like to return home and stand here again and be able to say this is the place where I stood with Atta and watched the comings and goings of the Lake. The fact is, in my time the Lake has been drained and the land put to other uses. It took a long time, that I do know, and the Legends of the Lake say that it will fill again, but how anyone would know that is anyone's guess. It's probably just a fable. Having said all that I can work it out by studying the map, I know I can.'

'We can do it together. I would like to help and I'm getting the hang of it, so how about this; you did say on the day you arrived that Glastonbury isn't an island any more, but that doesn't matter, it's very distinctive. We could work it out from there.'

'You're right, we could' George agreed. 'We'll do it together.'

Atta was pleased.

'Let me see,' he said, 'if we use the sun or your compass we can know where north is and then we can be certain the map is the right way up and we could use your compass again to draw a line between Glastonbury and where we are standing now. That won't tell us exactly where we are on your map but at least we will know we are somewhere along that line. It's a start. After that, and I'm not sure about this, but if I have my facts right we could use the little brown contour lines to mark out the extent of the Lake and its exact shape. I think we could go to an island like the herder's island for instance, because that is where the higher ground is and then we could work out which contour line is the right one to use for marking out the Lake. Does that sound right to you?'

George nodded. Atta was a fast learner.

'I'm already looking forward to doing it, I really am. Once we have two known fixed points it's just a short step from us being able to look at the map and say this is where Atta's house is and here is where the jetty is and so on. The people in my now will be overjoyed, and I'll certainly leave some of my maps for you. My maps and my compass too. In no time at all you'll have the whole of the Lake plotted. I know you have already accomplished most of it but if everyone who uses the Lake has the same map it would be useful for locating boundaries. That would be especially useful to the herders. You know Atta,' he added pensively, 'I'm glad to witness your science at first hand. It was one of the things that made me want to come here, once the decision was made as to who would be chosen.'

'I can say the same thing to you,' Atta replied, adding, 'we still have a fair way to go. I'd like to hear more about the big bang theory while we walk. It's a staggering notion that time and space all began with an enormous explosion. And matter, too. It is a puzzle to me how there could be nothing and then there was an explosion. What exploded?'

'That's a very good question and it has been the cause of a lot of speculation and argument. One of my pupils has a theory though, and I'll tell you about it some time. She's a very original thinker and when I heard her I felt as if she had hit me with her brain. I can't begin to tell you how pleased I was.'

'It's always a pleasure to have a pupil like that,' Atta agreed.

Engrossed in animated conversation the two scientists made their way down to the shore of the Lake and were mid-way through a patch of trees and scrubland when a cry of pain pulled them up sharply.

'Oww! Ouch! Jeepers Creepers! Oww!'

Slapping at his clothes with flailing arms a boy who George guessed to be about the same age as small Alfrid burst from the undergrowth.

'Ouch! Stop stinging me! Oww!' He howled.

Atta and George Green rushed forward and George collected a few stings himself. Together they brushed away the few remaining bees that clung to the boy's clothes.

'That's got rid of them,' Atta said as he carefully removed a sting from his own arm. 'What were you doing to set them off?'

'I wanted to collect some honey,' the boy replied unsteadily. 'Everyone knows where the nest is and I had to come this way because I have to carry some hides to the ferry. It's on the way now.'

'We saw it from the top of the ridge,' Atta informed him, 'but you've plenty of time.'

'You seem to have collected a few scratches as well,' George observed.

'I had to repair a hedge for the herders to stop the sheep straying, and there were whole heaps of brambles to plug the gap. When I've put the hides on the ferry I've some more to do.'

'You seem to be living a hard life,' George commented.

'It's the only life I've got,' the boy replied; rather sharply, George thought.

'Where are your hides now?' He enquired.

'By the nest. I suppose I'll be stung again when I go back for them. And I never got any honey either.'

'I'll fetch them for you,' George offered. 'How far is it?'

Atta answered for the boy.

'No more than a few paces. Just follow the path,' he told George, pointing the way.

The hides were easy to find, tied in a bundle that was heavy. Too heavy for the boy, George thought.

The youngster obviously found it a heavy burden.

'I'll watch out for you in the Dads and Lads games,' George told him.

A tear began to roll down the boy's cheek.

'I'm not in the games. I haven't got a dad, I'm a foundling, I haven't got anybody. I've got to go,' he added abruptly and hurried away as best he could with his burden.

'He's a prickly little fellow and no mistake,' George observed.

'He takes too much on himself,' Atta replied. 'I think it's to keep himself occupied, but he really should spend more time at play, it's an important part of growing up.'

'Who is he?' George enquired. 'I haven't seen him around before but he didn't seem surprised to see me.'

'His name is Arrad, and that tells you something about him. He's from the north, about as far north as you can go without getting wet feet in the sea. I've never met anyone with that name face to face but in the days before the stones stopped working I've spoken many times to the people in the north and Arrad was not a common name, but it wasn't especially uncommon either. I've spoken to at least three people named Arrad.'

'His relatives perhaps,' George suggested.

'I don't think so. He knows about the Western Isles too, and he's been taken to some of them. I think his parents or guardians had something to do with the stones, but that's only a guess. A guess based on what I know of the stones in the north. There are a lot of stones, some in circles and some not.'

'There still are,' George informed Atta, 'or I should say they will still be there when I return to my own time. The Vikings knew the Western Isles too, perhaps Beowulf and Freya mentioned them.'

'They did, but the stones had no real interest for the Vikings. They also said that the land they came from had standing stones too.'

'I should have brought a map of the North Sea with our countries shown on it,' George said thoughtfully. 'I can draw one myself from memory but it won't have the accuracy of the maps I did bring. I'll get Hilary to help me. Between the two of us I think we can put a fairly good map together.'

Atta thanked him.

'It will be welcome, and there are many people who will be interested.' He added, 'It occurs to me that perhaps small Alfrid can tell you something about young Arrad. Their ages are close enough and you never know... we'd better hurry ourselves, it's going to rain soon. There's a warm weather front moving in. Arrad won't be mending any more hedges today, but tomorrow it will be brighter and in two or three days it will be quite hot.'

***

It was the custom of the Lake People to eat a good breakfast very early in the morning, and some people saved a portion of their meal to eat in the middle of the day. Many people had work that took them too far from home to return for the mid-day break. Vocca the fisherman was one such, as were the ferrymen who transported passengers and cargoes of animals and heavy goods to their destinations all over the Lake.

The main meal of the day was eaten in the early evening, and George and Hilary Green had just enjoyed their portions of baked pike. The dish was a new experience for them and George was fairly sure that Hilary had the recipe and he wondered if the fish could be obtained in his own place it time. He thought it unlikely but he could hope, just as he hoped that Hilary had also been given the knowledge to make the cold infusion that he was drinking now. He wondered if Eathl's passion for infusions owed something to Freya. Possibly, he thought, but not necessarily. The Lake dwellers seemed to him to have a rich and varied diet, and that must include what they drank.

Outside, the rain that Atta had promised fell steadily. Sipping appreciatively at his beverage George raised the matter of the boy Arrad.

'He keeps himself to himself,' Alfrid told him.

'A bit too much if you ask me,' Eathl added. 'He ought to spend more time at play and a little less time at work. A lot less time,' she amended.

'He does like to play sometimes,' small Alfrid informed George, 'but he soon goes off to do more work. I think it's because he hasn't got a dad to play with him in the Dads and Lads Games. 'I like it when my dad plays with me and we always have a race when we come back from the cow field. I'm a good runner.'

'And so you should be,' Eathl said sternly, trying hard to suppress a smile, 'you get enough practice fleeing the scene of your capers.'

If small Alfrid was abashed he didn't show it.

'He was trying to get some honey from the bee's nest when I saw him, but all he got was stings,' George said.

He thought for a moment and then added, 'He shouted ouch and Jeepers Creepers. Does everyone on the Lake say Jeepers Creepers?'

'They do now,' Eathl told him. 'Beowulf and Freya said it all the time and it soon spread everywhere. I know they said it in your now and I expect people in the Viking Age started to say it too when they heard it from them.'

George thought that was probably true.

'He'll try again tomorrow, I know he will,' small Alfrid told him, 'because he wants to see where they go when they swarm and then he will know where to take more honey.'

'Hmm. He won't see them swarm tomorrow, the weather won't be right. Atta told me it will get hotter in a day or two, and they'll go in about six days. I had a feeling they were getting ready, and that's why young Arrad got stings instead of honey. You know, I think I'll wander over and see if I can find him at the nest in the morning. Perhaps I can get his honey for him.'

'Well, it's up to you,' Alfrid pulled a face, 'but I've been stung more times than enough myself. It's made me not want to try it again!'

***

The Lake in the morning was a strange place, mysterious and half-hidden by mist that the rising sun would soon drive away. Adopting the ways of the Lake, George Green saved some of his morning meal, which he now carried in a small pack on his back, along with some other things he might need.

The Lake dwellers were early risers and already he could hear the sound of men and women at work and play. Several people greeted him as he set out along the shore, making for the place where the ridge jutted out into the waters. Other travellers were on the track and he found himself overtaken by Atta, who slowed his pace to match his own. The old man walked with a staff but George had begun to suspect that this was more of a badge of office than an aid to walking despite Atta's complaints about the stiffness of his knees.

'On your way to find Arrad?' Atta guessed shrewdly.

'I might be able to help him get his honey,' George replied. 'I know a thing or two about bees.'

'I know they sting,' Atta chuckled.

'Hmm, they certainly do. Atta, that's what Alfrid said last night. Doesn't anyone know more than that? They make honey and they sting,' George said, echoing the words spoken by Copper Beach in the far future.

Atta shrugged his shoulders.

'That sums up all I know,' he acknowledged. 'I confess I've never given the matter more than a passing thought. I steer clear of them myself.'

'Perhaps I can teach young Arrad something then,' George said. He added, 'That reminds me, you said his name tells you that he came from the north. Can you tell by their names where all the people come from?'

'Good question.'

Atta thought for a moment.

'Atta is more common in the land to the west. If you travel eastwards you won't find many people named Atta. Actually my name is Siglattastin but only the middle part is normally used and everyone with that name is always called Atta. Dendric and Cadric are local names, never found far from the Lake, and Vocca is a name that is common wherever you go. Alfrid and Eathl have names that came from their homeland, so any Alfrids or Eathls you meet on the Lake came from outside like they did. They never have blue eyes either, but blue eyes are rare wherever you go. Then there's Gwenve, the Senior of the Healers. It's a name that's found everywhere but is never common in any one place.'

'How about Twiss?' George asked slyly.

'Twiss! That girl was trouble before she cut her first tooth! When she gets together with small Alfrid you can be sure they're up to something they shouldn't be doing. Hmmph! I suppose you've heard we're related. The relationship is distant but not distant enough for me. Bah, that girl... and that reminds me, young Arrad will kick you in the shins as soon as look at you. Don't say I didn't warn you.'

George became aware that a small urchin had grasped his trouser leg, which he was shaking to attract his attention. A group of schoolchildren had caught up with him and Atta. He looked down at the youngster.

'I know a joke,' the urchin said. 'Would you like to hear it?'

Before George could reply an older girl burst out, 'Wigstin, come on! We'll miss the raft and then you'll be in trouble!'

'I'm coming! Gerdin, you're always on at me. I want to talk to the green man. You don't look green to me.'

'It's my name. I'm George Green.'

'Wigstin! Will you get a move on!'

'I want to tell my joke first.'

'Then I'd better hear it,' George said, 'but you'd better be quick I think.'

'All right, I will.' Taking a deep breath the boy said, 'Where does the biggest and wildest boar there is go to sleep?'

'I don't know. Where does it sleep?'

'Wherever it likes! Ha ha! Is that a good joke do you think?'

'It's the best joke I've ever heard,' George informed the budding comedian, who looked pleased and scampered away as Gerdin scolded him some more.

'That joke was old long before I heard it, and that was a good many years ago,' Atta observed.

'It was a few thousand years older when I heard it for the first time.'

'Well, they do say the old ones are the best ones,'

Atta had business on the far shore of the Lake and their ways parted where the trail forked. The sound of a horn warned that a raft, invisible in the mist, was not far from the quay.

'I'd better get a move on,' Atta declared, 'or I'll miss my passage. It's going to rain before long by the way, almost as soon as the mist clears.' He chuckled slightly and added, 'Anywhere else it would stay sunny but on the Lake, well things are different on the Lake.'

As an afterthought he said, 'We won't see the sun for, umm, two days. There won't be a downpour and it won't rain continuously, but I wouldn't expect the bees to swarm until the weather turns. That's a guess,' he added honestly, 'because I really don't know much about bees.'

'It's a good guess,' George replied. 'I told Alfrid six days.'

George was in no hurry and as he strolled at a leisurely pace he reflected that life on the Lake was thoroughly enjoyable and there were many in his own time who would envy the people who lived here in this time. There was one thing he really did want to know, and that was how Wint managed to get around the language barrier. He doubted that he would ever know.

As he had expected, George Green found Arrad close to the tree where the wild honey bees had made their nest. Rather, Arrad found him first for George made more noise by himself than a score of hunters as he brushed wet undergrowth aside, and Arrad owed his life to his skill at avoiding detection. Every day of his long trek to the sanctuary of the Lake had been fraught with peril.

'I guessed you would be here,' George told him.

'I came to see if I could take some honey without getting stung this time,' Arrad admitted readily, adding, 'and if the bees swarm I want to know where they go before anybody else does.'

'Atta caught up with me while I was walking along the shore,' George informed him. 'He says it will rain shortly after the mist clears. Tomorrow and the day after will be the same and bees don't swarm in the rain.'

'Oh. I didn't know.'

Arrad sounded disappointed.

Odd, George thought. Atta didn't know either. Collecting honey seemed to be a chance affair on the Lake. He decided to learn more.

'Doesn't anyone keep bees?' He enquired.

'How could they?' Arrad retorted scornfully. 'You can't keep bees, they're not like cows and pigs. To begin with, you can't catch them, and if you did, how would anyone pen them in?'

'I think there might be ways,' George replied cautiously.

Years of experience in the classroom had taught him how to proceed with care and not make his questioning too obvious.

Slipping his rucksack from his shoulders he said, 'I could do with a drink after my walk here, and I've brought enough for two. Is there any place where we can sit down?'

Arrad pointed.

'Over there, if you don't mind sitting on a wet log. Or you can sit on the wet ground. Either way you'll end up with a cloak that's wet and dirty, and you haven't even got a cloak.'

'True,' George admitted, 'but I've something in my bag that might do just as well.'

So saying, he pulled a waterproof poncho from his pack.

'I can slip this over my head and pull the hood up,' he explained, 'or I can spread it on the ground and two people can sit on it and stay dry.'

Finding a patch of short grass he spread the poncho and sat down cross-legged.

'See?' He said as he patted the space beside him. 'Room for two.'

Arrad seated himself with caution and inspected the material.

'It's the same colour as my cloak, dark green. It's a good colour to wear in the forest because it makes you hard to see, but it isn't wool like my cloak.'

George agreed and pulled a flask from the pack.

'I'm ready for that drink I was talking about,' he said, unscrewing the cap while Arrad looked on intently.

'The cap is one cup,' George explained as he passed it to Arrad, 'and underneath the cap there is another cup.'

Arrad held both cups while George unscrewed the stopper.

'Hold steady and I'll do the pouring,' George said, and added, 'this flask keeps the drink hot so be careful.'

He took a cup from Arrad and sipped it carefully.

'Ah, delicious,' he said appreciatively. 'Give it a try.'

Arrad sniffed the hot beverage and took his first sip.

'It's an infusion,' he declared as he identified it, 'and I think it has honey in it to make it taste sweet. Now you can see why I want to collect honey, there's a good living to be made from it if anyone can find a steady supply. I can't see why this hasn't got cold, and I can't see why your cloak poncho thing doesn't get wet.'

George's eyes gleamed with pleasure. The challenge of explaining man-made materials and the workings of a vacuum flask to a boy who was born five thousand years before he was! Clearing his throat he began…

When the sky began to darken George realised with a shock that a considerable amount of time had passed while he was teaching his young pupil. Scrambling to his feet he said, 'We'd better move smartly or we'll be caught in the rain before we've collected your honey.'

Stuffing his flask into the rucksack and throwing his poncho over one shoulder he let Arrad lead the way to the place where the bees had their nest, which George saw was in easy reach of anyone standing on a low branch. He cast about for dry tinder.

'I want something to burn,' he told Arrad, 'and I want to make plenty of smoke.'

'We won't get anywhere by burning the tree down,' Arrad objected and gave George a hard kick on his shin.

George grimaced with pain.

'If you do that again I'll give you one back,' he declared angrily.

'You wouldn't dare.'

'Try me,' George challenged, and spent an uncomfortable moment wondering how Arrad would answer.

At last he said, 'Now watch and learn because the next time we do this you will be the one doing the work. These dry flower stems and a mix of damp grass should do the trick. Now, if I hold them in a tight bunch and set fire to it, hmm, I'll tell you what, you hold them while I set them alight and smoking and then hand them up to me when I've scrambled up onto that branch. Be ready with my lunch box to put the honey in.'

'Won't you be stung? I'm still sore from the stings I got yesterday,' Arrad queried anxiously.

'I might but you won't,' George replied cheerfully as he placed the tight bundle in Arrad's hands and produced a cigarette lighter from his pocket.

'I thought this might come in handy,' he said to the astonished boy.

Soon he was standing on the low branch and reaching down to take the smoking tinder. Leaning against the trunk in order to keep both hands free he fanned smoke into the nest while Arrad looked on and held the plastic box as he had been told. George dropped the smoking bundle and thrust his arm into the hole in the tree trunk. Feeling his way round he explored thoroughly with his fingertips and picked off a large piece of honeycomb. He passed it swiftly to Arrad who held up the box to receive it. George jumped down.

'There,' he declared with satisfaction, stamping out any remaining sparks that might have dropped.

The rain started as he watched Arrad carefully place the lid on the airtight container.

'Were you stung?' Arrad enquired.

'Just one.'

'Was that because the bees couldn't see you through the smoke?'

'Good question,' George replied with pleasure. The boy seemed alert and intelligent.

'There are two schools of thought about that,' he said, 'one says that the smoke makes the bees feel drowsy. There's an element of truth about that, I believe. Other people say that what really happens is that the bees are fooled into thinking the nest is about to go up in flames and that makes them eat all the honey they can because if they have to move out there's no other way they can carry it. Then they get too fat to sting because they can't bend enough to get the sting in, and those people are right too, I think.'

'You believe both things then?'

'I do and I don't know which is more right than the other. There's a lot I don't know about bees Arrad but the point is it works, and that's the acid test of anything. Does it work? If a method works then use it, but that doesn't mean it can't be improved.'

'I see. I think I see. I know I don't know much. I can learn though.'

'That's the spirit.'

Eathl watched from the shelter of the doorway as the pair arrived, laughing at something Arrad had said. George removed his poncho and shook off the rainwater while Arrad removed his cloak and hung it on one of the hooks under the eaves, which were built in for the purpose.

'Look,' Arrad showed Eathl, 'George Green knows how to get honey. Would you like some? I had a drink from the... the vacuum flask, that's the word, and I could taste the honey you put into it.'

Eathl had no need of honey but she was alert to the situation.

Producing a small pot and thanking Arrad she declared, 'I'll take only as much as I put into my infusion. The rest is yours.'

'You can keep the box to take your honey home and give it back to me tomorrow,' George told Arrad, adding, 'if you can tear yourself away from your work tomorrow I think I might have a surprise for you if you turn up nice and early.'

His only reply to Arrad's pleading was to give him a broad smile and tell him he would find out in the morning.

***

'Alfrid, what are the rules for taking honey and capturing bees?' George asked keenly as the conversation flowed after the evening meal.

Alfrid looked slightly surprised.

'Is that a question for Alfrid the shoemaker or Councillor Alfrid?' He queried.

'Councillor Alfrid.'

'I thought as much. Well, anyone who doesn't object to being stung can collect all the honey he can carry. Or she,' he added as an afterthought. 'I know of a woman in one of the other villages who collects honey and the stings that go with it. I can't remember her name but…'

'Megwin,' Eathl interrupted.

'Yes, that's her. Sooner her than me,' Alfrid ended with a laugh that was echoed by Eathl and small Alfrid.

'And capturing bees?'

This question made Alfrid look really startled.

'It's never been done and I wouldn't know where to begin. I wouldn't know why either, when all anyone has to do is find the nest and take the honey.'

'And the stings,' small Alfrid interjected.

'So there is no song for keeping bees,' George said thoughtfully.

'I think we might have overlooked something,' Eathl made her first contribution to the discussion. 'We all saw your bees, and Merlin's too when we went to your time in the future, so you must have caught them somehow.'

Small Alfrid looked puzzled.

'How can anyone catch that many bees?' He wanted to know.

'Ah. That's the trick of it.'

'Tell them George,' Hilary chided.

'All right. Well, I'd be an old man before I could catch a whole colony of bees, but I won't have to, it's not necessary. What I have to do is catch the queen bee and all the rest of the bees will follow, and that's how I can set young Arrad up as an apiarist. That's a posh word for bee-keeper. If I can find more bees nests I can get more bees for Arrad to keep. Three or four to start him off would be about right and

I'll teach him what to do as I go. There are a couple of things I need but I'll tell you what they are and how I mean to do it. I'm going to…'

'Wait a moment,' Alfrid interrupted. 'I need to fill my cup before you begin, I expect we all do, and then I'm all ears, as you say in the future.'

He talked while he filled his cup.

'If there are any nests nearby old Megwin will know where to find them and I've heard Dendric mention that the hunters know of one or two but they leave them well alone. I can have a word with Dendric at the next Council meeting or whenever I bump into him but Megwin is getting on in years and she doesn't travel much. All the same, I'll get a message to her.'

By the time George had outlined his plans it was late and small Alfrid had long since put himself to bed.

'Well that about sums it up,' Alfrid declared, 'and I think it will do young Arrad good to have an interest. And show a profit,' he added.

'He'll have a lot of work to do first,' Hilary said, 'but at this stage it's not important. He doesn't shy away from hard work though.'

***

Arrad appeared early in the day, looking forward with keen anticipation to whatever it was George Green was going to surprise him with.

Alfrid was already out of doors and making ready to accompany his son to the field where his cows, and those of others, were kept. Beowulf had turned him into a competent stockman but he still followed his old profession of shoemaker. What with making shoes, keeping cows, and his duties as Councillor, Alfrid was never short of things to do and he had often been heard to say that he would not be sorry when his term of office was over and he could be just plain Alfrid again. Eathl and small Alfrid were in whole-hearted agreement.

'Go straight in,' Alfrid told Arrad, 'George is nearly ready.'

'Do you know what we are going to do?' Arrad asked him.

Alfrid laughed.

'Perhaps I do, perhaps I don't. You'll have to wait and see.'

He refused to answer any more questions. Eathl could be heard calling for Arrad to come in, so in he went.

'I saved my honey in a jar like you told me to and I've brought your box back,' he told George, 'and look, Cartiwiss has put enough food for two in it so we can have something to eat later. I hope that's all right,' he finished anxiously.

'It was very kind of her,' Eathl reassured him. 'I'll tell her myself the next time I see her.'

Eathl and Hilary watched the pair go about their business, Arrad almost skipping with excitement.

'Arrad seems in good spirits this morning,' Eathl observed. 'He doesn't... well he doesn't seem to enjoy himself much. I've said it before and I'll say it again, he ought to spend less time working and more time playing, but he doesn't seem to want to play very much.'

Hilary looked thoughtful.

Interlude

At first light he had left the safety of the forest and climbed his way to the broad track that ran along the spine of the ridge. Too experienced to leave the leafy cover and walk straight into the open, he sought a hiding place from where he could see and not be seen and waited patiently, watching and listening.

Time passed and the sun rose higher in the sky. Noting the place of it's rising he knew that he was still travelling in the right direction. He listened to the gentle wind and sniffed the clean air that smelled subtly different from the usual smell of the forest. Water was nearby, perhaps he could reach it by nightfall or even by the middle of the day if he was lucky. He was eager to be on his way because he was sure that his long journey was nearly at an end, but he had learned to be patient. His mind was fully made up when a pair of ducks winged overhead.

Cautiously and with many backward glances he stepped into the open and resumed his steady walk. Distances were deceptive and as the ridge changed direction slightly he suddenly spotted a stretch of water below. It was water, but was it the Lake? He stopped and considered his position, then left the ridge and descended silently through the forest towards the water, remaining alert to the slightest movement or noise. He found a level stretch of ground in front of him and noticed that in some places the trees grew right down to the water's edge. After wondering whether to seek the cover they provided he decided that he was better off where he was now.

Somewhere a horn was blown. It was not so close that he needed to take much notice but it did mean that people were not too far away. It was a piece of information to be noted and remembered but it was no threat. He was as sure as he could be that he had found the Lake at last. It was supposed to be very big and he had no idea how many people lived there but he had been told that here he would find safety. Feeling relatively at ease he waited patiently, hoping to be noticed. It was a long wait and he had begun to wonder if he could catch a fish and start a fire.

Suddenly his attention was caught by the sight of a fisherman's canoe, paddled easily and expertly by a single occupant who allowed his craft to drift slightly while he put a net over the side. Spying the lone watcher on the shore the fisherman waved. Cautiously the boy waved back. The net was pulled out of the water and the canoeist paddled towards him until they were near enough to talk.

'I don't think I've seen you before, and I know most people who live in these parts. I'm called Vocca. Who are you?'

'Arrad,' he replied, and asked, 'is this the Lake? I was told to go to the Lake and I would be safe from Tarn.'

Vocca looked surprised.

'Tarn's dead lad, everybody is safe from him now. Didn't you know that?'

Arrad was not convinced that his safety was assured.

'He might still have followers,' he objected.

Vocca laughed.

'Well lad, um Arrad, even if Tarn has followers, which I doubt, they don't dare show their faces here. Haven't you heard of the Battle of the Lake?'

Arrad shook his head.

'Well then, this is the Lake you were seeking, and it was here that we had to make a choice between Tarn or freedom. The Lake chose freedom. Now then, will you stand here all day or shall I paddle you over to my village? It's not far away.'

'Is it safe?'

'It might be safer than standing here,' said a gritty voice behind him.

Arrad whirled and reached for his knife.

'Put it away lad, you don't want odds of three to one. I'm Dendric and these are Hirwerth and another Vocca. We've had you in our sight for the last four days, and if we had any doubts about you, you wouldn't have got this far.'

Dendric continued more kindly, 'You haven't eaten or had anything to drink today. Here's my water bottle and a little food. You can return the bottle later. Now lad, hop into Voccca's canoe and we'll meet at the village before sundown.'

Vocca had come close inshore and passed two good sized fish to Hirwerth as Arrad was helped into his canoe.

When the small craft rounded the point that hid the village Arrad let out a gasp of surprise.

'What are those… those?'

Having no word for what he saw he fluttered his hands in the air.

'Flags lad, they're called flags. They're a fine sight aren't they? The Vikings brought the idea of flags from the future when they came and gave Tarn a thrashing, which we could never have done without them to show us how. We learned fast and we learned well. It's behind us now but we haven't forgotten. It'll be a sad day if anyone's ever stupid enough to try us again and mark my words, for some it will be a short day and our flags will still fly at the end of it. Our flags, not somebody else's.'

Arrad made no reply. In his short life he had never seen flags and he had no idea who or what the Vikings were. It seemed he had a lot to learn.

Chapter 25

It seemed to George Green that his insistence that he wanted to immerse himself in the life and work of the Lake had been passed by word of mouth to every inhabitant.

He noticed that a wooden dock had been built at the water's edge and a raft had been steered into it. Two mooring ropes held it in place, leaving very little space between the raft and dry land. The deck was level with the dock to within an inch or two and George noticed wheel marks on the level ground. Alfrid had said that his people were not very good at making wheels but George remembered Eathl saying that they were leaning all the time. He guessed that water haulage played an important part in the economy and commercial traffic of the Lake. He likened it to roll on roll off in the style of cross channel ferrying in his own now. Ro-ro as they called it. For some reason the thought amused him.

Accompanied by Arrad he had timed his walk to the shore well. At the water's edge he found a wobbly calf being coaxed off the raft, followed by the mother cow. A man hailed him.

'This one was born last night, over there on the herder's island, and it hasn't quite got its sea legs yet.'

The man's female companion greeted him.

'I'm Morndale. We got word early this morning that two of you need to cross to the island.'

'And I'm Lerghwil,' the man added. 'We both know Arrad and they tell me you're called George Green. There aren't many folk on the Lake who have two names. How are you finding things in our time? It must be different from yours, very different if some of the things I've heard are true.'

A long pole was put in his hands and George listened carefully to the instructions about its use as the raft was pushed into open water.

'The Lake has many places where the water is shallow enough to use a pole but it takes an expert to know them all,' Lerghwil told him, 'and if anyone does claim to know them all that person doesn't know the Lake at all. Well, maybe Vocca the fisherman does but he's the only one. The Lake's a big place and some of the shallows are traps for the inexperienced or careless; your pole gets stuck in the mud and you have to make a quick choice between either hanging on or letting go. The right choice is to let go.'

'And then you drift until you either run into the shore or somebody rescues you,' George guessed.

Lerghwil laughed.

'It's happened to me more than once,' he chuckled, 'and in winter it's no joke, I can tell you.'

'Or the rain,' Morndale added, 'but even that isn't as bad as being lost in the mist.'

'That it's not,' Lerghwil agreed. 'The mist is a friend to the Lake people, but it has to be given the respect that's due to it. The thing is George, we carry a set of paddles to get us across deeper water or get us out of trouble if we have to let go of a pole. The shallows are mud-bottomed and we don't often lose a pole or go for a swim, but the mist is deceptive. Sometimes the mist has no depth so you can be out of the mist from the waist up but you can't see your own feet, and that means you can't judge the current either.'

'We used that to our advantage when we prepared for the Battle of the Lake,' Morndale added. 'More than one of Tarn's men thought we were trapped and all they had to do was come and get us. We picked places where the current was strong to play that trick on them,' Morndale shrugged her shoulders, 'and the Lake did the rest. Good riddance to bad rubbish; it was them or us. Nobody wasted pity on them.'

'I've seen you from the shore when the mist is like that,' Arrad piped up for the first time. 'It looks funny.'

Lerghwil agreed and said, 'It feels funny too. I remember the time when Shipmaster Cadric was out charting the Lake. He went aground more than once. So many times that he lost count.'

'Poles up,' Morndale announced suddenly, bringing her own pole aboard.

George quickly followed suit.

Lerghwil gauged the current and the way the raft drifted.

'No need for the paddles,' he decided, 'this is a sandbank. It's never in exactly the same place for more than a few days, especially after rain.'

Arrad looked puzzled when he and George Green stepped off the raft at the island where the herders cared for some of the animals that belonged to an astonishingly large number of Lake settlements.

'Why have we come here?' he asked as they walked along the well-built jetty, 'I can't see that this will help us catch any bees.'

George decided to end the secrecy about their mission but a cry of welcome from one of the herders caused him to wait until the man joined them.

'I'm Hernwil, Senior of the Herders,' he introduced himself confidently.

'I'm told that in your time when strangers meet they shake hands. Right hand I believe.'

Hernwil extended his right hand.

'I'm pleased to meet you Hernwil. I'm George Green, which I think you know already, and this is Arrad.'

Hernwil and Arrad shook hands.

Arrad's question was soon answered.

'I need some straw and I'm told this is the place to get some because you keep straw for the animals you look after,' George said to Hernwil.

'That shouldn't be a problem. How much and what for?'

George explained to Hernwil and Arrad.

'My intention is to catch a swarm of bees and keep them where I want them so that Arrad can collect the honey they make. The Lake will gain a regular and reliable supply of honey and Arrad will have something he can make a living from. What I want to do is make a straw hive for the bees to set up home in. I've never made a straw hive before but I know what they look like and the construction is simple. I can make a drawing on my sketch pad to give us something to work on but I don't know how much straw I shall need. I'm asking a lot, I know that but I would really appreciate your help,' he said.

'We have more straw than we need so I can give you as much as you want. All I need to know is what your hive will look like and how big it will be.'

George thanked Hernwil and reached for his sketch pad.

Chapter 26

Small Alfrid's claim that he was a fast runner was no idle boast. He returned from the pasture panting for breath but well ahead of his father.

'Whew, I'm puffed out,' he gasped as he threw himself down on the grass outside his home.

'I beat you again Dad,' he shouted to Alfrid.

Alfrid walked the last few yards, holding his hand to his side and breathing hard.

'First one home fetches a drink of water for both,' Alfrid replied as soon as he was able. He seated himself on the bench seat beneath the eaves and fanned his face with the sole of a shoe that he meant to stitch later to complete a pair for Gwenve, the Senior of the Healers.

Eathl appeared, carrying Elfrey on one arm and a mug of cold water in her free hand.

'We saw you coming,' she said as she watched Alfrid put aside his piece of leather and quench his thirst.

'Hilary has something to tell you and ask you as well. She's gone to speak to Cartiwiss about it. We've got a surprise for you, or I should say a surprise for George, and young Arrad too, when they get back from the herder's island.'

Small Alfrid accepted the half empty mug from his father and gulped it noisily, ignoring Eathl's stern look.

'I'm listening,' Alfrid replied.

'Hilary will tell you, it was her idea,' Eathl told him unhelpfully, 'and we must talk to Vocca as well, and he's out on the Lake.'

'I know. I saw his canoe when we were up in the fields with the cows.'

'So did I,' small Alfrid chipped in. He looked up as a cloud momentarily hid the sun.

'Atta says it will rain later,' he commented.

'Only showers, and it won't last all day, that's what he said to me,' Alfrid told him.

'It won't stop us going into the cow field,' Eathl said, and added to her son, 'and you too young man, it might keep you out of trouble for a little while at least. You can help us make a space in the corner of the field for George's bee thing. We're going to pull branches and brambles to make a space where the cows can't knock it over. Beehive, that's the word, I remember it now.'

'Can Twiss come too?' Small Alfrid asked. 'I'll go and tell her.' He raced away without waiting for an answer. Eathl sighed.

'Stay out of trouble with Twiss there too? Some hopes. If I'd said she couldn't come, if I'd had time to say anything, she'd turn up 'by accident' anyway.'

Alfrid rose to greet Hilary Green and Cartiwiss as they arrived.

'I imagine this is another matter for Councillor Alfrid,' he guessed, rightly as it turned out.

After listening to what Hilary had to say he looked thoughtful. 'Hmm.'

After some deliberation he said, 'I can't see anything against it. I'll have to talk it over with Vocca and George before it goes before the Council but speaking for myself I like the idea. I like it a lot!'

The three women looked pleased, Hilary especially so.

'Good,' she said. 'Cartiwiss thinks Vocca will agree and if I know anything about George, which I certainly do, I can tell you right now he'll be over the moon about it.'

'Over the moon? How…'

'It's just a saying. Like saying he'll be as pleased as Punch. Uh, I'm not explaining myself very well, am I?'

'Oh. I understand, I think. You're saying George Green will be very pleased, is that it?'

'He certainly will be, and so shall I,' Hilary replied sincerely.

Eathl reminded Hilary that she had something else to say. Hilary nodded and picked up Alfrid's piece of leatherwork.

'It came to me this morning when I saw the leather you're using to make shoes. Alfrid, why don't you put your mark on the leather the way they do in my time? Make some kind of mark on the leather, the way Copper Beach puts her mark on her clothes. I said to Cartiwiss…'

'I've seen it on your hats,' Cartiwiss said excitedly, 'and I'm putting my order in now. I want to be first in the queue for a new pair of shoes with Alfrid's mark on them!'

'But I haven't got a mark to put on my work,' Alfrid protested, 'and besides, everyone knows my shoes when they see them. I don't need to put a mark on them.'

'That's what you think,' Eathl retorted. 'Just you wait and see. Leave it to me and Cartiwiss to spread the word around and your prestige will go sky high, as they say in Hilary's time. And you can put your prices up,' she added significantly.

'Don't tell him that!' Cartiwiss wailed. 'Vocca says I spend too much on shoes already!'

When everyone had finished laughing Hilary said seriously, 'What does your flag look like, as if I didn't know already?'

Alfrid pointed to the flag he had raised early in the morning outside his house and was about to reply when small Alfrid and Twiss approached at a fast run. Twiss slowed down rapidly when she saw them and the pair made an abrupt change of direction.

Small Alfrid yelled, 'We'll wait for you in the cow's field!'

The pair sped off.

'I think we ought to get a move on,' Eathl commented, 'before they get into even more trouble, and I must drop Elfrey off at the playgroup for a while.'

'My flag has wavy blue and white bars, nearly everyone who was at the Battle of the Lake has those on their flags' Alfrid said, picking up the interrupted conversation. 'And it's got a brown hedgehog wearing boots because I make boots and shoes and my hair is as spiky as a hedgehog's prickles.'

'Not to mention your brown eyes and pointed nose,' Eathl added with a fond laugh at Alfrid's expense.

'There you are then,' Hilary told him, 'that little hedgehog is your trade mark, the mark of the House of Alfrid.'

'Oh. So it is.'

Alfrid sounded astonished.

'Oh,' he repeated, 'I'm beginning to understand the significance of flags. There's more to them than I thought. I mean, a flag says something about the person who flies it. Where they come from, what they do, what they have accomplished, where they belong, who their fellow people are, and whom they may depend on. And who might call on them for aid and, and, and...'

256

After a short silence and a period of deep thought he said, 'I knew the flags were important from an individual point of view but the more I think about it the more I sense their true meaning. I haven't put it into words before but it is plain to me now that the blue dragon flags that fly all over the Lake are a daily reminder to us that we are one people and that together we are stronger than we are as individuals. Together we get things done, things like the rafts and their docks, and the causeways.'

Alfrid's voice was rising and he sounded excited.

'Together we can think bigger thoughts and accomplish bigger things. We can care for each other, which is the Law of the Lake of course. We can dream and know that one day our dreams will become reality, and we will do it ourselves. We will! We will! And our dreams will not be small!'

More soberly he continued, 'I think I'd do well to talk with Atta and George and Vocca and...'

Alfrid lapsed into thoughtful silence. He was a visionary. Wessex already had then blue dragon banner and now, perhaps, it had taken another step towards becoming a kingdom.

Hilary knew that she had witnessed something that few people had ever seen, the first stirrings of a new nation. For the moment she kept the thought to herself.

GEORGE GREEN'S ADDRESS TO THE COUNCIL OF SENIORS

'Ladies and Gentlemen of the Council,' he began, and then half turned to face the many people who had found places to sit on the grassy slope that was a natural amphitheatre from where they could look down onto the levelled area where the Council of Seniors sat.

'Ladies and Gentlemen of the Lake. Before I state my request to the Council of Seniors may I first give my thanks to all of you for the hospitality you have shown to visitors from the future.'

'It is the Law of the Lake,' one of the Seniors reminded him.

'I'm aware of that Madam Councillor but my feeling is that you, all of you, have gone further than the Law requires. In my time we would say that you have put flesh on the bare bones of the Law.

'It was my expressed wish that when we arrived here I wanted to immerse myself fully into the life and culture of the Lake. I was unsure whether I could offer anything in return, but now I believe I can, and that is the reason I stand before you now. I want to gain your approval for a request I am going to make.'

'The Council of Seniors will consider any requests. That too is the Law.'

'Thank you. I have not come before you without first consulting those who will be most affected by my request, namely Vocca the Fisherman, and Arrad, whom I believe you all know. I have also raised the matter with Alfrid the Shoemaker. Alfrid and Vocca are of course Members of the Council of Seniors. I have been advised of the protocol for proceedings to be heard by you, and I say that although they have their opinions I will not state them to you. They will speak for themselves, as will Arrad. There is one other person to whom I have spoken, and that person is my wife Hilary who came with me to the Lake when Wint opened the gateway to us. The fact is, and I am almost ashamed to admit it, that Hilary was the one to think of doing the thing that is the subject of my request.'

'Alfrid, Vocca, Hilary, and Arrad will leave their seats and stand with you,' Atta directed as Leader of the Council, adding, 'you have failed to mention Eathl and Cartiwiss. I find it hard to believe they are unaware of the nature of your business.'

'They are aware,' George Green confirmed, 'but each of those ladies has an infant to take care of and each has deputed Hilary to speak for her.'

From his seat in the front row Atta turned to face the Council.

'Has the Council of Seniors any objection to that? A show of hands.'

No hands were raised.

'Very well,' Atta continued, 'George Green, you may make your request.'

'Thank you, I will. But before I do I wish to acquaint the Council with the facts that have led me to make this request. I have already said that I want to play my part in the daily lives of the People of the Lake, and I believe I have something to offer.

'A few days ago Arrad drew himself to my attention by his yells after he had attempted to raid a nest of bees for their honey and got severely stung for his efforts. I have since discovered that nobody on the Lake keeps bees.'

'How could anyone?' An elderly Councillor asked. 'Bees can't be penned like cattle.'

'Neither can fish,' George Green countered, 'but Vocca the fisherman harvests them for his living. Keeping bees can be done, as Councillor Alfrid can confirm.'

'Alfrid?'

Atta made a question of Alfrid's name.

'I can confirm that. In the far future have seen for myself that George Green and others can and do keep bees. George has more than one swarm, all in separate hives, which is the word for the… the little houses where the bees live, and I have tasted the honey they produce. At this stage of the meeting I will inform the Members of the Council that I have advised George Green that anyone who can collect honey may do so, and I see no reason why anyone who is able to capture a swarm of bees may not do so, and keep them for their honey.'

'Councillors? A show of hands,' Atta demanded, raising his own left hand.

The vote was unanimous. If George Green and Arrad could do as George claimed, the bees and the honey they produced would be theirs.

259

'I have a question for George Green. Gwenve, Senior of the Healers,' the questioner identified herself according to Council protocol, although she was known to all.

'George Green, are you saying you will be able to produce honey on demand?'

'Councillor, that is exactly what I am saying. I know how to catch a swarm and I can teach Arrad enough while I am here so that he will have honey to sell or trade for other goods or services,' George replied.

'I hoped that would be your reply,' Gwenve informed him.

'I have treated most of you with honey', she addressed the Council and all the People of the Lake, 'either internally or externally or both. It has strong medicinal properties. Arrad,' she continued, 'I would like you to take your first order of honey from me. As soon as you produce your honey I want some!'

'You may reply,' Atta prompted the youngster kindly.

'I... I... I will.' Arrad stammered.

'Will you treat my sweet tooth?' One of the older Councillors enquired of Gwenve.

Even Gwenve who was notorious for having no sense of humour where her profession was concerned, managed to join the laughter that followed.

George Green waited for silence and let a few long moments pass while he put his thoughts in order.

'You know,' he mused, 'in my own time I am a schoolteacher. It was the only thing I ever wanted to do and I have never regretted that I became one. When I was younger every school was marked by a sign that has since been replaced by another. It was, in my opinion, a very bad thing. The sign I am speaking of was a picture of a flaming torch. I have made a drawing of that torch to pass among you.'

He gave the sketch to Atta, who passed it to the Council.

'I'll keep talking while the drawing is passed around,' George said.

'That torch was known as the torch of learning. In that one picture the whole purpose of every school, and my life's purpose, is summed up. To grasp the torch of knowledge and pass it on. To pass on the desire for knowledge and understanding, and to shine the light of the torch into the dark corners of the unknown. It has never been my purpose or intention to tell anyone what to think, but I have always encouraged my pupils to think about what interests them. To explore the world around them, perhaps to uncover new knowledge, but above all to carry the torch of learning in here,' he tapped his head, 'and here,' he put his hand over his heart. 'To carry the torch and keep it burning brightly. To expand the limits of their thinking and to test those limits.'

'It is a noble aspiration.'

'Thank you. I have said this to Arrad, one way or another, and in the matter of keeping bees and the honey they make I believe I have lighted the torch of knowledge in him. I am still working with him to catch our first swarm, which I believe will happen soon, and the People of the Lake have kindly made a hive in which the bees will live. I will continue to teach Arrad all I can but my time here must be short and after I have gone Arrad will have to make his own decisions. This illustrates the point I made earlier, that I will not tell him what to think, but I will, I hope, have given him something to think about. There is a world of difference.'

'Arrad, you're a lucky young man,' one of the Councillors observed.

'Thank you sir, I think I am,' Arrad replied politely.

A Councillor raised his hand.

'Councillor Dendric?'

'Dendric, Senior of the Hunters,' the man began formally. 'I might be able to help George Green and Arrad find more bees. The hunters come across them from time to time and we give them a wide berth, as we do whenever we find a wasp nest. Anyone who has been stung as often as I have can tell you why but if George Green can really catch them I'll go with the hunters and take him and Arrad to two nests that I know about that are a bit off the beaten track but not too far from the one where Arrad got stung and when we've done that we'll find urgent business a long way off. I'll ask around and see if any hunters know of more nests but I've had enough stings to last me for a lifetime.'

George waited until a polite ripple of laughter died away before he voiced his thanks.

'Now I would like the Council to hear my request,' George said seriously. 'I have said I want to play as large a part as I can in the affairs of the Lake. So would Arrad, and I know that is important to him. Councillors, Ladies and Gentlemen of the Lake, in a few days the Dads and Lads Games will begin, an important event that has brought many who are present at this meeting from a considerable distance.

'However, I cannot take part, I have no Lad. Neither can Arrad, he has no Dad. Therefore I ask that Hilary Green and I formally adopt Arrad as a son of our own, and that as father and son we may both enter ourselves for the Games. That is my request.'

There was a collective gasp from his audience. Atta gestured for silence.

'Your case is well made, George Green. The Council of Seniors will decide. Alfrid, Vocca, Hilary, it is my decision that your depositions need not be heard. A show of hands,' he demanded.

Every Member except one signalled agreement.

'One objection,' Atta noted. 'Councillor Meglen.'

'Not an objection,' the Councillor denied, 'but before I cast my vote I want to know more. George Green,' she asked, 'how long is this arrangement to last? Is it to end when the Games end?'

'Hmm. A good question Councillor, and one that I had not thought to ask. George Green, how do you reply?'

'It will not end with the end of the Games,' George declared firmly, 'nor will it end when I return to my own time. I would like Arrad to know that although we will not meet again he has a mother and a father somewhere in time, parents who think of him every day. I want Arrad to know that, and I want the Lake to know it too. That is my answer.'

'It was well spoken.' Atta commended him.

Councillor Meglen agreed.

'Then may I propose that George and Hilary be granted the Freedom of the Lake? Freedom that will not end with their return to their own time. I ask this to acknowledge their committal to the affairs of the Lake.'

'Seconded! Motion carried!' Every Member yelled enthusiastically.

It was a long time before order was restored.

'Calling for a show of hands would be superfluous. I wish all Council decisions could be made as quickly,' Atta commented. 'I hardly need to declare that George Green and Hilary Green are granted the Freedom of the Lake.'

Pleasure was written all over his face.

'Alfrid and Vocca will take their places with the Council. Hilary Green will join George and Arrad. Arrad Green, you are recognised as the son of George Green and you may both take part in the games.'

'Two names!' Arrad gasped in surprise. 'But I'm not important.'

'It is the custom in George Green's time I am informed, and I have never heard you called unimportant. On the Lake nobody is unimportant!'

***

Ears ringing with the cries of well-wishers, George, Hilary, and Arrad Green left the arena, Arrad skipping with joy and singing, 'Arrad Green, Arrad Green, my name is Arrad Green,' over and over.

'That went well,' Vocca the Fisherman said from behind them as he hurried to catch up, 'and I can stop being Councillor for a while, I'm glad to say. I'd better warn Cartiwiss not to expect to sleep tonight, young Arrad will be singing until dawn.'

'Thanks for your coaching in the correct procedures, and Alfrid's too,' Hilary replied, 'I'm glad I wasn't asked to speak, my mouth was so dry.'

Vocca chuckled.

'That never goes away.'

Councillor Meglen sought out some people she knew. Clutched firmly in her hand was George Green's sketch of the torch of knowledge. She had a use for it.

Interlude

'I wonder what George Green is doing right now,' Copper said as the group that had made their farewells to Alfrid and his family waited for the gate to re-open and admit George and Hilary to their own time.

'Tell me when now is,' Clive Bowden replied, 'and I might be able to guess.'

'You know what I mean,' Copper scolded him.

'Sure do. The English language isn't adapted to handle the when's and where's of time travel,' Clive replied cheerfully.

'I'd think twice about guessing anything about George Green,' Edwin Mallory said, 'I've known him all my life and the one thing I can say for certain is that whatever he's doing he's going at it full blast, George has never been one to do anything by halves. I'd take bets that he'll surprise us all in a few minutes when he comes back.'

'That's a bet I won't take, I know him pretty well myself. But I'll wager he'll come back with a grin on his face that only surgery will shift!'

Chapter 27

The night had been a late one for everybody but work still needed doing and Alfrid had taken several orders for shoes that he wanted to start on. Some orders were placed by people who lived some distance away and Alfrid wanted them to be ready before they had to depart. At the very least he wanted to be able to give a trial fitting to each customer. He still had not decided how to put his mark on his work. He was not the only shoemaker on the Lake but his position as the Senior among them was undisputed and his shoes were always in demand.

George Green was making ready to accompany him to assist with care of his cows. The Herders looked after them well but Alfrid tried hard to be a good stockman in the way he had been taught by the Vikings.

Not infrequently he marvelled at the way his fortunes had changed when he was at his lowest ebb and he had suddenly been confronted by giants and he thought his death was just was just one breath away. He had never seen anyone or anything that looked as terrifying as Beowulf with his horned helmet and his sword unsheathed, and Freya who carried a double headed axe as lightly as a twig and looked ready to use it.

It was a bewildered man who unexpectedly found himself the owner of a cow and calf, and some of Tarn's men who had thought to ambush him lay dead in the grass. He was never sure, but he sometimes wondered if that was the time when he dared to think that Tarn might be beaten.

His reverie was shattered when Arrad arrived at the run, shouting, 'Dad! Dad!'

It was a cry of joy.

George appeared, beaming all over his face.

'Hello Son! Good morning!' George boomed as Hilary came out of doors, closely followed be Eathl carrying Elfrey. Small Alfrid was not far behind.

'I'm in the Games!' Arrad exclaimed to small Alfrid.

'I can run faster than you can,' small Alfrid bragged.

Arrad was ready for him.

'And I can skip stones on the Lake better than you,' he replied, 'and I nearly always hit the post.'

Watching the boys scamper off, followed at a more leisurely pace by Alfrid and George, Eathl remarked, 'You can already see the difference in Arrad. It's about time he had a new interest and if I'm any judge George has solved the problem of what he's going to do with his life.'

'It's not doing George any harm either,' Hilary replied. 'They're good for each other and it does mean that George can be well and truly involved with the affairs of the Lake, which is exactly what he wanted.'

'And it gives the Lake a chance to observe the two of you. Or perhaps I should say the three of you now,' Eathl said shrewdly.

***

As George remarked to Hilary that evening, he was not often lost for words but just for once he really didn't know what to say.

A cry from Alfrid saved him.

'Well George, what do you think?'

Collecting his thoughts George replied, 'I reckon the hive is ready for the bees as soon as we get a few fine days. Two days without rain ought to be enough for the bees to swarm. Maybe only one. I mean to have a chat with Atta as soon as I can because we don't want to miss the swarming, do we Arrad?'

'We don't, and I still have to learn how to catch them but my dad's going to show me,' Arrad told Alfrid confidently.

Arrad and small Alfrid raced away while George and Alfrid tidied the collection of branches and brambles that the ladies had collected, leaving plenty of space for George and Arrad to do their work.

'I haven't thanked anyone for lending us this space in the field,' George said as they walked away and Alfrid rubbed a scratch on his hand where a bramble had caught him.

'It's a small enough space but I'll speak to the Council about giving Arrad a plot of his own. As I understand it he'll need more than one plot if he can manage to catch more swarms,' Alfrid replied.

'The plot you've loaned us is big enough for more than one hive but I'm looking ahead a few years Alfrid. I'm going to make a few more hives as fast as I can. They won't be much more than wooden boxes but that will be enough. I want to lay the foundations of something that will keep the Lake supplied with honey for years to come. My dream for Arrad is for him to keep one or two hives in every village around the Lake, and that's a lot of villages. In addition to that I'd like to set up a hive or two close by Gwenve's infirmary to produce honey for medical use. It's a big ambition Alfrid, but I really believe Arrad is up to it. If I can leave the Lake knowing that I have secured a future for Arrad and a regular and reliable supply of honey for the Lake I shall know that I have done something useful with my time. As a Freeman of the Lake I shall have made my contribution.'

Interlude

It's incredible! Using mental arithmetic Arrad worked out how much straw is required to build a straw hive of a given height and diameter!

He knows the value of pi. Whether he uses 22/7 or 1.142 I don't know but I wouldn't be surprised to learn that he uses both in the same calculation. (I wonder how many decimal places figure in his calculations?).

He understands calculus (or a form of calculus) and uses it as another tool for performing mental arithmetic. Figure it out; the hive is conical, more or less, but the framework it is built around is made from bent sticks and straight ones and the value of the curve is not constant. I could have made a framework that is of course, but in any event the hive is a three dimentional artifice and Arrad still handled it!

He assigned a thickness to the rope of straw that winds around the frame. My eyeball measurements tell me that it is about one and a quarter inches in diameter. I have stated that in imperial measurements and why not, since I grew up with them? I could have used the metric system. I think Arrad uses only one system because measurements here seem to be standardised, but I don't know that for certain and I don't know what the units of measurement are. I must (will) make it my business to find out. Which leads me to a correction I must make.

I gave the value of pi in fractions; 22 over 7, and I guess that this is in Arrad's mental armoury. I also gave it the decimal value of 3.142. I've used only three places of decimals but it suffices most of the time. But, and it's a very big but, I have a suspicion that Arrad doesn't use decimals, which is to say base ten, because I do know that the commonly used base unit on the Lake is eight.

Base ten (decimal) mathematics throws up odd numbers very easily and as everybody knows, or should know, expressing 1/3 as a decimal with 100% accuracy is impossible. Base eight however, generates whole numbers and even numbers more readily and with complete accuracy, if a little clumsily sometimes. Reminder; eight bits equals one byte, and computer memories are measured in multiples of bytes.

So, as I have said, base eight is very convenient and, I suspect, no accident. The people of the Lake are using computer technology and they do it mentally. It is a humbling thought.

I can see that I shall have to expand on this and clarify my thinking but now is not the time.

MORNING

After a rather sleepless night spent testing my own ability to perform mental arithmetic I am forced to admit what I knew already; that I can't handle calculus in my head the way Arrad can. I don't even come close. I am not even sure whether Merlin can. I know that Wint has said that Merlin is the last pupil of a school that had lost a lot of knowledge that was familiar to the Old People. Merlin uses a pencil and paper the same as I do, except that he is a far better mathematician than I am.

Probably the best mathematician I know is Brian Gleaves. Brian is a natural born engineer who has, as he puts it, a sort of knack for figures. I know he won't mind me saying that his education during his school years was limited, but in that one subject he shone. (The limits were those of his teachers, not Brian. I happen to know that he is learning Latin along with Copper Beach, somewhat to his own surprise. Rumour has it that he is a very good pupil).

At this point I can hear voices from the future screaming at me to say something about the counting song. Before Hilary and I left our own time (our own now) we had instructions from everybody to discover all we could about the counting song and so yesterday I asked Arrad about it when he performed his mental gymnastics.

I did not understand a word he said.

Not a single word.

I don't mean his knowledge of mathematics is way above my head, although I'm sure it is. I mean that he sounded as if he was reciting meaningless garbled noises. When the news about Merlin and everybody else with extended lifespans leaks out as it is intended it should, we shall rightly be castigated for not asking Alfrid and Eathl and even small Alfrid to explain the counting song to us when they visited our own time or as I prefer to think of it, in our now.

269

With the benefit of hindsight it is easy to say what we ought to have done, but I am as sure as I can be that the results would have been the same. I shall make a point of talking to them in this now but I expect the outcome to be no different from my experience with Arrad.

Chapter 28

As he closed the pages of his journal George had the thought that Arrad might have navigated his way to the Lake by using mathematics. He had heard a little about the arduous journey the youngster had made and it occurred to him that his instructions as to how to reach his destination might have been given to him in the form or angles and distances. It was an impressive piece of navigation.

Let's see, George thought, the time taken for any journey is equal to the distance multiplied by the speed, or rate of travel. Arrad's journey must have been broken down into stages, probably the distance he could be expected to cover in a day. Hmm, that would mean that he had to recalculate his trip every time he went round a bend. I couldn't do that but I suspect Arrad can.

The stones probably helped. Arrad couldn't use them to communicate because they don't work any more but my guess is that they can be used as fixed points for triangulation, which when all is said and done was the method or drawing the Ordnance Survey maps of the British Isles in the first place. Imagine carrying sines, cosines, and tangents, in your head and mentally calculating speed, angles, and distances, as you travel. I can't. Arrad can. It beggars belief.

But to have as a pupil a boy who is far cleverer than myself! Wonderful! Brilliant! Marvellous! And what a privilege!

'Dad! Dad! What are we going to do today dad?'

George's updating of his journal was brought to an end by Arrad's eagerness to get busy at whatever George had in mind for the day.

'Collect some wood and bark and make more homes for any bees we can find. There's more than one way to make a hive and I don't want us to be caught short if Dendric and the hunters find us more bees. After that I thought we might visit the hive,' George replied, feeling the boy's excitement and sharing it.

'I want to check it to make sure it's dry inside. I'm sure it is but if any water is getting in I want to know so we can do something about it. Then I want to smear honey inside it so the bees will smell it and feel at home right from the start. You can do that job.'

'That's why you told me to keep some honey in your box when you showed me how to make smoke so you don't get stung the way I did!' Arrad exclaimed.

George beamed.

'It's no guarantee that you won't get a few stings but it does lessen the odds. The way I see it Arrad, a sting or two is the price you pay for what you take,' he replied. 'Pop the box in my bag with the other stuff. There's a plastic bottle of water in there along with my flask of a hot infusion that Eathl made for us, and something to eat in case we get hungry. The bottle isn't full but I thought we might work up a thirst so I put it in my bag.'

'I don't know about plastic. Is it something for bees?'

George chuckled and removed the bottle from his bag.

'That's plastic. We brought some water with us when we made the journey from the stone when Wint opened the gate for us. We knew everyone was thirsty from the walk to the stone because small Alfrid said so when he came through so we packed plenty of these bottles for the walk back.'

He put the bottle back in the bag.

'Can I carry it?'

'Sure, but the bag is heavy so we'll take turns. Slip it over your shoulders and we'll be on our way.'

Arrad adjusted the straps with care and together they set of, making a leisurely pace but overtaking a group of chattering children.

'Green Man! I know another joke,' Wigstin called out.

George smiled.

'I think it had better wait until another time,' he called back, 'or Gerdin will be on at you again.'

'Gerdin always is,' Wigstin answered.

'Well you ask for it,' Gerdin said severely.

'This is a good joke,' Wigstin said, ignoring the look of exasperation that crossed Gerdin's face.

'What's worse than being chased by a wild boar?' Wigstin asked.

'Being late for school' George suggested.

'No. I've done that.'

'I'm not surprised.'

'Have another guess.'

'Falling off the school raft?'

272

'I've done that too. It's not that.'

'Then I don't know what's worse than being chased by a wild boar. You'd better tell me.'

'Being chased by two wild boars!' Wigstin exclaimed triumphantly. 'Ha! Ha! Ha!'

'And what is worse than being chased by two wild boars?' Gerdin asked him with a look that said Wigstin had pushed his luck far enough.

'I'll tell you, it's being chased by me, and if I reach the raft before you do I'll throw you in the water myself and don't think I won't!'

Wigstin made a bolt for the raft.

Just another day on the Lake.

Engaged in earnest discussion George and Arrad continued on their way.

'Will it rain today do you think?' Arrad asked.

George searched the sky.

'I'm not sure,' he replied, 'but it does look as if it might and I hope it does.'

'Huh? Why?'

'Partly because I want our hive to be thoroughly tested and partly because we want to make sure that we will be ready when the bees swarm so we'll have a better chance of keeping them when we do catch them. What we don't want is to catch them and then lose them if they decide they don't like their new home and fly off somewhere else.'

'How will we know if they decide to stay? I mean, if they decide not to stay we'll know when we look at the hive and find them gone, but how will we know if they are going to stay?'

'That's a good question and well thought out,' George replied, 'and the answer is we wait and see. If they haven't left after, say, ten days to be on the safe side, then we can be confident that we have them for keeps.'

A loud cry startled them.

'Hey there! Hey! I want to talk to you!'

They whirled round. Neither had noticed Atta striding towards them, carrying his staff as he always did. George thought he detected a slight limp, but it was hard to tell. Perhaps Atta needed the support of his staff and perhaps he did not. George was sure that the staff was more than just a walking stick.

'I was hoping to catch you,' Atta gasped as he panted for breath after his hurried pace brought him near.

'Atta, Atta, what's the weather going to be like today?' Arrad demanded impatiently.

'The weather. Hmm. Well. No change for a day or two. It will rain a little but not much.' Atta held his thumb and forefinger close together. 'This much. You won't get a soaking but you won't see the sun either. A warm weather front is coming from the west but it won't make landfall for two days. When it does we'll see the summer again. If I understand correctly your bees won't swarm in the kind of weather we're having at the moment.'

George Green wondered how Atta knew the state of the weather far out in the Atlantic Ocean.

'Atta sir, how do know how much rain will fall. You can't measure it.'

'I'll tell you what, we'll make a rain gauge and you can see for yourself if Atta is right next time we have a good shower, if that suits you Atta,' George said before Atta was able to reply.

Atta took up the challenge.

'I'll be glad to make my forecast. I don't know how your measuring will be made but I will tell you how much rain will fall and we will see if I'm right and if I am it will cost you a small pot of honey when you have some. Arrad, how does that suit you?'

'Very well sir,' Arrad replied politely.

George slipped the bag from Arrad's shoulders and removed the two litre water bottle that had come with him from the future.

'This is easy to cut,' he told Arrad and Atta, 'so to make a rain gauge I'll simply cut it about half way up and then we can measure the depth of the rain that falls into it.'

Atta regarded the plastic bottle.

'Hmm… the bottom is not flat so we'll have to calculate for, oh! No we won't. There's an obvious solution!'

Arrad looked perplexed.

'I can't see how,' he said.

George chuckled.

'The answer is in front of you but you'll have to work it out for yourself,' he said. He added, 'There's no trickery. There really is an easy solution.'

'Your father is giving you the opportunity to experience the pleasure that comes with discovery,' Atta said. 'It is a valuable lesson.'

'Well, I … I will do it. I don't know how but I will do it.' Arrad displayed dogged determination.

George was pleased.

'I was hoping to catch you,' Atta repeated, returning to the reason for his hail. 'I have a message for you George. Work on the new causeway is due to begin in a shortly and the builders have invited you to join them and take some pictures with your picture device and help with the work if you like. The causeway is to be a bridge over a piece of ground that floods during the winter and doesn't ever really dry out. It's hard work and no mistake but it will provide an opportunity to see what goes on. I believe the people in your now are interested in how we go about things. It'll also mean a day or two away from the village but a place has already been made for you to stay with family of one of the builders.'

'I'll jump at the chance,' George declared enthusiastically.

'I'd like to see your new bees nest if I may,' Atta continued. 'Arrad Green, may I tag along with you when you, well I don't know what it is you do but I would like to poke my nose into your business and see what's going on. My curiosity as a scientist has me itching to learn more.'

George noted how Arrad looked pleased when Atta used both his names, and slightly bewildered when Atta directed his questions to him and not George.

'It's called a hive,' Arrad corrected Atta. 'That's the proper word for it and if you come with us now I can tell you all about it and my dad can test my knowledge at the same time and tell me if I go wrong. I've got to make sure I know what to do when dad goes home. Before he goes home, I mean.'

George nodded assent, felling pleased by the way his new foster-son behaved and his new self-assurance.

'I feel sure I'll learn a lot by watching what you do,' Atta commented. As an afterthought he added, 'I can't imagine why there has never been a song of knowledge for people to keep bees and make

275

honey. Because nobody wanted to be stung I suppose. A sting every now and again is one thing but it does seem folly to risk it too often.'

'I agree on one point,' George replied. 'Which reminds me, I've just told Arrad I want to collect a few bits and pieces for another hive, something that will be a bit different from the one we have now. I'll explain everything while we work. I want to make a box out of wood and bark because your bees nest in holes in trees Arrad, and I think we must make them feel at home right from the start. We can see what sort of hive they like best and then you can make more of the same kind. Learn by trial and error and don't be afraid to fail sometimes because finding out what not to do will add to your store of knowledge.'

'Knowledge is valuable. Knowledge sustains,' Atta said to Arrad, echoing the words spoken by Jack Smythe in the far future.

'I'm surprised there are no beekeepers because honey has always been prized. In my own now it's fairly well known that bees have been kept for their honey for thousands of years. I can tell you it gives me a funny feeling to think I might be about to change the course of history,' George continued.

As the trio moved on he continued, 'I nearly said I haven't altered the course of history half as much as Beowulf did but I'm more inclined to believe the real culprit is Wint.'

'I wouldn't be surprised, the knowing ones can do things that most people don't even know how to think about,' Atta replied, 'but your argument falls down because you told me yourself that Wint had nothing to do with choosing who would come from your now to ours.'

'I know. It's as big a riddle as knowing how we can understand each other's speech. We shouldn't be able to but I have a theory that might go some way to explaining it. It has been speculated that Wint comes from a different branch of the human race from ours.'

'Eathl mentioned that to me. Go on.'

'His kind know how to travel from one now to another; the discovery might have been accidental or it might not. I have imagined that his kind and our kind live side by side in every age, unknown to us but not to them. That would account for Wint knowing my language and yours through contact with his own kind in my time and your time. I know that seems improbable but it is a working theory. I then think that when I stepped through the gate from my time to yours the knowledge was somehow put into my mind by way of some form of hypnotism. I wouldn't have thought that possible but there's no denying that Gwenve could have put anything she wanted in my mind when she knocked me out. I remember Nerthi the healer telling me that Tarn was able to put in such a strong suggestion that any prisoners died before they could say anything even when it was obvious they were trying,' George said seriously.

'Hmm, I can see the possibility. Let's sleep on it; we're not likely to find an answer. I've a feeling you were going to tell me something about bees.'

'I was. I mean, I am,' George confirmed Atta's guess. 'Arrad won't be stung anything like as much as you seem to think he is. Besides, there's good reason to believe that anyone who does collect a few stings is less likely than most to suffer arthritic joints in later life.'

Atta looked startled.

'Is that a fact? Jeepers, Creepers, if I had only known that when I was Arrad's age!'

Chapter 29

George addressed his attentive audience of one.

'The first thing to know is why bees swarm. They have a good nest but they leave it to go somewhere else. Why?'

'Because the flowers are all used up?' Arrad suggested.

'Possibly but not likely. The real reason is to set up a new hive. Bees usually swarm in the spring but swarming can happen all through the summer as long as there are flowers, and you don't have to look far to see plenty of flowers all around us.'

'I can see that,' Arrad replied, 'and that makes this a good place for bees doesn't it? I sort of worked that out.'

'You got it right; this is a good place. The next question is why they should want to find a new home, and the answer to that is to have more colonies of bees. A colony is the name for a nest of bees. Or a hive of bees. What we are going to do is make sure the new colony is where we want it to be so you will be able to collect your honey without having to search for a colony that could be anywhere. Eventually we want you to have more than one hive. Perhaps twenty or more.'

Arrad spread his fingers.

'Two eights and half an eight,' George said helpfully.

'I don't know your counting song,' Arrad confessed.

'I don't know yours either but we can get along.'

Arrad agreed.

'A swarm happens when the old queen of the colony leaves the hive with about half the worker bees. Often it's more than half and I think the reason for that is because some bees might be lost along the way,' George continued.

'But I thought bees always know where they are,' Arrad objected.

George approved of Arrad's objection.

'Very good, but I have reasons for thinking the way I do. Swarming happens in three stages. First the old queen leaves the hive with her workers. Second, they cluster somewhere not too far away while a few bees search for a place for new nest. Third, the swarm flies off to the place they have found. That seems simple enough but the clustering stage when their new home is being found can last for up to three days and that is as long as the bees can last before they start to die off. Three days is an unusually long time but it can happen that way and so that's why I think more bees leave than stay behind,' he explained.

'I can see that makes sense,' Arrad agreed.

The boy mulled over all that he knew about bees and came to the conclusion that something was wrong.

'Dad, you said the queen bee leaves the nest when the bees swarm but that means there isn't a queen in the old nest and if there isn't a queen bee all the other bees die and there won't be any new ones because the queen isn't there to lay eggs. I'm sure you're right but it doesn't seem right to me,' Arrad said hesitantly.

'I did say that,' George agreed, 'but what I haven't said yet is that sometimes the worker bees make larger cells called queen cups. They do that all the time and when the queen is going to leave she lays eggs into them and when that is done she leaves the hive and the bees swarm. The eggs she laid in the queen cups become new queens and so the hive has a new queen after all.'

'That's all right then and so I will have one old nest and one new one. Two nests and twice as much honey!' Arrad said with mounting excitement.

'If all goes well, and in due course you will have as many hives as you can handle but a word of warning; in my now we say don't count your chickens before they are hatched. There are no chickens here but we can say don't count your honey until you have got it. Don't worry though, I'm getting you off to the best possible start I can manage.'

'I think you must be. I already know more about bees that anyone else, even Atta,' the boy said seriously.

This was the moment that George Green later described as one of the worst moments of his life. He had taken it upon himself to raise the hopes of a young boy and endeavour to set him up in a new and prosperous path in his life and he had precious little time and no equipment to do even half of what he thought he ought to do to give Arrad a fighting chance of making a success of it.

Was his legacy to be failure? George didn't want to think about that; to face the fact that he might be the cause of a young boy's failed ambition. He put the unpleasant thought to one side and returned to the subject of acquiring bees.

'There is another way to set up a new colony in a new hive and I was coming to that. Just now I mentioned the queen cups. Can you remember what they are?' He asked.

'They are bigger than the other cells and the eggs that are laid in them are the ones that will be the new queens,' Arrad replied promptly.

'That's right, and if we can find another nest and it has queen cups that have been capped we can remove some and put them in a new hive where they will hatch. There's a bit more to it than that but I think we can manage,' George said.

George drew pictures in his notebook to show what queen cups looked like and he drew life sized pictures of the queen and worker bees so that Arrad would be able to identify the queen of any swarm that he captured. His intention was to make a handbook of bee keeping in pictures, showing what went on in the hives, how to capture swarms, how big his hives should be and the best places to put them, and anything else he could think of.

The lesson continued.

Interlude

These jottings are for the vicar to add to his collection of fables, conjectures, idiotic theories, et cetera. This theory (no let's not call it a theory, let's just call it a silly idea, but an idea that has shaken me to the core). Well then, here goes:

Wolf children. Children that for whatever reason have been raised by animals, principally wolves. Rome is said to have been founded by Romulus who, along with his twin brother Remus, was raised by wolves. There is a statue in Rome that... well, ask Julia. I'm straying from my point. Avoiding it perhaps. Professor Land might want to comment.

Wolf children then. It seems from what little I know that the human ability to communicate with other humans with speech, facial expressions, actions, body language, and so on is hardwired into our brains; it is automatic, a function of being human. As with my heartbeat, I need it but I do not need to think about it to make it happen.

My point is though, and the wolf children are a perfect example, that the teaching of language and other forms of communication is done unconsciously by parents, and it must be started when their children are babies and continued through infancy in order for the ability to develop fully. It must be done at these stages because if it is not the individual never acquires the ability to communicate with other humans. Or perhaps can only acquire it imperfectly. (Another poser for Professor Land).

I had begun to think of the Lake People as wolf children because it seemed to me that they had lost, or not been taught, a vast body of knowledge. The standing stones offer a perfect example. Nobody seems to care about them, especially the younger ones. Trade and industry and all the old Songs of Knowledge are being reworked as many old skills are being rediscovered, skills and arts that had, to put it bluntly, been allowed to stagnate. I realised that this old knowledge has in fact been retained and with the end of the era of the standing stones it is re-emerging. My newly adopted son Arrad has brought this home to me quite forcefully. His knowledge of mathematics is almost without parallel in my own particular now, but not in his. At the time I failed to see the significance of this but I have now reached the conclusion that the wolf child phenomenon applies.

But not to the Lake People.

The Lake People can still use the old knowledge as Arrad did but they seem to have turned their backs on it so that today, (their today) they are consciously developing new methods, new working practices, technology, metals for example, social science/dynamics and so on. Whatever they undertake they are keen to find and explore new ways of doing things and they are not afraid to make mistakes. I thought them to be wolf children who had not been taught the things of the past. I thought there were wolf children and I still think there are but the Lake people are not the wolf children I thought I had identified.

It isn't them. It's us.

We are the ones who have never been taught the old technology, the physical and social sciences of pre-history. We can't even imagine what their communications systems were like and we never will. It is something we should have learned as infants and now it's too late. We are simply not equipped to understand.

Our best and perhaps our only hope is to re-learn it by trial and error, never knowing when we are exploring blind alleys, as we certainly will do, and test our results rigorously at every step of the way. Perhaps by doing this over many generations we may at last cease to be wolf children and be fully developed humans once again.

And there you have it vicar.

Crazy, crackpot, preposterous, and sheer bone-headed stupidity. Perhaps.

Addendum. The Lake People use a system of counting in multiples of eight. Very logical, modern computers are similar. I wonder if we had continued to ignore our thumbs when we count we might have had computers a long time before we actually did. How did their counting system develop? Did they use the ten finger decimal system and abandon it in favour of base eight? Was the abandonment deliberate? Over to you vicar. Interesting problem isn't it? Brian Gleaves is a whiz at figures. Let's ask his opinion.

Second Addendum. I set my new son Arrad the problem of making a rain gauge from a two litre plastic bottle. The base of these bottles is not flat; I suppose knobbly is a good description. After a false start

Atta spotted a solution to the problem. Arrad took the bottle home and somewhen during the night he figured it out. It's simple; nobody ever said you have to start with an empty bottle so all that needs to be done is fill it part way and begin to measure rainfall from the level you have filled it to. I intend to set the same problem to the new pupils when the autumn term begins.

Note to Clive Bowden, penned a few days after the foregoing nonsense; social stratification does exist but only just, and everyone on the Lake rates his or her worth as about the same as anyone else's. Atta is the principal member of the Council of Seniors but that only means that he is first among equals. As far as I can tell there is no official leader and (how I envy them!) there is no need of one.

I imagine that if Alfrid were approached by anyone who declared that he wanted to be king the reply would be 'Fine, you're king, now go away and be king somewhere else, I'm busy.' Atta would be more likely to crack his head with his staff, while Dendric would put a spear through him, but only if one of the other hunters didn't beat him to it.

One last thing Clive, I expected to find each community living in a small huddle of huts all crammed into a very small area. It transpires that the Lake is home to many communities (villages) and a lot of those are quite small but there is none of the huddling that I expected. Every house has various numbers of occupants and extended families are common, and each house is surrounded by plenty of open space which is used for play and keeping a few domestic animals, mostly goats and pigs and, more rarely, sheep, and for cultivating herbs and flowers. The animals are fenced in of course and not everybody keeps them. I suspect that the flowers are a result of Freya's passion for blossoms. I'll ask around.

The Lake also takes pride in its flags. Beowulf imported the idea of flags, as we know from Brother Scribe's account of the Viking's exploits on the Lake, and the flags are flown all the time. Anybody can have a flag of whatever design they choose, and many people have chosen to indicate their professions on their flags. It is the custom that when people spend a few days in another village their flag goes with them and announces the presence of a visitor. It seems an agreeable custom to me, and often the visitor brings some wares for trade so the flag lets everyone know there is a cloth maker or a potter with goods for sale. The tradespeople swap knowledge and techniques with each other as well, which in turn leads to development of goods. In sum, I would call the Lake a high-class residential area. Very high-class and populated by very high-class people.

Let it not be thought that I am looking through rose-tinted spectacles. There is still work that is hard, unpleasant, and for want of a better way of putting it, the Nimby factor kicks in. Not In My Back Yard. But waste disposal is a dirty smelly business and somebody must do it. My point is that it does get done and nobody, but nobody, is exempt. You helped make it, you help clear up. Do as you would be done by, and the reverse of the coin, be done by as you did.

When Alfrid makes the glue he needs for shoe-making he takes note of the wind direction and does his work at some distance from the houses. I have helped him, or observed him to be more precise, and the stench would etch glass. As for tanning hides to make leather, the less said the better. It is carried out as far as possible from the domestic centres. I think it could safely be called an industrial estate.

I must endeavour to knock these notes into shape at a later date. I had cherished the thought that as a scientist I could put my ideas down on paper in a cogent and logical manner, and in the physical sciences I hope I still can. The social sciences present me with a different class of problems that I regret I am ill-equipped to handle with the precision they deserve.

Chapter 30

The sound of somebody running on the path caused George to stop and turn round. Atta running? After the complaints he made about his knee joints? Well, it had to be seen to be believed but the evidence was plain. Atta slowed and stopped to a walk and adjusted the bag that he had slung over his shoulder.

'On your way to look at the bees?' Atta guessed. 'I wouldn't be surprised if they swarm any time now. Don't get me wrong, I know very little about them. Most people look on them as flying pests that are only useful for their honey if anyone is foolish enough to chance being stung all over. Having said that my guess is that same time between noon today and late tomorrow afternoon they will start to look for a new home.'

George agreed.

'I would have like Arrad to come along this morning but he wants to finish off a few jobs he had promised to do before I came along and spoiled his plans,' he replied.

'He's none the worse for that,' Atta declared positively. 'If anyone needed a new direction Arrad is that person. Has he found the solution to the rain gauge problem?'

'He has. You should have seen the look on his face when he told me.'

'He got a taste of what it is to feel the pleasure of discovery.'

Atta skipped a few paces and used his staff to take a swipe at a weed that had sprung upon the edge of the path.

'It's going to be a hot day,' he continued, 'and that's why I'm up early, and I know you've been getting up and about regularly to keep an eye on things as soon as it's light enough to see where you're going.'

'I don't want to miss the swarm. I'm not going to get many chances Atta and I'll never forgive myself if I can't set Arrad up. I've told him everything I can to get him going but there's a big difference between telling and showing,' George said seriously.

'Arrad can be sure of my support whatever happens,' Atta promised.

He pointed to a low bank that had a seat strategically placed to give a good view of the Lake and suggested they stop for a while. He scrambled nimbly up the bank.

'The sun hasn't driven the early morning mist from the Lake yet but it won't be long and by mid-day it will be hot. I was wondering if you have noticed anything?'

Atta glanced sideways at George as he posed the question.

'Apart from the fact that you look very pleased with yourself and you're as chirpy as a cricket to use a phrase from the now that I come from I really haven't noticed anything unusual,' George replied.

Lifting the flap of his bag Atta produced a three cornered hat and perched it on his head. George's jaw dropped.

'There, I've got a hat like the one you and Alfrid wear. Since the last time we talked I've had a visitor and this hat has something to do with it.'

'Wint!' George exclaimed.

'Correct. I never know when he will turn up but now and again we spend an evening in my house. We both enjoy a fine wine and I smoke my pipe and we talk about anything and everything. Naturally he is interested in you and Hilary and the attitude of the People of the Lake towards you and how you are adapting to a way of life that is outside anything you have ever known. I told him about you and young Arrad and your plan to see that the Lake has a ready and reliable supply of honey from now on. We have always had honey but it's never been a proper business. Do you think my new hat suits me?'

'As much as mine suits me. I don't wear mine at home except when I work in my own garden but here on the Lake it's a different matter. I'm wondering how Wint knew what colour of hat to bring, or was it just chance?'

'Ah, now that's the thing. He didn't. I had to go and make my own choice. I didn't get my hat in the now that you came from but I did get to go to other nows. I went to the country where you were born and while I was there I helped two young boys free their kite from a tree where it was caught on some branches. I asked them what their names were and they said -'

'George Green and Edwin Mallory!' George exclaimed. 'I remember that! It was a simple box kite that we made ourselves and the wind caught it and snagged it in the branches and our efforts to free it might have come to nothing if you hadn't come along. I owe you our belated thanks.'

'I was glad to help.'

'You were dressed in the clothes of our time. Not the clothes you wear on the Lake.'

Atta laughed.

'I didn't want to be conspicuous!' Atta declared with a wide smile. 'Years later I saw you again; in Bath this time. I think the year was nineteen ninety-five but I can't say for certain. You were waiting for Hilary at the corner of the North Bridge and you leaned on the parapet and watched two children at play in the gardens below. They had a piece of string about two metres long by your measuring. I wasn't able to see whether they were holding it or if they had tied their wrists together but they were running up and down and having the time of their lives. A woman told them to stop it and I need hardly say they took no notice!'

George thought back.

'A little black boy and a white girl. No, that's wrong; she was black and he... no, I can't remember which was which. I don't suppose it matters.'

'It didn't matter to them so why should it matter to anyone else? Then Hilary came along and you watched them together for a moment before you left.'

'You might have introduced yourself.'

'Hello George and Hilary. I'm Atta and I've arrived from five thousand years ago. How would that have gone down?'

'Like the proverbial lead balloon.'

Both men laughed as they imagined the improbable scene.

'I'll ask Hilary whether she remembers those children,' George declared. 'I wonder what happened to them and where they are?'

'It's an interesting thought. Intriguing.'

Atta paused for a while.

'It didn't end there. If I have a spring in my step it's because Matron Patti put new knees in me. Of course she doesn't know she's going to do that so...'

Atta tapped the side of his nose significantly.

'Keep it to myself. You bet I will!'

George wondered how far into the future that must have been.

'As it happens she had been expecting me for some time but I think you should not let on,' Atta said.

'You're full of surprises and I imagine Wint is at the bottom of it but I'll keep your secret.'

'How I would like to watch Gwenve's face when she finds out,' Atta said gleefully. 'I promised her my old bones when I'm done with them so she and the healers can learn from them. It will be the best prank I ever played. If only I could see it!'

Becoming serious again he said, 'It didn't end there George. I've brought back one or two things as well as my new hat.'

'Am I permitted to ask questions?' George enquired.

'Not at this stage. I can see it's going to take you a few minutes to catch your breath,' Atta added.

'Minutes? Since when did you mark time in minutes?'

'I had to move with the times, as Merlin often told me. I swear George, he's worse than that little pest Wigstin when he starts telling jokes!'

'I… I don't know what to say,' George croaked.

The two men sat in silence for a long while; each man immersed in his own thoughts.

The rising sun slowly burned away the early morning mist that rose from the surface of the Lake and ripples of water sparkled in the sunlight. Atta adjusted his new hat to shade his eyes and the sound of a distant horn signalled the departure of the school raft from its overnight moorings.

'No need for me to hurry; that only means the raft has cast off and it has to make a pick up before it is our turn, and from here we shall see it in plenty of time for me to walk to the jetty.'

'I'm still getting to grips with the horn blowing,' George admitted. 'Sometimes I can tell which horn is being blown but I'm never sure what the message is. Sometimes the horn is blown once, sometimes twice, and sometimes three times and it can be one long blow and two short ones or some other combination. The single blast we heard when the raft cast off was an alert signal to let people know the school raft is coming. Some children have a tendency to drag their feet just as I did when I was a boy. Then there is a single short blast that is used between rafts as a warning. I can make your writing for that.'

George Greens mouth hung open as Atta wrote the words long and short in his notebook.

'There,' Atta beamed. 'I saw something of your writing about five thousand years from now and I managed to grasp it quite easily when Angela Collins taught me how to read and write. I think you know her,' he ended with a grin that stretched from ear to ear.

'Jeepers Creepers and Odin's Ghost!' George exclaimed.

'I need hardly say that the same applies to Angela as to Matron Patti. They probably wouldn't believe you anyhow but I don't think it would be right to tell them anything.'

'I couldn't agree more,' George croaked.

'Those other things that I mentioned that I brought with me to give to you are going to have to wait until the Games are over. One thing I will say is that something I learned was the most wonderful surprise I have ever had. It was recorded and some pictures were made. They will hang on my wall for me to see and remind me of, shall we say somebody I met while I was away.'

'A small clue?' George hinted.

'No clue,' Atta replied firmly, 'but I do want you and Hilary to see them when the Games are over and I happen to know you didn't mention them to anyone and for that I give you my thanks.'

He drew in a deep breath and said slowly, 'It is a matter of no little importance. The person I insisted that I do tell you. And for the time being I insist that the matter is closed.'

'Very well.'

Returning to the subject of horn blowing George said, 'We used to send messages by the Morse Code which was a series of dots and dashes that could be used to put words together. In the same way you can blow any amount of combinations on the horn and anyone who knows their meaning can understand the message.'

'You catch on fast,' Atta said warmly. 'The children learn the Song of Knowledge for that in school. It takes a while but they get there eventually, and speaking of getting there it's time to make a move. Actually,' he added, 'although there are many ways to blow the horns to send messages most people forget them as soon as they learn them and only ever use a few.'

A short stroll led to a fork in the path.

'I go this way and you go that way and if you run for it you might miss Wigstin and his jokes,' Atta said wryly.

It was too late.

'Green Man! Green Man! I know another joke!' Wigstin shouted as soon as he saw them.

George was ready for him.

'It's my turn,' he said. He showed Wigstin his clenched fist.

'Have you ever noticed that you can never see these?' He asked and when Wigstin bent over for a closer look he slowly uncurled his fingers and showed an empty palm.

'I can't see anything. Oh! That's a good one! I must tell it to Lerghwil. Ha! Ha! Ha!'

'I hope he throws you in the water,' his sister Gerdin told him.

Wigstin scampered off.

'That joke will go round the Lake before two days are out,' Atta declared, 'and I'd best be on my way. If Lerghwil does throw Wigstin in the water I want to be there to see it!'

George strode off with his head in a whirl. He had almost forgotten the purpose of his walk but he had not far to go and he knew he was close when he heard the hum of bees. His approach was slow and cautious, then he suddenly turned and ran. The queen had left the nest and swarming had begun.

George was out of breath by the time he reached the village.

'Swarming,' he gasped to a passing villager who took his meaning at once.

'Catch your breath,' he advised. 'Leave it to me to fetch young Arrad and all his equipment; it's no bother, I was on my way to collect the reeds that should have been left for me at the jetty and they'll still be there. It's no problem.'

Panting heavily George sank down on the grass and clutched his side. He nodded weakly as the man departed.

He was still puffing when Arrad came running with the things he needed. It was not much; a box with a hinged lid that he had made to place the swarm into, a piece of cloth to cover it while the bees were being carried to their new home, a sharp stone knife, a small hatchet that George hoped he would not need, and the small box of honey that he had kept when George showed him how to waft smoke into the hive when he collected his honey.

Excitement showed all over his face.

'I didn't need to run all the way,' George said when he had recovered his breath. Arrad had been carrying firewood to one of the houses when George arrived but that could wait. Arrad had collected the things they would need and the pair were making their way to the swarm.

'I didn't know when the swarming started and I thought it would be later rather than sooner. I don't know where the bees will cluster and if we get there in time we won't have to go looking for them. We usually wouldn't have to go far but you never know for sure. Actually there is a time honoured way to get a swarm to cluster but I never got round to mentioning it.'

Arrad looked surprised.

'I know you can't just catch them but I can't see how anyone could stop them buzzing around,' he said.

'It's easy when you know how. The thing is, the swarm needs to be able to hear the queen when they are all flying around and if they can't hear her they settle so what you need to do is make a noise. The way people have done it for ages is to bang a metal tray but metal trays are in short supply in this now. Banging a drum would do just as well. Anything would do if it stops the bees hearing the queen.'

'I could do that Dad, I know I could. Would a whistle do? Vocca and Cartiwiss had whistles when Beowulf and Freya and Alfrid fought the Battle of the Lake. That was before I came here but they told me all about it. I can ask them to show me how to make a whistle,' Arrad said enthusiastically.

George thought about it.

'I think that would do nicely. I'll show you what a football fan's rattle looks like and at some time we can put one together. If the whistle doesn't work the rattle surely will.'

'We're in luck,' he said a little later. 'They've settled on a branch that's low enough to reach out and touch.'

'I know what to do Dad. I have to do it on my own and you can see if I go wrong but I don't think I will if I do what you told me'

'All right. I'll stand back.'

Time to put it to the test.

Arrad held his box beneath the swarm and with trembling hands he swept the swarm slowly and carefully into it. He placed it on the ground and closed the lid.

'Whew! They are heavier than I expected but I didn't get stung and I'm sure I saw the queen because one bee is much bigger than the others so that must be the one. I was a bit nervous but I remembered everything you told me and now I have a swarm of bees. I have a swarm of bees!'

Arrad could hardly contain himself.

He was still hopping with excitement when he introduced his bees to their new home. George was able to see the queen for himself.

'There. I've smeared some honey inside the hive like you said so they feel at home. Now we have to wait for a while before we know they won't go somewhere else don't we? Eight days and two more days.'

'That should do it. In my now we say don't count your chickens before they hatch. I told you that once before.'

'Vocca says don't count your catch before you land your fish. That means the same thing doesn't it?'

'Vocca is a wise man.'

'Dad?'

'Yes?'

'That time when I kicked you. You were never going to kick me back were you?'

George smiled.

'No, I never was.'

'I haven't kicked anyone since then and I never will again,' Arrad promised.

'That's the spirit.'

Father and son regarded their handiwork for a while and then retreated, satisfied with what they had accomplished.

Interlude

Two motionless figures watched and enjoyed the play of light as the setting sun sank slowly on a warm and windless evening.

'I shall miss this,' one remarked in a strange high-pitched voice, 'I will never see it again. Nothing works the way it did and our endeavour must be to preserve what we can and pass our knowledge to those who come after us.'

'Not all the knowledge,' his companion suggested.

The first speaker shrugged his shoulders.

'Many things will be hidden but we shall leave hints here and there and those hints will become the stuff of legend, believed by some and mocked by others. It is necessary. Much will be dismissed as fantasy and ridiculed but the one tiny spark of knowledge that reaches the right minds will suffice. It will inspire just a few to search for what was, what is, and what might be. It will take a long time.'

'Was it successful?'

'To a degree.'

The speakers seemed to have no concept of the passage of time, or perhaps they had the knowledge but not the words to describe it.

'They set their knowledge down in words for anyone to read but they have preferred to remain hidden, a wise precaution. The seek contact but only from such men and women who are able to find them. They will release more information as and when they find it.'

'I would like to know what from their writing takes.'

The first speaker, by far the smaller of the two, drew something from his rich dark blue coat.

'It is here. They have put a picture on the front of the work, a picture of water that has spilled out of a passage and into a pool that will be built many years from now. The corner of the pool that you can see is the place where the water comes in. The water is hot. It will be channelled by the builders for their own use for bathing and other purposes. The building behind it was built centuries later. The people who built called themselves Romans. Their work has lasted for centuries as they will count time. One century was ten years multiplied by ten. Their way of counting was strange. As strange as their writing.'

His listener took the book he was offered and regarded the picture.

'What are those marks?'

'That is a piece of their writing. There is more inside.'

The writing was given a cursory examination.

'Ugh! Nasty little squiggles.'

'It serves its purpose. In one form or another this way of writing was known throughout the world.'

'I prefer my own writing. To paint or draw a thing is to master it.'

'Your writing is known to your race. Few others will able to interpret it.'

'I would have it no other way.'

The conversation was halted while the speakers observed a marsupial wolf that had emerged to hunt in the cool of the evening. The beast ignored them.

'The sun is nearly set,' the small speaker interrupted the silence. 'I must return soon. I was wondering; will your kind and mine become one again?'

'That remains to be seen and perhaps we shall never know. One day the Guardians of the Rock will know. We are few but we shall endure, I feel certain of that, and we will pass our knowledge on as we always have by word of mouth and pictures drawn on rock and in the sand. There will always be some who can read them and they will be the ones with the wisdom to know what to do when the time comes. Was the person who made this writing that you have shown me an individual of some importance?'

'It was he who collected the information that is contained here and put it into some sort of order. He left a lot out but that will not be entirely his fault, there is much that he does not know, and some of what he does know he chose to conceal. He is aware of his ignorance.'

'Perhaps he will learn.'

'That remains to be seen.'

'Time will tell, as always. Speaking of time, are you intending to show them how to move between one time and another?'

'No more than you are. They will find it in their own good, uh, time. I'm beginning to make bad jokes, a deplorable habit I picked up from one of them. They will find the way themselves and when they do they will realise they have known how for a century or more. What will astonish them is how easy it is.'

'And how unnecessary.'

Chapter 31

'I'd like to know more about the Dads and Lads Games,' George told Atta as they strolled by the shore of the Lake, 'especially now I can take part. I'm looking forward to the day, and as for Arrad, he can hardly wait. The fact still remains that I don't know anything of the events.'

'Arrad's jumping like a grasshopper and telling everyone about it. You and Hilary are doing wonders for him.'

George waved to a passer-by who called to him from the Lake as he drifted by on a small raft.

'I was saying I'd like to know more about the Games. They're important, that I do know but I suspect there is more to them than meets the eye.'

Atta agreed.

'A lot more. It's not exactly the social event of the year but the Games have an important function as well as being an excuse for a little frivolity. To begin with, they are not exclusive to the Lake and the people who live here. It's a get together and a chance to do some trading. It's like this; after the Battle of the Lake it was decision time for some. Whether to stay on the Lake and make their homes here or whether to go back to wherever they came from when Tarn was smashing everything and everyone who stood in his way.'

Atta chuckled.

'The young men complained that all the prettiest girls left the Lake and went somewhere else, and everywhere else they complained that the pretty girls stayed here. And,' he added as an afterthought, 'the girls had their own take on that! Ah George, the folly of youth!'

'We were all young once,' George replied, 'and were we any different?'

'Not one bit,' Atta chuckled again, 'and old as I am I still have an eye for a pretty girl!'

They strolled on, pausing occasionally to look more closely at something.

'The Games serve many purposes,' Atta said, 'just as you guessed. As I said, they are a social event with the chance to see old friends and relatives and make new acquaintances, and many tradesmen will come together and see what's new. Some prefer to guard their secrets and others will demonstrate new techniques. We always set out tables to show off our wares and let visitors show and sell the things they bring with them, and family news is swapped and new additions to the family are showed off.'

'What games are played? I'm playing but I don't know what I'm playing.'

'Hmm, that is something of a predicament. Well, the Games that are played are serious in places and more for entertainment in others. For instance, any youngster who wants to be on a raft must show he can swim, and swim well, so the swimming events require you to be fully clothed except for your shirt or jacket. I seem to remember Beowulf telling me that you swim very well.'

'I'm fairly good for a man of my age,' George admitted, 'but I doubt whether I could beat the younger men.'

'On that score you only have Alfrid the shoemaker to worry about. Most men are competent but Alfrid is good, really good. Small Alfrid is good too, and I'm told he went to the swimming place with his friends in your now. The boy has the wind in his shoes as well, over any distance you like. I forgot to say that Alfrid goes into the water head first but he's the only one who does. Everyone else jumps in and the raft crews insist on that because if you do it right you can keep your head above water, which can be vital if you jump in to rescue somebody. It doesn't happen often because everyone can swim but some of the younger ones might easily be swept away in the current, and in the winter anyone could find themselves in trouble. Can you go in head first?'

'I can and I can do it from any height up to about my own height,' George confirmed.

'Can you really? Then I think Shipmaster Cadric might like to talk to you. I'll point him in your direction when he arrives with families and contestants from other places. Putting that to one side for a spell, I'll talk about the other games. Stone skipping for instance; you get three goes at throwing a stone so it skips at least twice on the water and strikes a pole that will be set up during the next few days. You can find your own stones or get your boy Arrad to collect some for you. I think he would be glad of the task.'

'I think so too,' George agreed.

'Then it's settled. Now then, spear throwing and arrow shooting. Dendric will have given orders to the hunters to watch out for the best lads there. It's a good career for a likely young lad. Then there's coracle paddling. They are usually single person craft and you push off from the bank and paddle round a pair of posts and come back to where you started if you stay afloat long enough and if you don't drift away, and if you do the safety boat comes to the rescue. It's a fun event for the most part because coracles aren't used on the Lake very much and they aren't easy to handle. Most dads and lads go round in circles or capsize or both and everyone has a good laugh. All the same, now and again someone turns out to be a natural born handler and there's no doubt coracles are handy for setting eel traps close to the reeds. I wasn't all that bad myself once but that was about eight eights of years ago and then some. Makes me wonder where the years went.'

George sympathised.

'Not everyone plays every game so you have an element of choice. Most people play the games they are good at and the over-all scores are based on points. The method is complicated but scrupulously fair. One game that anyone can enter is the one where you tie your ankles together and run over a short distance.'

George showed his astonishment.

'We call that the three legged race and we still have that in my own time! Who would have thought it!'

'Tried and tested evidently.'

'We have our own version of the Games in my time. They were started a very long time ago in a country we now call Greece and they were held every four years. They fell into decline but more recently they were brought back to life about a hundred years ago. I can't recall the exact date. It was a custom once for people who were victorious at anything were given a laurel wreath to wear. Awarding a wreath to the victors might actually have begun with the Romans but history is not my strong point. There are no laurel trees on the Lake as far as I know but if I stop and cut a piece from an oak tree I can fashion an oak wreath. We have quite a long history of those. I'll show you what I mean.'

George swiftly cut a small branch and wove an oak wreath which he placed on his head.

'It seems an amusing custom. I might introduce it into the Dads and Lads Games,' Atta commented.

***

George and Arrad had found a shady spot to sit and eat their packed lunch of coarse bread and meat that Eathl had prepared neatly, wrapping it in leaves to keep it fresh. George thought they were beech leaves but admitted his ignorance. He poured hot drinks from his flask and sniffed the brew appreciatively before taking a small sip.

'I don't know what went into this except that it has honey as a sweetener. What do you think?' He asked Arad.

Arad repeated George's performance.

'Mint,' he announced confidently,' and elder flowers that were dried and put away last year. There's a song for that. I think dried apples as well and perhaps other things.'

'Whatever it is it tastes delicious. You know Arad, in my time this kind of infusion has only become popular during the last, oh, twenty years or thereabouts, but Eathl could teach us a thing or two any day. Not just Eathl either, I've had these drinks given to me by lots of other people. Every drink has been different and each one has been a new experience. A very good experience I might add.'

'I've been told the Vikings liked these drinks a lot, hot or cold. I wish I had been here when they were here but I wasn't. Were they really as big as people say they were?'

George smiled indulgently at his new son.

'Every bit as big,' he confirmed, 'and it was all bone and muscle, not to mention brain. Beowulf and Freya were intelligent as well as big. They understood very well the use of axe and sword and they were fearless too.'

'Vocca says they were like the eagles that know that everything they see belongs to them and they were willing to face certain death to claim it and hold it.'

George laughed but quickly became serious.

'Does he now? Well, Vocca is right about that. The Vikings came from a race of warriors and death was neither sought nor avoided when they went to war. It was just another possible outcome but history shows they were damned difficult to kill. I suppose I mean history will show that. It hasn't happened yet and it won't, not for, um, I'm not sure when it will happen but I do know it won't be for a long time to come.'

He thought for a moment before he added, 'And when the day does come they found an adversary worthy of their respect when they came to the Lake.'

George fell silent and the pair sat and rested in the pleasant summer sun of, George thought, early June. It looked set to be a scorching hot summer.

Interlude

'A word in your ears everybody. Recorder please Jill, this might turn out to be important and it equally might not but either way I want to be able to refer back to it,' Peter Birkett addressed his team.

The graduate student did as she was asked.

'Here's an idea that struck me last night when I was washing the dinner dishes, which I'll have you know is something I do from time to time. I finished with a sink full of soap bubbles floating on the water and then it hit me that I've read that our universe is one of many floating in a sea of bubbles,' Peter Birkett said.

'Just one more bubble in a sea of bubbles. I've read the same thing. It was described as a raft of bubbles. I can look it up and reference it if you like,' the man with curly hair offered.

'Thanks but not yet Mac, not until we decide if we've got something. Out of the blue I realised that I could draw a straight line between the centres of any two adjacent universes regardless of whether they were arranged on a raft of water or all clumped together. Raft of water isn't much of a description but you know what I mean. OK so far?'

Peter Birkett regarded his fellow scientists.

'Ray,' he said, 'you haven't said anything yet but you've got your wheels turning.'

Thus prompted, Ray Marsh replied, 'I was thinking about soap bubbles and universe bubbles. The bubbles on the surface of the water are all dome shaped and their size depends on the volume of air inside them. Their internal pressure is the same in every bubble and we can ignore gravity and surface tension. The bubbles that are universes don't float on the surface of anything so they can't possibly be dome shaped. They are in a cluster all different sizes but their shapes must differ, depending on their volume…'

'Huh? Why?'

'Think about it Jill. Each bubble, be it soap or universe, is in contact with other bubbles but the bubble cluster is three dimensional and so little bubbles fill the spaces between larger bubbles and where there is contact between bubbles or adjacent universes, the region of contact is flat. It can't be anything else because of the equal pressure in each bubble but the number of bubbles that another bubble touches is variable because bubbles are not all the same size and the shape is dependent on the number of contacts. The pressures in each bubble have to be equal because any bubble with a greater or lesser pressure would expand or contract to equalise the pressures. Anything else would be like having say, one corner of this room with a higher pressure than the rest of the room. It doesn't happen. It can't happen.'

'Good answer,' Peter Birkett approved, 'up to a point, anyway. You haven't demonstrated that the internal pressures of each universe are equal but my gut feeling is that it is how things are but let's not forget the shape of the universe as we understand it has no corners or sharp edges, which your version would certainly have. Each of you has seen the email I sent to George Green where I suggested that the matter and anti-matter universes occupy the same space. Bear it in mind that when Christine Appleton described her conjectures about the universe she said that in her theory the big bang produced a universe made up of matter and another universe made up of anti-matter. Now then, I said I could draw a straight line between the centres of any two universes in the foam or on the flat surface of the, what shall I call it, the cosmological water. But in the cosmos that Spockette hypothesised the universes are hour glass shaped matter and anti-matter twins and it doesn't follow that they are all aligned the same way. Perhaps they never are; think of the difference between a row of hour glasses all standing on a shelf and the same number of hour glasses tossed into a bucket. So is it possible that the only way to draw a straight line between centres is to invoke the fifth dimension, whatever that is? She did say that cosmological theory demands a dozen or so dimensions which, she said, seem to be…'

'Like screwing up a sheet of paper!' Jill Lucas exclaimed.

'Very good. I call it a meta-universe, something that goes beyond what we usually think of as the universe. Now, have I flipped or am I on to something?'

'In my universe the answer is yes. Also no.'

'Thanks Mac. I'll remember that,' Peter Birkett said wryly.

'Maybe we should put it on hold and get on with the business of devising new ways to bash atoms together,' Ray Marsh suggested, 'and by the way, you called her Spockette. Did you realise that?'

'Uh, no, but I wasn't first. OK folks, back to the grindstone. Recorder off please Jill.'

Chapter 32

Work on the new elevated causeway that the Council of Seniors had ordered to be built was begun as soon as the task of surveying was completed. George Green had seen the planning that went into the project, including the time the work should take, the manpower and materials that would be required, and the craftsmanship that the job demanded. The causeway was to cross a permanently sodden and frequently flooded stretch of ground and it was meant to replace an existing path that was laid directly onto the ground. This path made it easy for materials to be brought up to where they were required but it was plainly in need of repair. It was plain to George that the work had been scheduled for the summer for good reason. The Council had stipulated that it should be wide enough for two people to pass or a cow to be led to a new pasture and be just high enough to be clear of winter flooding.

The work called for sharpened wooden piles to be driven deep into the soggy ground and the depth had been established through previous experience. Once they were in the next stage was to fix a large number of pre-cut planks into position. That was for the future; at present George was hauling a new upright and steadying it while it was driven into the ground by a man who stood on a moveable platform and wielded a large and heavy stone hammer. Dressed only in shorts and his three cornered hat and working above his knees in muddy water George was enjoying every minute. Two girls of about twenty years were bringing up more planks in readiness for their fixing.

The working day was as long as light permitted and there was no let-up except for very short refreshment breaks.

The hard work continued and by mid-afternoon the causeway had advanced further than the work plan called for and all agreed that they had been lucky with the weather. Towards the end of the day the work was stopped and all the tools were accounted for and made ready for use on the following day. The work party made for the local swimming place to freshen up and wash away the day's grime. Nudity was the order of the day and George was slowly becoming used to the custom. Men and women bathed together and as Hilary had said, everybody has seen everybody else without clothes and nobody takes any notice. It seemed to be true but George did have to remind himself that he was the one who had insisted on doing as the Lake dwellers did. Merlin had repeated his terrible joke a number of times; 'George is off to live in the past lane.'

Well then, when in Rome do as the Romans do, and when in Avalon do what is done in Avalon, even though the district had yet to be named. George looked all around him and wondered. Was he standing in the place where Avalon would arise? Avalon, the land of apples. A place of myth and fable whose name had rang down all through the ages and been a place of pilgrimage and inspiration. A place, but much more than a place. Through the centuries Avalon had kept the spirit of the Lake alive and if the Legends of the Lake were to be believed the Lake would flood once more and perhaps Avalon itself would rise again. And perhaps he, George Green was there at its founding!

His reverie was halted by a splash of water on his face. One of the girls who had carried the planks for the new causeway laughed.

'You were off with your own thoughts,' she said cheerfully, 'and I was asking you to see if I have washed all the mud off my back. And there's a raft coming to take us home.'

She turned round for George to see.

'You'll do,' he reported, 'there's no more mud to wash off.'

The girl swam away with easy strokes. George caught up with her and they waded to the shore where he had draped his clothes over a bush.

The evening was a pleasant affair. When everybody had eaten George showed off the photographs he had taken during the day whenever he got a chance. He had taken two cameras with him and the workers were free to take pictures too. George wanted to know what they thought worth recording and he was well aware that Clive Bowden would want to get his hands on them.

'I never knew I was so handsome,' one old man quipped.

'Your eyes are growing dim,' was the reply, 'I've seen better looking toads.'

The humour was rough and ready but none the less it made for an enjoyable end to a day of hard toil.

George was called on to tell more about the time he lived in. One of the girls had a lot to ask about the hairstyles of his day and openly asked George if he thought Eathl would show her the magazines she had brought to the Lake when she returned from the future.

George assured her that Eathl would be glad to share everything and he suspected than a hair dressing salon was about to spring into being.

'I heard from a raft man that you have a new son called Arrad Green and you are catching bees for their honey,' an elder commented.

George explained what he and Arrad were doing.

'Arrad is making new hives while I am away,' he said. 'The practice will stand him in good stead and I've described some new kinds of hives for him to try. Essentially a hive, which is what we call the places where our bees nest, a hive is a box where the bees can construct their honeycombs. Arrad will be able to reach inside the boxes and pull out the honey because he's going to make a little door so that he can reach inside.'

'I can speak for everyone here that when Arrad turns up here he and his bees will be welcome. Tell him to ask for me, Hanwed, and I will have seen to it that a place will be made for them and he will be welcome to spend as many days as he needs to put his things into place. I would go to the games and tell him myself but I have attended the last two games and not everybody can go.'

'Now the new causeway is nearly built I think the best place for them would be on the other side, away from the houses. I don't want my children to be stung,' one mother declared.

'I don't think you need worry about that,' George told her. 'Bees don't sting unless they are provoked. Arrad will be able to show all the children what he is doing. And all the parents,' he added hastily.

'Arrad will collect a few stings now and again, he knows that but I have always thought that a few stings are a fair price to pay for the honey I take,' George continued.

'Aye, anything that comes free is worth what you pay for it,' the woman's neighbour agreed with the wisdom of years to back her up.

The elder, Hanwed, suggested that breakfast be eaten early on the following day, with the prospect of an early finish when the causeway was completed. He estimated that by mid-afternoon the work would be over. Nobody disagreed with his estimate and it was soon settled that the evening meal would be something of a celebration and a barbecue with the whole village attending.

George found himself looking forward to it with keen anticipation.

***

As near as George could judge the raft arrived on time. Living in a world without timepieces the population of the Lake seemed to have an inbuilt sense of the passage of time. George supposed it was something they grew up with. He had made a point of leaving his wristwatch behind when he stepped into the past and he noted with satisfaction that it was not missed.

The raft was to make a number of scheduled stops along the shore of the Lake and there were several other passengers who had business in other places. A pig in its pen was taken aboard and it was apparent that the raft men were used to handling animals. A chorus of farewells sent them on their way as the raft was poled away from the shore.

'They're looking for a current,' a young man said to George. 'It speeds the passage and that means the raft has to tie up at the next stop so that it doesn't get ahead of schedule, but the real reason for catching the current is that it is easier to drift than to pole or paddle all the way. It only works if you happen to be going in the right direction. I'm going two stops along the shore because I've got to do some coppicing work and collect an order of willow for the furniture weavers. I'll be away from home for two nights, or maybe three, it depends on how much work I have to get through.'

'I'm looking forward to seeing how Arrad is getting on,' George replied.

'I've heard all about him. Could he put a bee's nest out in the woods? I'm thinking that there are lots of open places in the coppiced areas where flowers spring up. I know bees like flowers but that's all I know.'

It was an intelligent question. George was getting used to the mental alertness of all the people he met.

'That would be ideal,' he replied.

'Well, once he's got his business going I'm sure that the people who live close by would be pleased to have a supply of honey just a short walk away. I know I would. I'll tell you what; if I happen across a nest in the woods I'll get word to Arrad straight away, and if he can catch them they're his. I'll just watch from a safe distance,' the young man ended.

As far as the Lake and bees was concerned the watchword was caution. George thanked him sincerely.

A coracle appeared from behind the reeds that surrounded a small islet. Atta had mentioned that these craft were little used on the Lake. The occupant was very intent on the task of pulling an eel trap out of the water but she took the time to wave a greeting.

George waved back.

As the journey continued George decided to keep his diary up to date and he sat cross legged on the raft to do his writing, stopping from time to time to answer a question. The Lake was placid and the scenery slipped past. Sometimes there was a shouted greeting from the shore and one a group of young boys followed the raft for a while before they turned back to their homes. There were scheduled stops and George was engaged in more than one conversation. All in all it was a pleasant way of spending a morning.

Lunch was eaten at noon when the raft was moored alongside a quay. One of the men who poled the raft was replaced by another. George understood that the raft crews rotated their schedules when long journeys were undertaken. This was to ensure that nobody had to work a shift that was too long.

'Old lady Megril is going to be late as usual,' the replacement raft man observed. 'The old girl isn't as spry as she used to be but she has as much right as I have to get around and visit family and friends, and she's got plenty of both. We can make up lost time if we have to and if you want to know anything about old days on the Lake she's the one to talk to.'

'She's not short of juicy scandal either,' somebody added.

How times haven't changed, George mused.

Megril was helped to board the raft and seated next to George. She laid her walking stick beside her and George noticed it was skillfully made.

'My old legs aren't what they used to be,' she sighed. 'You must be George. They told me about you,' she added. 'You've been helping to build the new bridge.'

'I did what I could but I'm no expert,' George replied.

The old woman nodded.

'Nobody can do everything but everybody can do something. Sometimes it helps to fail because you learn a valuable lesson and then you get on with the things you can do. When I was a girl I wanted to make clay cooking pots but I soon discovered I had no talent for it so I gave it up. Not without regrets mind you. My mother nagged at me to try something else but I didn't know what to do or even what I wanted to do. My father wasn't pleased either I can tell you!' She told George.

'You wouldn't have been happy being a bad potter,' George replied, 'so what did you do?'

Megril was pleased to be asked.

'I sat by the shore of the Lake and I sulked,' she said happily, 'but then a boy from the village came along; he was someone I grew up with and he was off to collect willow sticks for a coracle he wanted to make. I was bored and so I tagged along for the sake of having somebody to talk to. I can't say that we knew each other all that well. He cut the willow with a good stone knife and I helped him carry it back to where he found me. That was as far as I wanted to walk so we stopped there and he started to weave the sticks for his coracle. It was as good a place as any to do the work and when he asked me to hold a strip of bark while he bent to pieces of wood together I did and I tied it with a good tight knot. After that I started to do some of the weaving and in no time at all the frame was finished and all he needed to do was put the seat in and cover it with hide. He said tomorrow would do and we sat and talked for a while until he decided to go home and I was left with his cast off pieces of willow and then I started to fiddle around with it and I made a basket to take home with me. It was only a little basket mind you but it got me thinking. I'm going on a bit aren't I?'

'It's an interesting story,' George replied, 'and there's more to it unless I'm very much mistaken. What happened next?'

Megril was keen to talk.

'My little basket got me into weaving,' she replied, 'and I often went with the boy to cut willow, and I started to watch to see if he was out on the water in his coracle because he used to set eel traps in among the reeds. I had the idea of weaving an eel trap for him; it's easy enough and it only takes a few sticks of willow. So I wove the trap and gave it to him and he came round to my house with an eel he caught in it. Well one thing led to another and I became a willow weaver and I made chairs and tables and beds and little cots for the babies and I made lots of baskets and the boy who made the coracle became my husband. My, the years roll back when I talk about it! You must think I'm a silly old woman who talks too much!'

'I think nothing of the sort,' George replied sincerely.

'I was a very lucky girl. My grandmother said I was flighty. Honestly, to hear her talk you would think she never chased a ball or a boy in her life. I'll have a few words to say to her when we meet again I can tell you!'

Was there ever a more pleasant way to spend a lazy afternoon? Megril was helped to her feet by George and one of the crew of the raft when her destination was reached and a small crowd was there to meet her.

'Her children and grandchildren,' a new passenger said to nobody in particular. It seemed that Megril was respected and known to everybody.

George divided his time by writing his notes and talking to anyone and everyone as passengers came and went. Sometimes he did nothing but watch the banks of the Lake as the raft slipped by on the current with only small adjustments from the raft men. It was plain that any journey in the opposite direction would go against the current, as had been the case when George was transported to the small village where the causeway building was to take place but by steering away from the main current good progress was made. As if on cue he spotted such a raft and recognized Lerghwil and Morndale who had ferried him and his new son Arrad to the herder's island. As their raft approached he saw that their cargo consisted of earthenware pots, large and small. Shouted greetings were exchanged, along with the information that Wigstin had fallen off the school raft again. It seemed to be a regular event. George reflected that he had drastically changed his opinion of the way people lived thousands of years in the past. The people who lived on the Lake were confident, comfortable, hard-working, healthy, educated, and enjoyed rewarding social lives. Atta was right when he declared that there had never been a better time to live.

A combination of the fatigue that was the result of the work he had been doing and the warmth of the afternoon sun made George drowsy.

By his reckoning it would be three hours at least before he reached Alfrid's village and it could easily be more. He was more asleep than awake as the raft steered away from the shores of the Lake and into a stretch of open water that covered many square miles. Or kilometres. More than once he had wondered what system of measurement would be commonly used in a future far removed from his own.

Time passed.

A boat appeared. A passenger was the first to spot it and she pointed it out to George and the crew.

'Somebody is in a hurry,' she commented, 'and look, it's turning towards us.'

She had sharp eyes.

'Four oars. It's the fast canoe from the infirmary. I can make out its flag. They always show a flag when there is an emergency and then all the other craft give way to them or get called on for assistance. When I was a girl I rowed one myself but in those days we never had flags like we do today,' she said knowledgeably.

The raft was hailed.

'Is George Green on board?' Somebody yelled through a megaphone.

'Eh? Me? What do they want with me?'

George soon found out when the canoe was expertly turned and matched the speed of the raft. It bumped the side of the raft.

'It's Hilary, she's been taken to the infirmary and we've been sent out to act as a fast ferry back to the healer's island. Jump aboard George and we'll be on our way.'

'But my, my baggage…' George stammered incoherently.

'It'll follow you. Hurry, we want to get you there fast. I'll tell you about it on the way.'

'Is she badly hurt?' George demanded as he was helped into the canoe which promptly sped off as fast as the oarsmen could manage.

There was no immediate answer. The rowers were busy.

Eventually; 'Hilary collapsed and the infirmary raft was sent for while she was being treated at the village. They knew her condition was serious and they kept her alive so Gwenve could treat her properly. It's a heart problem and Gwenve is going to operate. By now she probably has or maybe she hasn't finished yet, and that's all I know.'

'Land of my fathers,' George muttered as his face paled.

Then the implications hit him. He felt his world collapse.

'Operate!' He yelled. 'She can't do that. She'll kill her!'

'Steady on George or you'll have us over. Trust Gwenve, she knows what she's doing.'

The canoe rocked as George pounded the side of it in helpless despair.

Another oarsman grunted with the effort of rowing but gasped, 'She will have done operating by the time we reach the infirmary. You'll see. Hilary is in good hands.'

George Green doubted it. His face was drained of colour and he felt physically sick. He urged the crew to row faster while he inwardly admitted that they were speeding across the water faster than any craft he had seen so far and he knew he was being unreasonable.

'She'll kill her!' He raged out loud. 'Gwenve will kill her! What does she know about heart surgery?'

There was no answer. George had never felt so helpless. His world was collapsing and there was nothing he could do. He felt himself giving way to despair.

By his estimation it was an hour before the canoe was hailed from an approaching raft.

'Change of oars! Come alongside! Come alongside!'

With the speed and efficiency that only came with practice the four oarsmen in the canoe were on the raft and a fresh crew took over.

'The operation is going well,' was the terse reply to George's questioning.

It was plain that nobody was in any mood for conversation even if it had been possible. Time passed slowly for George. Trailed by a long wake the canoe sped on.

Sitting cross legged gave George cramp in one leg and caused him to grimace. Cautiously he straightened the limb and massaged his calf.

'Nearly there,' an oarsman said.

George wondered how he knew but he supposed that each man knew the shoreline and recognized landmarks along the way. Inconsequentially the thought crossed his mind that the taxi drivers of London must have something in common with the oarsmen. Perhaps and perhaps not. His mind was wandering. Even the sound of a horn blown by a teenaged boy on the quayside below the infirmary failed to gain his attention. Suddenly he found that the canoe was alongside. He had reached his destination and he was scared of what he might find there. With difficulty he struggled to his feet and was helped ashore where he promptly fell over. Solicitous hands helped him to his feet and he managed a shaky walk that became a run as he climbed the path to the infirmary. Twice he slipped and nearly fell and soon he was clutching his side and panting for breath.

The paved path led straight to the door. George found his way blocked by the healer he recognized from his previous visit as Nerthi.

'Steady there George, steady on. Hands into the bowl first, we don't want our patient to pick up anything nasty.'

The man was right but George showed his impatience.

'Gwenve is bringing Hilary round in easy stages. By now she should be wide awake but she'll be a bit drowsy. That's the way, right up to your elbows and try not to rub your eyes until it dries because it stings like blazes.'

Nerthi noticed George wince and continued with a wry smile, 'If you've got any cuts and scratches that'll find them but they'll heal all the better for it. Come with me and we'll see how our patient is getting on shall we?'

Hilary was lying still while a young orderly applied a clear sticky substance from her waist to her shoulders while Gwenve watched with approval. She managed a weak smile.

'This is my second or third coat of paint. It's to keep me still and it dries so hard it's like a suit of armour but it's see through so they can keep an eye on my progress.'

'What happened?'

'I had a dizzy spell and the next thing I knew I was here,' Hilary whispered, 'and Gwenve said she was going to have to do heart surgery. I was scared,' Hilary stopped to catch her breath and then continued, 'I was really frightened. Gwenve kept me awake while she made the first incisions and then she knocked me out so she could get on with the tricky bit. That was hours ago, I've only just woken up.'

'And you must rest. Sleep.' Gwenve ordered.

Hilary was sound asleep instantly. Like a light being switched off, George thought. He suspected that Gwenve had used her hand movements and hypnotic art to put her into trance although he had seen nothing.

'Hilary will sleep until dawn,' Gwenve told George. 'You can see where I have operated. The treatment that the orderly is applying will dry hard soon and keep her immobile. It allows me to monitor the healing process. After one eight of days it will have darkened too much for me to see through and it will be ready to come off. Hot water will wash it away and Hilary will be able to sit up. I expect a complete recovery.'

'Can I stay with her all night?' George asked.

'If you wish but it will serve no purpose. My advice is that you return home and come back in the morning. You may bring your camera, is that the right word? Your camera to make pictures. The orderlies can do that for you if you or Hilary shows them how. Bring Arrad with you, we had to turn him away while we got on with our work.'

Gwenve turned and walked away.

Nerthi chuckled.

'Gwenve is a little, uh, short on ceremony shall we say, but Hilary couldn't be in better hands. If I were you I'd take her advice. Take the rest of the day off and then get a good night's sleep, you look as if you need it.'

George knew when to give in. Nerthi's advice was to wait until after breakfast before putting in an appearance. Making his way to the quay he wondered how long he would have to wait before he could hail a raft or canoe. It turned out to be a short wait and he answered a barrage of questions as the crossing was made.

His luggage had not yet arrived but he was assured that it would not be long in coming. Arrad was there to meet him when he stepped ashore.

'Is mum going to be mended? They wouldn't let me stay,' he complained tearfully. It was obvious that the boy had been crying.

George reassured him.

He put his arm round his son's shoulder and said, 'She's going to be all right. I've seen her and she was awake and talking and Gwenve said she will sleep until the morning and then we can go and see her.'

To take his and Arrad's minds off the subject he asked about the hives that Arrad had been working on while he was away.

'I looked at the pictures you drew for me and I found some big pieces of dry bark and I have made three hives that I think will be all

313

right and I have enough bark left for more. Six or seven more; perhaps eight even. Vocca gave me some short pieces of string because he has no use for short lengths and he gave me some worn out fishing nets as well. I can use them to drape over a hive and help hold it together. When I was in the woods I found a tree with a hole in the trunk and I wondered if I could manage to get some bees to go there if I can find a swarm. Suppose I put a swarm in the hole and blocked the entrance with straw for a day so the bees would get used to being there, do you think that would work?'

Arrad looked enquiringly at George.

'I don't know but it's certainly worth trying. Sometimes it is good to know what doesn't work but never let that put you off. Trial and error is a tested method,' George replied.

'I talked to a man named Hanwed who lives where I was helping with the new causeway,' he continued. 'Hanwed told me he will look out for swarms where he lives and he said he will find a place for your hive if he spots any swarms. It seems to me that perhaps you should send a hive in advance. That way you will have everything in place. Do you know how to get a message to him to tell him that a hive is on the way and ask him to look after it for a little while until you can make the trip? You could get your hive ready for anything that turns up. What do you think?'

Arrad was pleased with the idea and he thought he could get a message delivered. He added that one of Vocca's old nets would be useful when the hive was moved, which he thought could be done the day after a message was sent to say it was on the way. Side by side they walked towards Alfrid's house and George found himself answering more questions. It occurred to him that Alfrid and Eathl were doing to him what he had done to Arrad. Take his mind off things. He felt grateful.

A horn sounded and Eathl looked up from the meal she was preparing.

'That's a raft, but not a regular one,' she said.

George remembered something.

'My luggage, I had to leave it on a raft when the canoe came for me. Perhaps it's my luggage.'

'I'll help you carry it Dad,' Arrad volunteered and added excitedly, 'I can ask the raft crew to tell everybody about my hives wherever they go and ask them to bring a message back to me to say when they are ready, which they will be if I can keep the bees away from their houses and make honey as well, and then I'd better go home and tell Cartiwiss all about it.'

Eathl considered that to be a good idea.

'The raft will be here before you reach the jetty if you don't hurry,' she said, and she was right.

Arrad proved to be right when he told the men on the raft what he proposed and they agreed to spread the word and pass any messages back to him. The thought that the supply of honey could be more that a hit or miss business was taking hold. George found his bags being unloaded when he and Arrad reached the shore. He felt he ought to offer a payment but he knew it would be refused because his status as a Freeman of the Lake guaranteed free passage anywhere. Perhaps he could write a note of appreciation. No, that was no use, they couldn't read or write. But hang on George, you could do it anyway. Why not? Yes George, why not? No reason. The note would never be read but it would be understood. He would do it.

Brainwave. I can make a get well card. I have all the paper I need, plus pens and pencils of all colours.

'Arrad,' he said, 'we're going to make a card for Hilary. I'll show you what I mean when we get my gear stowed away.'

George produced several sheets of blank paper and a number of coloured pencils and felt tip pens. He blessed his foresight for bringing them but wished he was using them for another purpose. He brushed the thought aside.

'When a person is ill in my now we send them a card to say get well soon,' he explained to his son. 'We're going to make Hilary a card and take it to her in the morning when we visit her in the infirmary.'

Folding the sheet in half he used a felt tip pen to write a message on the front of his card.

'This says get well soon,' he explained, 'and now we will sign it on the inside. My name is George and this is how I write it. Now I'll write Arrad on another piece of paper and you can copy it onto the card. Watch me and do it like this. Write Arrad a few times and when you are ready you can write it on the card.'

Carefully the boy wrote his name in capital letters. After a few attempts he told George he was ready to write on the card.

Soon George was holding a home made card signed by him and his son.

'Hilary will really like this,' he said with satisfaction and pride.

Alfrid and Eathl had watched with interest.

'We learned how to write our names in your now George. Can you let us make a card for Hilary too?'

George was delighted.

'Of course, and I'll tell you what. Spread the word around and tell everyone that I will help them make cards for Hilary and deliver them to her. She'll be at the infirmary for a few days yet. I'll ask Gwenve if she can have visitors and then people can deliver their own cards in person.'

***

George had really started something. He slipped the get well soon card into a plastic pocket and allowed Arrad to take it home with him. When the boy turned up in the morning he came accompanied by Cartiwiss and Vocca the fisherman.

Hesitantly Cartiwiss asked if she and Vocca could make a card for Hilary. Soon he was holding the finished article and Cartiwiss and Vocca were beaming with pride.

'Take your practice writing with you,' George told them, 'and from now on you will be able to write your names.'

'It is a good thing to be able to do,' Alfrid told them.

Arrad showed his impatience by hopping from one foot to the other as the raft neared the mooring of the island of the infirmary and he nearly lost his footing when he leapt ashore. Soon he and George were climbing the path with Arrad far ahead of George.

Nerthi greeted them.

'Gwenve told me to let George go in first,' he told Arrad, 'and for you to wait a while. It will be a short wait and the time won't be wasted because I want you to come with me to a place I have picked out for a hive. I'm told that you need to bring a hive here and then catch a swarm of bees to put in it, is that right? I've picked a spot not too close but not too far away either but it wouldn't take me long to tell you all I know about bees.'

'Arrad knows the right kind of place,' George reassured the healer.

He found Hilary and Gwenve inside. Gwenve pointed to the bowl that George saw was filled with the astringent antiseptic wash that had stung his scratched hands on his last visit. It stung just as much on his second.

Hilary smiled.

'I feel fine,' she replied in answer to George's question. 'I had some breakfast; it was a spicy sausage in a roll and I washed it down with something that had elder flower and other herbs and it was delicious. The orderly brought it in for me and she's called Cartiwiss like Vocca's wife.'

'You look well,' George replied.

'I'm being well looked after. I'll have a scar but Gwenve and Nerthi say I won't have any discomfort.'

'Your ribs will ache for a day or two,' Gwenve reminded her.

'I had to reach Hilary's heart quickly,' Gwenve explained to George, 'so her ribs suffered a little. It was unavoidable. Hilary tells me your healers are able to look inside their patients so they will be able to see what I did and we have discussed the possibility of Hilary doing a writing if I dictate the procedure I carried out, and I think I might be able to make a drawing for your healers to look at.'

'Splendid idea!' George enthused.

The orderly that Hilary had called Cartiwiss came and asked if anyone wanted more to drink.

'You and I will have something to drink in a few moments,' Gwenve replied, 'and Hilary must keep her fluids topped up. Will you bring in a large pot for George and Hilary and young Arrad who is not far away.'

'He's with Nerthi and they're deciding where to place a hive and he has one ready for delivery that he can bring across on the raft before the end of the day. If all goes well you will have a supply of honey right here on your doorstep. Arrad will know what to do to get it out of the hive,' George said to Cartiwiss.

Arrad soon arrived shaking his hands that were wet from the antiseptic wash that Nerthi had insisted he use before entering the infirmary.

'Mum! Mum! I've brought you a card and Dad showed me how to do my own writing. Look!'

Pride shone all over his face as he produced the get well card that he and George had made.

'Vocca and Cartiwiss made one as well,' Arrad said as he produced another card.

Even Gwenve was impressed and she said so before she and the orderly made their departure.

Arrad swelled with pride.

'I've brought you something,' Arrad continued. 'Would you like to have my toy? It might help you get better. It's my best thing.'

He produced his carved wooden tiger from inside his jacket.

Hilary was touched.

'You're so kind,' she said sincerely, 'but I'll just keep it by my bed until I leave the infirmary and then you must have it back. I'm sure it will help me get better.'

Interlude

GEORGE GREEN'S NOTES.

How should I begin? Hilary suffered a major heart attack while I was away working on a new causeway and she was taken across the Lake to the infirmary island where she was operated on by Gwenve, the Senior of the Healers.

I knew from what I have been told that skulls that are thousands of years old have been found showing evidence of healed trepanning operations. Ancient brain surgery? The evidence points that way. I believe that false teeth are not unknown either, and there are bones that show healed amputations. But heart surgery? I suppose that very little soft tissue has been discovered so whatever soft tissue surgery has been performed all traces have been lost.

Hilary seems to be well on the road to recovery. Gwenve has promised to dictate her procedures to me and suggested that I take photos so that I may present them to… um, there's the rub. Not to her regular doctor. Probably to Doctor Kate Fawcett first, and then to Doctor Andrew Simpson.

Gwenve used soluble stitching throughout; there will be nothing to remove and according to Gwenve her work will leave very little scarring. She's an amazing woman and I owe her an apology. The stitches were made from the same material as the stuff that was painted on Hilary to prevent infection and keep her immobile. I can say it was something with seaweed as its main ingredient (my guess is kelp, which is also a source of iodine) and that's all I can say. I hope to have the details later.

I'm avoiding the thing I should be talking about. Hilary has a heart condition. She knew about it shortly before we came here, by which time our plans were well advanced. If I had known I would have cancelled the trip. Hilary knew how much it meant to me so she kept it to herself.

Gwenve was aware as soon as she saw Hilary. How? By observation. The way Hilary walked up the path to the infirmary, her breathing, pulse, colouring, and later by feel, her temperature. Against her better judgment she kept the news from me. I would rather have known than been kept in ignorance.

Gwenve also warns that further surgery will not be possible. Not only that, but the outcome would have been the same if Hilary's heart attack had occurred in our own now. I don't want to believe that but believe it I do.

And there, for the time being, the matter rests.

HILARY GREEN'S NOTES

Today my straitjacket was washed off with hot water and I can sit up again. I have been very lucky, it seems. I did know about my heart but I couldn't spoil George's opportunity to come back to the tail end of the Stone Age and the beginning of the Bronze Age. Not to mention the Iron Age; it's early days yet but iron is becoming increasingly common. The Bronze Age seems to be squeezed between the Stone and Iron Ages and didn't last long. I might be wrong about that but history was never my strong point.

Gwenve and Nerthi, the other healer, have looked in on me every day. I mustn't do anything yet except sit up. The orderly helps me; today it is Cartiwiss. Not Vocca's wife; Cartiwiss is the name of several Lake women and girls. The girls are always called Twiss until they grow up. The orderly tomorrow will be Traff, a man of endless patience. With two sets of twins he says he has to be.

I'm trying to get to grips with people's names. The way they start and end has a meaning (Think Gerdin, Wigstin, Dendric, Cadric, Meglen, Megwin) but I don't fully understand it.

Nerthi is due to leave for another infirmary after the Games and a new junior healer will take his place. This is quite normal; it seems that junior healers rotate every six to eight months.

Cartiwiss has offered to do my hair next time she is on duty and I'm going to do hers in return. She wants to know all about hair styles in the place in the sphere of time that I come from. She doesn't think the way I do and to her it seems natural that people should shift from place to place. That might be because she used to be a stone turner when the stones still worked, which was a very high class profession. (Note for George and Merlin: place to place is correct, not shift from time to time. You figure it out).

320

Returning to the all-important subject of hair George mentioned a girl who helped with the bridge building that he was involved with who was also interested in hair styling. I never would have guessed that hairpieces are fairly common, though usually reserved for special occasions or by 'women of a certain age' who have stored their own hair against the day when greyness begins to show. Nearly everyone has dark hair and it seems to me that everyone who met Freya with her blonde Viking hair has a hankering to try hair lightening. I know George can make sodium stearate (soap to you and me) and I'm going to ask him if he can concoct a hair lightener. It'll make his fortune if he can but you can't take it with you as they say.

I'm going to stop now because I'm still a little frayed at the edges.

PS. Later. I didn't mean to imply there is no soap on the Lake. There is, and plenty of it and it is often scented herbal soap made with plant extract but I don't know which ones.

I will be out of here before the games.

Chapter 33

'That's the shore line pretty well marked Atta,' George Green said with a note of satisfaction, 'and thanks to your knowledge of the local area we've managed to put your village on the map that I brought with me. We can feel pleased with ourselves.'

'Is there anything remaining in your place in time?' Atta enquired. George was uncertain.

'A fair number of discoveries have been made over a wide area. The Lake is a big place and it was drained and flooded more than once, parts of it anyway. The Legends of the Lake say that one day it will fill again and become the Lake that we're looking at now but how that legend began is a mystery.'

'I have a sneaking suspicion that I can make a guess,' Atta replied shrewdly, 'and I have another suspicion that you are thinking the same as I am. Somebody has been to see for himself, that someone being me, but I have no intention of mentioning it to anybody and that includes you. Not yet anyway. My knees will give me away when Gwenve opens me up when I'm dead but… maybe somebody is going to piece things together from things I let drop. A little piece of information here and another little piece there and the next thing is the story comes out.'

'There's not much we can do about it. The knowledge did get out or will get out,' George said.

Atta agreed, 'Not that the knowledge will do any good. I'm just curious that's all. Curious about what will be said. And who will say it.'

'Getting back to your question about locating this village on the map… no wait, I'm getting it the wrong way round. First we must transfer the information we have as accurately as we can onto my maps and then we can see if there is anything that will let me say yes, this is the location of the house where Atta lived,' George said.

'Not very likely,' Atta replied.

'I'm not so sure. When I go back home I will at least know where to look. It's an intriguing notion. It is odd though. In my now the Lake has been drained so the features on the maps I brought with me are places that are under water in this now.'

Atta nodded his understanding.

'The brown contour lines on your map show that clearly,' he said.

George agreed.

'They'll be under water again someday but that day might be many years away from my now. The First Legend of the Lake says that three things are true. One, that the People of the Lake came from somewhere else. We know now that many of them did. Two, that there was a battle and the red and blue dragons went their separate ways. We know how that part of the First Legend came about and you know it at first hand; you fought in the Battle of the Lake. But the third part has a puzzle until now. That's where the Legends say the Lake will fill again. That hasn't happened yet in my now but its plain that it will happen and you have seen it. Puzzle solved but I'll never be able to talk about it to anyone in my own now.'

'For me the biggest puzzle is how that information was put into the Legends. I ought to say when it will be put in I suppose,' Atta said.

'I wonder. Let's imagine that Wint or someone decides to reactivate the stones some day, assuming that it can be done. That piece of information might be to let us know about it.'

'You're forgetting something. He did decide and that was how I came by my new knees,' Atta declared instantly.

'I agree, but I can't think of any other reason… ah, why should I? I'm trying to rationalize Wint's decision and I can't and what difference does it make anyway?'

Atta shook his head.

'None, and the fact is George I find myself asking if it would be a good thing if the stones are made to work again. It seems to me that too much reliance was placed on them and now we have to do without them and I for one feel more invigorated. Perhaps liberated even. In my opinion too much reliance on technology is not a good thing. We were lucky, when our system broke down we were quick to pick ourselves up and make the best of things. I would even go as far as to say we live in a better age now than we did a few years ago. Not everyone would agree but I think most people would. Perhaps our work is harder sometimes but it is more satisfying.'

'For my part I find myself asking if it would be a good thing if I knew more about your time in the future. I mean my future. I'm interested but if you do tell me more, well obviously I can say nothing to Patti or Angela Collins so I'll say nothing to anybody.'

'A wise decision.'

Not far away a handful of Councillors surveyed the array of tables and frames where the tradespeople would display their wares, take orders, and make business deals. The night was expected to be dry and calm so a few people had already begun to bring their goods to the trade fair and make their stall ready for an early start in the morning. Eathl had noticed some fine earthenware and planned a few purchases. There was a table where jewellery would be sold the following day and she would be sure to see what was on offer.

Councilor Meglen declared herself satisfied; she hoisted a shoulder bag and went off in search of George Green and his son. She was quick to find George, and Atta offered to walk the short distance to Alfrid's house and find Arrad.

'I think Hilary Green might like to hear what I have to say so it would be better if we all went to Alfrid's house. I heard from the orderly named Cartiwiss that her recovery has been all that Healer Gvenve said it would be but let us not make her come to us when we can easily go to her.'

The trio made small talk and as they made a leisurely stroll. Meglen enquired about the way Arrad was making progress with his new business of bee-keeping.

'While I was on my way here on the raft that belongs to Lerghwil and Morndale I was told by Lerghwil that you have managed to catch some bees and keep them to make honey for Arrad. I hope to see him with a stall at the games next year,' she said, 'and I'll be sure to tell him so.'

'If all goes well he'll have bees up and down the Lake,' George replied.

'I would like to see for myself how he will keep them. Atta has said they are in a box with a little door for Arrad to put his hand in and collect the honeycomb. He'll collect stings as well to my way of thinking.'

'It's the price you pay for the honey you collect when you keep bees,' George confirmed, 'but Arrad knows how to collect his honey and not be stung too often.'

He remembered giving his speech about paying for your honey with a few stings before; to Arrad and to an elder named Hanwed who had said that Arrad would be welcome to place a hive near his village.

Deep in consultation with two men who were unknown to George Green, Alfrid was startled to see his visitors approach. Introductions were soon made and George discovered that the men were shoemakers like Alfrid.

Hilary was taking part in the discussion.

'We were talking about the shoes we will put on our stall,' Alfrid told the trio. 'We will show styles that we copied from the pictures I brought with me from your now to mine. We don't expect high heels to sell but they are an example of what we can do. The lace holes with the coloured metal eyelets will be popular with the ladies, we know that already. It's a good thing I brought plenty for all the shoemakers.'

'And the hole puncher,' one shoemaker declared. 'My opinion is that we will be overrun with orders for sandals because they have always been popular and we've put in some new ideas from the pictures. I like to put metal buckles on mine but,' he nudged his companion, 'some people are more traditional and prefer laces.'

'I've dyed a selection of laces with colours that will have the ladies flocking to my workbench,' the man averred.

'One thing we feel sure of is that there will be work for every shoemaker on the Lake for a very long time,' Alfrid said. 'I don't know if I feel pleased or not about that,' he finished with a helpless shrug and a wide smile.

'I'm going to try high sided boots,' the first man said. 'I remember when Freya the Viking was here she wore boots like that sometimes and so did Beowulf. It's something of an experiment but it will extend my range. All I have to do is outsell Alfrid when he puts his on the market.'

'Like I said,' Alfrid repeated, 'there will be work for all of us for a long time to come.'

'Well, it will keep me out of the way of my wife and that will keep her happy!'

'It's going to keep me happy too George,' Hilary told him, 'because I've placed orders for sandals with everybody. We haven't much time but they will be ready by noon tomorrow.'

Everybody laughed.

'We could make it earlier and give ourselves more time to show off our workmanship,' Alfrid said, 'but I don't think we shall be short of customers.'

Councilor Meglen unshouldered her bag and laid it on Alfrid's bench.

'I have something for George and Arrad,' she said. 'Arrad first I think.'

The boy looked astonished.

'Some of the Council members have got together and made your flag Arrad. Everyone on the Lake will know it.'

She drew the folded flag from her bag and handed it over for Arrad to unfold.

'I have had eight wavy bars put on it; those represent the Lake.'

Clive Bowden's shield that Arthur of Britain declared he should have when Arthur made him Clive of the Lake bore the same number of bars.

'On the wavy bars of the Lake I have placed three bees. Anyone will know that you are Arrad, a person of the Lake and a beekeeper. Some say three is a lucky number and just for once I believe it.'

Arrad was ecstatic.

'Th… thank you.' He stammered. 'Look Dad, my flag. My own flag!'

George showed his own pleasure.

'That was a wonderful gift,' he said sincerely.

Meglen smiled with satisfaction.

'I haven't finished,' she declared.

She pulled another folded flag from her bag.

'It is the custom for entrants in the Dads and Lads games to fly their flags so I have taken the liberty of having a flag made for you. Unfurl it and tell me what you think.'

George's hands trembled.

'You have the same wavy bars of the Lake,' Meglen said, 'and I have had a red dragon placed on the flag because we are aware that in your now you were born in the land that the red dragon flags went to

326

after the Battle of the Lake. The dragon holds the torch of learning that you showed the Council at the time when you took Arrad as your own son. I have seen to it that the torch is black as was your picture, and it burns with a bright yellow flame to light up the dark corners of ignorance and bring enlightenment and education to everyone.'

Overcome with emotion George found himself unable even to say anything by way of thanks.

Chapter 34

Atta had promised a fine warm day for the games and his forecast was as correct as Merlin's were. George wondered how they were able to make their predictions as accurate as they were. The Lake sparkled under a blazing sun as all the contestants and their families made their way to the play area.

Despite Hilary's protests that she was fully recovered from her heart surgery George insisted that they walk slowly. Arrad carried the flat pebbles he had selected for the stone skipping event. He had more pebbles that he and George needed and he was almost bursting with excitement.

'Small Alfrid will come first in all the short distance running events that he goes in for and his dad will come second because he can run fast too. We can enter those races and we might get a place but the long races will go to the hunters and their lads or perhaps small Alfrid might get a place. I think we will get some points at the stone skipping even if we don't win. I've never done tug-of-war but I know you have entered us and I'll pull as hard as I can. Are we going to do coracles as well?' He chattered.

George told his new son that they would enter.

'I've never been in a coracle but I've been told not many people have so we stand as good a chance as anyone,' he replied and added with a chuckle, 'and a better than even chance of getting wet.'

'That won't matter if we do the running and the tug-of-war and the stone skipping first and then do the swimming and leave the coracle for the last event because we will already be wet from the swim,' Arrad replied seriously.

It was true. The swimmers were required to go fully clothed into the water because anyone could fall off a raft or a jetty and they had to be proficient enough to keep their heads above water until they were either pulled out or managed to pull themselves out.

'If we skip the stones first I can put down all the spare ones and not have to carry them,' Arrad said.

'Stones, swim, run, tug-of war, and coracle, and that's five events. When they are done our points will be added up and we will know how we got on. We are allowed to do other events and take the best scores but I don't know which ones to do even if we get a chance. Can you throw a spear?'

'I won't know until I've tried it,' George replied with a laugh.

Arrad matched his humour with the comment, 'Everyone will go to see Councillor Alfrid when he throws a spear but you have to stand well out of the way because nobody can tell where it will go. He always enters that contest and I know he doesn't expect to win but he's a good sport.'

'We have a saying that it's not the winning, it's the taking part. Competition is healthy but winning isn't everything and when Alfrid loses he shows that losing is not a disaster. It's a valuable lesson to learn,' George replied.

***

On the day of the games the weather was warm and dry, as Atta had predicted. All over the village tables of goods for sale were set out and from very early in the morning traders had begun to display their wares and services. The games were combined with what George could only think of as a trade fair. Alfrid had laid out a range of sandals, which were the favoured footwear of most people during the summer because they were light and roomy, especially important for growing feet. In the colder weather laced shoes and woven socks were worn and George told himself that he should not have been surprised that the socks were often brightly coloured. Freya the Viking had brought fashion socks to the Lake and they were swiftly copied.

The ladies were already touring the various exhibits and making purchases and when their husbands and sons were taking part in an event they would look after the stalls unless there were older children in the family who could stand in and let the wives and mothers cheer and shout encouragement.

Hilary was the centre of some attention and many well wishers asked after her health. Not to mention her clothes and hair style, she reported later when she rejoined her husband and their new son. George remembered that a girl who had been on the team that had laid the new causeway had shown an interest in hair styling when he had been away and working on it himself. If she was attending the games she might look for Hilary. Hair dressing was not a new profession but he felt sure the girl would not miss her chance. He had not expected so much interest would be shown. Typical of a man he thought inwardly. Guilty George; guilty of being male.

Arrad was questioned by a group of men and women from different villages who had heard about the prospect of obtaining regular and reliable supplies of honey and wanted to know more.

'I can't collect honey in the winter but I will be collecting it in the summer the way people do now,' he explained, 'but if I can get enough hives in every village I will be able to collect enough honey for everyone to store and use until it is summer again.'

'That's a lot of honey. I doubt you can collect that much.'

'I think I can lady, but not at first. I will make all the hives I can during the cold days and in the spring I will have enough for one or two in every village. I can bring them on a raft as far as I can and then carry them to wherever the village wants them and that is where I shall put them together because my dad has shown me how a hive can be, uh, flat packed is what they are. It means to bring all the pieces and put them together where I need them and the raft people worked it out that I can put three hives on a raft if they are flat packed instead of just one that is already put together, and a flat packed hive is easier to carry because I can carry it one or two pieces at a time if I have to go a long way.'

'We shall see.'

Arrad was confident it could be done.

'My dad says there are other things that could be made from flat packed parts,' he said, 'but he also says you figure it out.'

'Hmm. He might have a point.'

One or two thoughtful faces departed.

It was a time of buying and selling, re-unions, gossip, courtship, new acquaintances, reminiscences. Babies were shown off, health was talked about, knowing glances were exchanged. It was typical of daily life but more intense.

Time passed quickly and George was startled when he heard the sound of a horn. As if to leave no doubt another horn was blown, and then another. That signaled to the Dads and Lads that the sports events were getting under way.

Arrad carried his collection of flat stones to the edge of the Lake. Three poles had been erected some distance from the shore and the centre pole was the target for stone skipping while the outer ones were guides for the onlookers and scorers. Stone skipping was a simple game and some of the boys who played were quite young. George guessed that the underlying purpose of the game was to give the youngsters a chance to be involved and strengthen family bonds. And to make a contribution to the social structure of the community. I never thought of myself as a social scientist, he thought, I'm gaining a lot from my stay on the Lake.

Tug of war. George and Arrad found themselves teamed up with a Herder and a Thatcher and their boys. Opposing them were a Reed Cutter, a Hunter, and another Thatcher and the teams were evenly matched. Heaving and straining and with heels dug in the rope was pulled backwards and forwards but never far enough for victory until with one final effort the other team was caught off guard and George and his team lurched backwards and fell sprawling backwards onto the grass. They lay exhausted until the Reed Cutter helped them up with the comment that he felt as if his arms had been pulled off.

Taking time to get their breath back the men and boys sat and talked for a while and when a villager passed by with a camera they posed for pictures. George had been so immersed in life on the Lake that he had almost forgotten about the cameras that he and Hilary had distributed. The results were sure to add a lot to the knowledge of history. Metal working had been recorded, as had building and thatching, fishing, growing, hunting, herding, play, rafting, schooling; the list was endless. George had probably been photographed many times without him noticing, which he thought was a good thing because the pictures would not have been posed for.

There was no need to hurry for the next event that he and Arrad were to take part in but a young boy and girl raced up and between gasps for breath told them that a coracle was ready for George to paddle. He got to his feet and brushed himself down to remove some dried grass.

'It's a bit early to get dunked in the water but I'll do my best to stay afloat,' he commented.

'Everything I own says you'll go for a swim but good luck anyway,' a passer-by commented.

The man with the camera made sure he stayed close to George and Arrad as they made their way to the jetty and the coracle.

George was helped into the small craft and Arrad helped to steady it while he settled in and received some advice.

'Keep your upper body still. A coracle isn't like a canoe and you don't need to lean your body into your paddling. Take slow and steady strokes, short ones, and steer by angling the paddle. Slow and steady, that's the way of it.'

Dipping his paddle into the water with caution, George sat rigidly still and tried to keep his arms close to his sides as much as he could. It seemed to be a good technique but he was careful to keep his strokes short so as not to make the coracle spin round in circles. To his surprise he made steady progress. At the turning point George manoeuvred his craft round the first marker pole without bumping against it and losing marks. The judges exchanged looks of approval and the onlookers applauded. Things were going well. It crossed George's mind that he could make a living if he owned a coracle and some eel traps. He certainly had a knack for coracle handling.

Round the second marker post and still going strong. Then; 'Swarm! Swarm! George, there's a swarm in the village and its gone under the eaves of a house. You must come and get it, everyone's going crazy!'

Coracle event or swarm event? There could be only one decision. Arrad will miss the coracle event but his future lies with the bees. George dug his paddle deep and leaned into his stroke. And capsized.

Land of my fathers!

Willing hands dragged him onto the jetty and pointed him in the right direction. Caught unprepared he dumped the contents of his rucksack and together with Arrad he raced to the house where the bees had swarmed.

'I don't want them in my house,' the woman who lived there complained loudly. 'Take them away before they sting me!'

There was no danger of that provided the woman was restrained from trying to use her broom to shift them. George had arrived in the nick of time. Arrad held the rucksack open and George carefully dislodged the swarm.

'My bag isn't the best way to move the bees but needs must. Where shall we take them?' He said to Arrad.

'Nerthi the Healer found me a place near the infirmary if a raft will take us,' Arrad replied.

'And so,' George said later, 'we took the swarm across the Lake and we crossed our fingers. It never rains but it pours and the following day Dendric, who was the Senior of the Hunters came to tell us of two more nests that his men had found. Dendric guided Arrad to one of them and then beat a hasty retreat and one of his men took me to the other and the next thing we had captured two more swarms. Arrad really made me proud. The next swarm was taken more leisurely and Arrad insisted on taking the swarm himself and we thanked our lucky stars we had some flat packed hives ready for them.'

***

The games were over. All over the Lake people were packing their belongings and preparing to make an early departure the following morning. Many families had a long journey ahead of them, especially the ones who were to make the sea crossing to their homeland in the country they now knew would one day be called Wales.

Atta observed wryly, 'As usual the boys are complaining that all the prettiest girls live on the wrong side of the sea. Ever year is the same.'

'What's new?' Hilary replied.

'Nothing I suppose. It's been like that since time began, which I now know to be when the big bang started everything off. I know it even if I don't understand it.' Atta said in reply.

'I'd better get a move on,' he added. 'I'm overseeing the closing ceremony tonight and I want to be sure it all goes according to plan. When it's all over I can stop being Councillor Atta and Alfrid can stop being Councillor Alfrid. It's time to pass the job to somebody else and I for one will be relieved.'

'So will Alfrid, I know for sure. Who is going to be elected to the Council now?'

'Vocca the fisherman has wriggled out of the job for years but he can't dodge it forever. It'll serve him right if they make him head of the Council. I don't know who else is in the running,' Atta replied with a touch of humour in his voice.

He parted company with George and Hilary and made his departure, walking vigorously.

'Too bad we can't tell Patti Driscoll when we get back to our own now that the new knees she put in him have given him a new lease of life,' Hilary said, 'but it will be years before that happens.'

Hand in hand they strolled at a slow pace towards Alfrid's house.

'I'm trying to take it in one last time,' George said in a serious tone. 'I can't believe how privileged we've been. We've made our mark on the Lake, I know we have. I'll never forget all this.'

A wide swing of his free arm took in all their surroundings.

'The people. Their plans and wishes for the future. The buildings. The industry and the technology. So different from everything we are used to but it suits the time and place. I envy them in so many ways.'

'It's all been so refreshingly uncomplicated,' Hilary said seriously, 'and I know I might not still be here if Gwenve hadn't operated on me. I never guessed they had that level of medicine. I'll never forget her.'

Eathl greeted them at her door.

'Cartiwiss told me to tell you that your son Arrad will come round as soon as he has had something to eat and made himself presentable,' she said.

What she did not say was that Arrad had already called at her house and slipped something into one of the bags that George had packed in readiness for an early start in the morning when they would make the trek to the stone where they had arrived and Wint would open the gate to the future.

Small Alfrid arrived, panting for breath after a short but fast run. As usual, he was accompanied by Twiss. The girl had a request.

'Can I see the picture of my plant again?' She pleaded, and she added, 'I think I might be a grower one day. My dad has been to see Domric in the healers garden to see if I can be a grower like him and I think he said he will teach me all the songs about growing plants.'

Hilary collected the camera that George had used to take a picture of the potted plant that Jasmin Tyler had given her. Twiss had been given a space to plant it and with small Alfrid's help she had cleared the ground and turned the soil over. Hers was the first and so far the only flower garden on the Lake but George was sure there would soon be others. Jasmin's present to the Lake had been as many packets of seeds as she could cram in to the cart that George had hauled into the past.

Twiss admired the picture.

'It's growing taller already,' she told George and Hilary proudly. 'Will you be sure to show this picture to Jasmin?' She asked anxiously.

'Of course I will,' George promised.

By his reckoning it was about three hours later when he set out with Hilary and their son to attend the closing ceremony of the Dad's and Lad's games. He and Arrad wore the oak wreaths that all the participants of the games wore and were expected to wear for the ceremony. George thought he had begun a tradition that would last as long as the games were played. He really had made his mark. Many pictures had been taken of all the players, including himself. If only he had been able to make copies for everybody. Perhaps he ought to have brought his chemicals and some good old fashioned film but it was too late now.

'One last time,' a woman spoke from the centre of a group of people. 'One last time and then we will hand all your camera things back for you to take home tomorrow.'

George and Arrad posed for the photographers.

'These will be invaluable,' George told them, 'and they will let everyone know what you look like, especially if I take some last pictures of you. On behalf of all the people in my now I thank you for what you have done for us.'

'We didn't win anything,' George reminded Arrad as they collected the cameras. He would have liked the ceremony that closed the games to be photographed but it was prudent to collect the cameras in so as to be sure that none were accidently left behind.

'I know dad but we played didn't we? We did play. I think this must be the best day of my life,' he said happily.

People from all over the Lake flocked to the Council meeting place. George and his family found themselves ushered to a seat at the front of the crowd.

Atta called for quiet.

'We have some prizes to award,' he began, 'for what have been the best games I have ever had to pleasure to attend and officiate. As you all know I shall be standing down after tonight so next year somebody else will be standing where I am. Man or woman, I wish them the best of luck. And now, if the prize winners are ready, let the proceedings begin.'

One by one as their names were called the proud procession of Dads and Lads stepped forward to receive their prizes as their names were called. Each pair received loud and well deserved cheers.

Atta addressed the assembly again.

'All that remains to be done is for the ceremony to be closed. May I wish you all safe and pleasant journeys home and,' he chuckled, 'I can promise you fair weather for the next few days. Wigstin, step forward. I should have mentioned this before,' he addressed the crowd again, 'but Wigstin is going to tell one of his jokes first.'

Mock groans were heard from everybody, including George.

Wigstin looked pleased. Somehow, George thought, he always did.

'Here is my joke,' he said. 'Where is the best place to stand when Councillor Alfrid throws a spear?'

'In front of his target,' the crowd roared happily.

Wigstin waited for the laughter to die away and then with a solemnity that few knew he possessed he began:

Wigstin.
How many are the Laws of the Lake?

All.
The Lake has but one Law and by it we are bid
Do as you would be done by
Be done by as you did

Wigstin.
Who is the Law for?

All.
The Law is for the big
The Law is for the small
The Law is for the short
The Law is for the tall
The Law is for the one
The Law is for the all
This is the Law of the Lake

And by it we are bid
Do as you would be done by
Be done by as you did

Wigstin.
I have heard you say it two times
But I must hear it three
I ask of all who love the Lake
To say again with me
When it is said a third time
Of doubt we will be rid

All.
Do as you would be done by
Be done by as you did

It was over and there was no more to be said. Quietly the men and women and their children stood up and began to move off. Many had packed their belongings in preparation for an early start in the morning, as had George and Hilary.

Chapter 35

Doctor Andrew Simpson thought long and hard about the things he had to tell the couple who sat opposite him in his office. Hilary Green helped him out.

'Gwenve was right wasn't she? I'm alive thanks to her but if it happens again I won't live to tell the tale.'

Wearing an uncomfortable expression Andrew Simpson replied cautiously, 'I wouldn't be that certain. Gwenve was an outstanding surgeon but there's no way she could have had any knowledge of life support machines. Perhaps something could be done.'

'Frankly I doubt it,' Hilary said bluntly.

More gently she said, 'Admit it Andrew. I won't survive another attack will I?'

'While there's life there's hope,' Simpson countered, 'but I have to admit that in all probability Gwenve was right. To be honest I'm surprised you lasted long enough to undergo surgery at all.'

'Nearly everyone on the Lake has some knowledge of first aid,' George Green told him. He added, 'The healers will come at a moment's notice but whether the healer comes to the patient or the patient is taken to the healer it takes more time than it does in the here and now so any kind of immediate assistance can mean the difference between life and death.'

'Quad erat demonstrandum, as Julia would say.' Simpson said.

Hilary smiled.

'Julia and dozens of other people in our little society. Latin does tend to grow on you.'

Simpson agreed.

'As I myself have just demonstrated,' he replied.

He shuffled the papers on his desk.

'The pictures Gwenve drew and the notes she dictated to you George are invaluable. If she were here I would let her into the operating theatre without a second's hesitation and I'd give a lot to know how her hypnotism worked,' he said seriously.

'She could have sawed off my arms and legs when she tried it on me,' George agreed.

'Suppose we stop talking in circles,' Hilary said crisply. 'The question is how long have I got to live? Don't look so surprised Andrew, we know it could happen at any time and we're grown up people. How long have I got?'

'If it were anybody else,' Simpson began, and stopped abruptly.

'I don't know,' he admitted honestly. 'I believe everything Gwenve had to say and I'm on the verge of admitting she knows a lot more than I do but even Gwenve had no answer. I wish I could be more helpful.'

'That's the way we thought it is,' George Green replied.

He added, 'We've talked it over with our daughters.'

'We don't intend it to come as a surprise,' Hilary added, 'and we're prepared, all of us. Gwenve has given me more time and I'm eternally grateful but I'll accept my fate. I've given up driving but I'll make no other concession. I'm not an invalid and I won't behave like an invalid or be treated like an invalid. I don't see myself as any different from anyone else and I'm no worse off that millions of other people.'

Andrew Simpson nodded his agreement.

'It appears that everything has been said,' he acknowledged.

'Not quite,' George Green said with a wide grin on his face. 'Have you heard Merlin's joke about it?'

Merlin was known for his schoolboy jokes.

'Not yet. Is it a good one?'

'It made us laugh: a man went to his doctor to hear his diagnosis. All right, he said, we know about my condition so how long have I got? I'd say about ten, was the reply. Ten what? Ten months? Ten years? How long? The doctor looked at his watch and said, nine, eight, seven…'

***

Already younger in appearance than his years warranted Robert Robertson flipped through his notes one last time.

'Sorting and cataloguing all the photographs that George and Hilary brought back from the past is going to take years, especially bearing in mind that I'm an amateur at this business. I have managed to get every picture into the computer system and I have made sure to have back-up copies but there are so many photographs that I haven't even begun to categorise them. I haven't the qualifications to do that so I shall rely on George and Clive to lend a hand, not to mention Merlin and Julia,' he said.

'Those pictures are invaluable,' Clive Bowden commented. 'They bring an insight into pre-history that is unprecedented.'

'That's not all they have done,' Robert continued. 'We've been keeping this under wraps but Julia took one look at one particular picture and nearly fainted. She showed it to Merlin and they agree, but I'm going to let Julia tell the story.'

Julia stood up.

'There is a plaque in the city that states that the first king of all England was crowned here,' she said. 'That was King Edgar and I remember the occasion well because I attended the ceremony myself. The ceremony was performed by Dunstan, the man who was to become Saint Dunstan. I knew Dunstan when he was a boy who lived on the Lake and he was always up to some caper or other. It must have been hereditary because Dunstan was the spitting image of Wigstin! Robert said I nearly fainted when I saw Wigstin's photograph and that's not far from the truth.'

'I remember Dunstan too,' Merlin said when Julia returned to her seat. 'I don't know whether Lerghwil ever threw Wigstin into the Lake but there were times when I dearly wanted to throw Dunstan in! He spent a year or so in exile but Edgar asked him to return to England after a King Eadwig was shown the door. Eadwig was a regional king of, shall we say loose morals, and Dunstan had caught him at it with two of his harlots. Two out of many I might add. Dunstan found it expedient to do a bunk; anyone with an iota of common sense would have done the same. Anyway Edgar persuaded him to come back and the crowning ceremony that he performed has changed very little from that day on. Dunstan was the person who devised the form it should take and in my opinion he was the best of the English saints.

'Returning to the subject of the photographs, as Clive said, they are invaluable. We can interpret the photographs and draw conclusions from them and from the diaries that George and Hilary kept,' he continued. 'I never suspected that open heart surgery was possible five thousand years ago but it obviously was and Hilary is here to prove it. We must be cautious because we don't want to let our hearts rule our heads but I have spoken to George and Hilary and they claim that their guesses and opinions carry some weight because they are the ones who were there.'

'The people who live in Alfrid's now are a lot more educated and sophisticated than I would have expected,' Copper said.

'They were quick on the uptake, that's for sure. Until I showed them how to use a camera they had no idea, well of course they hadn't but hundreds of those pictures were taken by people of the Stone Age and early Iron Age. It's a good thing we took a lot of cameras with us, thanks to Alfrid and Eathl urging us to do so, and it's a good thing we took a good supply of batteries and memory storage,' George said.

Robert smiled.

'I did find one interesting picture of George that Hilary told me was taken when he had finished a day's work up to his knees in mud when they were building the new bridge. All the workers of both sexes went into the Lake to get cleaned up and I found a picture of George emerging starkers and talking to a very pretty girl who was as nude as he was.'

'What!' George spluttered. 'I didn't know about that! If this gets out Robert I swear here and now that someone else will be thrown in the Lake!'

'Spoil sport. I was thinking of giving out copies to…'

What Robert was about to say was drowned out by gales of laughter.

Merlin waited a long time for the room to settle down.

'The pictures of the past bring to light new facts that even I was unaware of. It's both remarkable and fascinating to see how people who lived five thousand years ago took to modern technology. I said lived; perhaps I ought to say live. We see them at work. We see them at play. We know their names and what they did. They have sent us a whole host of things; pottery, wicker work, carved wooden playthings, some pictures they drew with colouring pens. We even know the names of the artists because Hilary showed them how to pen their names on the pictures they drew when they gave them to her. They drew their houses and their schools, they drew pictures of rafts and canoes, swings and see-saws and skipping at the playing place, and so on. I could go on for hours but I won't because I'm going to let the vicar talk about one very special photograph.'

'Thank you Merlin.' The vicar stood up. 'I have a photograph that was taken by a man named Atta, who is the leader of the Council of Seniors. It was taken at the closing of the Dads and Lads games and Atta intended to step down when they were over. Alfrid was going to give up his seat on the Council too, and devote more time to being Alfrid and less time to being Councillor, much to the relief of Eathl and small Alfrid you will recall. The photograph is another picture of George and we have had it framed for George to hang on his wall. It's historic and cultural significance is outstanding. George, you are the Green Man.'

'I know. That was what Wigstin called me all the time.'

'George, you're missing the point. Look at the picture and you'll see what I mean because this is you wearing a wreath of oak leaves like all the entrants in the Games wore. Similar pictures have been used as inn signs for centuries. How many pubs do you think have been called The Green Man? The Green Man appears all over the place. In Europe his carved effigy can be found in churches, abbeys, cathedrals, and any amount of non-ecclesiastical buildings. He's been carved, painted, and as well as being found in Europe he can be found all over the world, perhaps because travellers and explorers took the legend of the Green Man with them or because visitors to our shores took the legend home when they returned. I really don't know but I expect it happened both ways. In wine growing countries the oak leaves have been substituted for vines.

'The Green Man comes from a time long before the great religions were established but we know the Romans adopted local deities and incorporated them into their own beliefs and although I am speaking of my own religion I can state that the early Christians did the same thing with the ceremonies they found. If they hadn't done so they would have alienated new converts. The Green Man is a symbol of rebirth and stability and the continuing viability of society. A good example is the harvest festival. It stands to reason that the gathering of the harvest is a cause for celebration, be that a harvest of grain, grapes, fish, vegetables, berries, and so on. Every society performs a service of thanksgiving of one form or another and it would be silly not to do so and let's not forget that ceremonies and celebrations reinforce the bonds of kinship at local and national level. Their importance cannot be overestimated.

342

'So the Green Man is undoubtedly and indisputably pagan in origin and yet he remains a part of our daily lives. And here he is; George Green, otherwise known as the Green Man!'

Notes from the journal of Robert Robertson

Some weeks have passed since nine of us were given the pseudo-virus. Me and Victoria my wife, Mr and Mrs Whiting, Mr and Mrs Rudd, Herr and Frau Pfaffinger, and Janet Smythe. The age rule was broken for Janet. It was done to match her apparent age with Jack Smythe who grew up with the virus in his blood. Another person for whom the rule was broken was Dr Kate Fawcett in an experiment to see if the virus could be put into anyone with her blood group which is not the same as Copper's. It was an illegal experiment and it worked and that is why some of the nine were given a different strain of the virus. The effects were instant but I will not go into details.

I have had several long conversations with Merlin, the vicar, and the chronicler, the subject being the chronicles themselves. Such a lot has happened during the last few months that it is impossible to include everything.

The major news item concerns George and Hilary Green. They are back at home and to put it in their own words they are enduring endless grilling and interrogation about the time they spent in the past. So much has yet to be said that the chronicles cannot tell the full story, which means that publication and information about many of their adventures will have to be postponed until it can be put into some sort of order. Future readers, whoever they may be, will be able to access everything on their computers. Original material will probably be placed in a museum but that is still under discussion.

There is general agreement that the inclusion of a group of young students into our society has been a success and likely to be of the greatest importance and interest to future readers and for that reason the chronicler has given them lots of room. He has omitted to mention that Marcel and Françoise Land came over on a flying visit from France for the opportunity to talk to Alfrid and his family. It was clear and above board; our visitors from the Stone Age/Iron Age were fully aware that the psychologists were interested in the minds and thought processes of a group of people who lived five thousand years ago.

Marcel and Françoise very soon found out that it was a two way process!

I have urged the chronicler to say more about Walter Pfaffinger. When our two countries were at war our paths crossed on at least two occasions when we exchanged shell fire, and Walter's transition from the commander of a German Mark Four Panzer Tank to a physiotherapist is a story in itself. He was made a prisoner of war when one of his tracks was blown off in the Ardennes and he was held until the war was over and before he was officially released he did a bunk. Technically he was still a prisoner and he was in deep trouble… but the story is his to tell, not mine. For the record, I served in a Guards Regiment. (Motto – Join the army and see the world. Join the Guards and scrub it! We were very spit and polish and proud of it). I told Marcel Land that being in the Guards was not at all the same as being in the army. It was a while before he caught on to the joke. That was some time ago.

We have a need to plan for our immediate futures. I have a good understanding of computers (take that you nerdy fourteen year olds!) and I intend to find work in that area. Walter wants to take up physiotherapy again and do volunteer work on a steam railway either here or in Germany. If they have any in Germany; I'm not clear about that. Annaliese Pfaffinger is going to be a hair stylist. I was unaware that she used to do that but Victoria talks to her a lot in conversations that are a mixture of English and German and I got my information from her. Henry Rudd is giving up dairy farming and considering studying architecture. Henry Whiting is picking up where he left off, working with wood.

How long I shall continue to work as our society archivist and record keeper is as yet undecided and so far nobody has come forward to take on the job. I keep the records as they are brought to me and I index them to the best of my amateur ability and thus it is that I see the chronicler whenever he comes to me for material and to keep abreast of events. As I think I have mentioned already the amount of material is colossal and I have photographed it, scanned it, and digitalised it. History will love me or hate me but I need the storage space.

It is plain that the chronicles do no more than skim the surface. What then are their purpose? My answer is that they were written to give a broad overview in a form that is easy to read and spread the word far and wide. They will provide a snapshot of our day-to-day affairs. It might turn out that the things that are considered important by us will be dismissed by future readers as unimportant and immaterial and naturally the reverse is true. I haven't got a crystal ball and neither has the chronicler! We simply do our best.

To get back on track and stop trying to justify myself, Alfrid and his family were shown Frank Holley's microlight aircraft but declined Frank's offer of a flight. To my eyes it is a flimsy contraption that I would not risk my life in! Frank took off and circled around and then flew off to keep an eye on some of the local farms which is something he often does.

While he was doing that it was observed that Lofty and Elizabeth Harrison appeared to be cooking something up with Brian Gleaves and Julia.

Knowing as I do just how much information the chronicler must digest and present to any reader I can fairly state that he is subjected to an information overload. It bothers him that he has neither the time nor the space to include everything that comes his way. Inevitably there will be critics demanding to know why this or that was never included. And why certain things were of course.

Case in point; Shipmaster Cadric. It is known that he heard from Beowulf and Freya that the Vikings had discovered a land to the west. In short, their longships crossed the Atlantic Ocean and they discovered America long before Christopher Columbus made his voyage. Cadric wondered if he might beat the Vikings to it and according to George Green the voyage has not been made yet but Cadric has not given up on the idea.

And another thing. Lofty Harrison was right about Jasmin Tyler when he made an instant decision to bring her on board. I have no idea how many people have been to see 'her' garden but I certainly have and when I did I learned a new word; HABDOTROPISM. In the plant world it means sensitive to touch. Jasmin explained how the word applies to cucumber plants that have tendrils that sense when they touch something and wrap themselves around it to anchor themselves and grow higher. Cucumbers grown commercially in greenhouses grow rapidly and the growth of their tendrils can be seen with the naked eye and a keen ear can hear a creaking noise as thousands of tendrils grow. Astonishing!

Alfrid and his family have returned home. Their visit was a raging success and they returned laden with gifts for themselves and everyone on the Lake. Jasmin Tyler went with them to Merlin's standing stone when they left and she stepped through very briefly with small Alfrid and gave his Stone Age/Iron Age friend Twiss a potted plant.

George Green stepped through and Clive Bowden's prediction that he would be wearing a grin that only surgery would remove was as close to the truth as made a difference. While he was on the Lake he adopted a son whom he set up with a number of bee hives and wrote a picture book for him showing various designs of hives and pictures of bees; queens, drones, and workers. He left the boy with five hives of bees established and settled in. In his own words it never rains but it pours and the nests of bees that had been found wild all swarmed at once or nearly so and when he and his new son were competing in the Dads and Lads games they were suddenly called away to deal with a swarm that had lodged under the eaves of a nearby house so they never competed in all the events they had wanted to have a go at and they never won any prizes. There was a sixth swarm but the bees decided to go elsewhere after a few days. Still, five out of six isn't bad.

At this point I must report that I will talk to George about the hives at the earliest opportunity because my information is that he left the Lake before he could be sure that the swarms of bees that he captured became established in his and Arrad's hives. I suspect that I have made a mistake or somebody else has.

George also brought back his own flag that was designed by a woman named Meglen and he is a Freeman of the Lake in perpetuity and on top of that he is the legendary Green Man. If ever I get the chance to go where/when George and Hilary went I'll go like a shot. Other people would like to visit other times and Copper has been heard to declare that she would pay anything for a ticket to ride in an open carriage behind Stephenson's Rocket steam engine. Future historians look it up for yourselves.

I imagine Walter Pfaffinger would like the same opportunity.

There. Have I broken up the log jam of over-information and cleared the way for the chronicler to continue with his narrative and bring it to a close? That goal has been my intention. Enough is enough as they say, and as one episode of the chronicle is closed another one will surely open.

Chapter 36

James Wilson stowed a few items into his school rucksack ant then frowned and patted his pockets.

'Mum, I can't find my compass. I had it ready to take with me but… I'll look in my bedroom but I'm sure I didn't leave it there.'

'On the kitchen table,' Mrs Wilson replied briefly. She added, 'Are you still testing the nail? I thought you'd given up on that.'

James shrugged his shoulders.

'We didn't give up but we don't do it as much as we did at the start but it rained for three days last week and Deke says there might be enough underground water to kick it off. Might be.'

'What do you think?'

'I doubt it but it's worth a go.'

'Tell me if anything does happen.'

'Mum, if anything happens I'll tell the whole world,' James replied with a broad smile.

The ringtone on his phone ended the conversation. James read the text message it carried.

'Christine is on the way. I'd better be going,' he said as he slipped his rucksack over his shoulders.

'Compass.'

'Oops! Nearly forgot. Thanks mum.'

He found Christine Appleton outside the corner shop and she had something to show him.

'Look James. I made a small version of my flag and sewed it onto me rucksack.'

James examined it.

'That's pretty much the way you drew it in small Alfrid's picture phone book when he was here,' he commented.

'I was doing the washing up and I realised the scouring pad was exactly the right oblong shape for a scaled down flag so I got some white material and cut it slightly oversize so I could turn the edges over to stop them fraying and then I used a permanent marker to ink in the design. It took longer than I expected but it secms to have worked. You could make one too because your flag is black and white like mine; a black cog wheel with white eyes on a white background,' Christine said and then added, 'I think light blue would be a better background colour for my flag and if I sacrifice a blue pillowcase I could get four flags out of it.'

Her rucksack was light and she carried it over one shoulder.

'I could if I could sew I could but I'd most likely make a mess of it. Have you asked Mrs Beach about making a full sized flag like Jasmin Tyler's?'

'No but I can make my own,' Christine replied.

Suddenly she asked, 'Have you heard about Mrs Green?'

'I've known for a couple of days but my parents said it's not for me to talk about,' James answered cautiously.

'Same as mine. They must have rung round to everybody. I can see why we aren't to talk about it but all our parents must know we will, just between ourselves. I'm not sure how we can face Mr Green when we see him at the start of the new term but I do know I'm not looking forward to it, I mean, having to pretend we don't know and I'm sure he knows we do know.'

James agreed.

Christine had more to talk about.

'Have you fed live food to your trilobites?' She asked.

'No, just fish flakes and pellets from the supermarket. They gobble them up like there was no tomorrow so I'm having to guess how much to give them. They live in the dark in Merlin's cave so I feed them as late as I can but I don't think it makes any difference what time I do it. You can see their luminous spots darting all over the place,' James replied.

'Like fireflies in the water. I've sat up in bed and watched them. Mine eat during the day and they seem to know which end of the aquarium to go to when I show them a coloured card so I think they can identify different colours but maybe any card will do. I need to do more experimenting. Anyway James, I've fed them live tubifex worms and it starts a feeding frenzy when I drop them in. They don't last long enough to reach the bottom of the tank!' Christine ended with a laugh.

'Umm. I've never heard of them.'

'You can get them from the aquarium shop. They're dark red and they come as a wriggling mass of worms. The assistant told me I can put them straight into my aquarium or keep them in fresh water for a

350

day or two before I put them in. That's what I did. I dropped a wriggling ball of worms into the water and the trilobites went mad for them,' Christine told James.

'I don't suppose Yo will be feeding worms to her trilobites,' James chuckled.

Christine laughed again.

Yolanda Walker hated anything that she described as a creep crawly she would have had hysterics at the thought of a mass of wriggling worms.

'What are they called again?' James asked.

'Tubifex. Tubifex worms.'

'I could give some to my trilobites and maybe I could get dad to feed some to his cave shrimps. They haven't turned anything down so far,' James said.

The covered market was not crowded and James produced his compass and laid it on the nail.

'Nothing happened,' Christine observed.

'Then we'll say the experiment was inconclusive shall we?'

The pair whirled round.

'Uh. Mrs Green. We didn't hear you coming,' James stammered.

Hilary Green smiled.

'Evidently,' she replied. 'I believe you have already heard about my heart condition and been instructed not to talk about it,' she continued.

The teenagers nodded dumbly.

'Ignore what you were told,' Hilary said briskly. 'I've said this before and no doubt I'll say it again but what happened to me could have happened to anyone. I was lucky to be in the right place at the right time, which is to say I was on the Lake a few thousand years ago and Gwenve was a first rate surgeon.

'I didn't come here to tell you that,' Hilary continued. 'Merlin and George and the vicar have arranged a meeting tonight in the Village Hall. Your parents will have been told by now I should think. There's a video to watch and there is a guest speaker who is an old boy of the school. More than that I can't say. I've some errands to run so I'll be off now and I'll see you again this evening.'

She turned away and was gone, hidden from view among the narrow alleyways of the indoor market.

James replaced his compass in his rucksack and the pair drifted off to meet their friends in the usual Saturday morning meeting place.

Deke Thorpe greeted them with the words, 'You've just missed a message from Alison about a meeting tonight. She wouldn't say why.'

'Mrs Green came up to us in the market and told us and our parents have all been tipped off.'

'Something's going on,' Yolanda Walker said, leaning forward, 'and I'll be sure to be there this time because I wasn't there when Mr Wint turned up from the past. I did see him though, and he looked through my telescope and showed me a place on the moon where something will happen one day but he wouldn't tell me what it is and when it will happen. Perhaps it will be a meteor impact or a landing site.'

'Is he Mr Wint?' Jasmin Tyler asked. 'I thought that was his name and title all rolled into one.'

Deke Thorpe confirmed that it was.

James and Christine had skipped breakfast to be at the nail before the market became crowded and they headed for the counter for muffins and fruit juice. James piled plates the others had used earlier onto an empty tray and carried it away.

Chapter 37

George and his passenger drew up in the car park outside the Village Hall and the car that had trailed them pulled up alongside.

'I'll make the introductions when we get inside,' George said briefly as he led the way.

'Good evening everybody,' he said to the dozen or so people who were seated with their backs toward him. Heads were turned as the trio strode down the centre aisle and turned to face their expectant audience.

George gestured to his guests to sit down before he began to speak.

'I see the vicar managed to bring you all together but you must be wondering why. The reasons will soon become clear but first let me introduce two people. First and on my left, is someone you have all heard of, namely the chronicler. His name appears thinly disguised in the book that was distributed to everyone so I won't bother to repeat it. The chronicler is here this morning to observe and record but he won't take any part in the proceedings. Secondly and on my left is Peter Birkett who is totally in the dark as to what we all know is going on.

'Peter I owe you an apology for omitting certain details from what I have told you so far and when the reason becomes clear I hope I shall be exonerated.'

Addressing the room at large he continued, 'Peter was one of my pupils who has gone on to do pioneering work in the world of quantum mechanics. In short, he devises new and better ways to bash sub-atomic particles together, and now you know as much as I do. Now we get to the nitty-gritty. Christine I owe you an apology as well.'

The girl looked startled. George continued speaking.

'During the evening when Jasmin and her father were brought into our society you were pressed into talking about your ideas about the universe. What you didn't know was that we had a couple of video recorders running and for that you can blame Julia when next you see her; she had heard you earlier in the day and you made something of an impression. It's not often that Julia is impressed,' he added.

'To continue. I posted a copy of the recording to Peter and we had a video chat about it during which time I told him that the video had been edited and I told him that the editing had simply removed some unimportant details, which I am afraid was another lie. I also happened, ahem, to mention that a few weeks previously you had been called Spockette, and now I'm going to show the video of out talk that was filmed at Peter's end and includes the reaction of a certain Doctor Sheldon Cooper. The vicar will pass out a transcript to everyone, along with a copy of an email that Peter sent me at a later date.'

'ASP 1, ASP 2, and the Appleton Interface Region,' Christine said in a faint voice after she read it and the laughter had died away.

For the first time Peter Birkett had something to say.

'When I was your age it never would have occurred to me to challenge Zeno of Elea. I had to look him up by the way. You're an original thinker but I understand you're not headed for a career in cosmology. Is that right?'

'Yes sir. I've decided to go in for marine biology and oceanography,' Christine replied in a voice that was still unsteady.

'Well if you ever change your mind... I made reference to the universe cold spot in the email you are holding. Did you know about it when you put your thoughts together?'

Christine shook her head in denial.

'No sir. I'm not into cosmology but Yo is.'

She leaned forward and glanced past Deke Thorpe to Yolanda Walker.

'It's a place in the universe that hasn't got as many stars as it should have but that's all I know about it,' Yolanda said.

Harry Tyler uncrossed his legs and indicated that he wanted to say something. At a nod from George he began.

'I'm Harry Tyler, Jasmin's father,' he pointed to his daughter and continued, 'I'm a painter and decorator and not a scientist so I might get a few things wrong. I was there in the room when Christine did her talk so I know Mr Green edited out any mention of a scientist called Wint. What Christine said in the unedited version was that Wint sees time as a sphere and it is possible to travel inside the sphere of time. I do know that travelling through time is possible in theory but that's not all I know about it because right here there are two people who have done it. One is the vicar who went back a few years and the other went back about five thousand years and spent a few weeks in the Stone Age. He's sitting next to you; it was Mr Green.'

'I went back too Dad. Only for a few seconds though.'

'I stand corrected. My daughter went back into the past for just long enough to give a plant to a Stone Age girl.'

…

'There was Alfrid and Eathl and their son who was called small Alfrid and they had a young daughter who was called Elfrey which was a name they made up and it was half Eathl and half Freya,' Jasmin Tyler said, 'and small Alfrid had a friend in his own Stone Age and her name was Twiss. I mean it is Twiss and I went through just for a second when they went home and I gave her a plant as a present,' she added.

…

'Came across Zeno's place paradox. Zeno maintained that everything that exists is in a place, which is fair enough, but he went on to say that a place must be somewhere; namely a place. Another place in other words, and that led him to say that every place must be in another place. Just thinking about that makes my head spin but taken to its logical conclusion there must be a limitless number of places. On the face of it that seems unlikely and I'm sure Zeno thought it so but in the light of what Mr Green has just told me there was or is a woman hospital worker called, um, Cartiwiss was it? Cartiwiss told Mrs Green that she, I don't know how to put this, she said that other times are just other places and all anyone has to do is walk round the corner and there you are. Well, that certainly binds time and space together. Does that accord with your reasoning?'

'I suppose it does, especially if there really is a multiverse but it's hard to follow,' Christine replied.

'And so say all of us.'

…

'I saw it in a junk shop and it had an instruction book so I bought it for about fifty pence. When I use the slide rule I can see every stage of what I'm doing in a way that I can't with a computer or calculator.'

'I gather the examiners didn't see it your way when you used it in an exam.'

James Wilson had an infectious grin.

'No sir, they didn't.'

…

'Grey background with the dark blue dragon of Wessex and a red trilobite motif. I'll keep my eyes peeled for anyone wearing a tie or scarf that matches it. Am I permitted to have flag too?'

'Everybody can have one. When I was on the Lake there were any number of personal flags and that was where I got mine. King Arthur wanted it that way and now they're catching on. I've counted half a dozen at least around the school as the word spreads and that's only a beginning. Mostly the students are trying out different designs on the covers of their exercise books. It's not heraldry and doesn't pretend to be but now it's started to take off I predict a big bang of flags.'

…

'I haven't got a hedgehog yet. If somebody doesn't help them they will all have gone in ten years time. Extinct. People keep cats and dogs for pets and they don't do anything useful for plants and nobody takes any notice of the little insects and animals that do good in their gardens and farms. I'm going to keep trying.'

…

'I can't do anything with this. I can't stop my work with my team and if I go public I'll be the laughing stock of the scientific community. What I can do is prevail on my long-suffering parents to put me up again in Bath as soon as I can get a couple of days off. I'll show my team the pictures you've provided and hope they take me seriously and come here to see for themselves. Whatever other artifacts you allow me to take might go some way to persuading them that I haven't gone raving mad and perhaps, and it's a big perhaps, they might give some attention to what's going on, and I'm none too sure what that something is. I'll have to tell my wife as well. Don't expect an immediate result. Thanks for getting me in in this. And finally; Jeepers Creepers!'

Interlude

PROFESSOR LAND'S NOTES

I've been giving some thought to something George Green raised with me. During a discussion about the talk that Christine Appleton gave, George said he could never have done what she did because he would have reached his boggling point. He termed it the point at which his mind would not accept what he was thinking. The mind boggles as they say.

To be honest my thoughts were anything but serious. Then I took a second swing at it and a whole raft of questions emerged, together with the possibility of writing a (fairly lighthearted) book on the subject.

Questions:

What is a boggling point?

What is your boggling point?

Why have you got a boggling point?

Does it serve a purpose?

Can you shift your boggling point?

Do you want to?

Would it be desirable to do so?

Does your boggling point hold you back?

(From anything – relationships, promotion, education, new projects, adventurous experiences, risk taking, new undertakings, the list is endless).

Is your boggling point holding back your colleagues, working team/group, your organisation and so on?

Is the possession of a boggling point a survival strategy?

Is it redundant?

How does it change as you age?

Those are my tentative thoughts and there may be others to come. Almost certainly there will be.

If I do write a book who should I write it for? Business? Education? Students? Scientists? Old Uncle Tom Cobley and all?

Perhaps the biggest question is whether or not an examination and identification of an individual's boggling point has any therapeutic value?

Later.

I slept on it and by the time I finished my breakfast I had decided not to proceed; not out of laziness but because I couldn't see any value in it.

Around eleven this morning it occurred to me that my own personal boggling point had been reached. That was not comfortable but in a way it was, I think and hope, liberating. I will proceed but as Julia and Copper Beach would say, festina lente, or in other words hasten slowly. And the title? The Mind Boggles.

Chapter 38

Deke Thorpe walked slowly out of the school building at the end of the day. It was Thursday and the weekend held the promise of rain. Hoping to spot Jasmin Tyler, Deke looked over his shoulder among the groups of pupils who followed him out. Jasmin had sent him a text message saying she wanted to talk to him urgently and he had replied that he would meet her at the end of lessons. Deke had other plans but he hid his annoyance and he intended to make their meeting a short one.

'I want to bring someone to do his homework with us on Saturday morning,' Jasmin said breathlessly as she caught up with him.

'Anybody I know?' Deke kept his answer short.

'Terry Mitchell. He is in my form and he wears glasses. He doesn't like it when people call him Tel or Mitch, he just likes to be called Terry. He's been told that he will be put back a year if his performance doesn't improve. He isn't a nimlet but he doesn't do his homework and he's quite shy. I think he had been crying but he said he hadn't. I've already told him he can come.' Jasmin replied.

'Fair enough, did you tell him about the Bell Curve?'

Jasmin shook her head emphatically.

'All right. I'll tell the others. What subject will he bring with him?'

'We've got geography assignments so I told him to bring that.'

'OK Jas, you can work together. I've got a language test to revise for and so has Yo but I don't know what James and Christine are doing. I've got to get a shift on or I'll miss my bus. See you on Saturday if not before.'

There were no rules about who could or could not join the homework group for the Saturday sessions Deke Thorpe mused while he rode the bus home. Some went on to higher education and others did not. Deke knew of one other group and possibly two, but there was something different about the group he belonged to and that was the knowledge they carried with them. Should this Terry Mitchell be left out? Emphatically no. Jasmin had declared that he wasn't a nimlet, a word that had come into their vocabulary after a local geography exercise when Deke himself had joked that the word sounded as if it described someone who wasn't very bright. One day the people who lived in the village of Nimlet might want to ask him some pointed questions about that. Deke put the thought to one side.

It didn't seem right for this Terry Mitchell to be kept in ignorance, and for another thing Jasmin Tyler was going to be left on her own sooner or later because she was two years behind the other group members. The study group had become important to him, he suddenly realised, and it meant that continuity would be maintained as far as the Bell Curve Society was concerned. That was what had brought his group into the Society in the first place so it seemed logical to expect it to be important to the people who had brought them in. Logical? He was starting to think like Spockette. Deke smiled inwardly and made up his mind what to do next. He would phone Merlin.

***

Refill pads covered the table when Jasmin came to the homework group's regular Saturday morning table in the burger bar with Terry Mitchell in tow. The boy looked nervous and Deke remembered Jasmin telling him he was the shy type. He put him at his ease.

'Make room everybody. I'm Deke Thorpe and these are James Wilson who is sitting next to Christine Appleton, and Yo Walker who is sitting next to me because we're revising for a language test. Jasmin said you have geography assignments. We've got a rule that it's up to you to do your own work but everybody helps everyone else. OK?'

Terry Mitchell nodded dumbly.

'Start off with a carton of orange juice first and drink it as you go along,' Yo Walker advised, 'and take a break every twenty minutes to let your lessons sink in,' she continued.

'It works for us,' James Wilson added.

'I can't see much use for geography,' Terry Mitchell declared.

'You'd be surprised. All our subjects join up together in a way but nobody ever tells you that. It makes each subject more interesting,' Christine Appleton told him.

Terry Mitchell was not convinced and it showed in his face but at least he wasn't openly hostile, Deke thought.

Each pupil had revision or assignment work to be ready for the coming week and the session got under way.

'I've got apps on my tablet so I can look up the geology and the type of soil anywhere in the British Isles,' Jasmin explained to Terry Mitchell as the session drew to an end. 'All the information comes from the National Geological Survey and it's useful for geography when you learn about moorlands and mountains and agriculture. It's just like Christine said, all the subjects come together. I use the app for my garden work. You must come and see my garden,' she said.

'No peace until you do,' James added.

'I've put gardening down as my career choice,' Jasmin continued. 'What did you put down?'

'Nothing,' Terry muttered. 'I'm good at sport but I'm not much good at anything else. I might get a job in a garage or something but I don't know.'

'It's early days,' Christine comforted him. 'I only made my choice a few weeks ago. I'm going in for marine biology. If you are interested in sport you should go to the sports centre and find out more about it. They do all sorts of things there and I know there are brochures. You might find more things.'

'Oh.'

Terry became more chatty during the short breaks they took.

'I've never done this much homework,' he admitted.

'Time goes faster when you work together and it's more interesting to do it here instead of doing it at home. I think so anyway,' James Wilson replied.

'I haven't written much about glaciation and truncated spurs yet,' Jasmin declared. 'Only about two lines.'

'It was the only bit that made sense to me,' was Terry's surprising reply.

'I'll write some more now I've jogged my own memory.'

They returned to their work for another short session until Deke Thorpe declared it was time to stop.

'I know it's a bit early but there's a couple of things to sort out. Terry, you're in the homework club now and it's up to you whether you stay or leave.'

'I'd like to stay. I really want to.'

'Good,' Deke approved, 'but there's a sort of club within a club, a society we really want you to, well, I'll show you. You see the scarf that

Yo is wearing? Well, society members all get a scarf like that. Girl members I should say. Men all get a tie.'

Deke reached into the rucksack that carried his school books and pulled out a tie.

'This is yours and it's a free introductory offer that's yours to keep even if you don't want to be a part of it.'

Christine Appleton produced her own scarf and made a neat knot as she tied it on.

'The motif is a dark blue dragon and a red trilobite on a grey background. That'd because the blue dragon was the symbol of the old kingdom of Wessex that covered southern England, and the trilobites lived in the sea until they all died out millions of years ago. Except they didn't, not quite. Jasmin hasn't got any but the rest of us have got some in our aquariums at home.'

'You can come round to my place and see them and my parents say your parents are invited too,' James said.

Terry Mitchell said nothing.

Deke produced a book from his rucksack.

'This is where it gets interesting. This book is about some of the members of the Society, which is called the Bell Curve Society and you'll see why when you read it but it would be best if your parents read it first. This is my copy but you will get a copy of your own next Saturday and you can give mine back to me. Some of our teachers are Society members; Mr Green and Mr Bowden are both in this book. Miss Collins isn't in the book but she is a member too. As a matter of fact there is a follow-up book that we are in but it hasn't been printed yet.'

'Oh. I don't wear a tie much.'

'Neither do we but now and again you see someone wearing a tie or scarf like ours.'

Jasmin produced something from her own rucksack.

'Look Terry. This is my flag. Anyone can have one. Christine has made a small version of hers and sewn it on her jacket and James has done the same with his.'

Terry Mitchell stared at the patches.

'I'm going to change the background colour of my flag but so far all I have is the patches I made. My rucksack has got one too,' Christine told him.

Deke produced a card.

'Here's my phone number and email address. We've all got these but don't flash them about to anyone, just put the numbers in your phone and we'll put your number in ours,' he said.

James gave Terry his own card and added, 'I can run these off on my computer and I'll make some for you.'

'Your card says colour aberration under your name. What does that mean?'

Yolanda told him.

'I got us detentions for that,' she added.

'My phone isn't very good.' Terry sounded embarrassed as he took the phone from his pocket.

Yolanda Walker laid hers on the table.

'Same as mine but yours takes photos and mine doesn't, it makes calls and texts and that's all. It's pay as you go and it costs ten pounds every three months or so to top it up. I don't need any more than that,' she declared.

Terry looked relieved but said nothing.

'There's one thing to remember Terry, and that's that we are all pupils and Mr Green and Mr Bowden and Miss Collins are our teachers and that's the way it is. They treat us as equals when we have special meetings sometimes but we still have to call them sir and miss and we don't get special treatment. A teacher is a teacher and a pupil is a pupil and that's that, so don't step out of line,' James warned.

Deke Thorpe stowed his homework away.

'That's it for me. I'm off to the market to check on the nail. It won't prove anything but you never know,' he said.

'Sports centre for us,' Yo said.

'No swimming for me this week,' Jasmin said. 'I have too much to do in my garden. Lettuce and radish to pull out for a salad first, then weeding and watering.'

Terry Mitchell left with a bemused expression on his face as the group split up and went their separate ways. Then he remembered what Christine had said about the sports centre. It would look too obvious if he followed the others but he made up his mind to go there later.

Chapter 39

The open space in front of the entrance to the Roman Baths was largely empty when Clive Bowden arrived and found a seat. It was Saturday and it would be crowded later but it was too early yet for the shoppers and visitors and sightseers who would throng the area later in the day. He kept his eye open for the people whom he knew had been told where and when to find him. The wait was shorter than he had expected it to be.

'Mr and Mrs Mitchell?' He greeted them. 'I'm Clive Bowden,' he added, 'and I teach history. I don't believe we have met before but even on parents evenings we never manage to see everybody. We can sit here and watch the world go by and I'll do my best to explain what's going on.'

'We read the book our Terry brought home with him. Skimmed through it, we haven't read it properly. If you and Mr Green and Miss Collins weren't in it we wouldn't have come along this morning,' Mrs Mitchell declared bluntly.

'Miss Collins isn't in the book,' her husband corrected her. 'Terry told us about her and she turned up at school with a scarf that matched the tie he brought home. It all seems a bit far-fetched to me. I think whoever wrote it used your names and invented everything else.'

'Far-fetched doesn't begin to describe it but there is a lot more truth in it than you might think,' Clive agreed with a broad grin. 'You will have a scarf and tie of your own shortly. We call it our introductory offer, and you each get a copy of the book that was written about us. My sources tell me that your son will be returning Deke Thorpe's book to him this morning at the homework club they hold in the same place every week on Saturday mornings. I need hardly say that Mr Green and Miss Collins and myself have put our careers on the line,' he said honestly.

'Deke seems a strange name. Is he a foreign student?'

'His name is Derek but you call him that at your peril,' Clive replied

'If that's what he wants, fair enough.'

'I suppose you have risked you careers if any of this is true but what we want to know is why our son Terry is mixed up in this whatever-it-is.'

'Naturally. It all began here at the Roman Baths when Mrs Shore as she was then dipped her fingers in the water and picked up something that got into her blood. Actually we haven't found anything in the water to account for it and I can tell you that quite a few samples have been sneaked out. People dip their fingers in the water, wipe them on a tissue, and pop the tissue into a plastic bag and nobody notices a thing, or if they do they think nothing of it.

'What happened next was that Mrs Shore began to shed over fifty years of her life and she went underground so to speak and after a while she was telling the world that her name was Copper Beach and she was thirty-five years old. Actually she could have easily claimed to be only thirty.

'You have read the book in part at least so I'm giving just a brief outline. Very brief. Anyway, I met Copper as she had become and after a while I persuaded her to marry me. We have a young son who we named Lawrence after my father.'

There was a sharp hiss of indrawn breath'

'That's not in the book!'

'Not the one you read but it will be in a later volume. The Chronicles didn't come to an end with that book; in fact they're still being written.'

'But she's … she's…'

'About a hundred years old. I won't reveal her actual age because as my father once said, all women lie about their ages.'

The wide grin was back on Clive's face.

'But you still haven't told us why our son is mixed up in all this.'

'I was coming to that in my own long-winded way. He was invited into a study group that meets every Saturday morning to revise and do homework and kick ideas around and I must say I'm pleased about it for two reasons. In the first place your son has been told that unless his grades improve between now and the end of term he will be put back a year…'

'We know he isn't doing well at school but we can't get him interested,' Mrs Mitchell protested. 'He has brought some information leaflets from the sports centre though and I think he might have started to think about sports coaching,' she added.

Clive nodded agreement.

'He's a boy in his early teens and all teenagers have their ups and downs. The group that invited him to join them are all top flight students and if he stays with them I will personally guarantee you will see an improvement. If I'm not mistaken your son is already putting more effort into his work. These things do not go unnoticed in the classroom,' he said.

'If only it lasts.'

'I think it will,' Clive told them. 'The group he has joined isn't the only one and in every group they tend to look after each other. They help each other with their revision and it shows in their marks. I did say there are two reasons why I am pleased that your son was invited into the group, and the second reason is that he has brought their number up to six, and four of them are two years ahead of him so they will be moving on sooner or later. They all want to go to university and in fact they more than qualify as things stand at the present time but they are staying on and taking more subjects.'

'Terry says there is a girl who is really brilliant.'

'He's talking about Christine Appleton and she's a lot cleverer than I am. She has a talent for letting her mind roam free and she has a rare ability to brush aside any preconceived ideas and not let the things she knows prevent her from following up her ideas that, on the face of it, don't make sense. I'm not explaining this at all well but I can provide evidence because she was filmed without her knowledge and that film went off to an old pupil of the school who is now leading a team of scientists who are doing things in particle physics that I don't pretend to understand. She made a big impression on them I can tell you, and she raised possibilities that will blow your mind away. I'll arrange for you to see the film for yourselves and when I do I think you will agree that your son is in very good company,' Clive said.

'I still can't understand what's going on,' Mr Mitchell said. 'I'm not complaining but I just don't get it.'

'It isn't easy,' Clive agreed, 'but we don't keep anything secret and everyone is on a level footing, including yourselves now, and Terry of course. You can talk to whoever you like and in fact it was Deke Thorpe who phoned Merlin and that led directly to where we are now, sitting outside the Roman Baths while the world pass by while the youngsters are in their usual meeting place.'

'Terry did seem to be looking forward to it,' Mr Mitchell admitted.

'That's good. We're all agreed that Terry isn't a high flier but he can be if he tries. He's no nimlet, uh, I don't know if you've heard that word?'

'We have since last week.' Mrs Mitchell managed a smile.

'He's also less shy with the group than he has been with anyone else and from now on I expect him to be more outgoing,' Clive added honestly. As an aside he remarked, 'It's going to get crowded here before long. Tourists and shoppers, the good weather brings them out on the streets.'

A man who carried a plastic bag approached and said, 'Would you mind if I join you and get the weight off my feet for a moment? My bag is getting heavy.'

He sat down as room was made for him.

'Ah, that feels better already,' he said with a sigh of relief.

Regarding his surroundings he gestured towards the entrance to the Roman Baths and continued, 'It's changed a lot from the time when the Romans built the Baths but can you imagine what it was like in the days when Bath was a Roman city? A bit like this I should think.'

Years seemed stripped away and the people who thronged the square were now dressed in Roman and Romano-British clothing. A family strode past and a young boy complained that he was thirsty and wanted to stop at a stall for a drink. A group of women who seemed to be strangers appeared to be deciding what to do next and it was plain that there was a difference of opinion, and the juggling skill of a street performer entertained the crowd.

Everything returned to normal. Mr and Mrs Mitchell looked stunned.

'That was fairly typical of things as they were back then. I neglected to introduce myself. I'm Merlin, and now I can relieve myself of my carrier bag. I've brought you copies of the book that was written about us, together with some more material that you might care to look at, including a fair amount of filmed material. Last and not least, our club tie and scarf.'

'I'm … I'm staggered. Gobsmacked.'

367

'Our son took a pair of scissors to his tie.'

'The tie was his. He can do what he likes with it and ties are replaceable,' Merlin said mildly.

'To be honest I thought it was an act of rebellion and I wasn't at all pleased so I said…'

'… why did you do that?' Deke Thorpe asked.

'Because you have got flags and patches and I wanted something so I took snipped the end off my tie to make a patch for my jacket and another one for my school bag. It wasn't me who sewed them on though.'

Terry Mitchell showed off his patches.

'Actually I haven't got a flag yet and neither has Yo because we haven't made up our minds about the design. I wish I'd thought of doing what you did,' Deke told him.

Christine leaned forward.

'You could do what Terry did. Most patches seem to be round or four sided but there's no logical reason for them not to be five sided like the one on Terry's jacket. It's shaped more or less like a shield because that's the end that Terry snipped off. That leaves Yo but our scarves would make good flags wouldn't they?' She said.

'Not mine,' Yolanda objected. 'The material is too good and I like my scarf the way it is.'

'Mmm. So do I but I wonder if Mrs Beach could make nylon dragon and trilobite flags that would stand a bit of wear and tear, like the flags people put on their cars.'

'Could everybody do what I did and have flags and patches with dragons and trilobites. I mean, it's like anyone can have a national flag but they can still have their own designs. I think,' Terry Mitchell finished uncertainly.

'Genius! There goes my tie!' Deke Thorpe exclaimed.

'Something tells me Terry's kicked something off,' James Wilson said thoughtfully.

Chapter 40

'I've been having a think about marine biology. We talked it over and not to mince words neither of us is sure about what comes afterwards. It won't be a life of watching shoals of coloured fish in clear warm water.'

Christine Appleton had half expected this.

'I know,' she agreed readily. 'I could watch them for hours at a time but there's a lot more to marine biology than that.'

'Such as that giant isopod you showed us,' her mother said.

'It's strange and I would like to see one in its natural habitat and find out more about it. Not all sea life is pretty and not all of it is fish. I think marine biology is an interesting subject and I want to study it and perhaps one day I will be able to go down to the sea bed in a submersible,' Christine replied.

'I agree it's interesting but you were never exactly an animal lover,' her father said.

'The sea is different and well, it's mysterious. We know more about the moon than we know about the sea and the things that live in it and I want to know more. There's lots of laboratory work too; things like tracking pollution and fish stocks and it has links to oceanography and the movements of currents and sea levels. There's so much to do.'

'You seem to have done your homework,' Christine's mother observed.

'It isn't the same as doing original research. I looked it up on my computer and I found two species of fish that are really interesting and they're not brightly coloured either. I downloaded some pictures and I can show you.'

Christine's father looked slightly amused as he replied, 'If they look anything like that giant isopod creature I've seen enough already. It looks like an invader from outer space or something, what with those weird eyes. Draw a picture on your refill pad and talk us through it.'

Christine retrieved her writing pad from her school bag.

'This fish is a lancelet and it isn't very big so I'll draw it oversize.'

'Don't you mean lancet?' Mr Appleton said.

'No.' Christine shook her head. 'There is a fish called a lancet but it's about two metres long and shaped like an eel. The lancelet is little and very different. Here.'

She made a neat sketch.

'There are lots of species of lancelets,' she said as she drew a picture. 'About thirty I think, and they live half buried in the sand or mud anywhere from the tropics right up to Scotland. I don't know how far north they go, which might be something to watch if global warming alters the sea temperatures. They aren't very big and mostly they're about as long as my little finger but I'm drawing it bigger.'

Christine's mother looked closely.

'It looks the same going backwards as forwards,' she said, 'and what are those finger things? Some sort of fin?'

Christine shook her head.

'You're looking at it the wrong way round, those are tentacles that filter the water the lancelet takes in and they trap tiny food particles. My drawing isn't very good,' she confessed.

'I might have got it right if I waited for you to draw its eyes,' her mother said.

'I can't. It hasn't any. It might have light sensitive cells but that is all it has. It hasn't got much of anything really, not even proper fins and it isn't even much of a swimmer.'

'So what is special about it?'

'This.'

Christine drew a line that ran about the whole length of the fish she had sketched.

'This is called a notochord and it is positioned above its innards, which I haven't drawn but they are very primitive. The lancelets haven't even got a heart. The notochord extends all the way into the head and that is where it is very slightly enlarged and it's the closest the lancelet comes to having a brain. Evolution seems to have left the lancelet behind but it has survived for millions of years so it isn't one of nature's failed experiments. I'll have to check my facts but about five hundred and forty million years ago the vertebrates broke away from the lancelets and that means that all the vertebrate species, mammals, birds, fish, and reptiles, are all descended from the lancelets.'

'Whew! If that isn't special I don't know what is,' Mrs Appleton admitted.

'I can't see any family resemblance,' Mr Appleton quipped cheerfully, 'but I'll take your word for it.'

'Perhaps if you stand sideways,' Christine suggested.

'I'll overlook that,' her father reciprocated with a beaming smile. 'Now, about the second fish you mentioned. Something predatory with a bad attitude and lots of teeth?'

Christine smiled.

'Nothing like that. Its little and brown and the best way to see why I like it is to watch a short piece of film I downloaded to my computer.'

While her computer came alive she removed the band that held her pony tail in place and shook her hair free.

'There,' she said. 'Mudskippers. This still shot shows you what they look like. They're amphibious fish and they breathe air and they even drown if they stay underwater so they keep a small pocket of air in their burrows when the high tide submerges them. They have to stay wet because they breathe though their skin and the lining of their mouths. You can see their eyes are on the top of their heads so they can bury themselves in mud and still see, and the strange thing is they can see better out of the water than they can in it. Most of the time they live out of water and they move in skips and jumps and they climb mangrove roots and trees.'

Christine tapped a key on her computer and continued, 'Here's the clip I downloaded and you can see them skipping on the mud, and watch this one blink. There! It sort of pulls its eyes downwards like frogs do. This one is going to climb a mangrove root.'

They watched the progress of the small creature until the clip ended.

'There,' Christine said, 'mudskippers are still fish but I think they might be on the way to becoming amphibians and perhaps leave the water for good. When I discovered them I thought they were funny little things but their lives aren't funny to them and it's not nice to laugh at them. I like them and I think the Vikings would have called them persons if they had ever seen them.'

'They do seem to have individual personalities,' Christine's mother said. 'Why don't you ask Suzanne Fluteplayer what she thinks. Thanks to Beowulf and Freya she thinks like a Viking.'

'Oh! I never thought of that!'

'I did notice they only have two legs, or fins that they use for legs. That doesn't seem like something that is likely to move onto dry land,' Mr Appleton said.

Christine disagreed.

'Those are pectoral fins and they will be the front legs but you can't see the back fins very well. They are the pelvic fins and they are close to the body and the mudskippers use them to climb roots and trees. Those fins hold tight while the mudskipper claws its way upwards with the pectoral fins, so there is a chance that one day a four legged creature will come out for good and go from fish to amphibian to mammal and perhaps something else even. Isn't that wonderful?'

Her parents had very little to say when Christine turned the computer off, put her writing pad away, and made ready for bed. The girl might have been surprised to know that they had looked up all they could find about marine biology and discovered that a lot of cutting edge research was being carried out within fairly easy reach of Bath.

'So there we are,' Mrs Appleton said when they were alone. 'Our daughter is going to be a scientist. Somehow that doesn't come as a surprise and it's plain that she has done her homework. She won't get home every night but she won't be too far away.'

'Her choice of a career wasn't what I expected but having said that I don't know what I did expect. Maybe in a hundred years from now she'll decide to try something else.'

'In a hundred years,' Mrs Appleton nearly choked. 'Do you really think so? I'm not so sure I would but, well...'

'Time will tell.'

'That sounds like a Merlin joke but you're right. Time alone will tell.'

Chapter 41

Frank Holley looked up from his work when he heard a woman calling him.

'Hello, is anybody there?'

He was using a wire brush on a piece of machinery, preparing it for a new coat of paint before it went back to its owner.

'Coming. Give me a few seconds.' He called back.

He was still wiping his hands when he greeted his visitors.

'Julia and Marge, I haven't seen either of you for a while. Brian and Jack can't be far away by this time. Four thirty at the latest was what Brian estimated. I was going to fill the kettle in a few minutes so I can rustle up two more mugs. Brian didn't mention you were dropping in.'

'That's an oblique question,' Julia accused him with a smile. 'You want to know what brings us here.'

'True; at heart I'm still a nosy copper,' the ex-Superintendent admitted shamelessly.

'It has to do with Brian's expansion. We've brought your new business plan. Part of it anyway. When the business gets bigger you'll be wanting to streamline the office.'

That much is true, Frank Holley admitted to himself. There was the question of extra staff to be considered as well. Frank was aware that Brian had put out a few feelers among his clients, with a hint that he might soon have a place for an apprentice engineer. If anyone had shown interest he was unaware of it. Still, it was early days.

Brian didn't seem to be surprised to see his visitors, a fact that made Frank Holley suspect that something was going on behind everyone's back. What Brian did with his business was up to him of course but Frank was a man who always endeavoured to make sure that he had thought out all the angles before he made a decision. It was a policy that had seen him through more than one sticky situation. It was to be hoped that Brian was doing the same.

***

'Any minute now,' Brian Gleaves said unsteadily.

Nobody replied. The office where the administration of Wolftamer Agricultural Engineering was carried out was overcrowded but hushed. Frank Holley compared the time displayed by the wall clock with the time shown by his wristwatch. The seconds crawled by. Jack Smythe raised himself very slightly by lifting his heels a fraction of an inch to ease his circulation. It was an old trick that he had been taught by his drill instructor early on in his career in the armed forces when he had to spend long periods standing at attention on the parade ground.

A watched pot never boils. The well-worn saying ran through Jack's head as he waited for the telephone call that was only seconds away if all was going according to a plan that was laid down a few days ago. Or a good many years ago, depending on your point of view. Nobody moved; it was as if the world was standing still. Brian reached out a trembling hand towards the phone, then snatched it back and bit his lower lip.

Once again Frank Holley looked hopefully at the clock on the wall, willing the second hand to move faster. There was no guarantee that the call they all waited for would ever be made but he kept that thought to himself. He shuffled his feet and felt annoyed with himself when he realised what he was doing.

He caught his breath when the phone rang shrilly. Nobody moved.

'Answer it Brian,' Julia prompted.

Slowly, almost reluctantly, Brian Gleaves lifted the handset.

'Hello,' he said hoarsely.

'Hello. My name is David Harrison. Am I speaking to Mr Brian Gleaves?'

'That's me mate. I'm Brian Gleaves.'

Brian looked up at the expectant faces.

'It's him. Them,' he whispered.

'Sorry, I didn't catch that.'

'I was just saying as how it's you. There's a lot of people here. We didn't know if you was going to call,' Brian explained.

'It's been in the family diary for years and half the family is here with me now. Is the vicar there?'

'He's here mate.'

'My grandfather Kenneth is looking forward to meeting him again and I'm to tell the vicar he's still driving the Rover.'

'Tell him now mate, I'll give the phone to him.'

The phone was almost snatched out of Brian's hand and hopping with excitement the vicar held a short conversation before he handed it back to Brian.

'He's something to tell you,' he said cryptically.

Brian held the phone so the conversation could be overheard.

'That's right mate. Lofty Harrison said as he had a garden centre, him and Elizabeth, and we had a chat about using a bit of land what I've got to open one up here. It'll need a bit of work so I'm looking a couple of years ahead.'

'I know. My great grandparents drew up a set of notes about the working of garden centres, including the layout, the buildings, the car park, and so on. There are a hundred pages more or less and they're worth their weight in gold. They wrote about their stay in Bath as well and left instructions for it to be given to a Mr Robert Robertson and I suppose he will pass it on to the chronicler. I know about them through the books they brought back when they came back. They're well thumbed by now because everyone in the family has read them over and over again. I could pop everything in the post but out of curiosity I'm booking into an hotel for a night or two and I'll motor over to your yard and make a pest of myself,' David Harrison said.

'No problem there mate, there's room at my house and Julia's got me smartened up a bit.'

'Julia? The Lady of the Lake? That Julia?'

'That's right mate. She's here with me now, we're all squeezed into my office.'

'Now more than ever I want to come. I'll take you up on your offer.'

'Any time mate, just turn up.'

***

Brian studied the information pack that Lofty and Elizabeth Harrison had put together.

'It's a lot to take in but I reckon I could do it all right. Blimey! Wait until I tell everyone! I'll be taking on more people, I can see that. I'll tell you what I'll do mate, and that's get Julia over to take a look. My sister Marge too, she knows how to do the books right and proper. I'm thinking maybe one bookkeeper could handle two businesses. Blimey! Brian Gleaves opening a garden centre!'

'My great-grandparents brought enough pictures from their stay that they could work out a scheme for landscaping your property. It's in the notes, near the back,' David Harrison replied. He added, 'It's quite a big job. We can take a walk around your place when you can spare the time and we can make an estimate of what needs to be done.'

Brian Gleaves agreed.

David Harrison continued, 'There's a girl I want to meet while I'm here, the one with the garden. She made my great-grandparents sit up and take notice and they left instructions that she is to be offered a work placement with us during the summer holiday next year. It will need parental permission of course but the offer is on the table.'

Brian chuckled.

'If you meet one you'll be meeting them all. There's six youngsters in their group an' I don't know a lot about the latest one what joined but the ones I do know are all brainy,' he told David Harrison.

He continued, 'Tell you what. I'm doing a bit of a barbecue next week an' if you can be here you can get to see everyone and we can go over the plan for the garden centre. The people what will be here ain't short of ideas neither so you'll most likely get your ears bent. Make it a long weekend and bring your misses. How about it?'

'Brian, you're on!'

Brian reached for the phone and dialled while he spoke.

'This here is Mr Tyler's mobile number so he might be too busy to answer but, oh, Mr Tyler, its Brian Gleaves here mate. I've got a couple of people staying at my place for a while and they are Mr and Mrs Harrison what are descended from Lofty and Elizabeth Harrison. Leastways, he is. The thing is mate, Lofty owned a garden centre and now the new Harrisons are in charge. He's called David and she's called Mary. Anyway mate, Lofty and Elizabeth and me had a talk about a garden centre at my place. I got the space for it. It turns out your Jasmin told Lofty she wants work experience in a garden centre and they could tell as how she knows her stuff so Lofty and Elizabeth left a note in their family diary so David and Mary came to tell us she can spend a few weeks at their place next summer, so I'm ringing to say if you drive over at the weekend you can talk about it. How about that? And I forgot to say all her friends are invited. Tell you what, make it Sunday afternoon and I'll lay on a bit of grub. I ain't as good at the barbecue as what Mrs Bradley is but I'll sort something out. What about it?'

'Wow!' Harry Tyler sounded startled.

'I forgot to say for Jasmin to bring her flag along with her. I told David about the flags.'

'I'll have a word with the other parents and see about doubling up on cars. Am I allowed to tell Jasmin what this is all about?'

'I reckon as how that would be all right but maybe David and Mary Harrison should be the ones. There's quite a bit of stuff to go over.'

'I'll go along with that. OK Brian, leave it with me.'

Interlude

Extract from the notes compiled by Lofty and Elizabeth Harrison after their return from the future that is our own now.

These writings are made for the family records and a copy is to be given to Mr Robert Robertson at a later date.

It began for us many years ago during our wartime service when we worked together to keep Mosquito bombers flying. Two of our friends, Flying Officer Henry Rudd and Sergeant Henry Whiting, flew one of our aircraft and we had a little game where we each put sixpence into a bag and after every flight the sixpences went to whichever one of us had most of our quarter of a marked tail wheel on the ground. Henry Whiting was the pilot and it was amazing how often he managed to claim the prize.

Towards the end of the war they failed to return from a raid and we were told they had been shot down and killed. Lofty was discharged before the war was over and Elizabeth managed to get her own discharge shortly afterwards. We married, set up a shop, worked all hours, raised a family, and got on with our lives.

Imagine our surprise when we were visited by a man from the future! The vicar turned up with the little bag of sixpences we thought was lost when the Mosquito was shot down. It turned out that Henry Rudd and Henry Whiting were alive after all and the vicar brought proof that he came from a future where they are still alive. That should be when, not where. It didn't take much guessing that we are not because if we are the vicar's journey would have been unnecessary.

We were offered the chance to go forward in time (or sideways into another time, we have never been sure how to put it) and we had a reunion with our wartime friends and met Walter Pfaffinger and his wife Anneleise, and Robert and Victoria Robertson. Walter had commanded a tank in the German Army and Robert had been a Guardsman and they had fought each other in Africa and Italy. Walter's story gave us an insight into the face to face warfare of soldiers.

The future is hard to describe. Television sets are enormous and nearly flat. They can almost be hung like a picture on the wall. We don't think the programmes are any better though.

We met and talked to some very bright schoolchildren who had a homework club and we were talking to them in their Saturday morning hangout when a girl named Jasmin Tyler walked in. We had heard her name mentioned before and she was invited to join us. Jasmin carried a gardening magazine and she showed us a letter she had written and the magazine printed. It was obvious that Jasmin really knows what she is talking about and Lofty made an instant decision that she should be invited into the select company that knows about Merlin and the Lady of the Lake. More of those in other parts of these writings. We never mentioned that we own a garden centre, but Jasmin is to be told later and she is to be offered work experience with our descendants, at the time we mention elsewhere.

The city of Bath was a new experience for us. Neither of us have been there so we did the usual tourist thing and bought some souvenirs that for obvious reasons cannot be shown to all and sundry. It was interesting to visit the Roman Baths and ride on an open topped tourist bus. (Painted bright red and yellow but we think we were told they used to be green).

Fashions have changed of course and rucksacks are universal. Everyone has one, even little tots who have brightly coloured ones. We soon found out how useful they are. Everyone carries a pocket phone. They are far smaller than anything we have seen and some can be linked to computers. Everybody owns a computer. They can send and receive pictures and all manner of things. It is our opinion that this is taking technology too far because a lot of people spend hours playing games on them, which seems to us to be a waste of time.

Harrison descendants take note!

Something that strikes us as strange was the coffee cup fad. We call it a fad because we cannot see it lasting but we could be wrong. Some people take large insulated coffee cups with them, filled with the coffee they made before they left home and others use paper cups brought straight from the shop. You see them everywhere.

We have brought a lot of information about all these things but they must not be shown to anyone outside the family.

Chapter 42

Brian had not given a thought to the weather and on Sunday afternoon it looked overcast but it was not cold and he thought there would be no rain. Without wasting time he addressed all his guests.

'Most of you know about when Lofty and Elizabeth Harrison was here a little while ago. Well, it weren't such a little while for some people you ain't met yet. This here is David and Mary Harrison. Lofty and Elizabeth was David's great-grandparents. What they did when they went back home was to write an account of what they did when they were here, and that's going to Robert Robertson for the records and he's going to pass it on to the chronicler so everyone can get a read of it. That was one thing they did and the other thing was to write up a sort of guide to setting up and running a garden centre, which I'm thinking about doing. We had a bit of a talk about it on account of they had a garden centre and they know what to do.'

His listeners looked at each other.

'I don't recall them mentioning that,' Mrs Wilson said.

Brian smiled.

'They didn't tell everyone but a few of us knew about it. David and Mary have something to tell Jasmin.'

Wearing an expression of bemusement the girl stepped forward.

'My great-grandparents set down some instructions for us some instructions years ago, as soon as they came back from here a few weeks ago, if that makes sense,' David Harrison began. 'What they said was when they first met you they saw your gardening magazine and the letter from you that they published and it was plain to them that you know your gardening. I saw the magazine myself years ago because they sneaked one back with them, which might have been against the rules. Straight away they wanted you to join your friends in their little group and that's what happened. They also said you wanted to gain work experience in a garden centre. What they didn't tell you is that they owned a garden centre and I'm to tell you Jasmin that they left instructions to our family to offer you a few weeks with us next summer. All we need to do is work out the details with your father.'

The stunned girl looked to her father for guidance.

'It's what you wanted isn't it, and it's a great opportunity so I think we can come to an arrangement and I'm sure I can take care of your garden for a little while,' Harry Tyler told her.

Jasmine could only nod dumbly.

'Well that seems to be settled,' David Harrison beamed.

Janet Smythe had been listening together with Brian's sister Marge. Now it was her turn to speak.

'We're going to light the barbecue in a few minutes. They do say too many cooks spoil the broth but together with Julia and Mary we might not make too bad a job of it.'

'I reckon as how I'll chance it,' Brian replied cheerfully.

Rubbing his hands together he continued, 'I just told you about my idea of putting a garden centre here. Well, it weren't all my idea because Lofty and Elizabeth had a hand in it. They had a bit of a look round and took some pictures and made sketches and I knew they were going to sort of lay the groundwork and I knew someone was going to ring me up. 'Course I didn't know it was David and Mary and they didn't either but they did know their garden centre was still going because we sort of looked it up and then we set a time and date for a phone call. And that's the way it were.

'David and Mary have drawn up a bit of a plan of the land and marked in some sort of lay out. It ain't hard and fast but it's a start. I expect everyone knows I'm making my engineering business bigger and I already know what building I'll have to do for that but nothing else is fixed.

'So the bottom line is I don't know for sure what's going where. There will have to be buildings and a car park and a bit of levelling out. There's going to be a whole lot of rock to be shifted and truck loads of stone to be taken away.'

'Not all of it,' Jasmin blurted out. 'I'm sorry, I didn't mean to interrupt,' she apologised.

'Some could be used as landfill maybe but there's going to be a lot left over,' Brian Gleaves said.

'I meant rockeries. Rockeries and stone walls. Some places have stones along their driveways and sometimes they paint then white. It's in my gardening books and magazines,' Jasmin told him.

'I'm blowed.'

'Everything is a commodity Brian,' his sister told him. 'I learned that when I was a bookkeeper. Whatever it is somebody is going to want it and pay for it. Wheeling and dealing.'

'So I save the cash what I might've spent on carting it away and I make a bit more from selling it. Well I can't say as it won't come in handy.'

Brian's sister addressed the teenagers.

'What Brian was going to say next is for you to see the plans and the photos that Lofty and Elizabeth made and see what ideas you come up with. What do you think?' She said.

'That's stretching them a bit,' Mrs Mitchell remarked as the group jostled around the plans.

'I didn't see anyone walking away,' Marge replied.

There was some talking and pointing and then the teenagers moved off, pushing through the scrub and undergrowth.

'This is where the buildings are supposed to go,' Christine Appleton said eventually, 'but it's only an outline plan so they might put them somewhere else. Ouch!'

She stumbled over a stone on the uneven ground.

'There's enough here for a dozen rockeries and a mile of stone walls,' James Wilson said.

'And milestones,' Terry Mitchell added.

'What?' Deke asked.

'Milestones. Jas said rockeries and stone walls and I don't see why anyone couldn't have a milestone,' Terry replied defensively.

'Hmm. You're right. Why couldn't they?' Deke conceded.

'They might want standing stones as well because I've seen them for sale in my gardening magazine. Mostly they are two metres or less but some are a lot bigger,' Jasmin told him.

'An interested contractor might take some stones for headstones,' Deke suggested. 'I'll see what the vicar thinks.'

'Little ones for pet cemeteries,' Yolanda Walker said. 'You could put some in a garden centre with Herbert Hamster or something written on them as an example.'

'That's a good one. I'll add it to the list. I think lots of people would like to mark the grave of a pet dog or cat.'

Terry Mitchell pointed at something.

'The map said there is a place where there used to be a quarry. It's just over there. I've always wanted to try rock climbing. Could a garden centre be an activity centre too?' He asked tentatively.

'Logically it could but from a practical point of view it might not be that easy but rule nothing in and rule nothing out. Put it on the list Deke,' Christine directed.

'And a restaurant. Garden centres have restaurants or cafés,' Jasmin Tyler said.

***

Deke Thorpe. Précis/summary/discussion re garden centre. Jas mentioned stone walls and rockeries and the uses of stone in gardens.

Jas. Boundary stones along driveways.

Christine. Stones that mark boundaries are a matter of history.

James. Global positioning by satellite could mark boundaries to a hairsbreadth. No disputes over who owns what.

Jas. Good fences make good neighbours. I saw that in one of my magazines.

Terry. Milestones too.

Jas. Standing stones in your garden.

Terry. There's a bit of a cliff. It could be an action centre.

Christine. Don't rule it out. We're already on a nature trail.

Deke. Marked by standing stones.

Yo. With signs showing compass directions and distances. That's orienteering.

Deke. Imagine if one of the stones turns out to be active. The compass would go all over the place.

Christine. So we tell the trail walkers what to watch out for.

Jas. Garden centres have restaurants and cafés too.

Christine. I know! If Mr Gleaves has standing stones for sale the garden centre could go all Stone Age and the café could sell Stone Age food and drink. I'm sure Mrs Bradley talked to Alfrid and Eathl and wrote down their recipes. Jas, could you grow Stone Age vegetables?

Jas. I could make a little garden next to the café and grow everything but I don't know what I should plant. Mrs Bradley would have to tell me. Small Alfrid told me they know how to make sausages and bacon and ham but they only eat eggs in the spring. I think their herbs were the same as ours and they used wild plants that we don't use now but if I could get the seeds I could grow them. I could put wild flowers on the table because they liked flowers. I gave Twiss a plant when small Alfrid went back.

Deke. Anything else anybody?

Yo. Bees and honey.

Terry. They kept cows, it says so in the book. They roasted them over open fires didn't they? One big barbecue.

James. Small Alfrid told me they minced the meat up sometimes and made Stone Age beefburgers and he said they were better than ours.

Deke. That's another one for Mrs Bradley.

Yo. Gravestones are standing stones aren't they? That's in the book too.

Deke. I'll pass that to the vicar.

Yo. Pet cemeteries or pets buried in your garden. Small headstones for pets.

Deke. Mr Gleaves will have to fell some trees. I think there is something in the rules about that, like if there is a preservation order on a tree it is not okay to fell it but otherwise you have to plant a tree for every one you cut down. I'll search the internet and see what it says.

Christine. That means timber. Another commodity.

Jas. Verge markers along driveways, the same as for stones.

Terry. Suppose you have a tree trunk that five or six people could sit on and then you could use some stones to hold it in place and keep it off the ground and when it isn't a seat it could be a seesaw.

James. That works for me.

Deke. And me. Hold on while I tot this up. Stones for boundary markers and standing stones and gravestones for pets and maybe for people too. Felled trees for seats, drive markers, and whatever else we can think of.

Jas. Bird boxes and places for hedgehogs and insects.

Deke. Right Jas, I'll get that in as well. Then the café and Stone Age menu, the nature trail or activity trail or activity centre. I like that. I'll get this typed up into some sort of order and pass it along. Is there anything else?

James. I can think of something else. The barbecue should be ready to dish up beefburgers and whatever else they've got.

Yo. Lead the way James, I'm right behind you.

James did lead the way and it was not long before then group was sitting at a table enjoying their beefburgers and drinking from cans. A typical group of teenagers.

Interlude

My parents have been on to me again about marine biology. I'm the last one to have made a career choice and they, well they don't try to put me off but they say it isn't all warm sea and tropical reef fish. They're really beautiful to look at but they're not the only thing in the sea. I said I know and I'm most likely to be looking at cold water marine life most of the time. I would like to see the tropical reefs and just sit for hours at a time watching brightly coloured fish but that isn't the be all and end all and I could do that as a tourist because lots of people do. Anyway, I've got to go to university first and qualify and then I'll know exactly what I want to do. There's so much that nobody knows about the seas and oceans and marine life so I might be spoilt for choice.

I still haven't asked Suzanne Fluteplayer whether the Vikings would have called mudskipper fish persons but I think they would have done.

Chapter 43

David Harrison and Brian Gleaves stared at each other.

'This ain't anything like what I was expecting,' Brian said as he read through the notes that Deke Thorpe had prepared.

'It's not what I expected either,' David replied.

'Well mate, I've met them before and I know they ain't stupid but...'

'Brian, they're full of surprises,' Julia reminded him, 'but all the same I never expected them to lay the groundwork for a themed garden centre. David, is there any mileage in this?'

'Mileage? I should say so. I'll take it on trust that your Mrs Bradley can turn out Stone Age snacks and meals and I'm already convinced that young Jasmin can grow anything,' David Harrison replied.

'Her Viking name is Jasmin Greenfingers,' Julia told him.

'It's going to take some thinking about,' Brian said seriously. 'I sort of thought they might say where they thought things ought to go after they saw the lay of the land but I got to admit that's up to me with a heap of help from David and Mary. It's a long term plan and I reckon maybe two years before we open the door. I should say that's about right and we can put it around the framework they came up with. Blimey, they could've charged me consultant's fees and no mistake.'

David laughed.

'Don't put ideas in my head Brian.'

***

James Wilson and Christine Appleton arrived later than the usual time.

'We stopped to talk to Suzanne Fluteplayer when we were walking past the Royal Crescent. She's practicing something with Pauline Grant and Pauline was playing while Suzanne was singing but they wouldn't tell us what the words meant but there's no prizes for guessing they would both be arrested if a passing policeman understood Old Danish,' Christine said.

'William of Salisbury might.'

Christine shook her head.

'Possibly but the Normans came after the Vikings so he probably doesn't.'

'I wouldn't chance it,' Deke asserted.

James and Christine agreed.

'I need help with my maths, we're doing triangles and I can't get the hang of some of this stuff about sines and cosines and tangents. Can you show me what I'm doing wrong?' Terry Mitchell asked and pointed to his exercise book. 'It doesn't explain it very well,' he complained.

'OK. You can do this on your calculator but I like to see what's going on so I use logarithm tables. It helps you understand each step of the way. Budge up a bit and I'll show you,' James replied.

'Not just yet. Terry has got a new interest but he won't say what it is,' Yolanda Walker said.

Jasmin prompted Terry by saying, 'We'll keep on at you until you give in so you might as well tell us.'

'What is it?' Yolanda demanded. 'James won't help you with your maths until you tell us, will you James?'

'Hey, don't put the pressure on me,' James protested.

Terry shrugged his shoulders in a gesture of defeat.

'All right, I'll tell you if you promise not to laugh.'

'We promise,' Deke told him.

'All right. You know I said I fancied doing rock climbing when we were at Mr Gleaves' place? I thought there might be a climbing wall at the sports centre so I just walked over North Bridge and went in and somebody there helped me get all the brochures and she said there isn't a climbing wall but perhaps there might be one day. I sort of wondered if that is where you took small Alfrid swimming and then I thought I might be able to do lifesaving or something but I haven't checked to see yet.'

'Now that's settled let's have a look at your homework,' James said practically.

***

Christine Appleton and James walked to their Saturday morning rendezvous.

'I've heard that Terry Mitchell has decided he wants to learn canoeing,' James told her. 'I don't know what put the idea in his head, it was just something I heard in school.'

Soon they were sitting at their usual place in the burger bar.

'I went to the sports centre again to have a look at the swimming pool and on the way back I saw a trailer load of canoes when I was on North Bridge. There's no climbing wall at the sports centre but canoeing is an outdoor activity and I looked on the internet for more information and I found paddle boarding and rafting and all sorts,' Terry told everyone.

As an afterthought he added, 'I'm trying to improve my marks and I got nearly everything right in my maths this week after James showed me how to work through the questions.'

'Are you going to take up canoeing?' Christine enquired.

'I want to do canoeing and the other water activities like the paddle boarding and rafting I said about but my parents told me I'm not to do any of it until my marks improve. Which they will,' Terry finished with a new determination.

'If you paddle a canoe along the river or the canal it will make it more interesting if you know the names of all the plants along the banks,' Deke Thorpe commented.

'I know and I can see why Christine said everything is all joined up. It makes sense now.'

Terry Mitchell had found the glimmerings of a new direction in his life.

INTERLUDE

Rain battered the window and dark looming clouds raced across the sky. Peter Birkett pursed his lips and pushed hi empty coffee cup away.

'They say it's going to get worse before it gets better,' he said gloomily as he regarded the view from the window.

'Would this be a good time for me to book a duvet day for the next three days?' His graduate student Jill Lucas asked brightly and with more optimism than expectation of receiving a favourable reply.

'Nope.'

'Slavedriver.'

Physicist Ray Marsh looked up from the day old newspaper that someone had left laying around.

'You said you wanted to run something by us,' he prompted. Peter Birkett nodded affirmative.

'This is for Mac really but I'd like to get everyone's impressions,' he replied.

Alistair Macdonald looked interested.

'I've been looking again at the material Mr Green sent me,' Peter Birkett explained. 'Mac said he thinks Spockette might be onto something when she said there ought to be time particles.'

'She didn't put it quite that way and neither did I,' Mac protested.

'Bear with me. You did say you bought into ASP2, which is the maybe time particle more than ASP1 which is the maybe particle that set off the big bang.'

'Peter, are you sure you're a scientist?' Jill enquired solicitously. 'That didn't sound scientific to me.'

'Nor me,' Peter Birkett admitted, 'but listen to this. I did a thought experiment of a kind and what I wondered was that assuming ASP2 really exists, what would be the result of a mass of time particles clumping together? That's what ordinary matter did and the result was the stars and planets and everything else.'

There was silence.

'Hmm. Time particles coming together and forming something. Interesting,' Ray Marsh commented at last.

'Forming what?'

'That's the big question isn't it? You know, I told Mr Green that JBS Haldane said the universe is not only queerer than we imagine, it's queerer than we can imagine. I guess this is an example of that queerness. Nowadays we would call it strange rather than queer but it still stands and the good news is that it gets even stranger. Imagine if these time particles repelled instead of attracted?'

'Uh. Like poles repel, unlike poles attract. I see what you are getting at,' Alistair Macdonald said.

'Exactly. Clumping together would not happen but maybe, just maybe, the particles would rush away from each other. Might that account for the expansion of the universe? We do know that it is expanding. Is the time dimension the driving force? Time expands and as a consequence the spacial dimensions are forced to expand in order to keep up with time, and the universe keeps getting bigger? Does that float anyone's boat?'

'Peter, it sinks mine. If you tell me to work on it I'll pack my bags and get a job in the canteen. How in the world do you and Christine manage to hypothesise anything so plausible in its own way but so outlandish that it's right off the scale of weird?'

'That's easy to answer. We had the good fortune and the privilege to be taught by George Green, and don't think for one minute the canteen job would fall in your lap. I've tasted your coffee. Better stick with what you know.'

Alistair Macdonald made a suggestion.

'If you want to get a little closer to finding an answer you could do worse than to ask for Christine's opinion.'

Peter Birkett's jaw dropped open.

'You know, I think I will. Not yet but one day perhaps.'

Interlude

I'm happy to report that Suzanne Fluteplayer is doing very well in spite of her occasional outbursts. Together we have begun a portfolio of Viking music and verse. (Frequently profane and very jolly).

That profanity triggered something in my mind, and that was the discovery in Germany about ninety or a hundred years ago of a set of verses written in Latin and German, but not modern German. They are as racy as anything the Vikings dreamed up. There was no musical score but music was written for the verses by Carl Orfe and the world knows the collection as Carmina Burana.

Taking a mental leap of faith it occurred to me that Alison is a repository of medieval bawdy ballads and raucousness so I intend to tap her up and persuade her to collect everything together. Whether the collection (and the Viking repertoire) will ever be performed publicly is problematical to say the very least!

Chapter 44

Years passed, some quickly, some slowly.

George Green spent a comfortable night and in the morning he ate a very light breakfast. His room was pleasant and airy and he managed to sit up against the pillows that the nurse had plumped up. There was a television for him to watch but he wasn't interested in anything that was showing.

He had visitors as often as Matron allowed and his affairs had put in order a long time ago. He closed his eyes and let his mind roam. He thought of Hilary and the day she died. It was at the breakfast table when she grasped his hand and said, 'I don't know what our Hall of Warriors will be like but that is where I will be.' They were the last words she spoke.

Life had been good. George thought back to his schooldays and the mistakes he had made and the apologies left unsaid as he groped his way to manhood. Oh yes George, you weren't perfect were you? But you tried and that is all a man can do. He had regrets but not many.

He opened his eyes at the sound of the door opening. It was Matron Patti.

'Ready to receive visitors?' She asked. 'Just for a few minutes,' she added, 'you mustn't get over excited.'

'Matron Patti I'll report you to the authorities if you shoo them away before we're finished,' George told her.

'In this hospital I am the authority,' Patti replied. It was true and they both enjoyed the light hearted exchange.

Patti ushered the visitors into the room. George gasped. His daughters and… Odin's Ghost! Arrad! He was aged about thirty years but George knew him instantly.

'We never thought to meet our brother but Wint opened the gate and here he is!' George's eldest daughter said.

'Hello Dad. It's been a long time.'

'About five thousand years,' his other daughter added.

'It's good to see you again. Are you keeping well?' George asked.

'Very well Dad, and the Lake sends its best wishes, even the ones who weren't born when you were there. I've got bees in every village and I've played in the Dads and Lads games. I've got a boy of my own now, and two girls,' Arrad said proudly.

'Do I know their mother?'

'Do you remember Gerdin who used to chivvy young Wigstin around?'

'Of course I do. You're a very lucky fellow.'

'My luck started on the day I got stung all over and you came along with Atta and you fetched the hides I dropped when I ran away,' Arrad declared positively.

'We've heard all about that from both of you now,' George's youngest daughter told him.

George pointed to his bedside table.

'You hid your toy in my luggage. I only found it when I came back to my own time,' he accused his son.

'I swore Alfrid and Eathl to secrecy,' Arrad said. 'I wanted you to have it as a present and something to remember me by.'

With a smile on his face George said, 'Well I've got a present for you. Take the dragon that stands next to your toy. It's the dragon that Meglen put on my flag and it is holding a black torch with a yellow flame. Atta brought it back from a time that hasn't happened yet but he couldn't give it to me before the games because Meglen still had to make my flag and I suppose she hadn't thought up the design. Now it's yours. Your toy is going to be a family heirloom for me and my girls and perhaps my dragon will be a family heirloom for you.'

It was quite a long speech from and old and frail man and George's voice grew weaker as he talked. He was interested in hearing what was going on in his own time and Arrad's time on the Lake and he took pleasure from the conversation between his children. Once in a while he asked a question but mostly he was content to listen. Time passed and Matron Patti put her head round the door.

'That's more than long enough. You must rest,' she told George.

'Matron Patti we all know I haven't got much longer. Let me enjoy what time I have left,' George whispered.

Patti intercepted an almost imperceptible nod from George's eldest daughter.

'Very well,' she relented.

The door closed silently behind her.

George's children talked some more about what they were doing and exchanged information about their families. Arrad told how he had wooed Gerdin and what their children were like.

At last George told them, 'I'm feeling a little tired. I think I'll rest for a while.'

He closed his eyes and his breathing slowed. His children fell silent.

Suddenly George opened his eyes again but he was not his children that he was seeing.

'She's here, they all are. Hilary, Atta, the Vikings, old friends and people I've shared with in the great adventure of life. Dearest Hilary...'

And George Green, husband, father, teacher, and Freeman of the Lake, passed away.

Chapter 45

Snap! The gate that Wint had opened for himself and Atta closed immediately after they stepped through.

'Many things have changed but there is much that has not changed so much that it is no longer recognisable,' Wint said in his high pitched voice.

Atta was slow to respond.

At length he said, 'The Lake. There was a jetty there where the rafts used to stop for passengers and cattle and anything else that needed to be ferried and I can see there is a jetty there now but this one is much bigger than the one I know. My guess is that a lot of years have passed since we left the city of Bath a few breaths ago.'

'Do you want to know how many years?'

'I don't think so. It would serve no purpose to know,' Atta replied to Wint's question. He continued, 'Vocca and Cartiwiss had their house just over there,' he pointed, 'and Alfrid and Eathl are a little further up the slope. I lived, hmm, just about where I am standing now and I suspect that it is from this spot I shall return to my own now. It would be convenient and logical.'

Wint confirmed that this was the case.

'I can see the place where the infirmary stood, across the Lake where a new building stands now, and if I walk around I might discover other things that are familiar, Atta continued.

'That new building is an infirmary. In this now it is called a hospital. It is not large but it is large enough to serve the local area which in this now is called the District of Avalon. You will have all the time you need to meet the people and see what they do here and I know you well enough to know that you will do as George Green is doing in your now and make yourself involved in the daily business of the Lake as it is now. This whole area is a school but much more than a school, as you will see. I have come to work with Merlin and others to discover what went wrong with the stones that made it possible for Tarn to use them for his own ends. Perhaps we might be able to merge our old sciences with their new ones but it will not be easy and there is no guarantee of success. Nevertheless we will try,' Wint said.

'I have seen for myself how advanced the new ways are and more than once the thought has crossed my mind that we were too dependent on the ways I grew up with. I don't like to admit it but we had stagnated and the collapse of the old way was a good thing in the very long term although it has to be said that much hardship was caused in the short term, if you can truly call the passing of so much time a short term,' Atta replied seriously.

Wint agreed.

'I thought it too dangerous to try until I could be sure that I would cause no more harm,' he said.

He stopped to view the shimmering waters of the Lake for a few brief moments.

'Our hosts are on their way and they will be here to greet us soon,' he added.

'I understand that you will stay here and I will go to Bath or somewhere nearby and I will come and go more or less as I please but what I do not know is your reason for bringing me here. Not that I'm ungrateful for the opportunity to see more of the way things have turned out,' Atta replied.

'The reason concerns George Green. Call it his legacy if you will. The fact that the school here is largely because of him, he was far more influential than he ever realised and there are certain things I would like you to give him when you return to your own time.'

'That I will be glad to do. George Green is making a name for himself in my time as well.'

'Is there anything you would like to take back for yourself?'

'Not for myself,' Atta replied resolutely. 'I have everything I need but perhaps I might take back more pictures. The ladies can't get enough pictures of clothes and shoes, not to mention hair styles. Some toys for the children perhaps. They like puzzles.'

'It will be arranged,' Wint told him.

'The people of the Lake will be grateful.'

Atta pointed with his staff at an approaching group of people.

'They seem to be expecting us. Our hosts perhaps?' He enquired.

Introductions were quickly made. A couple whose ages Atta guessed to be about his own age of eight eights of years plus two more years.

'Clive Bowden and Copper Beach,' they identified themselves.

'My father Merlin,' Copper added.

'Hello. I'm pleased to meet you. I believe that is the correct greeting,' Atta replied as he revised his estimate of his host's ages. He wondered how much time had passed and decided once again that it was of no consequence.

'I'm afraid we must make a move,' Copper said to Atta. 'We would like to have you as our guest for a while. We still live in the same house that we lived in when Alfrid and Eathl stayed with us,' she continued. 'It's a little larger now because we had extensions built,' she added.

'Thank you. I haven't really come prepared; all I have is my staff and a few things in the bag I have slung over my shoulder,' Atta replied.

'We expected that. I've called a buggy to pick us up and take us to the station to catch the train to Bath and then we jump into the car for the drive home,' Clive Bowden told him.

'I never rode in a train but Alfrid says he did when he was here. Him and all his family of course but I did see trains from a distance at the time when I saw George Green waiting for Hilary,' Atta said.

'This train isn't like the ones you saw,' Copper said cheerfully.

It was not. From his elevated position Atta regarded the scene as he passed.

'This train is without wheels,' Copper explained. 'It's a magnalev and the force that propels it is the same force that lifts it from the track.'

Atta turned to face her.

'I can see I have a lot to learn. The train that I can see seems to be on a bridge,' he observed.

'It's a viaduct, which is a bridge of a kind,' Clive Bowden explained. 'Trains travel best on level tracks so gradients are kept to a minimum. The railway engineers erected a series of pylons over low lying ground and the track is laid on the top of them. The pylons are T shaped,' Clive demonstrated by laying one forefinger across the top of another, 'and that makes it possible to run trains in both directions with one track going one way on one arm of the T and the other track going in the opposite direction on the other. Where the ground is higher the construction people cut a way through and so the track has little or no problems with gradients.'

'I must say I never expected anything like this,' Atta replied. 'So much is new and different in ways that I could never imagine. Has Bath altered much? I did see something of the city but it is plain that many years have passed since my very short stay when I saw George and Hilary Green by the North Bridge.'

'Some things have changed a lot, others not so much. The railway station is little different from the way it was first built. The bus station was moved back to its original site and the buildings that were there were demolished. I never liked them anyway. Bath is a world heritage site so there are rules about what can or cannot be done. The Roman Baths stayed the same and so has the Abbey. You will have plenty of time to see them for yourself,' Copper told him.

'I'm afraid my pace is a bit slow,' Atta replied. 'I ought to have gone to Healer Gwenve for something to ease my old knees but Wint arrived without warning and here I am with only the things I stand up in and the few things I managed to stow in the bag that I slung over my shoulder, but I've said that already.'

'I'm sure Doctor Kate or Matron Patti can do something for you,' Copper said confidently.

'I should be grateful.'

Once in the station Atta craned his neck to watch the approaching train. He stepped on board confidently and followed his hosts to some seats.

'The other people on the train seem interested in us,' he observed.

'We asked in advance that they give you a chance to catch your breath and get used to being here because so much is bound to be new to you and we thought it might be overwhelming,' Clive said.

'That was thoughtful but I'm a resilient old man. I feel that I would like to talk to them,' Atta replied.

'On your own head be it, as we say,' Copper said with a wide smile.

Clive turned in his seat and beckoned to the passengers who were mostly students of all ages and Atta was quickly surrounded. Everybody talked at once. Atta signed a dozen note pads, explaining, 'I learned this from George Green when he showed us how to make get well cards for Hilary Green when Gwenve operated on her.'

Of course, Clive thought. Hundreds of years have passed for us but for Atta it has been only days.

As Atta finished giving his autograph he explained, 'Atta is a shortened way of writing Siglattastin. I could never write my name in full but that doesn't matter because everyone calls me by the short version. Now I have a question that I have asked myself many times and it is this; can anybody tell me how it is that I can talk to you and you can talk to me and we understand each other? It doesn't seem possible.'

Not to Atta nor to anyone else it seemed.

'You aren't what I expected,' one youth admitted. 'I don't quite know what that was but I thought your interests were more limited. Now I'm changing my mind.'

'Up to a point you are correct. The fact is that to a certain extent we had lost our curiosity. Life went on with little changes year on year and we were content with that. Too content, I now realise. I had more curiosity than most and it got me into all sorts of trouble but not everyone was like me. The potential was there but it is not what you've got, it's what you do with what you've got. Our imaginations have been given a boost by the events of a few years ago when the Vikings came and we had to face up to Tarn and beat him. We never knew we were free until that freedom was nearly snatched away from us but now we do know what freedom is we shall never give it up, and knowledge is, it's hard to describe but we would have no access to knowledge and learning if we were not free. We would be told what to think, or more likely told not to think at all. Keeping people ignorant is a means of controlling them as we now know and through that knowledge we have found a new incentive for learning and discovery. We make mistakes but we always come back for more. Some of my discoveries have been useful and some might or might not be useful one day. I only wish I knew which is which!'

There was a ripple of appreciative amusement.

Atta is going to fit in as if he were born here, Copper thought.

A young boy looked to Clive as if asking for permission to speak. Clive interpreted the look and invited him to say something. With some amusement he noticed that the boy was named tRevor if his name badge was to be believed.

'I'm nine years old and I want to know if you really have knives and axes made out of stone instead of metal like my pocket knife,' the boy said.

'I see. Well, it is true,' Atta replied seriously. 'We have some metal and we seem to be finding new uses for it all the time but I grew up using a good stone knife and I like to use stone tools whenever I can. I think an apple cut with a stone knife tastes better that an apple cut with metal but I'm quite an old man and stone has always served me well. Would you like to see my stone knife?'

'Yes sir! Yes please sir!'

Atta drew his knife from his tunic.

'It's very sharp so I keep it in a sheath, like so. Be careful not to cut yourself,' he warned.

The boy examined Atta's knife with care before he returned it to its owner and then he pulled a knife from his trouser pocket.

'It's called a pocket knife because you keep it in your pocket,' he explained, 'and you put your thumbnail into the little groove to pull the blade out. I bought it from the school shop and it cost me nine pence and I paid an extra penny to ink my name into the blade. I made a mistake and made the second letter into a capital but I don't mind because if I should lose it everyone would know who it belongs to and I would get it back in no time as soon as anybody found it. And then I got a new name badge for my jacket so it is the same as my knife and I asked everyone to write it the same way. It still sounds the same.'

Well that explains tRevor's name badge, Clive thought, and if he wants it written that way so be it. The boy was an individualist and no mistake, and Atta has the ability to adapt his talking to suit the listener. He anticipated some interesting conversations.

Chapter 46

Atta puffed his pipe into life and carefully placed his spent match into an ashtray.

'It is good of you to permit me to smoke my pipe,' he said. 'I understand that smoking indoors is not the done thing but to sit outside with my pipe on an evening like this is one of life's pleasures.'

'My father used to say the same thing and Frank Holley still does. I never took to it myself but I know from what Frank has said that the quality of the tobacco is as good as it ever was but any harmful chemicals have been removed.'

Atta nodded. It seemed that gesture had not changed over the centuries.

'Wint told me that,' he agreed.

He raised another subject.

'When I saw you I thought your ages were close to mine but of course I learned from Alfrid that you are long life people and I have a feeling that there are many more like you. Is it passed on through the generations?'

'No,' Clive replied. 'Most people turn down the offer of an extended life if it is made. Our sons made it clear that they wanted nothing to do with it from a very early age and nobody in the family took up the offer until at last one of our great grandchildren did. We had two boys, the eldest was named Lawrence Bowden after my father and after a bit of a gap we had Jeffery Beowulf Bowden. Jeffery used to play with Julia and Brian's youngster when Julia eventually got Brian to the altar.'

'The Lady of the Lake,' Atta breathed.

'Julia and Merlin are going to the stones one more time, or maybe two. Already they are far older than anybody else and they say their work is done. Nobody wants to live forever.'

Atta agreed. He picked up the glass that sat on the table in front of him and studied the contents.

'Lemon squash. Alfrid told me about it but I confess it tastes even better than I expected. I know a number of people who make infusions for hot or cold drinks but this is so refreshing on a warm evening.'

'Did Alfrid tell you about ginger beer?' Copper asked him. 'My grandfather used to make ginger beer when I was a little girl and I'm sure I got in his way when he let me help him. Whenever I drank it the bubbles went up my nose!' She laughed lightly at the memory.

'We don't make, um, fizzy drinks, is that the word? We don't make them but small Alfrid tells everyone about them. Ginger beer and lemonade and I think orangeade as well but I'm not certain. We don't make milk shakes either but Beowulf and Freya did mention them and if I remember right Beowulf liked chocolate milk shakes while Freya banana milk shakes. Or it might be the other way round,' Atta replied.

'It was a very long time ago for us but I can look it up in the Chronicle database. It'll only take a minute,' Clive told him.

'I wouldn't go to the trouble, it won't prove anything or make a difference and it will spoil the daydreaming of an old man when I sit by my fire on a cold winter evening,' Atta replied with a touch of humour.

Copper agreed and was about to say more when the object that Atta had assumed was a table ornament emitted a short buzz and a voice said, 'Copper are you there? It's Patti.'

'I'm here Patti, with Clive and Atta.'

Copper pushed a button at the base of the communicator.

'Oh good. I've a message from Merlin.'

Patti's face appeared on a small screen.

'What has my father done now?' Copper asked suspiciously.

Patti laughed.

'Nothing this time. Actually the message came from Wint and Merlin relayed it. He told me that Atta has some trouble with his knees so if you can find time tomorrow, say at two o'clock, I'll see what we can do about it.'

Atta looked thoughtful.

'I see. Well, Matron Patti I'm more grateful than I can say about my knees but I don't want to put anyone to any trouble. I'm just an old man with the knees of an old man.'

'It's no trouble. I'll see you tomorrow. I'm looking forward to meeting you. Must dash, I've got a mountain of work to get through. Matron might have warned me,' she finished ruefully.

Atta put down his half empty glass.

'Correct me if I'm wrong,' he said, 'but I accuse you of knowing about this in advance. George Green told you something when he came back from my now didn't he? Something is going to happen to me isn't it?'

'Atta, have you ever been called too smart for your own good?' Clive replied.

'Heh! Once or twice I have!'

'Only once or twice. I know an understatement when I hear one, but I'll come clean. George Green did come back with a story. We don't know the details but we do know you went, will go, to the hospital to see Matron Patti and if George was only half as right as he usually was you will be glad you did,' Clive said.

'Then it seems I have no choice. I've always wanted to see what's round the next corner anyway. And now I've let my pipe go out.'

Copper pushed a box of matches across the table.

***

Clive misjudged the volume of traffic and the trio arrived at the hospital earlier than expected. The receptionist they spoke to confirmed their arrival and directed them to a waiting area where they made small talk while many curious glances were directed in their direction.

Two people approached.

'Hello Atta. I'm Matron Patti and this is Walter Pfaffinger. Come along with us and we will have a look at your knees and see what we can do for you.'

'I do feel somewhat stiff first thing in the morning,' Atta admitted in the examination room.

Walter Pfaffinger said nothing but looked thoughtful. Atta turned to speak to him.

'I know it isn't possible but I have a distinct feeling I have seen you before,' he said.

'You have. I was the guard on the train yesterday. I work on the line between Bath and the Avalon District for two days out of seven, one day as a guard and one day as a driver. I'm holding down more than one job,' Walter replied without disclosing the fact that he had been observing Atta very carefully and he had juggled his working hours to be on that train.

Atta was helped onto a low table which raised him higher when Matron Patti held a switch down.

'Oops! I didn't mean to startle you,' she apologised. 'I'm going to look at your knees and all your other bones. If you look at the screen above you when I begin you will be able to see everything I can see. It won't take long so try to keep still.'

The screen lit up and Atta wiggled his toes.

'I just wanted to see if that really is me,' he told Patti.

'I'll let you off that one. Now do try not to move.'

It was over in seconds.

'There, all done. Up you get and come and sit next to me and I'll take a longer look and explain everything as we go. I can already see you have a splendid set of teeth.'

She smiled at Atta's look of amazement. She talked Atta through the images on the screen and found his understanding not far short of miraculous. Beckoning Walter to look over her shoulder she said, 'Look at this. That must have hurt a lot.'

'It did hurt a lot,' Atta confirmed.

'What happened?'

'I was caught in a rock fall at a place not far from the Lake. There is a ravine with a pathway wide enough for two people to walk from the bottom to the top. It's quite a long walk and I hadn't gone far when some boulders came tumbling down. I put my hands up and the bag I carried protected my head but my right leg got a real whack and I was knocked over. I remember that but I'm a little hazy about what happened next but I was found unconscious and covered by small pieces of rock and it took a while to get me out. Then I spent more than two eights of days flat on my back and feeling sorry for myself.'

Atta grimaced at the memory.

Walter Pfaffinger took over.

'Back on the table Atta, and I want you to draw your knees up one at a time while I put a weighted bag over your ankles. Stop if it gets painful, which,' he added honestly, 'it will do at some stage so don't try to work through it,' he instructed.

Atta endured a series of exercises until Walter was satisfied.

'Up you get' he said. 'You have cartilage damage in both your knees. I thought as much. While I was working on you Matron Patti collected something from the printer next door and she has a present for you. Ta da…'

'This is your inner man, somewhat reduced in size and with articulated joints. It's a memento for you to take home,' Patti told him.

'I don't know what to say,' Atta stammered. He stared at the small model of his skeleton as he took it into his possession.

'I haven't done yet. Come on through to the printer and I'll show you something else and I'll talk you through it and discuss what I propose to do next.'

Atta was fascinated.

'These are your knees, printed oversize so we can see you in more detail. You see here how your right kneecap was shattered and you had hairline fractures in both legs, which have healed reasonably well. They didn't travel too far, thanks to the people who kept you flat on your back for a while.'

'I didn't thank them as much as I ought to have done. I was a very bad patient,' Atta confessed.

'Somehow that doesn't surprise me,' Patti smiled. She continued, 'Now the bad news is that sooner rather than later you will be almost unable to walk because your knees are worn out.'

'Gwenve has already told me that. I was hoping you were going to tell me she is wrong.'

Patti shook her head.

'She isn't, but now for the good news and you might need to brace yourself. I propose to remove your knees from here to here,' she indicated, 'and put in artificial replacements.'

'Can you really do that?' Atta blurted.

'I can, and I can give you a choice about what I will do. I can take a tissue sample and use the information in the computer to grow a new set of knees for you around a framework. They will be identical in every way to the knees you were born with. That will take a little while until they grow. That's your first choice. Your second choice is for me to remove your knees and replace them with artificial metal joints that I shall attach to your bones. I can do that as soon as you like; it won't take long for the computer to make sure I have perfect set of joints to put in you and you'll be up and about almost immediately. I'll keep you in overnight and the following morning Walter and I will run a series of examinations and send you on your way. Your choice.'

'I don't know how to make an informed choice but I told Gwenve a long time ago that she may have my carcass for teaching purposes when I have finished with it. I'd love to see her face when she finds something artificial in me. I suppose the scars will give the game away.'

'They won't,' Matron Patti declared, 'because I won't leave any scars.'

'In that case my choice is artificial knees and the shortest time of rest as possible.'

Patti nodded. This was not unexpected.

'The day after tomorrow then if that suits everyone. I'll ask Clive and Copper to bring you in at eight in the morning and when I've run a few tests I'll perform the operation in the afternoon. The following day I'll discharge you as soon as I'm satisfied you are fit to go. Let's go and tell Clive and Copper shall we?'

Clutching his precious scaled down copy of his own skeleton Atta dutifully followed Matron Patti and Walter.

He was half way home when Copper posed the question that he had been considering.

Indicating Atta's new possession she asked, 'What will you do with it?'

'I really don't know,' he replied honestly. 'I'll probably find shelf space for it. It will give my visitors something to talk about and it has just occurred to me that it will support any claim I make that I have been here in your now. I imagine that many people will want to see it and perhaps later Gwenve could find a use for it.'

'One way or another it will certainly make a talking point,' Clive said.

Atta agreed. An idea struck him.

'Clive! Copper! Listen to this! You have done so much for me and I wonder if I might do something in return. It's chancy but it might work. Freya the Viking left a hoard of Viking things for you to find and recover; George and Hilary told me all about it. I wonder if the People of the Lake might do the same. We could leave some things where they would not be found accidentally. I know of places in the hollow hills where the rocks gave me a battering. Merlin lives in such a place I believe. If we look around I might be able to find a feature we all recognise and there we might leave something. George and Hilary have said you are interested in the tools we use, and the pottery. We could leave cloth, perhaps some clothes, and Alfrid would be sure to donate a pair of shoes and I think the clothes would interest you, Copper.'

'A Stone Age collection! I could make a Stone Age collection!' Copper enthused.

'I know I speak for the Lake when I say that everyone will want to contribute something. It will be our way of saying we were here and this is what we did,' Atta expressed his thought out loud.

'That would be priceless,' Clive told him, 'but I wouldn't want to take anyone's prized possession and as you say yourself it is a bit of a gamble.'

'But could it be done? Has such a thing ever been found?' Atta questioned him.

'If it had I would know it. Merlin would too,' Clive declared.

'Then I shall speak to the Council of Seniors and we must find a place to leave it, and I'll be sure to stress that no man or woman or child shall be asked to give up a cherished possession. Will that do?'

'I think it will do very well,' Clive confirmed.

'Good, I shall see to it, and while we are talking about sending things from one time to another I should say that Wint has already mentioned that he wants me to take some things back with me when I go. It is plain to me that I am here for that reason but there is more to it than that, I suspect. I feel certain that you and Wint and Merlin and who knows how many others want me to... to do something. Not in your now but in mine. Am I close to the truth?' Atta said with a knowing look.

'Uncomfortably close,' Copper told him.

'I knew it! I knew it! And I consider it a fair exchange for all you are doing for me. Uh, I imagine Matron Patti knew all along that she is going to take my worn out knees and replace them.'

'Also close to the truth and Patti will tell you so, but nobody knew the details,' Copper confirmed.

'And now,' she added, 'I'm going to start dinner the moment we arrive home. I'll let you choose; chicken curry or steak and kidney pie.'

Clive looked to Atta.

'I remember the Vikings saying they liked curry and they did say there is more than one kind and the dish was, is, served with rice. I have no idea what rice is but what was good for the Vikings is surely good for Atta. I am bound to admit that I am curious about the food in this now. Eathl says eggs are available all year round too, she told everyone that. That seems odd but if Eathl say it is so then it is so,' Atta said.

'Settled then. Curry tonight and eggs for breakfast again tomorrow either boiled, fried, poached, or scrambled,' Copper declared.

'I recommend poached eggs on toast,' Clive advised, reminding Atta that today he had eaten fried eggs at breakfast time.

'You know, I'd forgotten that,' Atta declared.

It was later that evening when Atta relaxed with his pipe well alight.

'I really enjoyed my first taste of curry,' he complimented Copper, who looked pleased.

'I shall make more curry dishes so you can sample the different kinds. Some are quite hot and spicy and some are milder than the curry I made today. I prefer to sit somewhere in the middle. As to the hot and spicy dishes, they are good but all things in moderation. Mrs Bradley is inclined to say that any fool can make a curry that is too hot and a lot of fools do,' she said.

'I shall be guided by you,' Atta replied.

Clive had a piece of news for him.

'I've arranged a sightseeing tour of the Lake for tomorrow,' he announced. 'They do say the best way to see the Lake is from the Lake itself so I've booked cruise tickets. Bearing in mind that there have been many changes over the years I still think you will recognise some things.'

'Alfrid said the Lake is no more. It was all drained,' Atta said. He added, 'Evidently it is drained no longer. I'm curious to know what happened.'

'The Legends of the Lake do say it was drained and re-flooded. Alfrid and Eathl told us all they know of the Lake and we think one of the reasons you were brought here is to take back the knowledge that the Lake is restored and the story will become part of the Legends, which are a collection of stories that tell of the Lake and its events and the people. We have collected all we know of the Legends and to some extent they have transformed our view of the past,' Clive said.

'Our past and your present and future,' Copper added.

***

Standing in front of the railway station Atta observed, 'I can see changes have been made since I was here a few days ago but it is still almost as it was then. Where we stand now there was a place for public transport and behind us there were buildings.'

'Bath is a world heritage site so there wasn't much anyone could do to make alterations to the station,' Copper told him, 'and as for the buildings you mentioned I was glad to see the back of them.'

'Me too,' Clive added.

'I can see they have been replaced by other buildings but the new ones seem better somehow. To begin with they are not as high as the old ones and there is plenty of space in front of them. Space for some trees, and I think they are for people to live in because there are balconies and other things. I see a few shops at ground level. It seems to be a pleasant place. The people in this now have more space and less crowding,' Atta replied.

Two women rode their scooters to the station entrance and folded their machines to carry them to the train they would catch.

'Bella and Trix. Those are not their proper names but they work in astronomy and there is a star in the Orion constellation called Bellatrix so those names are a play on words,' Clive remarked with a casual nod in their direction as he identified them. 'They are mother and daughter. Would you care to say which is which?'

'I'm not caught out that easily,' Atta replied with humour.

Copper gurgled with delight.

'If we don't get a shift on the train come and go and leave without us,' Clive said practically.

Except for the staff he carried Atta looked no different from anyone else on the train but there was no doubt that everyone knew who he was.

'The news of your arrival was broadcast everywhere almost as soon as you stepped through the gate,' Copper explained.

'News always travels fast when an anticipated event occurs,' Atta said lightly. 'More often than not it is news of a new arrival; is it a boy or a girl? After that it is news about Wigstin and whatever caper he has been up to. I used to think small Alfrid was a pest but Wigstin is in a league of his own. His jokes are terrible and his antics beggar belief.'

Copper remembered something.

'George Green brought back pictures from your now and when Julia saw them she said Wigstin is the image of Dunstan who crowned the first king of all England in a ceremony in Bath. It was somewhere near to the Abbey and Julia was there to see it,' she told Atta.

'Julia the Lady of the Lake? I must meet her. I mean if it isn't too much trouble,' Atta added hastily.

Copper smiled.

'It won't be. Julia wants to meet you too.'

The journey on the train was nearing an end when Clive produced a tourist guide and a map that showed the places of interest.

'Alfrid never did grasp the concept of maps but George Green did record that you understood his ordnance survey map and you knew what contour lines mean so I don't expect this map will give you any trouble. The station where we will get off is here and we can walk the short distance to the pier where the boat picks up passengers. If you like we can call a buggy like the one we used when you arrived,' he said.

'My knees will stand it. It is mostly the cold winter weather that gives me trouble and in any event the knees I have now have only to last me one more day so I won't worry about wearing them out. I must say I'm looking forward to walking long distances again. Perhaps not as far as the distances I walked as a young man but a fair distance for an old one and a fair pace too,' Atta replied.

'Then we will walk,' Copper declared.

'And perhaps you will recognise a few places despite the changes that have been made,' Clive said hopefully.

'I can certainly show you where Wigstin fell off the raft,' Atta laughed, 'because there can't be many places where he hasn't fallen off yet and no doubt he will fall off in those places sooner or later. If fish could count they could tell you how many times he has fallen off but it must be more times than I have years.'

411

'We have our own fair share of Wigstins,' Clive said with a wry expression.

'As we say on the Lake, boys will be boys.'

The more things change the more they stay the same.

***

On board the Lake vessel Atta regarded his surroundings with keen interest.

At the shore was left behind them Copper explained, 'This craft has more than one purpose. It's a sightseeing trip for everyone because we get a whole host of tourists and visitors to the Lake and it's a regular service for public transport as you will see from the stops we make. It carries passengers and any amount of small freight because the Lake is home to people and industry and the school, plus the research institutions, and all of these are linked. The Lake is a bustling place I can tell you. The information I got at the pier says the children who boarded when we did are doing a survey of wildlife, mostly birds, and the crew of the vessel will bring up samples of water for them to study. They do a lot of that and... I'll tell you what, there will be more than one microscope on board. Hang on and I'll go and see if I can get some of the pupils to show you.'

Slightly breathless after her long sentence Copper hurried away.

Clive chuckled.

'There's no stopping Copper when she wants to get something done,' he said lightly.

'I can name an eight of women who are no different,' Atta replied. He added cautiously, 'The people of this now seem to me to be... to, to have more of a sense of purpose than the people I saw on my last trip to Bath which was a long time ago for you but only a few days for me. I'm not saying the people of that day were indifferent to what was going on around them but they lacked the urgency that I see around me now. That's not a good way of putting it but it's the best I can do. I hope I haven't given any offence.'

'None whatever,' Clive replied honestly, 'and I agree. It needs a lot of explanation but it is a subject I've taught any number of times. I'm not teaching at the present time, I've gone back to agricultural engineering which is one of my other occupations but I can lay on a presentation at the school whenever I like and I guarantee a big audience because I throw the lecture open to anyone who cares to attend. It's an object lesson that everyone ought to take on board and here on the Lake learning never stops. Men and women of all ages never really leave school here.'

'I look forward to it.'

'There will be a price to pay because the moment the news gets around that you are in attendance they will throw any amount of questions your way. How do you feel about that?'

'Flattered,' Atta replied thoughtfully, 'and a little scared.'

'So would anyone be, and to make even more scary it will be broadcast live around the world, I can see that coming because of the interest everyone is showing about you.'

'Something similar is happening to George and Hilary Green so I can hardly complain and I do want to participate in the affairs of, well the whole world I suppose.'

Copper returned and sat down.

'Some samples of water are on their way but not before a handful more have been taken up and examined. Say in about twenty minutes time,' she said.

Atta wondered what he was about to see but whatever it was he looked forward to a new experience. His curiosity had got him into trouble on more than one occasion as he had cheerfully admitted and he still remembered the whack of Vocca's grandfather's paddle but it was no more than he deserved and nobody's fault but his own. Then there was the matter of the wood ants in the clothing of the bathers…

Then he looked startled and pointed to something.

'That's a Viking ship!' He gasped. 'I know it is because I saw Beowulf's ship when we fought the Battle of the Lake, but I don't know, I mean, I thought the Age of the Vikings was over.'

'Not quite, and the evidence is right in front of you,' Clive answered him. 'The Viking Age as we know it came to an end a very long time ago but when everyone finally accepted that there are some people who lived through it, people like Merlin and Julia, that was when the people of Denmark which is where Beowulf and Freya came from, and the people of Norway who are descended from Viking raiders and traders, they all got together and built more ships. They already had but on a small scale. The ship over there belongs to

413

Northern Commerce, NorCom for short, and its one of a couple of dozen. Uh, three eights.'

'I can work with your way of counting,' Atta said,' even though I find it a little odd.'

Copper drew his attention to the building beside the road that led to the longship moorings.

'That's the Viking Long House,' she said. 'It's a hospitality centre among other things and it's a favourite venue for wedding receptions. The modern Vikings know how to throw a party too.'

'And tell tall stories,' Clive added, 'and what happened there once is a story worth telling. We'll show our noses there another day but today is just a trip on the Lake to get the feel of it.'

'I have been watching for anything I might recognise but so far I haven't been able to spot anything for certain. The landscape has changed a lot.'

Clive agreed and said, 'When it was certain that the Lake would flood again it was allowed to happen. Actually there was no way to stop it. Then the new industries began to move into the district, largely because of the school, and a deep water channel was dredged, you'll see why later. Anyway Atta, the material that was dredged amounted to thousands of tons. I can't give you a figure for either weight or volume but what was dredged up was used around the shores of the Lake and Jasmin Tyler did the landscaping and saw to a lot of the planting and...'

'Jasmin Tyler! I know that name!' Atta exclaimed. 'It is only a handful of days for me of course. Jasmin Tyler is the girl who stepped through the gate with a plant for Twiss. It has, um, unusual properties, and Twiss is so made up with it she means to become a grower herself. Her father has spoken to the Council of Seniors and the Senior of the Growers is going to find here a place. Jasmin's plant has changed the course of her life.'

'Jasmin will be pleased to hear it...'

'She's a long lifer too! Uh, sorry.'

'Jasmin more than earned it. The pupils from the school where George taught are all the same and small Alfrid knew them all and I'm sure each of the will have a message for you to take to Alfrid and his family. We shall never forget them. There is a later pupil who came after they left, a boy named Terry Mitchell and today he runs the sports centre, the canoe club, the indoor sports and so on, and in his spare time he acts in an amateur dramatic society.

'In his spare time?' Atta questioned. 'And when does that happen?'

'You might well ask, but he fits it in somehow.'

'Everybody seems to have more than one task and it appears that they are free to pick and choose what they do. We choose our own professions as well but it is the usual thing to stick to just one activity.'

'People today live longer than they did when I was born and there is a limit to how long anyone would want to do the same thing and it has become normal for people to have a change after a number of years and take away the skills they have gathered and make the most of the opportunity to learn to do more things,' Clive agreed. 'Often they return to education again to learn specialist skills and in part that is what the school in the District of Avalon is all about. Nearly everybody does that at one time or another so the students here are young, old, and very old.'

Copper added, 'My main occupations are costume design and I have my own business for that, and I'm a railway engineer for British Railways, currently on leave of absence. I can skipper a small ship too so I go to sea sometimes.'

'That is in accord with what I witnessed in Bath during my brief visit a long time ago. My thoughts are that when people live longer lives they somehow make as much of them as they can,' Atta said half to himself.

Something seen out of the corner of his eye caught his attention.

'What's that? I've never seen anything like it.'

Clive look in the direction Atta indicated.

'It's a drone, either remotely controlled or more likely pre-programmed to fly to where it is meant to go. They usually carry small items for delivery and my guess that's a prescription for a patient sent from the hospital.'

Whatever it was the small craft flew unerringly on its errand.

Atta studied his tourist map.

'This building that is close to the water's edge is very large and there is what I think must be a ship in the water,' he observed.

His ability impressed Clive and he remembered his father Lawrence Bowden remarking that when he was at school the teaching was that the people of Atta's time were little more than savages.

415

'That's the Marine Sciences Building, or one of them, and the ship is a research vessel that docks next to it. I wonder if Alfrid ever mentioned that Copper used to keep some small fish in a tank indoors?'

'Many times and small Alfrid thought they were for eating but you told him they were just for looking at. It seems odd but I'm sure some of the things we do would seem just as strange to you. George says as much,' Atta replied.

'My tank was little but the tanks in the Marine Sciences Building are enormous but Christine Appleton has sent a message that she will be the one to show them to you and at the moment she is in the airship and it won't be back for weeks. Christine was another friend of small Alfrid. She's a diver driver too.' Copper said.

'I'm sure she is, or I would be if I knew what a diver driver is,' Atta replied with a touch of humour. 'I do know her name though.'

'The diver is a small craft that goes under water for research purposes. It can sample the water at depth and bring up samples of the sea bed and small sea life for further study. The driver is the person at the controls,' Copper told him.

'I see. In the manner of driving a car?'

'It can't be set on auto like a car because obviously there are no roads and there is nothing to guide the diver so the driver has to control it manually all the time and it's quite complicated,' Copper replied. 'Can you see that space between the hills over there? That is a purposely made space for the airship to dock when it comes back.'

'A ship that flies is beyond my grasp,' Atta admitted.

'You will see it before you go home so I won't describe it. This one flies over the seas all over the world but I don't know how much of the surface it surveys each time it goes out. There is a satellite link which helps them locate places of special interest and the ship also carries astronomical equipment so the skies can be observed from different places, which can be important for things like eclipses that are only visible from the oceans. The whole thing is an enormous flying laboratory and it can stay away for as long as you like,' Clive said.

'Don't forget the North and South Poles,' Copper reminded him.

'I'm sort of coming to that but I need a globe and a lot more time.' Copper agreed.

'We've given Christine a mention and I expect Atta has heard of Yolanda Walker. She often flies when there is some special astronomical work involved. So do Bella and Trix, the ladies we saw catching the train.'

'Small Alfrid usually calls her Yo,' Atta confirmed. 'Yo and Christine took small Alfrid to the swimming place in Bath and there were others called Deke and James. Will I meet them too?'

'Deke is flying the airship. His big interest is botany, the study of plants including trees, mosses, and anything that grows, and he used to fly small airships to hard to get to places and quite often he flew below the treetops or alongside them to take cuttings or seeds. He collected soil samples and some other people on his airship collected insects and more than once they discovered insects that had never been seen before,' Copper said.

'Another one with more than one profession then. And James, what of him?'

'I was coming to that. James has always been interested in engineering materials and he helped develop the lightweight materials that make all types of aircraft including airships. At present he is probably on his way back from goodness knows where because he will have been told about your arrival and the group who knew Alfrid and his family make a point of staging reunions whenever they can.'

Clive might have said more but he was interrupted by a middle aged man who hurried up to them.

Holding a shallow dish with care he said excitedly, 'I've got some things that were pulled out of the water.'

'Take my place,' Clive told him, 'so Atta can get a good look.'

'I've got a dragonfly larva. They feed on other things in the water and they can even take small fish. Eventually it will come out of the water and climb up a reed or something and soon it will spread its new wings and fly off. I want to put it back in the water when you have had a look at it and then I'll get a microscope and show you some of the little things that live in the water,' the man said. 'By the way, my name is Josh. Josh Lehman from Australia, studying river and lake management. We used to think rivers were no more than stretches of moving water but now we include the land for a mile or more on each side to take account of the wildlife and vegetation.'

Atta regarded the specimen with interest.

'There are different kinds of dragonflies. Do you know which kind this is?' He asked.

'I don't,' Josh admitted, 'but I have taken a picture of it and weighed and measured it so I'm confident that I shall be able to identify it when I get back in the school. I'll pop it back in the water now and come back in a second or two with a microscope.'

He hurried off on his errand.

'The swimming place!' Atta exclaimed suddenly. 'That's where everyone goes to swim and exchange gossip as often as not.'

'Cripes, it still is! I mean it is now the Lake is flooded again. Can you use it as a reference point?'

'I certainly can, especially because I arrived at the place where my house is. Where it was. There is a jetty where the rafts docked and further along round the headland is where the Dads and Lads Games will be held soon after I go back. I'm getting my nows all mixed up aren't I, but you catch my meaning.'

'Avalon,' Copper breathed. 'That's exactly where Julia said Avalon was, the village with the swimming place. The village that was so important it gave its name to the whole district. And it still does.'

Clive left his seat to take pictures. So that was where Avalon stood. Julia had never pinpointed it although he was certain that she and Copper's father could easily have done if they so wished. Now he felt that he could refer to the centuries old photographs that George and Hilary Green had returned with centuries ago and use them to map the whole village and its surroundings. Atta could supply such details as the place where Alfrid made the glue for the shoes that he made. Alfrid had said it was a smelly process and small Alfrid also knew how to do it. Clive knew that wine had been made somewhere, and pottery, basket weaving, cloth manufacture and dying, furniture making, and so on. In short, anything and everything a self-supporting community needed. Returning to his seat he found that Josh Lehman had returned, accompanied by a younger girl and boy.

He stood back to observe and record the scene.

'These came up in the water samples,' Josh was explaining. 'They usually do where the current is not too fast for them. They are too tiny to see with the naked eye but with the microscope you can make out some single celled bacteria strands. There are protozoa in there too, the ones with tiny hairs and pseudopods.'

Atta was enthralled.

'I've got more,' the boy said eagerly. Pulling a face he added, 'I've got a picture of a squoink as well. That's what you get when you want to take a picture of something like a grasshopper and it jumps away just when you press the button and all you get is a picture of a leaf.'

He was younger than the girl by three years, Clive thought.

'Or flies away,' the girl said. 'Somebody said there ought to be a word for when that happens but there isn't one so we call it a squoink.'

You learn something every day, Clive thought, slightly amused.

'The little ones are called rotifers and they are free swimming and almost transparent and the big ones are waterfleas and they are a branch of a big family of arthropods. Their limbs are jointed and they are crustaceans the same as shrimps but much smaller,' the boy continued.

With a light laugh the girl added, 'They are harmless if you swallow one when you go swimming. I must have swallowed hundreds when I was learning to swim.'

'I imagine I must have done too,' Atta laughed back at her until she stopped and pointed to something.

'Oh look! It's a dragon boat!' She exclaimed.

Atta declared he had never seen anything like it.

The colourful craft was propelled through the water by paddles. Atta counted ten paddlers on the side if the boat that he could see and they were putting all they had into driving the craft swiftly across the water of the Lake.

Josh Lehman answered Atta's question.

'It's a Chinese tradition and they have dragon boat races and festivals all over the world. We've got them back home in Australia and anyone can have a go, same as here on the Lake. I reckon there must be about twenty boats here altogether,' he said.

'Mister Wang keeps his dragon boat moored by the Chinese Lucky House,' the young boy piped up. 'I know he does because I've been there. I can't use chopsticks very well though,' he added.

This required more explanation.

'You want to go there mate,' Josh Lehman concluded. 'Chinese grub is number one.'

Chopsticks? Grub? Atta concluded he had a lot to learn.

'What is lucky about the Chinese Lucky House?' Atta asked Josh Lehman.

'Uh, nothing really mate. I don't know what is was called when it opened but it got it's name on account of the fortune cookies they give you whenever you go there to eat. That's a sort of biscuit with a message inside it and the message is always about you getting good luck. The place belongs to Mr Wang or more like his company that's based in China where they make a whole load of components for the probes that the airship drops into the sea. Mr Wang organises this end of the business.'

Once again Atta concluded he had a lot to learn.

They sailed on. Atta had orientated himself in the landscape that had been altered so dramatically from the day when he lived on the Lake and he was able to identify other places.

'It's a lot more cultivated,' he observed.

'That was intentional,' Copper told him. 'There was space available and Deke Thorpe and Jasmin Tyler turned it into a garden so it would be a nice place to live as well as work and the industrial buildings are not all crowded together. Speaking of Deke and Jasmin they bred a new apple. It's called the Avalon Apple and when we get back to the Viking Longhouse we can pop in to the restaurant and sample Mrs Bradley's apple pie. It's out of this world.'

Atta evidently thought so after he had eaten a second helping. He also learned more about Chinese dishes and Copper promised they would eat at the Lucky House before too long had passed.

That evening he reminded his hosts, 'You said there is a story worth telling about the Viking Longhouse.'

'I'll say there is!' Clive exclaimed, 'and it involves me so I'll do the talking. It began after the population crash, which is a topic I'll reserve for a later day. On the far side of the North Sea is Denmark, the country that my ancestors Beowulf and Freya came from.'

'I heard about that from them. They sailed in something of a hurry with an angry Viking chief and his warriors hot on their heels. They thought it was hilarious,' Atta told Clive.

'That was typical of them. Anyway, next to Denmark is Norway and Viking raiders sailed from there as well. The Vikings from Norway tended to sail a northerly course round Scotland and strike on the west coast and the Danish Vikings favoured the direct approach and sailed straight across the North Sea and raided the east coast. There were no hard and fast rules about it but that was the way it usually happened. I'll call a map up on the screen and you can see for yourself what I mean.'

Atta regarded the map intelligently.

'The coastline shown here is the coast as it was when the Vikings raided,' Clive explained. 'Eventually they settled and after a while they integrated. The process took some time and battles were still fought but that's the essence of it. After the population crash the Danes and Norwegians did a bit of thinking and it wasn't long before a fleet of longships was built and they came across again to trade through the Scottish ports, down the east coast and through the English Channel here, then round the tip of Cornwall and into the Lake. It wasn't that they didn't have regular ships like freighters and passenger ships, they simply liked to sail in the way of their ancestors.

'Anyway, they came to the Lake because they knew about Beowulf and Freya and the fact that I'm descended from them. They built a traditional Viking longhouse and opened up for business and for residential purposes because they came to the school as well.'

'The school. I've heard a lot about the school. It must have been of utmost importance,' Atta commented.

Clive agreed.

'It was and it is. In a way the whole District of Avalon revolves around the school and it is the reason why so many industries came to the Lake. Nowadays education and industry go hand in hand. The Lake is at the core of Planetary Management which encompasses a whole variety of science, sociology, technology, and anything else you can think of. The importance of Avalon cannot be overstated,' he said seriously.

'Getting back to the subject in hand,' he continued, 'the modern day Vikings thought it would be a good idea to have some sort of ceremony to commemorate Beowulf and Freya and the Battle of the Lake, in which you yourself fought.'

'I wasn't much of a fighter,' Atta said, 'but I did make all the weather observations and forecasts and that enabled Beowulf to time his plans to the exact moment when the conditions he wanted were there. When the fighting began I banged a drum in Freya's band and tried not to look as scared as I felt.'

Clive nodded.

'That band was important. Freya knew what she was doing. She also made a promise to the Lake People that if ever they wanted help from the Vikings they should play their pipes and drums and the Vikings would come,' he said. 'We know that from the records that a man known only as Brother Scribe wrote down at Freya's dictation,' he added.

'I was there. It seemed a curious promise.'

'It seemed strange to us as well,' Copper interjected. 'We never knew what it meant.'

'I was talking of bands,' Clive continued his narrative. 'Well, during the rehearsal for the ceremony that the modern day Vikings planned we had a band of our own. Suzanne Fluteplayer knows all the Viking tunes and the words of the songs and together with Pauline Grant who is a musician she taught what she knew. The songs are, shall we say, very robust, and they went down well. You could hear roars of laughter from a long way off. So Suzanne played her flute and a chap named Andrew Simpson played his drums together with his fellow players. The noise of the rehearsals was indescribable.'

'I know of Suzanne Fluteplayer,' Atta affirmed. 'Beowulf and Freya spoke of her.'

'Suzanne learned their language in a matter of days. It was a talent she never knew she had. Anyway, when the final rehearsal was over and the musicians were packing up Pauline Grant was heard to say if that cacophony doesn't bring the Vikings nothing will. She knew of Freya's promise but made nothing of it.'

Clive paused to sip wine from the glass in front of him.

'That sets the scene,' he continued after a moment. 'Came the day and there we were, all assembled outside the Longhouse and ready to go in. I was wearing the Viking sword that I was given when Copper and I were married in a double wedding celebration with Beowulf and Freya as the other couple. The crew of the longship were all crowded round, having sailed in especially for the celebrations. We were starting to move indoors when two car loads of officials drove up, full of self-importance and hot air. It seemed that people in high places objected. There is no such title as Clive of the Lake, they said, and titles had long gone out of fashion. This last was true, there had been so many junk titles handed out in the past that nobody wanted them

422

any more and they served no purpose in the minds of most people. Nobody in the same high places was prepared to acknowledge Julia as Lady of the Lake either, they denied her position and her authority. Julia was furious and the new Vikings were having none of it. I lost my temper and so did they because when Arthur made me Clive of the Lake he used Beowulf's Viking sword Ravager to tap me on one shoulder and a Viking's sword is as much a part of him as his eyes and ears.

'The officials found themselves surrounded by a horde of very angry Vikings and they turned and fled. Everyone who witnessed what took place saw modern Vikings but many years later one of the officials confessed that he saw a Viking army straight out of history, all charging and yelling and ready to hack them to pieces. It was uncanny and no one has ever explained it but what is certain is that the sound of Viking laughter accompanied the rapid departure of officialdom.'

'Hoo hoo hoo.'

Atta gave a good imitation of Beowulf and Freya.

'Some say it's a trick of the wind in the eaves of the Longhouse and it is a fact that when the wind blows just right the sound of laughter can still be heard,' Clive said.

'Could it be that you and Copper have gained something of Merlin's power?' He speculated. 'I have heard what he can do. Not to mention the Lady.'

'Cripes,' Clive gasped, 'I never thought… I mean it never crossed my mind.'

'If it was us I hope we never have to do anything like it again. Merlin and Julia can control it but I can't and I've never really dared to do anything. I know I can to a limited extent and my father has promised to teach me more but I keep it to myself,' Copper said.

'The notion that anybody could have the power and not have complete control of it sends shivers down my spine,' Clive added.

'And mine,' Atta concurred.

He massaged his right knee thoughtfully.

'It's strange to think of having new knees even Gwenve can't do that for anyone,' he changed the subject, perhaps hastily.

'Given the advantage of years of dedicated research and development there's no doubt that she could. I remember how surprised everyone was when Hilary came back to us and we learned how Gwenve had saved her life with heart surgery. More than surprised; we were amazed. Nobody suspected that is possible in your now,' Copper replied.

The evening passed in light conversation until Atta declared it was time he went to bed.

Chapter 47

A bright and clear morning saw the car's computer deliver Atta, together with Clive and Copper, to the hospital at exactly eight o'clock. Matron Patti was there to greet them, which was something of a surprise because both Clive and Copper had expected her to be busy somewhere else. Surgeon Matrons did not usually see to admissions but it was plain to see that Atta's case was an exception.

The formalities were quickly dealt with and Copper and Patti brought each other up to date with their social lives until an orderly appeared with a wheelchair.

'No,' Atta declared firmly. 'I would like to take my last few steps with my old knees before you give me new ones.'

Matron Patti nodded to the orderly.

'Atta may walk. Take him to the ward and get him settled in and I'll be along shortly,' she said. 'Oh, and go through the menu with him. Light lunch, and for dinner he can eat as much as he likes of anything he wants.'

The orderly led the way to the ward and Atta spent the morning watching a series of educational programmes between talking to the nurses who made visits at intervals. The next time he saw Matron Patti he was in the operating room.

As he laid on the operating table a young man said, 'I'm going to put this cuff on your arm just below your elbow and it will let me and Matron Patti know all about your blood and how fast your heart is beating, what your temperature is, and anything else we need to know. You can see it on the screen.'

Atta looked at the monitor.

'Interesting,' he commented.

Matron Patti approached.

'We shall soon be ready to begin. In a moment or two you will be unconscious and when you wake up it will all be over,' she told her patient.

'No healer has ever had problems getting me to sleep but I notice you are not wearing a healer's badge. How will you hypnotise me?' He asked.

Patti smiled.

'Sometimes an operation can be done on a hypnotised patient but I am no hypnotist. There are other ways,' she said.

'Hmm. I see. My cuff thing tingles a little. Does it need adjusting? And how will you make me uncons…'

'Like that,' Matron Patti's assistant said. With a glance at the monitors he continued, 'He's all yours Matron.'

Patti's incisions were swift and sure. Robotic arms moved at her direction.

'The people who treated him when he was caught in a rock fall did a remarkable job,' she commented once.

'He was lucky and no mistake. He might never have walked again. Not without crutches anyway,' her assistant agreed.

One hour later Patti said, 'All done, you can wake him up now.'

'…cious? Jeepers Creepers! What happened?'

'The tingling feeling you got from your cuff was an anaesthetic being injected through your skin to send you to sleep. How do you feel?' Patti said.

'I feel fine and bewildered and I don't know what I feel most. Is it over? Have I got new knees? Can I get up and walk about?'

Matron Patti smiled.

'Not yet, it's the wheelchair back to your bed for you. In the morning we'll get you up on your feet and Walter Pfaffinger will walk you up and down the ward to see how well you bend your knees. If you can squat and stand up again without discomfort I will release you either before lunch or shortly afterwards, it depends on how much you like hospital food.'

'I ordered spaghetti for dinner tonight, I thought it would be a new experience. Which reminds me, you knew you were going to give me new knees even before I came, didn't you?'

'Yes and no,' Patti replied. 'When George Green came back from your now I was a junior nurse and in those days Surgeon Matrons were not even dreamed of so I thought he was having a joke at my expense. George never told me I would put metal knees in either. I did offer you other choices.'

'So you did,' Atta remembered. 'Either way I'm very grateful. Perhaps I can even play football again with some of the parents.'

'I see no reason why not,' Patti answered, 'and now it's back to the ward and rest for a while.'

Atta meekly allowed himself to be wheeled away. You didn't argue with healers.

***

Atta finished his breakfast and decided that Beowulf had a point when he described coffee as stinkwater but he acknowledged that some brands were better than others. He discovered his opinion was shared by Walter Pfaffinger.

The physiotherapist had completed his examination of Atta's ease of movement and he and Matron Patti were happy to discharge him from the hospital when Clive and Copper arrived to collect him. The man could hardly stop talking about his experience but Copper managed to get a word in at last.

'James Wilson arrived while you were in hospital and he has something to try on you but I'm not allowed to tell you what it is and I'm obliged to say that it is something you might not care to try but I have and so has Clive…'

'And once won't be enough,' Clive interrupted.

'Hmm. I'm intrigued,' Atta said.

Studying his staff he changed the subject.

'I won't need this to aid my walking, not for a few years anyway but Atta without his staff is like a Viking without his sword. It's part of me.'

'Because you no longer need it to walk with that's no reason to give it up,' Clive thought.

'True. I'll keep it with me wherever I go. I'll miss it if I don't.'

'It's a bit like my sword. I hardly ever wear it but my flag is never far away. Nearly everybody has a flag from the age of about fifteen and we wear them as patches on our jackets or we fly them from small poles. Your staff would make a fine flagpole.'

'I have no flag but I must consider it. I know there are kits to help with the design. Everyone knows where I live when I am at home but I could take my flag to anywhere else on the Lake and let everyone know I'm there. I must think about the design.'

That evening Atta enjoyed another curry dish and Copper declared she would try him with an array of recipes before he returned to his own time.

The table was cleared and the trio sat outside in the warm evening air.

'Two things puzzle me,' Atta declared. 'The first is what am I doing here, which we have discussed and the second is something you have said we would talk of. I mean the population crash. What happened? Why did it happen? Was nothing done to avoid it?'

Clive crossed and uncrossed his legs.

'We have said that one reason Wint brought you here is to take some things back and give them to George Green. I'll answer the first question easily but in a disjointed manner. We know you did this and I'll endeavour to explain why. Avalon today is unique and the school where George and I taught has a bearing on this. Perhaps my own efforts helped but it is George who should take the credit.

'George retired but his legacy lived on and eventually a second campus was secured at Avalon. Many of the pupils who studied there were snapped up by other educational establishments or industries and before long a new building was needed. Several new buildings in fact. Avalon became a seat of learning and one construction was the George Green Building. There is a statue of a dragon outside the building and small statuettes can be bought for use as ornaments or paperweights. That statue is based on the flag that a lady named Meglen made for George to fly at the Dads and Lads Games. The dragon is shown holding the torch of knowledge...'

'Meglen!' Atta sputtered. 'But she hasn't... she didn't...'

'She will and she did and George was tremendously proud of it. We would like you to take one of the statuettes and give it to George when you get home. Give it to him after the Games of course, and how you explained it to Meglen has always been a matter of conjecture,' Clive said.

'I expect I shall think of something but right now my head is spinning in all directions at once!' Atta gasped.

'There's a prospectus as well. The school at Avalon has them printed to give information about the many and varied educational courses to prospective students, who may be as young as some of the students you have met already or they might be hundreds of years old.

The prospectus is entitled The City and the Lake because Bath and the Avalon District are intertwined and a lot of the students live and in the city and there are classes there as well. The students go from one site to another, depending on their studies. The school has an open door policy so anyone who wants to study here may do so. The prospectus shows pictures against some of the school buildings and other facilities and some staff members have their pictures alongside some of the articles they have written about their departments. It's a fairly large prospectus and my piece is on page eight. We're sending it back so George may see for himself how much his life impacted on the affairs of the school and the Lake. I have a feeling he will be embarrassed but it's a chance I'll take. George never mentioned it to anyone so I had no idea of its existence until one of his daughters showed it to me about ten years after George died. I dismissed it as a joke but the chronicler of that time decided to release it for anyone to read. If any of those copies still exist they are hundreds of years old but I doubt that any have survived. I had forgotten about it until Wint and Merlin reminded me and asked me to get you to take a copy for George when you go home.'

'Time travel is a funny business but who am I to complain? I'll gladly take a copy for George and I wonder what he will make of it?'

'Hmm. I wonder.'

***

For a long time Atta was speechless.

'Am I really going to do that?' He asked. 'Am I really going to fly with the birds?'

The years had done nothing to diminish James Wilson's wide smile.

'I don't know if you will like it because it must seem strange and you have nothing to compare it with but it's quite safe and the people who live and work on the Lake all try their hand at it at one time or another. As you can see from the badge on the tail this one belongs to me.'

Atta had noticed the badge on James' right sleeve matched the design on the tail of the aircraft. He was aware that almost everybody wore a badge that was a small representation of their flags.

'To fly,' Atta breathed. 'To go where the birds go. To fly. All my life I have dreamed about flying and all I could do was stand and watch. And envy,' he added.

'Well now's your chance. Let's walk around my machine and I'll show you how things work. Ah, Pat,' James spoke to a young girl who approached, 'Nice timing. Thanks.'

He took a small model from her.

Atta looked at the girl and said, 'I've seen you before, it was on the boat before I got my new knees. You were the one who told me what a squoink is. No, it wasn't you, it was the boy you were with.'

'That's right sir. I'm Pat Daly and one of my jobs is to help here, which,' she wrinkled her nose, 'is mainly sweeping floors and making cups of tea. If I can stand it long enough it counts towards my Duke of Edinburgh's Bronze Award.'

'All good training,' James replied with his usual good humour.

He hasn't changed in hundreds of years, Clive reflected.

Another girl showed off her badge and said 'I'm Michelle Proctor but I'm not doing Duke of Edinburgh's. I do work at the hospital and this badge on my jacket is a replica of the old road signs for hospitals and it was especially chosen because George Green had the Torch of Knowledge on his flag and that came from a road sign too. I do more training when I'm on ambulance duty but I have to help out here because James is my four greats grandpop. It's not fair but you can't choose your ancestors,' she ended with a wide smile and pulled a face at James.

'Nor your descendants,' James replied with a smile that matched hers, 'which is lucky for you young lady. Carry on the way you do and you'll soon get your Nimlet's badge.'

Michelle stuck her tongue out at him.

'And now to business,' James said briskly as he led the way to his aircraft after poking his own tongue out at Michelle.

'It has two engines,' he explained, 'here under the wing and close to the fuselage which is this bit,' he tapped the aircraft to indicate what he meant. 'Moving along the wing we have the ailerons which move up and down,' James demonstrated with the model that Pat Daly had brought with her. 'The ailerons are controlled from the cockpit which I'll show you in a minute and what they do is let me bank the aircraft to the left or right when I make a change of direction. You see on the tail fin here, that is the rudder and I control that with my feet; left foot forward to turn left, right foot forward to turn right. The other moving surfaces are the elevators here on the tailplane. I move them upwards from the cockpit when I want to climb and downwards when I want to descend. All right so far?'

Atta nodded.

'I think so,' he said. 'The whole concept is new to me but it can be grasped with a little thought.'

'Actually it's fairly simple. I'll demonstrate when we are flying. Now for the engines. As I said there are two engines, one on either side. They are ducted fan engines, which means the blades are inside a sort of tube. They draw air in at the front and blow it out of the back a lot faster than it came in so the aircraft gets pushed along. They are solar and battery powered and they are very quiet. The solar panels that cover most of the upper surfaces provide electricity to charge the batteries and power the engines and the instruments in the cockpit that tell me all the information I need when I'm flying,' James told him.

'Now for the wheels,' he continued. 'There is one wheel in the fuselage near the front of the aircraft and two smaller wheels beneath the wings. The wheels are not powered so when I'm on the ground I use the engines to move around. All of that leads to the cockpit where you can see two seats side by side. If Clive or Copper will take my model we'll jump in. I'm giving you the left hand seat which is normally where the first pilot sits and Pat will help you in and get your straps adjusted. When that's done I'll talk you through the cockpit drill and close the canopy and away we will go. I'll just take off and land to see how you take it and if you like it we'll go up again and I'll show you the Lake as the birds see it.'

While he was being strapped in Atta learned that Pat Daly was the younger of twins whose parents had named them Patrick and Patricia, so Pat was known as Pat Daly Her and her brother was Pat Daly Him.

'It makes sense in a funny sort of way,' she said, 'but goodness only knows what our parents were thinking about,' she said as she fitted Atta's headphones. The canopy was closed and James unclipped a checklist and talked Atta through it.

'Controls. Batteries. Straps. Instruments. Trim. Canopy. Brakes,' he read while Atta watched keenly.

'Ready?'

'Ready,' Atta confirmed.

James thumbed a button on his control column.

'Avalon South. James ready for take off. Circuit and land. Two on board.'

'Cleared.' The reply was a single word.

Keeping a watch out of the corner of his eye James released the brake from his main wheel. The engines made an almost inaudible hum and Atta did his best to look in all directions at once as the small aircraft left the ground after a short run to gather speed.

Atta was enthralled. His flight lasted a little less than five minutes and there was no need for James to ask if he had enjoyed it.

'Shall we go up again? We can fly to the Lake in just a few minutes, you probably got a glimpse of it when I flew us back to the airfield.'

'I missed it,' Atta admitted. With rising excitement he was quick to add, 'Yes! Yes! Yes! I have gone where only the birds can go. It's a lifetime dream that I never thought would be fulfilled. Never for one moment!'

'I'll tell the tower we're going sightseeing then.'

James thumbed to button on his control column.

'Avalon South. James plus one, tour of the Lake, one thousand feet. Request radar advisory.'

'Roger that James. No traffic expected for, uh, two hours plus; the sky is yours. How did your passenger like his first flight?'

'Ask him.'

'Atta this is Avalon South. What do you think of flying?'

'Push the button on the control column on your side so they can hear you in the tower,' James said.

Atta did so.

'I enjoyed it I want to do it again,' Atta stammered.

'Good for you. James you are cleared to take off.'

At eight hundred feet James levelled off.

'When we climb we are on full power but that reduces automatically for level flight unless I want to increase my speed,' he told Atta.

He indicated the instrument display and Atta seemed to grasp the concept.

'I'll climb again and you will see how the engines draw more power,' James continued, and once more Atta showed his understanding.

'The drain on power shows here,' he said as he studied the instruments where a vertical red indicator got shorter. 'I think the writing must show a scale but I don't know about that.'

'You're right. The solar panels will soon have the batteries topped up again. Now I'll level us out at one thousand feet. What do you think will happen?'

'The engines will run more slowly and the red marker thing will stop getting shorter,' Atta replied confidently.

'Right, and if I lower the nose and we lose height, what then?'

'The reverse of climbing higher. The engines will draw less power. Less that flying level I think.'

'Right again. They will draw just enough to keep turning. I could shut them down altogether but I never do that unless I want to shorten my approach to the spot where I intend to land,' James said. 'It's the reason why this aircraft has no spoilers or airbrakes; we don't need them.'

'I'll take your word for it. You never mentioned spoilers and airbrakes before,' Atta replied.

'There was no need but I can explain it better when we back on the ground so for the time being we'll do a tour of the Lake and give you an overview of things the way they are now compared to what you are familiar with. Put your feet on the rudder bar and hold the control column lightly and follow me through on the controls.'

Gingerly, Atta did James' bidding.

'Left turn first to get us going in the right direction. That's good. Airspeed forty five knots, which is about fifty two miles an hour, the cruising speed for this aircraft. It's slow but it was never meant for long distance flying.'

Atta made no comment but continued to observe the things James did. He kept his hands and feet on the controls when James made small changes to their course.

'Viking Longhouse,' James said briefly as he pointed it out. 'I'm taking my hands and feet off the controls. Make a left turn to fly directly over it.'

Atta looked startled but with a hand that shook slightly he made his turn.

'Easy isn't it?' James grinned.

Atta's expression matched his.

'Over there is the Chinese Lucky House, all painted red and gold, which are considered to be lucky colours. While you have the chance you must try Chinese cooking; its delicious and even Mrs Bradley can't match their seafood dishes.'

Atta remembered that Josh Lehman had said as much. For the next hour he handled the controls and when James declared their time was up it was too soon for him.

James landed the aircraft and Atta followed him through on the controls all the way down.

Atta was almost dancing with excitement as he and James made their way to the group of people who waited for them. Some were known to Atta and some were strangers.

Clive made the introductions.

'This is Brian Gleaves who is my boss when I'm doing my work as an agricultural engineer and this if Frank Holley who also works for Brian. At present Frank is the Chief Flying Instructor at Avalon and Brian is working for him, and standing next to him is Jack Smythe who is an agricultural engineer too. Brian and Jack are aircraft engineers too and sometimes it's hard to tell who is in charge of what,' Clive ended with a wide smile.

Brian held out his hand and said, 'Wotcher mate.'

After hundreds of years Brian Gleaves still called everyone mate, Clive reflected with an inward smile.

'I'm, I'm pleased to meet you all,' Atta said honestly, still slightly in awe of his experience of flying. Turning to James he stammered, 'I have no right to ask this but if there is a chance for me to fly some more...'

Atta looked slightly embarrassed.

'You will fly as often as you wish,' a voice behind him said.

Atta spun round and his mouth dropped open. There was no need for the speaker to identify herself.

'L... L... Lady,' he stuttered, his head spinning. This was too much!

Then the robes were gone.

'Please call me Julia and remember the Lake was yours long before it became mine. You learned its ways and made it your own until such time as there was a new Lady.'

'It seemed so strange. There has always been a Lady of the Lake, as far back as I can remember and even farther back than my grandfather could remember. Sometimes they were knowing ones and sometimes they were not. Our tradition is that the Lady is never appointed, it just happens. The Lake and all its people greet you.'

Julia nodded.

'I welcome you to the Lake as we know it today. You shall come and go as you please and no place is barred to you, no doors are closed. There is much to see and you will find that everyone is ready to talk with you and explain what they are doing and how and why they do those things. I know for example that you have met Pat Daly Her, and Michelle Proctor, and young tRevor. He certainly has a mind of his own and in that he is typical of all the people who live and work on the Lake. Now I shall leave you with Frank Holley for a while. He has something to show you.'

He had. Atta found himself in a strange machine that matched the aircraft he had flown in except that is did not fly. It certainly felt like it though. It was called a flight simulator and it was used to instruct pilots in the use of instruments and the ways of flying. As always Atta was keen to know more and he was all attention.

Julia turned to James.

'Have you told him?' She asked.

James shook his head.

'Not a word but I don't think it would have made any difference if I had.'

Chapter 48

Wint was the first person to notice Clive and Copper and he pointed to the spot where Copper's father Merlin was engrossed with a task that was a mystery to them but appeared to have something to do with tuning his new standing stone.

'That was quick,' Merlin said. 'You haven't long left the airfield and Frank Holley's crew.'

'We thought we would come and say hello and poke our noses into your business,' Copper told him.

'There isn't much to see. Wint has sent and received audio and visual signals to one or two other stones so we feel sure our new stone will aid our understanding of the way the stones work. Wint is attaching monitoring equipment and meters and so on. We should be ready to start our experiments before long but before we do we will isolate this stone from all the others that still work,' Merlin replied.

Wint looked up from his business and said, 'We have measured electrical activity in and around the stone and through the ground. The readings are hard to detect but I think I can amplify them.'

His voice was high pitched but Copper was sure it had deepened and she wondered whether Wint's frequent contact with what was possibly a second branch of the human race had something to do with it. It scarcely mattered but it had been rumoured that the branches had begun to merge although it had never been confirmed. In any event the rumours came from Australia where Copper knew that the Guardians of the Rock had been working with up to a dozen knowing ones. She herself had only ever met Wint but she was aware that there were others.

The Guardians had an oral tradition that went back farther than anyone could remember but it was said that what they knew would keep an army of physicists occupied for decades.

'We should leave and let you get on with your work,' Clive declared. 'Atta is with Frank Holley for a couple of hours and when they are through Frank will put him on the shuttle bus with instructions to the driver to drop him off at the Longhouse for lunch before we show him round the George Green Building. He's really got the flying bug by the way. He was asking for more the moment James landed them back on the ground.'

Before they left to climb themselves out of the hollow where Wint and Merlin had erected their stone Copper declared that they must come to dinner with her and Clive before too long.

'Atta likes curry,' she added.

The Longhouse was reasonably empty when the pair arrived and found a table.

'We've all been watching the bulletin board to see Atta go flying. It must have been strange for an Iron Age man but the bulletin board said he enjoyed it,' the young waiter said as he took their order.

'Two cups of coffee,' Copper ordered, 'but nothing to eat. We're going to wait for Atta to come in around lunch time.'

'In other words, your usual. I'll have it here in seconds.'

'Morning coffee and afternoon tea. We are becoming predicable in our old age,' Copper remarked as the waiter sped away.

'Suits me,' Clive replied cheerfully.

He thought for a moment before he added, 'I can't believe how well Atta fits in with us. In his own now he never used metal if stone was available but in our now he doesn't think twice about it.'

'He's adaptable and I suspect he's a lot more adaptable than we would be, and there's no doubting his intelligence. I'm afraid my old schooling still colours my thoughts. We were taught about cave men. Mis-taught I should say. I never had any real notion of history before I met you and then I read everything I could find. It was a mixture of books and I bundled it all together in my own mind but I did learn. Gradually I admit but I did learn,' Copper replied.

Clive smiled at her recollection.

'I remember how you used to carry your library books in your old wicker basket before Peep made it his hiding place,' he said.

He opened his mouth to say more about the small dragon that had become Copper's pet but he stopped and said instead, 'Don't look now but I think someone is coming our way.'

'Atta? I wasn't expecting him yet.'

'Not Atta. Nobody I know.'

The stranger stopped and said hesitantly, 'I hope you will excuse me but I want to pick your brains.'

Copper instantly noticed his name badge.

'I see you have spotted my deliberate mistake. I'm tRevor's father and when he told me what he had done when he put his name on his knife I decided to stand by him and so I became eLberd as you see by my own badge. It's a father and son thing, or it was to begin with and now it's a mother and daughter thing as well. I can't see it catching on but it does no harm,' the stranger said.

Clive motioned him to sit down and join him and Copper.

'What do you think we know that you don't?' He asked good humouredly.

'A great deal probably but each to his own. The thing is, I'm mid-way between changing my work as a solar panel technician and installer. I'm nearly eighty years old and I don't want to spend the rest of my life doing the same thing over and over. I've still got about seventy years to go if I don't do something silly in the meantime. I haven't decided what I'm going to do but I made my way to the school library and rooted around a bit and came across an early edition of the Aqua book that was written when the news about you and the bell curve came out. It was skimped over in school but I had time on my hands and I read about what Mrs Beach said about the people who talked about sports on the old television programmes,' eLberd explained.

'I said they talked nonsense and they ought to be ashamed to take the money, or something like that. I could have got more and better informed opinion by gossiping in the queue at the post office,' Copper remembered.

'Well, I wasn't going to take anyone's word for it, even yours, so I made a nuisance of myself to the librarians and archivists and they managed to find quite a lot of old material for me. I set myself an arbitrary target of a hundred hours of television viewing and you were right Mrs Beach, it was rubbish. I found the football games entertaining. They still are of course but the stuff they spouted afterwards was pure drivel. And can you believe golf was a spectator sport? Well you were there and I wasn't but I can only conclude that the people who wanted to watch two people whack a ball round must have had time on their hands,' eLberd declared.

Warming to his theme he continued, 'Horse racing was another thing, just a few minutes of racing and hours of talk and a lot of people with silly hats and binoculars they didn't need. I don't wonder it came to an end the way motor racing did, even if the reasons were not the same.'

'You seem to have a low opinion of the sporting world,' Clive observed.

eLberd shook his head. 'I haven't,' he denied, 'but I have a low opinion of, what shall I call them, the fringe element perhaps; superannuated players and so-called experts who ought to have been shown the door. They spoilt the whole thing for me.'

'I agree,' Copper declared emphatically.

eLberd was visibly relieved.

'I'm glad I'm not alone,' he said. Continuing his narrative he added, 'It doesn't end there. I sat through endless hours of what they called game shows, reality shows, panel games, and can you believe it, celebrity programmes of every hue. There were talent shows that were little more than lighting displays and the entrants were kept waiting for the judgement of a panel of people who were often appointed for no reason that I could fathom. The wait for then judges verdict was stupidly long, it was enough to make you go spiral. The game shows were just as bad, the same people turned up on them again and again, switching from one show or game to another. Some were well educated and some even produced some good work but there were others who were there for no good reason that I can fathom and there were others who were well below average in the intelligence stakes. I was embarrassed at times and I think it would have been kinder to destroy the records but that would have been glossing it over and that would have been wrong. It happened and we must live with it.'

'They were what were called media savvy and they knew full well how to play to the cameras and the uncritical audiences,' Clive said.

'I can't understand why audiences turned up to watch these things unless it was to come in out of the rain. They laughed at puny jokes and witticisms that weren't in the least bit witty. I swear that if I had appeared as a guest and the host welcomed me as eLberd from the Avalon District I would have been applauded, and for what? It didn't make sense and there were countless broadcasting channels,' eLberd said scathingly.

'I still agree,' Copper told him.

'Then why?' eLberd gestured eloquently.

'Over to you Clive,' Copper said.

Clive Bowden crossed his legs and then uncrossed them while gazing thoughtfully at the rafters in the ceiling.

'There were several reasons and as always there is no simple answer. Firstly, people were starting to live longer, thanks to improved medicine and living conditions. At one time people's lives went through two stages; first there was the age of learning and then there was the age of working, and the second age began for girls as well as boys almost as soon as they could walk. Things improved gradually and then there was the third age, the age of leisure. Some people decided to enrich their lives by advancing their education. Perhaps you have run across the university of the third age as it was called, often abbreviated to U3A. It was informal and unstructured for the most part and it served its purpose well but education isn't for everyone and the fact is that many people were mentally lazy and all they wanted was bread and circuses, which is what the Roman Senate used to control the Roman mob.'

'I'm happy to say I can remember that from my history lessons and considering who I'm talking to I'm relieved as well but I have to admit I never made the connection but bread and circuses says it all. There were so many cooking programmes anyone would have thought that food was all they thought about. Food, sport, and game shows were the equivalent of bread and circuses,' eLberd declared.

'You're not alone in thinking that and if you like I'll ask Mrs Bradley to give you her thoughts about all those cookery programmes but you might want to cover your children's ears when she gets going. There was also the matter of employment and incentive. Work had become less labour intensive than previously and automation and improved production meant that labour forces in industry were reduced while at the same time the population increased. There was nothing for a lot of people to do so bread and circuses became the order of the day and the entertainment industry turned out more and more of less and less. It was a quick and easy fix and for some it's nice work if you can get it but only until the bottom drops out to coin an old phrase. In the end it did. The industry had its backers and its critics and what went on behind the scenes we might never know unless something turns up in the archives. In any event it was going to be a truly enormous task to turn things around. The sleepwalking public needed a good kick up the rear and in the end that was pretty much what they got.'

Copper reached for a napkin and found a pen in her bag. Then she scribbled a note and passed it to eLberd who looked puzzled by it.

'1984. I don't understand,' he told her.

'It's the title of a book that was written in the middle of the twentieth century by George Elliot. That was his pen name by the way. The book looked forward about twenty-five years, hence the date. It's no longer taught in the school curriculum but it wouldn't hurt if it were, and I'm sure you can find it on the database. It envisaged a time when the government, otherwise known as the party, oversaw the entertainment that was fed to the proletariat, in other words the masses, by Prolesec which was a section of the Ministry of Truth. Truth was far from, well, the truth. The stuff that was produced was superficial, deliberately so, and it covered films, music, literature, and the news which was often fake news because the governing party only told people what they wanted them to hear. There were departments set up to produce rubbishy newspapers that printed crime stories, sport, and horoscopes and not much else. The party held the belief that if the general public were allowed to have too much information and knowledge they would rise up against them. You mentioned talent shows, and in George Orwell's book he mentioned a machine called a versificator that churned out mechanical music. The talent shows never got that far but it was production line material that got through all the same. It has been claimed that the things you have been listening to and watching are very similar to what the book described.'

'Did nobody ever question it?'

'They did but to be honest the people who liked that sort of thing wanted to be kept happy and contented and they didn't go in for critical thinking,' Copper replied. 'Fake news and poor quality entertainment was all they asked for provided there was plenty of it. You could try and find a selection of the magazines that featured show business stories and kept the actors in the limelight and were boringly uninteresting and often figments of the imagination. There were far too many people who didn't know how to make better use of their leisure time and didn't even want to know. Fortunately not everybody was like that or the world would be in a real mess now.'

Copper stopped her discourse and pointed to the door that Atta had just walked through, accompanied by about a dozen girls and youths all dressed alike and carrying staffs. They were plainly on friendly terms and everyone including Atta talked at once. Eventually one youth brought an end to the noisy proceedings by indicating that Atta should join Clive and Copper while the rest of the group made for the self-service counter.

eLberd made to get up but Copper stopped him.

'Atta wants to talk to everyone on any subject. I expect he'll talk non-stop about his new knees and his flying experience and his new friends as like as not. He looks like the cat that's got the cream doesn't he?'

She introduced him to eLberd and her guess was soon confirmed.

'My son tRevor talked to you on the train when you first arrived. The children had been warned not to bother you but tRevor is a past master at making a nuisance of himself sometimes,' eLberd said.

'Isn't that what boys do?' Atta said with a touch of humour. 'I remember the time when I was a boy and I collected a box full of wood ants and then I piled up everyone's clothes at the swimming place and put the ants all over them. I tell you, you know about it when a wood ant bites you. You should have heard the yells! Unfortunately for me I was spotted and I got the punishment I deserved and I was made to prepare the ground for the growers for six whole eights of days and that put an end to my summer capers that year!'

Atta laughed uproariously at the memory of his past escapades, stopping only when their table waiter reappeared with an apology for his late service.

'Early delivery for the kitchen and nobody to handle it,' he explained. 'Would anyone like to order anything?'

'Another coffee,' Clive said. 'I'll think about lunch in a minute.'

Copper declined to order.

'Tea please,' eLberd said.

'I don't know,' Atta said. 'I might like to try one of your fruit drinks, the ones you mix with water.'

'Try lime,' Copper suggested.

'I talked to some people I came in with when I was on the shuttle bus because they all dressed alike and carried staffs like mine. They told me they belong to the Second Avalon Scout Troop. I'm not at all

442

sure what that is but there were two girls on the airfield and one was working for a Duke of Edinburgh Bronze badge, whatever that is, and another girl who is related to James works at the hospital sometimes has a badge for it and the Scouts seemed to be doing something similar. James told that girl she would get a Nimlet's badge but I think that was not serious. Perhaps you could tell me all about it later.'

'I must soon get back to work,' eLberd declared when his tea was finished. 'I haven't given up my job yet and I'm doing scheduled maintenance of the solar arrays when the Humboldt comes in so I'm getting my gear and servicing manuals in order before it arrives. It was a pleasure meeting you Atta.'

'Humboldt?' Atta made it a question as the technician prepared to depart.

'The airship is named after a German called Alexander von Humboldt who lived way back in the early part of the nineteenth century. They still teach lessons about him in school because of his work. He was the first person to understand how everything affects everything else and nothing happens in isolation. Nature is more than the sum of its parts and it is an interaction of all living things and all non-living things; geography, climate and the weather, the oceans, the mountains the seasons, and anything else you can think of. He was the first person by a long way to realise that human beings had the ability to upset the balance of nature by destroying the ecosystems such as rainforests. He claimed that the balance is a fine one and the destruction of one thing would inevitably lead to the destruction of other things,' Copper told him.

'That makes sense to me,' Atta agreed.

'Rainforests are a particularly good example,' Clive said. 'In South America the forests were destroyed to grow other crops because there was no understanding of the role they played. Rivers became torrents that washed away the soil because the roots of the trees were no longer here to bind it and towns and villages were washed away with it, and still the destruction of the forests went on, often illegally. The damage wasn't confined to the rainforests. The airship is named Humboldt to honour his work and to remind us of the damage that was caused through irresponsibility and sheer ignorance. It was a lesson to be learned the hard way.'

Copper agreed with Clive.

'Humboldt is Christine Appleton's hero. And,' she added, 'it wouldn't hurt us to eat something.'

'I met a man named Josh Lehman and he told me how soil was washed away when the trees along the river banks were cut down and now the river includes the land on each side of the river and not just the water. He said he comes from Australia,' Atta commented.

Sunlight sparkled on the Lake as the water taxi made the crossing after their light lunch. Atta stood against the rail and Clive and Copper pointed out the sights. A siren and a fast moving craft caught their attention. The hull was painted with green and yellow squares.

'Ambulance,' Clive said briefly. 'All other craft give way to them on land and water. They're amphibious and they can enter and leave the water almost anywhere and they only use the siren when they are in a hurry to reach a casualty or a sick person or if they are on their way back to the hospital. Usually it's for minor injury but the Lake has a good safety record.'

'The girl at the airfield who wears a hospital badge told me she goes in the ambulance for some of her training. Is that the same thing?' Atta asked.

'It is. I think that must have been James' fourth of fifth stage daughter,' Copper replied. 'Is her name Michelle Proctor?'

'Yes, that's her. She did say she and James are related.'

'I know her slightly,' Copper said. 'According to Terry Mitchell she plays a ferocious game of rugby.'

An hour later they caught the ferry to cross the Lake.

In no particular hurry they strolled onto dry land and made for the George Green Building.

'This is where the school in Bath first opened the campus on the Lake. The statue is George Green, holding the torch of learning aloft and it was based on the flag that Meglen made for him, or will make, I don't know which is the correct way to say it,' Clive said.

Inside the building the first thing that Clive wanted to show off was a wall mounted glass case that held a flag.

'George Green's own flag, sewn by Meglen for him to fly at the Dads and Lads Games. It's priceless and it's only on a sort of permanent loan to the school. Meglen made a flag for Arrad as well. She was clever with her needle and no mistake,' he said.

'I… I… I can see why I ought to say nothing to her or to George and Hilary but it will be a hard secret to keep,' Atta said.

'To the best of our knowledge you did kept it well but there are some things we would like you to give to George after the Games. We know you did that because his daughters discovered them after his death but he never mentioned them to us while he was alive and we believe that either he was too modest to say anything or he didn't want us to know what the future held. Probably a mixture of both,' Copper said.

'Go on,' Atta murmured.

'We are going to pick up a small replica of the statue of George from the school store where they sell them as souvenirs and for use as paperweights or ornaments or simply as a memento of time spent studying at Avalon. I mentioned those once. You took one back with you together with the prospectus that that I told you about, the one that describes the school and its purpose and methods; The City and the Lake. There are pictures of the Lake as George could never have imagined it. These things George never mentioned but he treasured them,' Clive said.

'If only you could read it,' Copper added.

'Why can't I? I'm sure I could manage a little learning while I'm here and it would add immeasurably to my experience. I know something of the numbers for flying; things like height and speed…'

'Jeepers Creepers!' Clive yelped. 'Why didn't anyone think of that? Of course we… it's Angela Collins' domain but I can get you started with the letters of the alphabet. I can. I will!'

The school store was extensive. Clive found shelves stacked with the statuettes he had described.

'This size,' he made his choice and continued, 'now for pens and lined paper and anything else that comes to mind.'

'Something comes to my mind,' Copper declared. 'I'll be back in a minute. Oh, and Atta might like a pen knife like tRevor's and he can ink his name into the blade and after that we had better go along to the registration office and register Atta as a student and get his registration documents all sorted out. They keep one copy for the records and you get a copy to prove you are a student now and you can prove it to anyone in the future. Or the past I suppose.'

445

She sped away. Clive and Atta made for the sales check out where Clive deposited the statuette and the assistant pointed in the direction of the stationery items he wanted.

'Five lined pads ought to do it,' he said to Atta.

'It's buy two and get one free, wide lined or narrow,' the assistant said helpfully.

'You've talked me into it. Six pads and some exercise books, all wide lined. I'll find my way.'

Clive selected a few more items. Before long Atta found himself inking his name into a new knife, spelling his name as George Green had taught him when he made a get well card for Hilary. He was feeling proud of his efforts when Copper arrived with some other things for him to see.

'Off the peg jackets, take your pick of black, blue, green, of beige, and then we can get your name badge sewn on before we go. It only takes a minute to make a badge and sew it on,' she told Atta.

'Umm, blue, but everybody seems to know who I am so do I really need a name badge?' Atta asked, sounding slightly bemused.

'Not strictly perhaps but it's something everyone does. We don't wear our jackets all the time and neither does anyone but everybody has one. Oh, and we must buy a flag kit. Everyone has a flag and they have a small replica sewn as a patch on their jackets. Mine is the bell curve and star and Clive's is a black boar pierced by a sword on a background of blue wavy bars,' Copper replied.

It was hard to tell if Atta was convinced but if that was the custom he felt bound by it. The future was a very strange place!

***

Angela Collins used the hologram link to contact Clive, Copper, and Atta, who showed off his grasp of the alphabet by writing the letters on his scribbling pad and singing the letters as he pointed them out afterwards. Angela was impressed with the way he took up knew knowledge so easily.

'I knew something of writing because George Green showed me how to write my name, and the alphabet letters were easy to learn because Clive sang them the way he says all the schoolchildren do when they learn to read and write. It's the same way we use the Songs of Knowledge to remember things and pass them on. It's a logical method and it works and it it's plain that its worth has been shown over many years,' Atta told her. Angela agreed, saying she had already booked a room in the George Green Building. Atta rubbed his hands in eager anticipation.

His own flag, hmm, that was a thought as well. He had never considered adopting a flag of his own. What should it say about him? What colours should he have? What designs? George Green had made every endeavour to fit into the Lake society as he found it and he must do the same but inwardly he admitted that he had no ideas. Perhaps that was best. Start from nothing and see what develops. First things first Atta, apply yourself to your reading. Well yes, but he had flown with the birds; should his flag show a soaring eagle or perhaps a small, well, a kingfisher perhaps. Kingfishers are brightly coloured and they do live on the Lake so a kingfisher might be the proper bird for him. But reading first. Reading! Reading! Reading!

Chapter 49

'Copper, come and look at this note from Angela Collins,' Clive Bowden called.

'Read it out Clive, I'm rolling out pastry and I'm up to my elbows in flour,' Copper called back.

Clive ambled into the kitchen with his communicator in his hand.

'Teaching Atta is just like teaching Christine Appleton used to be. She scared me then and she still does. Atta is the same and I guarantee that before the end of the week he will be a competent Level 2 reader. PS. No need to tell them what I said. Angela.'

Copper read out loud as Clive held the communicator for her to see. Brushing away a stray strand of hair she left a smear of flour on her face.

'Christine kept us all on her toes,' Clive agreed, 'and there's no doubt that Atta catches on fast. Christine scared me too sometimes, along with half the staff. She could run intellectual rings round every one of us, we knew it and she knew it too but somehow it didn't matter.'

In the early evening Atta puffed his pipe until it was going to his satisfaction as they sat in the garden in the early evening. Three glasses and a large jug of iced lemon juice sat on the table in front of them.

'Half of me says I shouldn't impose on your hospitality any longer than what is proper and the other half wants to stay and see everything and learn all I can,' Atta said.

'And do more flying if my information is correct,' Clive grinned.

Atta agreed. Enthusiasm showed all over his face.

'I never dreamed I might fly one day, or if I did it was only to wonder what it would be like. I tried to imagine it but all I could do was stand on high ground and look across the country. I could see a long way sometimes but I was firmly bound to the earth so for all I knew my imaginings fell far short of reality and as it turned out I was right. Thinking and doing didn't match,' he said.

'As is often the case,' Copper agreed, 'and as far as we are concerned there is no need for you to be in too much of a hurry to leave us, especially as there are more things that everyone is determined to show you. Jasmin Tyler wants to show off her plants and I wouldn't be surprised if she has another one for Twiss.'

'The one she gave her when small Alfrid came back is thriving. Twiss gave me a piece of the flower to chew and my mouth went numb. I've never known anything like it,' Atta declared.

Copper laughed. 'That's why it's called the toothache plant or the electric daisy,' she said.

'Toothache plant is an apt name for it.'

'Deke Thorpe will have something exotic to show off to you too. He's a botanist, a plant specialist if you like and he can talk non-stop about plant science for days at a time. He's piloting the airship so you won't get to meet him for a while. I don't know where it is at present but I can call it up on the tracker to show its position and a plot of where it has been. Somewhere out over the ocean is all I know. Deke can fly anything, he's a natural and nowadays everybody does more than one thing. Some tasks are mundane but necessary and even the heads of sciences take a turn at painting fences, clipping verges, keeping the drains clear, and so on,' Copper said.

'That's as it should be,' Atta declared positively.

'On that we all agree,' Clive said. 'Christine Appleton is on the airship as the mission director and she is head of marine sciences and I know she will drag you into the Marine Science building by the scruff of the neck if need be and give you a tour of the laboratories and aquariums.'

'Alfrid talks of aquariums and the little goldfish,' Atta reminded him.

'Christine's aquariums are different. Imagine a glass tank three times your height and as long and as wide as the lawn where we are sitting. That's how big some of her aquariums are.'

'Wow, that's big. I'd no idea,' Atta gasped.

'You wait till you see them.'

'I'm really looking forward to these wonders. They just keep on coming.'

'Yo Walker wants you to see how she looks at the stars. I don't know for certain but there is a rumour going round that Bella and Trix are getting things ready for that. Yo Walker is on her way back to Avalon where she can control any amount of telescopes from the astronomy building and she'll be sure to set up a link so you can see and talk to the crew on the space station,' Copper continued.

'I don't know what a space station is,' Atta replied.

Clive looked at his wristwatch.

'You will in about ten minutes from now,' he said enigmatically. 'I'll fetch the binoculars. You're going to love this but don't ask me what it is all about until you've seen it.'

'Over in that direction,' Copper pointed. 'It's so big you can see it in daylight if the sun is in the right place, and I know it is because Clive looked it up. It looks like a bright star but if you use the binoculars you will be able to see it better. Not in any detail, you need a telescope for that, but you will get an idea of what it is like.'

Silently and majestically the space station sailed across the sky and Atta was speechless.

'At present there are eighteen people on board. Usually they go up in threes and stay for six months but there is no hard and fast rule about it.'

'And I will be able to talk to them? That is what you said,' Atta gasped.

'Yo will make sure of it. Actually they know about you already and they are the ones who asked to talk to you and show you what they do and what it is like to be up there and what the earth looks like from the station.'

'Once again I don't know what to say. I have no words for it,' Atta said. 'There are things I never could have thought of. I've heard you mention a population crash and you did say we could talk about it at a later time. I understand there are fewer people all over the world now than there were when I was in Bath for a brief period. That was when I saw George Green waiting by the North Bridge for Hilary while he looked down to where the children played in the gardens. I can see it for myself. What happened?'

'Well, harking back to our conversation about Alexander von Humboldt when we were in the Longhouse, it was a dark period in our history and it's a long story but if I stick to just two things I can give you an overview. First thing; pollution, chiefly atmospheric pollution. Do you know anything about carbon dioxide?'

'Carbon dioxide? I have enough information to know carbon dioxide is a gas that is a product of industrial activity when the burning of coal and liquid fuel takes place. And everything that breathes exhales carbon dioxide. It can be absorbed or removed from the atmosphere by plants and the seas and oceans. Is that sufficient?' Atta replied.

'I'm impressed,' Clive admitted. 'George Green and Wint have given you a good scientific background and I have a sneaking feeling you already knew a lot more than you have let on.'

'Uh, I might be guilty.'

'I knew it! Anyway, the amount of carbon dioxide that was released into the atmosphere was staggering. Far more was produced than could be absorbed and the equilibrium of the global climate was threatened. It is a greenhouse gas and too much carbon dioxide in the atmosphere means the air gets retains more heat. It had been apparent for decades, ever since before the end of the twentieth century that little by little the climate was getting warmer. In some places the result was drought and in others it was increased rainfall because warm air holds more moisture than cold air and when it rained there was flooding. Pakistan was one of the worst hit places. Seasonal flooding there was the usual thing and there was always loss of life. Many people were left with nothing and they had little enough to begin with.'

'I've got images of some of the major cities and towns that were affected by rising sea levels,' Copper interjected. 'Here we are; Amsterdam on the other side of the North Sea from us. The Dutch had been aware for decades of the probable effects of rises in the sea level and they were prepared for it although they were taken by surprise by the amount of rising. Then there was Venice which was a city that had been flooded for hundreds of years because of sinking ground level. Venice had to be evacuated. In America Miami, San Francisco, and New York were badly affected and New Orleans simply disappeared. The Chinese copped it in Shanghai but managed very well. Manila in the Philipines just about coped, as did Calcutta and Mumbai in India, but in all those places there was wide spread damage.'

'Flooding was worldwide. Parts of Africa were engulfed by mudslides, parts of America were flooded, most of the South American continent, and all over Europe including the British Isles where the flooding was greatest in East Anglia and the Thames Basin, north to Lincolnshire and Yorkshire And North West Scotland. On the west side it was South Wales, which is opposite the Lake so the Lake was flooded too. It was a controlled flooding but nothing could have prevented it. The Lake is not exactly as it was when you saw it last but it is still a big place.' Clive continued.

'Wait a moment and I'll call up river flooding and flash floods and mud slides. They washed whole towns away or buried them under mud and boulders. We had our share of that in the United Kingdom but not on the scale that these clips show,' Copper said.

'Um, I've seen a small example of that in the ravine where I was injured by falling rocks but I've never dreamed of anything on that scale,' Atta said with a visible shudder.

'It was the cause of many deaths. I don't know if anyone ever calculated just how many,' Clive told him.

'In Russia the warming caused widespread melting of the permafrost that covered most of the country. Whole towns and cities were undermined and had to be abandoned. One town simply slid sideways for about three miles and miraculously it was a slow slide and nobody died but everybody left in a hurry.

'What was happening was called weather whiplash. It was going from one extreme to the other and we were very much afraid that the weather would reach its tipping point. Imagine a canoe rocking on the surface of the Lake. The rocking gets less and less until the canoe is stable again. That's the first scenario. The second is when the rocking neither decreases nor increases, which is stability of a kind but not pleasant. The third scenario is one where the rocking gets more and more intense until the canoe tips over. Most people thought the world would become unbearably hot and some predicted an age of ice. Things looked bad either way.'

Clive stopped to pour lemonade into his glass. Atta waited expectantly.

'The weather had been getting weird for decades. Drought, flood, tornados, violent storms, they had all become more frequent and millions of people were killed and then the weather really went wild. The scientists said afterwards it had been nature's last ditch effort to get back on an even keel.'

'Like the canoe you mentioned,' Atta commented.

'Exactly like that. Nature switched off the rain in some places that usually had plenty of water. It was claimed that any civilisation is only, um, three eights of days away from complete breakdown if there is no

452

food and water. Millions died of hunger and thirst and there were sandstorms that lasted for days in the desert countries. Dust got into engines and clogged them up and made surface travel impossible. Air travel was out of the question and in any event it was a one way ticket. Crews refused to fly there. One privately owned aircraft left without its owner but crammed with the families of the air and ground personnel who operated it and kept it flying. It was so overloaded it was a wonder it left the ground at all.

'The same thing happened with private yachts. Some were enormous and cost staggering sums of money and they were kept as floating boltholes in the event that their owners needed to do a run in a hurry, usually for political reasons or to avoid answering questions about their activities. Some owners and their retinue were unceremoniously thrown over the side and others found their ships had sailed without them.'

Clive added honestly, 'I'm cutting corners but there's a lot to tell. I'll skip to the desert countries. Deserts are a worldwide natural feature. In some places hundreds of years pass without a drop of rain but other places are inhabited and by careful management they have even been made to produce food. Imports were still needed but efforts were being made to minimise them. If Copper can bring up the equatorial belt you can see the extent of then deserts, or at least most of them.'

Soon Atta was studying the map.

'It's a very large area,' he said eventually.

'It is. If Copper can display the satellite images of India and China you can see what atmospheric pollution looked like from space,' Clive said. 'This is what atmospheric pollution looked like as seen from the orbiting satellites. These pictures were taken at different times but they show the extent of the pollution. You can scarcely see the ground.'

'Can you put a scale on that for me?' Atta requested.

'Sure. Here's a ten mile grid. Every square is one hundred square miles. I can change that so every square is ten thousand square miles.'

Atta gasped.

Copper had more to show. 'Each black dot represents a coal fired power station,' she said, 'and more were being built when the satellite images were taken.' After a short pause she changed the scene and added, 'And this is what that pollution looked like to the people on the ground, the ones who had to breathe all sorts of chemicals. It was estimated that seven million people died every year as a result of breathing the polluted air that resulted from fossil fuel burning.'

Clive took over the narrative. 'Visibility was down to a few yards in the coal mining towns and cities. No wonder millions died and it was not limited to India and China.'

Clive stopped talking and gazed skywards.

'The Chinese made heroic efforts to limit air pollution but their population was immense and they needed food and other goods. Nevertheless they closed down a vast number of inefficient factories and other production facilities, knowing that there was no short term solution to the problem. They set up a whole raft of green belts where development was halted. They laid down action plans and they stuck to them, but the fact remains that they were the consumers of half the world's coal and it was simply not possible to shut down all the power stations. Not only that, they still had to build more in order to survive. It was an impossible situation but they did everything they could.

'That covers pollution, not in any detail but enough to convey some sense of the damage that pollution was doing to the planet. Whichever way you look at it the root cause was overpopulation. It had been coming for some time but most people told themselves it would go away. I'll use a figure that I can remember because I wrote a history of the events myself. The population of the world was forecast to reach nine billion by the year twenty fifty. I'll write that down. Hang on while I fetch pen and... no, pass me your exercise book and a pen.'

In an aside to Copper he said, 'Copper, can you display a world atlas?'

Atta handed the requested items to Clive.

'Nine billion. That's a figure nine followed by nine noughts, like so.'

Clive showed Atta the figure written as 9,000,000,000. Atta studied it and Clive suspected he was mentally converting it to the system of numbering that he was more accustomed to.

'It's a figure too large to grasp,' he said eventually.

'It gets worse. Approximately every thirty five years the population doubled so by that reckoning it would reach eighteen billion by the year twenty eighty five.'

'Jeepers Creepers!'

'There's more. The projected increase in numbers meant that the demand for food would increase by seventy percent from the demand for the year twenty seventy. Actually it was estimated by some that the population would stabilise and level off at twelve billion. That was wishful thinking on a grand scale,' Clive told him.

Once again he was sure Atta was converting his figures to his own reckoning system.

Atta reached for the pen and wrote 12,000,000,000.

'Some of the figures I have used have been disputed but the fact remains that by twenty fifty over half a world population of nine billion were going to have to depend on imported food for their daily needs,' Clive continued. 'Sixty percent of the people who were going hungry lived in the belt of nations that included India and China to begin with, Ethiopia, which was in a very bad way, and then there were Bangladesh and Pakistan that were both bordered on India, plus Indonesia.'

'You left out the Democratic Republic of the Congo,' Copper reminded Clive as she highlighted that region on the atlas she had called up.

'So I did, and it has to be added that a whole raft of on-going wars only made things worse.'

Atta studied the atlas.

'You paint a bleak picture,' he commented.

'It was bleak and it was horrible,' Copper told him, 'and it got worse all the time. More and more people needed more and more living space and land that could have been used to grow food was used to build whole towns and cities. It was a downward spiral and it was out of control. The fact is that the root cause of all the world's troubles was over population and there were some people who were brave enough to say as much. Shortage of land, shortage of housing, shortage of resources, demand for more and more of all these things could all be traced back to the plain and simple fact that there too many people.'

'Couldn't the population be limited?'

'Up to a point the answer is yes it could and efforts were made to do just that, but not everywhere. There were barriers to overcome, things like social custom and beliefs, and resistance to any kind of birth control. Resources became scarcer. Slowing population growth might have at least provided a certain amount of breathing space; time to work out a long term sustainable solution.'

'And did it?' Atta asked pointedly. 'Everything I have heard so far points to failure.'

'That's partly because nothing ever happens in isolation as Humboldt was the first to point out,' Clive explained. 'More people use more resources including transport of goods and services, more energy use, more clean water, more of everything. They demanded higher living standards, more schools and leisure activities, more hospitals, more road and air transport. It was always more, more, more. And in return they produced more waste; production waste, chemical waste, more plastic waste, and perhaps most importantly, more carbon dioxide. Actually Christine Appleton might dispute that. The oceans had been a dumping ground for plastic waste that got everywhere and didn't break down. Millions and millions of tons of the filthy stuff and I hate to say it but we were part of it.'

'The oceans had been fished to exhaustion. Fish stocks everywhere were running out,' Copper added.

'But the oceans are so big,' Atta protested.

'And the fishing industry was big and too efficient. Everything was caught by trawlers with nets that were miles long and by dredgers that scraped the sea bottom clean. There were useless attempts to limit the damage by setting standards to govern the size of the mesh of the nets so younger fish could slip through and grow to maturity and keep the stocks replenished. It didn't work, any more than limiting the amount of fish that could be landed worked. It often happened that more fish than the permitted number were caught and they had to be thrown back into the sea because that was what the law demanded. They were dead so there was no point in throwing them back when they could have been sold for food, so that rule was plain stupid but the lawmakers weren't fishermen,' Copper said acidly.

'What the weather did was the cause of flooding all over the world, as I have already said,' Clive continued, 'and the mosquitos loved it. Malaria has always been the biggest killer of all and now it ran rampant; there was no stopping it. Drinking dirty water when there was no water that was fit to drink caused cholera outbreaks on a massive scale. All the resources in the world were not sufficient to halt the diseases that were out of control. Malaria and cholera were just two of many. Some were treatable if treatment was available but all too often it wasn't.'

'The worse disease was bubonic plague,' Copper interjected.

Clive agreed.

'I was coming to that. Bubonic plague was nothing new and it had been the death of millions of people in the past. I can quote dates and times because my chief occupation is history and I always has been. The outbreak that became known as the Black Death broke out when an Italian trading port was attacked by the Mongols during the autumn of thirteen forty-six. The Italians took to their ships in the spring of the following year to get away from it, as they thought. You have to remember that nothing was known about the transmission of disease in those days. The Italians sailed and took the Back Death with them. Their first stop was Istanbul and Turkey was the next country to feel the effects. From Turkey it made its way via the Silk Road and into China.'

'Stop for a moment Clive, I'm calling up a map,' Copper interrupted.

'That is the entire world as it was known then, I believe,' Atta commented while he studied the map.

'You're right. The disease spread through southern Europe from end to end in thirteen forty-eight and the following year it moved northwards and reached England and Scandinavia before it turned back on itself and infected Russia.

'I'll side-track myself here and discuss an important event that took place as a result of the plague. In thirteen eighty-one the English government passed a law to limit wage increases after the working classes of the day realised that their services carried a premium because of the shortage of labour. That government was made up of the landowners and they put their self-interest ahead of everything else. The outcome was the Peasants Revolt. A man named Wat Tyler was their leader, and to side-track myself again I'll mention that Jasmin Tyler's father insisted that he was never to be called Wat after suffering the nick-name during his schoolyears.

'To continue; the rebels made their way to London where the mayor allowed them in. Julia says this very act made Wat Tyler suspicious but that never got into the history books. The King, Richard the Second met with Wat at Mile End on the fourteenth of June and he agreed to the peasant's demands and promised to end serfdom and feudalism. The next day they met again at Smithfield and the Lord Mayor of London injured Wat with a dagger. That mayor was Sir William Walworth. Wat was taken to a hospital and on the orders of Walworth he was murdered by decapitation. It was a despicable and disgraceful act that should have seen Walworth hung. King Richard then declared that his promises were made under threat and were therefore invalid. Richard was only fifteen years old but he was acting in his own interests in the same way as his government ministers. Having said all that I shall return to the subject of the bubonic plague.

'In their ignorance the common practice was to find scapegoats and the targets of the mob were beggars, pilgrims, anybody with a skin condition, religious groups and anybody who didn't fit in. There can be little doubt that many people who denounced their neighbours had an eye on their property.

'Eventually the Black Death receded but it was not gone for good. Europe and the Mediterranian were never plague free throughout the fourteenth to the seventeenth centuries. There were continuous small outbreaks but the sixteenth century saw its return with a vengeance and it became known as the Great Plague of London. The thing is, bubonic plague never really went away. It came back again and this time it had mutated, uh, changed it's character. It was a monster with an incubation period of about ten days. In other words a person could be infected and pass it on to others without even knowing they had the disease. International travel was so widespread that the plague was world wide before it showed itself. It could be treated if I were caught early enough but time was short and anyone who showed the signs of plague usually died within two or three days. Some people recovered without treatment but that was rare.'

'Then the population crash was the result of climate changes and disease. I can see that on a worldwide scale there was nothing effective that could be done to halt it. Let me see if I have got it right; firstly the disease must be easily passed on to other people and secondly it must be passed on while the infected people can still get around and come into contact with more people to infect, which would mean they had about ten days to pass it on, using the figure you gave me and thirdly the people who are infected have to survive for long enough to pass the disease on to others. That would be ten days plus the two or three days it took someone to die once the plague showed itself. I imagine that locally in some places there were effective measures but they weren't enough to make a material difference. I know there were cities with a population of ten million or more people and even smaller communities must have made it possible for one infected person to come into contact with hundreds of others. I think I have heard enough. Tell me, how many people died?' Atta said.

'About half the total population of the world,' Clive said bleakly. 'Some nations just disappeared and vast areas were totally depopulated and I won't talk about the cleaning up that had to be done because you can imagine what it must have been like. It was a long time before anyone could begin to pick up the pieces and the world was changed forever. It was then that the Chinese and the Russians held a summit meeting. In essence each told the other you are in no condition to go to war and neither are we so let's accept that things have changed. They put that proposal to the Americans and the British, and all concerned agreed. There was to be no territorial expansion and as it happened Russia and China shortened their borders to suit the new conditions. Politics was to give way to science where global issues were at stake and the International Environment Watch Committee was established with a minimum of bureaucracy. It was acknowledged that the global climate had tipped and the purpose of the Committee is to work to ensure that the tipping goes no farther. It is advisory but it has the power to override politics and industry, which it has done more than once. It has headquarters in Italy and offices all over the world and some of George Green's pupils are members.'

'I see. I have one further question and it is this; I believe I am expected to pass on to George Green everything you have told me. I think it is also to be given to the chronicler of his time for distribution to anyone who cares to read it. Won't that alter everything?'

'You did pass it on and it made no difference. The events had been set in motion centuries before they all came together and the information was available to everyone, or almost everyone. As individuals people agreed that something should be done but those same individuals identified themselves with regions and nations or beliefs or social classes, and that was an altogether different matter so the measures that were taken came too late. We were lucky in one respect, and in one respect only; nature fought dirty but fast and thanks to the amount of air travel that I mentioned the plague spread so rapidly that it was all over in far less time than anyone had foreseen. It was as if nature didn't want to leave any loose ends and although it sounds heartless to say so it made reconstruction easier for those who did survive.'

'Mother Nature banged people's heads together and told them to sort themselves out,' Copper added. 'It was my grandmother's recipe for settling petty squabbles and it worked.'

As she often did when she spoke of the past Copper unconsciously rubbed her left upper arm where her inoculation scar had long since faded.

Chapter 50

It was evening and the weather was warm when a pair of canoes bumped together on the Lake and the occupants stopped and rested their paddles.

'I don't much feel like racing back,' Terry Mitchell declared. 'I'm in favour of taking it easy.'

'There's no need to hurry,' Angela Collins agreed.

'A little bird told me Atta can read and write already, thanks to your teaching. Who would ever have thought you would teach a Stone Age man? Or is he Iron Age? I'm a little confused about that.'

'He comes from a transition period somewhere between Iron Age and Stone Age as best as I can make out and I've never been quite sure where the Bronze Age fits in except that it is somewhere between them. Atta would never have thought of reading and writing but he did say he thought he could learn and I took it from there. I've said it before and I'll say it again that in many ways he reminds me of Christine Appleton. He even questioned the logic of English spelling, for instance the spelling of the school motto,' Angela replied.

'Knowledge Sustains.'

'It was the motto of the training school that Jack Smythe attended when he went into the armed forces of the day and a better motto I have yet to come across. That's by the way; what I'm getting at is the spelling of the word knowledge. It makes no sense but I wouldn't change it for anything because it carries the history of the language along with it. The English language carries a wealth of history and knowledge in words like that.'

'Atta is a better pupil than I was,' Terry observed wryly.

'You weren't the best of students,' Angela agreed.

'I improved when Jasmin Tyler brought me into the study group in the old burger bar. I suppose in a way you could say they got me where I am today because they made me think about rock climbing on the day we went to Brian Gleaves' place and when I went to the sports centre to see if they had a rock wall. They hadn't but I was on the way back when I saw a load of canoes on a trailer going over North Bridge and from that day onwards I was hooked on outdoor activities and all

461

of a sudden I knew what I wanted to do with my life. I never knew then of course that I would still be alive today and I've done a few other things along the way; we all have. I imagine you never thought you would put on plays and pantomimes in the George Green building one day. I don't suppose Merlin ever expected to appear in pantomimes either!'

Angela laughed.

'The children love it and so do the adults. Merlin in a wizard's outfit being chased by the Wicked Witch as played by Matron always goes down well. That pantomime almost wrote itself! I've been a hairdresser and a gardener as well and Pauline Grant made a musician out of me and taught me to weld and then Brian Gleaves turned me into an engineer. What did I do to deserve that?' She asked.

'I'm currently the Director of Outdoor Leisure Pursuits, or Dollop as I'm irreverently known, and I've been a farmer, a forester, a flight engineer on the airships, and a hospital orderly. We can't complain, can we?' Terry replied.

'Hardly. By the way, Henry Whiting is flying up to Hereford with Atta. Atta hasn't been told about it yet but he'll jump at the chance. He doesn't know he'll be doing most of the piloting either. They're picking up Jasmin because she's at the horticultural station in Hereford and Miranda Bradley as well. I don't know what Miranda is doing at the moment except that is something to do with electricity but I really look forward to seeing her again.'

'Me too.'

'It will be a huge reunion. Everyone wants to meet Atta, especially those who knew Alfrid and George Green,' Angela continued.

'I'd like him to tell George from me what a privilege it was to be taught by him,' Terry said seriously. 'It was a privilege and an honour, I've heard Christine say that more than once. Atta can take that message back from all of us. I've an idea! Let's make a card and all his old pupils will sign it. I know George never mentioned anything about the Lake as it is today but I also know Atta is going to take a lot of material with him when he returns home. I could never tell him before but better late than never.'

'I wouldn't say that's the best idea you ever had but none the less it is a good idea,' Angela said with a smile.

'I'll put the word out to the others. I know I never went in for the science stuff much but when I did decide what I was interested in he was right behind me. Come to think of it decide is the wrong word. I discovered, that's what I did. I discovered.'

'Discover to learn, learn to discover,' Angela quoted. 'Henry Whiting was in the same position as you were when his wartime flying was over. He had no desire to continue as a pilot and in any event the market was flooded with pilots all looking for flying jobs.'

As Henry had put it the Labour Exchange was overrun with returning servicemen.

'Line up alphabetical. Colonels and Cooks and Captains all go to Room 22. Divers and Drivers, down the hall to Room 23. Privates and Pilots come back on Thursday. That's the way it was, he used to say,' Terry remembered.

It was true. By chance an uncle put him on to a job with a building firm and Henry agreed to give it a try until he found something more suitable. He sawed wood and hammered nails and at the end of the three months deadline he had set himself he discovered that jobs were hard to come by and he rather enjoyed what he was doing.

He found some second hand tools and equipment and taught himself to turn wood on a lathe, to measure and plane with absolute accuracy, and make anything at all from wood. It took time but he managed to build a thriving business but he always maintained that his proudest moment was when he turned out a set of wooden skittles for his children.

A hail from the shore put an end to their conversation.

Waving back Angela said, 'Our grandchildren taking their own grandchildren for an evening walk. It doesn't seem so long ago that we used to do that.'

Terry Mitchell agreed.

'I'll be teaching then to sail and paddle canoes one day soon,' he prophesied. 'I think we ought to make for dry land and put the canoes away. There's a bit of work to be done before we can pack up for the day.'

'I'll make a light supper and then its off to bed.'

'I'll sleep like a log tonight,' Terry declared.

'Who said anything about sleeping?' Angela dug her paddle into the water. 'Come on, I'll race you. Last one to the slipway is a nimlet.'

Chapter 51

At the breakfast table Clive produced two message slips from his top pocket and talked out loud as he handed then out.

'One for me, two for Copper, one more for me, three for Atta and another one for Copper. They usually have only two or three lines,' he added to Atta, who looked puzzled.

'I don't know who, how, I don't understand why I should get these,' he stammered.

Clive grinned.

'It's one of the penalties of being able to read,' he quipped. 'What do they say?'

Atta read out loud.

'From Merlin and Wint

To Atta

Come and see what we are doing whenever you find the time.'

'Well done. And the next one?'

'From Terry Mitchell

To Atta

I think I said that right. I have a lot to learn but the way letters are put together to make a different sound. It seems illogical but if that's the way it is then so be it. The message is, umm, if you would like to come for a sail on the Lake come to the... the yatch, is that it? Yatch Club?'

'Yacht. It's a perfect example of the way some words are spelled in a very illogical fashion. It happens because so many of our words come from other languages. Our language changes as time goes on and new words come in and others are forgotten. Language isn't fixed and it has to adapt to new situations.'

'Oh. Like squoink?'

'I know I've heard that word somewhere but I can't remember what it means,' Copper said.

'There were students on the boat when we went round the Lake and one told me there was no word for the times when they took a picture of a thing and it jumped like a grasshopper or something and all they got was a picture of where it was and so they made up a word for it and it's a squoink,' Atta reminded her.

'I can't think of a better example. Whether it will catch on remains to be seen,' Clive said with humour. 'That's two messages. What is the third one?'

'From Henry Whiting

To Atta

I am going to fly to Hereford today to pick up two passengers and bring them back to the Lake. There is a spare seat in the aircraft. Would you like to take it?'

'Take it,' Clive urged unnecessarily. Atta's expression told him everything. 'Terry Mitchell won't mind waiting for a while to take you sailing,' he added.

On the kitchen wall the communicator beeped for attention and printed another message slip. Copper tore it off and read it.

'Another one for Atta. You're a popular man today,' she said as she handed the slip to Atta.

'From Emil the... the... I don't know this word,' Atta said. He showed the slip to Copper.

'Emil Thompson. I'm afraid it's another example of our illogical spelling,' she said.

'From Emil Thompson,' Atta continued, 'I am the troop leader of the Second Avalon Scout Troop. Some of my Scouts have met you and those who have not all want to. We are going on a Scouting Weekend and I would like to invite you to come with us. I will send more details later.'

Clive whistled.

'Wow! Take it!' He exclaimed. 'I don't know Emil Thompson but I'll get a reply off to him while you are on your way to Hereford with Henry Whiting'.

Copper stood up and cleared their empty plates with the remark that they had better make a start if Atta was to go flying again.

When he stepped confidently off the shuttle bus Atta was surprised to find two girls waiting for him. He recognised Pat Daly Her and Michelle Proctor.

'I'm doing more aircraft work today for my Duke of Edinburgh Bronze Award. Mr Gleaves says I'm nearly there,' Pat Daly Her told him.

'We'll get Nimlet Awards if we don't get a shift on,' Michelle Proctor said.

The girls giggled and Atta guessed that a Nimlet Award was either to be avoided or perhaps it was some sort of joke. He had meant to ask about it before now but it had slipped his mind. An image of Wigstin came into his head but he put the thought to one side. There would be time for that sort of thing later.

Soon Henry Whiting introduced him to the aircraft they were to fly.

'It's identical to James' machine except that is a four seater and it has four engines instead of two and as you see the extra engines outboard are built side to side with the inboard engines and the reason for that is to keep the air that is pushed out of the back of them as close as possible to the centre line of the aircraft. Some of the big passenger aircraft hang the engines under the wings and spread them apart. Those engines are somewhat different and you could stand up in the air intakes,' Henry told Atta.

'I think I have seen them but they fly too high for me to pick out any details even if I knew what to look for,' Atta replied.

Henry Whiting agreed. By way of explanation he added, 'There's not much chance that you will ever see one up close. They can't use these little airfields so the biggest aircraft you will see here is the one we're standing next to. You might see an airship here though; they can land anywhere.'

'But I thought there was a special place for them where the land was made into a hollow place close to the Lake.'

'That's where the big research airship comes in because the science people need it to be close to the water and the Marine Sciences Buildings. Everything else comes into the airfield here but there is no regular schedule. Now we'd better do a walk around check and you can tell me what you remember.'

It seemed that Atta remembered absolutely everything and Henry Whiting found himself mightily impressed and had to remind himself that Atta came from a time when the Stone Age was merging into the Ages of Metal and until a short time ago he had no knowledge of technology. Not as he knew it, Henry thought wryly.

Atta ran through the cockpit drill perfectly.

'That leaves just one more thing,' Henry told him as he uncovered an instrument that was new to Atta.

'This is a route map and it's more or less the same as the ones that are fitted in cars. I've already programmed our destination into it and entered Bath as a way station. It's not the most direct route but who cares? The red line on the screen is the way to Bath and the dotted red line shows the direction we are pointed in now so all we have to do is point ourselves in the right direction when we're off the ground and hey presto! When the lines merge we know we're going the right way.'

Atta said he understood and when Henry took his hands and feet off the controls shortly after take-off he demonstrated his ability.

'You have control Atta. Take us to two thousand feet and point us in the right direction,' Henry said.

Atta's confidence and pride in his new skills shone through his every action.

'I can see the railway station,' he soon reported. 'It is easy because of the track, and I can see two trains going in opposite directions.'

'Anything else?'

'The Abbey and the Roman Baths.'

A short beep in his earphones caused him to look questioningly to Henry, who tapped the instrument that displayed the route map.

Atta turned the aircraft and matched the dotted and unbroken lines and whooped with delight.

'I did it! I did it!' He yelled enthusiastically.

'You sure did.'

Henry might have added that not every trainee pilot flew as accurately as Atta in the initial stages but he knew that Atta was unaware that he was being taught to fly. He was as impressed as James had been.

The time passed too quickly for Atta.

Then; 'James says you have landed his machine. I'll handle the radio and you have a go with this one. It's no different.'

Atta's landing was perfect. Henry Whiting had been ready to take over the controls if necessary but Atta's performance left him speechless.

***

Copper tapped her fingers impatiently while she waited for her step-mother to reply.

Matron took her time but at last she answered and listened to what Copper had to say.

'It's a long shot but I'll talk to Doctor Simpson and Doctor Mallory and I'd better include Doctor Kate as well.'

'If you would Matron. Can you lean on them just a little?'

'Who, me?' Matron chuckled. 'I'll do what I can Copper but if I were a betting woman I would only bet a very small sum on getting a result. I believe it is impossible or supposed to be' she added honestly.

'I knew you would. And can you keep quiet about it? I don't want it to be made public,' Copper asked.

'Obviously. All right Copper, I'll see to it.'

Copper uttered her grateful thanks and ended the call.

Interlude

This is written by me, Attta. I know how to write my name in full and it is Siglattastin but I am always called Atta. The words are mine and Angela Collins is helping me with my spelling and my punctuation and she prompts me when I have to stop my writing and ask her about a word because sometimes I am not sure if the word I am going to use is the right word.

I am making this writing because I have been told by Copper and Clive that there is a series of books that have been written during the course of centuries. They are called a chronicle and they tell of the Lake and it's People and the events and affairs of the Lake. I am a Lake Person and therefore of much interest. This I know because the entire population seems to want to talk to me. They want to hear about my life and what I have done and what I would like to do in the years that are left to me. That seems reasonable and logical because in this way they gain first hand information.

I stop and think for long periods while I put my thoughts together and I might not always get things in the order that I should. A previous chronicler said that he faced the same problem when he was taken to task about the way he wrote.

(Is that right Angela? Taken to task is something that I have heard. It is correct Atta).

I have written this to make it plain to anybody who reads my writing that I often have to seek advice. My writing is a new skill that I never expected to gain. I never gave it a thought but it is a wonderful thing. Perhaps I mean accomplishment and not skill but I think my meaning is clear. I know about the use of brackets but the reader who has got this far will have noticed that. I do feel that I have been given a sufficient number of words to make a (coherent) account.

All of my life has been spent on the Lake. A few times I have travelled I think about a hundred miles but I soon came back to my home. I grew up as children do. I went to school and my education, I mean the pattern of my education, closely matched the way the children of this now become educated. I had a mix of learning and doing and from the age of about eight years my learning was what I wanted to know about (self directed) and the children of this now do as I did. This has not always been the way of education and the children of this now do not usually self direct until they reach an age of fourteen years.

This might be a good place for me to write that everyone lives and studies and works at (a very fast pace) and they use their leisure time actively. In many respects they are like the people of my now and unlike the people who lived in 1995.

(Write the date in full in a work of composition Atta).

Nineteen ninety-five. Thank you again for helping me with my writing.

My best friend was Meglen. We found our marriage partners and we were happy with our choices. Today (my today) we are each alone and perhaps I shall chase Meglen and my new knees will help me catch her!

What I wanted to know was everything! I built houses all over the Lake. I learned how to measure (the building site) and mark the places for the wooden posts and the door. Then I dug the holes. A house needs a roof and that is work for the thatchers. It needs walls and a hearth so you see I was just one part of a team and no one person or task was better than another. I enjoyed my work but I always wanted more so I became a weather watcher (meteorologist) and I tried my hand and my mind at anything. In one respect I have failed and that is in my mistrust of metal, which I thought was no more than a passing fad. I shall remedy this.

My thanks to Angela and I shall return to this writing at another time.

Chapter 52

Water lapped at the small jetty where the small craft with a single sail bumped against it. Atta had been told that these craft were used for recreation and to teach the art of sailing. Terry Mitchell passed his staff to him as he sprang ashore.

'This is as close as I can get you but if you follow the path up the hill and turn left you will find Merlin and Wint and their new standing stone about half a mile away,' Terry told him.

'I shall enjoy the walk now I have my new knees,' Atta replied, 'and perhaps I might meet a fellow traveller along the way. In my now we often catch up on events that way and pass on information and gossip as we walk along together and then we pass it on and if for instance a house needs a new thatch or a girl wants, oh, anything; shoes, work, a friend of her own age in another village to share clothes, well that's the way the Lake works.'

'If it works don't fiddle with it,' Terry responded as he pushed his craft away.

Atta gave him a brief wave and strode off with confidence. It seemed strange but he remembered the thought that he had once had that there had never been a better time to live. That was in the time that followed the defeat of Tarn when the Vikings had formed and trained an army and lured Tarn into a well disguised trap. Fast and dirty, that was the way Beowulf had wanted to fight the Battle of the Lake and under his direction that was how it was fought. It is important to do wars properly Freya had declared, because it saves time and lives. It was a pragmatic approach to warfare and she was right.

Where was his train of thought taking him? Ah, yes, it had never been a better time to live. Well, it seemed to Atta that the wheel had turned full circle and he found himself in a now that matched his own. There were differences, big differences, but it seemed not to matter. Atta felt that anyone he met in this now, the boy tRevor for instance, could fit into his own now with ease and even small Alfrid and Twiss could fit into this now although it might take some time. Mind you, he wasn't so sure about Wigstin!

'Atta!'

Startled, he whirled round.

'I… I didn't hear you coming,' he stammered.

'I know. You were miles away.'

'I was thinking.'

'It must have been a deep thought.'

eLberd indicated to Atta that he should join him on the bench where Atta had just passed him as he sat.

'I was thinking too. This is a quiet place to sit and stare at the Lake and turn things over in your mind. I expect you are on your way to see what Wint and Merlin are up to?'

Atta confirmed eLberd's speculation and added, 'I was thinking about the way the people of your now and the people of my now are no so different from each other but I was here several hundred years ago, I'm not sure how many, and I don't think the people I saw then, an admittedly small number, I don't think they would fit in quite so well in your time or mine. Some would but I'm as sure as I can be that half of them or perhaps more than that even would not… well let's say they would have been slow to adapt.'

'You have the advantage over me, all I know from personal experience comes from the eighty years I have lived. I've done a little travelling but I've never stayed away for long. Perhaps I can claim second hand knowledge gained from watching endless hours of the old television entertainment and I make no bones about it, I rate a high percentage of that as worthless. It had no merit whatever,' eLberd declared.

'Hmm. That echoes Beowulf's opinion. The Vikings did like to see anything about farming and cows and they had a thing about brass bands, which they liked loud. Freya formed us into a band when they showed us how to fight Tarn. I'm a bit old for fighting but I banged my drum in that band. It united the Lake like never before and the sound of it made Tarn fly into a rage whenever it was mentioned. Freya knew exactly what she was doing. Then we had our flags. Tarn didn't like those either. We fought their bodies and their minds and we made the Lake ours, all thanks to Beowulf and Freya,' Atta said.

'I've read the Chronicles but you were there, and that makes a difference. The television was not all bad and I suppose that if the Vikings had not seen the television and the brass bands the Battle of the Lake would have been very different. We both have a lot to thank

472

them for. There were educational programmes as well; the farming programmes that the Vikings liked are a case in point. I notice you are wearing a name badge but no flag badge. Haven't you got a flag? I thought everyone in your now had a flag.' eLberd said.

'I never got round to it but I have a flag making kit and I know a smaller version goes on the right sleeve but I really haven't decided what my flag should look like,' Atta replied.

'It can be a difficult decision. Its supposed to say something about you so you could start with the blue wavy bars of the Lake. When all is said and done you are more of a Lake person that any of us,' eLberd thought.

'I shall consider it. Perhaps I shall add the torch of knowledge as well,' Atta replied.

'Good idea, and while you are about it you might add a bird in flight. The whole world knows you have done a bit of flying and they say you can't get enough of it.'

'True,' Atta declared warmly. 'It was something I never dreamed I would do.'

'Wavy bars for the Lake, the torch of knowledge, and a flying bird. It's a start.'

'I'll sleep on it but as you rightly say, it's a start. Sleeping on a problem often brings a solution. You did say you were sitting and thinking when I walked past you,' Atta prompted.

'So I did. I was wondering about my work after I finish my job with solar panels. I'll carry on doing that until I finish the work on the Humboldt airship when it comes in and then I'll be off. I'm buying into a cycle business, which will kill two birds with one stone. I have a boy and a girl at school here and my wife goes to Bristol where she works on airship engine installation and maintenance. Its only a train journey away but one of us has to be nearby and Sylvia, that's my wife, has to work long hours sometimes.

'Nearly everyone rides a bike and the business buys in the parts and does the assembly work and now and again they build bikes from scratch. I know quite a bit about the work and I can top up my knowledge in no time because of my background. I'll have to write my name properly when it goes on the paperwork but that was going to happen sooner or later anyway. So our problems are solved in one throw,' eLberd finished.

Atta agreed and made the comment that it would be nice if every problem could be solved so easily.

'Nice but boring. What would we have left to moan about?'

'The weather?' Atta suggested.

'Aye, there's always the weather.'

Both men laughed.

Atta continued on his way, walking briskly uphill and giving mental thanks to Matron Patti and the rest of the team who had given him his new knees. He still used his staff and he always would; it was part of who he was. I might use it as a small flagpole one day, he thought. That was what people did and they often left their flags outside buildings so any passer-by would see them and know who was inside. It seemed a useful and logical way to say, for instance, that Atta is inside and he invites anyone to come in and join him for a chat and perhaps a glass of ginger beer. He wondered if the brewers back home could make a refreshing drink like it.

When he reached the brow of the hill he turned to look back at the Lake. The water sparkled as a light breeze rippled the sun-lit surface. Some small sailing boats were out and a distant ferry tooted. He shaded his eyes when something else caught his attention. Ah, the Viking longship was out on the water too, rowed expertly and smoothly by a crew of students from the Scandinavian countries. The red and white said was raised as well, to catch whatever wind it could.

The sight of it brought back memories of the time not many years ago when a ship like that fought in the Battle of the Lake and landed a Viking trained army on the shore of Alfrid's homeland where Beowulf fought and defeated Tarn in a one to one struggle that was the saving of civilisation itself. Beowulf sacrificed his own life in order to give Tarn to the stones, which was the only way Tarn could be killed. The backlash killed Beowulf instantly and the longship brought his body back to the Lake. In a Viking funeral ceremony the ship was fired by Freya, and Beowulf was carried to the open sea and the Hall of Warriors.

He could stand by the Lake all day with his memories but Atta brought himself back to the present and stepped forward on the last leg of the journey to the place where Merlin and Wint had erected their standing stone.

There was more equipment than he had been told to expect. A row of metal cabinets had been placed to one side of it, the side that faced the Lake. The stone stood in a hollow, out of the line of sight of the complex of buildings that Atta had been able to see as he approached. He remembered that the site had been chosen because of the constant flow of water that drained through the ground. It was little more than a trickle but it was enough. Wint noticed him first and beckoned to him to approach.

***

Copper's communicator demanded her attention; an unwelcome interruption that broke her concentration but it was her policy to accept any call immediately whenever she was working alone. It was a different matter if the caller expected her to take calls when she was engaged with other people. It would be bad manners towards the people she worked with and that was something she would not tolerate. If it was urgent the caller would try later and if it was not her time was not wasted.

It was Matron and the call was important.

'Copper, there's no need to be alarmed but I've got Merlin in hospital. Merlin and Wint and Atta. They are all right but I'm keeping them in for observation.'

Copper sat down heavily.

'What… what happened?' She gasped.

'I'm not sure,' Matron replied honestly, 'but it had something to do with the new standing stone they put up and there was an explosion that was heard all over the Lake. That's all I know except that the new knees that Surgeon Matron Patti put in Atta need attention.'

'I'm coming over,' Copper said decisively.

'Very well. Leave it to me to contact Clive.'

Copper's absolute trust in her step-mother did nothing to stop her racing to the station. She took a three-wheeled scooter from the public charging rank and raced through the city, suspecting that she violated several traffic laws but not caring. When she left the machine at the station rank she noted that if she hurried she might just catch the train that was scheduled to leave in two minutes time. Out of breath, she found a seat and used a public communicator to contact Clive Bowden.

'Matron told me. I'm about half way across the Lake on the ferry and I should arrive at about the same time as you,' Clive told her.

'Do you know what happened?' Copper demanded.

'No, except that there was an almighty bang. The word on the Lake is that nobody was hurt and I think that item of news came from the ambulance crew. More than that I don't know and let's be honest, its no more than a rumour,' Clive replied.

With that Copper had to be content.

Michelle Proctor was taking orders from the three men for their evening meal when Copper arrived. She introduced herself and informed Copper that she knew Atta because she had seen him when he went flying with James Wilson and Henry Whiting. She added that Pat Daly Her was coming because she knew him too. Copper nodded dumbly and Michelle dived past Matron and raced away to the kitchen.

Atta leaned back on his recliner, his knees bent.

'Are you going to tell me what happened?' Copper demanded.

Merlin beamed.

'Meet the hero of the hour,' he said. 'Atta saved our necks.'

'He did? How?' Copper asked suspiciously.

'Well, to begin with…'

… Atta made his way down the slope into the hollow where the new stone stood. It was not a large stone, barely the height of a man but Atta knew that the size of a stone had little bearing on it's power.

'The stone is active,' Wint told him, 'but once we knew that we isolated it so whatever happens here will remain here because we aren't sure what we can do.'

'Why do anything?' Atta questioned him. 'In this now there is surely no need of them.'

'True up to a point,' Wint concurred, 'but what really interests us is why the system broke down so suddenly and so completely when it did. Tarn took advantage of the situation but he had nothing to do with the collapse. We want to know what happened because it shouldn't have done.'

'I see, and now I understand why you have separated this stone from all the others which are still active when the right things are done. You don't want to lose control again.'

'That's it in a nutshell,' Wint agreed.

'I notice all your instruments and I know from my flying that instruments are there to measure something or to record measurements,' Atta said.

'Right in one. These metal cabinets are chock full of recording equipment and data storage banks. It was a bit of a job getting everything together and levelling a spot where we could put them but we got there in the end. Each cabinet weighs about five hundred pounds and it was hard work but eventually we got what we wanted,' Wint replied.

Speaking for the first time Merlin added, 'You arrived just at the right time. Look at this; we drilled a hole into the stone in fourteen places and inserted probes to a depth of twelve inches to measure things like temperature, pressure changes if the probes get squeezed, electrical conductivity and connectivity, and a host of other things. I finished connecting the probes to the recording equipment about ten minutes ago, which is what all those cables that link the stone to the cabinets are all about.

'Wint is going to throw the switch to set things going and we hope to get our first readings on the instruments you can see on the cabinets so all we need to do is stand where we can see the instruments and the stone and make any adjustments if we need to.'

'What do you think will happen?' Atta asked.

Merlin smiled a very wide smile.

'That's the beauty of it,' he said as he guided Atta closer to the cabinets. 'We don't quite know what to expect.'

Wint took up his station and glanced at Merlin as he grasped the switch and pulled it sharply. A low humming noise built up, rising in pitch.

'That's the sort of thing I meant,' Merlin said. 'I've never heard that noise before. It seems to be coming from the stones. I wonder if...'

A violent push between his shoulder blades stopped him.

'What? Atta, what...?'

'Down! Get down!' Atta yelled and sent Merlin and Wint crashing to the ground as he threw himself on top of them.

'What the hell do you think...!'

'Stay down!' Atta barked.

Bang! The ear-splitting sound of a loud crack shook the air and something struck the cabinets hard enough to topple two of them to the ground. One cabinet was hurled into the air to come crashing down yards away.

Merlin yelped. 'Ouch! That hurt!'

One cabinet had given him a hard knock as it fell.

'I have a broken arm,' Wint gasped. 'Atta, what about you? Are you all right?'

'I'm unhurt but I have a tingling feeling and numbness all over,' Atta replied. He stopped for a moment before he added, 'I can't tell if I have any other injuries because of the numbness but my staff is broken.'

Merlin interrupted. 'One of my ribs is broken. Maybe two...'

A hail of gravel rattled against the fallen cabinets like bullets and tore up the grass around them.

'Stay down,' Merlin urged. 'I wonder what went wrong?' He speculated.

There was no reply.

A drone appeared as if from nowhere and a mechanical voice said, 'No hazardous material detected. I count three people. Are there injuries?'

'Some broken bones and I have a cabinet laying across one of my feet but I think I can wriggle free.' Merlin replied.

'If you are in no danger you would do better to remain still. An ambulance has been summoned. Your breathing, temperature, and pulse are normal. Is there nausea?'

'None. We are all shaken up but apart from minor injuries we seem to be in good shape.'

'That is noted. The ambulance will arrive in,' pause for calculation, 'four and a half minutes. This drone will continue to monitor and record.'

The ambulance carried a crew of four.

'Hold still while we get you out,' an ambulanceman directed.

'As if I had a choice,' Merlin grimaced.

Atta recognised on of the crew as Michelle Proctor, one of the girls whom he had met when he was going flying. He remembered her telling him about her St John's Ambulance badge but he had not appreciated the significance of it until now. Michelle was small for her age but she was tough, as she demonstrated when the weight of a cabinet was lifted from Merlin. Atta noticed that she was particularly attentive to Wint.

'That should do it.'

The speaker offered his hand and helped Merlin to his feet.

'Keep as still as you can. The drone signal said you have some broken ribs and we don't want to risk a punctured lung,' he added.

'I don't think I'm that badly injured,' Merlin protested.

'I don't think is a long way from being sure so take my advice. I'll snitch on you to Matron if you don't.'

'Aw,' Merlin growled but wisely he did as he was told.

Michelle helped Wint to his feet.

'Hold your arm just so and it will be more comfortable,' she directed. 'I'll help you to the ambulance and put it in a sling.'

Wint was more compliant than Merlin.

'Atta, you told the drone you aren't injured,' the ambulanceman said. 'Can you get up?'

'Actually I can't,' Atta said calmly. 'I don't hurt anywhere and I can move everything except my knees. My legs are bent and I can't straighten them. I didn't want to make a fuss.'

Two of the crew swiftly fetched a stretcher from the ambulance and …

'… that's what happened,' Merlin said.

Matron heard him out and turned to address Copper.

'I'm keeping all three of them in for the night whether they like it or not,' she said crisply. 'Merlin has broken ribs but he will heal overnight and he doesn't need treatment but I'll want to see him tomorrow before I send him home. Wint has a broken arm which fortunately for him is a clean break. If it wasn't and it healed crookedly it would have to be broken again and reset. Our St John's Ambulance girl Michelle knew exactly what to do when she put his arm in a sling.

'As for Atta, I scanned his knees and found that his metal joints have been welded together but it is a very small weld, about the thickness of a small sewing needle. Surgeon Matron Patti is pleased that she will not have to remove and replace them and in a two minute operation later this evening she will un-weld him and tomorrow after breakfast he will be able to walk out of here.'

'I thought Patti was in Bath,' Copper said.

'She was here to look at a broken wrist on another ward. That patient will be taken to Bath but she will perform Atta's operation here.'

Michelle Proctor appeared again, with Clive Bowden in tow. She handed a message slip to Matron who read it with pursed lips and passed it to Copper.

'Perhaps you would like to read this to your father,' she said pithily.

'Um, yes. Father listen to this, and you too Wint. It's from the Guardians of the Rock who are still on their way from Australia and I quote, "We recommend that you do not proceed with the experiment you propose." I hope that's taught you both a lesson,' she said severely.

Michelle moved closer to Wint while Merlin pulled a face but said nothing. Discretion is the better part of valour, he reminded himself and inwardly admitted that he and Wint had been lucky not to have been seriously injured.

Clive directed a question at Atta.

'From what I hear I understand you knew what was happening and you pushed Wint and Merlin out of the way. How did you know?'

Heads turned towards Atta.

'I didn't know,' he admitted, 'but there has been talk on the Lake about the things that happened when Tarn used the stones for his own ends. Tarn wasn't a stone turner and all he knew was what he had heard but that didn't stop him and there was a price to pay. His actions usually ended in disaster for the unfortunate souls he forced to attempt to turn the stones over to him and these disasters were often preceded by a humming noise and when I heard that sound I was alerted. My hair stood on end the way Alfrid's does and I felt a tingling in my knees. I guessed something had gone wrong and I acted on instinct.'

'And it's a good thing you did,' Copper said warmly.

She seemed about to say more but the arrival of a flustered nurse stopped her. She closed her mouth.

'Matron, there's visitors for… for everybody,' she stuttered.

'Show them in,' Matron said briskly.

'All of the Matron?'

'All of them Nurse.'

All of them turned out to be a coach load with the promise of more to come according to one visitor.

'The word went round the Lake and someone had the idea of making get well cards the way they did on the Lake when George Green went back to Atta's time. Its written in the Chronicles and one good turn deserves another and this is the result. The children all got to work and made cards,' she said. 'Atta and Merlin and Wint are all getting cards.'

'It's a kind thought. Copper and Clive, we shall leave them to it. Nurse, you and Michelle will stay and keep some sort of order if you can,' Matron ordered.

'I still make tea in my office regardless of the rules,' she added.

She poured tea and declared, 'There are times when I truly believe Merlin should have a man with a red flag walking in front of him wherever he goes to warn people he is coming and give them then chance to steer clear of him the way they did with cars when they first appeared on the streets.'

'You didn't have to marry him, but he's my father and I'm stuck with him,' Copper replied.

'As are my children. Life can be so unfair sometimes.'

Copper and Matron dissolved into laughter.

'There is one thing,' Copper said when she regained her breath, 'did anyone else notice how Wint and the St John's Ambulance girl were looking at each other?'

'Her name is Michelle and now you mention it, yes, I did.'

'And?'

'Uh. I don't know.'

'Well I'm not blind,' Copper said, 'and they had big eyes for each other. They did.'

'Interesting.'

'Cross time marriages are not unheard of if rumour can be believed. Michelle is young and Wint is goodness knows how old but what's the hurry and there's no disputing the fact that love at first sight has worked for the three of us. We might be witness to… well I know for certain I have Neanderthal genes so…'

'Its awesome,' Copper whispered.

'It also begs the question of where they will live. And when.'

'Right here and right now,' Matron declared. 'I want those miscreants where I can keep an eye on them and put a stop to any more harebrained schemes they might dream up.'

***

Accompanied by the entire 2nd Avalon Scout Pack, Atta walked unaided from the hospital shortly after an early breakfast. Word had spread that his staff had been found in pieces and the Scouts were keen to see him use his stone knife to fashion a new one. For his part he was only too keen to do so. On more than one occasion he had stated that without a staff he felt somehow incomplete.

He left his get well cards with Matron to be neatly packed and she had estimated that they numbered a hundred at the very least.

One of the Scouts made a recording as he selected a suitable length of wood and used his stone blade to cut and fashion it. From the other Scouts he learned that each of their staffs was five feet long and the measurements were marked with notches. At the upper end of the staff the final foot was sub-divided into intervals of one inch. Atta matched his new staff to theirs.

'Its part of Scout Lore,' one youth explained. 'When the Scouting movement started off hundreds of years ago every Scout made a staff and the pattern was laid down in the Rules of Scouting. Then the staffs were more or less banned for some reason but the ban was lifted centuries ago. The same thing happened with sheath knives. Every Scout carries a knife but they were banned too.'

'Another part of Scouting is that the Scout salute is like this,' a Girl Scout demonstrated, 'and we always shake hands with out left hands.'

'Out hats are the same,' another youth told him. 'We wear the same hats that the original Scouts wore. They are called Mountie hats because the Royal Canadian Mounted Police wore the same kind of hat and they still do. They just went out of fashion in the Scouts but they came back later when Chief Scout O'Brian-Huang reinstated them. That was ages ago.'

'I have noticed that you all wear badges on your Scout clothes and some of you have your personal small flags on the right shoulder but there lots of small badges that I haven't seen anybody else wear, except perhaps the one below your name badges,' Atta told the group.

'That's the Scout badge and its usually the only Scout badge that's worn on our everyday jackets. Scouting is a life long thing in a way and everyone knows you were a Scout once. The badge is the fleur de lis badge and every Scouting country wears it,' a girl informed him.

482

She added, 'It used to be just plain Scouts and one day some girls turned up and joined. Then it became Boy Scouts and Girl Guides but it all merged back together eventually. Anyone can join the Scouts nowadays because there's no age limit like there used to be. My granddad didn't joint until he was a hundred and three years old. He's in the First Avalon Troop.'

'Hmm… It seems like a good idea.'

'There are other organisations and the Scouts are not even the oldest because the Boys Brigade came first. The records do say they didn't always get on together and there were a few fights. The girls joined that too but it took a while. Then there is the Duke of Edinburgh's Award Scheme and Junior Science and all sorts of others. You don't have to join any of them but most people do and you can even join more than one group but hardly anyone does because that's taking on too much. There's always something to do.'

Atta declared that he was very impressed.

It was evening when Atta finished what he was told was a traditional meal of baked beans and sausages.

When the plates and cutlery had been washed and put away Scoutmaster Emil Thompson declared that it was time for a sing song. Atta had learned that Scoutmasters were always called Skipper.

'Time for a Scout song that was made at the beginning of Scouting. The words were made up so that any Scout could sing it regardless of what their native languages were. They're easy to pick up and you'll be singing along in no time and I'm going to record it. Ready everybody, one, two, three…

Ging gang goolie goolie goolie goolie wotcha
Ging gang goo
Ging gang goolie goolie goolie goolie wotcha
Ging gang goo
Ging gang goo
Haylo, oh haylo shaylo, haylo ho
Haylo, oh haylo shaylo, oh haylo shaylo haylo ho
Shallawalla shallawalla shallawalla shallawalla
Oompah oompah oompah oompah…'

'And the second verse is the same as the first, ready Atta,
Ging gang goolie goolie goolie goolie wotcha…'

Chapter 53

Merlin and Wint surveyed the site of their latest misadventure.

'Angela Collins has threatened to write another play about me. You're in it too and she won't let us off easily, you may depend on it,' Merlin observed.

Wint replied with an expressive shrug and the comment, 'I suppose we deserve it. We can claim that we now know what not to do.'

'Even if we don't know what went wrong and why we ought not to have done it,' Merlin replied. 'I doubt whether we will get away with it but we can try.'

Everything was smashed and Merlin doubted that any useful information could be gleaned from the wreckage except, he thought morosely, it might be possible to calculate the speed at which the fragments of stone had perforated the metal cabinets and in some instances had gone all the way through them.

'We were lucky. The big chunks of stone that were thrown off would have been the end of us and as it was they knocked some of the cabinets clean over and you know how much they weigh. Michelle made sure my arm was held properly and that saved me from having to have it broken again and re-set,' Wint said.

He added, 'I must be sure to see her again and thank her properly.'

You can't fool me Merlin thought as he struggled to keep a straight face.

***

'James, I've heard a lot about the airship, the one they call the Humboldt. I've been told that it is big and I have seen the place where the ground was shaped to make a landing space for it but I might not have understood because that place is surely too big,' Atta commented.

'Actually Atta, it is that big. Its named after Alexander von Humboldt and its truly enormous. All the airships are big of course because the bigger they are the more efficient they are and some have to carry heavy loads. Others, like the Humboldt often stay airborne for weeks at a time and have to carry a large crew and a lot of equipment so there is sleeping accommodation and food preparation, which means a kitchen and a canteen. They have to be big. Some are for carrying people and an air cruise can last for weeks, stopping at various locations. They can land anywhere there is room for them. The Humboldt is a science airship and it needs all the facilities that are built into it's landing spot. You haven't seen all that yet but there are mobile servicing platforms for loading and unloading equipment and carrying out work on the engines and outer hull, and on top of that there is always work to be done internally. It's a big operation,' James replied.

Without being asked he projected an image onto a wall screen.

'This is a third angle projection that shows the Humboldt from above, that's what we call the plan view, and the view from the front and one side,' he said.

Atta was quick to grasp the concept.

'Right. This next picture is one I took myself from my aircraft.'

'Oh! I never thought about the colour.'

'Mostly silver-grey. The whole surface is a solar panel. Actually a series of solar panels that are linked. Solar panels have come a very long way since they were first invented and they are tremendously efficient. The blue painted stripes show it to be a marine science airship, the same as the stripes on the sea ships. Other markings on other airships are there to show who they belong to and what they do,' James explained.

'Logical and even necessary at times I imagine,' Atta commented. 'Am I right in thinking that bigger is better because bigger airships have more surface than small ones and therefore more solar panels and more power for the engines and all the other things inside the airship and more space for the, umm, the helium gas?'

'Right again. Notice how the eight engines are arranged so that the upper engines on either side are set a little way behind the lower four because when they are all be swivelled to give downwards thrust the lower engines are not affected by the upper ones. The two fins at the rear do the same thing as the fin and rudder on my small aircraft, its just a different way of doing things. See how they stick upwards and outwards? They have control surfaces just like I have. The four upper engines can also be swivelled independently when necessary. It all adds up to very precise control,' James said.

'I can't wait to see it,' Atta said with enthusiasm.

'They can't wait to see you, especially Spockette. That's Christine to everyone else but she got the nickname while we were all still at school.'

Atta listened attentively while James gave an explanation.

'Deke Thorpe crashed an airship once, about two hundred years ago,' James continued.

'Did he? What happened?' Atta exclaimed.

'It was a science machine and smaller by far than the eight engine craft but still quite big and it had four engines. It was operating over the norther polar ice cap and I don't know what it was doing apart from the fact that it had something to do with the search for ASP1 and ASP2.'

'I know something of them from what George Green told me a little while ago,' Atta said.

That was news to James but it saved the need for lengthy explanations.

'It started with a call from a science station when…

'Skipper, we're showing snow on the screen. On our present course and speed it should be with us in twenty minutes,' a voice in Deke Thorpe's earphones told him.

'Roger that,' Deke replied laconically.

There was nothing unusual about it.

'That dry stuff just bounces off us,' the flight engineer on duty commented. 'I'll hold off on the de-icing.'

Deke thumbed his intercom button.

'Jill, isn't there a satellite that could check this out?' He asked.

Jill Lucas was quick to answer.

'I thought of that and there is but the science station wants a closer look. There's a temperature inversion and we've been given the task of climbing up through it into the warm air layer and then back down into the cold. They want us to repeat that for at least nine times. Where that figure came from is anyone's guess,' she replied.

'Temperature inversion? They don't happen at this latitude,' somebody said.

'They do now.'

'OK. We'll do what they want or we won't hear the end of it but I don't like it,' Deke said. 'I'm due to hand over in half an hour but I'll pilot this myself. Jill, will this mess up what you're doing?'

'Negative Captain. It takes more than a little weather to stop the particles I'm looking for. What I really want is measurements from the aurora borealis but solar activity is a bit slow today. I can help to monitor the atmospherics if you want.'

'I never thought of that. Do it and see if you can get me a depth reading for the inversion. I need to know the height where the temperature starts to rise and the height where it falls off. Also I want to know the temperature variation, and how far the inversion has spread,' Deke ordered.

'Working on it,' Jill replied.

Unconcerned by the changes to his schedule Deke Thorpe climbed up through the temperature inversion and the readings showed that the change of temperature was unexpectedly large. He descended and repeated the operation. And again. And again.

'Now I know how a porpoise feels,' the flight engineer commented wryly.

Suddenly; 'Its raining! Jeepers Creepers! Its raining!'

The engineer's hands went straight to the windscreen de-icing switch.

'Glaze ice. We're in an ice storm.'

Deke made a mental review of what he knew about ice storms. Snow falling through a layer of warm air melts and turns to rain and when that rain falls through a layer of cold air at below freezing temperatures the raindrops become supercooled and they will freeze on contact with anything they fall on and that creates a layer of clear ice. Glaze ice. Record thickness, umm, can't remember but in excess of seven inches. Bad news.

'Engineer keep the control surfaces, engine intakes and fan blades de-iced.'

'Roger that. Its going to drain a lot of power.'

'No choice. One cubic foot of water weight sixty two pounds, take my word for it, so one inch of glaze ice on an area of twelve square feet will weigh sixty two pounds. Glaze ice is dense so to all intents and purposes the figure still stands. I don't need to tell you how many square feet this airship measures. If the ice forms on the upper surfaces only it will add a lot of weight even if it only amounts to one inch thickness and I don't think it will stop at one inch,' Deke said in a level tone.

He thumbed the intercom button.

'All crew, all crew. We're in an ice storm and the ship is icing up. There's no way out of it so I'm taking us down. Our best hope is to sit it out on the ground but the ship is getting heavier fast and the controls will ice up before long, even with de-icing going full blast. Crew on duty, seat belts on. Off duty crew to bracing positions. It's going to be a rough ride.'

It was.

Deke and the flight engineer fought the ship and the ice all the way down but the weight of the ice was too much and there were signs that the ship was going to roll over. It might turn completely upside down, which Deke thought likely, or only roll part way. That would still render it unstable.

Deke slammed the ship down on the ice just as the roll began. It was a crash, not a landing, and some equipment tore loose but there were no serious injuries. That was due to pure luck, Deke admitted.

'… and that was how Deke crashed his airship. There was an enquiry and a fistful of computer simulations and so on and the result was that every simulation ended with a rollover and a crash, mostly when attempts were made to keep the ship in the air, and the board of enquiry was forced to admit that Deke had averted a disaster that could have ended with loss of life,' James said at the end of his narration.

'It must have been an unpleasant experience,' Atta commented.

'Not as unpleasant as the two days they spent with very little heat while they waited for a rescue. No other airship was to be sent into an ice storm until matters were resolved. It took the clean up crews more than a month to recover the ship and it's contents, mostly one piece at a time, and the whole area was cleaned up.'

'Yes, I see that.'

'Anyway Atta, you've had a few days away from flying since your knees had to be repaired so we can get you back into my aircraft tomorrow afternoon if you're willing.'

'Willing! I can hardly wait!'

***

Atta landed James' aircraft perfectly.

'Three in a row,' James complimented him. 'You could do this on your own now.'

'Could I? Yes, I suppose I could,' the unsuspecting man replied.

'Good.' James unstrapped himself and raised the transparent cockpit canopy. He climbed out and said, 'Tell the tower you are making a solo flight. Take off and land while I wait here for a couple of minutes.

'Well I... I see...'

'Off you go.'

If Atta only knew how many people are watching this, James thought. His second thought was that any watcher who was unaware who was piloting the aircraft would never have guessed it was a man from an age when stone technology was giving way to an age of metal and they would have been even less likely to guess how quickly Atta had become ready to fly solo. His third and somewhat rueful thought was that Atta had needed less instruction than he had.

Back on the ground Atta could hardly contain himself. Grinning from ear to ear he literally jumped for joy.

'I did it! I did it!' He exclaimed over and over again.

He spent the whole day describing his experience with hand gestures to anyone who would listen.

***

Atta was attacking his second bacon rasher when realisation dawned.

'You were teaching me to fly from the very first,' he said to James in the small kitchen area inside the hangar where the aircraft were housed.

James smiled widely and replied, 'Not quite but almost. Nobody knew how you would take to it or even if you would fly at all. Alfrid turned down an offer from Frank Holley in the thing he used to fly hundreds of years ago. We decided to give you the chance and I knew from the start you would come back for more and from then on I was teaching you what to do. Henry Whiting told me you handled the four engined machine as if you were born to it and he admitted he was impressed. I hate to have to say this but you were a better student pilot than I was.'

'Was I really?' Atta looked pleased. 'But you grew up when flying was commonplace. Alfrid told me about aeroplanes but never in my wildest dreams did I expect to see one for myself and as for flying one... Whew!'

'It comes down to aptitude. Some have it and some don't.'

'Hmm, I'll have to take your word for it. I wonder what else I could do?'

'Catch the shuttle bus and find your way around the Lake on your own. Step aboard the train the same as anyone else does who has spent a lifetime doing it. Use a communicator. Read and write. How's that for a start?' James replied.

'I was eased into it and I never realised what was going on,' the astounded man admitted.

'It would never had happened if you weren't up to it,' James told him. 'Intelligence is intelligence no matter where or when you were born and that applies to adaptability and the readiness to try new experiences,' he added.

It was Atta's turn to smile.

'I have always been prepared to try something new and find out about things but as far as intelligence is concerned I have to tell you I have done my share of stupid things. Casting Wint adrift on the Lake was a really stupid act and I got my backside whacked with a paddle for it and I can't say I didn't deserve it,' he said.

Both men laughed at Atta's recollection of boyhood misdemeanour.

'As soon as you finish what passes for lunch in this place we'll get ourselves kitted out with lifejackets and I'll run you through the drill, which we have to do because today we're going to fly over the sea. It's a formality because I've never heard of any aircraft like mine ever having to make a forced landing but regulations are regulations. You'll do the flying. I filed a flight plan last night and the research people okayed it,' James said.

'Over the sea? Will we see seagulls?'

'Sure. There are a dozen or more fishing boats that all come from the Cornish fishing ports as you can tell from their black and white flags. I thought you might like to take a look at them so I loaded in a course that follows the coast for a while and then turns out to sea. Most of our fish comes from Cornish waters and the skippers pass on information about fish stocks and sea conditions to the marine science people. It's not unusual for the scientists to go to sea as deck hands; I've done that and so has Christine Appleton. Deke Thorpe tried it and swore never to set foot on a fishing boat again. He can fly anything but he's no sailor. That was about eighty years ago or maybe a bit more. Copper Beach goes now and again and she's actually a qualified skipper. Her grandfather was a sailor in his younger days and he passed on his love of the sea to her.'

'I believe she mentioned that once,' Atta recalled. 'Even Shipmaster Cadric has been known to be seasick,' he added. 'I expect it will get you sooner or later if you go to sea often enough.'

'I hope not,' James replied sincerely.

Evidently he meant to sail again someday.

Atta flew accurately and confidently as he followed the track that his instruments displayed.

'Ship!' He exclaimed suddenly.

It took James a few seconds to spot it.

'Steer to your right to get him on your side of the aircraft and waggle your wings,' James instructed.

'They're waving back!' Atta soon reported.

'He's been fishing in the Irish Sea and by the look of the course he's steering I'd say he's on his way back to Penzance to land his catch. You wanted to see seagulls and there they are, the fishing ships are always followed by gulls. That's Skipper Trehearne's ship, I know it well. The airships patrol our fishing waters and the skippers always give them a wave. I don't come this way often but the four engined aircraft do. Not the one you flew with Henry Whiting but specially build maritime patrol aircraft. Anyone who fishes where he shouldn't is soon warned off. The foreign skippers know the score and their regulars stick to the rules and they've been known to tip us the wink if there's anything we should know about. They've got their own air patrols so everyone looks after everyone else and everyone reaps the rewards,' James said.

Atta circled the ship twice before resuming his original course. James noted that he constantly scanned the weather and the sea. He knew there was a research vessel just over the horizon and he wondered if he would see it before Atta did. To his amazement Atta spotted something else.

'James, there's something flying that I don't recognise,' he reported.

He indicated what he meant.

'It isn't as high above the sea as we are so I don't think I need to do anything but what is it?'

'It's a helicopter from a foreign research vessel and you saw it before I did. Well done. The ship is too small for airships to land on but the helicopter can take off and land vertically and it doesn't take up a lot of deck space. They aren't as easy to fly as this aircraft but the ship often needs to lay a pattern of instruments into the sea and the helicopter can do that much faster than as ship can and it can recover them as well.'

James hoped his short explanation was sufficient.

'It's likely that the foreign ship will sail into the Lake when it has finished whatever it is doing. Our ships sail into foreign ports to exchange data and it works both ways' he added.

'I see now that the, umm, the helicopter uses the same principles of flight as the drones that cross the Lake,' Atta said.

'Got it in one. Have you ever been told you are too smart for your own good?'

'Frequently,' Atta sighed with a wide smile that showed he regretted nothing.

James was inwardly relieved when he spotted the ship before Atta did, acknowledging that he had the advantage of knowing where to look and what he was looking for. He told Atta to circle the ship as he had done with Skipper Trehearne's fishing vessel.

'It's a big ship. Bigger than I expected and much bigger than the fishing ship,' Atta observed.

James agreed.

'The deep channel on the Lake had to be dredged and widened for ships like this to come into the Lake and dock at Marine Sciences. They carry some automated submersibles that take up a lot of space and some have a manned submersible that can reach the bottom of, well, nearly everywhere. Christine Appleton is what they call a diver driver and she has been to the bottom of the sea all over the world. Her discoveries include some fish species that nobody had ever seen until she found them. I know for sure that she wants to give you a tour of a science ship like this one and the airship when the Humboldt comes in, and then there are the Marine Science buildings and the aquarium,' he said.

'Clive and Copper told me the aquarium is big,' Atta commented. James laughed.

'I think they were economical the truth. Its way bigger than anything they told you. Its huge,' he said.

'I see. I believe it is a popular attraction as well as a learning centre,' Atta replied. 'I'm learning to take surprises in my stride,' he added.

'I could spend hours doing nothing but look at the fish. You're going to love it.'

'I am looking forward to it and I'm sure Alfrid and Eathl will be pleased to hear all about you and the things you do. They still talk about you and Twiss looks after her plant as if it were a member of her family.'

Atta might have said more but a voice in his earphones said, 'Atta this is radar advisory. An unscheduled aircraft is coming to the Lake from Goonhilly Observatory down in Cornwall. I can give you an interception course.'

'Go ahead radar,' James replied for Atta.

'It's worth taking time out,' he explained to Atta. 'It means you will get to see another aircraft in flight. We won't get too close but we'll give it a couple of minutes and then get on with a bit of sightseeing.'

'Four engines,' Atta soon reported. 'Is it Henry Whiting?'

'Possibly, or it could be anybody.'

They returned to their original plan of observing some of the ships at sea.

***

'Copper, I can report some progress and if all goes well we should be able to give you an answer shortly. I can't say any more than that but I'm optimistic,' Andrew Simpson said.

Copper Beach leaned forward over her desk. The pencil that she had been using to sketch out a special order for a customer fell to the floor.

'That's wonderful!' She enthused.

'Don't get carried away just yet,' Andrew Simpson cautioned her.

'You wouldn't have phoned me if you were anything less that ninety nine percent sure,' Copper replied.

Doctor Simpson chuckled.

'Well, perhaps not, but keep it under your hat, okay?'

'Whatever you say. And thanks. Thanks a million times.'

***

Atta brought the aircraft to a halt outside the hangar where he had been directed to park. He found a reception committee waiting for him when he walked in though the open door.

'I'm Yo Walker and this is Bella and Trix and Peter Birkett. I was a pupil of George Green and so was Peter but Bella and Trix came later.'

Atta recognised the women he had previously see outside the railway station in Bath.

'I wanted to get to you before Christine does,' Yo continued, 'so I'm whisking you off to the astronomy building and Peter will tell you about the work he is doing and I'm going to show you the stars as you've never seen them.'

'Wint told me about your looking device,' Atta commented.

'Wait until you see what I have now,' Yo said with a huge smile. 'James, you are coming too. It's far too long since we last saw each other.'

Atta looked with interest at his surroundings.

'We haven't got a telescope here but we don't need one because I can tune in to telescopes all over the world and control them so can point them at any part of the sky I want to. Not only optical telescopes but radio and other telescopes that let us see what the universe is up to,' Yo Walker told him.

'George Green has been telling me about the big bang and I don't claim to understand it but I do know it was the big bang that started the universe off,' Atta replied.

'I'm glad he did because I'm going to show you a recording of something that Christine Appleton said a long time ago when we were young. George Green was there when she said it but I was not because I had already got an astronomy night booked. Wint managed somehow

494

to come and see me and then he went to see everyone else but he saw us in the wrong order. I mean he came to see me after it was quite dark and then he saw the others while it was still fairly light. I told him about the others and I mentioned them by name so when James said it was too early for me to do any astronomy Wint told him he didn't always do things in the same order and afterwards James said how did he know I'm James and not Deke and his mother asked him if he had looked in a mirror recently. I bet James never told you about that.'

'I've never been allowed to forget it,' James said ruefully.

While Christine's presentation was shown Atta watched with interest, along with Peter Birkett and a girl who had been introduced as Jill Lucas. Atta recalled that she had been a member of the crew of the airship that Deke Thorpe had crashed some hundreds of years previously.

'Christine had her own ideas about the big bang and she was a bit shaky about it because she found herself saying that the big bang didn't explain everything. What makes it ever more astonishing is that she was in her mid-teens at the time. Christine thought there might be two more particles involved. One particle we called ASP 1, the particle that Christine thought was the particle that started it all off, and the other particle we called ASP 2, which was a time particle. It's hard to imagine time as a series of solid particles. No wonder Christine was a bit shaky about it,' Peter Birkett said.

'Christine's theory had nothing to do with the work we were doing at the time,' Jill Lucas took up the narrative, 'but we couldn't leave it alone. More correctly, the theory wouldn't leave us alone and eventually we plucked up enough courage to talk about it to other scientists. Most of them didn't want to know but you saw what Christine said about symmetry and that grabbed the attention of some others and after a bit of head scratching they decided to take a closer look at it. On the face of it time particles seemed impossible but there was a lot of number crunching and a theory of time emerged and this theory says that there is a time particle and it breaks down into either three or eleven smaller particles. We don't know which and it doesn't seem to matter. They can't truly be called particles but we have to call them something. Anyway Atta, the crunch bit is that these three or eleven particles form five pairs plus a spare, or two double pairs plus a spare, which doesn't make sense and that's more weird than we can imagine. We just can't but it was said a long time ago that we can't imagine how weird the universe is. The pairings make and break in, well, in no time and so one particle is always spare and it wants to pair up and it does that by joining with another group of three or eleven particles or a double pair and it's spare particle. The result of this is that any time is connected to any other time and because space and time are interdependent that means that if we can somehow grab hold of these particles we could go anywhere in the universe that we want to and we could do it instantly. Imagine that if you can!'

'I can't,' Atta said unsteadily.

'Nobody really believes we could go everywhere exactly. It's more likely that it could be done in small jumps, but how far the jumps would take us is an unknown,' Yo continued. 'And it begs the question of whether you will be able to travel in time to whenever you want to go.'

'Talking to you is like talking to Christine,' Yo declared, 'and the answer is that all our research says we won't be able to do that. You saw what Christine had to say about symmetry when George Green filmed her. The same thing applies. It appears that in our universe all the time particles spin in one direction like wheels all turning the same way, and in the other universe they all spin the other way but the particle clumps are not aligned the same way so time travel is likely to be limited at best. To my way of thinking that is a good thing.'

'And to mine.'

'It also begs the question of how Wint manages to travel to his future and then return but our belief is that his ability is even more limited than the theory suggests. Impressive I grant you but limited. Our best theory is that the time particles are everywhere, which they must be or nothing would be happening anywhere, and Wint somehow latches on to them but even he doesn't know how it all works. We simply haven't the ability or the mental development to handle it, so you're in good company if that's any consolation.'

Chapter 54

Deke Thorpe steered his way between the tables.

'Move your paperwork and make room for your breakfast,' he told Christine Appleton. 'One poached egg on a muffin and two rounds of toast with two pots of cape gooseberry jam so you can spread it a quarter of an inch thick the way you always do. Why don't you eat marmalade like any civilised person?'

Christine put her work aside.

'I do eat marmalade and you know it,' she responded, 'and where is my fruit juice?'

'On my tray. I'm going back for it now. I'm having it chilled.'

Deke soon returned with his own tray and Christine's orange juice.

'I was completing my log of the trip,' Christine said as he sat down opposite her.

'Mmm, we've never stayed out this long before. You had us pass over every square mile of the Atlantic Ocean and that's a lot of square miles. You must have measured everything that could be measured and your sea-bed probes brought up twenty zillion microbes.'

'The more the merrier. We still don't know for certain how some of them adapted to eat up the plastic junk that was dumped in the ocean but its lucky for us they did. The plastic that floated on every sea amounted to over twelve million tons when it was all scooped up. Most of it anyway. Twelve million tons! The seas were dying; over fished and polluted and who knows what was regularly dumped when nobody was looking?' Christine said heatedly. As if it were an afterthought she added, 'It was reckoned there were a million species faced with extinction because we humans had destroyed their habitats by illegal logging, uprooting hedges, indiscriminate chemical spraying that had the chemicals leaking into the rivers and seas and killing off whatever insects they came into contact with. The fools knew what they were doing and they just didn't care.'

She stabbed a fork into her poached egg as if it had offended her.

'I'm a botanist so I have my own take on it. We were losing more species than I care to think about; flowers and their all-important pollen, trees of all kinds, lichens, grasses, all of those were species habitats, we were destroying them all over the world and the underlying cause was over population pure and simple but all most people wanted to do was paper over the cracks. It was madness. More than one scientist has written that the population crash was a good thing if you take the long term view,' Deke said.

'Including me,' Christine replied, 'as you well know. It was horrible while it lasted but it was over as quickly as it began.'

'Nature's surgical strike, as they say. Thanks to the sheer volume of international travel the plague spread globally before the first deaths. The human race was second guessed because what was expected was a flu pandemic because it was well known that the flu virus mutates like nobody's business and the old vaccines become ineffective. Its on the record that it was expected to be contained or at least slowed down long enough to get new vaccines out. Bubonic plague was considered but thought to be more easily treated but it was out of control before anyone knew it was there. It had mutated and it gave no warning and it had gone round the world before the first deaths happened. By then it was too late and people were already dying in their millions.'

Cutting into his scrambled egg on toast he continued, 'Let's talk about something more pleasant. I'll land this thing at ten o'clock precisely, which is about four hours away. What are your plans?'

'Three months of family time and after that I'll divide my time between examining my microbes and being to be a farm girl. Actually a host of specialists will do most of the work with the microbes while I lay hedges and dig ditches. I need a long break from academic work to recharge my batteries but I'll still be in touch.' Christine told him. 'What will you be doing?' She added.

'Much the same. Three months of family time and then botanical pharmacy but I'm a minor player in a big team, same as you,' Deke replied.

'Aren't we all,' Christine smiled. 'By the way, I forgot to tell you I shall be giving a guided tour of the Marine Sciences to a very special person.'

'Let me guess. Atta?'

'Right first time. It will take a slice out of my family time but I shall make up for it. He only has a couple of weeks left so I want to spend all the time I can with him and I know you do too. Yo has already shown him the Astronomy Department and he talked to some of the space station people including one of her, let's see, fifth generation grandsons, and to the station on the moon and by all accounts he asked some very intelligent questions. James even taught him to fly! Can you imagine that?'

'I bet he couldn't, and that reminds me, the jump seat is free if you want to sit up front and watch a maestro at work when I bring us in.'

'Yes. On second thoughts no. I mean I would like to but I've been there before and Axelle has dropped a few hints and in any event I still have some things hanging up to dry in the wind tunnel. They should be dry by now.'

Christine gave a slight nod in the direction of the serving hatch.

'OK, I'll see how she feels when I take the trays back. Are we about to lose our best canteen manager?' Deke said.

'I wouldn't be surprised. I've seen her talking to the SONRAD operators more than once.'

'I've never been one to stand in the way of ambition. And my fruit juice is getting warm.'

***

Avril Downwood read the message slip as it rolled out of the wall communicator and she passed it to her husband as she joined him at the breakfast table.

'For you Hugh. From Emil Thompson,' she said briefly. 'Its interesting.'

Hugh Downwood read the slip and his mouth dropped open.

'The man's a genius!' He exclaimed. 'I wish I'd thought of it first. What do you think?'

'The same as you.'

Avril was known to use words sparingly.

'The media people will have to go along with it but I think they will. They're all over the Lake because the whole world is interested in Atta, what with the daily bulletins and news items and interviews with the people he has met. Atta knows but it doesn't bother him and the media crews keep their distance. You know, Emil is really on to something.'

499

Deke Thorpe indicated the jump seat and Axelle dit-Turner sat down. Deke leaned towards her and told her to put on the headphones that hung on the side of the seat.

'That's better, now you can hear the flight deck chatter and ask any questions you like. Things are quiet at the moment and we have an hour to go before we dock,' he said.

'There seems to be an awful lot of information on the screens,' Axelle said cautiously.

'There is and that's the reason for two pilots and a flight engineer to be on station twenty-four hours a day.'

'Which accounts for the number of mouths you have to feed,' the flight engineer commented.

Axelle managed a faint smile. She knew a dozen SONRAD operators and there were two medical staff, two physical fitness trainers who doubled up as canteen staff, and then there were communications, meteorology... the list went on and on.

***

Clive and Copper and Atta had been offered places on the Viking longship to watch the arrival of the Alexander von Humboldt airship on the condition that Clive wore his Viking sword, which he was glad to do. The crew insisted on calling him Clive Boarslayer which was the name given to him by Beowulf and Freya, his Viking ancestors. Brian Wolftamer was on board with Julia, the Lady of the Lake. Wolftamer was another name given by the Vikings so Brian's place was assured.

Every crew member was armed to the teeth; axes, swords, and fighting knives were in evidence everywhere. Pauline Grant and Suzanne Fluteplayer, another Viking name, had long since arranged one of the Old Danish drinking and feasting songs into a rowing song and as Clive pulled an oar his voice could be heard with the rest of the crew. Copper reflected that a longship was no place for the faint hearted as she translated the words for Atta who's laughter threatened to split his sides.

Clive was relieved of his oar and sent to join Copper as the ship glided to a halt and was kept on station by just two rowers on either side.

'Not long now,' Copper commented with a glance at her watch.

While they waited expectantly Clive explained what was going to happen.

***

Axelle dit-Turner listened intently to what Deke was telling her.

'I'm going to fly over the Lake for the benefit of all the observers who always turn out to welcome us and then I'll fly east and line us up for landing and docking. That means we will end up facing the prevailing westerly winds which are barely blowing today. Watch out for the Viking longship because they tell me Atta the man from the past is on board and I'll steer a course that will put him on your side.'

'I shall look out for him but I know from experience how many boats and canoes will be out on the water. I did it myself once because I'm a canoe club member and Terry Mitchell drew my name out of the hat,' Axelle replied.

'Lucky you,' the co-pilot commented, 'there's always a lot of competition for that.'

Axelle agreed.

'I'm hoping to bring us in without the lasers having to guide the docking clamps. I've only managed it once and so have a few other pilots but the ship is so long that you only have to be off for a fraction of a degree for the lasers to kick in.'

'I see. I never thought of that before.'

'Only one pilot has done it twice,' Dag Rajaratnam said from his co-pilot's seat.

'What Mr Rajaratnam is trying to say is that he is that pilot.'

'Sheer skill captain, sheer skill.'

'Sheer luck.'

Dag Rajaratnam puffed his chest out.

A voice in her earphones reeled off a set of instructions that Axelle did not understand but she guessed were instructions from the ground.

'Roger that,' Deke said briefly and added to Axelle, 'I must ask you not to talk from now on Axelle. This is where we start to earn our keep.'

Axelle wondered whether to acknowledge but decided not to. Later she was to find out that it was the right decision; brevity was the rule and talk was kept to a minimum when the airship was manoeuvring at a low altitude and the flight deck crew were concentrating on their work.

She spent time looking out of the window as the scene below unfolded. Her eye was drawn to a fleet of small craft which included the colourful dragon boat that was sponsored by the Chinese Lucky House but where was the longship? She strained to see it and suddenly it was there when Deke altered his course so it could be seen from her side window. Everyone on board seemed to brandish a sword or an axe and… surely that was Copper Beach with an axe. Well, she thought, I never knew that! Atta must be the man waving a staff and the sight of a small launch with a battery of cameras trained on the longship confirmed her suspicion. She wondered what he made of it as she waved furiously when they passed by.

Deke's attempt to land without the lasers direction the docking clamps was unsuccessful but only a handful of pilots had even done it once. Everyone remained seated while the gangway was connected and then there was a rapid exodus. Deke motioned Axelle to stay behind.

'Christine told me you want to change your airship badge from the green outline of ancillary crew to operational orange,' he said.

'I would like to. I talked to some of the SONRAD operators,' Axelle replied seriously.

'I see no reason for you not to except for the fact that it means the loss of the best canteen manager and cook we ever had but our loss is your gain and I'm going back to my day job of botany and good home cooking for a while so I won't be affected. You won't make any of the next two patrols but I'll see to it that you start ground school and simulator training, which is how all the operators start off and then you will do two patrols as a supernumerary operator before you get signed off. Good luck with it and the next time I take the airship out I hope to have you on my crew as a SONRAD operator.'

**

'Emil? Emil, this is Hugh Downwood. I read your slip this morning and I got really carried away and I contacted the media people and

502

they went spiral! They love it! I've had messages coming in all day and they're still coming. I tell you Emil, Avril had to change the roll tape three times and then have more droned in. I'm up to my knees in them, from London, Hong Kong, all over the United States, Melbourne, Sydney, Shanghai, Ottowa, the list is endless! The coverage will be world wide and the wheels are in motion in places I've never heard of!'

**

Christine Appleton supervised the transfer of samples to the Marine Sciences. It was necessary but at last she was free to join her family. Bliss!

Hold on a minute Christine, aren't you forgetting something? No, but I have pushed it to the back of my mind. My excuse; the sheer volume of the work I had to do on the long oceanic patrol and survey.

Very well, sort your thoughts out.

The reunion. Everyone who was there at the start when Copper Beach went public about her condition (or very soon afterwards Christine) makes a point of getting together every ten years or so. Many, like her, had homes in the city of Bath and travelled to the Lake by train, and some spent long periods away. James for instance, you never knew where he was going to turn up next. James was at home at present but next week or the week after? Then there was the matter of Atta, the man from the past. An intriguing thought. She was going to show him the aquarium and all the behind the scenes work that was carried out there. It was a must!

And then more family time.

**

Deke Thorpe was another crew member who would be late getting home. As gantries and servicing platforms were positioned Deke was going through the snag sheet with Ket Ketley the ground engineering chief.

'I expected more after the long patrol, there's not much on the sheet that will give me any problems when I get my people on the job,' the engineer declared.

'We've been running with a small helium loss in the number four cell for the last three weeks. It's not the valves because I had them checked so I'd say we have a small leak. Very small, it will take a lot of finding,' Deke replied.

'I'll get some good old fashioned soapy water on it and look for the bubbles. I've got a crown that says I'll locate it within half an hour.'

'Cheapskate. Let's make it dinner at the Lucky House for two families, loser pays.'

'Its your money, you're on. Eat up everyone this ones on Deke, that's what I'll be saying!'

***

Clive found a message slip when he and Copper arrived home. Reading it as he tore it off the communicator he said, 'For you. Its from Andrew Simpson and it's a bit weird, all it says is eureka.'

Copper snatched the slip from him.

'I must talk to him straight away!' She exclaimed.

'Why?'

Copper explained in a few words.

'Cripes, Jeepers Creepers and Odin's Ghost!' Clive yelped.

Chapter 55

Clive, Copper, and Atta stepped of the shuttle bus outside the Marine Sciences building. As usual, Atta carried his staff. It was a warm morning that promised to get warmer as the day wore on and everyone wore light summer wear. Apart from his staff Atta looked like anyone else. The other passengers scattered to the main building and to a number of other smaller buildings. Copper told Atta that those buildings housed breeding aquariums and other research facilities and one was a pumping station that descended through several levels and it circulated clean and filtered water to the many aquariums of the facility.

Christine Appleton stood near the entrance of the main building, talking to a man who was on his knees tending to the plants that bordered it. His wheelbarrow held a rake and a lawn edging tool and as many as twenty empty flower pots, so he must have been planting whatever had been in them. He stood up when the visitors arrived and fanned himself with the three cornered hat he wore.

Christine greeted them.

'I've been waiting to meet you ever since you arrived and if I could have dropped what I was doing I would have done and come straight back to the Lake,' she said, 'although that would have been difficult in the middle of the Atlantic Ocean.'

She introduced the gardener. 'This is Mikhail Patel, on loan to us from the Russian Academy of Science in Vladivostok.'

'Call me Mik. Most people do.'

'I'm called Atta.'

'I know. The whole world knew who you are from the day you arrived. If you hopped on a bus in Vladivostok everyone on the bus would recognise you even without your staff.'

'I would sooner go without shoes than go without my staff,' Atta declared.

Christine smiled.

'Shall we go inside? There is a lot to see but we will have the place to ourselves until the door opens and we get a rush of students and visitors who just come to look at the fish in the aquariums,' she said.

'Not us Christine, we have a lot to do today,' Copper apologised. 'We will leave you and Atta to go round together and we will meet both of you at the station in Bath when you get off the train if that suits you, 'she said.

'It does. Mikhail, are you coming in?'

'I'll be in when I've watered the plants I've bedded in. If I don't do that Jasmin Tyler will speed me on my way to the Hall of Warriors and have my head for a garden decoration.'

'I don't think she would go that far,' Christine said with a smile as she and Atta headed for an exhibition in the main entrance hall.

'We put these here to show people the difference between fish and the mammals that resemble fish and live in the sea like them. Those are the whales and porpoises and dolphins. Once they were land animals but they returned to the sea, probably because their main diet was fish, and over millions of years they lost their rear legs and their front legs became fins. The models show them with four legs as they were on land and then with tails like fish and front fins. The scaled down model of a skeleton of a whale shows two tiny triangular bones that are all that is left of the pelvis and rear legs. You can see how the bones of the spine change where what remains of these bones are and those other bones behind them are the bones of the tail, which is how they were before the whales went back to the sea,' she said.

'I'm intrigued. I never considered how thing change over millions of years. Could the whales come back out of the sea and regrow their back legs, do you think?' Atta said.

Christine shook her head.

'No. Once a limb or any part of the body is gone it is gone for good,' she replied. There are many creatures that live deep underground in caves and they have lost their colour because nothing can see them so they have no need to blend into the background, and other creatures have lost their eyes altogether and live by touch.'

The tour continued and Atta was fascinated by the things he saw. In a cylinder that rose ten feet from the floor a column of jellyfish held him spellbound while Christine talked about them. He discovered that there were many kinds of jellyfish and some had a very nasty sting. Seahorses he described as having to be seen to be believed! Some of the tropical fish were beautiful to look at but their poisonous spines could kill a human being. Others were less beautiful but no less deadly.

Atta realised that he knew almost nothing about what lived in the sea but he understood why Christine had chosen to study marine life and it's environment. When he was a boy he had sat by the side of the Lake with other children and watch fish rise to the surface and occasionally one would swim by close enough to be seen but neither he nor his companions had any idea of what went on beneath the surface.

In some way he felt his mind growing closer to Christine's.

The colourful reef fish held Atta spellbound.

'So many different kinds of fish and so many shapes. Fish with flat sides that are a bit like the bream that Vocca catches sometimes and fish that are shaped like the trout and the sea fish. I ought to say most of the sea fish because Vocca fishes from the shore of the sea and even from the ships sometimes as well as fishing on the Lake and he catches strange looking fish that are flat and their eyes are both on one side of their heads and their mouths are on sideways,' he said to Christine.

'We have those in other aquariums,' Christine told him.

Atta was intrigued.

'How many aquariums are there?' He enquired.

The answer left him speechless.

'I don't know for certain but including everything in this and the other buildings there must be at least three hundred.'

Christine gave Atta time to digest this and the suggested that they continue the tour.

'There are so many things I want to show you. I have been to the bottom of the deepest seas and there is a submersible on display that is an earlier model of the one that I have taken down about twenty times. I was the driver on most descents and on others I was a photographer or sample grabber collecting samples of the sea bed for analysis and sometimes I collected some of the creatures that live at those depths,' Christine explained as she led Atta to the vessel .

'I would like to take you down with me to see it for yourself but there is no submersible available at the moment,' she added with regret.

'It would be a wonderful experience but I'm already overwhelmed. What else have you got in store for me?' Atta replied.

Atta became aware of other visitors who had come in when the doors were opened to the public. Some had undoubtedly been listening to Christine while she talked to Atta and he hopped they had gained as much from it as he had.

'I'll show you some plankton next. They are tiny shrimp-like creatures for the most part and we have a screen set up so they can be seen in real time enlarged many times over. There, you can see some of the many different kinds of plankton swimming and drifting in the water. They are at the bottom of the food chain and they're important because bigger creatures feed on them and the bigger things are eaten by even bigger things, and so on,' Christine said.

Leading the way past more aquariums she spoke over her shoulder.

'The next exhibits are special to me. The first one is for mudskippers and beside it there is a tank for blennies. See how the mudskippers move in jumps on the mud where they live. They spend a lot of time buried in the mud with only their eyes looking out when the tide is out and they snap at anything they can eat comes along. They spend time actively seeking food, which is what they are doing now. They can see better out of water than in it and they seem to have little personalities.'

'Can they breathe when they come out of the water?' Atta asked. 'It seems unlikely.'

'They can and they do because they can't breathe under water any more and when the tide goes out they take a bubble of air under the mud with them. They have to stay wet but I think one day they will come out of the water for good and stop being fish,' Christine replied.

The next exhibit was a rock pool with water splashing in it.

'These are blennies. I didn't know about them when I first found out about the mudskippers but you can see how their eyes are on the tops of their heads just like the mudskippers. They must stay wet and they are more scaly than the mudskippers but their fins move separately like taking steps instead of jumping and one day perhaps they might come out of the water and stay out.'

'I wonder which will be the first?' Atta said thoughtfully.

'There's no way of telling,' Christine replied.

'Perhaps another fish will beat them both to it,' Atta speculated.

They told me he is fast, Christine thought, and that was an understatement.

She promised there was more to come after a little light refreshment. Atta wondered what he was going to be shown but because he had insufficient knowledge of her science he decided it was useless to speculate.

'I usually eat a light mid-day meal,' he told Christine when she asked him, 'but a cup of tea and some fruit juice would be nice.' He studied the menu and obviously hesitated over some words. 'I don't like coffee very much but I have tried ginger beer which was like no drink I ever had. I didn't know what to expect but it wasn't that. Perhaps orange or grapefruit juice to drink and let me see, a sausage roll to eat.'

'Make it grapefruit juice and I will have the same,' Christine declared and added that she had been told that Angela Collins has taught him to read.

'You picked it up quickly,' she complimented him.

'I had a very good teacher,' Atta replied seriously, 'and I practice reading and writing whenever I can. Some of the spellings I find strange but Angela told me that the spelling of a word sometimes carries information about the way language develops and the history of the people who speak it. She told me that attempts had been made to simplify it but they were opposed again and again.'

'Not least by Angela,' Christine replied with a smile.

They had a lot to talk about; each was fascinated by the other. They spoke of their childhoods, their growing up, the people they knew, the things they did. There was so much to say and very little time, as they knew too well.

'Your now is like mine in many ways,' Atta declared. 'Everyone does work and sometimes they do very hard work but they play, especially with their children, and they study and pass on knowledge and keep active. People walk when they might ride and they all seem to be learning new things. In my now we walk because we have no cars and buses and trains, but we often walk when we could take a raft if our destination is not to another bank of a river or lake.'

'It wasn't always like that,' Christine replied seriously. 'When I was a young girl there were so many people who spent their time uselessly. You could see them with the communicators we had in those days and they constantly sent text messages back and forth to each other. Text is writing printed on a screen, I don't know if you know that.'

'I'm coming to grips with it. I seem to be learning history and sociology all the time.'

Christine looked pleased with Atta's reply.

'They talked on their communicators as well, but most conversations were trivial at best and so were their lives and they just didn't care, or maybe they hadn't the wit to see how they were wasting their time. Some never did earn their keep or a decent place in society. There were women in their twenties with two or more children who didn't know who their

fathers were and as often as not neither did their mothers.'

Atta's mouth dropped open.

'Not everyone was like that of course and it wasn't fair when other people called them humanity's background detail. That wasn't nice. Atta, I got scared, really scared when I learned about the animals that had abandoned their limbs or their eyes and I thought the day would come when humans would lose their brains because they wouldn't use them. Cows and sheep eat grass and reproduce but they do it by instinct and there were people who ate and slept and reproduced by instinct just like cows and sheep. I cried myself to sleep more times than I can remember because the thought of losing my ability to think distressed me and scared me more than I want to admit,' Christine continued.

'It would scare me too,' Atta declared.

'I think we should get round the table with Mrs Bradley a dozen or so others who have made a study of the times and get her to talk about the reasons for so much unemployment and the role that the government and economics played,' Christine decided.

'The same Mrs Bradley who made the recipe for those delicious pork and apple pies?'

'They are delicious aren't they?'

'Then I really must meet her!'

Time passed quickly while they talked and explored each other's minds, oblivious to their surroundings. There was so much to talk about. So different and so alike, Atta thought. Eventually Christine suggested they continue their tour of the building and it's exhibits.

'There is more here than can anyone can see in a day or even a month,' she declared, 'but I have something special to show you and its going to take the rest of the day.'

Atta carried their trays to the rack which was ready to be rolled to the kitchen where the plates and cutlery would be washed. He looked forward to whatever it was that he was going to see. No hint had been dropped while they were at lunch.

He soon found himself standing in front of an aquarium that was large enough to hold two of Shipmaster Cadric's ships and a Viking longship. Clive Bowden had told him it was big and James had claimed that it was bigger than Clive's estimate but this was truly staggering. Shoals of tropical fish of all colours swam in the clear water. Some were small, about the length of Atta's hand. Mentally visualising the feet and inches that his new staff measured he estimated other fish to be up to two feet long, and some were even longer. A pair of large ray fish flapped unhurriedly by and a solitary shark patrolled a reef that was somewhere near the middle of the aquarium.

'It's quite harmless,' Christine told the astonished man.

She approached a console that Atta had not noticed while his attention was focussed on the aquarium. He hadn't noticed a dozen and a half schoolchildren either, listening attentively to what the man at the console was saying. The man handed them both a pair of headphones that were identical to the ones Atta wore when he was flying and he thought that perhaps they were part of an interactive lesson. Christine donned hers and ushered Atta back to the aquarium and the startled man heard her say, 'Mikhail are you in there?'

'Behind one of the reefs by the back wall. I'll be with you in a few seconds,' came the reply.

What was a man to think? A strange figure swam from behind the reef. It was a man but his face looked out of a window and there was something attached to his back and he had feet like a frog.

'Hello Atta, its nice to see you again. I've finished my gardening and come back to my day job,' Mikhail Patel said.

It must be Mikhail, I hear his voice and hear him speak but, but…

'Mikhail can hear us. Just talk normally,' Christine advised.

'And call me Mik like everyone else. Even Christine most of the time,' Mikhail Patel insisted.

'I, hello,' Atta said haltingly and, he felt, inadequately, but…

'Mik, show Atta your gear and talk him through it,' Christine instructed.

'Sure. I'm wearing flippers on my feet to help me swim. These are the short ones we wear in the aquarium so we can swim or we can walk on the bottom, like this,' Mikhail demonstrated.

'Walking under water is a slow process,' he chuckled. 'When we dive in the sea we wear longer flippers and don't do any walking. I'm breathing air which is stored in the cylinder strapped to my back. It's no different from breathing on dry land and the cylinder holds enough air for three hours. I got into the water a few minutes ago so I've plenty of time and I'll get a warning when there is only twenty minutes of air left and then I'll come out because that twenty minutes is a reserve. That's standard practice. I can swim and do somersaults and rolls and pretend to be a seal and I can get among the shoals of reef fish and observe them up close.'

Mikhail demonstrated his underwater acrobatics.

'I've never seen anything like it,' Atta admitted. 'I really don't know what to say.'

'It's very easy really. Anyone can pick it up in no time. Come this way and Mikhail will get you geared up and I'll be waiting for you in the aquarium,' Christine said.

'I can swim with the fish? I can be like a fish! Oh my, I, I, I...'

'I did tell you I had something special for you,' Christine said happily.

Atta could only agree.

When he gingerly made his way down the ladder he hesitated before he fully submerged but when the water rose over his faceplate and he found he was still breathing he continued to descend. As she had promised Christine was waiting and she helped him put the flippers on his feet.

'We put these on before we jump into the sea but in here we come and go by the ladder so as not to make a splash. The fish don't really mind but we do it anyway,' she explained.

If Atta had been asked he would have admitted to some apprehension but this disappeared as Christine and Mikhail steered him towards the reef and he became more accustomed to his strange surroundings.

Fish surrounded him. So many shapes, and what colours! His companions identified them and showed him things like sea anemonies, some crabs and starfish, and harmless jellyfish. The aquarium was so vast that there must be hundreds more wonderful things. More than anyone could see in many eights of days of swimming with the fish. Unconsciously Atta began to relax and explore his environment and test his ability to swim as seals do. It was like being a small boy again!

Christine and Mik showed him more wonders of the sea than he had ever dreamed of. His questions were intelligent and were answered in full whenever possible but sometimes his guides admitted they simply did not know.

Mik Patel explained, 'That's the wonder of the ocean Atta. There is so much still waiting to be learned and discovered. Sure, we have explored but the oceans are big and I hope we will never be able to claim there is nothing more that the oceans can teach us.'

Christine Appleton agreed.

'We never will explore everywhere and there will always be new fish and other living things to find,' she said.

'That's the beauty of science,' Atta replied. 'To learn and to discover and to know you will never know everything. What could we pass on to our children and grandchildren? What would they find to do? They would hate us and despise us and rightly so,' he declared.

The sound of applause in his helmet startled him. A voice from outside the aquarium told him that his experiences were being observed by as many people who could crowd into the building and the media crew had been recording and broadcasting everything. Atta's reply had been well received.

'They have been pestering me to ask you to ask Atta to come to the front of the aquarium and talk to them,' the voice continued.

'I don't speak for Atta,' Christine said with more than a trace of disapproval in her voice.

'Understood and I apologise. Atta sir, would you come and talk to the media?'

'I will but I would like to make it a short session. I have little time left to do all the things I want to do and although you will have guessed that I wish never to achieve all my ambitions I do want to fill my time by educating myself and being educated,' Atta replied.

'Very well. I'm closing all the media microphones and earphones except for just one and I do not know which microphone I have left open. One two three four five; will the person who heard that raise a hand?'

'I did.'

A hand was raised as the three swimmers came to the front of the aquarium; Christine, then Atta, then Mikhail, and the hand raiser who appeared to be in his mid-twenties was ushered forward.

'What would you like to talk about?' Atta asked him.

The man shuffled his feet.

'Sir, I really don't know,' he answered honestly. 'I never expected this and I had a list of prepared questions to ask if I had the chance but now they seem trivial or even stupid. The eyes of the world have been on you since your arrival and I don't know if there is anything new to ask you. Perhaps if you would tell me how it feels to be inside the aquarium? I mean tell everyone,' he added hastily.

'That is a very good question. Uh, I don't know your name?'

'Pierre, sir. Pierre Nissen.'

'I'll call you Pierre and you call me Atta. To answer your question Pierre let me liken my experience of flying with what I am doing now in the aquarium. When I fly with the birds I am up in the sky with them and I can see further than I have ever seen in my life and when I look down I see people and animals, vehicles, houses, ships, roads and rivers and trees and so on. It is amazing and if I could take an aircraft back to my own now believe me I would. Flying is a wonderful thing but at all times I am in the aircraft and I am seeing things through the window.

'Compare that to swimming with the fish. I can reach out and touch the reef that they swim around and I can swim among a shoal of fish as if I were a fish myself and the water that surrounds them also surrounds me. I am almost at one with the fish and all the other creatures that live here and nothing comes between me and their environment the way that being in an aircraft separates me from the air and the birds outside. I can stop still in the water and float at any depth. It is as if I have no weight; at once strange and exciting.'

'Is it better to swim with the fish than to fly with the birds?' Pierre asked.

'I can't say that. I don't think there is an answer, or perhaps I ought to say there is no answer that would satisfy me. I can only say I believe it to be a matter of personal opinion.'

'Is there any point in my asking you what you will miss most when you return to your own time? Your now? I suspect there is no easy answer to that either.'

'And you are right. I cannot choose one experience over another. Should I talk about objects or buildings or people? Each has it's own qualities and attractions and none is inseparable from the other. That does not mean I find your question without merit and I would be happy to discuss it further with you, time permitting. Unfortunately for both of us time does not permit, so I shall say that is one regret I shall take with me. It will occupy my mind during the long evenings of winter and perhaps I shall gain some inner knowledge of the workings of my own mind.'

'You say that time is running out and you will soon return home. Sir, wouldn't you like to stay for longer. Permanently even?'

'Stay for longer perhaps but not permanently. My place is on the Lake as I know it. I grew up there. I know the people. I knew people who are no longer with us; I grew up with them and we played and sometimes I got into trouble with them. I know their families and their histories as they know mine. I cannot desert them, it would not be right. I shall always wonder what else I might have experienced if I had more time but I shall have the pleasure of wondering. There is no price that could be put on that.'

Atta's answer drew applause.

Christine Appleton said, 'I wish Atta could stay but he is right. I shall always regret that I couldn't spend more time with him and take him to the bottom of the sea. I have been many times and there is always something new and more discoveries to be made. I am like Atta, I shall never see all there is to see and I would have to no other way.'

There were a few more questions before Pierre Nissen thanked Atta on his own behalf and on behalf of the media crews.

Christine's hair streamed behind her as she led the way back to the reef they had been exploring.

'Will you take a bet on how long it will take for Pierre Nissen to apply to learn marine biology?' Mikhail asked.

'I'd as soon take a bet with Ket Ketley,' Christine replied lightly.

The remaining time was spent on exploration, aquabatics, and play, until Mikhail announced that his twenty minute warning had sounded.

'Time's up for all of us,' Christine replied, 'and I have to catch the train back to Bath with Atta and meet Clive and Copper at the station.'

'I'll stay and re-charge our air cylinders and generally make myself useful,' Mikhail declared.

Atta ushered Christine onto the train and they quickly found seats. Most of the passengers greeted them with a brief hello that was warmly returned.

One called out, 'Christine you left some laundry in the wind tunnel when you left the airship. I would have brought it along if I'd known you would be on the train but my crew have lodged it in the mail and it will probably be waiting for you when you arrive home.'

'I always manage to leave something behind,' Christine replied ruefully. 'Thank you.'

Atta was curious.

'I think I have heard mention of a wind tunnel on the airship but I'm at a loss to understand what it is,' he commented.

'It's a longish room on an upper deck where the laundry is hung up to dry after it has been through the washers. There is a vent for air to come in from outside and it blows through at a steady ten miles an hour most of the time but it can be adjusted and then it leaves the airship after it has blown past all the laundry and dried it,' Christine explained. 'It should be called the drying room but nobody ever calls it that.'

'The question of washing and drying everything had never occurred to me,' Atta admitted.

Christine asked him if he had noticed a large scaffold that was being erected on one of the football pitches on the Lake.

He had.

'I know about them. The media people are going to record my going away ceremony in the George Green Building an eight of days before I return home and everyone will be able to watch it on the screens that will be attached to the scaffold. I'm told it will be broadcast all over the world as it takes place. I hope it will be a simple affair. After the ceremony all the recording devices will be packed away and I will be left unobserved. I haven't minded their attention and they have never made nuisances of themselves but I do look forward to just strolling around and saying goodbyes here and there and I mean to visit the aquarium again and do nothing except sit and wonder,' he replied.

After some thought he added, 'I have wondered about a flag and an arm patch. I have a flag making kit and I thought I might have a flag with a bird on it because I have been flying. Now I wonder about having a fish.'

'I often swim in the aquarium for pure pleasure,' Christine told him, 'but I think perhaps a simple design would suit you better. What do you say to a man with a staff in one hand and the torch of knowledge held in the other? The background could be the wavy bars of the Lake. What do you think?'

Atta looked stunned.

'That would be ideal,' he stuttered.

'It will say to the world that you are a man of the Lake and your staff shows that you are a person of some importance. The torch of knowledge will be like to one on George Green's flag and it will show your interest in teaching and learning. I haven't known you nearly as long as I would have liked to but I think that flag and a patch on our sleeve sums you up perfectly,' Christine said.

When they stepped off the train and found Clive and Copper waiting for their arrival Atta could hardly contain himself.

'I swam,' he babbled. 'I swam like a fish and with the fish. I was in the water and I could talk and swim and fish were all around me. It was… It was…'

Plainly Atta had run out of words.

Not quite: 'My flag! I almost forgot. My flag will have wavy bars on it and a man with a staff in one hand and he is to hold the torch of knowledge on the other. Christine had the idea for me but I wish I had thought of it first!'

After dinner, (chicken curry, a favourite), Copper set produced a sketch pad and she and Atta worked on the design for the flag until they were satisfied with it.

Chapter 56

Clive Bowden faced audience, half of whom were strangers to him. Nervously he licked his dry lips and started to address them.

'If Emil's scheme is to work it must go world wide and at the same time it must not reach the ears of the wrong people. You all know which people I'm referring to of course,' Clive Bowden reminded the group who had gathered at a long table in the conference room in the Brunel Hotel in Bath where some of the assembly were staying.

They looked to each other and nodded agreement. There was nobody present in the specially selected group who was known personally to each of the others but short introductions had been made. Some were known by reputation or position, others were not but it was easy to guess that their presence rested on their abilities.

'Each of you is here because you know what the outline plans are with regard to Atta's leaving bash, uh, ceremony, call it what you like. The plans are no more that outlines and any suggestions will be listened to and considered. The only stipulation is rule nothing in, rule nothing out. Everything is on the table and very soon it will be on the wall because we have lined the room with white boards and given coloured marker pens to everyone. That ends my welcoming speech. Are there any questions?'

One man half raised his left hand.

'Is Atta likely to walk in on us? He has the freedom to come and go as he pleases. Do you know his whereabouts? I'm asking because if he is in Bath he might find out that we are here and decide to pay us a visit.'

'At moment Atta is on the Lake at the aquarium with Christine Appleton and later today he will be doing more flying. I imagine everyone is aware that he has learned to pilot an aircraft,' Julia replied for Clive. She added, 'Emil, you didn't identify yourself, though I hardly think it is necessary in your case. Emil's suggestion is what brought us here this morning. Half of what brought us here that is. The other half was stated by Copper Beach some time ago. What we want to do is bring Emil's ideas and Copper's ideas together and decide how the ceremony is to go.'

'Among the media the secret is out already,' one man commented, 'but I have placed calls, uh, I ought to have identified myself. I'm Dmitri Braden, London and National Broadcasting. L and N has the ear of all the national and international broadcasters including most of the obscure local stations. As of now I can't say for sure that everyone has been contacted but when they are they will be fully briefed and I think we may count on their cooperation, not to mention their howls of rage but they will also be told in no uncertain terms that either they fall into line or they risk being cut out of the network when Mr Thompson's plan falls into place. I admit it's heavy handed and I'll never be allowed to forget it but on this occasion the end justifies the means as far as I'm concerned.'

'What about the social network?' A woman enquired. 'Simone van Kleef,' she identified herself. 'From the Lake,' she added briefly as if that were sufficient. It was.

'Tricky but manageable Simone. There is no possible way the activity on the Lake will pass without notice, which I guess was where your question was going, but we can put it down to normal preparations for the big event and even the huge outdoor screens where the broadcast from the George Green building will be shown won't cause much comment if the details of the event are not revealed. Petrel Goodman, also from the Lake,' she ended.

'Translators.' Avril Downwood used words with typical economy.

'Best done locally. The words will appear on the screens all over the world when the show is broadcast. That's an awful lot of languages,' Clive thought.

'Another one for L and N Broadcasting,' Dmitri Braden said. 'Our service calls for a host of translators and linguists and I can get word to stations where some languages or dialects are only spoken by a handful of people, for example the click language in Africa and Navaho and the other Indian Nation languages on the other side of the Atlantic.'

'Almost everybody in the Pan-African Conglomerate can speak English as a second language or even a first but the suggestion that the native languages are screened will be appreciated. I can tell you now that the outdoor screen that is going up in Rift Valley City is going to be the biggest in the world. Unless of course that someone puts up a bigger one,' Jackson Nbonne said with a broad smile.

'I'm booked in to this hotel for two more nights including tonight before I return to my embassy but I can start the ball rolling with a message on my communicator,' Jackson added with a longing glance at the pipe that rested on the table in front of him, a Tyrolean pipe with the bowl covered by a silver cap, one of a collection that Jackson owned. 'My government has already contacted the heads of the Pan-African States,' he added.

'Spire Elmerstone, temporarily representing All Ireland. Screens are going up in every park and stadium in the world and every theatre will be packed,' Spire Elmerstone said while he scribbled a note. 'Petrel is right and so are Avril and Simone. We cannot pretend that nothing unusual is happening but we can keep a tight lid on the information that we don't want made public. That means each and every one of us must play our cards close to our chests and make sure that the only people who are told are the ones who need to know. As an afterthought I might add that if any of us finds out that an, umm, unauthorised person has found out that person must be spoken to. We must avoid rumours or the whole plan will spoil.'

'The Lake will take care of that,' Petrel Goodman declared.

'L and N Broadcasting will want to everyone to wear their jackets,' Dmitri Braden said, 'and I don't mean the day to day jackets with nothing more on them but name badges and miniature flags. I mean the full works. There's always a lot of interest and discussion about the jackets and their wearers and what the badges indicate, for instance the different edge colours on the airship crew badges. It's more than just a Lake thing. My guess is that everyone of us in this room has a badged up jacket.'

Jackson Nbonne gave the thumbs up sign. Others followed.

Small groups of two or three people arranged themselves in front of the boards. Notes were made and suggestions offered. Some notes were discarded; others were developed. The groups split and re-formed as ideas were talked over.

Starting time?
Finishing time?
All day event?
Entertainments?
Transport?
Waste disposal?

Catering?
Media?
Shuttle service?
Exhibits?
Showcase the Lake?
Involvement of…?
Events?
Regatta?
Lake industries?
Competitions?
Raffles?
Prises?
Emergency services?

***

The meeting continued past it's scheduled time while the details of the programme of events were thrashed out. Clive and Julia remained to clear away the debris while everyone else left the room. Clive became aware that someone was tapping his shoulder.

'Coffee?'

'Uh. Thanks Julia. Give me a few more seconds to hold my head in my hands.'

He straightened slowly and accepted the cup that was offered.

'We're making a real gala of this aren't we? I've never seen this place in such a mess.'

'Cleaning up won't take long. I knew this would be big. Anyone could see it coming but even I could never have guessed what today would turn up,' Julia said.

Clive nodded and cautiously sipped his beverage.

'There's a lot to be done to organise the day but looking on the credit side we won't have to worry about keeping Atta out of the way and in the dark about what's going on,' he said.

'He will have his own programme of activity in the run up to the day of the ceremony. And come to think of it he'll be kept busy afterwards but he'll be writing his own programme as he goes along in a manner of speaking,' Julia commented.

'Will he suspect anything?' Clive wondered.

'I think not. He's clever but he's inexperienced in the ways of our time. Our now,' Julia replied.

'That doesn't reassure me. Christine Appleton is an altogether different matter,' Clive said.

'Christine could be a problem but it's no secret that a ceremony is going to take place and we can hope that she doesn't read anything into it except for what information is there for everyone. She has a lot to keep her occupied, what with the analysis of the data that was collected by the Humboldt on it's last patrol. She was the mission director so she is heavily involved, and don't forget the time she is spending at the aquarium with Atta. At it or in it. I think we're safe.'

Julia held up crossed fingers.

'I hope so Julia, I really do hope so. I know you won't pull a stunt on them and neither will Merlin but I feel as if I were walking on eggs. It won't look good if anything goes wrong, and that reminds me of something I haven't wanted to think about and neither has Copper. Julia we think that Copper is, I mean she can…'

'You don't want to say it any more than you want to think it so I'll say it for you. She can. Her abilities are emerging and however much she tries to suppress them it is inevitable. If you think back to the time when those overblown dignitaries were chased away by what they saw as a Viking army out for blood, that was when it started.'

'It scared Copper when she thought it might have been her doing. She had no control over it.'

'Good. She should be scared. That ability is not to be taken lightly. Shall we return to the matter in hand? Suppose we run through the events of the day.'

'Is there anything we've forgotten?'

'Only everything.'

'That's what I'm afraid of.'

Chapter 57

Clive led the way past the statue of a red dragon holding a torch and into the George Green Building. Atta was familiar with some of the classrooms that lined the main hall but his mouth dropped open when he saw a man on a step ladder putting the finishing touches to a painted flag on one of the wall panels. His flag!

'Hello Atta, I'm pleased to meet you at last. I'm Harry Tyler, painter and decorator, signwriter, geographer, shopkeeper, and canal boat builder. My daughter is Jasmin Tyler and you've met her already. What do you think of my artwork?' The man asked.

'I like it. I only made the design last night with a lot of help from Copper,' Atta replied. 'The idea for the flag came from Christine Appleton,' he added.

'Things move fast on the Lake when we put our minds to it. I painted most of the flags along this wall; Copper Beach's Bell Curve and Star, Clive's pierced boar, my daughter's Ace of Spades, Deke's flag, your flag, I painted them all. The one next to Jasmin's belongs to Walter Pfaffinger, the man who had you doing exercises when your knees were replaced. Walter was a tank driver in a long ago war and he always had a hankering to be a train driver so his flag and arm patch shows a picture of a train that is a direct copy of an old road sign for a level crossing but the wheels of the train have been changed to the tracks of a tank. Over there is James' skull and crossbones, and so on. Christine's flag, Deke's flag, Yo's flag, I painted them all,' Harry Tyler repeated.

'I never expected this,' Atta said haltingly.

'Your place is earned. The Lake owes you a debt that can never be paid.'

Nobody had noticed Julia's arrival.

'I'm bringing a message from Deke Thorpe to say he very much wants to show you round the Humboldt airship this morning. There are technicians and crews working in and around the ship and they will be happy for you to observe and ask questions and Deke intends to have you sit at a SONRAD station while they re-run an actual exercise that was recorded about ten days ago. It is interactive so you can stop the programme at any time and question whether the operator made the right decision based on the information that comes through. I can tell you that the operators are not infallible and from time to time they have so much information that it isn't easy to decide what is important and what may be ignored. I ought to know, I am an operator myself sometimes.'

'I look forward to it very much Lady, uh, Julia,' Atta said unsteadily.

'It is an experience not to be missed,' Julia told him, 'and now if you will slip your jacket off I have brought you a new one. One that has your badge on the right sleeve.'

Atta was speechless.

Julia had anticipated this and she continued, 'When you have finished seeing the airship you can collect your new flag from the school office, and some more arm patches.'

***

The airship was running on it's own power and some of the electricity generated by the solar panels was being diverted into the British Grid. Deke thought it was being used to charge the batteries of other users but there was no way of knowing than without contacting the power authorities and it was of no consequence.

'We generate more energy than we can use and even with all eight engines at maximum performance we are never short of power,' he told Atta. 'When we operate at night we use the power of our own batteries which have been fully charged during the day. In some respects we are over-powered but we like to think of it as an emergency reserve. Back in the old days when solar power was still under development nobody would ever have believed how good the solar panels are. They probably would never have believed that most of the panels on this ship are painted on either. Technology has come a long way since then.'

'The airship seems even bigger from the inside that it does from the outside,' Atta said.

Deke agreed.

'Other people have said that,' he replied. 'The bottom of the ship is where the batteries are, plus the ballast tanks, plus some automatic power converters, plus some stores for the kitchen, and plus some of the probes that we launch into the sea and others that we recover. That's just the start. Next floor up is where the equipment operators have their stations. SONRAD, communications, meteorology, atmospheric monitoring, probe launching and recovery, and some systems management, and some crew accommodation. Upwards of that is where we are now. Kitchen, recreation and rest areas, laundry, more crew accommodation, referencing computers and study areas. Some senior pupils often go on patrols to further their education so we have our own onboard tutors. Then we have the physical fitness and gymnasium areas and the cockpit. This is where I sit when I am piloting the airship and the co-pilot sits where you are, and the flight engineer sits slightly behind us so that the crew who do the actual flying sit higher than the other operators and get a better view,' he continued as he turned on his instrument panel.

'There isn't much to see at the moment but the display shows height, speed, wind strength and direction, outside air temperature, navigation information, and the course I'm steering, and a host of other things. One of the student pilots had a shot at landing the airship on a flight simulator and he forgot to account for the force of a side wind and he was blown sideways into an aircraft hangar when he tried to land it. It would have been a very costly mistake in a real situation.'

Atta looked surprised.

'Does he know nothing about cows?' He said.

It was Deke's turn to look surprised.

'You've lost me,' he admitted.

'Cows turn to face the wind in the winter when the snow and rain is blowing sideways. Actually they often face away from it. The reason is that a cow is, uh, bigger when you look at it from the side than it is when you look at it from in front or behind and so the wind has more effect on the animal and the same thing applies to the airship. It has to,' Atta explained. 'The ship will more easily be blown sideways unless it is turned to face the wind. Or away from it of course,' he continued.

'That isn't the way its taught at flying school but it's a good way of putting the message across,' Deke told him. 'The student ought to have known better. Actually it is harder to fly an airship as big as the

Humboldt than it is to fly most aircraft. Most people don't understand that.'

'I hadn't realised how much work goes into the running of an airship,' Atta commented.

'It can be stressful at times,' Deke admitted, 'but it never fails to be exhilarating. I don't usually go out on long trips like our last one because I'm a botanist before I'm anything else but its good to take a break now and again.'

'To recharge your own batteries,' Atta commented shrewdly.

'That's a good way of putting it. Most people have a wide set of skills and we like to add to them whenever we can.'

Atta was full of questions as his tour of the airship continued.

'You know what?' One technician said. 'I've seen him from a distance and I heard he's good but I reckon he could pin down a slot on a patrol any time he fancies doing the training.'

'He's not going to be around long enough,' his companion replied while she screwed a cover plate over a junction box.

'Yep. Too bad. Are you flying on the next patrol?'

'Thinking about it. You?'

'Thinking about it.'

A new romance? Maybe.

***

Ket Ketley ushered his family into the Chinese Lucky House. 'Eat up everybody. This one's on Deke!'

Interlude

This is more of my writing. I have practiced whenever I can and Angela Collins has shown me how to use a dictionary which I find useful though I have yet to explore it's possibilities. It contains lots of new words and I know how to find a word and discover the proper way to spell it. I find some spelling illogical but Christine (I'll write about her later) and Angela have told me how the spelling of a word holds information about where it came from in other countries and who spoke it and what they were like. They brought their own thoughts and customs.

I have met some new people (Christine is one) and spoken some more times to people I have met before. eLberd is one of those people and he has told me that his investigation of past entertainments has inspired him to stage an act (performance? I am not sure) in the George Green Building and present some songs from (1) the nineteen thirties and forties and (2) the nineteen fifties and sixties. He has had a set of clothes made that are characteristic (representative?) of those years and he has given small performances which have been well received and now he wants to play to a larger audience. For reasons I do not understand he calls himself the stinging detective when he is on the stage. Entrance will cost two crowns.

(Capitals Atta. It is his stage name. Thank you Angela). The Stinging Detective.

His new work will keep him busy. He is buying into a bicycle business when his work on the airship is done. The airship is named after Alexander von Humboldt who is a hero of Christine's.

I met Mrs Bradley and I told her how much I enjoyed the pork and apple pie that is made to her recipe. Those pies are really delicious. My dictionary is a great help when I write words like delicious. We also talked about the differences between the people of this now and the people I observed at the time I saw George and Hilary Green on my brief visit which was only a few eights of days ago for me.

I learned that the change dates back to the aftermath of the population crash (I ought to have mentioned that I have a thesaurus as well as a dictionary). James had already told me that about half the people in the world died of the illness. Mrs Bradley thinks it was more.

James also said that the heads of the governments of China and Russia made sure there would not be a fight as a result of the crash. She repeated a story which is not official but it claims that heads of the fighting forces had a hot line (a communications link) to each other that their governments were not aware of and it was they who refused to do any fighting because they knew better than their governors what that would mean. It is said that the Chinese took the lead in this but it has also been said it was the Russians. Each has claimed to have set things going and each has denied it from time to time. I cannot say that Mrs Bradley was right or wrong.

The human race needs something to kick against, Mrs Bradley told me, and after the population crash the people who were left (Mrs Bradley says only four out of every ten which is less (fewer Atta) than James told me) the survivors had to rebuild and it was a global rebuilding and rethinking of the direction that humanity should take. What came about was an appreciation of hard work, preservation and conservation, and education. Not everyone was happy about that because they found that wealth and worth are not the same thing and they suddenly found that they had to do useful work to pay their way and all some of them had ever done was push buttons and tell themselves they were creating wealth. That was rubbish. The process of rebuilding was rapid. Mrs Bradley said needs must so we got on with it. The plague time was terrible but short and though it might sound harsh and unfeeling we can't say they weren't warned. Mrs Bradley told me that when she said that she included herself. Eventually people came to see the population crash as a good thing. That needs further thought and discussion.

I shall not write anything about social upheaval except that some people sought to take advantage of the situation and they were firmly and not always gently punished. Mrs Bradley told me I should look up the Do As You Would Be Done By Laws (which are also known as the Tit-For-Tat Laws), and the New Levellers in the school computers if I am to understand the social upheaval that took place following an earlier outbreak of the plague and the upheaval that took place after the crash. Ultimately the first Levellers were unsuccessful. The New Levellers were not. This (according to Copper) goes back to the late twentieth and early twenty fist centuries when the so-called elite did all they could to overturn the expressed and legal wishes of the common people.

In this now nobody is ever called a common person. It would result in the social exclusion of anyone who uses that expression. Complete social exclusion with all that it implies. It has happened and there is no appeal. (That is not entirely correct Atta. To be a commoner is one thing. Social exclusion is the punishment for calling a person common, which implies that one group of people is inferior to another. It is neither acceptable nor tolerated).

On to more pleasant matters. Christine Appleton is a name I have heard spoken more than once and I met her and I became a fish! Let me start at the beginning. The Marine Sciences building (in reality a complex of buildings) houses a large number of aquariums with many kinds of fish and other sea creatures. One aquarium is much taller than I am and it is very wide and it goes back a long way. It is like a sea packed into a box. The walls are like windows so anyone can see into the aquarium and there are reefs and fish of all colours because it presents (represents, Atta) a tropical sea.

Inside the aquarium there was a man named Mikhail Patel who was dressed strangely with aids to swimming and breathing underwater. Yes, breathing underwater!

Christine talked to him and he came out of the water and helped me 'get geared up.' Then I went into the water with Mik and Christine and I swam like a fish. I stopped motionless and I did not sink to the bottom or float to the surface. I played like the seals play and Christine showed me the wonders of life in the seas and oceans and we could talk to each other and there were people who had come to see the fish and I talked to them when I was in the water and they were outside!!!! Those marks are to show it was a special experience and it was too soon for me when I had to come out of the water.

Then I got a badge for my jacket and my own flag. I told Christine that I had wondered what to put on my flag and I had thought about having a bird because I have done flying in a device called an aircraft and I have done it on my own. Christine says (said, I mean) that I should keep it simple and a flag with wavy bars for the Lake and a man holding a staff in one hand and the Torch of Knowledge in the other would make it possible (ensure) that anyone would know about me.

Later writing.

Christine looks half my age but of course she is far older than I am. There is a man named Marcel Land and a lady called Françoise Land who want to talk to me about that. I can't think why but if there is a reason for it I want to know what it is.

(What you described as a little squiggle below one of the letters is called a cedilla. It's presence modifies the sound of the letter. Françoise is a French name and that accounts for the way it is pronounced. Thank you Angela).

Chapter 58

'I understand your concerns and interest but only in an intellectual way,' Atta said after a period spent in thought.

'I have spoken to many people who are far older than I am and many more who are not, including some young children and the question of age has never been raised. Some of those children might live long lives and others, probably most, will not but even those may expect to live twice as long as I will and I am already an old man. Clive and Copper did tell me that their sons wanted nothing to do with extended lives and I am led to believe that is normal. People in this now do live much longer than they did at the time when I first came to the city. I have talked with eLberd and he expects to live to a century and a half, which is not unusual. My own age is about sixty-eight years by your reckoning so I might have six or seven years left. That is a short life in this now but not in my now. It suits me because I am a child of my time, as the saying goes.

'My conclusion is that your questions have little or no meaning when the era and the society are not taken into consideration. It needs further investigation but as a starting position I suggest that the culture that a person grows up in gets carried with them into whatever now they go to. I cite myself as an example. Would you object if I smoke my pipe?'

Atta's answer stopped Marcel Land's train of thought.

'You threw my question back at me,' he said.

'I simply stated my point of view,' Atta replied.

'I was not criticising. Hmm, I was but I was criticising myself for asking questions from my point of view and that is a mistake I shall endeavour not to repeat. I ought to have known better. Age was a major topic around the time when I encountered Copper and Merlin for the first time and I let it colour my thoughts. It could be that I am not as mentally adaptable as I like to believe I am,' Marcel admitted.

'Hmm. The prejudice that anyone gathers in their formative years is hard to ignore and even harder to discard and I believe your history has more examples than mine. My now has few prejudices and this now is the same. It is your misfortune that you grew up in an era when prejudice was the norm. I think that is the biggest difference between us but we are intelligent men who can argue for and against our beliefs. I think we stand a good chance of reaching a mutually satisfactory position,' Atta suggested.

Marcel Land felt his mind reel.

'I'm inclined to agree. I have spent most of my life in the study of the mind but the minds I studied have all been minds that grew up with the things I grew up with; we are familiar with the same things. I want to know more about the meeting of minds like ours, minds that grew up in vastly different times and were subjected to vastly different values. What you have told me will set me on a trail of exploration, a trail along which I shall study some of the greatest thinkers in history, and some of the worst ones, in the context of their own times,' he said.

'It will be a huge task. An understanding of the worst minds might explain their actions. I don't mean that it would exonerate them or excuse their guilt in any way. I have experience of Tarn if you remember,' Atta replied.

'It would! It would! It would be instructive in areas of war, medicine, commerce, in education, perhaps especially in education, and…and…'

'I advise caution. A tainted mind may spread it's influence.'

'That is a point I was going to mention. I shall ask my wife to monitor me at all times and watch for signs that I might have been influenced. I must maintain objectivity and remain dispassionate in the face of, well, pure evil in some cases.'

'I look forward to further discussions. For the time being may I leave you with the thought that my mind is my greatest possession, but from what I have learned from Christine there have been many people who either would not or could not use the gift of sentience. Granted, some people are more capable that others but that piece of information made me feel uncomfortable,' Atta said.

'Mention of Christine reminds me. Atta, I want to get you and Christine together with me for a three way conversation. No, that's not right. What I mean is that I have talked with Yo Walker and she has said that talking to you is like talking to Christine. I'll be honest with you Atta, I want to study the two of you together.'

'Hmm. I'm sure we will have a lot to talk about.'

Interlude

PROFESSOR LAND'S NOTES

Cripes!
Jeepers Creepers!
Odin's Ghost!

***

DOCTOR LAND'S NOTES

What my husband means is that he talked to Atta, the man from the past, and he listened to one of his conversations with Christine Appleton and he could not keep up with them. We have some experience of Christine but neither Marcel nor I were prepared for the weight of intellect that Atta brought with him. We were warned what to expect, if warned is the right word, and our failure to comprehend the full extent of his mental ability was complete. We are licking our wounds.

Chapter 59

'The hall is filling and the crowd on the football pitch must be seen to be believed,' Clive said to Emil Thompson, 'and Dmitri Braden from L and N Broadcasting was right about getting everyone to wear their jackets with all the badges sewn on. The media love it.'

'So I heard from a staff member who also suggested that some sort of handbook of badges would be a good idea if someone wants to put one together. The school database would be a good starting point. The media people are still setting up a monitor screen so we can see what's going on outside and the side screens are going to show scenes of audiences all over the world. The programme director is upstairs in one of the classrooms and he has dozens of screens to watch and he will send broadcasts from place to place at random unless anything happens that he wants to focus on. Nobody seems to know for certain how the events are going to happen or even what they are,' Emil replied.

'You don't have to tell me,' Clive replied. 'I've never done anything like this and I never want to do it again. I've been through it over and over with the stage director but all anybody knows is the broad outline. For obvious reasons this has to go out live and unrehearsed and if I make a mess of it the whole world is going to see me make a fool of myself.'

'When I first got the idea for this I knew I was on to something but I had no idea it would take off the way it did. The Second Avalon Scout Troop has been briefed to come on the stage from the rear when the call comes. We all know what we have to do,' Emil said.

'I wish I had your confidence. I'm nervous bordering on panic stricken and I don't mind admitting it. I've been to see eLberd Stoke's act twice this week to take my mind off it.'

'The Stinging Detective, huh? I don't know why he adopted that as a stage name but the two crowns entrance fee was money well spent when I went with Avril to see the show.'

'I thought so too.'

Emil continued, 'Every day for the past week I've been working with the media and every time the question of glitches and hiccups arose I repeated the Scout motto. Be Prepared. Prepare for the unexpected because it's going to happen no matter what we do. Every day of our lives is like that so it's worth bearing in mind. Let's call it the anticipated unexpected; you know something will happen but you never know what it will be.'

'I hope I don't find out too late to do anything about it,' Clive muttered.

Hugh Downwood spoke for the first time.

'The stage hands are getting edgy and they want you to get on stage. I've just noticed them,' he commented. 'I think the hand signals they are making mean they want to get you fixed up with your earpiece so the stage director can tell you what's coming next and keep you informed. And give instructions I imagine,' he continued with a glance at the clock on the wall.

Clive swallowed noisily and led the way. The stage curtains were still drawn together while Clive received his last minute instructions and he could see some of the monitors hat showed scenes from all over the world; indoor scenes from theatres and halls, outdoor scenes from sports arena and farmer's fields, it seemed that anywhere a screen could be erected it was erected. It was night time in some places and daytime in others. Clive had the feeling that time had been put on hold.

Finally a voice in his ear enquired, 'Are you ready Clive?'

Licking his dry lips Clive nodded.

'Yes. No. Yes.'

'Good man. Curtains in ten seconds. Five, four, three, two, one. Curtains!'

Clive took a pace forward.

'I'm speaking from the George Green Building in the District of Avalon. My name is Clive Bowden and I will be hosting this event. Millions of viewers will have stayed up late to watch the events as they unfold and many others will have set their alarms to wake up early. Wherever you are watching there is a main screen and several side screens, which means that viewers will be able to watch what is taking place at other locations. For example, viewers in Vancouver will be able to see the scenes in Singapore City. The locations will change from time to time.

'Thanks to instantaneous translation viewers everywhere are receiving this broadcast in their own languages and there will be times when the main screens will show the written language in the Cyrillic or Chinese scripts to name two of many. However you write it the words will sound the same. In other words if a Russian and a Chinese speaker read what they see on the screen the words will sound the same. Why that is important will become apparent.

'At the present time your main screens are showing the scene from inside this building and some people in this audience are waving to their screen selves, and one of the side screens is showing a live broadcast from the space station that outside viewers in Moscow might see if they look up. They tell me the night sky is clear and the station is tracking from north west to south east. Give us a wave space crew and viewers in Moscow please wave back.'

Clive stopped talking while the exchange of greeting was screened. So far so good, he thought.

'Stay on the line Moscow, there are some people a little further away who want to say hello to the folks back home. Remember it takes two seconds for a signal to reach the moon and another two seconds for a reply to come back.

'Atta has already talked with some of the Lunar Research personnel so he knows that from experience and I'm sure many of you know it too. I'm getting ahead of myself. A few weeks ago we had the privilege of receiving a visitor from the past. Atta has stayed with me and Copper Beach and we have shown him something of the way the world looks today and in exchange we have learned more of life on the Lake as it was some thousands of years ago. He has thrown himself into the affairs of modern society and the media have followed him closely every step of the way. Tonight is his leaving appearance because the media have agreed not to record his doings any more so as to give him a week to be himself like any other person.

'Ladies and gentlemen of the world, please give a big welcome to Atta!'

Dressed in the clothing of an earlier age Atta came to join Clive on the stage.

Clive gestured him to sit down and for the first time he seated himself. The applause that had greeted Atta died away.

'You know many of the people in tonight's audience in the George Green Building and just as many outside who are watching on the screens on one of the football pitches. You have met and talked and done as many things as possible to experience what life is like in and around the city of Bath and the Avalon District. I may say you left a lasting impression,' Clive said.

'The people left a lasting impression on me,' Atta declared. 'I have seen and done things I had never dreamed were possible,' he continued.

'Including flying,' Clive prompted him.

'To go where only the birds can go was always a source of speculation and dreams. What must it be like to be a bird? What do birds see? All I could do was guess and my guesses fell far short of reality,' Atta replied.

'You got into that almost from the day you arrived when James Wilson put you into his two seater aircraft and from the very start you wanted more.'

'I did! I really did!'

'You never knew it but your first flight was filmed from the control tower at Avalon South. Let's have a look at it,' Clive said.

The first flight only for as long as it took for James to take off and fly a circuit of the airfield and land the aircraft back at the point where it had begun.

'I never realised that James was teaching me to do it for myself from the moment I saw his aircraft,' Atta told his audience.

Wearing a huge smile Clive said, 'You can take it up with him now. Come in James. Give him a welcome everybody.'

Irrepressible as ever James strode onto the stage. One set of cameras followed him and focussed on his arm patch that bore the crossed spanners below a gear wheel, his own version of a skull and crossbones, while a side screen showed the same badge on the tail of his aircraft. James waved to the audience as he was ushered to a seat.

'Nobody knew how Atta would take to flying so for the first few seconds I was ready to bang us down on the grass. I soon found out there was no need to worry,' James said.

'I enjoyed every moment. James explained all the things that needed to be done and how the engines work and he made it easy for me,' Atta declared.

'You earned your flying badge, and here is Chief Flying Instructor Frank Holley to award it,' Clive told the astonished man.

'One pilot's log book with all your flights recorded,' Frank Holley said. 'It shows who was the first pilot and who was the second, the destination and duration of the flight, and it's purpose. It only lacks your signature as first pilot for the flights you made on your own and from now on you keep it up to date yourself, and this is the pilot's wings badge for your jacket. These badges come in different designs depending on the type and who awarded them which is why your badge is different from mine. Yours is the badge that is given to the pilots who qualify on the Lake.'

'I'm overcome,' Atta stammered. 'I never thought to thank you. I don't know what to say,' he said as Frank Holley and James Wilson took seats at the in the second row on stage.

Responding to a prompt in his earpiece Clive said, 'History has shown us that George Green was welcomed into your now and it was as if he were born in your own time. We wanted to do the same for you and,' Clive smiled, 'not only because you will soon be able to tell him about us.'

'I shall have nothing bad to say,' Atta declared.

'Don't forget to put modesty aside and tell George about the way you saved Merlin and Wint from serious injury or worse. Some people' Clive smiled again, 'might say you saved them from their own folly.'

'I didn't know what was going to happen,' Atta admitted, 'but I have heard things about what happened when Tarn tried to turn the stones for his own use and I acted on instinct,' he said.

Screens all over the world showed the scene that the recconaissance drone had recorded after the explosion that destroyed Merlin and Wint's new standing stone, with the two of them managing to scramble to their feet while Atta was flat on his back with his knees bent. The amphibian ambulance appeared and one of the crew was Michelle Proctor, who helped Wint to the ambulance where she told him she would put his broken arm in a sling. Atta was taken to the ambulance on a stretcher. The drone backed off after the ambulance departed and the audience could see the full extent of the damage that had been caused. Flying chips of stone had destroyed the recording instruments and the heavy metal cabinets that had housed them. An electro-magnetic pulse had fused the new metal knees that Surgeon Matron Patti Driscoll had given him to replace his natural knees that had been shattered by a rock fall thousands of years ago. Atta's staff lay broken among the wreckage. The stage became full of medical personnel; everyone who had been involved with Atta was there. Merlin and Wint were there too and it was very noticeable that Wint and Michelle Proctor always managed to be close to each other as greetings were exchanged.

'While you were in hospital waiting for your knees to be put back into working order you had visitors coming in by the coach load,' Clive reminded Atta.

'They brought me cards that they had made especially for me,' Atta recalled happily. 'I shall take them with me when I return home and thanks to Angela Collins I am able to read them all, which I shall do again and again. The cards will give a lot of pleasure to an old man as I sit by the fire and smoke my pipe in the long afternoons and I shall remember the faces of the children who brought them into the hospital to give to me. There were so many children.'

All over the Lake children and parents waved their greeting to the many cameras of the media. There were roars of approval when Atta waved back.

'What did you think when Angela Collins offered to teach you to read?' Clive asked.

'I was, well, excited. Apprehensive perhaps. It had never crossed my mind that I might read until Copper Beach pointed it out to me that I can't. I mean I couldn't. I immediately wondered why I couldn't and I was sure I could manage to learn a little. Angela Collins showed me how the letters make different noises and how they make words when they are arranged the right way. Once I got started I found that it was not difficult, or not too difficult anyway, and my eagerness to learn about reading and writing was a big help. Thanks to Angela I can read and write but I find some of the spelling illogical. I know now that the spelling of a word often carries information about it's origins; where it came from and who spoke it. In that way I could see the links between language, history, geography, and perhaps other things that a serious student could discover. I regret that I shall not have the time to explore that further but I have a dictionary and a thesaurus and they have more than enough information on their pages to keep me going for a very long time. I shall be eternally grateful to Angela Collins.'

'You were a good pupil.'

Atta spun round to see Angela Collins step from behind the curtains.

'You were a good pupil,' she repeated.

'You made it interesting. I knew from my own experience that everything is connected in some way to everything else but your teaching made me broaden the way I look at things.'

Atta spread his hands apart to indicate what he meant and an idea struck him.

'I know what I can do!' He exclaimed. 'I can! I will! I have been wondering if there is anything I can do to repay everyone for the welcome I was given and all the things that have been done for me. Flying! Trains! People! Swimming like a fish! Wonderful things! I want to do something in return. I had thought about leaving certain things to be found by you at a later date and I might yet manage to do that but I believe I can make a bigger contribution if I take my reading and writing and together with the pens and paper I have been given I can write about the Lake. I can write the words in the English language that I am speaking now if Wint will permit me to keep that knowledge I can write on the, um, the alternate lines with the words I grew up to speak. If I draw some pictures it will be of some help to the people who read it and make it more possible for them to grasp the way of life on the Lake. My Lake. I must ask Wint to pass my writings on to you…'

'Yes!' The crowd roared. 'Yes! Yes! Yes!'

All eyes turned to Wint.

'How could I refuse?' He said with an expressive gesture that drew more applause.

Michelle Proctor shuffled closer to him, a move that was not lost on many viewers.

'That seems to be settled then and I must say I can hardly wait to read more of the history of the Lake and the British Isles straight from the pen of one who was there before any written history came our way but I suspect that I shall have to stand at the back of a very long queue. Angela Collins must surely have first claim,' Clive Bowden declared.

Referring to a prompting screen he continued, 'As all know Atta has demonstrated some of his skills to the Second Avalon Scout Troop. He approached them because they carried staffs and Troop Leader Emil Thompson was quick to invite him to go on a Scout Camp with his troop. Recordings were made and despite the fact that they have been screened almost as soon as they were made I'm bringing them on again.'

Viewers watched as Atta selected the piece of wood he needed and cut it down with his stone blade. He cut it to the same length as the Scout staffs and notched it with measurements of feet and inches and very soon his new staff matched those that each Scout carried.

'I felt much better when I had a staff again,' Atta declared.

The filming continued. Atta was show singing a camp fire song with the rest of the Scouts.

Troop Leader Emil Thompson and his Scouts were ushered onto the stage and to be greeted warmly Atta.

'I have a presentation to make,' Emil declared. 'Atta has been shown to have all the best qualities of a Scout and so the Troop has voted to admit him as a member of the Second Avalon Scout Troop.'

A Scout stepped forward.

'Here I have the fleur-de-lis badge of the Scout Movement, a Scout hat, the maroon and green scarf of our Troop, complete with a woggle to hold it in place. For those who don't know, the woggle is a small band that the ends of the scarf loop through to hold it in position.'

The media focussed on Emil's scarf and woggle.

'I also bring a copy of the Scout Handbook, the same as all Scouts have. Atta's name has been entered and I have asked District Commissioner Hugh Downland to present it to him. All our signatures are in the book Atta, and there is a set of photographs of our camp to remember us by.'

Hugh Downland was cheered onto the stage to be given the Scout salute by Emil Thompson and the Scouts; right hand held to the temple, palm outwards, little finger held down by the thumb.

'I'm honoured,' Atta declared as he tried on his new hat, 'and now I'm a Scout I can give you the Scout salute and shake hands with my left hand. I'm a Scout. Me, Atta, a real Scout! When I get home I must get my badges sewn on my jacket.'

Copper stepped from behind a curtain.

'We have already done that with a new jacket. Slip it on and let's see how you look,' she said. 'It has your pilot's badge sewn on as well,' she added.

The jacket was a perfect fit and it crossed Atta's mind that Copper Beach had supplied the Scouts with his measurements for his new hat. More than likely, he thought.

Emil Thompson took over.

'Now I shall conduct everybody in the singing of the campfire song that was shown on your screens a few minutes ago,' he said. 'You know the tune and the words are going to be shown on your screens in the script that is used wherever you are so that everybody can sing the same words. Lunar Research Station start first and the rest of us start four seconds later to get us all in synch.

'Go, Lunar Station, and, one, two, three, four…

Ging gang goolie goolie goolie goolie wotcha

Ging gang goo

Ging gang goolie goolie goolie goolie wotcha

Ging gang goo

Ging gang goo

Haylo, oh haylo shaylo, haylo ho

Haylo, oh haylo shaylo, oh haylo shaylo haylo ho

Shallawalla shallawalla shallawalla shallawalla

Oompah oompah oompah oompah…'

Emil Thompson encouraged the audience.

'And the second verse is the same as the first, but louder. Shake the tiles off the roof!'

'Ging gang goolie goolie goolie goolie wotcha

Ging gang goo

Ging gang goolie goolie goolie goolie wotcha

Ging gang goo

Ging gang goo

Haylo, oh haylo shaylo, haylo ho

Haylo, oh haylo shaylo, oh haylo shaylo haylo ho

Shallawalla shallawalla shallawalla shallawalla

Oompah oompah oompah oompah…'

Restoring order took some time.

Clive's head was still spinning when the stage director's voice in his ear told him to watch the monitor screen.

'This is going out world wide,' he informed Clive.

Inside the Lunar Research Station a scientist held a sheet of paper to his forehead and Clive saw a hastily drawn picture of a Scout hat.

542

Another researcher held up a sign. Clive read it out loud; '1st Lunar Scout Troop (Unofficial).'

Things are getting out of control, he thought desperately.

Hugh Downwood was the first person to comment. Coming to Clive's rescue he said, 'I haven't the power to make that official but what I can do is make you the Lunar Pack of the Second Avalon Scout Troop. Leader, Emil Thompson. Will that do?'

Four seconds later the reply came; that would do nicely.

Emil Thompson looked as stunned as Clive.

The screens changed to show Atta dressed in underwater gear and swimming with Christine Appleton in the large aquarium.

'I never expected anything like that,' Atta told the world. 'I think it must feel much the same as the people on the space station feel when they sort of swim in the air. If I closed my eyes I had no way of knowing if up was up and down was down.'

'A lot of training for space is done underwater. I expect you want to do it again.' Clive said.

'I do. Again and again and again,' Atta replied enthusiastically. 'Christine showed me all the coloured fish and they were like nothing I could have imagined and there were crabs and some fish that can come out of the water, and all sorts of things. All that and more, and Christine told me how there are fish that live at the bottom of the deepest seas. I never guessed how deep the sea is. Christine has been to the bottom and she showed me one of the diving things that she has been down in and now it is on display,' he said with an inward feeling that his enthusiasm was getting the better of him.

'Is Christine here?' He asked. 'I would like to see her again.'

'And she wants to see you,' Clive told him. 'Come in Christine.'

Clive wondered if there was any one person who lived or worked on the Lake who did not know Christine Appleton. It seemed unlikely. Atta greeted her warmly.

'I have only shown Atta a very small part of what the oceans are like. There is so much to see and so much to learn. Sometimes I could spend days or even weeks doing nothing but sit and look at the big aquarium and I love to swim there,' she said.

'It was something I shall never forget. I still find it hard to believe I was in the water and swimming like the fish.'

'We shall do it again,' Christine promised.

'I very much want to take Atta to the bottom of the sea,' she continued, 'but time is catching up with us and there is no submersible ready. If only… well you can't have everything.'

'I have already been given far more than I could ever ask for,' Atta protested.

Clive saw his chance.

'Christine and Atta, we have something for both of you,' he said. 'I played no part in this but I've been in the know for the past few weeks. Doctor Andrew Simpson is here to tell you all about it.'

Christine and Atta looked at each other. What was this?

'Some time ago I was asked by Copper Beach to do the impossible. I said it couldn't be done and everyone I talked to agreed. However, Copper doesn't take no for an answer and a small army set to work. Copper noticed early on that Atta and Christine think alike and they share a love of logic and they each have tissue samples stored in the hospital laboratories. A lot of medical jiggery-pokery went on. I won't bore you with that but now I can say with absolute certainty that Christine Appleton is a direct descendant of Atta!'

Christine and Atta flung themselves at each other and the crowd went wild.

With tear filled eyes Christine said, 'Family time. The rest of your stay must be family time.'

'Is there… have I more…?'

Christine beckoned to the audience in the hall and Atta watched as men, women and children made their way to the stage and one of the Scouts moved from the rear to the front. An old man was helped up the steps. Atta guessed him to be close to three times his own age but as to his relationship, who could tell?

At some time one or more members of Christine's family, his family, had merged with James' family or was it Mrs Bradley's family? He was going to learn a lot before he returned home.

***

The Second Volume of the Aqua Chronicles ends here.

544

Epilogue

The story of Atta and Christine Appleton did not end with the ending of the Second Volume.

Atta returned to his own time, taking all his possessions save for his stone knife which he gave to tRevor, the boy who was one of the first people to talk to him when he arrived. He took things to pass on to George Green and years after George died it emerged that one item was a copy of the small volume entitled 'The City and the Lake,' a prospectus of a kind, that was written as a guide for anyone who thought of working or studying in or around the city of Bath and the District of Avalon.

Copies were made and put on sale.

There have been changes. I, Michelle Proctor, became the Lady of the Lake some two hundred years after Atta's departure. I have none of the mental power that was possessed by Julia, nor do I wish for it but the word of the Lady is still law.

All these writings will be sent back to an earlier period and readers may make what they like of them, as indeed some did. Many had bizarre theories about them but some more serious scholars began to wonder, and the ability to wonder is the greatest gift that humanity possesses.